**Chloe Walsh** is the bestselling author of The Boys of Tommen series, which exploded in popularity on TikTok, Goodreads, and Amazon. She has been writing and publishing New Adult and Adult contemporary romance for a decade. Her books have been translated into multiple languages. Animal lover, music addict, TV junkie, Chloe loves spending time with her family and is a passionate advocate for mental health awareness. Chloe lives in Cork, Ireland with her family.

To find out more, visit
www.chloewalshauthor.com.

*Also by Chloe Walsh*

BOYS OF TOMMEN

# KEEPING 13

## CHLOE WALSH

PIATKUS

PIATKUS

First published in Great Britain in 2023 by Piatkus

10

Copyright © 2014 by Chloe Walsh

The moral right of the author has been asserted.

A CIP catalogue record for this book
is available from the British Library.

ISBN: 978-0-349-43927-3

Typeset in Garamond by M Rules

Printed and bound in Great Britain by
Clays Ltd, Elcograf S.p.A.

Papers used by Piatkus are from well-managed forests
and other responsible sources.

Piatkus
An imprint of
Little, Brown Book Group
Carmelite House
50 Victoria Embankment
London EC4Y 0DZ

An Hachette UK Company
www.hachette.co.uk

www.littlebrown.co.uk

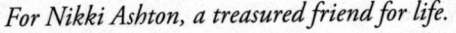

*For Nikki Ashton, a treasured friend for life.*

# Name Pronunciations

| | |
|---|---|
| **Aoife:** | E-fa |
| **Aoif:** | (like reef without the r) |
| **Sean:** | Shawn |
| **Gardaí:** | Gar-Dee |
| **Caoimhe:** | Kee-va |
| **Sadhbh:** | Sigh-ve |
| **Sinead:** | Shin-aid |
| **Neasa:** | Nasa |
| **Eoghan:** | Owen |
| **Tadhg:** | Tie-g (like Tiger but without the 'r' at the end) |

# Author Note

*Keeping 13* is the second installment in the Boys of Tommen series, and the second book for Johnny and Shannon.

Some scenes in this book may be extremely upsetting, therefore reader discretion is advised.

Because of its **explicit** sexual content, graphic violence, mature themes, triggers, and bad language, it is suitable for readers of 18+.

It is based in the south of Ireland, set during the timeframe of 2005, and contains Irish dialogue and slang.

A detailed glossary can be found at the back of the book.

Thank you so much for joining me on this adventure.

Lots of love,

Chlo xxx

# Him or Us

## SHANNON

"Make a choice, Mam," Joey said. "Him or us?"

Numb to the bone, I sat on the rickety chair at our kitchen table, with a tea towel pressed to my cheek, and held my breath for two reasons.

First, my father was less than four feet away from me, and that particular piece of knowledge caused my body to switch into shutdown.

Second, it hurt to breathe.

Dropping the blood-soaked towel on the table, I twisted sideways and tried to rest my side against the back of the chair, only to groan in agony when a surge of pain coursed through my body.

My flesh felt like it had been doused in gasoline and set on fire.

Every inch of my body was *burning*, screaming out in protest every time I inhaled too deeply. I was in trouble, I realized. Something was seriously wrong with me and, still, I remained exactly where I was, exactly where Joey had placed me, without an ounce of fight left inside of me.

*This is bad.*

*This is really bad, Shannon.*

The sounds of my little brothers' sobs and sniffles as they huddled behind Joey were almost too much to bear.

I couldn't look at them, though.

If I did, I knew I would break.

Instead, I focused my attention on Joey, taking strength from his bravery as he stared our parents down and demanded *more*.

*As he tried to save us from a life that none of us were getting out of.*

"Joey, if you just calm down for a moment—" Mam began to say, but my brother didn't let her finish.

Wholly enraged, Joey erupted like a volcano right there in the middle of our rundown kitchen. "Don't you fucking dare try and talk your way out of this!" Pointing an accusatory finger at our mother, he snarled, "Just do the right thing for once in your fucking life and put him *out*."

I could hear the desperation in his voice, the last sparks of his faith in her fading out fast, as he implored her to *hear* him.

Mam just sat on the kitchen floor, her gaze flickering over each one of us, but never once moving to go to us.

No, she remained exactly where she was.

By *his* side.

I knew she was afraid of him; I understood what it felt like to be petrified of the man in our kitchen, but *she* was the grown-up. She was supposed to be the adult, the mother, the protector, not the eighteen-year-old boy whose shoulders that role had fallen onto.

"Joey," she whispered, giving him a pleading look. "Can we just—"

"Him or us." Joey repeated the same question over and over, tone growing colder. "Him or us, Mam?"

Him or us.

Three words that should have held more meaning and importance than any other question I'd ever heard. Problem was, I knew in my heart that whatever answer was given, whatever lie she told herself, and us, the end result would be the same.

It was *always* the same.

I think in this moment my brothers realized that, too.

Joey certainly did.

He looked so disappointed with himself as he stood in front of our mother, waiting for an answer that wouldn't change a thing because actions spoke louder than words and our mother was a living, breathing puppet with strings that our father held the reins to.

She couldn't make a decision.

Not without *his* permission first.

I knew that even though my younger brothers were praying for a resolution, this was going to be an anti-climactic moment.

Nothing would change.

Nothing would be fixed.

The first-aid kit would be brought out, the blood would be mopped up, the tears would be wiped away, the cover-up story would be invented, our father would disappear for a day or two, and then everything would go right back to the way it always was.

*Promises made, promises broken* – the Lynch family motto.

We were all shackled to this house like a great oak to its roots. There was no escaping this. Not until we all came of age and got out.

Too worn out to think about it, I slumped in the chair, taking in everything and taking in nothing at all. It was almost like a prison sentence with no parole.

Sagging forwards, I clutched my ribs and waited for it to be over. The adrenalin inside of me was dissipating at a rapid pace, replaced with more pain than I could consciously endure. The taste of blood in my mouth was thick and potent; the lack of air in my lungs was making me feel lightheaded and woozy. My fingertips danced between numb and tingling.

Everything hurt and I was done.

I was so completely done with the pain and the bullshit.

I didn't want this life I had been born into.

I didn't want this family.

I didn't want this town or the people in it.

I didn't want any of it.

"I want you to know something," Joey finally bit out when she didn't answer him. His tone was ice cold as he spat out the words I knew were churning around inside of him like poison that needed to be exorcised from the pits of his fractured heart. I knew because I felt the same way. "I want you to know that I hate you more right now than I have *ever* hated him." His body was shaking, his hands balled into fists at his sides. "I want you to know that you are no longer my mother – not that I ever had one of those to begin with." He clenched his jaw, striving to keep the pain inside of him from expelling. His pride refused to allow him to show emotion in front of these people. "From this moment on, you are *dead* to me. All your shit? Handle it yourself. The next time he hits you? I won't be there to shield you. The next time he drinks all the money and you can't feed the kids or get the electricity switched back on? Find some other asshole to get cash from. The next time he throws you down the staircase or breaks your fucking arm in one of his whiskey tantrums? I'll turn a blind eye just like you did right here in this kitchen. From this day on, I won't be there to protect you from him just like you weren't there to protect us."

I cringed with every word that poured from his lips, feeling his pain in the deepest part of my soul as it mixed together with mine.

"Don't talk to your mother like that," our father snarled, tone menacing, as he hauled himself to his feet, all six feet and two hundred pounds of him. "You ungrateful, little—"

"Don't even think about speaking to me, you scummy piece of shit," Joey warned, glowering at Dad. "I might share your blood but that's as far as it goes. You and me are done, old man. You can burn in hell for all I care. In fact, I sincerely fucking hope you both do."

I felt a hand clamp gently down on my shoulder then, startling me, and causing me to groan in pain. "It's okay," Tadhg whispered, keeping his hand on my shoulder. "I'm here."

I closed my eyes as tears trickled down my cheeks.

"You think you can talk to me like that?" Dad wiped his face with the back of his hand and, in doing so, smeared a trail of blood up his arm. "You need to settle the fuck down, boy—"

"You're calling *me* boy?" Joey threw his head back and laughed humorlessly. "Me? The one who's been raising your fucking kids for most of my life? The one who's been cleaning up both of your messes, taking care of both of your responsibilities, picking up the slack for two worthless, piece-of-shit parents?" Joey threw his hands up in outrage. "I might be only eighteen, but I'm more of a man than you'll *ever* be!"

"Don't push your luck," Dad growled, red-eyed and sobering fast. "I'm warning ya—"

"Or fucking what?" Joey taunted with a careless shrug. "You'll knock me around? Hit me? Kick me? Get your belt out? Take a hurley to my legs? Bust a bottle over my head? Terrorize me?" He shook his head and sneered. "Guess what? I'm not a scared little boy anymore, old man. I'm not a defenseless child, I'm not a scared teenage girl, and I'm not your battered wife." Narrowing his green eyes, he added, "So, whatever you do to me, I can promise you that I'll return it tenfold."

"Get out of my house," Dad hissed in a deathly quiet tone. "Now, boy."

"Teddy, stop!" Mam wailed, hurrying towards him. "You can't—"

"Shut the fuck up, woman!" Dad roared, turning his fury on our mother. "I'll break your face for ya! Do ya hear me?"

Flinching, Mam looked to Joey, expression helpless.

Joey remained rigid, clearly fighting an internal battle, but he didn't go to her.

"You can't throw him out ..." Mam's words drifted away as she stared up in pure, unadulterated fear at the man she had married. "Please." Tears dripped down her pale cheeks. "He's my son—"

"Oh, so now I'm your son?" Joey threw his head back and laughed. "Don't do me any favors."

"This is your fault, girl," Dad barked then, turning to glare at me. "Whoring around the fucking town, making trouble for this family! You're the problem in this—"

"Don't even go there," Joey warned, voice rising. "Keep your goddamn eyes off her."

"It's the truth," Dad snarled, keeping his brown eyes locked on my face. "You're a waste of space and you always have been." With a cruel expression etched on his face, he added, "I told your mother about ya, but she wouldn't hear it. I knew, though. Even when you were small, I knew what kind you were. A fucking runt." Glowering at me, he spat, "Don't know where you came from."

I stared back at the man who'd spent my entire life terrorizing me. He stood in the middle of the kitchen, a formidable force to be reckoned with, two strong arms attached to fists that caused more damage to my body than I could remember. But it was his words, his tongue, that had damaged me so much deeper.

"That's a lie, Teddy!" Mam, strangled out. "Shannon, baby, that's not—"

"We never wanted you." Dad continued to torment me with his words. "Did ya know that? Your mother left you for a week in the hospital, debating whether or not to give you up until the guilt got the better of her. But I never changed my mind. I couldn't even stand the sight of you, let alone love you."

"Shannon, don't listen to him," Joey commanded, tone thick with emotion now. "It's not true. The bastard's unhinged. Just block it out. Do ya hear me, Shan? Block *him* out."

"I didn't want you either," Dad snarled, turning his glare on Joey.

"My heart's bleeding," Joey shot back mockingly.

"Well, we feel the same about you," Tadhg growled, hand shaking on my shoulder as he stared at our father. "None of us want *you*!"

"Tadhg," Joey said in a low, warning tone, panic lighting his eyes. "Be quiet. I've got this."

"No, I won't be quiet, Joe," Tadhg strangled out, filled with more rage than any eleven-year-old boy should be carrying. "He's the fucking problem in this family and he needs to hear it."

"Get him out of my sight!" Dad roared, turning his attention to Mam, who was hovering slightly apart from both of them. "Now, Marie!" he bellowed, pointing a finger at her. "Get him out before I do away with the little bastard."

"I'd like to see you fucking try," Joey taunted, shifting both Ollie and Sean, who were clinging to his sides, behind him.

"No!" Sniffling, Mam moved to stand between our father and Joey. "*You* need to go."

Dad took a step towards her and Mam automatically cowered away, hands shooting out in front of her face.

It was the epitome of pathetic.

None of us ever had a fighting chance with these people.

How could love and fear coincide in one human heart?

How could she *love* him when she feared him so much?

"What did you say to me?" he hissed, turning his fury on our mother. "What the *fuck* did you say to me!"

"Leave," Mam choked out, shaking from head to toe, as she backed up a couple of steps. "It's over, Teddy. I'm done – we're done. I can't . . . I need you to *go away*!"

"You're done?" Dad sneered, glaring at her. "You think you're leaving me?" He laughed cruelly. "You're mine, Marie. Do ya hear me? You're fucking mine." He took another step towards my mother. "Think you can throw me out? Walk away from me?"

"Just go," Mam strangled out. "I want you gone, Teddy! Get out of our lives."

"You think you have a life without me? You are *nothing* without me, bitch!" Dad roared, eyes wild and full of unrestrained madness. "The only way you're leaving me is in a box, girl! I'll kill you before I let you leave me. Do ya hear me? I'll burn this fucking house to the ground with you and your cunts in it before I let you go."

"Stop." A small cry tore from Ollie's throat as he clutched Joey's leg. "Make him stop," he sobbed, clinging to our brother like he held all the answers. "Please."

"Are you a girl now?" Dad demanded, looking disgusted. "Toughen up, Ollie, ya little bollox!"

"That's enough, Teddy!" Mam screamed, clutching her chest. "Get out!"

"This is my fucking house," Dad roared back. "I'm going nowhere!"

"That's fine," Joey stated in a cool tone before turning to look at our brothers. "Ollie, go outside and take Sean with you." Sliding his hand into his jeans pocket, he pulled out his phone and handed it to him. "Here – take this and phone Aoife, okay? Call her up and she'll come get us."

"No, no, no!" Mam began to panic. "Joey, please, don't take them away from me."

Nodding once, Ollie caught ahold of Sean's hand and hurried from the kitchen, running past the outstretched arms of our mother without hesitation.

At nine and three years old, they didn't trust her. Because they knew, even at their tender, young ages, whether she meant to or not, their mother would inevitably let them down.

"I told him to go – I told him, Joey. Please, I choose you. Of course, *of course*, I choose you!" Hurrying towards my brother, Mam fisted Joey's hoodie in her frail hands and looked up at him. "Please don't do this . . . please, Joey. Don't take my children."

"What good are you to them when you can't keep them safe?" Joey demanded, unmoving. His voice was shaking, though, as our mother clung to him, begging him for one more chance to let us down. "You're a fucking ghost in this house," he bit out. "You're wallpaper, Mam. A mouse." He ran a shaky hand through his blond hair and hissed, "You are *not good* for us!"

"Joey, wait – wait! Please don't do this." Clutching my brother's hands, she dropped to her knees and began to beg. "Don't take them from me."

"I can't leave them here," Joey strangled out, chest heaving. "And you've made your choice."

"You don't understand," she cried, shaking her head. "You don't see."

"Then get up, Mam," Joey choked out, tone pleading. "Get up off your knees and walk *out* of this house with me."

"I can't." Shaking her head, Mam exhaled a broken sob. "He'll kill me."

"Then die," was all Joey replied, tone void of all emotion.

"Let him go, Marie," Dad barked, tone laced with malice. "He'll be back with his tail between his legs. Cunt is useless. Won't survive a day on his own—"

"Shut up!" Mam screamed, louder than I had ever heard her. Sniffling, she scrambled to her feet and swung around to glare at Dad. "Just shut up! This is all your fault. You've ruined my life. You've destroyed my children. You're a fucking madman—"

Whack.

Our mother's words morphed into a wailed cry as our father's fist connected full force with her face. She dropped to the floor like a sack of stones.

"Think you can talk to me like that?" Dad snarled, glowering down at Mam. "You're the worst of the lot, you fucking whore!"

It took Joey all of two seconds to backtrack on what he had just said, because his hands shot out as he roughly shoved Dad away from her. "Keep your fucking hands off my mother." He shoved him hard again. "Don't touch her!" Crouching down, Joey attempted to pull Mam to her feet. "Mam, please—" His voice cracked as he knelt on the ground and brushed her hair back off her face. "Just *walk away* from him." He cupped her face in his bloodied hands. "We'll figure something out, okay? We'll sort this, but we can't stay here. I'll take care of you—"

"Who the fuck do you think you are?" Dad roared menacingly, lunging for Joey. "Think you know it all, boy? Think you're better than me?" Clamping his huge hand around the back of Joey's neck, he forced him onto his knees. "Think you can take her away from me? She's going nowhere!" Dad pressed down harder, shoving Joey's forehead to the tiled floor. "I told you I'd put manners on you, ya ungrateful, little bastard." He pressed his knee into Joey's lower back, rendering him helpless. "Think you're a man now, boy? Show your mother what kind of a man you are, crying on your knees like a little bitch."

"Stop it!" Mam screamed and pulled at my father's shoulders. "Get off him, Teddy."

"I'm more of a man than you," Joey hissed, voice muffled from the force it was taking to hold himself up with the weight of our father looming over him.

"Oh, you think so?" Dad grabbed a fistful of Joey's hair, reined back, and then slammed his face into the tiles. "You're a piece of shit, boy."

Spitting out a mouthful of blood, Joey planted his hands on the tiles once more and heaved his body up, desperately trying and failing to break free of our father's hold, as he continued to slam his face against the tiles. The sound of bone crunching filled my ears and my stomach churned, but Joey refused to give in. "That all you got?" He bared his teeth, blood glistening over white, as he snarled and fought wildly against Dad's hold. "You're losing your touch, old man!"

"Get off him!" Mam continued to scream as she pulled at Dad's shoulders. "Teddy, you're going to kill him!"

"Good!" Dad roared, throwing an arm back and knocking Mam away once more. "And you're next, ya turncoat whore!"

Trembling violently, I moved to do something, but I *couldn't*.

I couldn't get my limbs to *move*.

I didn't have the strength left inside of me to get back up.

Years of mistreatment, mixed with the beating I had just taken, had driven me to the point where, at sixteen years old, I couldn't stand up on my own two feet.

Pathetic, I remained slumped on the chair Joey had set me in, with blood flowing freely down my face, and my heart slowing in my chest.

I was dying, I realized. That, or my body had gone into shock. Either way, something was very wrong with me, and I couldn't help the one person who had never failed to help me.

With my head spinning wildly, I watched through glazed eyes as Joey managed to twist his body sideways, only for them to both end up wrestling on the floor.

My heart plummeted into the pit of my stomach when Dad came out on top once more. With his hand curled around Joey's throat, he closed his fist and began to hit him repeatedly in the face. Joey bucked wildly beneath him, desperately trying to get out from beneath him, but it was no use. Our father had at least forty pounds on him.

*He's going to die,* the fire in my heart screamed, *save him.*

I tried.

Panic-ridden, I tried to get to Joey, but I just couldn't move.

I felt like I had been paralyzed.

"Help her," I could hear Joey strangle out, coughing and spluttering. "Fucking help her!"

*Help who?*

*Help who, Joe?*

Every few seconds my vision went blank and I knew that meant I must be drifting in and out of consciousness. I also knew that this was a bad sign, alerting me to the fact that he had hurt me worse than before.

*So much worse.*

Out of the corner of my eye, I noticed Tadhg move for the cupboard. Yanking open one of the drawers, he withdrew a knife, and without a hint of hesitation, he lunged.

*Do it*, I sent a silent plea to the heavens above to give my brother the courage to *just do it*.

"Get off my brother!" Tadhg screamed as he held the tip of the knife to our father's throat, hand steady as a rock, eyes locked on him.

"Tadhg, put down the knife," Mam cried, moving slowly towards him. "Please, baby."

"Fuck you," Tadhg shot back, never taking his eyes off our father. "Get. Off. My. Brother."

*Do it, Tadhg*, I silently prayed, *make him stop forever.*

"Don't be stupid, boy," Dad laughed, but there was no humor in his voice now – just apprehension.

*Good.*

*Be afraid.*

"I'm not stupid," Tadhg replied, his voice deathly cold. "And I'm not Joey." He stepped closer, pressing the tip of the knife that bit closer. "I won't stop because Shannon says so."

My heart broke.

He was eleven years old and this was what they had turned him into.

I was praying for him to kill our father, to finish this off.

What the hell did that make me?

A part of me wanted to beg my brother to just stick that knife through me so I could be done with it all.

They were all so strong and I was weak.

I wasn't tough enough.

I couldn't bounce back like the rest of them.

I was defected.

"Tadhg," Joey panted from the floor, chest rising and falling quickly as he drew breath after desperate breath into his lungs, our father's hand still wrapped around his throat, "it's okay." His face was covered in blood, his nose clearly broken again. Both of his hands were wrapped around the one hand Dad had pinning his throat. "Just take it easy—"

"It's not okay, Joe," Tadhg replied, voice void of all emotion. "None of this is okay."

"What are you going to do, boy?" Dad sneered, still straddling Joey, but his bloodshot eyes were full of anxiety and locked on my little brother. "Stab me?"

"Yes."

Calling his bluff, Dad reached a hand up to take the knife, but quickly flinched away as a trickle of blood ran down the side of his neck. "Jesus Christ, Tadhg!" he bellowed, throat bobbing nervously. "You cut me."

"This ends now," Tadhg replied, taking another step forward. "Get off my brother and get out of this house for good, or I'll slit your throat and you can die."

I wasn't sure if it was immense relief or bitter regret I felt when I watched my father release Joey and climb to his feet.

A mixture of both, I suspected, though it was hard to form coherent thoughts anymore so I couldn't be sure.

Too tired to hold up my own body weight, I leaned forward and rested my cheek on the table. Taking in quick, short breaths, I tried to hold still, to not move and jostle my bones.

Everything hurt so bad.

The taste of blood in my mouth made me gag.

Shuddering, I whimpered from the reflex and just stopped moving altogether.

I resigned myself to the sensation of it sliding down the back of my throat, to the metallic taste of copper on my tongue.

Feeling woozy and disconnected, I allowed my eyelids to flutter shut, blocking out their voices as they shouted at one another by concentrating on the erratic beat of my heart as it thundered in my ears.

"Fucking help her, will ya!"

Thump, thump, thump.

"I'm going to kill you, Marie."

Th-thump . . . thump, thump, thump.

"Get the fuck out!"

Thump . . . thump . . . thu . . . thump . . .

"You're a dead woman walking."

Thump . . . thump . . . thu . . . thump . . .

Door slamming.

Thuuuuump . . . thu . . . thu . . . thump . . .

*"I love you, Shannon like the river . . . "*

Thump, thump, thump, thump . . .

Devastation flooded my body, joined by deep regret. Johnny's face a beacon of lost hope behind my closed eyelids, as I accepted the hand I had been dealt.

Hot tears of bitterness and regret dripped from my lashes, splashing onto my cheeks and mixing with the dried blood.

I felt so sad, like I had been robbed.

Maybe in another life things could have been different.

I could have been happy.

*"I think I need you for keeps . . . "*

"What's wrong with her?" I heard someone demand then, someone who sounded an awful lot like Joey's girlfriend, Aoife. "Why is she bleeding out of her mouth?"

*"Don't look so scared. I won't hurt you . . . "*

"Shannon! Shannon! Jesus Christ, do something!"

*"Tell me who put their hands on you and I'll make it better . . . "*

"Look what you've done!" I heard my mother scream.

*"I'll look after you . . . "*

"Call an ambulance."

*"You're safe with me . . . "*

"She's dying. He killed my sister. And you're doing nothing!"

*"I won't let you fall . . . it's okay, I've got you . . . "*

"Call a fucking ambulance!"

*"Stay with me . . . "*

I could feel the warmth of two hands against my face and reveled in the gentle touch. "Can you hear me?" Joey's voice filled my ears. "I'm going to get you out of here, okay?"

*"Just keep kissing me . . . "*

"Shannon, can you hear me?"

*"I love you, Shannon like the river . . . "*

"Shan?" I felt something poke at my eyes then: Joey's fingers, I realized, as he lifted my lids. "Shannon, come on, talk to me."

Eyelids fluttering open, I forced myself to focus on his terrified looking face as he stared right back at me. "I'm going to get you help, okay?" He exhaled a ragged breath. "The ambulance is on the way."

I opened my mouth to respond but nothing came out.

My lips couldn't form the words I needed.

"Shannon, breathe." My mother crouched in front of me then, kneeling beside Joey's feet, touching my face with one hand as she held a bag of frozen peas to my chest with the other. "Breathe, Shannon," she kept repeating. "Breathe, baby."

Was it helping?

Was it making it worse?

I didn't know.

I only knew that I *couldn't* breathe.

The scariest thing was that I didn't care.

I wasn't panicking.

I wasn't scared.

I was just . . . done.

"Shan," Joey repeated, voice rising as fear enveloped his features.

"Shannon, please." Crouching down in front of me, he placed both hands on my shoulders and gently shook me. "Jesus Christ, Shannon, talk to me!"

I tried, but nothing came out.

Coughing, I began to gag against the foreign taste of metallic as it spilled out of my mouth in a thick, oozy gush.

My head lolled to one side, brought back to an upright position when Joey held my face in his hands. "Aoife, give me your keys," he strangled out, green eyes glued to mine. Releasing my face, he moved out of sight. "I'll take her myself."

"Joey, don't move her. She could have internal—"

"Give me the fucking keys, baby!"

Without the strength of his hands holding me up, I automatically slumped forward, only to sag heavily against my mother.

"It's okay," she whispered, wrapping her arms around me, fingers moving through my hair. "Everything's going to be fine."

I wished I could hold my own weight and not lean on my mother. I didn't want her touch but I had nothing left inside of me.

The last thing I remembered before darkness enveloped me was my brother's touch as he folded me into his arms, followed by the sound of his voice as he whispered the words, "don't leave me," in my ear.

# Balls High

## JOHNNY

*No rugby for at least six weeks.*

Father.

*Bed rest for seven to ten days.*

Father.

*Your feet won't be touching grass until May.*

Father.

*Torn adductor, adhesions, and Athletic Pubalgia.*

Father.

*Rehabilitation.*

"Fuck!" Fisting the blankets around my body, I threw my head back and stifled a roar, knowing that if I had another outburst, I was going to get bleeding sedated again. I was on thin ice with the nurses stationed down the corridor from my room. Getting out of bed to take a piss and collapsing on the floor beside my bed had rendered me blacklisted. I'd been given a huge bollocking for not asking for help, reminded I had a catheter in place, and then given another shot of whatever the hell it was they kept flushing into my IV. They told me it was for pain, but I was suspicious. I was high as a kite. Nobody needed that volume of drugs in their system. Not even me, the eejit with the self-proclaimed broken dick. "Jesus fucking Christ!"

Blinking away the blurriness, I tried to focus on the wall opposite my bed with the television mounted to it, and Pat Kenny hosting *The Late Late Show,* but it was no use. I kept zoning out, my thoughts leading me back to that one word that had been haunting me, playing around in my brain like a broken record.

*Father.*

*Father.*

*Father.*

"Stop!" I growled angrily, even though I was alone in the room. "Just fucking stop talking."

My mind was playing tricks on me, making me feel anxious and on edge, and I had the worst feeling in the pit of my stomach.

My anxiety was so strong I could taste it.

Painkillers, my ass.

This was something that fucked with my head.

Nobody was listening to me.

I kept telling everyone that something wasn't right and they responded by telling me that everything was fine and then dosing me up with more of whatever the hell was currently flushing through my veins.

I knew they were wrong, but I couldn't see straight, never mind make sense of my worry.

The more they didn't take me seriously, the more anxious I grew until I was drowning in concern over something I couldn't quite put my finger on.

It was a horrendous fucking feeling.

My mind was reeling; only one word playing inside my head like a broken record.

*Father.*

And only one voice repeating that same word over and over again.

*Shannon.*

I had no idea why I was reacting the way I was, but my heart was going ninety. I knew this because every time I thought about her, the machine I was hooked up to started beeping and flashing.

I didn't cope well with anxiety. It just wasn't in me. Adrenalin, absolutely, but fear? No, I didn't fucking do well with fear. Especially when the fear in my heart was for another person.

When I did manage to train my eyes on the television, I kept thinking, 'what the fuck is Pat doing on the telly? *The Late Late Show* was a Friday night program, but hey – what the hell did I know? Not a lot apparently, since I couldn't distinguish between what night of the week it was.

Sagging back on the mattress, I blinked away the drowsiness and tried to think clearly.

Furious, I twisted my head from side to side, seeking more.

Something wasn't right.

In my head.

In my body.

I felt like I was trapped, a prisoner of this bleeding bed, and it sucked balls.

Furious with the world and everyone in it, I tapped my fingers against the mattress and did a recount of the ceiling tiles.

One hundred and thirty-nine.

Christ, I needed out of this room.

I wanted to go home.

To *Cork*.

Yeah, I was that fucking desperate that I didn't want to be in Dublin anymore. I was having a come-to-Jesus moment and wanted nothing more than to be back home in Ballylaggin, surrounded by all that was familiar to me.

To be back home with Shannon.

Jesus, I'd messed up real bad with her.

I'd reacted horribly.

I was an eejit.

Anger swelled up inside of me again, joined by the depression and devastation that followed every time I thought about what my future held – which was every minute of the day.

Pain? I was in a hell of a lot of pain, but my body was the least of my worries right now. Because I had lost hold of my bleeding senses. My head was gone, lost, back in Cork with a fucking girl.

Bored and restless, I glanced out the hospital window at the darkened sky and then back to the television screen.

Fuck this.

Reaching for my phone, I shakily scrolled through my contacts, struggling to make out the names through the haze, until I found the number I had dialed at least twelve times in the past god knows how many hours or days, and pressed call.

With a great deal of effort, I managed to hold the phone to my ear and waited, with bated breath, listening to the obnoxious *ring ring* sound, until I was greeted by his monotone voicemail.

"Joey." Sitting forward, I tried to shift my body into an upright position, only to end up pulling on some wires attached to my body that had no business being there. "Call me back." Exhaling a pained grunt when I felt a stinging sensation shoot up my legs, I focused on getting the next sentence out without slurring. "I need to talk to her." I was fairly sure I slurred my words anyway considering my voice sounded foreign to me. "I don't know what's happening, Joey. Maybe I'm fucked in the head, I'm high as balls, but I'm worried. I've got this bad fucking feeling—"

Beep.

"Well, shite." Feeling thoroughly defeated, I ended the call and dropped my phone down beside me before slumping back on the pillows.

Was I hallucinating this whole thing?

No, I knew I was in the hospital.

I knew she had been here to see me.

But maybe I was concentrating on the word father because I had been so surprised to see my own father here when I'd opened my eyes.

Mashing my lips together, I ignored the tingling, numbing sensation and tried to think clearly.

I was missing something.

When it came to Shannon Lynch, I felt like I was always three steps behind.

Drowsy, I tried to keep my head clear, but it was impossible with the warm, tingling feeling inside of me demanding I close my eyes and absorb the feeling of nothing.

*". . . If you want to know what goes on inside that head of hers, then be worth it . . ."*

"Fuck you, Joey *the hurler*," I slurred, throwing the covers off my body. "I *am* worth it." Dropping my feet to the floor, I caught ahold of the IV pole and pulled myself into a standing position. Every muscle in my body painfully protested the movement, but I forced it down and staggered towards the door.

"Johnny!" Mam exclaimed when she found me in the hallway a few minutes later. She was holding two plastic cups in her hands and staring at me with a horrified look on her face. "What are you doing out of bed, love?"

"I need to go home," I grunted, dragging my IV along with me, as I bared my ass to the world in the cloth hospital gown held up only by my broad shoulders. "Right now, Ma," I added, as I pushed off the wall I had been temporarily resting against, ignored the searing pain coursing through my body, and stumbled clumsily down the corridor. "I need to go."

"Go?" Mam balked at me. "You've just had surgery." Rushing to intercept me, Mam placed her hands on my chest and glared up at me. "You're not going anywhere."

"I am." I shook my head and tried to step around her. "I'm going back to Cork."

"Why?" Mam demanded, as she once again intercepted my move and blocked my path. "What's the matter?"

"Something's wrong," I bit out, feeling woozy and lightheaded. "Shannon."

"What?" Concern flashed in Mam's eyes. "What's wrong with Shannon?"

"I don't know," I snapped, feeling agitated and helpless. "But I *know* something's wrong." Frowning, I tried to chase my thoughts, to make sense of what I was feeling, but only managed to come up with, "I have to help her."

"Baby, it's the meds," she replied, looking at me with this fucked-up sympathetic gaze. "You're not feeling yourself."

I shook my head, at a complete loss. "Ma," I croaked out hoarsely, "I'm telling you, there's something *wrong*."

"What makes you so sure?"

"Because—" Exhaling heavily, I sagged against the wall and shrugged helplessly, "I can *feel* it."

"Johnny, love, you need to lie down and rest."

"You're not listening to me," I growled. "I know, Ma. I fucking know, okay?"

"What do you know?"

I sagged in defeat. "I don't know what I know, but I know I *should* know!" Frustrated and confused, I blurted, "But she knows, and I know, and she won't tell me, but I swear they all fucking know, Ma!"

"Okay, love," Mam coaxed, wrapping her arm around me, "I believe you."

"You do?" I croaked out, feeling drowsy but slightly sated. "Thank Jesus, 'cause nobody's listening to me around here."

"Of course I believe you," she replied, patting my chest as she led me back to my room. "And I'm always listening to you, pet."

"You are?"

"Mmm-hmm."

"I hate being lied to, Ma," I added, resting far too much of my weight on her slim body. "And she's always lying to me." My nose twitched and I mashed my lips together, trying to fight off the numbness in my face as a familiar scent wafted up my nostrils. "I like the smell coming off you, Ma." I sniffed again, inhaling the scent. "Smells like home."

"Jean Paul Gaultier," Mam replied, pushing the door of my room inwards. "Same as I always wear."

"It's a good smell," I agreed, nodding to myself, as Mam dragged me back into my room.

"I'm glad you approve," Mam chuckled.

"What am I supposed to do now?" I frowned at my bed, watching through a blurred haze as my mother pulled back the sheets and patted the mattress. "Sleep?"

"Yes, you're supposed to go to sleep, love," Mam encouraged, tone coaxing. "Everything will be a lot clearer in the morning."

I scrunched my nose up. "I'm hungry."

"Go to sleep, Jonathan."

"I don't like Dublin anymore," I grumbled, flopping back onto my bed. "They're starving me to death in this place." I closed my eyes, body sinking deep into the mattress. "And all the bleeding drugs."

I felt the covers being draped over my body once more and then a soft kiss on my forehead. "Go to sleep, love."

"Father," I mumbled, drifting off. "I hate that word."

# Keep Breathing

## SHANNON

"Shan, can you hear me?"

*Joey?*

"I'm right here."

*I can't see you.*

I felt a hand slip into mine. "Just stay with me, okay?"

*I'm scared.*

"Please don't leave me."

*I don't want to.*

"We're nearly there, Shan."

*Nearly where?*

"Just keep breathing, okay?"

*Don't let me die here, Joey.*

"Is she breathing? Aoife – is she breathing, baby?"

*Please . . .*

"I don't know, Joe . . . there's a lot of blood."

*Help me!*

"Just help her—" Sobs. "Make her fucking breathe!"

*I don't want to die . . .*

# Dropping Pennies and Bombshells

## JOHNNY

When I woke up Monday morning, it was to a clear head and a tsunami of pain.

Regardless of how much pain I was in, I knew I wasn't going to complain about it. Not when there was a high chance they would shoot me up again.

Pain relief of the liquid kind that was flushed through your veins was a bad idea.

No joke, I'd been mostly out on my ass since my surgery, high as a bleeding kite, because every time a damn doctor or nurse checked in on me, they deemed it necessary to click the fucking button attached to the line in my hand and flush more of the crazy into my system.

According to the team of doctors I had met earlier this morning: aside from the holes in my body from the surgery, I had been so distressed and uncooperative on Saturday, pulling at my wires and trying to leave the hospital, that it had been safer to keep me partially sedated so I could rest up and heal.

My parents and Gibsie had been in and out all weekend, visiting my crazy ass, but I'd been completely out of it, ranting and raving like a demented lunatic, screaming about fathers and rugby balls.

Yeah, that was bleeding embarrassing.

I was grateful that I couldn't remember.

Feeling aware for the first time in over forty-eight hours, I pulled myself into an upright position, ignored the shooting pain in my thighs, and reached for my phone off the nightstand. Thankfully, someone had had the good sense to put it on charge for me.

Ignoring the plate of food the nurses had left on my bed tray, I blinked the sleep from my eyes and scrolled through the million missed calls and texts I had received since my life had fallen apart late Friday evening.

Four missed calls and one voicemail from Coach Dennehy.

*Jesus . . .*

I shuddered at the thought of what he had to say to me.

Deciding against being a masochist, I quickly moved on, checking through the others instead.

Three texts from Feely. Five calls from Hughie. A couple of dozen messages in the group text from the lads at The Academy. A million more from the lads from school. My physiotherapist. One from Scott Hogan, one of my buddies at Royce. My P.T. Several more from lads I played with at the club in Ballylaggin. Many more from unknown numbers, or numbers I didn't have saved in my contacts list. Two from Mr. Twomey, the principal at Tommen. One from Coach Mulcahy. Seven texts and twelve missed calls from Bella.

"Fucking Bella." Frustrated, I ignored the voicemails and read through the countless *get-well* messages, deleting each one as I went until I was left with a blank screen.

Nothing from Shannon.

Not one measly text message.

Fair enough, she didn't have a phone right now, but Joey did and he had my number.

Pissed off, I scrolled down my contacts, found the name *Joey the hurler,* and pressed call. The anger inside of me increased with every ring that went unanswered. When I was connected to his voicemail, I felt like I was two seconds off exploding.

Drugged up or not, I knew I'd called him at least a dozen times over the weekend – I remembered that much – and being ignored didn't sit well with me.

"Joey." Gripping my phone with more force than necessary, I strived to keep my tone neutral even though I was peppering with anger. "I need to talk to her." I didn't give a shite how he interpreted this. I didn't give a fuck what anyone thought anymore. I had a niggling feeling in the pit of my stomach, one that no amount of sleep or hospital drugs could dissipate. "Listen . . ." Clenching my eyes shut, I attempted to be diplomatic and failed miserably, "I know there's something fucked up going on." *Nice one, Johnny.* "That sounds nuts. I know. I *know*, okay. But I've got this terrible feeling." Jesus, I was a headcase. "Shannon said something to me, or I dreamt she said something to me, but it's stuck in my head and I can't . . . look, I'm not even sure anymore, but I need to talk to her. I need to clear some shite up, okay? So just answer my fucking calls—"

A beep sounded in my ear, letting me know that I had run out of time.

"Asshole," I grumbled and then dropped my phone on my lap only to flinch in pain at the contact. Gingerly, I removed my phone, placing it back on my nightstand before lifting the covers, pulling back my hospital gown, and taking my first sober, clear-headed look at the damage.

*Hmm.* I tilted my head to one side studying myself. *Not bad.*

My hips, both thighs, and groin were all swollen, ugly and bruised, with bandages covering the parts of me that had been cut open, but my three favorite body parts were still very much in one piece, so to speak. My dick was there and my balls were keeping it company.

Frowning, I studied myself, feeling oddly violated that someone had shaved my balls without permission, but decided against being pissed about this. I was sporting an impressive semi, probably due to the excitement of still being in one piece, so I was taking this as a win.

*Thank you, Jesus.*

Covering myself back up, I exhaled a sigh of relief and pulled the tray laden down with food towards me, feeling my appetite return with a vengeance.

*You're okay*, I continued to mentally chant to myself as I chowed down on a rasher, *you'll heal, you'll get back on the pitch, and everything will be okay.*

*But she won't be*, a small voice in the back of my head hissed, *and you know why.*

Tearing viciously into another rasher, I continued to dwell and mull over every moment I had spent with Shannon Lynch from the day I knocked her out with my ball to the moment I sent her away from this room.

I figured it was a coping mechanism. Avoiding my feelings about my impending therapy and prospect of losing out on the U20's. I couldn't think about rugby right now. If I did, there was a very good chance I would have a meltdown, therefore I locked my focus on Shannon Lynch, obsessing about every teeny, tiny, insignificant detail until I was sure I would explode.

*Something's wrong.*

*Something's wrong and you know it.*

*Open your fucking mind and* think*!*

Dropping my fork and knife, I shoved the tray away and reached for my phone again. Redialing Joey's number, I clutched the phone and prayed for an answer. My anxiety was festering inside of me to the point where I couldn't think beyond anything other than her. When I was greeted with his voicemail again, I lost it.

"Listen, fucker, I know you're getting my messages, so you can either answer your bleeding phone or text me back. I'm not going away until I talk to her. Do you hear me? I'm not going the fuck away—"

"Morning, love," Mam chirped as she walked into my hospital room, interrupting me from the one-way conversation I was having with Joey Lynch's voicemail. "How's your penis today?"

*Give me strength . . .*

"Call me back," I muttered before ending the call and gaping at my mother.

"I brought you some flowers," she continued without waiting for an answer, setting a bouquet of I had no idea what the hell they were called on my bed tray. "You've been so upset." Smiling, she padded over to my bed and fussed with my blankets. "I thought these might cheer you up."

"*How's my penis?*" Gripping the sheets around me, I yanked them up to my chest, not trusting that she wouldn't pull them off and check for herself. "Do you think that's a normal thing to ask your son?"

Mam shrugged. "Would you prefer if I called it a willy, love?"

Jesus Christ.

"Well, I'm not six years old, Ma, so no, I wouldn't prefer that," I bit out, eyeing her warily as she hovered at the side of my bed. "And it's fine."

Mam worried her lip. "Are you sure—"

"I'm sure!" I snapped, batting her hand away when she, like I had predicted, tried to pull down my blanket. "Christ, Ma, we've talked about this before. You need to start respecting my boundaries!"

Huffing out a breath, Mam sank down on the edge of my bed and patted my cheek. "Will you at least show your father?" She gave me a pleading look. "I'm so worried."

"There's nothing to worry about," I grumbled. "It's fine. I'm fine. We're both fucking fine, Ma. I'm in a hospital, you know."

"Yes, but—"

"Trust me, I'm fine." I gave her a thumbs up. "It's all good, Ma."

Mam sighed heavily. "Honestly, I don't know if I'll ever trust another word that comes out of your mouth." She bit down on her lip and gave me that horrific, wounded-mother look – the one that always cut me deep, designed to make a son feel like a piece of shit. "You really let me down, Johnny."

*Christ, twist the knife, why don't you . . .*

"I know, Ma. Christ." And I did. "I really am sorry." Knowing she wouldn't let it go until I compromised, I forced out, "So if it'll make you feel better, I'll show Da when he stops by."

Mam smiled, appeased, and I sagged back on my pillows, grateful to have dodged that particular bullet. "Were the doctors in this morning?"

I nodded. "Yeah, they were in first thing."

She looked at me expectantly. "And?"

"They're letting me home in the morning."

"That soon?"

I rolled my eyes. "It's been three days and I didn't have heart surgery."

"I know, but . . ." Concern flittered her features, "I think you should stay another few days, love. The rest will do you the world of good." She leaned over and stroked my cheek. "You're looking so much more rested as it stands. Imagine what another few days could do for you?"

"It's going to be okay," I told her, feeling like shit for putting unnecessary stress on her shoulders. "I know the rules."

"But will you follow them?" she muttered under her breath.

"I won't mess this up," I told her, looking her straight in the eye. "I won't, Ma. I'll do the bedrest. I'll do the rehab. But then I'll be going back."

Her face fell.

I steeled my spine, knowing I couldn't give into the puppy eyes.

"I don't think you should play anymore, Johnny."

"I'm going to play, Ma," I replied quietly.

"No."

"Yes, Ma."

"Johnny, please."

"I'm playing."

"I can't stand the thought of you getting hurt again."

"Ma, this is what I'm going to do," I explained, trying to keep my tone gentle. "I know it's not what you'd have chosen for me, but it's what I've chosen for myself, okay? I'm good, Ma. I'm better than good. This is what I was meant to do with my life. I can't *not* play because you're afraid I'll get hurt." I shrugged. "That could happen crossing the road."

"But it didn't happen crossing the road," Mam shot back. "Every hospital bed you've ever occupied, and there has been more of those than I can count on two hands, has been a direct result of you playing rugby." She shook her head. "I don't understand why you're so hell-bent on injuring yourself."

"You don't have to understand," I replied, knowing there was zero point in trying to explain this when she was determined to stop me from playing. "You just have to support me."

"Why couldn't you take up golf?" Mam sobbed, dropping her head in her hands. "You're good at golf, love. Or swimming, or tennis?"

I reached over and patted her shoulder. "Because I'm a rugby player."

"Oh, Johnny—"

"Just support me, Ma," I said gruffly. Sitting up straight, I pulled her in for an awkward half-hug. "And I promise, I'll make you proud."

"I'm already proud of you, ya big eejit," she sniffled, batting away her tears. "And that has nothing to do with bleeding rugby."

"Good to know," I muttered. "I think?"

"Now, enough of making your ma cry," Mam said as she forced a smile and stood up. "Tell me how you're feeling."

"I'm fine," I replied, wary again. "I just told you."

"Emotionally," she replied, pushing the tray with my food back to me. "I want to know how you're feeling in your heart." Pulling open a napkin, she set it down on my lap and poured a cup of tea from the pot. "Eat up, Johnny, love. 'Tis out of your belly your mickey grows."

"Scarred," I choked out, grabbing my fork. "I feel emotionally fucking scarred, Ma."

"Mind your language," she scolded, swatting the back of my head with that left hand I'd been dodging like the bleeding *Matrix* most of my life. "You were raised, not dragged up."

Biting my tongue, I shoved a stone-cold rasher into my mouth and chewed viciously.

"Good boy," Mam praised, ruffling my hair.

*Dear Jesus, save me.*

*Please save me from this fucking woman …*

"How's the man of the moment?" Gibsie's familiar voice filled my ears, giving me a much-needed reprieve from the woman hovering around me like a bleeding helicopter.

"Alright, lad," I replied, locking eyes on the blond eejit who had been my best friend and partner in crime since childhood, as he stood in the doorway of my hospital room.

"Good morning, Gerard," Mam chirped happily. "Did you have a nice sleep, love? I left a fresh change of clothes outside your door this morning—" Mam paused and gave Gibsie a quick once-over before smiling in approval. "Ah good, you found them. The beige goes lovely with your complexion, pet."

"I did, Mammy K," he replied with a butter-wouldn't-melt smile. "You're too good to me."

I rolled my eyes.

"Well, I'll leave you two boys to it – give you a chance to catch up." Pressing a kiss to the top of my head, Mam strolled over to the door, where she received a kiss on the cheek from Gibsie. "I'll be in the canteen if you need me."

"I love that woman," Gibsie announced when Mam was gone.

I narrowed my eyes. "Forks make good weapons, you know."

"She's so fucking—"

"You'll have no eyes left in your head if you finish that sentence," I warned, yielding my cutlery like a weapon.

Gibsie chuckled. "How are you feeling?"

"Like I got mowed down by a truck on Friday night," I grumbled, lowering my fork.

"That good, huh?"

"Don't start, Gibs." Relaxing my shoulders, I grabbed a sausage and took a bite. "I'm in a shit ton of pain and feel like I haven't slept in a month. I can't do humor today."

"Well, at least your appetite is still intact," he offered, eyeing the huge plate of rashers, sausages, and toast I was inhaling.

"Don't judge me," I grumbled. "I took a knife to the balls for this." Swallowing a mouthful of pork, I reached for a rasher. "I deserve the grease."

He grimaced. "Fair point."

"Yeah," I deadpanned, "I know."

"So?" he asked, eyeing me with barely contained excitement. "Would you say that you're back to your full senses now?"

I shrugged. "Unfortunately."

Gibsie nodded. "And your heart?"

I narrowed my eyes. "What about it?"

"It's not going boom, boom, fucking boom today?"

"No," I replied slowly, knowing I was somehow walking myself into a trap but clueless as to how. "It's fine."

"Excellent," he replied. "Because I've been sitting on more material than I can handle. It's burning a hole inside of me, lad. Seriously, I can't sleep at night with the excitement. Waiting for you to come down from your buzz was like waiting for Christmas morning – and you know how much I love Christmas, Cap."

*For fuck's sake.*

"Come on." Waving a hand, I gestured him inside. "Get it over with."

Clearly delighted with life, Gibsie barreled into the room, not stopping until he was sitting on the foot of my bed. Clearing his throat, he said, "Before I start, I need to ask your preferences on where we should hold your stag."

I gaped at him. "*What?*"

"I was thinking Kilkenny," he explained, tone light and full of humor. "But we could do Killarney if you prefer to stay closer to home."

"The fuck are you talking about?"

"Well, funny you should ask that." Grinning, he settled down on my bed and began to spur more shite at me than I could take in. "You're engaged, or maybe you're betrothed. I'm not sure of the terminology – although, according to you, you're already married."

I stared blankly back at him. "Come again?"

"Ah, lad." He threw his head back and laughed. "You really don't remember?"

"Look at me." Dropping my fork on the plate, I pointed to my face. "Does this look like the face of a person who knows what's going on?"

My response only caused him to laugh harder. "I love it," he laughed, thoroughly enjoying my discomfort. "The wait was worth it. This is the best day."

"Explain, Gibs," I snapped, flustered. "Now – before I stick you with one of these bleeding needles in my arm."

"Shannon," he snickered. "Came with me to see you Friday night."

"Yeah, I know," I growled, rubbing my forehead. "I remember that much."

"And do you remember the conversation you had with her?" he countered, eyes dancing with mischief. "With anyone who would look at you?"

"No," I bit out. "Everything from that night is a haze." I could only remember small parts of Saturday morning. Parts where I acted like a complete tool towards Shannon. I let my pride get the better of me and sent her away. After that, I'd lost my shit and panicked, demanded to be taken home. My pain had been so severe that I'd been given enough meds to knock me out. "What did I do?"

"It's not what you did," he snickered. "It's what you *said*."

"Gibs, I swear to Christ, if you don't tell me what's going on—"

"Lad, you told her you were in love with her," he laughed, slapping his hand against his thigh. "Right before you asked her to have your babies."

My eyes widened. "No!"

His grin deepened. "Yes!"

"Jesus Christ, Gibs," I hissed, voice rising higher than normal. "Why didn't you *stop* me?"

"Because it was brilliant." Laughing, he added, "I thought you were going to make her sign something you were so fucking adamant about it."

I dropped my head in my hands. "What the fuck is wrong with me?"

"No clue," Gibs chuckled. "But if I had to put money on it, I'd say you were speaking your true feelings."

"What are you *talking* about?" I gaped at him, appalled. "I don't want any bleeding babies."

Gibsie winked. "Could've fooled me."

"Stop it," I grumbled, suppressing a shudder. "You know I don't."

"You begged her."

My mouth fell open. "I didn't."

"Shannon, please have my babies!" he mimicked. "I'm begging you, Shannon. Grow my spawn and touch my dick—"

"Stop," I begged. "Please. Don't tell me anything else."

"You told the nurse she was your wife." He added salt to my wounds by saying, "You told your mother all about how nice her tits were and how you couldn't wait to fu—"

"Oh, Jesus," I choked out, cutting him off before he could ruin my life even further. "That's why she's avoiding me, isn't it?" I demanded, horrified. "She probably thinks I'm going to try and fucking impregnate her the first chance I get."

"Well, your dick *is* working now," Gibsie offered, thoroughly enjoying my torment. "A little snippet of information you decided to announce to her, *stud*."

No wonder Joey wasn't answering my calls.

If Shannon had told her brother half of what I had apparently said to her, there was no doubt he'd be waiting for me in Ballylaggin with a vendetta and a sawed-off bleeding shotgun.

"I'm so fucked," I croaked out, dropping my head.

"Nah." Slapping my shoulder, Gibsie said, "Girl loves you back. Told you so Friday night."

I groaned loudly, feeling shame in the deepest parts of my soul. "Because I coerced her."

"No, because she just does," he corrected.

"Doubtful," I grumbled. "Very fucking doubtful, lad."

"Listen, Johnny, I'm going to give it to you straight here, lad," Gibsie added, tone slightly more serious now. "You've spent months lying to yourself and everyone else about your feelings. It was too much. All of that pent-up frustration had to come out of you sooner or later." Shrugging, he added, "The anesthesia and morphine just helped the process along – forced the truth out of you."

"I'm not," I denied, knowing it was pointless, but feeling like I needed something to cling onto. "I didn't mean any of that."

Gibsie arched a brow. "Don't piss down my back and tell me it's raining."

My shoulders slumped in defeat. "Yeah, okay, I meant it. Happy now?"

"Are *you*?" he asked, unblinking.

"Am I what?"

"Happy?"

"No, I'm not *happy*, Gibs." I glared at him. "Look at me," I demanded, slapping my chest for emphasis. "I'm bleeding *terrified*!"

"About your dick?"

"My dick, my balls, the girl, the game—" I paused and exhaled a shaky breath, "I'm losing my fucking mind here." Pushing the tray away, I slumped back on my pillows and sighed. "And I'm worried."

"Understandable," he agreed. "But you're going to be fine—"

"About *her*," I reiterated with a pained growl. "I'm worried about *her*, Gibs."

"Why?"

"She said something to me the other night," I admitted, feeling at a loss. "And I can't remember." Running a hand through my hair, I confided in my best friend the doubts I was having. "It was something about her da, lad." Grimacing, I tried to snatch up the memory but it continued to float just out of my reach. Frustrated, I let out a sigh. "I think . . . " Stopping short, I pinched the bridge of my nose, knowing that once it was said, I couldn't take it back.

"You think?" Gibsie coaxed.

"This stays between us," I warned him.

He nodded. "Always, lad."

Releasing another sigh, I sat up and brushed my hair back with both hands, feeling restless and uneasy. "I've been seeing things," I slowly began, watching him carefully, testing out his loyalty even though I knew I didn't have to.

"Dead people?"

"Fuck right off!"

"Okay, okay, I'm sorry," he coaxed, sobering his features. "Tell me."

I stared hard at him, waiting until his face was void of amusement before continuing. "On her."

His brows furrowed. "On her?"

Dropping my hands to my lap, I fidgeted restlessly. "On her body."

Guiltily, I looked up at him and blurted, "Too many things that have happened too many times and are too coincidental to be explained away as an accident."

Gibsie's eyes narrowed as awareness dawned on him. "Things like bruises?"

I nodded slowly.

"Where?"

"Everywhere." I released a pained sigh. "All over her body, Gibs."

"Shit."

"At first, I thought she was being bullied again—" I paused and scrunched my nose up, feeling like a piece of shit for breaking her confidence, but this was eating me up. "She had a shitty time at BCS, Gibs. A real fucking bad time, lad. So, I fixed it – or at least I thought I had, but . . . "

"But?"

"But I know it's *more* than that, Gibs. I know I'm sounding like a madman, but this is real to me. I know there's something going on. I remember her telling me something the other night," I growled, furious with myself for not retaining the crucial piece of the jigsaw. Because I knew in my bones I was missing something vitally important. "And now I think I've figured it out."

"You have?" Gibsie asked, sounding more serious than I'd ever heard him speak. "You've got a name?"

Nodding slowly, I looked him in the eyes, begging him to not judge me for saying what I was about to say. There was a chance that I was off the mark – a huge, colossal, Grand Canyon-sized chance, but I didn't think so, and the risk was worth her safety.

"I think it's her da, Gibs." Swallowing down my uncertainty, I looked my best friend straight in the eyes and said, "I think Shannon's father is abusing her."

I was a mathematician by nature and the common denominator in every problem I tried to solve regarding Shannon Lynch was her father.

She'd said father.

She'd told me that.

I *knew* she had.

She'd told me something about her fucking father.

I just couldn't be certain.

For days, my mind had reeled, going back over every single conversation I'd had with her, trying to find something I knew I was missing.

No matter what I did, or how hard I thought about it, my mind kept returning to that first day, to the conversation we'd had when she'd been only semi-aware of what she was saying:

*"Here." I trailed my finger over the old mark. "What's this from?"*

*"My dad," she replied, breathing out a heavy sigh.*

*"My dad's going to kill me," she continued to choke out, clutching her torn skirt. "My uniform's ruined."*

*"Johnny," she groaned and then winced. "Johnny. Johnny. Johnny. This is bad . . . "*

*"What?" I urged. "What's bad?"*

*"My dad," she whispered.*

If I was wrong about this, and there was a huge chance that I was, she would never forgive me. I figured I was already in the doghouse over the way I'd acted, but accusing her father of abusing her would be the nail in the potential coffin for us.

*You've probably already fucked yourself over there, too, Johnny, lad . . .*

Fuck.

I was losing my bleeding mind as my brain concocted up the most depraving, disgusting, inhuman, drug-induced thoughts.

Was Shannon's father hurting her?

Was I being ridiculous?

I was ashamed of thinking the thoughts I had, but they were there, in my head, loud and proud and driving me batshit with anxiety.

Was he abusing her?

Was that what was happening?

I'd never met the guy, but surely her brother or mother would have stepped in.

I'd met Shannon's mother once; granted it wasn't the friendliest of encounters, but the woman genuinely seemed to love her daughter.

She looked well.

Healthy and pregnant.

Her brother was strong and fit.

Her other brothers were practically babies.

That left the dad.

"Fuck." Gibsie shook his head. "That's a big accusation, Johnny, lad."

"I know," I groaned, feeling thoroughly disgusted. "And I know if I'm wrong, then I'll be opening a huge ass can of worms, but I just . . . " I shook my head and clenched my fists. "I can't get it out of my head. I think that's what happened to me," I added. "Why I lost my shit all weekend. I was trying to go home *to her*, Gibs. Because I'm scared *for her*." I shrugged, feeling helpless. "I know it's a hunch, but I can't sit back on this, Gibs. I can't ignore this or pretend it's not happening. Something's happening to her and I'm not prepared to sit back and do nothing." I exhaled a ragged breath. "She means too much to me to brush this under the carpet. Even if I'm wrong, it's worth checking, right? That's the right thing to do here, isn't it?"

"Just give me a minute to process this." Leaning forward, Gibsie pressed his fingers to his temples. "This is a lot to take in, lad."

No shit.

Meanwhile, I couldn't sit still. Pain was consuming me but my thoughts were worse, plaguing me to the point that I was a restless bundle of nerves and anxiety.

Something was wrong.

I could feel it.

"I need to go," I announced, unwilling to wait for him to process a damn thing. "I'm serious, Gibs. You need to get me out of here, lad. I need to go home and check."

"You can't walk out of the hospital on a hunch," Gibsie shot back, glaring at me. "Christ, Johnny, you can't even walk without help. How do you propose I smuggle you down to Cork, ya langer? Under my fucking jumper?"

"Something's happening to her, Gibs," I strangled out, feeling my heart hammer against my chest. "I can feel it in my bones."

"Hold up a sec, I've got an idea—" Pausing, Gibsie pulled his phone out of his pocket and clicked a few buttons before placing it on loud-speaker and setting it down on the bed between us.

"Hello?" Claire's voice filled the silence after three short rings.

"Claire-bear," Gibsie replied, holding out a hand towards me, gesturing for me to stay quiet when I opened my mouth to ask him what the hell he thought he was doing.

"Gerard." Relief filled her tone as she spoke. "Are you okay? How's Johnny?"

Keeping his eyes on me, Gibs ignored her questions and asked, "Why didn't you tell me?"

"T-tell you what?" Claire asked, sounded worried.

"About Shannon's father."

"What the fuck!" I mouthed, ready to kill him.

"Wait," he mouthed back, holding a hand up to keep me back. "Trust me."

"What are you t-talking about?" was Claire's hesitant response.

"You know exactly what I mean," he bluffed, slapping a hand over my mouth.

"She told Johnny, didn't she?" Claire sobbed. "Oh god, and he told you."

My heart stopped dead in my chest.

My entire world collapsed.

I was right.

I was fucking right!

"Yeah, she told him," Gibsie said, sounding furious. "What I want to know is why *you* didn't tell anyone, Claire?"

"I didn't know for sure," she hurried to say, sounding devastated. "She never confirmed anything, but all the bruises . . . I knew he was doing something to her. I was afraid, Gerard. I was scared, okay?"

And then it hit me like a goddamn freight train.

*"Who's hurting you, baby? I'll fix it."*

*"It's a secret."*

*"I won't tell."*

*"My father."*

Moving on instinct, I grabbed my phone off the nightstand and ripped off my covers. Sliding out of bed, I hobbled towards the bathroom door with 999 already dialed.

"Johnny, what are you doing, lad?" Gibsie called after me.

"The right thing," I hissed, furious.

"Should we talk to your dad first?" he asked. Climbing off the bed, he moved towards me. "He's the barrister, lad, and we don't know what's—"

Holding a hand up to ward Gibs off, I pressed my phone to my ear and concentrated on the operator's voice. "999, what is your emergency?"

"My girlfriend's in danger," I hissed down the line, losing the fight to control my emotions. "She's only sixteen years old. She's a minor and she needs your help. She lives at 95 Elk Terrace in Ballylaggin, County Cork, okay? Did you get that? 95 Elk Terrace. She's really small, okay? Fucking tiny. She can't defend herself and I can't get to her—" Trembling from head to toe, I pressed my forehead against the cool tiles in the bathroom, clenched my jaw, and growled, "I need you to send someone over to the house right away because her scumbag father has been beating the shite out of her."

"Well," Gibsie said grimly from the bathroom doorway when I had ended the call. Folding his arms across his chest, he gave me a nod of approval. "You are the definition of the cat amongst the pigeons."

"Christ, Gibs." Exhaling a ragged breath, I pressed the heel of my hand to my forehead and hissed, "How did I not see this?"

"In all fairness, lad, how were you supposed to?" Gibsie offered with a sigh. "Look at your parents, Johnny. Hell, I'd put money on John having never raised a hand to you before."

*True.*

"Exactly," Gibsie filled in, reading my thoughts. "It's hard to imagine something like that happening when it's so beyond the scale of normal for you that it's pretty much incomprehensible."

"It didn't click," I choked out, wrestling with the huge tsunami of guilt rising up inside of me. "I just . . . I didn't see this in my head."

"Listen, I texted your dad," he replied. "He's on the way, Johnny, lad. He'll help us."

"Good," I replied, tone clipped, as I tried to catch my breath and process this. "I'm going to need him to take my case when I go down for murder."

"Think he'll represent me, too?" Gibsie asked. Shrugging, he added, "When you're embarking on hell, it's always good to have a buddy."

# I'm Your Brother

## SHANNON

When I opened my eyes again, the first thing that assaulted my senses was the sunshine beaming in from the window, mixing in with the sound of beeping monitors, and bringing with it a throbbing in my brain.

*Thud. Thud. Thud.*

Confused, I looked for Johnny, but came up empty.

*He wasn't here.*

Panicking, I patted the mattress, twisting my head from side to side as I tried to scope out Mr. and Mrs. Kavanagh or Gibsie.

"Hey – hey, it's okay." A large hand wrapped around mine. "I'm here."

"Joe?" I croaked out anxiously, feeling my heart race at a hundred miles an hour, as I desperately sought him out. "Joe?"

"Shh, take it easy," a vaguely familiar male voice replied. "I'm right here, Shannon."

Rejecting the stranger's voice, I shook my head and reached for the wires in my nose. "Joey?" I croaked out, voice barely more than a hoarse whisper. Yanking the wires free, I inhaled a deep breath, gasping for precious air, something my brain demanded I do. The minute I did, pain seared through my entire chest and I cried out, my hands automatically moving to my side.

My *bandaged* side?

Startled at the contact, I pulled at the gown I was draped in to reveal a white bandage strapped between the left side of my ribcage and my breast. What the hell was happening to me? "Oh god, Joey—"

"Relax." A hand moved to cup my chin and I clenched my eyes shut, body turning to stone in the bed, as fear spiraled inside of me. "Take some nice, slow breaths."

*Relax, it's a gentle touch*, I slowly registered, but I couldn't be certain of anything anymore.

Struggling to remain in control and not let the panic consume me, I drew in short, slow breaths, flinching when my chest burned in protest. My head was throbbing so hard it felt like it was going to burst. I raised my free hand to hold my forehead, only to freeze when my fingers grazed what felt like gauze on my cheek.

And then I remembered.

*Dad.*

Dread seized my heart, my pulse rising erratically, as memories of my father beating me, beating Joey, hitting Tadhg, hurting Mam, all filled my mind in one fell swoop.

Was he here?

Was he close by?

Was I in trouble?

"It's okay," the voice continued to say, tone soft and coaxing. "You're in the hospital, but you're safe now, okay? Nobody is going to hurt you."

Safe now.

I felt like laughing at the empty promise.

Words.

All words.

Reluctantly, I tore my eyes open and just laid there, ice-cold and heart frozen, as I stared up at the man looking down at me.

"Hey, kid," he said, voice familiar and warm like Christmas morning. "It's been awhile."

I didn't respond.

I couldn't.

Instead, I just stared back at him.

Exhaling a shaky breath, he released my chin and reached for my hand again.

I quickly snatched it away, not wanting his touch.

Not wanting anything to do with his touch.

"Where's Joey?" I asked when I finally found my voice again. It didn't sound like it belonged to me. It was cracked and hoarse, but the words were coming from my lips, so I pushed on. "I need to talk to Joey." I needed to know what I was supposed to say if someone asked me what happened. *I didn't know the story.* "Is he here?" Kicking off the covers holding me to the bed, I scrambled up the mattress until my back was aligned with the metal headboard, and dragged in another pained breath. Ignoring the fire in my chest, I glanced around the bright room, wary and fearful. "I really need Joey, please."

"Shannon, you need to calm down—"

"I need *Joey*," I croaked out, flinching away when he tried to touch me.

"I'm here, Shannon." Blue eyes so similar to mine implored me to understand something I never could. "I'm coming home. For good."

"I don't care," I said, voice void of all emotion, as I wrestled with my anxiety. "I need my brother."

"I'm your brother, too," he said sadly.

"No." I shook my head, refuting his claims. "You left us there. You're not my—"

"Shan!" Joey's voice filled my ears, followed by the sound of a door banging loudly. "I told you to stay the fuck away from her." Stalking into the room like someone wired to NASA, Joey shouldered Darren out of the way and sank down on the edge of my bed. "She just woke up, asshole," he added, knees bobbing restlessly as he fussed with the blankets around my feet, covering up my bare legs. "The last thing she needs is another fucking drama."

"Joe." My hands shot out of their own accord, steadying his jittering arm. "What's happening?"

The moment my eyes landed on his face, I let out a pained sob. The skin below his eyes was black and blue, his nose was clearly broken again, and his bottom lip busted and swollen.

"Oh, Joe." Reaching up, I brushed his hair off his face, revealing two bloodshot eyes with pupils so dilated the green in his eyes was almost absent. Fear enveloped me. I knew what those bloodshot and blackened eyes represented and it wasn't one of our father's beatings. It represented something much worse, something I thought he had gotten a handle on last year. "Tell me you didn't—"

"Don't worry about it," he hurried to say, tone gruff, as he captured my hand and set it back down on my lap. "I'm fine."

No, he wasn't fine.

He was high.

"I'm *fine*, Shannon," Joey repeated, giving me a look that told me to *drop it*.

Clasping my hands together, I remained silent, swallowing down a million unspoken words to join the others festering inside of me. "What's going on?"

"You're okay," Joey said, twisting around to face me, giving me his full attention. "You've been in and out of it for two days. Docs gave you something so they could put the—" his words broke off and he flailed his hands out, shaking from head to toe "—the—" running his hands through his hair, he shook his head, and snapped his fingers. "Fuck, I can't remember the words."

"You were brought into the hospital on Saturday evening," Darren explained in a much more together tone of voice. "Today is Tuesday, Shannon. You've been in and out for a few days."

"Yeah, by me," Joey snarled, shoulders stiffening. "She was brought in here by *me*. Where the fuck were *you*, *Golden Boy*?"

"You were treated for a severe concussion and a traumatic pneumothorax," Darren continued to explain, ignoring Joey's comments. "You were pretty banged up when you got here. You've had some stitches on your cheek to close a cut and some bruised ribs."

"Bruised ribs," Joey sneered mockingly. "Open your eyes, Darren. She's bruised *everywhere*!"

"What the hell is wrong with you, Joey?" Darren demanded, glaring at my brother with narrowed eyes. "Are you high? Is that it? Did you take something?"

"Yeah, I took something," Joey shot back, turning his rage on Darren. "I took a lot of fucking beatings. That's what I took, asshole."

"Joe, relax." Anxious, I placed a hand on Joey's hand to calm him and looked to Darren. "What does a traumatic pneumothorax mean?"

"It means that bastard kicked you so hard he collapsed your lung," Joey filled in, pulsing with anger. "It means they had to shove a fucking pipe through your body to help you breathe."

"Oh god." Panic-stricken, I looked down at my body and whimpered. "Am I okay?" I placed a trembling hand over the wound. "Is that bad?"

"It's not serious," Darren hurried to console. "You didn't have surgery – they were able to relieve the pressure and help you breathe by inserting a small tube into your—"

"Not serious?" Joey demanded. "Are you fucking *kidding* me?"

"Joey," Darren growled. "*Calm down.*"

"Is there a hole?" I strangled out, peeking under my gown. "Is it still inside me?"

"No, Shannon," Darren soothed. "They removed it yesterday morning. You've had chest x-rays and CT scans. Everything looks great, okay?"

I nodded, feeling numb.

"But you'll be sore for a couple of weeks," he added with a grimace. "And you're on a course of antibiotics to prevent infection." Shaking his head, Darren added, "The nurses will explain everything better than I can."

"Really?" Joey sniped. "I thought you were great at everything."

"Whatever they prescribed you for your pain, consider it out of bounds," Darren growled, glaring at Joey. "I'm cutting you off."

Joey laughed. "Paracetamol?"

"You're not fooling anyone," Darren shot back, tone even.

"Why are you here?" I croaked out, feeling the panic lodge in my chest.

"I'm here to help, Shannon," Darren replied. "I'm here to take care of you – all of you." He cast a glance in Joey's direction and sighed. "Even you."

"Don't do me any favors," Joey spat.

"Why?" Clasping my hands together, I exhaled slowly and asked, "How did you know about what happened?"

"Mam called him," Joey replied, casting another menacing glare in

Darren's direction. "Apparently, the bitch had the bastard's number this whole time." His tone was dripping with venomous sarcasm. "They lied to us, Shan. Imagine that?"

Darren released a pained groan. "Come on, Joey, don't say that." Pinching his brow, he added, "That's our mother you're talking about—"

"Our mother?" Joey laughed humorlessly, feet bobbing restlessly. "We have one of those? Fuck, and here's me thinking mothers were mythical creatures like unicorns, because I sure as shit never met one in the flesh."

"You were in contact with Mam the whole time?" I croaked out, reeling. "For five and a half years?"

"He sure was," Joey filled in before Darren could. "Couldn't pick up the phone and check on us, but he was in close contact with Mommy dearest."

Darren shook his head. "You need to simmer down on the angst, Joe. It's not working for you."

"And you need to *not* walk back into our lives and think you can call the shots," Joey retorted, trembling with what I knew was barely restrained anger. "It doesn't work that way. You don't get to go, Darren; you don't get to walk in and out of our lives!"

*Call the shots?* "What shots?"

"Brother dearest thinks he's in charge now." Jerking to his feet, Joey paced the small room, looking like a caged wild animal. "Thinks he can walk out the door, abandon us for half a decade, and then stroll back in with his flashy car and fat wallet and lay down the law."

Darren glared at our brother. "That's not fair, Joey."

"What did you expect, *Darren*?" Joey countered, glaring. "A welcome home party? Some balloons and cake? You roll back into town and think we're going to fall at your feet because you're *saving us*?" He shook his head and sneered, "You forgot about us. You walked the fuck out. Left us with them. So as far as I'm concerned, you can keep walking. I've got this."

"You've got shit, Joey," Darren snapped. "Look at her."

"Look at *you*," Joey shot back, furious. Clapping his hands, he added,

"Nice fucking suit, Darren. You look well. Nicely groomed and well fed. Good for you." Glowering, he raised a hand and gestured to himself and then me. "Congrats on the success, big brother."

"I was eighteen," Darren whispered, running a hand through his dark hair. "I couldn't deal."

"Yeah, well I'm eighteen, too, asshole," Joey spat unsympathetically. "And guess what? I stepped up and *dealt*. I stayed!"

"Then you're a stronger man than I am."

"I'm not stronger than you," Joey strangled out, voice breaking. "I just happen to possess a conscience."

"Stop," I pleaded, clutching my head with my hands. "Please just stop fighting. I can't deal with this."

"I'm sorry." Darren ran a hand through his hair, clearly exasperated. "Can you tone it down for her sake, Joey? We need to explain this to her and fighting with each other isn't going to help."

Joey bared his teeth and gave Darren the middle finger, but he managed to keep his opinions to himself.

"Dad's gone, Shannon," Darren explained in a calm tone.

An emotion that felt suspiciously like hope washed through me. "He is?"

"He's not gone," Joey piped up. "He's hiding. Big difference."

And there went my hope.

"Can you give it a rest?" Darren growled.

"Can you not give her false hope?" Joey countered hotly. "It won't do her any fucking good in the long run."

"For now," Darren was quick to add, casting a warning glare in Joey's direction. "The Guards will find him and he'll go down for this, guys. I'll make sure of it."

"Sure, you will," Joey sneered. "*Saint Darren* to the rescue." Twisting his neck from side to side, he drummed his fingers on the mattress, clearly frustrated. "The justice system is a fucking joke in this country and we all know it. Even when they do find him, chances are that he'll get a suspended sentence, a slap on the wrist, and a bottle of whiskey, courtesy of the social welfare, for his troubles and you're lying to yourself if you believe any different."

"I went to court with Mam yesterday," Darren pushed on, ignoring Joey's comments. "We applied for a safety order against him. There'll be a hearing in three weeks' time, one he'll be expected to attend, but we were issued with a temporary protection order against him. He's barred from the house, from making contact with any of you."

"He should be done for attempted fucking murder," Joey spat.

"I agree," Darren replied. "I want him gone, too, Joe. I hate him just as much as you do."

"Doubtful," Joey sneered. "Very fucking doubtful."

Darren sighed heavily. "You want to do this, Joe? Have a competition over who had it hardest? Or do you want to get this family back on track?"

"There is *no* family," Joey countered heatedly. "That's what you're missing."

"We're still a family," Darren said quietly. "And we'll be a stronger one if we're all united."

"With her," Joey strangled out, looking truly distressed. "Finish what you started," he demanded. "We'll be stronger with *her*." He shook his head and laughed humorlessly. "What a fucking joke."

"Where is she?" I asked nervously.

"At home with Nanny and your brothers."

My heart sank. "*Why*?"

"Why?" Darren frowned. "What do you mean why?"

"I mean why is she still *here*?" I strangled out, fisting the sheets beneath me.

"Finally!" Joey chorused, throwing his hands up in the air. "Finally, someone gets it!"

"She's as much of a victim as any of us," Darren said slowly. "I know you guys don't feel that way right now, and I completely get that, but you have to understand that she's been through—"

"Bullshit," Joey sneered. "Bull-fucking-shit, Darren! She's not a victim. She's an enabler. She enabled him to do this." He pointed to where I was sitting. "She's as much to blame for Shannon being in here as he is."

"Joey, come on."

"No." Joey shook his head. "Maybe she was a victim the first time he put his hands on her. Hell, maybe the first ten. I'll give her that. She was young and thick. But twenty-four *years*?" He shook his head. "No, she did this to us, Darren. She had a hand in this."

"Have you ever thought about why there's so many of us? Why she kept having children with that man? Why she wouldn't leave?" Darren snapped, glaring at the both of us. "Or why she's all fucked up in the head like she is? Have you ever thought maybe she stayed because she was terrified he would follow through on his threats? We've all heard the 'I'll kill you and the children if you leave me' speech he's been feeding her – since she was *fifteen* year's old! For Christ's sake, that man spent two decades breaking her down and telling her that he would kill her if she left! Don't you think that might have fucked her up in the head? Did you ever consider that she was there against her will? Having children against her will? Being raped and beaten and mentally abused to the point where she lost touch with reality? She was fifteen year's old when she had me – fourteen when she was pregnant!" he added. "Think about that for a minute. Think about how fucking frightened she must have been when she was thrown into a life with that monster. She doesn't have a mother or father to show her the way. All she had in the whole fucking world was him. She was a baby having babies and it broke her!"

"I don't want to hear it," Joey barked. "I'm not listening to any more excuses."

"Have either of you ever thought about why she voluntarily put us into care?" Darren pressed, tone hard. "Well, have you?"

"She was *sick*," Joey sneered.

"She wasn't sick," Darren snarled. "She was trying to get us away from him. She was trying to save us from something she couldn't save herself from."

"Then why didn't she leave us there?" Joey roared. "Maybe we would have had a fighting fucking chance."

"You *know* why," Darren shot back, shaking now. "You know!" He inhaled several calming breaths before continuing. "She was afraid that it would happen to you, too. She was scared and pregnant with Tadhg—"

"So, because you got raped, we got brought home to be tortured?" Joey demanded. "Is that it? Two wrongs make a right? Because that's some fucked up logic, if you ask me."

"Joey!" I strangled out. "Don't!"

"I'm *sorry* that happened to him," Joey said. "I'm so fucking sorry that happened to you, Darren, I really am. But I got punished for it." He waved a hand between us. "We all did."

"It's okay, Joe," I coaxed, desperate to comfort him. "Don't get upset."

"It's not okay!" he strangled out. "Jesus Christ, I should have taken you all out of that house years ago. I should have called it in. I knew this would happen—" His voice cracked and he dragged in a harsh breath. "But they *scared* me – made me doubt myself!" He glared at Darren. "You *terrorized* me into believing that living with him was better than what was out there." Tears burned in his green eyes but he blinked them away. "I had the best six months of my life with that family. So did she—" he pointed a finger at me. "We were happy with that family. We were safe! But you and Mam convinced me there was danger, that it was safer at home." Slamming the heel of his hand against his forehead, he hissed, "I was six years old and you fucked my head so bad that I can't trust *anything* now. I can't even trust my own fucking instincts."

"I was afraid of it happening to you," Darren strangled out. "I thought I was doing the right thing. I was trying to keep you *safe*—"

"By *terrorizing* me! You made me believe you and you *left*!" Joey roared, shaking from head to toe. "You made me trust you! I was twelve and you walked out that door and dropped it all on my shoulders. And then *I* terrorized them! I told them all the same shit you told me, filled them up with all the same fears and paranoia, because that's all I knew. And look at us now!"

"I'm sorry for leaving you, Joe." Shuddering, Darren dropped his head. "But I had to go—"

"Yeah, and I'm sorry for believing you!" Shaking violently, Joey hissed, "I won't make the same mistake twice."

There was a long stretch of silence before Darren spoke again. "Look," he said gruffly, "I don't have all the answers for you guys, but I know I can't turn my back on our mother."

"I can," Joey offered tersely. "Easily."

"For the first time in her life, she is fighting back," Darren bit out. "She is *trying* to do the right thing by us. She's not a bad person and you both know that. She's a frightened woman who let her fears make terrible decisions for her."

"Her bad decisions nearly killed us," Joey shot back. "They put my sister in a hospital bed."

"Our *father* put our sister in a hospital bed," Darren corrected. "Don't let your anger cloud your logic, Joey."

"I'm not doing this," Joey hissed, throwing his hands up. "I'm not. I'm not going to listen to you justify her reasons for letting that bastard do this to us."

"All I'm saying is that it's not all black and white," Darren replied before turning back to me. "The Gardaí will be here later on in the day to take your statement. You'll either need Mam or me to be present with you when that happens."

"No." Anxiety was churning inside of me, festering away at all that was good and pure until I was nothing but a trembling mess. "I don't want to do this."

"It's okay," Darren said gently. "We'll talk it through and you'll have nothing to worry about."

"It can be me if you want, Shan," Joey interjected. "Doesn't have to be them."

"The last thing you need is to be around Gardaí in your condition," Darren growled. "What was it this time? Are you back on the—"

"Glad to hear your special phone calls with Mam kept you in the family loop," Joey spat. "Pity she didn't tell you about the *actual* problems we were having – oh wait, she probably did, and you just went right ahead and blocked it out. Must be nice to have a conscience with an off-switch. Selective hearing must feel fucking fabulous."

"Stop," I groaned. "Please."

"There's a social worker lurking around outside," Darren announced, turning back to me and dutifully ignoring Joey. He pulled at his blue tie and popped the top button of his crisp, white shirt before continuing, "You'll have to talk to her alone, of course, but once we all have our story straight, it should be fairly straightforward."

"Our *story* straight?" Whatever ounce of self-restraint Joey had been clinging to evaporated the moment those words came out of Darren's mouth. "Fuck that!" Jerking to his feet, he began to pace the room. "No more goddamn stories." Running a hand through his blond hair, he tugged at the ends and growled. "No more."

"I'm not asking any of you to lie," Darren replied. "I'm simply saying we need to rally around Mam—"

"You're asking her to omit the truth," Joey countered. "To leave out the parts where Mam covered up what he did to us – where she stood by and watched. Where she did *nothing*. And in my book, an omission of truth is a fucking lie."

"Well, if you want to stay together, then I suggest you accept her and get with the fucking program," Darren barked, losing his cool. "Because this is how I keep you guys together, okay? If we don't have her, if she's seen as anything other than what she is – a victim of domestic violence who did her best for her children – then Shannon, Ollie, Tadhg, and Sean might as well pack their bags now. And god knows where they'll send you. It'll be new schools, new homes, new friends, new fucking strangers. If you want that, then go right ahead and fight me on this, but it doesn't have to be that way. We can make this work, guys."

"I can't." Joey walked over and gripped the windowsill with so much force, I was surprised he didn't tear it off. "I can't *do this* anymore," he muttered to himself. "I can't keep living like *this*."

"Joe," I croaked out. "It's okay—"

"No," his voice cracked. "No, Shan," he whispered, keeping his back to me. "It's really not."

"We have another issue," Darren added, breaking the palpable tension.

Tearing my eyes off Joey's back, I looked back to Darren. "What?"

"Johnny Kavanagh."

Joey grunted in what sounded like approval.

"Wh-what?" Shaking my head, I fought down the tsunami of butterflies trying to claw their way out of my throat. "What does Johnny have to do with any of this?"

"Fucker figured it out on his own," Joey muttered to himself, keeping his back to us. "Must be worth something after all."

"He's making a right nuisance of himself," Darren confirmed grimly. "Calling the Garda station morning, noon, and night. He's had four Garda cars out to the house since yesterday."

"Wh-what?" Now I did clutch my temples as the throbbing in my brain threatened to kill me. "How does he know?"

"Don't worry, Shan. It's a good thing he knows," Joey piped up. "You don't have to lie for these people anymore."

"Can you just shut the hell up?" Darren snapped. "I'm trying to fix this and you're not helping matters."

"Because this isn't fixable," Joey tossed back. "I know it, Shannon knows it – Christ, even Sean knows it, and he's three!"

"I don't know what you told your boyfriend, Shannon, but you need to make him stop," Darren stated, turning his attention back to me. "He's interfering in something he knows nothing about."

"I haven't told him anything," I breathed, heart racing at the thought of Johnny. "And he's not my—"

"You're barking up the wrong tree if you think you'll keep her fella quiet," Joey scoffed. "Not everyone can be put in a box, Darren."

"Joey, for the love of god, can you just stop talking!" Darren snarled. "If you're not here to help, then go home."

"Fine, I'll go," Joey hissed. "Because I'm having no part in this." Swinging around, he glared at Darren. "If you want to lie and fuck these kids up further by keeping that woman in their lives, then go right ahead, I clearly can't stop you, but I'm done being a pawn in this game. I've done my time."

"It's not a game, Joey," Darren growled. "This is our lives."

"Then I don't want this life," Joey strangled out, face flushed. "If this is how we have to live, then I don't want to be *here*."

"Joe—"

"I'll see ya later, Shan," Joey croaked out before stalking towards the door. "I'm out."

I watched, frozen to the bed, as Joey stormed out, letting the door slam shut behind him. I didn't want him to go. Being left alone with Darren was the last thing I wanted to happen; not because I feared him, but because I didn't know him. He was a man now; a man who, by the look of his designer suit and expensive-looking watch, I had very little in common with.

"What are you now?" I asked, disappointed with myself for allowing my curiosity to get the better of me. With my wire-clad hand, I gestured to his clothes. "What do you do?"

Darren leaned back in his chair, eyes locked on mine. "I work for an international IT company." Shifting in his chair, he pulled on his tie again. "I'm based in their Belfast branch."

"So, that's where you've been?" I breathed, swallowing down the pain. "All this time and you've been a six-hour car drive away?"

"Yeah." He nodded slowly and then stopped. "Well, no, I spent the first four years in Birmingham, getting my degree and working an apprenticeship. I moved to Belfast in late 2003."

"Oh." I wasn't sure what else to say so I remained quiet. In truth, I wasn't sure there was anything else *to* say. He left. We stayed. His life improved. Ours worsened. End of story.

"I had to get out, Shannon," he added quietly.

I knew that.

But so did we.

"Did it get better for you?" I heard myself ask. I glanced up at him. "Did you find peace?"

Darren hesitated before saying, "I found a way to cope."

Exhaling shakily, I nodded. "Good."

"I have a partner," he offered, sounding a little uncertain. "His name is Alex. We've been together three years. We share a small apartment on the outskirts of the city center."

"Does he love you?" I asked.

Darren nodded. "Yeah, he loves me, Shan."

"I'm glad." Dropping my gaze to my hands, I cracked my knuckles and tried to find the right words. "I was always on your side." My voice was small. "I wanted you to be happy – to find someone who loves you. I never cared about whether that was a boy or a girl. I always wanted you to know that." I shrugged helplessly. "I was afraid you didn't."

"Shannon," Darren said with a sigh, "I didn't want to leave you behind."

"But you did, Darren," I whispered, forcing myself not to blink. "You *did* leave us behind."

"Do you hate me?"

"No." I sighed. "But I don't know who are you anymore." I lifted my gaze to meet his. "And you don't know me, either."

"I know who you are, Shannon," he said, voice trembling. "You're my baby sister who loves to sing and dance and read – and you're smart. You're so smart, Shannon. You've got the best school marks out of all of us. You love to play basketball. You love animals. Your favorite color is pink. You're always bringing home injured animals and birds and nursing them back to health. You want to go to University College Dublin to study be a veterinarian, and your ultimate ambition in life has always been to travel the world."

"I don't sing anymore and I don't dance. My favorite color is green and I haven't picked up a basketball since he stuck a knife through mine for bouncing it against the side of the house. I stopped bringing home animals a long time ago because I realized I didn't want them to be caged with me – when I realized they were safer in the wild than with me. I'm not going to go to college and become a vet because I've failed every single one of my classes for the last three years." I kept my gaze trained on his as I spoke. "Even if, by some miraculous intervention, I managed to pull my school marks up and pass my exams, I'm not naïve enough to believe I could ever afford to go to college. I don't want to travel the world anymore, and my ultimate ambition is to survive." He flinched but I forced myself to finish. "The girl you remember is gone, Darren. I'm not her anymore. Whatever I used to be, he beat it out of me a long time ago."

"I'm sorry, Shannon," was all he said.

"Yeah." I sighed. "I'm sorry, too, Darren."

"We need to talk about what's going to happen next," he said after a long pause. His tone was hesitant, his eyes wary. "It's important."

Swallowing deeply, I nodded. "Okay."

"Do you trust me?"

"No."

Darren flinched. "I deserve that."

"It's not about what you deserve," I croaked out, voice raspy. "It's how I feel."

"Fair enough," he mumbled, rubbing his jaw. "But social services are breathing down Mam's neck. You know what that means."

Yeah, I did.

I wasn't entirely sure I cared anymore, but I definitely knew what it meant for *us*.

"I'm prepared to move back home and take care of you guys until Mam gets back on her feet and we get this whole mess cleared up. The social workers involved in the case are supportive of this arrangement and are confident enough to allow you to come home to us," Darren continued. "I've spoken to Alex and he understands, and my boss is willing to let me work mostly from home. I will be required to make an appearance at the office once a week, but we can work around that once you guys go back to school after the Easter holidays. But none of this works without Mam. Without one decent parent in the mix. We need to support her, too, Shan. Regardless of what Joey says, we need to show a united front."

"When you say support her, what do you mean?" I wasn't sure why I asked that question when the answer was obvious.

"Basically, when they ask you about your relationship with Mam, you need to remind them that she's a good mother who tried her best for you, provided as stable a home as she could, and financially supported the five of you on her own. Tell them about how she enrolled you in Tommen when she found out you were being bullied at BCS, and how she loves you very much."

"So, you want me to lie?" I whispered.

"It's not a lie. She's a victim, too, Shannon," he said with a weary sigh. "And right now, she's about all that stands between you and the foster care system." His eyes darkened then and he looked away. "And whatever Joey says, trust me when I tell you that you don't want that."

Pain churned inside of me for all he'd been through. "Are you okay?"

He blinked at me, looking a little startled by my question. "Me?"

I nodded.

"I'm okay." He blew out a harsh breath. "I'm just worried."

"Me too," I squeezed out.

"I don't want you to go into care," he added, voice torn. "Aside from all my own issues, it's not a good place for any of you. You're doing well at Tommen. If they take you, you'll be moved to a new school and have to start all over again."

My heart seized with dread. "I want to stay at Tommen," I strangled out.

"I know," he agreed. "And I'm going to make sure you do. I'll cover the fees. I'll do whatever it takes, but I need you to support me on this."

"Joey won't." My hands shook as I spoke. "He won't live under the same roof as her, Darren. You don't know what it's been like for him."

"Joey's irrelevant in this," Darren muttered, pinching his temples. "He's over eighteen."

"That doesn't make him irrelevant," I snapped, glaring at my oldest brother. "He's the most relevant thing in our lives, *Darren*."

He sighed heavily. "I know, I know. I didn't mean it to come out like that—"

"Did you know that Sean called Joey 'Da-Da' until he was two?" I interrupted sharply. My eyes were wide and full of unshed tears, my hands balled into fists and shaking at my sides. "Sean actually thought his brother was his *daddy*. I suppose it would be an easy mistake to make, you know, considering Joey sat up most nights doing his night feeds and changing his nappies when Mam was working nights or drowning in her depression. So, go ahead and tell Sean how irrelevant Joey is. Or better still, tell Ollie and Tadhg that every time Joey slept outside their bedroom door, for fear our father would go after them, was irrelevant. Tell them about how all the beatings Joey took for them were irrelevant. Tell me how *irrelevant* the brother was who fed us when we were starving, stuck up for us when we had no one, gave us money when we needed it for school—" my voice cracked and I dragged in several deep breaths before I could continue. "Tell *me* how irrelevant he is, Darren," I strangled out, feeling the burning protest of my lungs from the sudden exertion. "Go right ahead and do it!"

"You know I didn't mean it like that," he sighed. "Of course he's not irrelevant. That was a shitty thing for me to say."

"Yeah," I strangled out, chest heaving. "It was."

"What I was trying to say is that Joey's over eighteen. Legally, he's an adult and the social workers aren't interested in him. They're concentrating on the minor children – you, Tadhg, Ollie, and Sean. He's not on their radar."

"Have you met Sean yet?" I heard myself ask, tone harder than I knew I was capable of. "Ollie got big, didn't he? Tadhg, too. What age were they when you last saw them? Three and six, wasn't it?" I knew I should stop and rein it in, but I couldn't. I was so furious that he could be so flippant with his words. It hurt to hear him call Joey *irrelevant* because I knew that was exactly how Joey was feeling when he'd stormed out earlier. "I was ten. Joey was twelve – barely older than Tadhg is now. Do you think we have changed, Darren?"

"A lot has changed," he whispered.

"Yeah, it has," I agreed, voice warbling. "And the mother that was so good to *you*, the Mam *you* remember, isn't the one *we* experienced."

"She's still your mother."

"See, you keep calling her that, but I only remember having *one* of those."

"Shannon—"

"His name is *Joey*," I choked out, fisting the sheets. "The *irrelevant* one. *He's* been our mother, Darren, when our real one checked out." Tears pooled down my cheeks as I spoke, forcing myself to get it out and for him to hear it, "When you left, something *died* inside of her. She wasn't the same. Everything went dark. You think you know, but you don't. You can't know because you didn't see . . . "

"I've seen enough, Shannon," he replied wearily. "Believe me."

"Whatever you saw, it was during a time when she was *present*," I bit out. I wasn't saying any of this to hurt him. I just needed him to *get it*. "She hasn't been present in a very long time."

"Look, I'm not going to force your hand here," he finally replied. "Whatever you want to do is your choice."

*But . . .*

"But this isn't just about you," he filled in. "Tadhg, Ollie, and Sean's futures are at stake here, too."

*So, you have no choice . . .*

"Mam is trying, Shan," he coaxed. "She's willing to do whatever it takes to make this work."

*You're trapped . . .*

"She just needs some guidance," he whispered. "So, if you just trust me and follow my lead on this, I promise you that I can give you guys a better life. You won't have to worry about him coming back because I won't let that happen ever again. And once the Guards get your statement and this goes to court, you'll never have to worry about—"

"Wh-what? I'm not going to court," I strangled out, hurrying to get there first. "I'm not going against him, Darren." I shook my head, body shaking violently. "No way."

"Shannon, he can't hurt you anymore," Darren urged. "I swear, this will be—"

"You just told me that he wasn't arrested for this," I bit out. "That means he's out there." I bit back the urge to scream and gripped the mattress. "This is bad, Darren. You don't get it, but I do. I *see*. This will all go away, she'll take him back, and then he'll make me pay for getting him into t-trouble." Sniffling, I reached up and roughly wiped away the tears from my cheeks. "Joey's right; there's no justice for people like us. He'll get a slap on the wrist – and that's if we're really lucky. No, I'm not saying anything about him."

"He has to pay, Shannon."

"Easy for you to say," I shot back, trembling. "When you're not the price."

"What?" Darren frowned. "Shannon, that makes no sense."

"Whatever, Darren, you wouldn't understand," I sniffled. "He loved you best."

Darren balked like he couldn't believe the words that had just come out of my mouth. "You couldn't be more wrong," he strangled out. "You're so fucking wrong, Shannon."

"You got *words*," I hissed defensively. "Cruel words, horrible words, things that never should have been said to you, and I am so sorry for that, but you didn't get what we got—" I had to stop and take a few steadying breaths before I could finish. "However bad you think it was when you lived at home, however many slaps you think *you* took, I promise that it got a million times worse after you left. I promise you that Joey and I took *more*."

"And neither of you got what I got," he snarled, losing his cool with me. "You got a nice little family for six months. You got ice-creams and fucking hugs. You didn't get what I got, Shannon, and be very fucking glad about that!"

I flinched at his words.

Darren dropped his head in hands. "I'm sorry."

"Yeah," I whispered. "Me, too."

# I'm Not A Liar

## JOHNNY

I had been lured into a false sense of security yesterday by the very people that had brought me into this world with promises of action. However, the minute I was helped back into my bed and the nurse was called, it became pretty clear to me that I had been duped. It became even clearer when I was told that a *good night's sleep in my own bed would clear my crazy thoughts*.

Fuckers.

Sleep didn't ease a damn thing in my mind. When I woke up this morning, it was to thoughts of Shannon and a rage so hot in my stomach that I was sure I would develop an ulcer.

My body was restless, my mind shot to hell, the entire drive home from Dublin. When we finally crossed the border and re-entered Cork, I swear, I had never been happier to return to the rebel country, which was beyond ironic considering I'd spent the last seven years plotting and scheming to get out of this place.

But things were different now.

*I* was different.

I had people to see and shit to attend to.

My first priority being Shannon.

In the past twenty-four hours, I had called the local Garda Station in Ballylaggin more times than I could count. After the seventh or eighth phone call with zero information being sent my way, relations had broken down between myself and Garda Daly, who had warned me that I was 'skating on thin ice' and to 'call one more time if I wanted to spend the night in the barracks'.

I had plenty I wanted to say right back to him but my parents had confiscated both mine and Gibsie's phones before I could cause any more damage.

Nobody was telling me a damn thing and that was the problem. All they had to say was 'we checked on her and she's fine'. That's it. That's all I wanted to hear and I would have been appeased. Instead, I received the standard, 'we're looking into it,' and 'I'm afraid we're not at liberty to discuss this with you' over and over again.

It was complete bullshit.

"This is bullshit," I verbalized my feelings aloud when my father pulled the Mercedes up outside our house and *not* Shannon's like I had been promised, before killing the engine. I should have known better than to trust a lawyer, especially when said lawyer dropped Gibsie home and then proceeded to take the back road to our house and *not* the main road to Ballylaggin town. "I need to see her."

"No," Mam answered for him as she turned in the passenger seat to give me a stern look. "You need to lie down and rest. Doctor's orders."

Resisting the urge to roar, I gripped the leather interior beneath me and hissed, "I'm fine."

"And we want you to stay that way," Mam agreed, "which is why you're heading straight to bed."

"You're not listening to me." Scrubbing my face with my hands, I shook my head and looked out the window at the rain hammering down outside. "Why is nobody fucking listening to me?"

"Because you've been under the world of stress, Johnny," Dad explained calmly. "Not to mention the world of medication."

"Exactly." Smiling sympathetically at me, Mam added, "You've had a terrible setback with the rugby, love. It's okay if you're not feeling yourself right now."

"I know what I'm saying," I shot back, furious. "I know he's hurting her."

Mam groaned loudly and Dad turned in his seat, leveling me with a hard look. "Johnny, you're throwing a lot of accusations around and you need to settle down before you get yourself into trouble."

"They're not accusations when there's proof," I spat, glaring back at him. "I have proof."

My father rolled his eyes – literally fucking rolled his eyes at me. "Friday night, you were so delirious that you were convinced Pat Kenny was in the room with you. Saturday night, it was the Russian from the *Rocky* film."

"Sunday night, you accused the nurses of trying to poison you," Mam offered with a grimace.

"Now, it's Shannon's father?" Dad finished and expelled a frustrated breath. "What are we supposed to believe?"

"You're supposed to *believe me*," I growled. "Because I'm telling the bleeding truth, Da."

Dad arched a disbelieving brow.

I threw my hands up, exasperated. "Obviously, I was wrong about Pat Kenny and the Russian – although the nurse's trying to poison me is still up for debate." I shook my head, forcing myself to stay on track. "But I'm clearheaded now, and I'm telling you that I'm right about this – I'm right about *him*."

"Fine." Dad nodded stiffly. "You say you have proof. Show it to me."

"Oh, yeah," I sneered. "Let me just go pull Shannon's body out of the boot for ya."

"Less of the attitude, Jonathan," Mam warned. "We're trying to help you."

"And who's helping Shannon?" I demanded, voice cracking. "Who's helping *her*?"

"Johnny—"

"I'm telling you both that if you don't take me over there, I'll find my own way."

"You're not—"

"I'm not a child," I roared, unbuckling my seatbelt and pushing open the car door. "I'm almost eighteen, dammit! So don't push me into a corner and expect me not to push back." Grabbing my crutches, I clumsily maneuvered out of the car. "You may be unsure, but I *know*," I insisted. "I fucking know! And if you won't help me, I'll sort this myself."

"Where are you going?" they both demanded in unison as they filed out of the car after me.

Ignoring them both, I leaned heavily on my crutches and wrestled with my pocket for my phone. Yanking it out, I unlocked the screen and dialed Gibsie's number.

"Don't even think about it," Mam warned. "You're not going anywhere—"

"I need you to come and get me," I said the second he answered, not giving him a chance to greet me. "Please?"

"Say no more," was his automatic response. "I'm already on the way."

"Thanks, lad." Ending the call, I gripped my phone with more force than necessary and stared right back at my parents who were gaping at me in disbelief. I knew why. This wasn't me. I didn't act like this. I didn't speak to my parents like I just had. "I'm not a liar," I told them. "Never have been, never will be." Trembling, I added, "I know what I've seen – what I've heard. I'm right about this and you're making a very dangerous mistake by not listening to me."

"We don't think you're a liar, Johnny," Mam sobbed. "But we *are* worried about you."

"And I'm worried about *her*," I tossed back, voice thick with emotion. Rain was hammering down on all of us, but I wasn't moving. I *couldn't*. "I'm terrified for her."

"Fine, I'll make you an offer," Dad said, clearing his throat. "Go inside and lie down, and I'll make some calls and see what I can find out."

I slumped in relief. "Really?"

My father nodded and pushed his damp hair out of his eyes. "If you're that concerned, I'll drive down to the station myself and make some inquiries."

"You're not fucking with me?" I asked, mirroring his actions. "You'll check on her?"

Dad nodded stiffly. "But I sincerely hope you're wrong, son."

"Yeah," I croaked out, feeling my mother's arm come around my waist. "Me, too—"

The sound of my phone ringing caused me to pause mid-sentence.

Glancing down at my phone, I read *Joey the hurler* flash across the screen and my blood began to boil.

"Where the fuck have you been?" I demanded the minute I accepted his call. "I've been calling you non-stop for days, Joey. Jesus Christ!"

"Yeah, I know," he replied in what sounded like a hushed tone. "It's been a complicated few days here."

"*Complicated*?" I balked and almost smashed my phone. "Yeah, see that word doesn't work for me," I snarled. "*Complicated* doesn't explain or excuse the marks on your sister's body." Staggering towards the car, I ignored the horrified looks etched on my parents' faces and continued to rant, "*Complicated* doesn't explain why she constantly flinches and cowers away from confrontation at school. And *complicated* doesn't fucking explain why, when I asked her who was beating the shit out of her, she said your *father*!"

"Johnny—"

"You told me to tell your sister that there was a family emergency that day you left her at my house," I continued, interrupting him, unable to restrain myself as my rage consumed me. "Do you remember that? You told me to tell Shannon that her *father* was back. And do you know what happened, Joey? Do you know she did—" I had to inhale several calming breaths before continuing, "She broke down and cried. She shook so fucking bad I didn't know what to do to make it better! I *couldn't* make it better! Because you lied to me. I asked you straight to your face who was hurting her and you lied to me!"

"I didn't lie," was his clipped response, and it only infuriated me further.

"You didn't tell me the truth," I snarled, furious. "I was standing right there, asking you, fucking *begging* you to just tell me what was happening to her and you didn't!"

"I couldn't—"

"You asked me to look after her, and then you took her away from me! You took her back to *him*," I roared, chest heaving.

"Because I had no choice," he hissed. "You have no idea what I've been dealing with."

"That's a cop-out answer," I spat, running a hand through my hair. "Everyone has a choice."

"And every fucker has an answer for every other fucker's problem – until it's their own fucking problem and then they're fucked," Joey sneered. "You think you know, but you have no idea."

"This has been going on for years, hasn't it?" I demanded. "And you all just . . . buried it."

"It wasn't an everyday thing," he snarled down the line. "Our old man has a drinking problem. I'm usually there to prevent shit going down. I try! I fucking try, okay? But I wasn't on Saturday. I had training. I didn't know – I didn't expect anything to happen. How was I supposed to know? I thought she was safe. I thought she was in Dublin with *you!* His bad day is Wednesday—"

"Oh, *I'm sorry*," I sneered, sinking down in the backseat of the car. "I wasn't aware that he had a beating schedule! Is it only Wednesdays he likes to knock her around? Should I pick her up on Tuesdays and drop her back on Thursdays? Would that suit him?"

"Listen to me—"

"Where is she now?" I demanded. "Are you with her? At your house? Is he there, too?" I knew I was going to lose my mind if he gave me the wrong answer. In my mind, there was only one answer to this fucked-up question. Their father needed to *not* be there. He needed to be as far away from her as humanly possible. I couldn't fucking bear the thought of it. Putting his hands on her. Looking at her. *Touching her . . .* "Is he near her?" I strangled out. "Has he touched her?"

"Would you just stop talking and *listen* to—"

"I should have trusted my gut," I spat, interrupting him again. "I knew there was something off about your family. I bleeding knew it. That night you came and picked her up? Everything inside of me was screaming to keep her with me. And instead of listening to the red flags shooting up in my head, instead of opening my goddamn eyes, I pushed it down. Because I kept thinking, no – no, this guy loves his sister. He wouldn't stand by and let anything happen to her." I had to bite my knuckles to stop myself from driving my fist through the window of my father's car. "More fool me!"

"Fuck you, rich boy!" he strangled out. "It's easy for you to judge me. You've never seen hardship a day in your entitled life. I did everything I could for my family."

"Except for the right thing," I shot back, livid. "You are aware that's how he has so much power over you, right?" I gripped the phone tighter. "Keeping quiet solves *nothing* for you and *everything* for him!"

"She's sixteen, asshole!" Joey roared down the line. "What do you think would have happened to Shannon if I went running to the Guards? She'd have been thrown into a care home, that's what! And there's more than just her to think about. I have three little brothers to look out for."

I opened my mouth to protest and then quickly stopped.

He was right.

I dropped my head. "Fuck."

"Yeah. Fuck," Joey sneered. "This isn't a movie, Kavanagh. This is our life. It's real, it sucks, and you don't know a damn thing about it. We've been in care. We've lived through that. For Christ's sake, our brother was—" he stopped short and exhaled a ragged breath. "We've been in the system, we know the score, so before you throw blame at me for not doing something, ask yourself why we would prefer to stay with him than go back!"

It took me a moment to absorb his words before speaking again. "Well, here's what I do know. I know that I'm on the way to your house right now, and I know that if I find him there, if he's anywhere near your sister, I'm going to bring the world of trouble to the scumbag's doorstep—"

"She's not at the house, asshole," Joey erupted in my ear. "That's what I've been trying to tell you. She's at the fucking hospital!"

My heart stopped dead in my chest.

"I took her there myself on Saturday evening," he strangled out. "After our old man beat her to within an inch of her life for messing around with *you*. Some asshole teacher from Tommen called the house and reported that he'd found her getting off with you in a changing room, so fuck you back, Johnny Kavanagh. If this is on me, then it's on you, too!"

The line went dead and I just sat there, numb to the bone, feeling a million different emotions invade my body, and stared blankly at the phone in my hands.

I could hear my parents talking rapidly to each other, but I couldn't make sense of what they were saying. A few seconds later, my father climbed into the driver's seat and cranked the engine.

"I told you," I said, eyes locked on the back of his head as the car tore off down the driveway. "I'm not a liar."

# Not Today

## SHANNON

I spent the rest of the day in a state of barely contained panic. The headache I had been nursing since I opened my eyes had intensified to epic proportions, made worse by the constant stream of questions being thrown my way. First, by the Gardaí and then Patricia, a social worker who wanted me to think of her as a *friend*.

Yeah, *sure* she was my friend. I knew what her friendship would bring me. I wasn't *that* naïve.

Darren had remained in the room the entire time the Gardaí were present, a silent watch owl, keeping guard over my tongue, making sure I didn't mess this up. This wasn't the first time I'd been in this position, facing the threat of authority with a family member lurking close by, making sure I knew what my role was in this. Usually, it was my father or mother standing by to make sure I minded my P's and Q's. Today, it had been Darren.

He didn't need to worry. I knew my role. I had perfected it down through the years. I said all the right things, hid all the bad things, and remained silent for the ones I knew were trick questions – the ones I knew were traps.

Doctors and nurses had come and gone from my room all day, poking and prodding at me, and asking me questions they didn't want the answers to. Disheartened, I did what I had to do to keep our mother out of trouble, wanting nothing more than to just be left alone. When they finally finished questioning me, and the nurses gave up on probing me, I felt worse than I had in a very long time.

Through it all, only one thing stood out to me, and all I could think was: I hoped Tadhg, Ollie, and Sean found the Easter Eggs in my school bag on Easter Sunday. I knew they wouldn't have any otherwise. Dad had spent the children's allowance money at the beginning of the month. There wouldn't have been any money spare to set aside for eggs.

Joey didn't come back that evening to visit me, but Mam did.

My heart sank at the sight of her.

Because I knew what was coming.

"Hello, Shannon." With teary eyes and a blotchy face, she walked over to my bed and enveloped me in her arms, holding on to me like I was something of importance to her. In a way, I knew that I was, because she needed to keep me quiet. She was coddling me because she was afraid of what I might do.

She didn't need to worry. It wasn't her life that would be ruined if social services got involved. It would be ours.

When I didn't reciprocate or make any move to return her hug, Mam released me and took the seat Darren had vacated when he'd left an hour ago. "How are you feeling?"

Unwilling to answer her, I remained rigid and motionless, my eyes taking in the faint bruising on her cheekbone on her gaunt face. *Why do you do this to yourself?* I wanted to ask, *why do you let him treat you this way?*

"I spoke to your doctors," Mam said in a shaky tone as she fiddled with the sleeves of her oversized raincoat. "They're talking about letting you come home the day after tomorrow, or maybe even tomorrow if your next round of tests look good."

"Home?" I asked, giving her a blank stare. "Or *care?*"

"Home, Shannon." Mam exhaled a ragged breath and nodded. "You're coming home." Tears filled her eyes as she spoke. "I'm so sorry, baby. For all of this."

I dropped my gaze to stare at my fingers. What did she expect me to say? That it was okay and I forgave her? Nothing about our lives was *okay.* "And Dad?" I forced myself to ask, keeping my eyes trained on my trimmed fingernails. "What happens now?"

"Your father won't be coming back."

*Lies.* "Yeah," I muttered under my breath. "Sure."

"It's true," Mam urged, voice thick with emotion. "I went to court. There's a temporary protection order in place to stop him from contacting any of us. I-I go back to court in three weeks. My solicitor assured us that we'll have no problem getting a permanent order against him."

*More lies.* "Until you decide you don't want a permanent order," I shot back, feeling empty inside. "Until you decide that you want to brush this under the table – like you always do."

"I mean it this time," she assured, voice hoarse and cracked. "I won't take him back again. I won't. Christ, look at what he did to you—"

"What he *did to me*?" I strangled out, outraged. "What he did to me *this time*, Mam." I blinked back the traitorous tears that were blurring my vision. "What he did to me *this time*!"

"Baby, I'm so sorry."

I didn't respond.

"Everything is going to be different from here on out." Her voice sounded weak, just like she was. Weak and broken and undependable. "Darren's home now and he'll help us get back on our feet. I promise it's going to get better."

I shook my head, furious with her words. "I don't give a shit about your precious *Darren*," I spat, hating myself for crying in front of her. "He means *nothing* to me."

"That's your anger talking," Mam choked out. "Not you."

"My anger talking?" Blinking away my tears, I glared at her. "What planet are you living on, Mam? I don't know Darren. I have nothing to do with him and I don't want to."

"Shannon," Mam sobbed. "That's not fair."

"Not *fair*? Have you even checked on Joey?" I demanded, voice raspy. She had always been about Darren. *Darren this and Darren that.* Joey never got a look in. Our father was the one who had been obsessed with Joey, but again, that notion had only sparked *after* Darren left. Joey was simply tossed into a role no one wanted him to play, least of all Joey. "You haven't, have you?" I continued. "You just left him out of this. You went right ahead and made decisions about our lives with Darren – a person none of us have heard from in over half a decade – and you never once thought to ask what your son who *actually* stepped up and raised us might think!" Hiccupping, I wiped my nose with the back of my hand and forced myself to continue. "I might be the one in a hospital bed, Mam, but Joey's the one you and Dad both broke."

"He won't speak to me," she sniffed. "He hasn't come home in days."

"I wonder why," was all I replied.

"I don't know what to do," she choked out. "How can I fix this if he won't speak to me?"

"You can't fix this, Mam," I replied, trembling. "It's like that story about Humpty Dumpty. Nothing will put him back together again. Dad threw him off the wall and you lost the pieces to put him back together."

"Oh god." She dropped her head in her hands and sobbed. "I'm so sorry."

"You should have seen him today," I said, wincing when a jolt of pain shot through me. "He was completely shattered."

"Shannon," Mam sobbed. *Weak, weak, fucking weak.* "Just give me a chance to make this right, baby, please." *You can't. You'll never fix this.* "I know I can turn this around for all of us."

"See, you're talking, you're saying all the right things, but it's just words." Shaking my head, I lifted my gaze to hers. "It's all words with you," I croaked out bitterly. "All the same words I've heard a million times before, to go with all the same promises you've repeatedly broken."

"So, what are you saying?" she cried, dabbing her cheeks with a crumpled-up tissue. "You don't want to be with me anymore?"

"I'm saying that I'll do what I need to for Ollie, Tadhg, and Sean," I choked out, drowning in my feelings. "To keep them safe and out of care, I'll give this plan of Darren's a chance. And I hope you're right, Mam. I really hope you are telling the truth this time, but I hope that for the boys' sakes, not mine. I *pray* that you can turn this around for them and be the mother they deserve, but it's too late to turn this around for us."

"I don't know what to say," she sobbed. "I'm just so sorry, Shannon. I know I can't fix this, but I ... God, I just don't know what to do anymore."

"I know you're not a bad person, Mam," I whispered, snatching my traitorous hand back when it moved of its own accord to comfort her. "And I know he hurt you, too, in ways I don't understand, and I am *sorry* that happened to you. I know you were scared, and I am so sorry that you had to live in fear for all these years—" furious with myself, I angrily swatted my tears away and exhaled slowly before continuing, "but that doesn't mean you get a free pass from us." I sniffled and wiped my nose with the back of my hand. "It doesn't make it okay because you *knew* what he was doing, you *saw* it, and you did *nothing*. You just left us, Mam. You were there, but you weren't. Joey was right when he called you a ghost. And I don't know, maybe it was your way of surviving, making it through each day in one piece, but you had more power than us. You were the grown-up. You were our *mother*. And you just ... " I shrugged helplessly. "Checked out on us."

"Do you think, in time, you'll forgive me?" she whispered, looking up at me with lonesome, tear-filled blue eyes. "Do you think you ever could?"

"Maybe?" I shrugged again. "But I know that I don't forgive you today."

# Bulldozer

## JOHNNY

"I need you to keep your head," Dad instructed as he walked down the corridor of CUH to ward 1A with his hand clamped on the back of my arm. "No outbursts," he added in a low tone. "And for the love of god, no accusations."

"What's there to accuse?" I growled, hobbling along with my crutches. "We both know what happened to her." Like I told him. Like I told *everyone*. "Jesus, he put her in the fucking hospital, Da!"

"Johnny—" Pulling me to a stop in the middle of a bustling corridor, Dad pinched his brow and then turned to look at me. "You're upset, I understand. I get it. I'm sorry for doubting you, okay? You were right and I was wrong, but *this*—" he waved a hand around, gesturing to where we were standing "—is a sensitive situation – one you have zero experience with. This is a domestic violence issue, Jonathan. The Gardaí and social services will already be all over this. Do you understand? There will be a criminal investigation – one you cannot interfere with. Emotions will be running high and the last thing you need to do is run in there all guns a-blazing. It might feel good and justifiable, but it won't help Shannon in the long run. So, if you want to see her then I strongly suggest you keep your opinions and feelings to yourself, and let me do the talking."

I gaped at him. "I'm *going* to see her; there's no if about it." My father gave a look that said *not likely*. "I am going to see her, Da," I repeated, furious.

"Then keep your head and *don't* bulldoze," he replied before releasing my arm and walking on ahead of me.

Glaring at the back of his head, I adjusted my crutches and hurried to catch up. "I don't bleeding bulldoze."

I rounded the corner, hunting my father's silhouette as he slipped through another set of double doors and out of sight.

Fuck my dick and these bleeding crutches.

He was clearly walking ahead of me on purpose. He wanted to get there before me so he could assess the situation in that cool, unfeeling, calculated way of his without his headstrong son there to make a hash of things.

When I finally caught sight of him again, standing at the nurses' station at the far end of the long corridor, I upped my pace, using my upper body strength to sling myself along on the metal sticks, peeking through the glass windows of each door as I went.

I was passing the sixth door on the left when my body came to an abrupt halt and my heart jackknifed in my chest.

Shannon was lying on the bed with her eyes closed and her hands tucked under her cheek.

She was facing the door, and at the sight of her, I had to stop and catch my breath.

A million and one emotions battered through me as my eyes took in the bruising dusting her face. She was black and blue to the point of being almost unrecognizable. Almost. I'd know that face anywhere.

I felt it now; the deep sense of guilt drowning me. The sadness on her face every time I dropped her back to that house. The fear in her eyes when I knocked on her door that first time – the second and third time, too. She was always so skittish, so demure and obliging. She asked permission for just about everything. She wasn't allowed to go anywhere. She told me that once – said her folks were protective. But she went with me anyway.

*"Can you save me?"*
  *"Do you need me to save you?"*
  *"Mmm hmm."*

*"What happened here? What's this from?"*
  *"My dad."*

The signs were there, had been for months, and I just bulldozed past them. My eyes were open but I had been looking in the wrong direction. I didn't hear her. I didn't listen. I didn't pay enough attention. I didn't take it in, I didn't see the hints, I couldn't hear the cries for help, but I was hearing and seeing them now.

And now? She was lying in this hospital bed because I'd kissed her. Because I'd kissed the shite out of her and got us into trouble. That's what Joey had said. Their father did this because she was messing around with *me*.

My mind drifted to Joey. Every time I'd met Shannon's brother he'd been sporting some fresh bruise on his face. I never thought twice about it, though. I had just put it down to hurling and brushed it under the table. God knows I spent most of my time nursing wounds. But this? My father was right. I could never understand *this*.

My heart galloped wildly in my chest, my hand moving of its own accord, as I reached out and clicked open the door. Casting a quick glance towards my father, who was still at the nurses' station, speaking to who I presumed was the ward sister, I pushed the door open and slipped inside.

# Don't Let Me Down

## SHANNON

The sound of metal clanging loudly caused me to jerk out of a fitful sleep. A chair scraping against the tiled floor came next. For a few uncertain moments I wasn't sure where I was. A part of me felt like I was back in my kitchen, so I kept my eyes clenched shut and braced myself for the impact. When it came in the form of a hand covering mine, I peeked up and found myself staring into a pair of achingly familiar blue eyes.

"Hi, Shannon."

Was this real?

Was I imagining this?

The wild, erratic beat of my heart and the heat of his hands on mine assured me that I was very much awake.

Stunned, I looked down to where my hand was taped with wires and wrapped tightly in both of his before returning my gaze to meet his. "Hi, Johnny."

"When did we suddenly switch places?" Johnny teased. His tone was light but his eyes were dark and stormy. "Are you trying to steal my thunder, Shannon *like the river*?"

I cracked a smile. "I guess I wanted some of those drugs for myself."

"Stay away from those drugs. They'll fuck with your head." He gave me a sad smile before looking around. "So, are you here on your own?" A deep frown was etched on his face. "Alone?"

I shook my head. "My mother is around here somewhere. She might be outside smoking."

Johnny leaned forward and opened his mouth to speak, only to stop himself short. Blowing out a breath, he rolled his lips between his teeth and asked, "So, when are you getting out of here?"

"Maybe tomorrow," I replied with a small smile. "Or the day after."

Johnny nodded stiffly and I knew he wanted to say more, but he stopped himself. "I'm not supposed to be here," he said then, shifting his gaze back to me. "At least, I don't think I am."

"I'm glad you are," I whispered. Having him here, hearing his voice and seeing his face, settled something deep inside of me. Something shifted into place, an almost relieved sensation fluttered over my skin, soothing something deep inside of me. I felt like I was home. I knew that sounded crazy. It was more than crazy. It was downright insane, but I felt it. It was real, raw, and pushing me to move closer, be closer, keep him.

In this moment, I felt something align itself deep inside of my body, and when it did, the weight I was feeling, the heaviness in my heart and the pressure on my shoulders, just fell away.

"Me, too," he replied gruffly.

"So, when did you get home?" I asked, feeling hoarse and off-balance.

"This evening." He raised my hand and pressed a kiss to my knuckles. "Took me forever to get back to you."

His words caused a shiver to roll through my body.

"I'm glad you're back to me." I knew I was opening myself up to heartache, not to mention the world of pain if he rejected me again, but I had to say it. "I really missed you, Johnny."

"Christ, Shannon, I don't know what to—" Johnny exhaled a huge breath, and then proceeded to lift my hand to his mouth. "You're okay," he whispered, pressing a kiss to the back of my hand, wires and all. Inhaling deeply, he placed my hand on his cheek and leaned into the touch. "You'll be okay, won't you?"

Nodding, I cradled his cheek in my hand and whispered, "Are *you* okay?"

"Don't ask me that." His blue eyes burned holes inside of me so deep I felt like I could never be repaired as he said, "Not when you're the one lying in here."

"I'm sorry."

"Don't be sorry." Clenching his eyes shut, he bowed his head, still clutching my hand to his cheek. "I'm the sorry one." He released a pained groan and pushed into my touch, rubbing his cheek against my palm. "I just need you to be okay," he croaked out. His lashes were so thick and hooded, I could hardly see the blue hidden beneath them. "I know I was a complete spanner when I came around after the surgery and I'm sorry. I'm so fucking sorry for pushing you away. I was just embarrassed and ashamed . . . and I was petrified of scaring you off, but I should have stopped you from leaving. I should have *handled* myself better. I should have asked you to stay with me." Twisting his face, he pressed a kiss to my palm and whispered, "I wanted you to stay with me."

My heart skipped a beat. "You did?"

"I always want you to stay with me, Shannon," he replied, clearly agitated. "And if I'd just manned the fuck up about my feelings and asked you to stay, I could have stopped this from happening—"

"No, you couldn't," I interrupted him, trembling. "I would have had to go home at some stage. Staying an extra day or two would have only made things a million times worse."

"Worse?" He clenched his jaw and balked. "Shannon, look where you are. How can it get any *worse*?"

"Things can always get worse, Johnny," I whispered.

"So, he did *this* to you?" he came straight out and asked me. "Your da?"

I opened my mouth to respond, but Johnny got there first.

"Before you say anything, I want you to know that Joey called me and told me everything I needed to know," he said, staring into my eyes. "Not that I needed him to. I figured it out on my own." His hand tightened around mine. "All those times you came into school black and blue and all fucked up—" his voice broke off and I watched as a vein in his neck bulged and pulsed. "All those times you lied to me? It was to protect *him*?"

"I don't want to talk about it," I whispered, falling into my life-long learned pattern of avoidance.

"No, no, we're not doing that." Johnny stared hard at me, calling me right out on it. "You don't get to shut me out, Shannon. You don't get to do that to me again, because I won't go this time. Do you hear me? I'm here, I'm in, I care, and I'm not going the fuck away."

My mind was reeling, struggling to make sense of what he was saying. Did he mean . . . ? Was he . . . ? Did he want . . . ? "You care?"

A pained groan tore from his throat. "Yeah, I care." He leaned closer. "I care so fucking much I can hardly breathe."

My breath hitched. "What do you want to know?"

"How about you start with telling me what's wrong with you," he suggested, blue eyes glued to mine. "What's the damage?"

"A few cuts and bruises," I admitted. "And a collapsed lung."

"Jesus Christ." I watched with my heart in my mouth as Johnny's face drained of color before returning with blood-red vengeance. "Fuck."

Releasing my hand, he leaned back in his chair and pressed the heels of his hands against his forehead, putting space between our bodies and his temper. He didn't say a word. He just sat there for several moments, breathing deep and hard, obviously wrestling with his emotions.

His dark hair was cocking up in forty different directions and he was sporting several days' worth of stubble on his jaw. Unsurprisingly, the disheveled look worked for him. He had on a pair of loose, grey sweatpants and a navy hoodie. The hospital admission band he'd been wearing the last time I saw him was still strapped to his left hand, and a set of metal crutches lay at his feet.

"You should've told me the truth," he finally said. "What was happening to you." Dropping his hands from his face, he leaned forward and snatched my hand back up. "I could have helped you."

"You couldn't," I breathed. "And I couldn't."

"No?" His voice was sad, matching his eyes. "Why not?"

"Because . . ." My heart was hammering violently against my ribcage. "Because . . ."

"Because?" Johnny offered, voice gentle and coaxing as he shifted closer to rest his elbows on the edge of the mattress. "Did you think that I wouldn't believe you?" He leaned closer, settling his chin on top of our joined hands. "Because I would. Every single time."

"Because he's an alcoholic," I squeezed out, feeling suddenly starved of oxygen. "And I was trying to keep my family safe."

"Safe?" he continued to probe, luring me into security with his irresistible coaxing, with the promise of *safety*. "From him?"

I shook my head, eyes wide and full of unspoken fear. "The foster system." My heart felt like it had climbed into my throat, making it hard to get the next part out. "Been there before." Releasing a pained exhale, I held onto his hand, taking comfort in the way he made me feel grounded. "Don't want to go back."

"When?"

"When I was little." I swallowed deeply, feeling the burn. "It wasn't . . . good."

Johnny nodded, and the heated interest in his eyes told me that he was committing my words to memory. Everything about this boy was intense and larger than life. He was far too intelligent to insult him with any more lies or watered-down truths, so I didn't.

Instead, I went with the truth. "They don't want me to talk about it with anyone." *And especially not with you.*

"Who's them?"

"My mother," I told him, feeling uncertain and wary. "And Darren."

Johnny's brows creased in confusion. "Darren, as in the brother who doesn't live in Cork anymore?"

I nodded. "He's back."

His brows shot up. "Since when?"

"Since this." I gestured to myself, feeling embarrassed. "He says he's home now, and that he's going to help Mam with the kids and, ah, and my . . . my f-father." I cringed at the last part –the father part.

"He says?" Johnny narrowed his eyes. See, too intuitive for his own good. "So, you don't believe him?"

"I don't know what I believe anymore." I shrugged wearily, too tired to put up a barrier between us. "A lot of grownups are saying a lot of things, they're all talking around me and above me, and I'm just—"

"Done with the bullshit?" he offered, squeezing my hand.

"Yes." I nodded, grateful for his acute interpretation skills. "I'm so done with the bullshit, Johnny."

"Where's your father now?"

I shrugged my shoulders. "I don't know."

"What do you mean you don't know?" His tone was sharp, even outraged. "He wasn't arrested?"

"He's missing – slipped out after it happened and hasn't been seen since," I whispered, feeling panicky at the thought of my father being out there somewhere. "Darren says he will be found and charged, but Joey isn't so sure. Nobody's telling me anything . . . well, except for Joey. Joe reckons that Dad's probably staying with friends of his in Waterford, keeping his head down until the dust settles and Mam takes him—" I expelled a defeated breath and mumbled, "back."

"Back?"

Numb, I shrugged. "I'm really not supposed to talk about this with—"

"It's me," he told me, tipping my chin up with his fingers. Meeting my gaze, he added, "You can tell me anything, okay?"

"I'm scared," I confessed, biting down on my bottom lip. "And I don't want to go home."

"With your ma?"

I nodded stiffly.

"Because she let you down," he said quietly. "Because you don't trust her."

"She makes promises but that's all they are; *empty* promises." Shaking, I moved to wrap my arms around myself, only to think better of it and latch on to his warm arm instead. "We're supposed to feel *sorry* for her because of what she went through, because she's a victim too, and I know that, I truly do, but I just . . . I can't find it in me to *feel* that way." The usual fear and uncertainty that consumed me whenever I was in his presence was absent now. I felt stripped down to the bone and laid bare to this boy, and he was still here, still looking at me with the same eyes, still wanting *more* from me. "She's getting support now, and the Gardaí and Social Services are obviously confident in her ability to parent us – that's why they're working with her. They're setting her up with all types of services and counseling."

"But you don't?" Johnny asked. "You don't think she can?"

"I know she would never hurt us," I whispered. "Not on purpose at least. She's not violent, Johnny, and she's not cruel. She's just *weak*. Darren keeps saying that we need to have patience and give her a chance, but I just … I can't get my hopes up." Gripping his forearm with both hands, I squeezed. "Because I've seen this all before. She'll take him back – I know she will – and then what? What happens then, huh?" Shaking my head, I furiously fought with my emotions, blinking away traitorous tears. "*Nothing*. Nothing will happen just like always, and I'm just so done with it all, Johnny." I exhaled a ragged breath. "I want to get out of this town, go far, far away, and *never* come back."

"Can you tell them?" he asked. "That you don't want to go back with her?"

"And where would I go? What would happen to my little brothers if I did that? They *want* to stay with her."

"Are you sure?"

"Ollie and Sean do. I don't know about Tadhg, he's not saying much, and Joey's over eighteen so he can legally live wherever he wants." I sighed in defeat. "If I push back on this, if I tell them that I don't feel safe with her, they'll whip us all into care and we'll be split up." My brows furrowed and I cringed before admitting, "I tell lies like I breathe air. Even to myself. Half of the time, I don't even know what's the truth or a lie. I have to actually think long and hard about it because that's all I've known. I've been covering things up for so long that I'm not even sure if *I'm* thinking clearly. And now, I'm doubting myself because I keep thinking what if I'm wrong about her? What if I'm wrong to think badly of her?"

Johnny was silent for a long time, not making a sound, just being there, being with me, sharing the weight, shouldering the pain with silent support. And I think I loved him more for what he *didn't* say in that moment. He didn't make the promises he couldn't keep. He didn't offer more than he could give. He just *stayed*.

Several minutes passed before he spoke again. "When did it start?"

"I don't remember a time when it wasn't like this," I admitted, feeling exposed and helpless.

"And me?" Johnny swallowed deeply. "When did it start because of me?"

"He was always paranoid," I told him, deciding I had nothing left to lose. "But once that picture of us was published in the paper, he had his own version of proof."

Johnny dropped his head. "Fuck, Shannon, that was months ago."

"I know," I sighed wearily.

"I made it worse for you," he strangled out.

"You made it bearable," I whispered.

"Where else?" Two words that seemed to be torn from deep within him. His gaze roamed over me slowly, unabashedly, darkening, until finally settling back on my face. "Is there more?" His fingers trailed over my cheek. "Show me where he hurt you."

I hesitated to respond, feeling cautious and uncertain.

"You can trust me," he said in a voice so low it was barely audible. "I'm not like him, Shannon. I won't ever hurt you – I couldn't. Not in any shape or form."

I knew this.

Aside from Joey, Johnny Kavanagh was the only other person I did trust.

It was with this knowledge that I slowly pulled my aching body into a sitting position.

"Take it easy," he coaxed, leaning over to help me sit up. "You okay?"

"Yeah." Letting my legs dangle off the side of the bed, I sat facing him, and reached for the hem of my pajama blouse I had changed into earlier. Gingerly, I lifted the fabric up to reveal the left side of my black and blue ribcage.

Johnny sucked in a sharp breath at the sight. "Fucking bastard," he snarled and then seemed to check himself because he swallowed down whatever else he was about to say, clenched his jaw, and whispered, "I need to see everything. Show me everything. I need to see it all."

So, I did.

I showed him my arms and legs, my neck and thighs, and with every bruise and cut I revealed, I felt a weight lift off my shoulders.

"And they made a hole here," I explained in a shaky voice, clumsily unbuttoning my pajama blouse to reveal the fresh bandage strapped to my chest and side. Shivering, I cupped my tiny breasts and twisted sideways to show him. "To help me breathe."

Johnny's eyes flicked to the bandage and I watched his entire frame stiffen. He wasn't looking at me in a sexual way. No, it was a look of pure horror. "Jesus Christ." He dragged his chair closer to the bed until my legs were nestled between his knees. "Is it sore?" Resting one hand on my thigh, he gently grazed the bandage with his free hand. "Are you in pain?"

*Yes.* "I'll be okay," I replied, turning back to face him. "The doctor told me it will heal in a week or two."

"He did this to you because of me—" Pausing, Johnny caught ahold of the fabric on either side of my chest and began to snap the buttons back into place, keeping his eyes on mine the entire time. "Because of what happened in the changing room?" When he was finished re-doing my blouse, he shook his head, expression torn. "Because you're not supposed to be with me?"

I shrugged helplessly. I couldn't lie anymore. Not to him, at least. He saw it anyway, the truth in my eyes, and it caused a low, pained groan to tear from his chest. "I'm so sorry, Shannon." Resting his forehead against my stomach, he wrapped his huge arms around my waist and whispered, "I'm so fucking sorry."

My body was shaking so hard, I was struggling to hold it all back, to keep my feelings buried down, when all I wanted to do was fold into this boy and never come back up for air. Trembling, I cradled his face to my stomach and exhaled a broken sob. "It's not your fault," I choked out, feeling the sting of hot, salty tears as they trickled down my cheeks. "It's not. If it wasn't you, he would have found something else to hate me for. That's the way it is in my family. My father doesn't need a reason to do the things he does, Johnny. He just needs a *notion*." Shaking, I trailed my fingers through his hair, forcing myself to keep my touch gentle and not cling to him and beg him to take me away like I so desperately yearned to do. "Don't be sad for me."

"Sad? I'm not sad, Shannon. I'm fucking devastated," he strangled out, lifting his head. "I was positive it was someone at school. Fuck, I was obsessed with figuring this out and I was looking in the wrong direction the entire time."

"Johnny . . ."

"I drove you back to that house," he groaned, distressed. "I watched you walk into that fucking house and I went home to a warm, safe bed, knowing in my heart something wasn't right but not opening my mind enough to see it!" Shaking his head, he released a frustrated growl. "I am so fucking sorry. You didn't deserve to have another person let you down."

"It's okay," I croaked out.

"No, it's not. It's *not* okay." He exhaled a heavy sigh and whispered, "Shannon, did he—" Johnny blew out a breath and shook his head before trying again. "Did he . . ." Flinching, he closed his eyes. "He hurt you." It was a statement, not a question. "Physically." He opened his eyes and looked at me once more. "Did he do anything else to you?"

"What do you mean?"

"I need to know if he . . . " his voice was pained as he struggled to get the words out. "Did he . . . ever make you do things that you didn't want to do?"

"Like what?" I strangled out, panicking.

"Did he ever touch you?" The words came out of his mouth in a rush. "Sexually." He closed his eyes as a pained groan tore through him. "Did he do that to you?" Opening his eyes, he looked at me, expression torn, and said, "Did he rape you, baby?"

"No."

"No?" Relief flooded his eyes for the briefest of moments before doubt poured back in. "You can't lie to me, okay? Not about this. I need you to tell me the truth."

"He didn't touch me like that," I croaked out, heart bucking wildly in my chest. "Nothing like *that* ever happened to me."

Johnny stared hard at me for the longest moment before releasing a shaky breath. "Okay." Nodding to himself, he whispered, "Okay," several more times as his shoulders sagged. "I'm sorry for asking you that, but I *had* to."

"It's okay."

"But I need you to know that you're not on your own in this. Not anymore." His voice was steady and strong now. "You have me."

My heart leapt in my chest. "I have?"

"Absolutely." His brow touched mine then, achingly soft, and his blue eyes bore into mine, silently asking for permission. To do what, I had no clue, but I was willing to say yes to whatever he asked of me. "I'm here," he whispered, stroking my nose with his. "And I'm going nowhere."

*Oh god . . .*

"Johnny?" My hands moved of their own accord, knotting in the fabric of his hoodie. "If you're going to let me down—" dropping my head, I closed my eyes and inhaled several shaky breaths before tipping my chin up and opening my eyes, "then I need you to do it now, okay? Don't wait until it's too late, and *please* . . . please don't make it hurt—"

Johnny silenced me by putting his lips on mine. Stunned, I could do nothing but sag against him, giving him all of my weight and trusting him not to break me.

It was a soft, innocent, almost featherlike peck on the lips, but it was everything in this moment, and it meant *everything* to me because it was from him. Because for the very first time he kissed me *first*.

"I won't," Johnny whispered, brows touching, lips gliding against mine as he spoke. "I'll always be careful with you, Shannon *like the river*." Exhaling a shaky breath, he tucked my hair behind my ears and cupped my face in his hands. "I promise."

"I'll be careful with you, too," I told him, trembling from head to toe.

He smiled. "That's good to know, because I've got a feeling you could do some serious damage to my—"

"I'm not sure where he is now, he *was* right behind me, but if he could just have a minute with her . . . never mind," a familiar voice said. "I've found him."

"Shite," Johnny mumbled. Releasing my face, he leaned back in his chair and offered a half-hearted salute with his hand. "Hi, Da."

"Glad to see that your listening ears are as absent as always, son," Mr. Kavanagh replied in a mild tone. "Shannon." He gave me a sad smile. "It's lovely to see you again, although the circumstances aren't ideal."

"Hi, Mr. Kavanagh," I whispered, feeling my walls rise up at a rapid pace. I wasn't sure if it was the sight of Johnny's mild-mannered father that caused this reaction or the furious look on my mother's face as she stood in the doorway beside him.

"Well," Mam strangled out, clearly upset, "I think he's had more than a minute."

"Mam—" I began to protest, but Mr. Kavanagh interrupted me.

"Understood." He looked at Johnny and inclined his head. "Let's go, son."

"What?" I stared in horror at my mother. "*Why?*"

"Because I said so," Mam replied, tone shaky.

"No." I shook my head and looked to Johnny. "No, you don't have to go anywhere."

"Yes, he does, Shannon," Mr. Kavanagh interjected. "Come on, Johnny."

Johnny looked how I felt, completely torn, as he looked from his father to me. Several long moments passed in tense silence before Johnny finally nodded in defeat. My heart sank as I watched him retrieve his crutches and climb unsteadily to his feet. "I'll be back, Shannon."

"I would prefer it if you didn't," Mam was quick to say. "Come back, that is. At least for a while. We're going through a deeply personal issue, it's a family matter, and I really don't feel like it's appropriate for you to be here."

My jaw fell open. "Mam!"

"Oh no?" Johnny shot back, not masking the anger in his voice. "Well, I would *prefer* if you shoved your *feelings* up the highest part of your—"

"Jonathan!" Mr. Kavanagh barked. "Time to *go*."

"You've done enough damage to this family already," Mam snapped, trembling. "Whether you realize it or not, so don't show your face around here again. You're not welcome."

"Mrs. Lynch," Mr. Kavanagh interjected calmly. "I think we all need to calm down—"

"Keep your son away from my daughter," Mam snapped. "She's sixteen years old and I don't want her messing around with him. She's in here because of him! Because he wouldn't stay away. So, *keep him away*. Do you understand me? Keep that boy *away* from my daughter!"

"What are you *talking* about?" I strangled out, feeling my heart gallop to the point where I felt dizzy. "He hasn't done anything wrong."

"I'm coming back to see your daughter," Johnny growled, eyes locked on my mother. "I played by your rules once before and look where it got her. So, you can rest assured that I won't be doing that again."

"Johnny, let's go," Mr. Kavanagh barked. "Now."

"Jesus Christ, Da!"

"Now!"

Tearing his heated gaze off my mother, Johnny turned to look at me. Ignoring our parents, he closed the space between us, cupped the back of my head with one hand and leaned down. "I'll be back," he whispered before pressing a lingering kiss to my forehead. Straightening up, he looked down at me and winked. "I promise."

Wide-eyed, I stared up at him and whispered, "I'll be waiting."

Johnny turned back to my mother and hissed, "I'm watching you."

"Come on." Mr. Kavanagh sighed wearily and placed a hand on the back of Johnny's neck. "Get out of the room before I take your crutch and beat you with it."

"Nice choice of words, Da," Johnny groaned, allowing his father to lead him out of the room. "Real fucking tactful."

"Oh Jesus," Mr. Kavanagh muttered, turning in the doorway. His face was a deep shade of red as he said, "My sincerest apologies for the tasteless remark," before closing the door behind them.

"What was *that*?" Mam asked, tone accusing, eyes narrowed on me.

"That was Johnny," I replied, daring her back with my eyes. "What was *that*?" I asked her right back. "What the hell, Mam? He came to see me and you ran him off."

"He had no business being here."

"What?" I gaped at her. "He's my *friend*!"

"And is your *friend* planning on making a habit of kissing you?" she demanded. "In front of your mother?"

*God, I hoped so.* I shrugged noncommittally.

"He's too old for you."

"He's seventeen," I shot back defiantly. "I'm sixteen."

"I don't like this, Shannon," she muttered, looking concerned. "Him. I don't like *him*. There's something about him. He's too . . . he's too . . . "

"He's too what, Mam?"

"Much for you," she filled in. "He's too old and too experienced and definitely too arrogant."

"Well, he's not your choice," I told her. "He's mine."

"Does he know?" Mam whispered, eyeing me with extreme wariness. "About our family?"

"He knows everything," I confirmed quietly, feeling a tsunami of misplaced guilt rise up in me. Logic told me I didn't need to feel bad, but my heart was confused. My heart called me a traitor. "I had to tell him," I choked out, explaining myself. "He saw the marks."

"Jesus, Shannon," Mam strangled out. "No." She shook her head. "No, no, no, this isn't right."

"Look where I am." My cheeks burned. "I couldn't keep lying to him."

"Not that!" Mam snapped. "I mean you and him." She shook her head again. "No, you're vulnerable and he's taking advantage of a bad situation."

"What?" I gaped at her. "I can't believe you just said that."

"Are you sleeping with him?"

"*What?*"

"Are you having sex with that boy?"

"Oh my god! You're so unbelievably disconnected." I bit back a scream. "Darren was right. You need *help*."

"He *hurt* you, Shannon," Mam choked out. "He knocked you out – put you in the hospital."

"Accidentally," I spat. "Unlike the man who you left in our lives, who likes to hurt us on *purpose*." I gestured wildly to myself. "I'm in the hospital again, Mam. Are you going to blame this on Johnny, too?"

Mam flinched. "If he had left you alone in the first place then your father wouldn't have had a reason to—"

"Don't!" I warned, voice cracking. "Don't you dare blame me for what he did to me."

"I'm not," she sobbed, crying again. "I'm sorry . . . I'm just *terrified* for you." Hurrying towards me, she sank down on the bed beside me. "Your father knows about him. What if he tries to find you through him? What if he sees you with him and it makes things worse?"

"He already knows where we live, Mam," I said with a weary sigh. "If Dad wants to get me, he will."

"Shannon . . ." Mam sobbed loudly. "Don't say that."

"It's the truth," I replied, feeling emotionally drained. "If he wants to hurt us, he doesn't need to go through my friends to do it. All he has to do is knock on the door and you'll welcome him in with open arms."

"No," she sniffled. "I won't do that again."

"We'll see."

"I knew this would happen," she whispered, reaching for my hand.

"You knew what would happen?" I asked, snatching my hand away.

"I saw the way he looked at you that day. At the school when I came to pick you up?" She exhaled a broken sob. "I knew he was going to be trouble."

"He's not trouble," I urged. "He's a good person, Mam – a great one. He's training to be a professional rugby player, for god's sake. He already plays for his *country*. He's smart and driven and kind. He's so kind, Mam. He doesn't take drugs or mess around like everyone else his age. He's not the monster you've invented in your head."

"Do you think I don't know what it's like; to turn the head of a boy like that?" she asked. "Your father was all of those things. He wasn't a bad man when I first knew him. He was wonderful. He was a star in his own right with the hurling. Everyone wanted to know him. He was adored, you know. Ballylaggin's golden boy."

"It's not the same thing," I strangled out, feeling my body grow hot and panicky. "None of *this* is the same."

"It's *all* the same," she shot back brokenly. "And look at me now, Shannon." She waved a hand aimlessly around the room. "Look where boys like that get girls like us. One mistake is all it takes. One slip up and your life is over. You'll be saddled down with more responsibility than you can cope with and he'll blame you for everything. He'll blame you for taking his future from him. For changing the course of his life. For making him a father when he's still a boy. Repeat my mistakes, Shannon, and that boy will blame you and resent you and break you until there's nothing of you left to hurt."

"I'm not you," I choked out. "And he's not Dad."

"*Yet*," she replied sadly. "Not yet."

"Stop talking."

Mam balked. "Wh-what?"

"You don't get to do this to me," I said, shaking. "You don't get to scare me away from the one *good* thing in my life."

"I'm not trying to scare you, Shannon. I'm trying to help you," she pleaded. "Trying to *protect* you."

"Yeah, from the wrong person."

"No." She shook her head. "From making the same mistakes as me."

"Well, you asked me earlier if there was a chance I'd ever forgive you?" Swallowing deeply, I clutched the edge of the mattress, looked my mother dead in the eyes, and whispered, "Drive him away and the answer will be *never again*."

# Accusations

## JOHNNY

"I am sorry, Johnny," my father said when he parked the car at the back of our house beside my Audi later that night. "I should have listened to you."

"I know, Da." Exhausted, I unfastened my seatbelt and swung the door open. He should have listened to me, but I couldn't talk about it now. I was struggling with my feelings, desperately trying to hold the fuck onto my emotions and not lose it. It wasn't easy though, and every time I thought about Shannon lying in that hospital, when I thought about those marks on her body, I slid closer to the edge.

I couldn't get her out of my head, which, to be fair, was nothing new, but now it was different. I was confused, my feelings all fucked up and laced with nervous desperation. I didn't want to leave her back there. If I had my way, I'd steal her away from that horrendous fucking family and keep her all to myself.

Helping me out of the passenger seat, Dad closed the door behind me and hooked an arm around my waist. I was glad of his help. My head was in pieces, my body weary and sore, and I didn't think I had a whole pile of juice left in the tank. "I won't make that mistake again, son."

Grateful for the boost, I gave up on using my crutches and threw my right arm around his shoulders instead, leaning heavily against him. "I'm in bits, Da," I admitted through clenched teeth, feeling the red-hot burn in my thighs and lower abdomen. "My body's wrecked."

"Good lad," Dad coaxed as he tucked my crutches under one arm and guided me to the door. "That's it – mind the step, son."

"I've got it," I bit out, forcing down a scream as I struggled over the doorstep. "I'm good."

When we stepped into the kitchen, Mam was standing beside the cooker with her apron on and a wooden spoon in her hands. The minute she noticed us, she dropped her spoon into the pot of stew, her stirring forgotten, and hurried over to me. "Are you okay, love?" she asked, cupping my face in her hands, brown eyes warm and laced with maternal concern. "Are you sore? What about Shannon? Did you see her? Is it true? Did you get to talk to her—"

"Edel, love," Dad interjected with a small shake of his head, "not tonight. The lad is dead on his feet."

Mam's expression caved. "Oh god." Her hands dropped to her sides as she stared up at me and Dad in horror. "It's true, isn't it?"

"It's true, love," Dad confirmed grimly. "He was right all along."

Mam covered her mouth with her hands. "Her father?"

Dad nodded stiffly.

"Oh, John." Tears filled my mother's eyes. "That poor child."

"It's not just her, though, is it?" I snapped, bristling with agitation. "There's a fucking ocean of children in that house."

Mam flinched. "And you think . . . "

"I don't know what I think anymore." Swallowing down a surge of anger at the complete fucking injustice that it was to be a teenager in this world, I swiped my crutches from my father and growled, "I have no bleeding clue." Brushing past them, I hobbled to the door. "I'm going to bed."

"Do you want to talk about it?" Mam called after me. "Johnny?"

"I need some space," I muttered, not looking back. "I need some time to process this . . . shitstorm."

"Johnny, love—"

"Edel, leave him be."

"But, John, he can't manage the stairs on his own—"

"Edel, let the boy be."

At a snail's pace, I made it down the hallway to the staircase, ignoring my parents as they argued between themselves. My breathing was labored from the sheer exertion it took to get my body to comply and *move*.

When I finally made it to the top of the stairs, having deserted my crutches three steps up, I felt faint. Digging deep into the storage tank of will inside of me, I steeled my spine and pushed on. It wasn't until I was inside my bedroom, with my door closed behind me, that I let it out.

Staggering over to my bed, I sank down on the edge and dropped my head in my hands. Sookie, my Labrador, stirred from her perch at the foot of my bed and bounded towards me, closing the space between us, clearly thrilled to see me again.

"How's my baby, huh? Did Ma leave you in here? Good girl." Bone weary, I scratched her ears and neck, while my attention shifted to the newspaper lying open on my nightstand. Leaning over my dog, I grabbed it and flicked it over to the page it was open to.

The minute my eyes landed on Shannon's smiling, un-marked face as she snuggled into my side, I felt like I had been sucker punched in the chest.

"I fucked up, Sook." Wrapping an arm around my dog, I buried my face in her neck. Exhaling a pained growl, I blinked away the sting of tears as my mind frantically flicked through every bad memory I had of Shannon until I felt like I would explode. "I fucked up so bad, girl," I confessed, clenching my eyes shut as a harsh sob tore from my chest. "Christ."

A low knock sounded from my bedroom door. "Johnny, can I come in?"

"No," I bit out, tensing up. I was surprised that my mother was actually asking my permission for once in her life. "Just ... just leave me be, Ma. *Please*."

There was a long pause and then the sound of footsteps retreating filled the silence, getting quieter and quieter, before spinning around and growing in volume. My bedroom door flew inwards and Mam strode in. "I'm sorry, love, but I can't do that."

And they called *me* a bulldozer.

"I know you're mad at me," she said, closing the space and sitting down beside me. "And you have every right to feel that way. I'm mad at me, too." Reaching out, Mam ruffled Sookie's ears before rolling her out of the way and shifting closer to me. "But you've been through hell these past few days." Placing her hand on my shoulder, she added, "I need you to know that I am *here*. I *need* to be here for *you*."

"I know you're here, Ma," I muttered, focusing my gaze on the door of my en suite bathroom. "Never thought you weren't."

"I talked to Dad about what happened to Shannon," she added gently, squeezing my shoulder. "I know you must be feeling confused right now."

I sighed heavily. "That's one way of putting it."

"It's *okay* to feel off-balance over this."

"I don't know how I'm feeling anymore," I mumbled, pinching the bridge of my nose. "Everything's just ... railroading." Dropping my head, I inhaled several calming breaths, wondering how in the hell my life had taken on this fucked-up route. "I feel like I'm drowning in their pain, Ma," I admitted hoarsely. *I feel like I'm drowning in* her.

"You're a smart boy, Johnny, but you're not emotionally equipped to deal with what you were exposed to tonight, and that's *okay*."

"There's nothing okay about *any* of this," I bit out through clenched teeth. "A grown man beats the living daylights out his daughter, fucking terrorizes her for *years*, puts her in a hospital bed, and just slips away into hiding?" I threw my hands up in frustration. "Do you think *Shannon* is emotionally equipped to deal with that? Because I honestly can't see how." I leaned my head back, more upset than I could handle. "I don't get it, Ma," I hissed, feeling the anger rise up in me once more. "I don't understand how a man could do that to his kid—" I clenched my jaw and inhaled through my nose, needing to keep my cool more than anything right now. "How anyone could do that to *her*."

"Sometimes people do horrendous and unexplainable things, love," Mam replied softly. "There's no sane way of understanding madness, love, so don't drive yourself crazy trying to."

"But I just—"

"Care about her?" Mam interjected gently. "We know, Johnny, pet."

"Months, Ma," I choked out, feeling anxious. "I've known Shannon for *months*, and knowing that every day of those months she was going home from school to that piece of—" I shook my head and took several deep, calming breaths before continuing, "I let her down. I'm just one more on a long list of people who let her down."

"You didn't let her down, Johnny. You didn't know."

"I knew *something* was wrong," I argued. "I knew that much!"

"Because you've always had a good sense of what was right and wrong," Mam replied. "That's what makes you special, love. You've always drummed to your own beat. Defended the underdog. You've never been one to fall into line or follow the crowd. Even when you were little, you walked your own line, Johnny."

"That's not really helping, Ma," I grumbled.

"What I'm trying to say is you obviously saw something in Shannon. Something that you wanted to protect. But it's not your job to save the world, Johnny. You weren't to know what was happening to her, so don't put this on your shoulders."

"Yeah, well, apparently, he's an *alcoholic*," I sneered. "Like that's an excuse to use your kids as a punching bag."

"It's not an excuse," Mam agreed. "It's a crime."

"I *hate* him," I spat, practically choking on my outrage. "I want to hunt the creep down and do some serious harm to him."

"But you won't."

"No, I won't." I glared down at my legs. "Because I can hardly take a piss on my own right now."

"No," Mam corrected, rubbing my back, "because you're on the cusp of a career you've worked your entire life to have, and that's not worth throwing away for a punch up, no matter how satisfying it might feel in the moment."

"You know, Ma, I *knew* something was off the very first day I met Shannon. I fucking knew something wasn't right, like she had secrets, but I just . . . " I let my words trail off and shrugged. "I didn't think they were *this*."

"How could you know, Johnny?"

"And *her*," I continued, glaring at nothing in particular. "I don't trust *her*."

"Her?"

"Shannon's ma," I spat out. "There's something seriously *off* about her. Like how – *how* in the name of god do you let your kids live in a home like that?" I looked to my mother for the answers. "How, Ma? How does that work?"

"I don't know, Johnny."

"Shouldn't she be in some sort of trouble?" I balled my hands into fists at the thought. "For not stepping in? Isn't that neglect . . . or failure to step the fuck up?"

"Mind your language."

"Really?" I arched my brow. "You're going to lecture me tonight of all nights? *Really*?"

Mam sighed heavily. "What did Shannon say about it? About her mother?"

"Stuff," I muttered, dropping my gaze to my lap.

"Stuff?"

"I'm not talking about what she says to me, Ma," I replied. "It's private. But I've got a bad feeling about that woman." Dropping my hand to my thigh, I began to smooth the ache that was building up in my body. "She's supposed to come home either tomorrow or Thursday, but that means she'll go back there. To that house. With that *woman*." I looked to my mother and asked, "How the fuck does that even happen?"

"I don't know, love," Mam replied, voice turning hard. "But your father told me how that woman spoke to you tonight. She had no bleeding right!"

"Jesus," I muttered, mentally cursing my father for telling her. "It doesn't even matter."

"It *does* matter," she corrected hotly. "She has no right to look down her nose at *my* son."

"She wasn't looking down her nose," I muttered. "She was pissed that I was there." Shrugging, I added, "The woman doesn't like me. She never has." Exhaling heavily, I shifted around, trying to get somewhat comfortable. "Not since I hit Shannon with that bleeding ball." I cringed at the memory, still feeling guilty. "She doesn't want me near her daughter."

"Well, she needs to step the fuck back from *my* son," Mam growled, visibly trembling with anger. "I won't have it, Johnny. Do you hear me? I won't *have it*! She's a very lucky lady that it was your father with you tonight and not me!"

"*Step the fuck back*?" My mouth fell open. "You planning on throwing down, Ma?"

"She tried to have you suspended in January," Mam growled, cheeks turning pink. "She put her hands on *my* minor child, on school grounds – something Mr. Twomey conveniently forgot to disclose when I spoke to him about it." She narrowed her eyes. "No one messes with my kid."

I frowned. "When did you talk to Twomey about this?"

Mam bristled. "I phoned him up after Shannon told me what happened – before I went back to London."

I gaped at her. "*Why*?"

"Because I'm your mother and I had a right to be notified of any issues involving my child at school," she shot back snippily. "I know that woman has been making trouble for you. I also know they threatened you with impending suspension because she pushed for it – that they made you out to be a *bully*!" Mam balled her small hands into fists. "I might not like the rugby, but how dare anyone put all you've worked for in jeopardy because of an accident? It's completely unacceptable. The school had no right to do that to you – and no grounds. I made that perfectly clear to your principal." Smirking, she added, "Before I threatened to pull both you, and our family's generous funding donations, from Tommen."

"Ah Jaysus, Ma." Running my hand through my hair in exasperation, I looked up at the ceiling and groaned. "Just so you know, she barely touched me."

"She *put her hands on you*," Mam repeated angrily. "She *pushed* you. She *threatened* you. She lashed out at you in anger. That might fly in her household, Jonathan, but it sure as hell doesn't in mine."

I arched a brow. "Says the woman always clipping me around the ear."

"Those are clips of love," Mam corrected. "And you're missing the point."

"Fine." I shrugged in defeat. "What's the point?"

"The point, love, is that she had no right to treat my son the way she did. She has no god-given right to lay down the law where you're concerned. That's my job. She needs to take stock of the glass walls surrounding her house before casting stones at mine. Your father should've told her just that, but he's too bleeding diplomatic." Huffing out a breath, she added, "It's the culchie in him."

I smirked at her comment. "I think it's the lawyer in him, Ma."

Mam huffed again. "Well, had your father spent thirty-six hours on the flat of his back, trying to push all eight pounds twelve ounces of you out of his arse, he might feel different."

"Jesus Christ." I shuddered at the glorious visual of my entry into the world. "Thanks for the mental image."

Mam smirked. "I know you think that I'm an overbearing nag, but I can't help it. That's what mothers do. We nag and worry and hover until we're cold in the ground." She leaned over and rested her cheek on my shoulder. "You're my boy, Johnny." She sighed heavily. "You might be towering over me now, but no matter what happens, or how far you go in life, you'll always be *my* baby."

"You know I love ya back," I mumbled, embarrassed and uncomfortable. "You might drive me demented most days, but I'd be lost without ya."

"I know, love." Mam sighed and patted my hand. "I know."

"Ma, please don't hate Shannon over this," I added, my words barely more than a mumble. "I know you're pissed with her mother, but don't hold it against her."

"Oh god, I don't hate Shannon, love," she hurried to soothe. "She's a smashing girl and I would never judge a child based on my feelings towards their parents." Reaching over, she pressed a hand to my back. "After all, your Nana and Granda Kavanagh never judged me and look at what I came from."

"True."

My mother's side of the family were *colorful* to say the least. She'd been dragged up, literally dragged from pillar to post, and passed between various relatives until, at the age of sixteen, she'd finally had enough and split from Dublin. Without a penny in her pocket and only her wits to get by, she smuggled herself onto a Bus Eireann coach with no destination in mind and landed in Cork. Hitching a ride to Ballylaggin, she landed on my grandparents' farm with a serious attitude problem and a willingness to earn her keep. Four years later, she was living in London, attending college, and married to my father.

"But I will say this," Mam added, nudging my shoulder with hers. "If Marie Lynch wants to start trouble with you, she'll have to go through me first."

"Ma ... " I shook my head and sighed heavily. "I'm defending the woman, but she's probably just projecting." Shrugging, I added, "They're all going through the wringer right now."

"I understand that, Johnny," Mam agreed. "I do, love. I can't comprehend how her poor children must be feeling." Standing up, she smoothed her apron down before adding, "But she won't be projecting onto you." Her eyes narrowed. "Over my dead body."

"I need to go back tomorrow." I watched my mother as she pottered around my room, sweeping up clothes off the floor. "To the hospital."

Mam didn't respond.

"Ma," I pushed. "I need to go back."

She sighed heavily. "I don't want you going anywhere near that woman, Johnny. Not when she's throwing around accusations about you."

"I'm not going for her sake," I snapped, bristling. "I'm going for Shannon – wait." I narrowed my eyes. "What do you mean accusations? Are you talking about the fucking ball again? Because I've already explained that was a bleeding accident."

Mam shook her head. "No, love."

"Then what?" I snapped, bristling. "What's she saying about me?"

"She said some things to your dad," she replied. "Some things that make your father and I uncomfortable about letting you go over there."

"Like what?"

"Look, Johnny, you need to steer clear for a while," she finally said, not elaborating any further. "I'm not saying forever, but until the dust settles, it would be best if you gave that family some space."

*The fuck did she say about me?* "I haven't done anything, Ma," I growled, feeling defensive and on edge. "So whatever she's saying about me, it's complete bullshit."

"Look, just get some sleep and we'll talk about it in the morning," she replied, not meeting my eyes. "You still need to rest, Johnny. You're running on empty."

I was running on empty all right; an empty tank of patience. "Ma?" I watched my mother as she walked over to my door. "Ma, what did she say?"

"Get some sleep, love," was all she replied. She moved to close the door behind her only to stop in her tracks. "Oh, I almost forgot—" Sliding her hand into the front pocket of her apron, she retrieved a small, folded-up piece of paper. "I found this when I was washing your clothes from Dublin." Walking back over to me, she handed me the paper. "You're a sweet boy." Smiling, she stroked my cheek with her hand before turning back for the door. "I'm proud of you," she added before closing my bedroom door out behind her.

Confused, I unfolded the piece of paper and stared down, feeling a swell of emotion hit me straight in the chest.

*Shannon like the river, will you please be my friend?*

The friendship contract.

Fuck.

Carefully refolding the letter, I tucked it into my bedside locker and sighed.

*Be okay,* I mentally prayed. *Please be okay, Shannon like the river.*

# Homeward Bound

## SHANNON

I had always felt unsteady. For most of my life, I remained in a state of constant unease, trying and failing to predict the next bad move, the move that would bring pain and misery.

As I stood in the doorway of my childhood bedroom on Thursday afternoon, I felt more unnerved and doubtful than ever before, because I couldn't predict the danger. I just knew it was lurking somewhere.

My body was on high-alert, the survival instinct inside of my head was screaming at me that I wasn't safe. Feeling powerless, I took stock of my room and noted that it looked exactly the same as it always did; small, neat, and tidy.

"I'll get you some new stuff for in here," Darren announced as he stepped around me and placed my hospital bag on the foot of my single bed. "Some new paint and curtains. A new bedspread. Whatever you want, Shannon. Just tell me what colors you'd like and I'll get it done."

*How about a new life? Or a new family? Or just some inner peace?* "I'm fine," I replied, throat still raw and hoarse. "I don't need you to buy me anything." Forcing my legs to move, something I was finding difficult since stepping through the front door earlier, I walked over to my bed and sat down.

My mind automatically shifted to the memory of Johnny sprawled out on my mattress, teaching me maths, and my lips tipped up. But then I made the mistake of glancing at the wall beside the door and my one good memory of this house obliterated into thin air, replaced with the memory of my father throwing me against the wall so hard, my head made a dent in the plaster. I was seven at the time and had refused to hand over my holy communion money. That had been a mistake. One I had paid for with both my money and my body.

"Are you okay?" Darren asked, dragging me from my dark thoughts. "Shannon?"

"Where is everyone?" I asked, forcing the memories back down.

"The boys are over at Nanny's," he explained. "I couldn't take them with me to pick you up, and Mam's at that class Patricia organized."

Patricia, being the social worker assigned to our family, and the class, being a parenting skills group.

I almost rolled my eyes at the notion. What were they going to teach her there? Not to let her husband beat her children? Not to run off for days and leave her children without food? Not to take to the bed for weeks on end and leave us to fend for ourselves?

Common sense should have told her all that.

Of course, the social workers didn't know all this. They were fed the " 'poor, battered wife trying desperately to keep her children safe" line Darren had made us rehearse until we were blue in the face. I cringed at the thought of how he worded that spiel to the younger boys. They must be feeling so confused.

*She's as much of a victim as the rest of us,* Darren had said. To a point, I agreed with him, or at least, I used to. But there came a time in life when I stopped making excuses for my mother, and that time came and went months ago.

"Do you want to talk?" Darren asked, hovering in the doorway now. "About Dad?"

I shook my head.

"Are you sure?"

I gave him a blank stare. I wasn't sure what he was expecting me to do. Confide in him? I didn't think so. He was as much of a stranger to me as the countless authority figures I'd been forced to speak to. *To lie to.*

"What about Joey?" I asked the question that was most important to me. "Where is he?"

Darren sighed heavily. "I don't know."

"Well, has he been home?" I asked, my tone hardening with my outrage. "Has he slept here since you got back?"

He shook his head. "Haven't seen him since the hospital."

"Did you call his girlfriend?" I demanded, feeling my pulse flutter wildly. "Do you know if he's with Aoife?"

"Joey's his own man," Darren replied. "He's an adult. Over eighteen—"

"Barely," I strangled out. It suited them for Joey to be gone. Without Joey, everything would fall back into place. Joey was a complication neither Mam or Darren seemed to want to deal with. "He turned eighteen at Christmas – and he's still in school. That hardly makes him an adult."

"Shannon, if he wants to stay out, there's nothing I can do about it."

"He doesn't want to stay out, Darren," I snapped. We were all a product of our environment. And Joey? Joey was *angry*. "He wants to not be in a house with her!"

"Well, whether he likes it or not, she happens to be his mother," Darren snapped. "He has a room in this house if he wants it. The door is always open to him. It's his choice if he wants to act out and not cooperate. I can't make him stay."

"Act out? Not cooperate?" I narrowed my eyes and forced down the urge to scream. "He's doing this because he's in pain and nobody is hearing him." *And especially not you!*

"Then he needs to sit down and talk about how he's feeling," Darren groaned. "Not run around banging his fists on his bloody chest." He ran a hand through his dark hair, clearly frustrated. "I want to help him, Shannon. I do. But I can't do that if he won't *let* me."

I opened my mouth to respond, but just shook my head instead.

There was no point in continuing with this conversation. Darren didn't get it. He either couldn't or wouldn't see this from Joey's perspective, and I wasn't wasting any more of my energy trying to make him.

"You're failing him," I whispered, unable to stop the words from pouring out, "Just like they did."

"Shannon." Darren flinched like I had physically hit him, and I guess I had – with the truth. "I'm here for all of you," he choked out. "For whatever you need. Day or night."

*Yeah, all of us except for Joey.*

"Then can I use your phone?" I asked, already knowing the answer before asking. Narrowing my eyes, I added, "You said you'd be there for whatever I need. Well, right now I need to make a phone call."

My brother stiffened. "If it's to call him, then no. You heard Mam."

I didn't need him to elaborate on who he was referring to. We both knew he meant Johnny. "Then can I get a phone of my own?"

Darren let out an exasperated sigh. "Shannon, we need to focus on the family right now. We have social workers breathing down our necks and the Gardaí up our asses. We don't need any more hassle. I know you think we're being unfair, but it has to be this way for now."

"Then I don't need anything from you," I replied coldly. "Except to close the door behind you."

"Shannon—"

"She's wrong about him," I hissed, having heard it all before. It had been three days since I'd seen Johnny. Three days since he'd arrived at the hospital to see me. And three days since my family had decided he was a bad idea. Mam never liked Johnny and now I knew why. He made her nervous. He knew too much and it scared her. *It should.* "And you're listening to it."

"I'm not listening to anything," he replied, tone weary. "I don't even know the lad."

"Exactly," I hissed. "You don't know him."

"I do know that Mam is right about you being in a vulnerable state of mind right now," he interjected. "It's not healthy to attach yourself to him."

"Oh my god." I closed my eyes and fought back the urge to reach out and break something. "You're both disgusting." Snapping my eyes open, I glared at my brother. "He's my *friend*, Darren. I'm allowed to have friends, you know!"

"A friend that you were caught straddling, with your skirt around your waist, in some changing room by your teacher?"

I flushed beetroot red. *Damn you, Mr. Mulcahy.* "We were kissing," I choked out. "That's *it.*"

"I'm not *judging* you, Shannon, I'm questioning your judgment. There's a difference," he was quick to say. "It would be very easy for someone in your position, who's been through severe trauma and neglect, to dive head first into something you're not emotionally ready for because you've had a taste of affection. And . . ." he added cautiously, "it would be very easy for someone to take advantage of a person in that state of mind, too."

"You are so wrong about him—"

"Just hear me out on this, okay?" he interrupted again. "I'm not saying this to hurt you. I'm just trying to make you *aware*." His tone of voice was soft and gentle but his words were patronizing and made me feel sick. "You're sixteen," he continued. "You've been through hell, and suddenly there's a young-fella knocking around, saying all the right things, making you feel wanted and alive. I get that, Shannon, I do. We've all been there. But you need to take a step back, think about what you're doing, and *why* you're feeling the way you are before you jump over a ledge you can't come back from. I don't want you doing anything that you're going to regret later on."

"You don't get it," I whispered.

"I get it. Everyone in the history of the world gets it. You think you're in love. You're convinced this boy will be the boy that saves you. But it's not real. It's all hormones and growing pains." Darren sighed wearily. "Your emotions are heightened when you're a teenager, and yours are especially because of what you've been through."

"I can't believe these words are actually coming out of your mouth," I hissed, feeling like I was being attacked. "You of all people."

"It's trauma bonding," he continued. "Maybe not completely, but you're definitely attaching yourself to him."

"Because I love him," I snapped, losing my cool. Blinking wildly when I realized what I had said, I debated taking it back before steeling my resolve. "I love him," I repeated, firmer this time. "And that has *nothing* to do with trauma or my family and everything to do with *him*!"

"You're a baby, Shannon," Darren sighed, belittling me once more. "You don't even know what love means yet."

"Are you finished?" I deadpanned, feeling the hot sting of tears. "Because you can go now."

Darren stood in the doorway for a solid minute longer, looking at me like he wanted to say something, but didn't. Eventually, he shook his head and turned to leave. "I'll be downstairs if you need me."

# I'm Alone

## SHANNON

I had been home from the hospital less than a week and already the cracks were starting to show in our newly formed family unit. Mam was withdrawn, and when she wasn't at work, she spent most of her time locked away in her bedroom or sitting like a zombie at the kitchen table, smoking cigarettes and staring off into nothing. This wasn't anything new to us, but without Joey around to compensate, the household was falling into a state of anarchy.

It didn't seem to matter what Darren said or did; Ollie and Tadhg weren't impressed and constantly challenged him. Even little Sean was resisting our new setup. He hadn't spoken a word to anyone since Dad left. I knew Darren was trying, and a part of me felt bad for my oldest brother, but a bigger part of me held infallible allegiance towards Joey.

Joey hadn't come home in days and with his noticeable absence from our younger brothers' daily routine, something they had been used to, came confusion and rebellion. I had a feeling Darren was regretting ever coming home. He was snowballing under the pressure of the role he had taken on, drowning in the bills and debts our parents had recklessly amassed, and smothering in the responsibility of caring for younger siblings and a weak mother.

On top of the meetings with solicitors, sessions with counselors, and house visits from social services and the Gardaí, the boys still had training sessions and matches most evenings. They had routines to uphold and even with Nanny helping out, it was a lot for one person to manage.

The pressure was immense and without Joey around to smooth everything over like he usually did, and steer Darren in the right direction, cracks were showing and tempers were rising.

The only good part about the whole mess was that our father was still missing. The bad part was that I knew in my heart that my mother was pining for him. She was pining for the man who'd made our lives a misery. That gave me little hope for a long-term future without him in it.

Without a phone or Joey, I had no way of contacting the outside world. Four months ago, that wouldn't have bothered me in the slightest. Four months ago, I would have been grateful to curl up under my duvet and hide from the big, bad world. But that was before Tommen. *That was before Johnny.*

Something was happening to me, I realized, something was shifting deep inside of my mind, and for the first time in my life, I felt *restless*. I felt like I wanted to pull on the chains shackling me to this house and *break free.* I had no idea where the notion had come from, but it was there, it was real, and it was encouraging me to dust myself off and *fight back.* To be brave and turn this life around for myself.

Not even the warnings from the Gardaí, encouraging me to stay at home while they searched for my father, or the constant whispering in my ear from Mam and Darren, could dissuade the yearning I had inside of my heart to break free.

I found it strange that now, with more bruises on my body than ever before, I wanted to push the boundaries, but that's what was happening.

"Have you heard from Joey?" Tadhg's voice cut through my thoughts, bringing me back to the present.

I swung around to find him leaning against the bathroom wall, his arms folded across his chest, watching me.

"No," I replied, turning back to face the mirror I had been staring into before he distracted me. "I haven't." Using my free hand, I ran my fingers through my hair, flinching when pain ricocheted through my scalp. "I haven't seen him since the hospital. You know this."

"And you're not worried?" he pushed, tone hardening. "Or do you not give a fuck like the rest of them?"

"You know I care, Tadhg." Forcing my hand to steady, I reached up with the scissors I was holding and tried again. "I give a lot of fucks."

"Why isn't he coming home, Shan?"

I wanted to scream *because she's here*, but I held it back and forced out, "I don't know, Tadhg," instead.

"What are you doing?" he asked then, sounding distracted.

Setting down the scissors on the sink, I turned around and gave him my attention. "I'm trying to fix my hair."

He arched a sardonic brow. "By hacking it off?"

"I'm not hacking it off, Tadhg."

"Then what are you doing?" he repeated, tone challenging.

I released a heavy sigh. "I'm bald."

"How'd you figure that?" His brows furrowed. "Your hair looks the same as always to me."

Walking over to the toilet, I closed the lid and sat down. "Come here."

"Why?"

"So I can show you."

Looking rather hesitant, Tadhg walked over to me. "Fine. Show me."

"Here." I lowered my head. "See the side part?"

I felt his fingers brush against my scalp before stilling. "There's a chunk gone," he deadpanned, yanking his hand away. "The size of a fist."

"I know." Swallowing deeply, I battled down my emotions and cupped the side of my head. "I was *trying* to bring some hair from the other side of my parting over to cover it up, but it's all uneven at the ends."

He was silent for a long time before asking, "Do you have a comb?"

I nodded. "On the sink."

Without a word, Tadhg walked over to the sink and grabbed both the comb and scissors.

"Whoa," I spluttered, eyeing the scissors warily. "Wh-what are you doing?"

"Fixing it," he growled. "Do you want my help or not?"

I debated the dangers of letting my eleven-year-old brother loose with scissors on my hair for the briefest of moments before shrugging in resignation. "Go for it." Whatever he did couldn't look worse than walking around with all of my hair tossed over one side. "I'm trusting you."

Tadhg's response to that was a clipped '*Hmm*', but his fingers were achingly gentle as he worked. "Do you think she'll take him back?" he asked after a long stretch of silence. "When the dust settles?"

*Yes.* "No."

"Liar," was all he replied.

Twenty minutes later and I was staring in the mirror and admiring his handy work.

"I moved it over," he explained, still scowling, as he stood behind me and stared at the mirror. "And then I just evened out the ends on both sides so you don't look stupid."

Instead of my elbow-length hair parting down the middle of my scalp like it always had, it now parted on the right, with the extra hair concealing the bald patch from where my father had torn clumps of my hair off.

"Thanks," I squeezed out, feeling a huge swell of emotion surge up inside of me. I turned around to face him. "I owe you one."

Tadhg shifted around, looking uncomfortable. "Yeah, well, if you want to do me a favor then find my brother."

My heart cracked. "He'll come back, Tadhg." Tears filled my eyes as I said, "Joey would never leave us."

"We're alone," he whispered, dropping his gaze to his feet.

"No." I shook my head and moved towards him. "We're not."

"Don't you get it yet?" he spat, backing away from me. "Haven't you figured it out by now? We are *all* alone." He shook his head and glared at me. "All of us. On our own. By ourselves. And that's that."

"Tadhg, that's not true—"

"No one fucking cares, Shannon," he told me, voice flat and void of all emotion. "Not about us. If they did, they would have come by now. And Joey doesn't care, either," he cried before storming away.

# Cashing In On Favors

## JOHNNY

Days had passed without a word from Shannon and I was going out of my mind with worry.

Between that and being banned from training and the gym, I was at a complete loss. Seriously, I had no fucking clue what to do with myself. I attended my physio and OT sessions, but without the distraction of my usual jam-packed schedule, my mood was worsening.

I also received a huge-ass bollocking, via phone, from my coaches at The Academy for putting my body at risk the way I had. What had seemed like a good idea at the time had come back to bite me in the ass. My doctors and coaches didn't trust me anymore, and I knew that it would be a very long time before they would again.

It was depressing.

The one upside to my downtime, and I begrudgingly admitted this, was that my body seemed to be thriving with the rest, recuperating at a much more rapid pace than I had anticipated. I could move more freely now, and the bruising and swelling in my balls and groin that had plagued me since Halloween was slowly beginning to fade. It also didn't hurt to take a piss anymore. I still wasn't taking any chances on the whole pulling my dick thing, but the morning hard-on I sported on a daily basis didn't cause me the discomfort it once had.

None of that consoled me because my entire focus was on *Shannon*.

Because of my father and his anal attitude towards upholding the law, I hadn't been able to see her. Apparently, Shannon's brother, Darren, had called my parents, making it clear, in no uncertain terms, that I wasn't to return to the hospital.

I understood that my father dealt with this kind of thing on a daily basis, he was used to watching dysfunction unfold around him, but I wasn't. This was personal for me – *she* was personal for me – and being kept in the dark was driving me insane.

My mother, the turncoat, was on my father's side, but she had her own agenda. She didn't want me going anywhere near Mrs. Lynch. Her back was up over the whole suspension threat and she didn't want me going next to nor near *a woman like that* – her words, not mine.

Because of my inability to get myself from A to B since my surgery, I couldn't get there without my parents' help, leaving me pissed off and car-less.

Betrayed and sulking, I remained in bed for most of the week, ignoring my mother every time she popped her head around the door to check on me – which happened to be every twenty bleeding minutes – and mulling in my bad mood.

I was smothering inside my house. Fucking losing my mind with the restlessness inside of my body. I wasn't used to sitting still and doing nothing. I was cranky and on edge, driven deeper into my own head with every passing day and no word from Shannon.

By the following Monday, I was resigned to my bad mood.

After an intense physiotherapy session with Janice this morning, followed by a further two hours in the pool, I was depressed and agitated. On the flat of my back, with Sookie tucked at my side, I wasted the rest of the day tossing a rugby ball into the air and catching it, all the while contemplating the worst possible scenarios that had been relentlessly plaguing me.

What if Shannon's dad came back and he didn't get prosecuted?

What if my body didn't heal in time for the tour?

What if he came back and her mother took him back?

What if the coaches overlooked me for that Danny Miller kid from Galway?

What if she didn't come back to school next week?

What if this was it for me?

What if she was put into care and had to change schools?

What if I'd played my last game in Dublin?

What if she got hurt again?

*What if, what if, what if . . .*

"I should have kept her in this room with us, Sook," I muttered. "I should have kept her, period!"

My faithful Labrador's response was to nuzzle into my side and yodel softly.

"Yeah I know, baby." Exhaling heavily, I tossed the ball across the room and wrapped my arm around her. "I fucked up real bad."

"Johnny, something's come up and Dad's had to go back to Dublin," Mam's voice filled the room moments before she arrived in my doorway. "Cillian called – you remember Cillian, don't you, love? Cillian Moore?"

One of the bloodthirsty solicitors who worked under my father? "Yeah, I remember him." *Hotshot little fucker.*

"Well, there's been some issue with a client's bail hearing and your dad needs to be there to clear it up. Cillian was handling the case, but something's popped up and your father is on better terms with Judge O'Leary."

I snorted loudly. "Glad to know where his priorities lie. As usual."

"Don't be like that," Mam said with a sigh. "He spent half the night on the phone last night – *again* – calling around for your benefit."

Arching a brow, I leveled her with a stare. "And?"

"And nothing," Mam replied. "He's not at liberty to discuss anything he found out with us – if he even found anything out." She sighed again. "You know all of this, Johnny."

Not bothering to respond, I turned my glare to the ceiling above me.

"He left some paperwork in his study and I need to drop it up to him," Mam continued to say. "I'll only be a few hours – I'll definitely be back tonight, but just in case, I've called Gerard to come over and keep you company while I'm gone. He knows you're not to leave the house, love, so don't even try and coax him into doing the wrong thing or there will be consequences for the both of you."

My ears perked up at the sound of Gibsie's name, and instantly, I was plotting mutiny.

I cared about a grand total of two things in my life: rugby and Shannon. And right now, both had been taken away from me without warning. I was losing control of the reins of my own life and it was making me crazy. What the fuck was I supposed to do? Stay in my bed and take my medicine like a good little boy with a broken dick? *I think fucking not.*

"Stay in bed," Mam added sternly. "Gerard can let himself in, so don't trouble yourself with the stairs, love. And I know you said you're not hungry, but there's a pot of soup on the stove and some fresh bread rolls on the table if you're feeling peckish later."

Yeah, my mother might not have gotten the pram she wanted with my discharge papers from the hospital, but she had gained more control over my life than she'd had in years and she was exercising that newfound power. I was out of commission and she was thrilled to have me under her maternal watch 24/7.

"Are you listening to me, Johnny?" Mam pushed. "Did you hear a word of what I just said?"

"I heard ya," I grumbled. "Gibsie's coming over to babysit me because I, apparently, can't be trusted to be left on my own for an hour." I rolled my eyes. "Even though I've taken care of myself for months on end without either one of my folks around."

Mam rolled her eyes right back at me. "Don't be such a drama queen."

I gaped at her, resisting the urge to scream and prove her right.

"Enjoy your *trip*," I said instead.

Mam arched a brow. "Enjoy your *strop*."

*Give me strength . . .*

"Goodbye, Mother," I bit out.

Mam smirked. "Farewell, my bouncing baby boy."

Jesus.

I waited until Mam had closed my bedroom door behind her before throwing the covers off myself.

Twenty minutes later, I was fresh from a shower and wrestling with a pair of jocks when my bedroom door flew inwards. "I'm so fucking bored," Gibsie announced, strolling into my room. "We're on our Easter break and how am I spending it? Locked up in my room, studying for an exam I'm not even sure I can spell, let alone take next year, and all because *you* decided to break your dick and leave me alone." Dropping his overnight bag on the floor, he flopped down on my bed and exhaled a dramatic sigh. "You're so selfish."

"Sorry for inconveniencing you," I grumbled as I balanced against the bathroom doorframe and tried to tuck myself in without causing harm. My stitches were healing nicely, but I was still sore and bruised. "I forgot it's all about you, Gibs—"

"*Whoa*, that's a lot of swollen dick!" Gibsie groaned, dropping a hand over his face. "You're all there, aren't ya, lad! Kind of wish I didn't come over now. Feeling kind of emasculated. And a little hard done by. Maybe I should learn to knock—"

"Stop talking," I muttered, settling the waistband on my hips. "You're being all fucked up again and I need you to be normal for an hour."

He arched a brow. "Only an hour?"

"Gibs!" I snapped, impatient.

"Okay!" He held his hands up. "I'm being normal."

"Good." I sighed. "Because I need you to take me somewhere."

"Oh, no, no, no." He sat straight up and pointed at me. "Bedrest, Johnny. For seven to ten days, lad."

"Yeah, and it's been ten days," I shot back.

"Nine days, if we're being technical," he huffed as he stood up and began to pace. "And your mother specifically mentioned ten days' bedrest when she called me earlier – not to mention the serious physical pain she would inflict on me if I so much as thought about aiding and abetting you in leaving the house!"

"Well, I need to see her." Shrugging on the loosest pair of sweatpants I owned, I reached for a fresh t-shirt and quickly threw it on. "I can't drive for at least another week, and they took my bleeding car keys, so I need you to take me."

"No can do," Gibs shot back with a firm shake of his head. "Mammy

Kavanagh will have my balls and I'll end up sharing a surgeon with you." He shook his head again to emphasize his displeasure. "I love you, buddy, but not that much."

"Come on, Gibs," I snapped, frustrated. "*Help me.*"

"I'm always fucking helping you," he groaned.

"Yeah," I deadpanned, "because I'm always helping you right back."

"You need to let her family deal with this, lad," he said, tone serious. "I'm not joking around here, Johnny. You need to take a step back here. You told me what they said – how her mother *warned* you to stay away." He threw his hands up in despair. "So just stay away for a while. They obviously want to handle it themselves. Give her some space, and you'll see her when we go back to school."

"And what if I don't see her?" I demanded. "What if she doesn't come back to Tommen?"

"Of course she'll be back."

"How do you know?"

Gibsie rolled his eyes. "Maybe because she goes to school there!"

Sinking down on the bed, I exhaled a pained breath and tried to wrestle in my emotions before speaking again. "Listen," I began, slightly calmer now, "I'm not asking you to take me to the gym. I'm not going near a bleeding rugby ball, and I'm not asking you to lie for me." Looking him dead in the eyes, I said, "I am asking you to take me to her because I can't fucking get there on my own. And I need to . . . and she needs me to . . . " my words broke off and I pinched the bridge of my nose. "If you don't help me and something happens to her, I swear, I'll never forgive you for it, Gibs." *I'll never forgive me.*

"That's emotional blackmail."

"That's the only hand I have," I replied steadily.

"She'll kill me," Gibsie pointed out. "You do get that, don't you? Your mother will *murder* me."

"I'll take full responsibility," I countered. "Just do this for me, Gibs."

"Fine," he snapped, throwing his hands up. "Call your fucking doctors. Ask them if they're familiar with surgery that involves removal of a woman's high heel from someone's asshole, because that's what's going to happen to me when I take her baby out of this house, Johnny. She is going to *hurt me*." Groaning, he added, "Tell them to book me a bloody bed. I'm going to need one."

# Jailbreak

## JOHNNY

"Okay, we need to think this through," Gibsie announced as he pulled onto the main road near my house. "Bring some sort of deflection with us – a carrot to dangle in case they turn us away."

"A carrot?" I turned my head and glared at him. "The fuck are you talking about? We don't need carrots and deflections, Gibs. We're going to drive over to her house, park the car, and knock on the bleeding door."

Gibsie rolled his eyes. "You have no tact. Here, pull my phone out – it's in my pocket."

"I don't need tact," I grumbled, but I did as he asked. He took the phone from my hands and I steered while he dialed. "You'll get points on your license for this," I muttered, grateful to be in control of something for once, even if it was only a steering wheel.

Gibsie grinned and pressed the phone to his ear. "Only if I get caught – hey, how's it going, babe? I need you to be outside in five – yeah, five minutes. Why? Because I'm picking you up, that's why. Yeah, don't waste time asking questions. Just put your coat on and meet me at the bottom of your driveway. It's cold outside so wear the red one." He grinned, clearly getting a mouthful down the line before saying, "I know you're at home because I saw you watching me from my bedroom window earlier – yeah, I know you stalk me, too. Yeah, you hate me. I know. I've heard it all before, babe. I love you, too."

"We're bringing Claire?" I asked when he ended the call.

Gibsie nodded. "It makes more sense than two lads showing up on their own." Shrugging, he added, "Shannon's her best friend, lad. She hasn't been able to make contact with her since Dublin. Girl's a nervous wreck over it all."

I shrugged. "Fair enough."

Five minutes later, we pulled onto Hughie and Gibsie's street and were greeted by a scowling Claire, who was standing at the bottom of her driveway, holding a neon-pink umbrella to protect herself from the March downpour.

"What's this about, Gerard? What's the big emergency?" she asked, climbing into the back seat when Gibsie pulled up beside her. "Oh, hey Johnny," she added, softening her tone a little. "I hope you're feeling better."

"All good," I replied, feeling uncomfortable knowing that she knew.

"Kav here has coerced me into driving over to Shannon's house," Gibsie said. "Thought you'd want to come."

"I do." Leaning forward, Claire poked her head out between our seats. "But they won't let you through the front door. I had Hughie drive me over there on Friday to see her, but her mother told me she was in bed." Claire scrunched her nose up as she spoke. "She wouldn't even hear me out, guys. She said Shan was too tired for visitors and just dismissed me."

Fury raced through me.

No goddamn way was I going to be dismissed by that woman or any member of their family.

"Simmer down, Cap," Gibsie instructed calmly. It was only then that I noticed my knuckles had turned white from the force of clenching them. "We'll see her."

"You're damn fucking straight we will."

"I know she lives in Elk Terrace," Gibsie said. "But that's a huge terrace—"

"95 – she lives at 95," Claire and I said in unison.

"Jinx," Claire chuckled.

"You know, Claire-bear, if you want to un-jinx yourself, you can always touch my wood," Gibsie offered.

"No thanks, I don't like wood," Claire shot back. "Or penises."

"I remember," Gibsie chuckled. "Wait – is that the plural for penis? Penises?"

"Probably," Claire replied, placing a hand on his shoulder. "I mean, plural for vagina is vaginas, so it sort of has to be, doesn't it?"

"I thought the plural for vagina was vaginae," he offered, and then after a thoughtful pause, added, "You know what, I think plural for penis is penii."

"Oh my god, Gerard, literally nobody says penii or vaginae," Claire scoffed. "It's penises and vaginas."

"Hmm," he mused. "Sounds weird, though."

"When it comes to human genitalia, I think it all sounds a little weird, Gerard."

I zoned out of their conversation, too concerned about Shannon to entertain either of them. Instead, I cranked the stereo and drowned my thoughts out with one of Gibsie's eclectic mix-CDs. I kept my eyes trained on the windscreen, not blinking and barely breathing until we ascended the huge hill and pulled onto her street.

"Shit," Gibsie muttered when we pulled up outside her run-down house in Elk's Terrace. "Bad luck, huh?"

"Yeah, lad," I muttered. "You have no idea."

"Turn down the music, Gerard," Claire scolded when Gibsie pulled up outside the house.

"What's wrong with my music?" he asked, looking comically wounded.

"'Knockin' On Heaven's Door?'" Glaring, Claire slapped his shoulder. "Really? After what just happened to her?" Leaning between the seats, she switched off the stereo. "That's so insensitive."

"But ... but she's not here?" Killing the engine, Gibsie turned to look at her. Confusion was etched on his face when he said, "And it's Guns N' Roses."

"It's a bad song choice."

"Hang on, what about this one—" His words trailed off as he switched the stereo back on and flicked to track 7. The guitar rift of Thin Lizzy's "Jailbreak" blasted from the speakers. "Better?" Gibsie asked, waggling his brows. "More suited for the occasion, sweet-pea?"

"Much," Claire replied, tone approving. "Good job, snuffle-bunny."

"Thanks, babe."

"You're both bleeding ridiculous." Shaking my head, I shoved the car door open and used my crutches to pull myself out. "This is serious."

"I know, lad," Gibsie replied, joining me on the footpath. "I know."

"So, what's the plan?" Claire asked, climbing out after us. "Do we just . . . " She shrugged helplessly. "Go in there?"

"Well, I'm going in there," I told her. Not waiting for either of them to respond, I rounded the wall that separated the overgrown garden from the footpath and hopped awkwardly to the door. Tension was emanating from my body in waves as I slipped my hand out of one of my crutches and rapped my knuckles against the door.

"Keep the head, Cap," Gibsie instructed quietly in my ear. Reaching around him, he caught ahold of Claire and shoved her in front of both of us. "Smile, Claire-bear," he coaxed, keeping his hand on her hip. "No one could say no to the sun."

Finally, after what felt like an age, the front door swung inwards and we were greeted by what I could only describe as the male version of Shannon. Dark-brown hair, piercing midnight-blue eyes full of secrets. "Yes?" he asked politely. "Can I help you?"

"Who are you?" I decided to come right out and ask. I already knew this was Darren, but I wanted him to confirm it.

"You're at my door," the man replied. "Who are you?"

Fighting down the urge to reach over and drag him out of my way, I asked, "Is Shannon here?"

Darren leaned against the doorframe and folded his arms across his chest. "Who wants to know?"

"Me."

He arched a brow. "And who is me?"

"I'm her—"

"He's her Johnny," Claire blurted out.

"Nice," Gibsie chuckled, tucking her under his arm. "And since we're making introductions, she's my Claire-bear and I'm his Flanker."

"I remember you," Darren said, giving Claire a curious look. "You've grown up."

"Look, is Shannon here or not?" I snapped, clinging to my patience by the skin of my teeth. "I need to see her."

"No."

*Goddammit!* "Well, can you tell me when she'll be back?" I bit out through clenched teeth. "So I know how long I'll be waiting in my car." *Because I'm not going anywhere, fucker.*

"No."

Furious, I leaned on my crutch and hissed, "Where is she, Darren?"

He shook his head and reached for the door. "Go home, Johnny."

"Don't do it, Cap," Gibsie warned, placing his hand on my shoulder. "Don't fucking bulldoze."

I heard him. I did. But I couldn't see beyond the red-hazed fog in my mind, smothering me, making it hard to think clearly.

"Nope," I growled, shaking off his hand. "I'm not going anywhere." I shoved a crutch in the doorway to block Darren from slamming the door in my face. "I know all about your family." I glared behind him. "About the shite that goes on in this house, and if you think I'm walking away without seeing her, then you have another thing coming!"

"You don't have a clue," he growled. "You *think* you do, but you have no goddamn idea!"

"Johnny, maybe we should just go—"

"I'm going nowhere!" I roared, feeling furious and sore from standing. "I'll stand right fucking here until he either lets me in or brings her down!" Straightening, I looked him dead in the eyes and said, "You decide. I'm good with either."

"Do you have any idea of what my family is dealing with here?" he demanded then, his cool façade slipping. "What we're all going through right now? Trying to work through?" He glared at me before continuing, "I am holding my family together by the skin of my teeth here, kid. I spent the best part of a week at my sister's hospital bedside, trying to manage the shitstorm that I've walked back in to. My family has enough problems right now, issues more complicated than you could ever understand, so I need you to back the fuck up and give us some breathing space."

"I'll give you all the space you need," I shot back hotly. "*After* I see Shannon."

"The last thing Shannon needs is you rolling up and *confusing* her," he snapped. "She's been through hell. She needs rest and peace. I'm trying to give her that. I'm trying to make her life *better*, and you storming in and bombarding her with questions is only going to traumatize her even further."

"Then Shannon can tell me that herself," I countered, unwilling to give an inch. "To my face."

Darren shook his head. "Jesus Christ, Johnny, my mother already explained this to you. I spoke to your father and explained this to him. What aren't you getting here? Why can't you understand that what's happening in our family is private and we need time to process everything?"

"What are you so afraid of?" I taunted. "That she'll talk to me? Confide in me? Tell me all the shite she *should* be telling the authorities but *isn't* because you're keeping her locked up like a fucking prisoner?" I looked him up and down and sneered, "Yeah, I know there's more. I know that fucking much. And I also know that you might be able to control her, but you can't control me, and I have no problem with blowing the roof off your dirty little secrets. And here's another thing you can't do." I straightened my spine. "You can't make me leave."

"You need to calm down," he instructed. "Stop puffing your chest out and looking for a fight, Johnny. My sister's fine and you need to leave."

"She was neglected and abused in her own home. She was tortured outside of it. It's a fucking miracle she's still standing. So no, I won't fucking *calm down!*" I snarled. "I want to see her and I'm not going until I do."

"If you don't leave, I'll phone the Gardaí," he replied. "I don't want to, but I will if you don't go."

"Then go for it, because I'm not going anywhere, asshole!" I roared, losing all touch with my self-control. "Go right ahead and call the fucking Guards, because quite frankly, I'd love to speak to them."

"Oh Jesus, his mother's going to kill me," Gibsie groaned. "It's bad enough that I took him out behind her back, but now he's going to be arrested, and then I'll be arrested because I'm a good friend and it's just bad form to let him go to prison on his own, but she won't see it that way. No, she'll see her baby in a cell and I'll be the dead, ball-less eejit beside him. Ugh!"

"Shut up, Gibs!" I barked.

"Stop the world," Gibsie groaned. "I want to get off."

"Gerard, calm down. Nobody is going to prison. Johnny—" Claire placed a hand on my arm, "Come on. Let's just go."

"I'm going nowhere," I hissed for the fiftieth fucking time, keeping my eyes locked on Darren. "Not until I see her."

"*See*?" Gibsie croaked out. "You heard him. He's going nowhere, and I'm going to heaven."

"What are you hiding?" I asked, narrowing my eyes.

"Nothing."

"Then why can't she see me?" I demanded. "Why can't I see her? What is your fucking problem with me—"

My words broke off when a small figure darted out from under Darren's arm and sprang towards me. My brain barely had the chance to process that the figure I was seeing was Shannon before she lunged at me, wrapping her arms around my neck and causing me to stagger back a step.

"Hi, Johnny," she whispered, tumbling off the doorstep as she clung to me. "You came back."

"Hi, Shannon." My crutches fell to the ground as I wrapped my arms around her body, holding her in place. "I promised I would," I replied, keeping my eyes narrowed and locked on her brother.

# Beautiful Boys and Broken Brothers

## SHANNON

At first, I ignored the angry voices penetrating the quiet bubble of my bedroom, presuming Darren and Tadhg were going head to head again downstairs, but then I remembered Tadhg and Ollie were at a birthday party. Sean was with Nanny, Joey was AWOL, and Mam was at work. That left Darren and . . .

*Dad?*

My breath hitched in my throat and I dropped the pen I had been using to scribble revision notes into my copybook with.

For a moment, I just sat there on my bed and held my breath, waiting for my bedroom door to fly inward and my father to appear. When it didn't happen, my anxiety lowered to the point where moving my limbs was possible again.

Unnerved, I climbed out of bed and walked over to my window to investigate. Pushing it open, I leaned out, rested my elbows on the sill, and searched for trouble.

The sight of the familiar silver Ford Focus parked outside my house caused my heart to thud rapidly.

I knew that car.

It belonged to Gerard Gibson.

*And wherever Gibsie was . . .*

"Then go for it, because I'm not going anywhere, asshole!" an achingly familiar voice with a thick Dublin accent boomed. "Go right ahead and call the fucking Guards, because quite frankly, I'd love to speak to them."

*Johnny.*

Because of the veranda under my window blocking my view of the front door, I couldn't see him, but I could hear him, and oh god, my heart thundered violently at the sound of his voice.

For a long moment I stood there, in a state of shock, absorbing his voice and the realization that he was actually *here* before my brain kicked into gear and my legs started to move.

Every inch of my body was aching, and the bruising on my face was darker now, more purple and prominent, but I didn't care. I pushed past my pain, forced down my insecurities, and got dressed in record time. The jeans I threw on were loose and needed the support of a belt, but I knew I wouldn't find one in my wardrobe, so I used my hair tie to hold them up. Slipping my feet into my runners, I grabbed one of Joey's hoodies off the back of my door before hurrying into the landing.

Feeling skittish, I clutched the bannister and half-stumbled down the stairs in my haste to get to him. When I reached the bottom step, I had to stop for a moment and catch my breath; my lungs protesting against the sudden movement.

Darren was standing in the doorway, obstructing my view of him, as they both argued back and forth.

Moving purely on instinct, I hurried over to the door and slipped under Darren's arm. Johnny's brows shot up in surprise at the sight of me, but I didn't give him a chance to say anything. Instead, I practically fell over the step of the door as I threw my arms around his neck and clung to him, feeling a rapid sense of instant relief spread across my skin like a hot flush absorbing me. "Hi, Johnny." Clenching my eyes shut, I held onto his body for dear life. "You came back."

"Hi, Shannon." I heard his crutches clatter to the ground as his arms came around me and then I was enveloped in the warmth and security I felt like I had been chasing my whole life. "I promised I would."

*This isn't safe for you*, my mind protested, *you feel too much for this boy, too deeply. Getting attached to him is a bad idea . . .*

"Shan!" Claire's voice filled my ears and my head snapped up. It was only then that I noticed her and Gibsie standing slightly back from the door. She looked back at me, brown eyes filled with tears, and waved awkwardly. "Hi!"

At the sight of her, something snapped inside of me and a sob tore from my throat. "Hi," I strangled out, as I detangled myself from Johnny and moved for her.

"God!" She met me halfway, wrapping me up in a hug so tight, I flinched. "Are you okay?" she demanded. Sniffling loudly, she released me and stepped back, letting her gaze trail over my body. "Oh my god, Shan, what happened – I can't – I don't even know what to – girl, you better be okay!" Grabbing my hoodie, she dragged me back in for a monster hug. "I'm so mad at you," she hissed as tears dripped freely down her cheeks. "And I'm so mad at me – and him." She glared at Darren, who was still standing in the doorway. "He's not as nice as I remember."

"I'm okay," I squeezed out, patting her back. "Just please be gentle."

"Of course," she sobbed, loosening her hold once more. "Oh god—" her words broke off and her face contorted in pain. "Your face."

"I'm *okay*, Claire," I gently reminded her. "I'm here." *I'm alive.*

"I just love you so much," she cried. "You don't even get how important you are to me!"

"Can I get in on this action?" Gibsie asked and then wrapped his arms around the both of us. "Group hugs," he mused, ruffling both our heads before stepping back and pulling out a box of cigarettes from his jeans pocket. "Good for the soul." Smiling to himself, he placed a cigarette between his lips and sparked up.

"Hi, Gibsie," I sniffled, wiping my eyes with my sleeve.

"Little Shannon," he replied with a wink. "You good?"

I nodded weakly.

"Damn straight you are," he said, tone encouraging. "Little fighter."

"You look like a panda bear," Claire croaked out, touching the dark circles under my eyes. "Are you sleeping?"

*Not a wink because I'm tortured with nightmares.* "It's just bruising." She flinched. "I'm sorry."

"It's okay," I whispered, offering her a watery smile. "I'll be okay."

"Ask her now," Johnny barked, drawing all of our attention back to where he was still locked in a stare-down with my brother. "Ask your sister what she wants. Ask her if she wants us to leave. Go on. Fucking ask her!"

"I've already told you," Darren growled. "She's not—"

"I want to stay with my friends for a while," I mumbled, surprising everyone. I felt four pairs of eyes land on my face and my cheeks burned. Stiffening my spine, I looked at my brother and said, "I'm going to spend some time with my friends."

Darren looked at me in defeat. "You shouldn't be outside after your procedure." He ran a hand through his hair and stifled a groan. "You shouldn't be going anywhere without me or Joey." He gave me a meaningful stare. "Think about this."

I didn't need to think about it. I already knew what he was referring to.

*Dad.*

He was out there somewhere and Darren was terrified of him getting ahold of one of us.

My old friend fear roared to life, sucker punching me in the gut, and I physically flinched.

*What if he finds you?*

*What if he comes back?*

*What if she takes him back while you're gone and he's in the house when you get home?*

*What if –*

"I'll look after her," Johnny announced in a tone so sincere, there left no room for doubt. Darren didn't respond to him so Johnny turned his heated gaze on me. "I'll look after you," he repeated, blue eyes locked on mine. "I will."

Exhaling a ragged breath, I nodded. "Okay."

Relief flooded his features. "Okay?"

"Yeah," I breathed, nervously clasping my hands together. "I want to go with you." I flicked my gaze back to Darren and saw the disappointment in his eyes, but held my nerve. "I'm going with him, Darren."

Darren shook his head, muttered something unintelligible under his breath, and then stepped outside. Retrieving Johnny's crutches off the ground, Darren handed them to him and hissed, "You better mean that because this isn't a game, kid," before walking back inside. "Remember what I said, Shannon," he added.

When the front door slammed shut behind him, I released the breath I hadn't realized I'd been holding.

Claire beamed at me. "Girl, my pride levels are so high right now they could not possibly be measured." She took my hands in hers and squeezed. "How does it feel to finally stick up for yourself and *win*?"

I shrugged, feeling confused. "Unnerving?"

"I know the appropriate song for this," Gibsie said, draping an arm over Claire's shoulder. Tossing his cigarette butt in the neighbor's garden, he waved a hand in front of them and said, "Bon Jovi – 'It's My Life'."

"Perfect!" Claire chirped, wrapping an arm around his waist as they strolled down the garden path towards his car. "You know what, Gerard? You can be pretty smart when you're not being pretty stupid."

Laughing, he pulled her into his side. "I know, right?"

"Shannon." Johnny's deep voice came from behind me, causing a shiver to roll through my body. "Are you okay?"

"I'm not sure," I admitted quietly, resisting the urge to lean back and feel his body pressed to mine.

"Do you still want to come with me?" he asked, standing so close to me that I could feel the heat emanating from his body. "It's okay if you don't. I'm just happy that I got to see you."

Nodding, I turned to look up at him. "That's the one thing I am sure of."

The sound of car tires screeching loudly caused me to startle and I stiffened, instantly panicked and on edge. Johnny shifted closer to me and I automatically burrowed into his side. "It's okay," he coaxed, frowning at something over my head. "I think it's your *brother*?"

"My brother?" Frowning, I spun around to see Joey stumbling face-first out of the back of a moving car. "Joey?" I called out, hurrying towards him. "Joe!"

The car that had deposited my brother beeped twice before speeding off down the terrace. I narrowed my eyes and glared at the black, souped-up Honda Civic as it tore off out of sight.

Awareness dawned on me, cold and ugly, as I registered who that car belonged to and what said person represented to my brother.

*Nothing good.*

"Was that Shane Holland?" I demanded when I reached him, out of breath and panting. "What the hell, Joey! I thought you left that behind you."

"Shan," Joey slurred, laughing to himself, as he rolled onto his back and sighed in contentment. "How's it going?"

"Get off the road, you idiot," I growled, feeling a mixture of relief and terror course through me. "Joey, get up right now!"

He mashed his lips together and sighed. "I missed ya."

"You're going to get killed," I hissed, glaring down at my brother. "Get up before someone drives over you!"

"Let them," he laughed. "I don't give a fuck anymore."

"Clearly," I grumbled, dropping to my knees beside him. "Does Aoife know about this?"

"Shh," he groaned, covering his face with his hands. "Don't."

"No, of course she doesn't." Reaching over, I checked his pockets and groaned in despair. "Well, your wallet's gone," I informed him. "And your phone!"

"I fucked up, Shan," he whispered then. "I'm always fucking up."

My heart cracked in my chest.

"Joe, just get up off the road and I'll help you, okay?"

Groaning, he shook his head. "I'm done."

"What did you take?" I asked in a hushed tone, leaning close to his ear. "What was it, Joe? What did they give you?"

"He's high?" Johnny asked, standing over us.

I debated denying it and lying, but then thought better of it. What was the point? My brother was lying in the middle of the road in broad daylight. I could hardly pass this off as an accident. "Yeah," I choked out, shoulders sagging in defeat.

Sighing heavily, Johnny handed me his crutches and reached down. "You're going to have to help me out here, lad," he grumbled as he caught ahold of Joey's hand and pulled him into a sitting position. The movement caused Johnny to hiss loudly and release Joey's hand. The moment he did, Joey flopped back down on the tarmac. "Fuck."

"Mister rugby," Joey slurred.

"Joey *the hurler*," Johnny acknowledged as he reached for Joey's hand again.

"Joey, get up!" I ordered, feeling flustered and embarrassed. I had tried so hard to keep our demons hidden and now here they were, on full display. I couldn't cope with it. It was too much. I felt too exposed. "*Please*."

"Come on, lad," Johnny grunted as he tried and failed to pull Joey to his feet once more. He was seeing the worst part of my life and he was wading in, throwing himself into the mix, crutches and all. "You need to work with me here."

"What have we got here?" Gibsie asked. Kneeling down beside me, he reached over and pulled Joey's eyelids open. "Woo, you're good and stoned, aren't ya, Lynchy?" he mused and then patted his chest.

"Aw fuck," Joey groaned, twisting away from us. "Not that mad bastard."

Gibsie laughed. "Glad to see I made an impression."

"I need to get him out of here," I strangled out, panicked. "Those guys might come back, and I don't trust Darren not to call the—"

"No worries, Little Shannon. I've got him." Catching ahold of Joey's shoulders, Gibsie dragged him off the ground in one clean sweep. "Now it's *your* turn not to puke in my car," he told Joey as he carted him over to his car and deposited him in the back seat.

Mortified, I wrapped my arms around myself and just stood there, frozen to the bone, and drowning in my emotions.

"Does he do that a lot?" Johnny asked, coming to stand beside me.

I shook my head and handed his crutches back to him. "Not usually."

He arched a brow. "Not usually?"

I blew out a harsh breath. "Not for a long time."

Nodding in silent understanding, Johnny adjusted his crutches and gently nudged my shoulder with his. "Come on, Shannon *like the river*."

# Back to The Manor

## SHANNON

Feeling completely exposed, I sat in the backseat of Gibsie's car with Johnny and Gibsie in the front and Claire and Joey beside me. The radio was off, not one single word had been uttered since we pulled away from my house, and if I had a knife at my disposal, I was fairly sure I could have cut the tension enveloping the five of us.

Joey was sprawled across the back seat, with his legs on top of Claire and his head in my lap. To her credit, Claire didn't complain or shove him off her. Instead, she proved the theory I had that she was the kindest person in the world by removing her coat and draping it over his trembling body.

Numb, I kept my eyes glued to his face, watching as his features contorted every time Gibsie hit a pothole or took a sharp turn. "You're so stupid," I whispered, gently pushing his blond hair out of his eyes. "Do you hear me? Hanging around with Shane Holland and his friends again? You know he's bad news for you. They don't care about you, Joey. They never did. They only care about what they can *get* from you. They'll bleed you dry." I stroked his cheek, my fingers tracing the discoloration on his face. "God, I'm so mad at you, Joey."

"Shan." Groaning, he clenched his eyes shut and stiffened. "Fuck."

"Yeah, fuck," I muttered, wrapping an arm around him when Gibsie took the turn-off for Johnny's house. "What did you take?" I leaned closer, keeping my voice low. "I know you're drunk, and I can smell the weed off you, but there's more, isn't there? What was it? What did they give you?"

He groaned again and clutched his stomach. "Sorry."

"Stop saying sorry and start telling me what you took!" I hissed. "Was it tablets or something more? Joey, tell me, dammit!"

"Please don't hate me," was all he replied, his words a muffled slur as he shook violently in my arms.

Devastated, I glanced around the car and felt my cheeks burn in embarrassment. Gibsie and Johnny were both staring straight ahead and Claire was dutifully looking out the window, but I knew they were listening to us. They couldn't *not*.

Tightening my hold on my brother, I remained silent for the rest of the journey, holding back the emotions threatening to overpower me, as I debated the bleak future that was laid out in front us.

*No money.*

*Shitty parents.*

*Painful memories.*

*Fear and resentment.*

*Always the fear . . .*

By the time we pulled up outside Johnny's house a little while later, I was completely disheartened and beginning to understand my brother's need to just *forget* for a while. I knew that's why he did this. *Escape and forget . . .*

Killing the engine, Gibsie climbed out and walked around to Claire's door. "Kav, give Claire your keys to unlock the door," he instructed, helping her out from underneath my brother's body. "You good, Claire-bear?"

"All good, Gerard."

Johnny, who was outside the car and wrestling with his crutches, slipped a hand into his pocket and retrieved a set of keys before tossing them over the bonnet and pulling my door open. "It's the silver one – in the middle."

"On it." Snagging the keys mid-air, Claire rushed ahead of Gibsie to unlock the door.

"Thanks," I croaked as I scrambled out of the car and closed the door behind me.

"Are you okay?" Johnny asked quietly, watching my every move with sharp, intelligent eyes.

"Where are your dogs?"

"Huh?"

"Bonnie and Cupcake?"

"Oh right, yeah, they're out back in their run." He gestured to his crutches and grimaced. "Can't exactly fend them off at the moment."

I shrugged, unable to form a response, and turned my attention back to Joey.

"Okay, buddy, let's do this." Reaching inside, Gibsie dragged Joey out of the car. Tossing him over his shoulder, Gibsie proceeded to carry my brother towards the house. "Don't puke on my—" The words weren't out of Gibsie's mouth when Joey began to vomit profusely what I could only describe as a black, charcoal substance. "Back." Gibsie groaned in defeat. "Don't puke on my *back*."

"That's a good thing," Johnny said, clearly noticing my horrified expression. "It's better out than in."

"I am so sorry about this." Shaking my head, I wrapped my arms around myself and fell into step beside him as he hobbled towards the house. "I seem to bring a constant stream of trouble into your life."

"Don't worry about it." Pressing a crutch against the door to keep it open, he gestured for me to go inside. "I'm growing fond of your trouble."

"You shouldn't." Sadness was blooming inside of me; the cold, hard reality of my brother's current predicament eclipsing the excitement I had felt when I saw him at my door earlier. "It's not a good thing."

Johnny frowned but didn't object. "Come on," he said instead, inclining his head towards the entry hall.

I hurried inside from the rain, too worn out to worry or ask questions that I didn't need the answers to. It didn't matter if his parents were home or not. It didn't matter if my insecurities made me question whether he truly wanted me here or not.

The facts were my brother had taken some type of illegal drug, probably an obscene amount of illegal drugs, and was currently being carried up the staircase of Johnny's house. Whether I was mad with him or not was quite frankly irrelevant. He needed me and I would be there.

*God knows, I owed him one.*

"Do you want to tell me about it?" Abandoning his crutches, Johnny held on to the bannister and climbed the stairs at a snail's pace. "Joey, I mean?" he added, stopping, mid-step. "What happened back there?"

"I don't know."

"Don't lie," Johnny said quietly. "Not to me."

Scrunching my nose up, I blurted, "He was going down a bad path last year. Hanging around all the wrong places with the wrong people, and accepting all the wrong kinds of things."

"Last year?"

I nodded. "Before Aoife came along."

"She steadied him up?"

*Apparently not.* I shrugged helplessly. "I thought so?"

"What was he on?"

"I don't know," I replied, and this time it was the truth. "He was definitely going out drinking with his friends, and I know he was smoking weed, but I'm not sure about the rest. Maybe yolks? Like ecstasy or some form of tablet? I heard my parents talking about it once, and I'm not sure how he would get his hands on anything else. He wouldn't have the money." I shrugged, feeling at a loss. "But I know he used to go off in that car during big break at school and come back for the last three classes with bloodshot eyes and a faraway look," I heard myself explain. "I think he was trying to escape? Things weren't great, and it was his way of coping with what was happening at ... uh ... at ... well, you know." Tucking my hair behind my ear, I let my shoulders sag in defeat. "It's not like we had anybody to talk to about that kind of stuff."

Johnny watched me carefully as I spoke, taking in every word I was speaking. "Was it a problem?"

"I don't know," I replied, sticking with the truth. "Joey doesn't *talk*. Not to anyone. Not even me. All I know is things were bad for him, worse than usual, and he was getting into more fights at school." *More fights at home.* "He was having trouble at training. Our f-father—" my throat bobbed and I had to swallow several times before I could continue

"—well, he was furious because there was talk of Joey being thrown off the team. But then Aoife came along and within a few weeks he had cleaned up his act. He wasn't walking around with bloodshot eyes or bouncing off the walls. He wasn't fighting as much at school. He was just …" I shook my head, trying to find the words to explain all of this. "She settled something inside of him. It was like she grounded him somehow – gave him something he clearly wasn't getting from …" I let my words trail off.

I didn't need to finish that sentence. Johnny's eyes were locked on mine and the word *home* hung heavily between us, unspoken and painful. Feeling exposed and vulnerable, I tore my eyes away and climbed the rest of the steps.

Concern roared to life inside of me as I watched Johnny struggle up the remaining steps. "Hey – are *you* okay?" I asked when he finally reached me, jaw tight and shoulders rigid.

He stiffened, and for a moment, I expected the same cold brush-off I was used to receiving when I asked him about his pain. But he surprised me by turning to face me. "I'm okay." His tone was soft, eyes gentle. Leaning against the bannister railing, he released another heavy sigh. "I'm sore," he offered with a small, vulnerable shrug. "I'm stiff, and I despise being slowed down, but I'm on the mend, okay?"

I studied his face, looked for the lies, and when I didn't find any, I nodded. "Yeah, okay."

"What about you?"

"Me?"

"Yeah, you." Reaching out, he traced his thumb across my cheekbone. "How are *you* feeling?"

"Same as you," I offered in a small voice, unable to suppress the shiver that rolled through my body when he put his hands on me. "Stiff and sore, but on the mend." I paused, thinking of something positive to say. "I can breathe again," I blurted and then cringed when I said it. "Sorry."

Pain flickered in his blue eyes. "It's killing me," he admitted, voice low and gruff. "Knowing what happened to you, seeing what that bastard did every time I look at your face, and not being able to fix it."

I released a shaky breath. "Johnny."

"I've spent days waiting for this," he quickly hurried on, his words coming fast, his accent thickening as he spoke. "To get time with you. To just *be* with you, and now I have you here?" His hand snaked out and entwined with mine. "Where I know you're safe? All I want to do is just . . . " Shaking his head, he pulled me closer. "Keep you right here with me and never give you back."

*Oh god, I want that, too.*

*I want you to keep me.*

"I know you have a lot of stuff going on in your life right now with your family, and there's a shitstorm falling down around us," he added, voice gruff. "I know there's a conversation we need to have, Shannon, an important one, but I just want you to know – no, I *need* you to know that I'm—"

"A little help, Kav!" Gibsie's voice boomed down the landing. "We have a code puke situation going on in here."

"Jesus Christ," Johnny hissed, throwing his head back. "I can't catch a bleeding break."

"I'm sorry," Claire croaked out as she barreled towards us, holding her stomach. "But I'm a sympathetic vomiter and that boy is spewing his guts up in there." Flustered, she gagged before adding, "Honestly, I'd love to help, really I would, but I had a heavy meal before I came here and if I stay in that room, it will be *carnage*."

"Oh god." Turning, I moved to go check on my brother, but Johnny tugged my hand and pulled me back to him.

"Don't go in there," he said, releasing my hand. "He doesn't need his sister seeing him like that."

"Yeah, Shan," Claire agreed, coming to stand beside me. "Let the boys take care of him."

"He's my brother," I countered shakily.

"Your *naked* brother," Claire shot back. "Gerard had to take his clothes off because he's covered in—" She paused to gawk. "Ugh, it smells so bad. He needs a shower and you can't do that in your condition."

"You remember the layout of the downstairs?" Johnny asked, directing his question to me. "Where everything is?"

I nodded, flustered. "I think so?"

"Take Claire downstairs with you," he instructed calmly. "Make whatever you want in the kitchen or chill out in the sitting room. Whatever you want. Gibs and I will sort him out."

"Are you sure?" I asked, not feeling very sure at all.

"Positive." He gave me one last, final look and then walked stiffly in the direction of his bedroom. "I've got this."

"You know," Claire mused, "when I signed up for this jailbreak, I didn't anticipate vomit." Wrapping an arm around my shoulders, she led me down the impressive staircase to the entrance hall. "Or penises."

"Penii," I corrected with a defeated sigh.

"Huh?"

"Mrs. O'Leary, our science teacher, says that's the appropriate plural." Not that it even mattered.

"Oh." She scrunched her nose up at the notion. "Well, I don't know anything about *penii*, I must have zoned out during class, but this house is *amazing*. It's like . . . Muckross or something."

"That's what I said," I whispered, taking comfort in having her with me.

"He'll be okay, Shan," she added quietly. "You both will."

"Yeah." *I hope so.*

"Now, come on," she said, tightening her hold on me. "I want to know everything."

# Dangerous Pussy

## JOHNNY

I had no explanation for how my life had unraveled to the point where I was showering a semi-comatose, drugged-up hurler other than this: I fell in love with a girl who had more layers and complications attached to her life than a Rubik's Cube.

A Rubik's Cube, I could solve.

Shannon Lynch's life, not so much.

"Did you get under his arms?" Gibsie asked as he stood fully clothed in my shower, holding a very naked Joey the hurler up. "Make sure you get the creases."

"How is this happening to us, Gibs?" I asked my best friend. "One minute, we're playing rugby for Tommen, hanging out at Biddies with the lads and running drills, and the next, we're hosing puke off a hurler from BCS." Shaking my head at the absolute lunacy of the situation, I squirted another dollop of body wash on Joey's chest and aimed the shower hose, careful to avoid the bruising. "How did we fall into this, lad?"

"You love his sister, and I love his sister's best friend," Gibsie replied, scrubbing Joey down with a sponge. "It's safe to say that pussy got us into this, Kav."

Wasn't that the fucking truth . . .

"Here," Gibs said as he turned Joey in his arms. "Make sure you get the back of him again."

Bile rose in my throat as my eyes took in the sight of bruise after discolored bruise, and scar after faded scar on his body.

His entire back was *littered* with a mixture of blemishes, faint lines, and scars.

*Jesus Christ.*

I studied his bare skin with cool, calculated eyes. It didn't take a genius to figure out who had put those marks on his body.

Their piece-of-shit father.

Maybe he used a belt, or maybe he used something worse. Fuck, I didn't know. But he had scars *everywhere*.

How the fuck had this gone unnoticed?

What about his girlfriend? Or their mother? His trainers?

Did nobody *see* him?

"This is so wrong," Gibsie grumbled, voicing my thoughts aloud. He turned him back to face me and wrapped an arm around his chest to hold him up. "So fucking wrong, Johnny."

"Yeah, lad," I bit out, careful not to spray the areas on his stomach with fresh bruises. "I know."

"Stop," Joey groaned, shivering violently, as he pushed against the arm Gibsie had wrapped around him. "I'm gonna be—"

Gibsie swung them both around just in time for Joey to shower the wall with a fresh coating of chunks. "Lad," Gibs said as he scrubbed the sponge over Joey's face, "you don't ever mix your drugs."

"Like you'd know," I scoffed.

"Well, I presume it's similar to mixing your drink," Gibsie shot back. "A big, fat no-no!"

"It's better he gets it all out of his system." Leaning around them both, I hosed down the vomit on the wall before retackling the never-ending stream of vomit coming from Joey. "They'd only pump him out in the hospital anyway."

"Exactly," Gibsie agreed, patting Joey's cheek. "Consider this your own personal, free-range stomach pumping session – Gibsie-style."

"Fuck off, ya creepy bastard," Joey groaned, shaking from head to toe.

"Normally, I would take offense to that," Gibsie huffed, "but considering we're in a shower together and your naked ass is pressed to my dick, I'm going to let that comment slide, because I, too, find this situation slightly creepy."

"He's saving your neck," I growled. "We both are, so why don't you show your appreciation by shutting the fuck up and puking out the poison."

"Fuck you, Kav—"

More vomiting.

"That's it," Gibsie coaxed, dabbing his mouth once more. "Puke out all the expensive, class A drugs. Good job. Let the water wash your sins and wages down the drain."

My phone began to ring loudly in my pocket and I frowned, my eyes shifting to Gibsie. "You're here."

Gibsie rolled his eyes. "I'm not the only one with your number."

Wiping my hand on my t-shirt, I slipped my hand into my pocket and dragged out my phone. "Shite." I stared at the name flashing on the screen and groaned. "It's my ma."

"Oh, Jesus," Gibsie joined me in groaning. "She knows, doesn't she? Of course she fucking does." He continued to scrub Joey down as he ranted. "She probably has a tracker on your ass."

"Get off me," Joey slurred, slapping at Gibsie's hand. "Christ."

"Keep him quiet," I warned, eye-balling Gibsie as I clicked accept and put the phone on loudspeaker. "Ma, how's it going?"

"Johnny, love," Mam sighed down the phone. "Are you alright? You took a long time answering me."

"I'm grand, Ma. What's up?"

"Oh, love, I was calling to let you know that I might not—"

"Stop!" Joey groaned loudly. "It burns."

Gibsie and I both froze and stared at each other in horror.

"What burns?" Mam demanded. "Are you okay?"

"Fuck me!' Joey continued to flinch and hiss. "It's too hot."

Glaring at Gibsie, I mouthed, "*Shut him up*."

Gibsie gaped back at me, whisper-hissing, "*How?*"

*Give me strength . . .* I aimed the hose at his face and mouthed, "*With your hand, genius!*"

With water spluttering from his own lips, Gibsie slapped a hand over Joey's mouth and I nodded in approval. Leaning over the tub, I adjusted the setting on the shower and lowered the temperature of the water. "*Happy now?*" I mouthed, glaring at Joey as I hosed him down.

"Johnny? Is Gerard messing with the cooker again?" Mam asked, sounding flustered. "Tell that boy he better not touch the matches. There's a hole melted into the extractor fan from his last outing with flammables."

"*That was* you!" Gibsie mouthed, outraged.

"No, Ma, he's not cooking." Shaking my head, I looked up to the ceiling and blurted the first thing that came to mind, "That was just some fella on the television."

"The television?"

"Yeah, we're, ah—" Narrowing my eyes, I aimed the hose at a stubborn chunk of puke on Joey's shoulder. "We're watching a film."

"Oh, Johnny," Mam grumbled. "Not one of those dirty ones. The doctors warned you to avoid interfering with yourself until your stitches heal completely."

Gibsie snickered.

*Jesus Christ.* I let my head fall back in silent despair. "No, Ma, we're watching . . . "

"You're watching what, Johnny?"

"*My Left Foot!*" Gibsie blurted out loudly. "For the leaving cert, Mammy K!"

"*I'm doing Gatsby, ya bollox,*" I mouthed, glaring.

"Ah, that's lovely," Mam cooed, mollified. "Good boy, Gerard! Very educational."

Gibsie arched a brow and grinned.

"Did you need something?" I asked, getting back to the point. "Because I'm trying to watch Christy Brown here."

"Oh, right, well here's the thing, love," Mam said, tone hesitant. I rolled my eyes with impatience and waited for her to get to the point. "I might not make it back home tonight."

*Thank you, Jesus!* "That's a shame."

"Traffic was insane getting up here and the thought of driving back down in bumper-to-bumper backlog is more than I can handle."

Gibsie gleamed in approval.

"Then you should definitely stop over at the old house with Da," I replied, tone soothing. "You're tired, Ma – too tired to be making that journey."

"On your own in the dark," Gibsie offered. *"Alone and female."*

"Gibs," I warned.

"Sounds too dangerous if you ask me, Mammy K," he continued, ignoring me. "Driving through Dublin city at night, all by your lonesome."

"She's from Ballymun, ya spanner," I grumbled. "She'd take your culchie arse out in a heartbeat."

"Boys!" Mam snapped and then sighed heavily down the line. "I'll be home no later than lunchtime tomorrow to take you to your physio appointment . . . if you're sure you'll be okay without me—"

"I'm sure," I quickly interjected, leaving out the snippet that I had been just fine without either of them for years. "I'll be grand." Leaning over the tub, I reached up and switched off the shower. "We both will." Grabbing two towels off the rack, I tossed one to Gibs and tucked the other under my arm. "No worries."

"I love you, Johnny," Mam finally said.

"Yeah—" Balancing my phone on the side of the tub, I draped the towel over Joey's shoulders before snatching my phone back up. "Love ya, too, Ma."

"Oh, before I forget—"

"Gotta go, Ma. Bye, bye, bye—" Ending the call, I slipped my phone back into my pocket and exhaled a huge sigh. "Thank Christ for that."

"I'll say," Gibsie agreed, dropping his hand from Joey's mouth. "I'd say we're in the clear, lad."

"Jesus," Joey hissed, teeth chattering, "you're a mammy's boy, aren't ya?"

"Do you want to be gagged again?" I narrowed my eyes. "Because that can be arranged."

"Fuck you both," Joey mumbled, breathing hard. "Don't do me any favors."

My mouth fell open. "Are you shitting me right now, Joey?"

"I think the word you're looking for is *thank* you both," Gibsie interjected cheerfully. He cast me a meaningful look and shook his head in warning. "And you are more than *welcome*, Joseph."

Holding my tongue and reining in my temper, I took a step back and watched as Gibsie helped him out of the tub.

"Don't fucking touch me!" Roughly shoving Gibsie away, Joey staggered backwards and collapsed on the floor. "I don't need your help."

"Well, tough shit because you're getting it," I snapped. "Whether you want it or not."

"You're a little fucked up, Joey the hurler," Gibsie mused. "You know that, right?"

"Yeah, I'm fucked up," Joey sneered, shaking from head to toe. "And you're just plain fucked in the head."

"Indeed," Gibsie agreed solemnly.

Breathing hard, Joey dropped his head in his hands and pulled on his hair. "Where's my phone?" Exhaling a choked breath, he hissed, "I need my *phone*. I need to call my . . . fuck!"

"You don't have a phone anymore, lad – or a wallet," Gibsie replied calmly. "Your sister said you sold it, right along with your dignity, for that horrendous pain you're in." Grabbing another towel off the rack, Gibsie tossed it on his lap, covering him up. "All that shit flushing its way out of your system right now? Everything you puked out of your body? It cost you exactly one wallet, one phone, and one soul. Pretty high price, huh? I sure hope it was worth it." He patted his shoulder. "Now, if you'll both excuse me, I need a shower of my own." Peeling his drenched shirt over his head, Gibsie tossed it in the laundry hamper next to the door before strolling out of the bathroom.

I half expected Joey Lynch to erupt right there in the middle of my bathroom, but he didn't do a thing. Instead, he wrapped his arms around his knees and dropped his head. "Fuck." Cupping the back of his neck with one hand, he rocked back and forth, muttering the word "fuck" over and over.

"What did you take?"

Silence.

"*Okay*." Lowering myself onto the edge of the tub, I rubbed a hand down my thigh and tried a different approach. "Why did you do it?"

"Don't judge me," he hissed, swinging his gaze to meet me. "Don't you dare fucking judge me ..." Squeezing his eyes shut, he balled his hands into fists and made a hitched sound in his throat as his body trembled violently. "Not until you've been in my shoes. Seen what I've seen. Heard what I've heard."

I remained still as a statue and resisted the urge to reach over and steady him. "I'm not judging you, lad."

"No?" Tortured green eyes locked on mine. "You saw her. Saw what *he* did to her. And I didn't ... I couldn't—" His words broke off and he dropped his head in his hands. "Fuck it. What's the point?"

"It's not your fault," I replied slowly, brows furrowing. "You have to know that."

More silence.

"I didn't mean it," I tried again. "What I said on the phone? It was my panic talking, lad."

Nothing.

His lack of response caused a trickle of unease to creep up my spine. "You are not responsible for your father's actions," I repeated, fighting down the huge swell of sympathy flooding my body. "You're not, so don't fuck up your life and your future by thinking you are."

Dropping his gaze to his knees, he whispered, "I couldn't protect her." Shaking his head, he exhaled a broken sob. "I couldn't protect any of them."

"That's not your job." My heart hammered wildly in my chest. *Jesus.* I felt like I was drowning in his pain. "You're not supposed to protect them. *They're* supposed to protect them. They're supposed to protect *all* of you, lad. Including you."

"I thought she was dead," he confessed in a voice so low it was barely audible. "All the blood? On the floor? On the walls? On my clothes?

Coming out of her mouth? Those gargling sounds she was making because she couldn't breathe? Because she was fucking *dying*! And then the silence? The sound of *nothing* at all?" He pressed the heels of his hands against his eyes and hissed, "I can't get the image out of my head – and believe me, I've tried."

*Jesus Christ.*

Reeling, I sat there, cold to the bone, and listened to his truth.

"I couldn't get him off me," he strangled out, chest heaving. "I knew she needed help – I fucking *knew* it – but I couldn't fight him off. I couldn't do *anything*!" Shaking his head, he let out a humorless laugh as tears trickled down his cheeks. "And my brother, *my eleven-year-old baby brother*, had to get him off me." Sniffing, he wiped his nose with the back of his hand and choked out a harsh sob. "While *she* stood by and did *nothing*."

"Your mother?"

"Who else."

I let that sink in for a moment before asking, "And now?" My voice was thick with emotion, but I forced myself to keep my shit together and continue. "What happens now?"

"The same thing that always happens," he muttered. "Nothing."

"With your ma?" I pushed, pressing my hand to my knee to stop it from shaking. "I mean, the Guards obviously know what your da was doing to ye, and they'll arrest him when they find him, but her?" I shook my head, struggling to take it all in. "There's no consequences for taking a backseat? You're just supposed to go back and live with her?" I swallowed down my anger and hissed, "In that house?"

Joey shrugged. "Didn't you hear? She's a victim, too. She needs to be *supported*."

"Shannon told me," I muttered, rubbing my jaw. "That's so messed up, lad."

"Yeah, well, it's on Darren now," Joey spat, blinking back his tears. "He can figure it all out because I'm done. I c-can't f-fucking—" his words broke off and he exhaled another hitched sob. "D-do this any-more," he finished with a sniffle. "I c-can't forget and I won't *ever* forgive."

I didn't know what to say to that. I didn't know what to say to any of it. Nothing in my life had prepared me for this conversation. For these people and their pain.

"Your sister loves you," I told him, feeling the need to tell him that, so that he knew at least one person in his world cared.

"My sister loves *you*," he replied wearily.

"She needs you," I added, ignoring the way my heart slammed wildly in my chest. "And from what I hear, your little brothers need you too, lad."

"Because I'm foundations," he choked out. "That's it – that's all I am to them."

"Foundations?" I frowned. "What does that mean?"

"It means I'm the guy who goes around cleaning up everyone else in my family's shit." He dropped his head and clasped the back of his neck. "It means I'm the fucking mother."

"Well," I exhaled heavily and stretched my legs out, trying to ease the burn in my thighs, "you're one hell of a mother, Joey the hurler."

"Someone has to be," he muttered as he ran a hand through his hair.

"Well, you did a good job," I told him. "And you've come too far to throw it all away on a temporary high, lad."

"The fuck would you know about it?" he sneered.

"I know you're trying to escape," I shot back. "That much is perfectly clear. You want to forget about the shite for a while – and Jesus, I don't blame you – but it's temporary. It' not *real,* Joey. And it's not going to fix anything. All of your problems will still be there waiting for you, regardless of how much powder you snort up your nose or how many tablets you toss back your throat. You can smoke all the weed you want, drown yourself in a bottle of whiskey, shoot yourself up with every drug known to mankind and it won't change a damn thing because life will *still* be waiting in the wings to kick your ass when you come to. I also know that if you keep going down this road, you'll get to a point where you won't be able to find your way back."

"Easy for you to say," he shot back, tone bitter. "You've never seen a hard day in your life."

"You're absolutely right," I agreed. "I don't know what you're going through. I have no fucking clue what it feels like to be you, and I'm damn glad for that. But I have my own demons, lad. My own choices I had to make, where it would have been so much easier to pop a few tablets to kill the pain when my body was falling the fuck apart from the inside out, or use steroids to build up my body instead of grafting in the gym six hours a day. I know that sounds like nothing in the grand scheme of things, not compared to your family shite, but I didn't do it, Joey, not one single time. Because I *knew* that putting that shite in my body would only be a choice for so long before it *stopped* being a *choice* and started being a *necessity*."

"Shit," he choked out, and then laughed humorlessly. "Where the fuck were you when I was sixteen, Kavanagh?" Sniffing, he wiped his eyes and sighed dejectedly. "Could've done with the pep talk back then."

"Wrong school," I offered with a halfhearted shrug.

"Wrong life," he whispered.

I sighed heavily. "Yeah."

There was a long stretch of silence before I spoke again.

"Can I help?" I finally asked, feeling like a spare prick. "Can I do something for *you*?"

"Yeah." With shaky hands, Joey clutched the basin of the sink and pulled himself to his feet. "You can loan me some clothes."

We both knew that *clothes* wasn't what I meant, but I didn't push him – not when he seemed to be clinging to the edge.

Without saying another word, I stood up and walked back into my room. Pulling random items of clothing out of my dresser, I tossed them into the bathroom and left him to it.

Confused and on edge, I walked stiffly over to my window and stared out into the darkness while I waited for him to come back out, watching as droplets of rain pelted against the pane of glass.

*So this is their life,* I thought to myself, *this is what she was hiding from you.*

Gripping the windowsill, I ignored the pain in my body and

concentrated on my whirling thoughts, desperately trying to find a solution for something I wasn't entirely sure could be solved. One thing I knew for sure was that I could never untangle myself from this girl. And what's more, I didn't want to.

I knew this wasn't good. Jesus, a blind man could see I needed to run far, *far* away from this situation, but I *couldn't*. Fucked up as it all seemed, I was quite content to remain right here, wrapped up in her personal breakdown. More than that, I wanted to wade in and do something, anything, to help her brother. It wasn't even just about Shannon for me anymore. It was about Joey and three other little kids I hadn't even laid eyes on. I wanted to help them all. My conscience demanded nothing less from me.

Several minutes passed by before the bathroom door swung open and Joey appeared in the doorway. He was dressed in a pair of my grey sweats and a white t-shirt, and looking like absolute shite. *Clean shite*, I mentally acknowledged, *minus the vomit and smell.*

"Thanks for the clothes," he muttered, eyes bloodshot, face deathly pale. "Do you have a phone I could use?"

My jaw ticked. I wasn't sure about this. Was he planning on busting out of here? "Why?"

"Because I need to call my girlfriend."

I eyed him warily. "Your girlfriend?"

"Yeah, my girlfriend," he hissed. "Can I use your phone or not?"

Uncertain, I took my phone out and handed it to him. "You don't have to leave. You can stay, lad. For as long as you need."

Ignoring me, Joey leaned against the dresser and stabbed his trembling finger against the keypad of my phone, messing up repeatedly to the point where he threw his head back and roared. "Come the fuck on!"

"What's her number?" I asked, taking the phone from him. "Call it out and I'll dial it for you."

"I warned her off you, you know," he said, handing the phone back to me. "Told her you'd be leaving – told her not to get her hopes up on you."

I shrugged, not one bit surprised given my current popularity status with his family. "What's her number?"

He muttered a string of numbers before saying, "Don't let her down. Whatever you're doing, Kavanagh, don't fuck my sister over."

I tapped in the number and pressed call before handing it back to him and saying, "I won't."

With wary, mistrustful eyes, Joey placed the phone to his ear, body shaking and jolting violently. "Aoife?" he whispered a few seconds later. "It's me."

Whatever his girlfriend said in response to that caused Joey to shudder.

Like visibly fucking *shudder*.

"I know," he whispered, clenching his eyes shut. "I know, okay? I *know* I promised. I fucked up." Turning his back to me, he ran a hand through his hair and choked out, "I'm so fucking sorry, baby."

Feeling uncomfortable, I decided to go downstairs in search of the others and leave Joey Lynch to his phone call/groveling. I wasn't sure I wanted to hear it anyway, not when my head was already bursting to the seams with more information than I could process.

Gibsie was shoveling coal into an already roaring fire when I walked into the sitting room, and the girls were curled up on the couch. Correction; Claire was curled up on the couch with her legs tucked beneath her. Shannon, on the other hand, was sitting as straight as a poker on the edge of the seat beside her friend. Gibsie had obviously dragged the couch over to the fire, something we always did when the weather was bad out, and I was grateful. I wanted her to be warm. I *needed* the peace of mind.

I cleared my throat before stepping inside, making a conscious effort not to startle her. She jumped clean out of her skin anyway and sprang off the couch, but the small smile she gave me assured me that I was a welcome surprise. "Is he okay?" she asked, wide-eyed and panicked.

*Not even close.* Nodding, I forced a smile.

"Oh, thank god." Her small shoulders sagged and she pressed a hand to her chest. "Are you sure?"

*No.*

"He's sure," Gibsie answered for me. Placing the shovel back into the coal bucket, he stood up, stretched his arms over his head, and winked over at me. "All's well in the world again."

"See?" Claire added, giving her an encouraging smile. "I told you that you had nothing to worry about."

Shannon didn't look so convinced. Her gaze flicked between Gibs and Claire before returning to me. "Are *you* sure?" she asked, looking at me with those haunting blue eyes.

I opened my mouth to lie, to tell her what she needed to hear, that everything was okay and she had nothing to worry about, but the words, "No, I'm not sure," came out instead. I fucked it even further by saying, "He's in a bad way, actually. A really bad way," and then I topped it off with, "I'm worried about him."

Shannon's face fell and both Claire and Gibsie groaned in unison.

"Nice one, Cap," Gibsie muttered. "We only spent the last hour telling her different."

"Yeah, very comforting, Johnny," Claire added sulkily.

"Well, I'm not going to *lie* to her," I snapped. Running a hand through my hair in frustration, I looked at Shannon. "I'm not going to do that, okay?"

Shannon nodded stiffly. "I should go check on him." She hurried past me, only to pause in the doorway. "Is it okay if I go up and check—"

"Go," I told her before she finished. "Don't ask for my permission, Shannon. You don't need it."

She nodded once more before slipping out of the room.

"Maybe once in a while, you could attempt to twist the truth," Gibsie offered, waving a finger around aimlessly. "You know, romance a situation up a tad to spare feelings and unnecessary *stress*."

"By lying to her?" I narrowed my eyes at him. "Yeah, lad, that sounds like real solid advice. Tell me how that's going to work for me?"

Gibsie shrugged. "Fuck if I know, lad, but that girl is buckling under the weight of some pretty heavy issues right now, so I'm thinking a few white lies might be easier to take than the blunt truth."

I opened my mouth to protest but stopped myself. "You're right."

"Yeah, I know," Gibsie mused. "Contrary to popular belief – mostly my mother's – it does happen sometimes."

The "Crazy Frog/Axel F" song blasted through the room then, loud and annoying as fuck, and causing Gibsie to reach for his phone and me to groan in sheer fucking despair.

"It's mine," Claire chirped, holding her phone up. She glanced at the phone and grimaced. "It's my mam *again*."

"Don't tell her that you're with me," Gibsie warned. "Whatever you do, babe, do *not* tell that woman that I'm with you."

Claire glared at him. "Who else would I be with? Besides, there's no point since she saw me getting into your car!"

He shrugged uncomfortably. "She'll kill you."

"Yeah, Gerard, I know," she hissed before clicking receive and putting the phone to her ear. "Hi, Mam – yeah, I know what you said . . . yeah, I know, Mam, but it's not what you think . . . " Putting her head down, Claire hurried past me, speaking so low and fast that I couldn't make out a word of it.

"Why will her mother kill her?" I asked, eyeing Gibsie with suspicion. "What have you done that you haven't told me about?"

Looking everywhere but my face, Gibsie muttered something about *'a huge fucking mistake'* before bolting after her.

I hoped for Gibsie's sake he didn't make *that* kind of mistake with Claire because Hughie Biggs had a temper on him when the notion took him, and I wasn't in any fit state to stop them from killing each other.

"Well, shite," I mumbled, staring after them both, "the drama just keeps on coming."

# Stay With Me

## SHANNON

I wasn't sure what I was expecting to find when I walked into Johnny's bedroom, but my brother passed out on his bed wasn't it. He was lying diagonally across the foot of Johnny's huge bed, but his feet were still planted on the floor.

Slipping inside, I quietly padded over to the bed and stared down at Joey's sleeping form. His lips were slightly parted and his breathing was deep and even. I sagged in relief. For a moment, I'd feared he was dead.

My gaze flicked to where he was still clutching Johnny's phone. Reaching out, I gently pried it out of his hand, careful not to wake him. I was terrified of what would happen when he did wake. Where would he go? Would he come home? Go to Aoife's? Go back to Shane Holland and his scumbag friends?

I honestly didn't know, and the uncertainty worried me more than my father's disappearance. Because I cared about Joey. He was important to me. For most of my life, he was the most important person in it. The thought of something happening to him was unbearable. It was too much to take, and I honestly didn't think I could take a whole lot more of anything.

I remembered how it was last year. The fighting at home had been terrible – the mood exceptionally arctic. Dad was spending all of his time at the pub, and Mam was rotating between working herself into the ground and falling apart in her bedroom.

You see, Dad had been having yet another affair with one of the barmaids, an affair that had come out in glorious fashion a few short months later, and Mam knew. She knew and instead of throwing him out, she took to the bed. Sean hadn't yet turned two, and was a handful. Between cutting his back teeth and screaming through the night, all of us were exhausted.

Things were getting worse for me at BCS, and Joey was losing his temper more often. Talking back to teachers, getting into brawls at school and even bigger brawls at home, until one day, he had a new group of *friends*. Friends who were too old to be hanging around with a school boy. Friends who had no business showing up to the school for drop-offs.

After that, Joey began to withdraw. He turned secretive and disconnected. He didn't care about anything. Not school or hurling. He was just disappearing.

Until one day at school, one of the girls from his class, the pretty blonde who always watched him, a girl I was sure Joey had never spoken more than two words to, chased him outside to the school yard and stopped him from climbing into that car. I knew this because I, too, had followed at a distance. The girl had caused an unmerciful scene in the carpark and had waved her phone around at those older boys in the car. And then she did something that had shocked me. She fisted his school jumper in both hands and dragged his face down to hers, kissing him right there, without thought for suspension had they been caught.

I never did find out what Aoife said that day, but whatever it was, it caused Joey to walk away from the car and climb into hers instead.

After that, things slowly started to change for him. *He* started to come back to us, piece by piece. Because Aoife gave him something that day, something to cling to. Hope for the future.

And then my father took that something away from him again.

*He took his hope.*

I saw it in his eyes when he visited me at the hospital; the light bulb Aoife had switched on inside of him had been slowly dimmed out to the point where he was back to darkness.

If he could just sleep it off, sleep whatever he had taken right out of his system, then maybe he would wake up with some clarity. A clear head and the ability to do some calm, rational thinking. Maybe he could—

"Shan? My mam called and I need to go home." Claire's voice cut through my thoughts and I swung around to find her standing in the doorway. Pressing my finger to my lips, I begged her with my eyes not to make a sound as I slowly crept out of the room.

"Sorry," she whispered when we were both standing in the landing with the bedroom door closed behind us. "I didn't realize he was asleep."

I didn't respond until we were at the top of the staircase and far away from the door. "It's okay. Neither did I." On shaky legs, I descended the steps, feeling the burn in my lungs as I moved. Since leaving the hospital, I'd spent the majority of my time holed up in my room. All the walking today had taken it out of my body. Niggling pains and aches were resurfacing and without the prescribed pain relief I had forgotten to take before I left my house, I was feeling every one of them. "What were you going to tell me?"

"I need to go home," Claire replied in a huffy tone. "My mam's been calling non-stop." She rolled her eyes for emphasis. "She says if Gerard doesn't bring me home by ten, she's locking me out of the house." Huffing out a breath, she added, "It a quarter to ten now."

"Would that be such a bad thing?" Gibsie waggled his brows, joining us in the hallway. "You could always stay with me."

Claire rolled her eyes again. "It's an empty threat, she would never lock me out, but *he* needs to take me home," she continued, wisely refraining from going back and forth with Gibsie. "And I was wondering if you wanted to sleep over?"

"Sleep over?" I squeezed out.

"Yeah." Claire nodded. "I mean, it's totally fine if you'd prefer to go home or whatever." She scrunched her nose up at that, making it very clear that she thought me going home was anything but *fine*. "But I can get my mam to call your mam if you'd rather stay with me?"

"I won't be allowed," I admitted with a sigh. Going home was the very last thing I wanted to do right now, but I couldn't exactly *not* either. "They'll hit the roof if I don't go back." I thought about all the trouble we were going through with the authorities, and while nobody had said I couldn't spend the night at a friend's house, I knew it wouldn't go down well with Mam. No, because she would spend the whole night wide-awake, stewing in her own panicked paranoia until I returned. "It's probably easier for everyone if I just go home."

"With all due respect, Shan, fuck them."

My eyes widened.

It was beyond rare to hear Claire curse, and *never* about parents.

"*Fuck. Them*," she added with a meaningful stare.

"Yes! Fuck them," Gibsie cheered. "You tell her, babe."

"Shush, Gerard," Claire said before turning her attention back to me. "You are sixteen years old, *we* are on our last week of Easter break from school, and *you* should be having normal teenage-girl experiences like staying over at your best friend's house. Instead, you've spent the first week of break lying in a hospital and dealing with more crap than anyone our age should have to. So, you do you, Shan. If you want to stay with me, then dammit, you stay with me."

"Darren will get upset." I didn't agree with a lot of what he said, and I wasn't pleased that he felt he could order me about, but I knew his heart was in the right place. And I didn't want to hurt him. I didn't want to hurt anyone. That was the problem.

"Darren will get over it," Claire shot back, rolling her eyes. "He's your brother, not your keeper. You had one of those and look where it got you. Look what he did to you!" I grimaced and Claire cringed. "Okay," she soothed. "Maybe I worded that wrong and was a tad insensitive given the circumstances, but you know what I mean. I'm saying this because I care about you, because I love you, Shan, and I'm done with watching people push you around. And, quite frankly, you should be done, too. Stop worrying about everyone else and think about yourself for a change. *Live* your life."

She was right, but it was hard to break the habit of a lifetime. Especially when the consequences had always resulted in pain.

I was programmed to do as I was told. It was a basic survival skill that I had honed to perfection.

*It was what had kept me alive up to this point.*

"What about Joey?" I asked, glancing nervously at the staircase behind me. Excitement mixed with a huge dollop of anxiety rose up inside of me; the prospect of not going home tonight growing more tempting by the second. "He's asleep and I don't think I should leave him—"

"He can stay here," Johnny announced, joining us in the hall. "You both can." His blue eyes locked on mine. "If you want?"

"Whoa there, stallion," Claire said, waving a hand in the air. "Steady up. I said she needed normal teenage experiences, but don't go jumping the gun here."

Gibsie snickered. "Boom."

"I'm not jumping the bleeding gun," Johnny shot back, tone defensive. "My folks are in Dublin, and I have an empty house. Her brother's already here. She's already here." His cheeks turned a deep shade of pink as he shrugged. "I was offering the obvious solution."

"Solution." Claire arched. "Uh-huh. Yeah, if that's what you're calling it."

"I was," Johnny replied with a frown.

"Yeah," Claire scoffed. "You were *jumping the gun*."

"No, I bleeding wasn't." Johnny looked to me for help. "I swear, I *wasn't*."

"I believe you," I offered up.

"Sure," Claire drawled. "Keep telling yourself that."

"Why don't we all stay here?" Gibsie piped up. "Call it a solution, or a compromise, or a slumber party, or whatever the hell ye want. We can even order a pizza. Just stop addling my brain with all the back and forth."

"I can't," Claire said with a heavy sigh. "Not since Mam found out that you—" She snapped her mouth shut. Her face turned a deep shade of red and she gave Gibsie a look that said *'and you know why'* before hurrying on, "I just can't."

I was surprised to see that Gibsie actually blushed, too.

"Well, well, well," Johnny mused, voice dripping with sarcasm. "Looks like someone else—" he paused to make air quotations "—jumped the gun."

"I most certainly did not," Claire huffed, folding her arms across her chest. "The only thing I jump, Johnny Kavanagh, is a skipping rope."

"Uh-huh." Johnny arched a brow and mimicked her earlier words back to her. "You keep telling yourself that."

"We don't all think with our genitals," she countered.

"Considering *my* genitals were recently sewn back on with a needle and thread, I'd say that's very true," he shot back huffily.

"Needle and thread," Gibsie snickered. "Nice visual, lad."

"Shut up, Gerard!" Johnny and Claire both growled in unison.

"You know, if you're looking for a stallion, you can always saddle me up," Gibsie tossed back.

"*Shut up*, Gerard!"

"Shutting up, Claire-bear."

"I think I'll stay here," I blurted out, partially because I wanted to defuse the situation and partially because I wanted to help my friend. Whatever was happening with her and Gibsie, Claire was deeply private about it. She would talk when she wanted to. Until then, I wasn't going to push it. After all, I owed her years' worth of not pushing for information.

Johnny visibly relaxed. "You'll stay?"

I nodded slowly. "If you want me to?"

"I want you here," he told me, never taking his eyes off mine. "I want you to stay with me."

*Oh god.*

*My heart.*

*These words.*

*This boy.*

"Are you sure?" Claire asked, giving me a look that relayed she was both grateful for my intervention and disappointed by my response.

"I'd rather stay and make sure Joey's okay." I turned to Johnny and my heart rate spiked. *Liar, liar. You want to stay with him.* "If you're sure that's okay?"

Johnny was grinning triumphantly at Claire but quickly sobered his features to a somber nod when he noticed me staring. "Absolutely," he replied. "I want you."

Gibsie snickered. "Boom, boom."

"*Here*," Johnny quickly amended, casting a warning glare in Gibsie's direction. He looked back to me. "I want you here with me."

My heart rate jumped clean off the Richter scale. "Thank you."

"Fine," Claire huffed, pulling me in for a hug. "But you call me if you need me, okay?"

"Okay," I replied, not bothering to tell her that I no longer had a phone. Knowing Claire, she would go right out tomorrow and spend all of the money she'd earned from babysitting to buy me a new one, and I didn't want that kind of relationship with anyone.

As depressing as it sounded, I would much prefer to be alone than to be with people purely because they pitied my circumstances. I wasn't entirely sure who I was as a person yet, or where I fit in the world, but I did know that I needed my friends to like me for me and not because they felt sorry for me.

"I'll see you soon, okay?" Releasing me, she walked over to Gibsie who was standing at the front door with it held open for her, only to stop in her tracks. "And you—" Turning back to Johnny, she gave him a scathing look. "Jump skipping ropes, not bones."

"Won't be jumping those either," Johnny shot back sarcastically. "Needle and thread, remember?"

"Yeah, well, just keep your penis in your pants," she replied, flustered. "And don't get any notions – that's all I'm saying." Having said that, she spun back around and practically floated out of the front door with Gibsie hot on her heels.

The door closed behind them and I was alone for the first time in what felt like forever with Johnny Kavanagh.

"Hi, Shannon," he said with an awkward half shrug, giving me his full attention.

Feeling shy, I tucked my hair behind my ear and smiled back at him. "Hi, Johnny."

"So . . . " Sliding his hands into his pockets, he looked around briefly before locking eyes with me. My heart sped up as awareness of our surroundings consumed me. I could feel it in the air; the electricity crackled around us. "What do you want to do?"

*Everything.*

"Whatever you want to do." Remembering I was still clutching Johnny's phone in my hand, I closed the space between us and thrust it against his chest. "I'm, ah, thank you for helping my brother." My cheeks burned when he reached up to take it and his fingers brushed against mine. "And me." Taking a step back, I clasped my hands together in front of myself and exhaled a pained sigh. "For helping me, too." It was pained because I was so socially awkward, I could hardly stand it. "And for letting us stay here," I added, taking another uncertain step, this time to the side. "So, uh, yeah, thanks."

Johnny stared down at me with a look of puzzlement. "Are you okay?"

I nodded eagerly. "It's good."

He smirked. "*It's* good?"

"Me," I corrected with a heavy sigh and dropped my head. "I'm good."

"What are you thinking?"

I shrugged and kept my gaze trained on my runners. "I don't know."

Johnny sighed heavily. "What am I going to do with you, huh?" Snaking a hand out, he clamped my waist and pulled me flush against him. My head snapped up of its own accord, my breath escaping my lungs in a rush. "Keep that pretty head of yours up, Shannon *like the river*." Tucking a strand of hair behind my ear, he grazed my cheek with his knuckles. "It makes it kind of hard for me to know what to do when I can't take your measure." He traced my chin with his thumb, heated blue eyes locked on mine. "I can't read you if you don't look at me."

"Okay," I agreed and then backpedaled. "Wait – huh?"

"Your eyes," he said, tone gruff. "I need them on me."

I blew out a shaky breath. "You do?"

Johnny nodded slowly, tightening his hold on my waist. "How else am I supposed to know what you're thinking?"

"I don't know," I breathed, chest rising and falling a little faster now, his close proximity wreaking havoc to my internal wiring. Unable to stop myself, I reached up and placed my hands on his chest, resisting the urge to knot my fingers in the fabric of his hoodie. "You could just ask me?"

"I *did* ask you, but you wouldn't tell me," he corrected, tone gentle and coaxing. "I asked you what you wanted to do, but you wouldn't tell me that, either." My pulse galloped wildly when he leaned closer and lowered his forehead to rest against mine. The featherlight contact was too much and not nearly enough all in one breath. "I need you to take the lead here, Shannon," he whispered. "You need to tell me what you want from me." I could feel his heart hammering hard in his chest. The rhythm seemed to match mine. "Because I'm not making any mistakes with you."

*Kiss me, Johnny.*

*Kiss me.*

*I want you to kiss me!*

When I didn't respond, because quite frankly, I couldn't get the words I had formed in my head to come out of my mouth, Johnny smiled and took a step back.

"Come on," he said with a small, rueful shake of his head. Taking my hand in his, he led me towards the sitting room. "There's no rush." His movements were stiff and slow without his crutches. "You can tell me when you're ready." Pushing the sitting room door open, he gestured for me to go ahead of him. "I'm not going anywhere."

Feeling lightheaded, a little breathless, and a lot disappointed, I released his hand and walked inside, feeling the absence of his touch all the way down to my toes.

"You can sit down, Shannon," Johnny said when I hovered near the couch. He walked stiffly over to the window and drew the curtains, cloaking us in semi-darkness before moving for the television. "It's okay."

Wordlessly, I dropped onto the couch and kept my gaze trained on the roaring fire, soaking up the heat and peace and quiet.

"What's your favorite pizza topping?"

I looked up at him. "Huh?"

"Pizza," he repeated as he pulled his phone out of his pocket and tapped at the screen. "What's your favorite topping?" Standing in front of the fire, he flicked on the huge TV and then turned back to face me with his phone pressed to his ear.

"Uh, pineapple," I mumbled. "Why?"

He gaped at me in horror. "Are you serious?"

"What?" I blushed. "It's delicious."

Suppressing a shudder, he began to speak into the phone. "Hey, can I place an order for delivery?"

"Wha– wait, you don't have to do that—"

"Pick a film," he mouthed, gesturing to the remote on the coffee table, before continuing calling out his food order to the person on the other line.

Stunned, I picked up the remote and did exactly what I was told, scrolling through the bazillion channels he had and settling on the first film I found.

"The food will be here in half an hour," Johnny announced when his phone call had ended.

"You didn't have to do that," I whispered, mortified. "Buy me food, I mean."

Johnny stared at me for a long moment before blowing out a breath. "Yeah, we're not doing this anymore."

"Huh?" I stared at him, wide-eyed and petrified. "Wh-what do you mean?"

"I'm going to buy you dinner, Shannon." Closing the space between us, he lowered himself down on the couch and turned to face me. "Sometimes we'll eat here and sometimes we'll go out, but it's going to be a regular occurrence, so don't overthink it, okay?"

I had no clue how to respond to that so I just nodded. "Okay."

"Tonight, it's a shitty pizza," he sighed. "Because I can't drive and all the good spots in town are closed early on Mondays, but I'll do better next time."

"I don't need better," I said softly. "I like pizza." *But I love you*.

"Maybe not, but you deserve better," he said quietly.

"I can't give you anything back," I blurted out, feeling heat creep up my neck. "I can't buy you dinner or pay for the cinema," I added, thinking back to the film he took me to see. "I want to." I dropped my head, too exposed in this moment to keep his gaze. "But I just can't."

"If you had a million quid in your arse pocket, I wouldn't have you pay for me," Johnny interrupted, tipping my chin up with his fingers. His blue eyes bored holes in mine as he spoke. "And you can call that a sexist or an old-fashioned way of thinking, but in all honesty, I don't give a shite. If we're eating together, I'm feeding you."

"It is a bit," I offered quietly. "Old-fashioned, I mean."

"Yeah?" Johnny shrugged. "Then you can blame my ma for that."

"I'd say she did a pretty good job," I breathed, shivering when he stroked my chin with his thumb.

"Yeah?" He smiled and leaned closer. "How good of a job, would you say?"

"I'd give her full marks," I whispered. "Definitely ten of ten."

His eyes blazed. "And I'd give *you* full marks."

"Me?"

"Always you," he whispered, eyes flicking to my mouth. "I love this." His thumb traced the tiny dimple in my chin. "It's fucking adorable." His gaze flicked back to my mouth and he dragged his bottom lip between his teeth, biting down hard, before releasing it on a groan and leaning back.

I stifled a groan of my own, devastated to lose his touch.

Tearing his eyes off mine, Johnny turned his attention to the television mounted above the fireplace. "*Love, Actually*?" A ghost of a smile crept over his face. "Really?"

"That was the first film I found," I said, flapping my hands around nervously. "You can change it if you want." Tucking my hair behind my ears, I bunched up my sleeves only to watch in dismay when they rolled back down. "I won't mind."

"No, it's grand," he chuckled, settling back on the couch. "Have you seen it?"

"No." I shook my head and followed his lead, settling back on the seat. "Have you?"

Johnny nodded, still smirking. "Gibsie made me go see this with him at the cinema back when it first came out."

This time I smiled. "Are you serious?"

"Deadly. We looked like two spanners sitting in the cinema surrounded by couples." Reaching behind us, he pulled a blanket off the back of the couch and draped it over my legs. "He was going through his Keira Knightly phase at the time and was so pissed when he realized how little she appears in this." He laughed softly, clearly thinking about something amusing. "He got so into it that he fucking wept during the part with the necklace—" he stopped himself before he could finish. "Sorry." He gave me a sheepish smile. "I almost gave the plot away."

"Why did you go with him?" Smiling back at him, I slipped my hands under the woolen blanket and snuggled deeper into the couch. "If you're not into these kinds of films?"

"Because he's my best friend," he replied, chuckling to himself, as he stretched his legs out on the coffee table. "And he's done worse for me."

"Like what?"

"Like breaking out of hotel rooms in the middle of the night to come see me." Johnny turned to look at me then. "Like bringing me to see you today."

"Thank you," I breathed, feeling something shift inside of me, pulling me towards him. "For coming back."

"Shannon, I . . . " He stopped himself short and released a heavy sigh. "Come here," he said instead, lifting his arm. "Let me keep you warm."

Desperate for physical contact, I closed the space between us and burrowed into his side. His arm came around me and a shiver rolled through me when I felt his lips brush the top of my head. "Let's do this," he whispered, turning the volume up on the television.

We didn't say anything else after that.

# Are You Going To Kiss Me Or Not?

## JOHNNY

I won the battle of the best-friend versus boyfriend, and it felt fucking fabulous.

*Round one to me.*

Except I wasn't even sure if I was her boyfriend.

*Boyfriend*; that was a stupid word.

Jesus, I needed to get a handle on myself.

Now I *finally* had Shannon alone, I didn't know what to do. She looked so uncertain earlier that it chipped away at my conscience to the point where I pulled back. I *wanted* to kiss her, but I didn't know if *she* wanted me to, and that was a problem for me. Because contrary to Claire's assumptions, I *didn't* want to jump the gun. I didn't want to dump my feelings on top of her and take advantage.

Everything about Shannon's life had changed so drastically and in such a short succession of time, that I didn't want to make a mistake with her. Most of all, I didn't want her to regret *me*.

And now here we were, back on my couch, with no secrets standing between us or training to rush off to. No, all that stood between us now was fear of the unknown.

For the first time in almost eighteen years, I felt like I was standing at a pivotal crossroad in my life. I didn't need to ask myself which path I was going to take – my feet were already moving towards her – but I was conflicted because I knew the path was a short one. If my father and doctors were right, and I did manage to make it onto the team in June, then that meant I had two months left with her. Two months and I would be out of here. Come June, I would veer off that path.

Suddenly, the prospect of the U20's wasn't as appealing as before. The tunnel vision I had lived by my whole life, the one with only rugby in sight, was clouded and blurry now. Trying to do the right thing for my future and doing what was right for my *present* was the reason I felt so fucking torn up over this girl.

I just wanted *time* with her. Away from her family and rugby. Away from everything. Just me and her. I wanted to hit pause on my life and just *keep* her. Strong words for a person my age, but I trusted my instincts and my gut. All of those were encouraging me, assuring me that I was dead on the money because this girl was the girl for me. The one I was supposed to keep. I could make my way through a mountain of pussy and it wouldn't mean a thing because I had caught feelings for her.

"Are you okay?" Shannon's voice cut through my thoughts and I shifted my gaze from the flames crackling in the fireplace to her face. She was sitting with her back resting against the arm of the couch, buried beneath the blanket I had dumped on top of her hours ago. She had her arms hooked loosely around her knees and was looking at me expectantly.

Unable to recall a word of what she had just said to me, I ran a hand through my hair and stretched. "Sorry, what was that?"

"You got up to put coal in the fire an hour ago and you've been staring at the mantel piece ever since," she explained in that soft voice of hers. "The film's over, Johnny, and the telly's gone blank."

"Shite, it has?" I looked around and noticed we were sitting in the darkness with only the fire illuminating the room. "Sorry. I must have zoned out."

Shannon frowned in concern and I felt her foot stroke the side of my thigh. "Is it the medication you're taking?" Her voice was laced with sympathy, her toes stroking my thigh soothingly. "Does it make you drowsy?"

"No, it's not the meds." *It's the fact that I've spent days rehearsing what I want to say to you in my head and now I can't get the words out.* "I don't know what happened to me." *You happened to me, and now I'm completely fucked.* "I'm just running on empty, I guess." *Because we've been sitting here all night and still haven't addressed the elephant in the room.* "Sorry, Shan."

Whatever I said caused her to smile and I arched a brow. "Something funny about that?"

"You called me Shan," she said, grinning.

"*Yeah* . . ." I grinned back at her. "So?"

"My friends call me Shan," she explained. "Well, the girls and Joey."

"Am I not your friend?" I teased, shifting around to face her. "Or is that pet name reserved only for members of your *inner circle*?"

"No, no, you are my circle," she blurted out and then grimaced. "I meant you're *in* my circle. *In* my circle – not *are* my circle." She dropped her head in her hands and groaned. "Ugh, I'm bad with people."

Laughing, I reached under the blanket and snatched her foot. Fuck knows why I did it, but I had her bleeding foot in my hand now so I went with it. *Gibsie was right; I had an issue with taking things that weren't mine.* "Relax," I said, setting her foot down on my lap. "I know what you meant."

Shannon's eyes flicked to where I was holding her foot on my lap, and I waited to see what she would do next.

If she pulled back, I would let her. But she *didn't*.

Instead she poked her other foot out from under the blanket and placed it on my lap with the other. Her eyes flicked back to mine, clearly waiting to gauge my reaction.

I reacted by draping my arm across her legs and loosely clasping her knee, keeping my eyes on hers the entire time, watching for the smallest hint of anything that might look like doubt.

"Can I ask you a question?" I plucked up the courage to say. When she nodded, I forced the words out. "How are you feeling . . . about me?"

Her eyes widened. "About you?"

"Yeah." I swallowed deeply. "About me."

Shannon was silent for so long that I was afraid she wasn't going to answer me, but then she started to speak.

"Sometimes I feel like I'm stranded," she confessed in a small voice, dropping her gaze to where I was holding her legs. "Like I'm stuck in the same place and I'm drowning." Clasping her hands together, she continued to speak, to gut me with her truth. "It's like I'm watching the water rising, and it's coming higher and higher. I can see it closing in on me, taking me under." Shivering, she bit down on her lip. "It's terrifying."

"I bet," I replied gruffly, trailing my fingertips up and down her jean-clad knee, unsure of what else to say, and terrified of saying the wrong thing.

"And then you walk in and it recedes." Tipping her chin up, she looked me dead in the eyes and exhaled a shaky breath. "You show up and all the bad just . . . goes away for a little while."

I could feel her eyes on me, and it caused a slow burn to ignite inside of me. My skin was hot, my body was coiled tight with frustration and excitement.

I was so *fucked.*

"That's how you make me feel," she whispered, blue eyes burning their way right down to my soul. "Better. Alive. Free. Safe. Important. I feel like I can breathe for the first time in days and that's only because you're here – because I'm with *you*." She grimaced then, like a painful thought had just come to her. "But I'm derailing your life," she added, voice small. "I've dragged you into my family's mess and I'm so sorry for that."

*Careful, Johnny.*

*Be really fucking careful with your words here, lad.*

She was a closed book that I had miraculously managed to pry open. I wasn't about to make a mistake and have the pages closed in my face. "I can't remember how this started or when I got wrapped up in you to the point where I feel like I'm strangling in your grief," I finally said when words found me again. "But I know that I don't ever want to go back to how it was before you."

She was so strong, so resilient, and she didn't even know it. I couldn't imagine going through what she had and just getting back up again. But here she was, ready to put her trust in me, leaving her house this evening even though her father was still around. I mean, that had to fuck with her head, right? But she didn't let it take her down. The girl was the definition of fall down seven times and stand up eight. No matter what seemed to be thrown her way, she always dusted herself off, climbed back up on her feet, and tried again.

"I'm just so tired of being here," she confessed in a small voice. "I'm trying, you know – to just get on with it. To not dwell, and to just be grateful, but I'm *not* grateful and I *can't* move on. I feel like I'm still trapped, and every day, I'm getting closer to the day where I won't be here anymore."

I didn't understand, so I wasn't going to tell her that I did. I had no idea about what she was dealing with or how she was even coping. All I could say was, "I'm here." And I would be.

"He's giving me rules, Johnny." Shannon scrunched up her nose, took a few shallow breaths, and then blurted out, "More rules. More laws—" she exhaled heavily and added, "More orders to obey."

Yeah, I was going to lose it.

*Breathe, Johnny.*

*Take a fucking breath, lad.*

It took me a moment to process what she had said, and many more to rein in my emotions and the sudden and desperate need I had inside of me to attack. "Darren?" I finally managed to ask.

She nodded weakly. "And I know he has good intentions, but I'm just . . . I'm so done with being controlled." Shivering, she added, "When I woke up in that hospital bed, alive and breathing, I promised myself that I wouldn't let anyone control me like he had. I *swore* that I would never let that happen again."

"You didn't let happen in the first place, Shan," I told her, voice hoarse. "It was out of your control."

"That's the thing," she replied. "I'm sick of *things* being out of my control, Johnny."

"Yeah." I sighed heavily. "I bet."

"You know, I still remember how I felt the first time I took a shower in this house," she said then, smiling softly to herself. "I just stood in your bathroom for the longest time and listened."

"To what?"

"The silence."

"Shan ..."

"It's hard to explain," she hurried to explain. "But I never wanted to leave that bathroom, because I felt safe – I *feel* safe with you." Shaking her head, she blew out a shaky breath and said, "and that's awful because it puts pressure on you."

Reeling, I began to rack my brain for the words I knew I needed to put her mind at ease. To piece her back together again. I didn't know. I just had feelings. Huge fucking feelings that were choking me and drowning me in a simultaneous pattern of addictive destruction.

My walls had crumbled. Everything I had built up in my bid to protect myself from the girl I *knew* would take me down had disintegrated. "Nobody's making me do anything," I finally said, feeling at a loss. "You're in my house because I want you here."

"Yeah?"

"One hundred percent," I told her. "And that has nothing to do with anything other than the fact that I just *want* you here with me, Shannon."

"Are you sure?" she whispered.

"Listen," I said, turning my body to give her my full attention. "There's something you should know about me, and it's that I don't do feelings fleetingly. I'm not a fleeting fucking anything – that's not how I work. So, when I tell you something, or when I do something, I mean it – I've thought it through. And I'm telling you that I *want* you here with me."

Her mouth fell open, her pouty lips forming a perfect little O.

"Yeah." I smirked, resisting the urge to reach over and tip her chin back up. "Oh."

"Johnny?" she asked then, shimmying closer. "Can I ask you one more thing?"

"Yeah—" the word came out all gruff and I had to clear my throat before trying again, "Yeah, Shan. You can ask me anything."

"Are you ever going to kiss me?"

Holy fuck.

*Keep the head, Kav.*

*Keep your cool and do not scare her off.*

*You've got her back, now* keep *her here.*

*Don't lunge, lad. Hold it back . . .*

I took me a few seconds to process her words before I could speak. "Do you *want* me to kiss you?"

"It would be nice to not have to make the first move and then run away." Her voice was barely more than a whisper and she ducked her face for the briefest of moments before looking back up at me, those blue eyes sucking me right in. "It would save me a lot of panicking," she added with a small shrug. "That's what I want – to not have to panic." She chewed on her bottom lip for a moment before continuing, "To know where I stand with you."

"I want to kiss you, Shannon." Ignoring the pain in my groin, I twisted my body around to face her. "I *will* kiss you," I amended, feeling all hot and flustered. "If that's what you want?"

Shannon blew out a shaky breath. "Okay."

I eyed her warily. "Okay."

She remained perfectly still, eyes locked on mine, cheeks flushed, expression *expectant*?

"What – like right now?" I asked, feeling a little fucking panicky at being put on the spot myself. "You want me to do it now?" Christ, I was making a hash of this. "I just thought you might, you know, want to talk some more."

"I don't want to do any more talking, Johnny," she whispered. "I've done enough of that to last me a lifetime."

"I just don't want to pressure you," I strangled out, hearing the nervousness in my own bleeding voice. "All the shite you've been through with your da, and now Joey. And your ma and her drama. And Jesus, your face is all hurt and sore, and your body—" I shrugged, at a complete loss. "I'm just . . . I think we should keep talking? Fuck, Shannon, I don't want you to feel like I'm taking advantage of you—"

"Are you going to kiss me or not?" Shannon stunned me by asking.

"I just . . . I don't . . . I'm trying . . ." My words broke off and I exhaled a pained sigh as I watched her watch me, those sucker-punching blue eyes wide and welcoming. "Fuck it—"

Unable to take another second of this, I cupped the back of her neck, closed the space between us, and crushed my lips to hers.

Moaning into my mouth, her hands moved to the front of my jumper, fingers knotting in the fabric as she tugged and pulled and encouraged me to come closer.

*Ah, fuck.*

Capturing her hands with mine, I repressed every fucked-up urge inside of me and just kissed her back, desperately trying to keep my cool and not push for too much. All I wanted to do was pick her up and wrap her body around mine, make a better angle for myself, but I couldn't do any of that.

*Take it slowly,* my brain, clouded by hormones, warned. *Don't fuck this up, lad.*

However, the minute I felt her tongue take a tentative swipe against mine, I knew I was completely fucked.

I couldn't take it.

I honest to god couldn't *take* the pressure in my chest. It caused a vital circuit attached to my self-control to crash and burn.

My brain switched off and my body took over.

My dick was sitting firmly in the driver's seat, and I was moving purely on instinct, kissing her back deeply, knowing there was a reason I needed to stop, but not finding the willpower to put the brakes on.

My hands moved to tangle in her hair and *her* hands moved to my waist, pulling at my flesh and encouraging me to come with her as she fell onto her back. And Christ if I wasn't right there with her, diving in like a fucking maniac, desperate for the taste of her as our tongues dueled together for what was, without a doubt, the best kiss of my life.

Kissing her was different because there were feelings involved.

Big, huge, terrifying fucking feelings that I knew she felt, too.

It was different because it *mattered* – because we mattered to *each other*.

My body was burning up, partially from the agonizing pain that was made worse with every reckless thrust of my hips against hers, but mostly from sheer fucking excitement of having her hands on my skin.

I felt like she had taken a knife to my chest, cut me right open, and every bit of me was bleeding into her.

I was hard, painfully fucking hard, and not in the good way that could be relieved, but right now, it didn't matter.

I didn't care if I was broken.

I didn't even care if I burst a stitch.

I didn't care about anything but the girl moaning and writhing on the couch beneath me.

# A Crazy Fucking Amount

## SHANNON

Johnny told me to tell him what I wanted. It took me four hours to get the words out, and when I finally did, I stunned us both with my bluntness.

The mortification I was feeling over how uncharacteristically forward I had been faded more and more with every thrust of his tongue as he kissed me deeply.

I could hardly breathe, my lungs were screaming in protest, but I knew I would rather die than go up for air. I felt like I was starving for him and the emotions driving me forward were overwhelming.

He was so much bigger than me, so much broader, and it thrilled me. The weight of his body on top of mine was too much and not enough all at the same time. Every time I thought I couldn't take the pressure, my hands dragged him down harder.

Breaking the kiss, he pulled himself up on his elbow. "Are you okay? Am I too heavy?" His chest was rising and falling rapidly, his hard breathing mirroring mine. "Am I hurting you?"

Reaching up, I snaked a hand around the back of his neck and tugged his face back down to mine. My hands were wrapped so tightly around his neck, I was sure I was cutting off circulation somewhere, but I couldn't release him.

I physically *couldn't* let him go.

I was frightened, unsure, and *sore*.

And the only true thing I knew in this moment was that I *trusted* this boy.

"Don't talk," I begged. "Just keep kissing me." Clutching him like a lifeline, I locked my legs around his waist and begged, "Just *stay* with me."

"Fuck . . . " He groaned deep in his throat. "I am." Exhaling a shaky breath, he pressed his lips to mine. "I'm staying." His lips brushed against mine as he spoke and the sensation caused a shiver of pleasure to roll through me. "And I'm so fucking with you," he whispered before sinking back down on me, pressing me deeper into the couch cushions, as he settled heavily between my legs.

My breath hitched in my throat when his lips landed back on mine, hot and probing as he parted his lips and blew my mind with his skilled tongue.

Closing my eyes, I tightened my legs that were around his waist, clinging to him for all I was worth. The move caused a pained growl to erupt from Johnny's chest. I knew I was hurting him and that I should let go, but I physically couldn't detangle myself from him.

My body felt like it had attached itself to his and, short of a tornado blowing through the room, I doubted anything could pry me off him.

He had one hand tangled in my hair and other clamped down on my hip, fingers flexing against my flesh every time I met his skillful thrust with a tentative one of my own. His hips were moving in a slow, drugging rhythm against my crotch, circling and rocking against me, making me ache and yearn for something hidden deep inside of me, something that with every brush of his lips and every stroke of his tongue, moved closer to my reach.

"I just feel like we should have a conversation—" Johnny tried again, breathing hard against my lips. "About where we both stand." Resting his brow against mine, he lightly kissed me again before finishing, "Just so we're on the same page."

"Really?" I breathed, sliding my hands under the hem of his t-shirt and shivering when I was greeted with hot, toned flesh. I had to stifle a moan when I felt his abdominal muscles tighten and contract beneath my touch. "I, uh . . . I guess . . . " Distracted and overheated, I shook my head, desperately trying to clear my lust-filled thoughts. "Are you sure?"

"No," he groaned, sounding pained and conflicted. "I just think that maybe we should?" He continued to rock against me as he spoke, angling those magic hips to cause maximum damage to my nerves. "Talk, that is." He stared hard at me for a long, strained beat before exhaling heavily. "About us." A huge tremor rolled through his powerful body. "Ah, fuck it—" and then he was back; kissing me, moving against me, making me shiver and tremble.

We stayed like that for what felt like hours, fully clothed, just kissing and grinding, touching and whispering, until I honestly didn't have an ounce of energy left in my body.

"You okay?" he whispered, nuzzling my cheek with his nose.

Nodding, I sighed in contentment and flexed my fingertips against his waist, wanting nothing more than to keep him here with me forever. "Just tired."

Burying his face in my neck, Johnny inhaled a deep breath before pulling back to kneel between my legs. A cold shiver swept through me at the sudden lack of contact. The fire was almost out now, only the rogue orange ember remained, and the night air was seeping into my bones.

Leaning sideways, he grabbed his phone off the coffee table, knocking the empty pizza box over in the process. "Shite," he muttered, and turned the screen to face me. "It's half three in the morning." He flicked on the torch on his phone so we could see in the darkness before setting it back down on the table and climbing stiffly off the couch. "I didn't realize the time."

I felt achingly shy as I pulled myself to my feet and watched him stretch his powerful arms over his head before shamelessly slipping a hand inside his sweatpants to readjust *himself.*

"Do you want to go upstairs?" he asked, yawning sleepily. "There's like half a dozen spare rooms. I can set you up in one?"

*No, I want to stay with you.*

I shifted uncomfortably, moving from foot to foot. "I don't mind."

"Do you want to stay down here with me?" he asked then, tone a little gruffer now. "Joey's in my room so I was just going to crash on the couch and I—"

"With you," I croaked out, already nodding in agreement. "I'd rather stay with you."

"Just to sleep," Johnny added, voice strained. "Okay?"

"Okay."

"Okay." Nodding to himself, he reached a hand behind his head and pulled both his hoodie and t-shirt off.

I was glad of the darkness in this moment because I knew my cheeks were glowing bright red at the sight of him.

He was so beautiful it hurt to look.

*All finely carved muscles and toned flesh . . .*

"I'm not getting any ideas, I promise," he told me as he pushed his sweatpants down and stepped out of them, leaving him standing in a pair of fitted boxers that were pitched at the front. "I just can't sleep in my clothes or I'll turn into a furnace."

"O-okay." He wasn't going to get any complaints from me. "I understand."

Riveted to the spot, I watched as he grabbed both his phone and the blanket and then climbed awkwardly onto the couch, wincing with every stiff movement until he was lying on his side against the back of the couch with the blanket covering his waist.

"You coming?" he asked, holding the blanket with one hand and patting the space in front of him with the other.

Gingerly, I lowered myself down to lie with my back to him.

Johnny switched off the torch on his phone and tossed it on the floor before draping the blanket around our bodies. "Relax," he whispered, pulling me closer with the hand he had tucked under me. "We're just sleeping." He wrapped his other arm around me then, enveloping me in the tightest cocoon. "You're safe." I felt his lips brush against the back of my head and a shiver rolled through my body. "I promise."

I curled both of my hands around his forearm and just held onto him, absorbing the feel of his body aligned with mine. The strength of him, his smell, his touch, the sound of his breathing . . . I devoured every second of this moment and locked it away in a treasure time capsule in the back of my mind, keeping it safe with all the others and praying I would have more to add to it. "Don't let go, okay?"

"I won't," he promised, tightening his hold on me.

I knew I was going to be in trouble tomorrow. When I got home it would be to stony-faced expressions and heated lectures, but tonight I couldn't find it in my heart to care.

Johnny trailed his hand over my side, back and forth, over and over, his touch featherlight.

"How did it feel?" he asked, lips brushing against my earlobe as he spoke. His fingers lingered on my side. "That day?"

I knew exactly what he was referring to; that day in the kitchen. "Um . . ." I closed my eyes and thought long and hard before I responded. "It felt . . . unfair."

"Unfair?"

I gave a small nod and tightened my hold on him. "Because I thought it was over and I wasn't ready for it to be."

"It?"

"My life."

He sucked in a sharp breath. "It's not over, Shannon."

"No." I clenched my eyes shut and battled down a surge of sadness, knowing in my heart that we were thinking two opposite things. "It's not."

"I'm sorry this happened to you," he whispered. "I know that doesn't mean shit, and it's probably the worst thing I could say to a person in your situation, but I am." He buried his face in my neck and whispered, "I am so fucking sorry that you were given those people as parents."

A traitorous tear slipped down my cheek, followed by another and then another after that. "I thought about you when it was happening," I confessed, biting down on my lip so hard I felt the familiar metallic taste in my mouth.

"Me?"

Nodding, I wiped my tearstained cheek against his forearm. "I knew what was happening to me, I knew I couldn't stop it, so I just thought up my happiest memory and clung to it."

"What was it?"

"You and me," I whispered, shivering. "Those things you said to me at the hospital. All those other times, too. I conjured you up in my mind and I concentrated on your face. I imagined your voice in my head and just kept you there – in my mind. Talking to me. Keeping me calm. Making me feel—" my breath hitched and I had to take a steadying breath before finishing, "safe."

"Jesus, Shannon," he strangled out, gripping me even tighter. "You'll never know how badly I wish I had been there."

Silence fell around us then, but it wasn't strained or tense.

Instead, it was comforting.

*Deeply* comforting.

Johnny took his time to process what I had told him. He didn't bombard me with questions. He just *stayed* right there beside me, asking one question at a time and then giving himself time to process my response and me time to process my life.

"All I remember is the constant shouting and fear of pain," I replied, several hours later, when Johnny asked about my early childhood. Dawn was breaking outside, illuminating the room in an eerie grayish hue, and neither of us had closed an eye. The light gradually pouring through the enormous windows helped me to see the freckles on his forearm, the scars on his knuckles, and the veins that seemed to just bulge from his taut, sun-kissed skin. "And that feeling in the pit of my stomach, the dread – it's the most familiar feeling I have. I almost feel like I'm not okay when I'm not worried. I'm not okay with feeling okay." I sighed heavily and concentrated on his fingers. He had long fingers, with rough and calloused fingertips and I couldn't stop touching them. "I'm constantly on edge, all the time, waiting for the sadness because that's what I'm used to – what I'm programed to feel, expect, and live with." Grimacing, I trailed my finger over the pad of his thumb and added, "Well, at least that's what Patricia and Carmel say."

"Patricia, the social worker," Johnny said, remembering her name from one of his earlier questions, as he captured my hand in his and entwined our fingers, *steadying* me. "And Carmel is the . . ."

"Counselor from the hospital," I filled in, stroking my nose against his arm. "Although, I've only met her twice and I'm not going back."

The hand he had been trailing up and down my ribcage stilled. "Why not?"

"Because I'm supposed to trust someone who is only there because she's being *paid* to listen to me? Someone who, once five pm rolls by, doesn't give a damn about me or my brothers?" I shook my head. "No, no way."

Johnny sighed and resumed his finger trailing. He was quiet for a long time before saying, "I think you should talk to someone about what happened in that house."

"I just did," I whispered.

"No, Shan, not me," he replied sadly. "A professional with the credentials to make a difference in your life."

"There's no point," I whispered.

"I think there is."

"I think you're wrong."

"What about Joey?" Johnny asked then, switching things up.

I froze for a moment before twisting around to face him. "What did you say?"

"I said what about Joey? Who's helping him?" Johnny asked, brushing his thumb over my cheek. "You said the kids are in counseling and doing play therapy. Your ma's in her own trauma counseling and doing some fucked parenting course. Darren's doing whatever Darren does, and your piece of shit da is on the run. But what about Joey? Is he seeing someone? If he is, then they need to find the lad a new therapist because he was all kinds of fucked up earlier."

*What about Joey.*

*He asked about Joey!*

Three words that meant more to me than anything else he could have said in this moment.

Pulling myself up on my elbow, I leaned over and pressed my lips to his. "Thank you," I whispered, pulling back to look at him.

Johnny frowned in confusion. "For what?"

"Asking the right questions."

"Uh, no problem?"

Something sparked to life in my head then, a question that had been torturing me for days. Rolling back onto my side, I resumed my holding of his arm while I fought to wrangle the courage to ask it. "Can I ask you another question?" I could hear the tremor in my voice, but I forced myself to not backpedal.

"Of course." I heard him yawn behind me, felt the heat of his breath on my neck as he tightened his arms around me, snuggling into my back. "Ask away."

*Here it goes . . .* "Why do you like me?"

Johnny stiffened behind me. "Why do I . . . *what*?"

"Like me," I filled in, my voice barely more than a whisper. "Why?"

I needed to know. I didn't want him to think I was a charity case, or worse, be with me because he felt sorry for me. The prospect left a sour taste in my mouth.

"Is this a . . ." His words trailed off and he slipped out from behind me, shifting into a sitting position on the couch. "Are you being serious?"

I nodded, wishing I wasn't serious, wanting more than anything to play this off as a joke, but knowing I never could because the answer was too important to me. "Yeah." Pulling myself onto my knees, I turned to face him and said, "I need to know."

"I don't just *like* you, I fucking—" Shaking his head, Johnny rubbed his jaw before looking back at me. "Shannon, I love you."

I stopped breathing. "You love me?"

He nodded slowly, blue eyes locked on mine. "Like a crazy fucking amount."

"Really?"

"Really," he confirmed. "And I'd ask your permission, but I didn't even ask mine."

"Oh . . . " I exhaled shakily and nodded. "Okay."

Johnny arched a brow. "*Okay?*"

"I just . . . I thought you were high when you said it that night," I blurted out, shifting closer until my knees brushed against his bare thigh. "I didn't think you meant it."

"I was definitely high that night," he agreed, twisting around to face me. "And I definitely meant it that night."

My heart galloped wildly. "You did?"

"I *love* you," he went right ahead and rocked my world by saying again. "Present tense – as in I mean it now. And maybe I shouldn't be saying that – maybe I'm fucking everything up by telling you that when you're in the middle of your family stuff, but it's the truth." He shrugged helplessly. "I'm *in* love with you. I think I've been that way for a while now – a long fucking while, if we're being totally honest." Exhaling shakily, he added, "And that scares the shit out of me worse than the thought of not making the U20's. *You* scare me more than anyone I've ever come up against on a pitch."

"Wow." I released a shaky breath. "I can't believe you just said all that."

"I know." He looked a little sick when he said, "Dick move, huh?"

"I love you back," I blurted out, feeling a flood of heat rush through my body. "Like a crazy fucking amount," I added, giving his words back to him.

"Yeah?" Johnny's smile was a breath-taking, full dimpled one, and it took the air clean out of my lungs. "Really?"

I nodded solemnly. "It's true."

Still smiling, he shook his head as if to clear his thoughts, and said, "And going back to your earlier question, I like you because you're you, Shannon. I've never met another girl like you."

I scrunched my nose up. "You mean another girl as screwed up as me."

"*No*, I mean a girl as kind, and caring, and trustworthy, and loyal as *you*," he countered gruffly. "And beautiful? Jesus Christ, you are so fucking beautiful that it's *painful* to look at you. I've never seen anything like you in my life."

I felt like melting into the couch. "Johnny—"

"No, no, just let me get this out before I lose my nerve, okay?" he hurried to say, sounding flustered.

I snapped my mouth shut and nodded.

Exhaling another shaky breath, Johnny continued, "It's like you *see* me – and I see you. Christ, I think you saw through me that very first day on the pitch at school, because I sure as hell haven't been the same since, Shannon. You don't give a shite about rugby. It never fazed you and that *threw* me because I'm not used to that. I'm not used to having someone want me for . . . well, for me – but you did. And you took the time to notice me. To see things that no one else was seeing – things I didn't want to acknowledge to myself." He ran a hand through his hair and slumped, his broad shoulders bowing. "And I was scared, Shannon. I was so fucking afraid of how I felt for you. I still am. You scare the absolute shite out of me – for reasons I'm still not entirely sure of, because in all honesty, I don't know what the fuck is happening here. My head is in pieces and I'm so far out of my comfort zone that I feel like I'm balancing on thin ice, but I know that there's no other person I would *willingly* put myself out there for like I have with you." He shrugged helplessly. "Like I'm doing right now."

"Johnny, I—" I opened my mouth to say something, *anything*, but I couldn't speak. I felt like I was drowning in my feelings. I *knew* that I was drowning in *him*. "I . . ."

"And I know what you're thinking," he added, sounding agitated. "You think I'm sticking around because of your da. You think I feel sorry for you."

My breath hitched in my throat. "No."

"You little liar." Leaning closer, he cupped my cheek with his big hand and pressed his forehead to mine. "I can read you like a book."

"Yeah," I admitted. "Kind of."

"Well, you're wrong." His breath fanned my face as he spoke, making me feel lightheaded. "I want you because you drive me fucking crazy. And yeah, I'm not going to lie, I feel sorry for you," he added gruffly. "I'd be a cold-hearted bastard if I didn't, but that's got nothing to do with why I want to be with you. I'm sticking around because I need you."

My heart beat so fast I feared it would burst. "You need me?"

"You think it's the other way around, but it's not," he told me. "I need you, too, because you calm something inside of me. You make me feel *good*. Like I don't have to . . . " his voice trailed off for a moment as he clearly pondered what he was trying to say. "You make me feel like I'm enough as I am," he finally admitted. "Like if this is the furthest I go, if I don't make the squad, then it's okay."

"You *are* enough," I breathed, wrapping my hand around his neck. "Just as you are right now." Desperate to comfort him, I hitched a leg over his and scrambled onto his lap, knowing I shouldn't, he was still healing, but not having the self-control to stop. "You're so good," I told him, knotting my fingers in his hair and pulling him closer to me. "You're such a *good* person, Johnny Kavanagh, and you don't even know it. You don't see how little rugby has to do with how special you are. But I do. I see it, and I know."

"See?" He clamped his hands on my hips and exhaled shakily. "You say it and I believe you."

"Because it's *true*," I strangled out, breathing hard and fast. "I just . . . god, you have no idea how lovely you are."

"What do you need from me, Shannon?" he croaked out, voice thick and husky. "I'll give you anything you need, baby." Shaking his head, he groaned like he was in pain. "I just . . . I want to make you happy."

"You," I whispered. "All of you."

"I'm already yours," he groaned again, before covering my lips with his.

My heart hammered hard in my chest and my body ached and pulsed. It was a deep aching inside of me that only he could sate. In fact, I was fairly sure I would never sate the need I had to just *be* with him. Closing my eyes, I held onto his arms and kissed him back, drowning in the sensations ripping through me.

Maybe Darren was right and I was in too deep, but I couldn't find it in my heart to care.

Everything inside of me was swept up in him, and I couldn't see beyond it – I couldn't think beyond the surge of feelings I had for him. Even my brain, the part of me that was supposed to heed caution, was encouraging me to be reckless with my heart; to throw it all in with this boy and trust him not to break me.

And I was all in.

# Tears, Threats, and Teapots

## JOHNNY

I knew I was in trouble before I even opened an eyelid.

The tone of my mother's voice as she screamed my name from the rooftops was proof of that. "Jonathan Kavanagh!" Her voice cut through the silence, followed by high heels clicking on tiles. "You better come out from wherever you're hiding and explain what the hell is going on!"

Startled, I sprung up, still half-asleep, and blinked rapidly as I tried to process what the fuck was happening.

"There you are!" Mam barked. "What are you doing sleeping in the sitting room?"

*I was in the sitting room?*

Resting an arm on the back of the couch, I looked over at her, feeling at a loss. "I, ah . . . " I yawned loudly and rolled the kinks from my shoulders. "Huh?"

"Do you have any idea why Marie Lynch left a message on your father's phone first thing this morning looking for her daughter?" Mam demanded, standing in the doorway with her hands on her hips.

"*What?*" Scratching my chest, I asked, "Marie who?"

"Marie Lynch!" Mam snapped. "Shannon's mother."

*Oh shite.*

"Well? I'm waiting for an explanation here, Johnny!"

The small ball of heat pressed to my side began to stir and a pair of midnight-blue eyes peeked out from under the blanket.

*Double shite.*

Last night's events came flooding back in a rush, bringing with it a flush of heat straight to my dick.

"*Hi,*" Shannon mouthed, looking wide-eyed and terrified, as she clasped the blanket between her fingers and stared up at me. "*Help.*"

From my mother's standing point, she could only see the back of the couch. I could have wept from the momentary relief that flooded me.

"*What do I do?*" she mouthed, breathing hard. "*Should I get up?*"

*Fuck no!*

"Would you believe me if I said I didn't know?" I called out to my mother as I pulled the blanket back over Shannon's head and awkwardly clambered over her, biting back the urge to scream when pain shot through me like a bullet to the cock.

*Stay down,* I mentally begged Shannon as I got to my feet, *please stay the fuck down.*

"Not in the slightest," Mam shot back, watching me like a hawk. "Why are you naked?"

I glanced down at my jocks and shrugged, feigning nonchalance. "I'm not naked."

Her eyes narrowed. "Then why are you lounging on my good leather in your underpants?"

"Underpants?" I gave her an indignant look. "Am I ten?"

"No, you're nearly eighteen and partially naked," Mam shot back angrily. "And there's a girl I can't account for – one who you're particularly fond of, and one whose mother has been hopping off my phone."

I scratched my head, knowing that I was completely fucked, but wrestling for a way out all the same. "I thought you said she called Da's phone."

"And your father gave her *my* number," Mam bit out, turning purple now.

*Jesus, I was so fucking dead.*

"I've been on the phone, listening to that bleeding woman drone on the entire drive down from Dublin, demanding I return her sixteen-year-old daughter before she calls the Gardaí on you."

"You shouldn't answer your phone when you're driving, Ma," I poked the bear by saying. "It's bad form."

"Bluetooth headsets, Jonathan," Mam growled. "Now, do you know where she is or not?"

"No idea," I lied through my teeth. "Sorry."

"If you know where she is, you need to tell me now," Mam countered, giving me one of those "don't bullshit me" looks.

"No clue," I shot back. "Sorry."

"Do you know what statutory rape is, Johnny?" she growled, sounding furious. "Because Marie Lynch threw that term around an awful lot on the phone to me! And if you've been with Shannon – if she's here now and you're lying to me, then you're going to be in some serious trouble, laddie."

"What the actual *fuck*?" I barked, horrified. "She said that? Are you being serious?"

"Yes, she said that, and it's not the first time," Mam said, voice shaking. "Do you have any idea how damaging an accusation like that could be to a boy's future – and especially one in your position?" She threw her hands up for emphasis. "You could kiss goodbye to a career in rugby, that's for sure!"

"I *didn't* do *anything*," I choked out.

"She's *underage*, Johnny," Mam snarled right back. "Her brother swore down that she left her house with you yesterday and she conveniently didn't go back home last night." Glaring, she added, "You're the mathematician in the family, so do the bleeding maths!"

I glared right back at her, furious. "So, because her brother thinks she's with me, that makes me a fucking rapist?"

"It means that if she doesn't show up at home, her mother will have the Gardaí up to this house and you'll be the first one—"

"Don't let her call the Guards on him, Mrs. Kavanagh."

I dropped my head.

*Fuck. My. Life.*

Springing out from under the blanket, Shannon jumped to her feet. "I'm here." Breathing a little harder than normal, Shannon grimaced and clutched her side. "And I'm so sorry. I know I'm not supposed to be, but I just . . . I didn't mean to . . . we didn't . . . "

Mam's mouth fell open in horror. "*Shannon?*"

"It's not how it looks," I hurried to defuse the situation, if that was even possible. "We fell asleep watching a film. We didn't do anything, Ma—"

"Shannon," Mam strangled out, moving towards us.

"We were sleeping," I repeated, stepping in front of Shannon. "Just sleeping. I didn't touch her. I swear, I didn't lay a finger—"

"Shut up, Johnny!" Mam choked out.

I swiftly snapped my mouth shut and eyed my mother warily as she approached us.

On shaky legs, Mam walked over to the mantel piece and leaned a hand against it. She still had her other hand pressed to her mouth and tears were filling her eyes.

"We didn't do anything," I offered once more, brows furrowed. "And look—" I pointed to the blue jeans and slightly askew white vest top Shannon was sporting. "She's fully clothed, so just relax, okay?" *And don't kill me too much.*

Shaking her head, Mam moved to the coffee table and lowered herself down. "Oh god," she strangled, dropping her head in her hands, voice strained. "Jesus, Mary, and Joseph."

It took me a few moments to figure out what the fuck was happening, and why my mother wasn't dragging me away by the ear, when it dawned on me that this was her first time seeing Shannon since the attack. Yeah, I was calling it an attack because that's exactly what the fuck it was. An *attack*.

Shannon's whole face was a map of bruises and discoloration, and it was hitting my mother hard.

*Good,* I thought to myself, *put yourself in my shoes and tell me what you'd do. Tell me how you'd take her back to that house?*

"I'm so sorry, Mrs. Kavanagh," Shannon choked out, flailing anxiously beside me.

"Hey—" I captured one of her hands in mine and smoothed a thumb over her knuckles, desperate to soothe her. "Shh, it's okay."

Shannon glanced down at our joined hands and then looked up at me. "I'm so sorry, Johnny."

"You didn't do anything wrong," I told her, tone gruff.

"I just . . . I didn't want to go home last night," she continued, breathing hard, as she looked to my mother. "I'm so sorry for causing trouble, Mrs. Kavanagh. I didn't mean to upset you—"

"I'm not upset with you, love," Mam interrupted, sounding slightly more composed, as she stood up. "Don't be worrying."

"I'll go," Shannon hurried to say. "Right now, I promise."

Mam sighed heavily. "You don't have to do that, Shannon, love."

"She doesn't?"

"I don't?"

"Let's all just have a cup of tea first." Wiping her cheeks with the back of her hand, Mam smiled warmly at Shannon. "And then we'll figure this all out, okay, love?"

"Yeah." Shannon blew out a shaky breath and nodded. "Okay."

"Now—" Turning to face me, Mam said, "do you have any more surprises for me?" There was a teasing lilt to her voice. "You don't have any more of her children hiding in my house, do you?"

I shifted around awkwardly. "Ah, maybe one or two."

Mam laughed.

I didn't.

"Thanks for the bed, Kavanagh," a familiar voice called out from down the hallway, choosing the worst possible time to wake from his stoned slumber. "Can I borrow a hoodie?"

*For fuck's sake.*

Mam's eyes bugged in her head. "And who is that?"

"Ah, that would be Joey," I muttered, rubbing my jaw.

"And who is Joey?"

"My brother," Shannon offered weakly.

"Are there any more Lynch children in my house, Jonathan?"

"No," I muttered, not meeting her eye. "I only took two."

"Jesus, Mary, Joseph, and the donkey," Mam wailed as she bounded for the hallway. "What am I going to do with you?"

"Is she mad?" Shannon asked, drawing my attention back to her. Her eyes were wide and laced with panic. Her entire frame had stiffened to stone. "Are you going to be in trouble over me?"

*Probably.*

"No," I replied, keeping my tone gentle. "She's just worried."

"Are you?" She swallowed deeply. "Mad?"

My brows furrowed. "With you?"

Shannon nodded, looking sick now.

"No, Shan," I said slowly. "I'm not mad at you."

"I won't let my mam do anything to you," she blurted then, clutching my hand tightly in both of hers. Her chest was rising and falling quickly as she spoke and I had a feeling she was either going to puke or have a panic attack. "Whatever she says ... I swear, Johnny, I won't let her get you into trouble ... I promise, I'll fix this ... Just please don't hate me—"

I leaned down and kissed her, knowing no other way to ease her panic.

Shannon went lax in my arms, I could feel the tension leaving her body as her limbs loosened out and her hands rested on my waist.

"I'm not scared of your mother," I told her, resting my forehead against hers. "And I could never hate you." I brushed my lips against hers again. "Not in a million years."

"But she's—"

I kissed her again, harder this time, making my point with my tongue.

"Your ma can say whatever she wants." Straightening to my full height, I tucked a rogue strand of hair behind her ear and rested my hands on her bone-thin shoulders. "She can make all the threats she wants. It doesn't change anything for me." Sighing at her forlorn expression, I cupped her face in my hands and leaned close. "Because I'm not going anywhere."

"Really?" Shannon whispered, staring up at me with those lonesome eyes. Her fingers were digging into my sides so hard I had a feeling she was going to leave a mark on me. "You promise?"

There she went asking for promises I wasn't sure I could keep, and there I went making them anyway.

"Yeah, Shan," I croaked out. "I promise."

Our lips touched again, brushing gently, and I knew right there and then that I was done for. It was a soft, gentle, innocent kiss that packed the punch of a lifetime because, with that minimal contact, she free-wheeled my hormones out of control and KO'd my heart.

Knowing that I needed to stop while I still could, I broke the kiss, breathing hard, and reached for my clothes, deciding it would be safer facing her brother with my pants on.

"Come on," I said, reaching for Shannon's hand when I was dressed. Tugging gently, I led her out of my sitting room and straight to my slaughter – which just so happened to be my kitchen. *Where my mother had a wide range of knives and other sharp appliances . . .*

Fuck.

Reaching the kitchen door, I stalled when the sound of voices echoed from behind the partially closed door.

"Oh my god, is he talking to her?" Shannon whispered, wide-eyed, when she heard Joey's voice.

Well, he wasn't shouting, which was a good thing because as sorry as I felt for Shannon's brother, if he planned on speaking to my mother the way he spoke to me and Gibsie yesterday, I was going to lose my shit. There was a line in a man's life that no one crossed. That line for me was my ma. No one fucked with her.

Pushing the kitchen door inwards, I stepped inside with Shannon clutching my hand like a lifeline.

My eyes immediately sought out and landed on Joey, who was leaning against the utility room door, looking cornered and feral, and yet, he was watching my mother with an almost reluctant curiosity.

He was clearly all fucked up, coming down from whatever he'd taken, and there my mother was, heating up bleeding scones and talking to him about god knows what.

The most shocking thing of it all was that I got the distinct impression that Joey was actually listening to her.

Frowning, I studied him closer. Jesus, he was *absolutely* listening to her.

Mam had her back to the door, not noticing mine and Shannon's presence, and was droning on about something or other. Joey, on the other hand, was concentrating so hard on whatever my mother was saying that he seemed oblivious to everything around him.

"You know, love, I'm sure I've heard of that garage," Mam said as she slid a plate of scones into the microwave and switched it on. "I'll definitely bring the car down the next time it needs a service."

"Really?" he asked her, voice low and uncertain. He pulled at his sleeves, twitching nervously. "You don't have to."

"I'd like to," Mam responded as she pulled various pots of jam out of the overhead cupboard. "How long have you worked there?"

"Since I was twelve or thirteen," he mumbled, shifting around uncomfortably, wary eyes still trained on my mother. "Been on the books since third year."

Mam froze for a moment before quickly recovering. "That young?"

He shrugged unapologetically. "Needed the money."

"And you like it?" she asked, reaching for the kettle. "Mechanics? That's something you might be interested in pursuing after you're done with school?"

He shrugged stiffly. "Money's decent."

"Well, I think you are a credit to yourself, Joey Lynch," Mam coaxed, dropping a few teabags into the pot. "Working all those hours after school." She filled the teapot with boiling water. "And in your leaving cert year." She set the kettle down and beamed at him. "You should be so proud of yourself."

Joey's brows furrowed so deeply, he looked like he was in the throes of a migraine. "Why?"

"Why what, love?" Mam asked kindly.

"Nothing." He shifted around again, pulling his sleeves down over his knuckles only to roll them back up a few moments later. "Doesn't even matter."

"I think it does," Mam replied softly. "Say what you were going to say, love. I'm listening."

"I, uh ... I—" Joey's wild green eyes flicked to me then, before swiftly shifting to Shannon. Instant relief engulfed his features. "Alright, Shan?" he croaked out, showing the first sign of genuine affection I'd seen since yesterday. "How's it going?" I watched him watch her, his eyes roaming over her face and a mixture of guilt and pain flickered in his eyes. "You okay?"

"Hey, Joe," Shannon replied in a tone thick with emotion. She nodded before adding, "Are you?"

"All good," was his response – his full-of-shite response because the lad was about as far from *good* as anyone could get. "Kavanagh," he said then, offering me a stiff nod. "Thanks again."

"Joey," I responded. "Anytime."

Feeling the need to do something, I released Shannon's hand and strolled towards my mother, grabbing the plate of scones from the microwave as I went. "These smell savage, Ma."

Scooping one off the plate, I stuffed it into my mouth, ignoring the burn as it scalded my tongue, as I moved for the island. The scones did smell great, but that's not why I was choking myself trying to stuff one down. It was because I wanted these two to fucking eat something.

"Manners, Johnny," Mam scolded, and then, in a much softer tone, said, "Joey, Shannon, why don't you both sit down and have some breakfast."

Neither one moved.

I glanced back at Shannon's wary face and then to her brother, and my blood heated to the point of turning to lava in my veins.

*Jesus Christ, what the fuck did those people do to these kids?*

Dropping the plate down on the marble island top, I pulled out a stool, carefully sat down, patted the stool beside me, and then mentally counted down from five.

*Four, three, two, one ...*

Like a skittish baby foal, Shannon moved her legs towards me, like I had hoped she would, and took the stool beside me. It took her three tries to hoist herself onto the stool, but unlike last time when we were alone, I didn't move to lift her for two very obvious reasons.

First, my mother was taking this incredibly well, given the circumstances, and I didn't want to push my luck.

Second, her brother was watching me like he didn't know if he wanted to trust me or throttle me.

When Shannon finally managed to get herself seated, I smirked down at her. She flushed bright pink and dropped her gaze to the counter, shoulders bunched together tightly.

Christ, she was back to being jittery.

It was like last night hadn't happened, and if she wasn't sitting right here beside me, I would have thought I'd conjured the whole thing up in my head.

Joey waited a solid minute longer before blowing out a breath and walking over to the island. Pulling out a stool beside his sister, he sank down and rested his elbows on the counter, shaking his head to himself and drumming his fingers restlessly.

"Now." Setting a pot of tea down in front of us, Mam went back and forth to the cupboards, laying out cups and side plates in front of us until the kitchen island resembled a high tea at a bleeding hotel. "Eat up," she encouraged, sinking down on the stool across from us.

Not needing any encouragement, I happily stuffed my face, drowning myself in food I would never touch during training, but they didn't make a move.

"Come on." Nudging the plate towards Shannon and Joey, Mam smiled encouragingly. "I'll be insulted if you don't try one."

Out of the corner of my eye, I watched as they silently communicated with one another. Not one word was spoken, but I knew something was passing between them.

And then they both moved in synchrony for the scones.

*Thank Christ for that.*

Relief flickered in my mother's eyes as she observed the Lynchs devouring the scones from behind the rim of her coffee mug. Her tear-filled eyes shifted to me and I gave her a *'I know'* look.

With a small shake of her head, Mam slapped on a bright smile and began to do what she did best: talk and meddle. The woman was gifted with her mouth, and could make conversation out of anything. I had no fucking clue where I went wrong or why that particular gene skipped over me, but as I watched my mother make small talk with the both of them, I was grateful.

Grateful that she was here.

Grateful she wasn't losing her shit with me for a having a girl sleep over.

Grateful that *she* was my ma.

"Johnny," Mam said after what had to be an hour of idle chit-chat, "we'll have to get going soon. You have physio in an hour, love."

My heart plummeted into my ass.

"I . . . " Pausing, I glanced at Shannon and then my mother. "I don't have to go."

Mam's brows shot up in surprise. "You don't?"

I hesitated for a split second and that was all it took for Shannon to spring off her stool and announce, "We should get going, Joe."

"Yeah." With a shake of his head, Joey stood up. "We should."

"You don't have to," I hurried to say, feeling panicked at the prospect of letting her go. "I don't have to go to physio. It's not that important. I can miss one day. It won't kill me."

"No, you need to go," Shannon replied. "And we need to go home." She glanced up at her brother. "Right?"

Now Joey was the one to hesitate as he stood in the middle of my kitchen, looking like he was fighting an internal battle of his own. "Right," he finally replied, tone tight. "Home."

"I'll drive you both," Mam interjected, shaking her head at me when I opened my mouth to protest.

I ran a hand through my hair in agitation. "But I just—"

"It's grand, Kavanagh," Joey said, giving me a meaningful look. "You've done enough, lad."

No, I hadn't.

I hadn't done enough by half.

# Throwing Down

## JOHNNY

I held her hand tighter than I knew I should, but I couldn't help it. Taking her back there felt all fucking wrong. Even now, sitting in the back of my mother's Range Rover with Shannon beside me and Joey up front, I was struggling to cope with the feelings battering me. *Wrong, wrong, wrong.* That was all I could think as Mam took the familiar turn off to their council estate.

Sweat beaded my brow as my body literally thrummed with more emotions than I knew how to handle. I felt like I was going to explode and I wanted to scream *don't go back.* I wanted to beg my mother to *do something.* To just *stop this.*

Logic told me to go to my physio, get my shit done, and stick to the bleeding plan. Problem was, my heart was screaming another plan entirely. I needed to think about the consequences, but they just wouldn't come to me.

*Fuck, this family was going to ruin me.*

Joey was silent for the entire drive, his body rigid, and it was as plain as the nose on his face that going home was the very last thing he wanted to do.

But he was doing it anyway.

For *her.*

Shannon's entire focus was on our joined hands. She had my hand pulled onto her lap and she was holding it just as tightly as I was holding hers.

With her free hand, she trailed her slender fingers over the scar on the back of my hand, the one I'd gotten in a rugby match years ago. She kept touching that scar over and over again, trailing her fingers up and down and over it until I felt like snatching it away because her anxiety was palpable and drowning me. Her hair was falling forward, her small face hidden behind her dark locks, as she bent her head and studied that scar.

Several times, I reached over and stopped her hand, but the minute I let go, she started right back up. In the end, I just gave in and let her do what she wanted to me.

When my mother parked the Range Rover outside their house, neither Joey nor Shannon moved a muscle.

Switching off the engine, Mam sighed heavily and then unfastened her seatbelt. "Okay, you two," she announced, voice strained from the effort it was taking her to sound happy. "Let's go."

I wanted to roar at her, beg her to do something I knew in my heart she had no power to do, because the panic rising up in me at the prospect of not seeing Shannon again, of not knowing whether she was okay or not, was driving me insane.

"Thanks for the spin, Mrs. Kavanagh," Shannon finally said. With a small nod to herself, she released my hand, gave me a small smile, and then moved for her seatbelt. "And for the scones."

"Yeah," Joey added, tone low, pushing the door open. "Thank you both."

"You're both more than welcome," Mam replied, voice thick now. "Come on, I'll walk you to the door. I need to have a little chat with your mother."

"Wait," I strangled out when Joey and Mam had climbed out. Catching ahold of Shannon's hand, I pulled her back into the Range Rover. "Don't go."

Shannon's eyes were wide and full of confusion when she said, "I have to."

"Don't," I said it again, knowing I was asking for the impossible, but asking for it anyway. I shook my head and bit back a growl. "I don't like this."

"It's okay, Johnny," she replied with a small sigh. "I'm okay."

*No, no, no!* "Just . . ." Exhaling a pained breath, I leaned back on my seat and tried to think of something, anything, to stop this, but came up empty. "You're sure he's not coming back?" I finally asked, still holding onto her hand. "You're sure you're safe?" I turned to look at her. "I can't take it." My voice cracked. "Not knowing."

"I . . ." She closed her mouth and glanced down at my hand before turning her attention back to me. "I'll be safe."

She wasn't sure.

She wasn't fucking sure and neither was I.

*Dammit to hell.*

"Here." Digging into my pocket, I pulled out my phone and handed it to her. "Take this with you."

"Wh-what are you doing?" Blinking down at the phone in her hands, she whispered, "Why are you giving me your phone?"

"So you can call me."

"But this is *your* phone, Johnny." Her brows furrowed. "How am I supposed to—"

"I'll call you, okay?" My heart was hammering in my chest. "I'll get ahold of another phone and I'll call you."

She started to shake her head. "No, no, no, you don't have to do that for me—"

"I need you to do this for *me*," I said, interrupting her. "I need you to take my phone, Shannon." I begged her with my eyes to just do what I was asking. "*Please.*"

"Okay, but I'm giving it back to you," she replied shakily. "Because I can't keep this, Johnny."

"Okay, that's fine," I told her, sagging in relief as I watched her pocket the phone in her baggy jeans. "Whatever you want. Just take it for now."

"How dare you!" a shrill female voice echoed through the air, causing Shannon to jump. "Where is my daughter?"

"Oh god." Shannon's panicked eyes locked on me. "Johnny, I'm so sorry," she choked out before bolting from the Range Rover.

Swinging around to stare out the window, I bit back a groan when I spotted Shannon's mother pointing a finger in my mother's face.

Mrs. Lynch was crying and screaming at the top of her lungs. They were in the middle of the garden with Darren standing between them, holding his hands up. Joey was leaning against the wall that separated their garden from their next-door neighbor's, unmoving.

"You need to calm down," Mam barked, although she sounded far from calm herself. "Your children are watching you."

It was only then that I noticed the three smaller versions of Joey standing under their porch veranda, looking on emotionlessly.

"And you need to control your son!" Mrs. Lynch countered, shaking violently. "Apparently, he has a problem with the word no."

"What did you say?" Mam hissed, taking a step towards Shannon's mother.

"Fuck," I muttered as I threw open my door and dragged my defected arse out of the Range Rover.

"What are you doing?" Shannon was running down the footpath ahead of me. "Mam!" she cried out as she rounded the corner and hurried into the garden, clutching her side. "Mam, stop!"

"Shannon!" Mrs. Lynch sobbed, moving to wrap her arms around Shannon.

"Don't," Shannon hissed, scrambling away from her mother's arm. "Don't touch me."

Her mother flinched. "How could you do that to me?" she sobbed. "How could you not come home, Shannon?" She hiccupped loudly. "How could you not even call to let us know where you were?"

"Why would I *want* to come back here?" Shannon choked out, glaring at her mother. "Look at this." She waved a hand at her mother. "Look at what you're doing right now!"

"I was worried about you," Mrs. Lynch cried. "I was petrified."

"I was *fine*," Shannon countered, trembling. "I was better than fine, Mam. I was *safe*!"

"Shannon, love, calm down," Mam instructed softly as she smoothed a hand down Shannon's arm. "Don't get yourself worked up, pet."

"Who the hell do you think you are? Keeping two of my children in your home without my consent!" Mrs. Lynch practically screamed, face turning red. "And don't you dare touch my daughter," she added, yanking Shannon out of Mam's reach.

*Oh no.*

*Oh fuck no.*

*Don't do it, Ma.*

*Take the high road . . .*

"Maybe you should have said that to your husband," Mam shot back heatedly. "When he was battering the shite out of the girl!"

*Oh Jesus, she went there . . .*

"How dare you!" Mrs. Lynch screamed. "You have no idea about what we've been through. No fucking idea."

"Mam, you need to calm down," Darren instructed calmly. "And you need to go," he said to my mother. "Now."

"I'm so sorry." Shannon sobbed loudly and pressed her hands to her face. "I'm so, so sorry, Mrs. Kavanagh."

"Don't you dare come on my property!" Mrs. Lynch hissed, when I moved to walk into the garden. "Stay away."

"Relax." I held my hands up like a fucking criminal, but despite the warning, I kept walking towards them because leaving my mother on her own was out of the question. "I don't know what you think I did, Mrs. Lynch," I added cautiously, "but I swear, I didn't do it."

"I told you to leave her alone," she hissed at me. "I told you to go away and what did you do? You took my sixteen-year-old daughter out of my home and kept her out all night." Sneering, she added, "I've a good mind to call the Gardaí on you."

"Leave him alone," Shannon sobbed, making a beeline for me. "Oh god, Johnny, I'm so sorry."

"I didn't do anything," I repeated slowly, wrapping an arm around Shannon when she flung herself at me.

"I'm sorry," she just kept saying over and over again. "Johnny, I'm so sorry."

"It's okay," I whispered, tightening my hold on her. "Don't worry."

She was crying hard against my chest. She was bleeding through her tears. Releasing pain and angst, devastation and fear, and I wanted to save her from it all. Her tears rained down on me, drowning me right along with her, and that's the exact moment I felt the shift; the switch from this being something sweet and innocent, to deeply complicated with the hint of forever.

*I was in so much fucking trouble.*

"Don't worry?" Mrs. Lynch hissed. "You'll have a lot to worry about if you don't leave my daughter alone."

"I don't want him to leave me alone!" Shannon screamed, literally fucking screamed at the top of her lungs. "I *love* him!" Her voice cracked. "I'm in love with him, Mam!"

For a moment, I just stood there, staring down at her in pure shock.

She said it again.

She said she loved me in front of her entire family.

*Well, shite . . .*

"He's taking advantage of you, Shannon," Mrs. Lynch wailed. "Why can't you see that?"

Surprisingly, I wasn't even angry at her mother. All I felt in this moment for the woman was pity. Sheer fucking pity for being as damaged as she clearly was. "I wouldn't do that, Mrs. Lynch," I said, keeping my tone soft and coaxing. "I would never hurt your daughter."

"Are you accusing my son of something?" Mam demanded then. "Because if you are, then you go right ahead and say it to my face, lady."

*Oh sweet Jesus . . .*

"Ma, just leave it," I called out.

"No, Jonathan, I will not leave it," Mam shot back, furious now. "If she wants to accuse you of something then she can damn well say it to my face!"

"You need to leave, Johnny," Darren warned, eyes locked on me this time. "Take your mother and go."

"If your son has had sex with my daughter, then that's statutory rape," Mrs. Lynch shot back. "Shannon is underage and can't legally give consent."

"No, it's not!" Shannon screamed, looking humiliated. "Oh my god, you need to stop talking!"

"Mam, stop," Darren had the good grace to say, cheeks red. "You're going over a line here."

"A big fucking line," my own mother hissed through clenched teeth, vibrating with tension.

"If I find out that your son has put a hand on my daughter, I'll have him arrested," Mrs. Lynch cried. "Don't think you're above the law because you have money and your husband's a barrister." Sniffling, she added, "If I get wind that he has taken advantage of my child, I'll press charges on him."

"Mam!" Shannon screamed at the same time that I dove for my own mother.

"Ma, no!" Stitches or not, I moved like a bullet, intercepting her just as her hand flew out. "Don't," I hissed, wrapping both hands around her middle and pulling her away. "It's not worth it."

"You bitch!" Mam snarled, pushing against me, trying to break out of my hold. "Who the hell do you think you are, threatening *my* child?" Battling against me, she hissed, "He's a good boy! Too good for the likes of you! You need to take a fucking good look at your own family, lady, because if you so much as think about bringing trouble to my son's door, I'll take you down. Do you hear me? I'll take you *down*, Marie, and I won't need my husband or any other man to do that for me."

"I'm sorry!" Shannon continued to cry, flailing helplessly. "Oh god, I'm so sorry!"

"It's okay," I called back as I carted my mother out of the garden, kicking and lashing out. "It's not your fault."

"Johnny ..." Her voice broke off and she cried hard. "I ... I'm ... sorry."

Not stopping until I was at the driver's side of the Rover, I yanked the door open, and bundled my mother inside. "Stop!" I barked, breathing hard from exertion. "Jesus Christ, Ma, settle down!"

Chest heaving, Mam slumped into the driver's seat, shaking from head to toe. "Alright." Nodding stiffly, she sat in the driver's seat and reached for her seatbelt. "Okay."

"Okay," I confirmed with a sigh. Slamming the door shut, I rounded the Range Rover, hobbling every step of the way as pain scorched its way through my body.

"Don't come back here!" Mrs. Lynch called out in a shaky voice from where she was still standing in the garden, watching me. "Or there will be trouble."

Shaking my head, I swallowed down a million *fuck yous* and turned to look at Shannon who was hugging Joey. "Shannon Lynch?" I called out, ignoring the rest of her fucked-up family. "I love you back."

Sniffling, she lifted her chin from Joey's chest and looked at me all red-eyed and blotchy. "S-still?"

"Still." I nodded in confirmation. "Like a crazy fucking amount."

And then I turned around and climbed into the Range Rover before my mother decided to take another leave of her senses.

# Dirty Laundry

## SHANNON

I felt like I was standing waist deep in the debris from the storm that had just blown through my world, and clueless as to how to proceed.

Reeling, I tried to make sense of the events of the last sixteen years of my life, but kept honing in on the last twenty-four hours.

*Mam, Darren, Joey, Johnny, Gibsie, Claire, Mrs. Kavanagh … my father.*

*Always my father.*

It had been the most uncomfortable cup of tea I'd ever slurped my way through in Mrs. Kavanagh's kitchen earlier, with Joey looking like something hell had thrown up sitting beside me, staring in confusion at the scone and clotted cream on his side plate. I had no idea what to say to Johnny's mother, and it was made worse again by the sobbing fits that took her over every time she looked at me and Joey.

The drive back to our house was equally as uncomfortable, made marginally better by the feel of Johnny's hand on mine and the sound of the light flow of conversation between Mrs. Kavanagh and my brother. I think Joey was so startled by Mrs. Kavanagh fussing over him, so completely caught off guard by her kindness, that when she told him to climb into the front seat of her Range Rover, he complied without a fuss.

I had no idea how she had the ability to get words out of Joey, but whenever she asked him a question, he dutifully answered her. She kept the tone light, never once asking either of us a thing about our father, choosing safer topics to discuss – like school, hurling, and his girlfriend, and Joey had responded with genuine, un-snappy answers that were completely un-Joey-like.

However, my elation over having my brother come home with me was overthrown by conflict the minute we pulled up outside my house.

What I presumed would be a civilized conversation between two mothers had quickly gone to hell the moment my mother made a derogatory suggestion that Johnny had somehow taken advantage of me.

I'd never seen a woman lose her cool as quickly as Mrs. Kavanagh had.

All it had taken was those two words and Johnny's mother had blown a head gasket.

It was shocking to watch a usually mild-mannered woman morph into full-blown mama-bear mode and attack.

I'd never seen a woman defend her child as fiercely as she had.

*None of us had . . .*

Not even Darren, who seemed to have a knack of calming a situation, could settle our mothers down as all hell had broken out right there and then in our front garden, in full view of my little brothers, with Johnny having to physically carry his mother out of the garden before they came to blows.

Terrible things had been said, our dirty laundry had been aired loudly, and the entire time Joey had leaned against the garden wall with his arms folded across his chest, silently taking it all in, never once moving to intercept the drama.

The rage swelling up inside of my body, even now, hours later, was both a foreign emotion and a dominant one.

Never in my life had I felt so *furious*.

*Statutory rape.* Two words that were swirling around in my head, making it hard for me to function.

How could she say that?

How could my mother even *think* that?

I was so embarrassed; so completely taken apart by it all.

*"Shannon Lynch? I love you back . . . "*

My heart slammed wildly against my ribcage and I snapped.

"How could you do that to me?" I demanded for the millionth time, glaring at my mother who was now sitting at the kitchen table with her mandatory cigarette balancing between her bony fingers.

She didn't answer me.

She hadn't answered a single one of my questions for over an hour, but I couldn't let it go.

I *couldn't* walk away.

Not this time.

"*Why*, Mam?" I hissed, tears dripping down my cheeks. "Do you hate me *that* much?"

She shuddered, her frail shoulders jerking violently, as she stubbed out her cigarette in the ashtray before quickly sparking up another one.

"Answer me!" I screamed, barely managing to restrain myself from reaching across the table and shaking her. "You owe me that much, dammit!"

"He's not safe for you, Shannon," was all she said, and her words were barely more than a broken whisper.

"You're going crazy," I choked out, shaking my head in horror. "You are losing your bloody mind!"

"I did the right thing. I did the right thing," Mam whispered over and over, as she sucked on her cigarette. "I protected you."

"He's *not* a problem for me," I choked out. "Johnny's a good person." A huge sob tore through my throat and I heaved, feeling so much pain and resentment that I felt I was drowning. "And *you* scared him away. You pushed the one good thing in my life away from me." Sniffling, I batted my tears away, furious with myself, my mother, and the whole damn world. "He'll never talk to me again," I strangled out, feeling the threat of a panic attack nip at my heels. "You ruined everything for me!"

"No." She shook her head. "You'll see, I did the right thing."

"Mam," Darren, who was sitting opposite our mother, interjected, "you're not making any sense here."

"She *can't* make sense of it," I strangled out, pointing an accusing finger at her. "Because she knows she's wrong."

"I'm not wrong," Mam whispered, trembling. "He's just like your father."

"Mam!" Darren snapped. "Don't say that."

"It's true," she whispered, flicking ash into the ashtray and taking another deep drag. "He'll be just like her father."

"Stop it!" I screamed. "Stop trying to do that to him."

"You'll be glad I stopped it," she continued. "Stopped you from making my mistakes."

"You're wrong," I hissed, blinking back the hot, scalding tears. "You're a fucking liar and I *hate* you!"

"Shannon, that's enough!"

"It's not enough." Backing away, I put some distance between our bodies, because I honestly didn't feel like I was in control of myself in this moment. "Joey was right." I blinked away my tears. "You're not good for us."

"Come on, Shannon." Darren groaned, rubbing his jaw. "Screaming and name-calling isn't helping anyone—"

"Then stop sitting there and *do* something," I begged, shaking so hard, I felt like I was about to convulse. "You know this is wrong." My breath hitched and I hiccupped a pained sob. "You know what she did was *awful*, and you're just letting her get away with it."

"No, I'm not," he countered. "She knows she was wrong, don't you, Mam?"

Silence.

"Mam," Darren pushed, tone harder now. "Tell Shannon that you know you were wrong."

Nothing.

"Mam!" Darren barked, voice cracking. "Answer us."

"Don't bother." Joey's voice cut through the stony silence and I spun around to find him leaning against the doorframe, casually observing the situation. "She can't hear you," he added, tone emotionless. "Because she's broken." He looked Darren square in the eyes and said, "You'll figure that out soon enough."

"Joe." Crying hard, I barreled towards him, not stopping until my face was buried in his chest. His chest that smelled like Johnny because he was still wearing his clothes. "Make this stop."

"This is what you wanted, Darren," Joey said in an eerily calm tone as he wrapped an arm around my shoulders. "You wanted her home with us. One big, happy family." Tilting his head to one side, he gestured towards our mother and said, "I hope we've met your expectations."

I half expected Darren to say something defensive, but he didn't. He didn't say a word.

Instead, he looked at our mother who was staring into her coffee-stained mug and released a ragged breath. Shoving his chair back, he stood up and walked out of the kitchen without so much as a backwards glance.

A few seconds later, the sound of the front door slamming filled the air.

I threw my hands out and choked out a humorless laugh. "I don't know why I'm surprised anymore."

Exhaling heavily, Joey released his hold on me and walked into the kitchen, heading straight for the cooker. I watched as he silently went to work, filling a saucepan of water and then pouring the contents of a bag of pasta into it. Setting the saucepan down on the hob, he switched on the heat and flicked on the extractor fan overhead.

When he was done, he wiped his hands on the tea towel on the draining board before turning to face our mother. "Get up and take a shower," he ordered, tone void of all emotion. "I need to feed the boys and they don't need to see you like this."

She flinched but didn't move.

Like the million other times I'd watched this exact scenario unfold through the years, Joey walked over to the table, snatched the cigarette from her lips and stubbed it out. He then proceeded to place both the ashtray and coffee cup on the draining board before returning to her side. "Get up," he repeated. "You stink of smoke and cider."

Mam dropped her head in her hands and cried.

"Get up," he said for the third time.

Once again, Mam made no move to stand. Instead, she snaked a hand out and grabbed his hand, clutching it tightly in both of hers. "Joey," she sobbed, clinging to him. "Joey."

With a resigned sigh, Joey swooped down and gently helped her out of her seat. A thousand different emotions played across my brother's face as Mam leaned heavily on his rigid body, sniffling and sobbing against his chest.

"Keep an eye on the dinner, Shan," was all Joey said as he guided our mother out of the kitchen and up the old, wooden staircase.

*And here we are,* I thought to myself, *back to square one.*

I took a few minutes to compose myself, wiping my eyes and blowing my nose, and then drained the pasta and mixed in the jar of sauce before calling the boys in from the front room. "Dinner."

Wordlessly, Ollie and Sean ambled over to the table, taking their usual seats. Dishing up their plates, I set them down in front of them with a glass of water each.

I waited for them to tuck into their food before turning to face Tadhg who was leaning against the fridge with his arms folded across his chest. "Are you hungry?" I asked, holding a plate out to him.

He glared at the pasta in my hands for a long moment before turning around and walking away.

Tadhg's silence spoke volumes and it matched my feelings. I knew he was furious, so was I, but he was reining it in because we had something back in our house, something that we were both desperate to not push away.

Not feeling one morsel of hunger, I sat at the table, in the chair my mother had vacated, and waited for the boys to finish before cleaning off the table and washing the dishes.

Numb, I fell into the age-old pattern that was my life, as I tidied up after the boys and helped Sean get dressed for bed. All the while, Joey dealt with Mam upstairs.

I found myself checking both the front and back door over and over again, making sure they were locked and then panicking when the sound of a car whizzing past outside filled my ears.

*Breathe, Shannon.*

*You're fine.*

*Everything's going to be okay.*

A little over an hour later, Joey returned to the kitchen. "She's asleep," he stated, moving for the plate of dinner I had set aside for him. "I gave her a couple of her Valiums."

Nodding, I curled my fingers around my cup of tea and blew into the rim, never once taking my eyes off my brother as he heated his plate in the microwave.

Joey joined me at the table, where he ate in complete silence.

"Are you okay?" I finally asked.

"No," he replied quietly, setting his fork down on his empty plate. "Are you?"

"No."

He looked up at me then. "It's going to be okay, Shan."

"Which part?" I whispered.

"The Kavanagh part," he replied.

I exhaled a shaky breath and shook my head. "No, it won't be."

Resting his elbows on the table, Joey drummed his fingers together. "Aoife's pissed with me."

My head snapped up. "Since when?"

He stared hard at his hands. "Since I fucked everything up."

My heart sank.

*Damn you, Shane Holland . . .*

"She loves you," I offered, reaching for his hand. "She'll forgive you, Joe, and you guys will sort it out."

He shook his head. "Maybe I don't want her to."

I frowned. "What are you saying?"

"I'm saying I'm a fucking disaster, Shannon." He pushed his hair back with both hands and exhaled brokenly. "And she deserves better."

"Are you two broken up?"

He shook his head slowly. "No."

"Then it's okay," I coaxed, desperate to comfort him. "It *will* be okay."

Joey shrugged. "I just . . . I don't want her to watch me turn into hi—"

A loud sound floated through the air, startling the both of us, and causing Joey to close his mouth.

Frowning, I patted my leg that was vibrating for a moment before remembering.

*His phone.*

Shaking, I dragged the phone out of my pocket and stared at the screen. It was a text from *Ma*.

"Who owns that?" Joey asked, frowning.

"It's Johnny's," I whispered, staring down at the expensive piece of equipment in my hands. "He gave it to me." I looked at my brother. "It's a message from his mother."

"Read it."

"What?" I gaped at him. "I can't."

Joey rolled his eyes. "It's obviously him."

"Really?"

Joey gave me a knowing look. "Read the fucking message, Shannon."

Heart fluttering wildly, I clicked into the message.

A CRAZY FUCKING AMOUNT. X

"You're right." I blew out a shaky breath. "It's him."

"Told you," Joey replied. "He's not running on you, Shan."

"Are you?" I asked, looking at my brother. "Running on Aoife?"

Guilt clouded his eyes, but he didn't respond.

And just like earlier with Tadhg, Joey's silence spoke volumes.

# Pull Your Balls

## JOHNNY

"Lose the pants."

Three words I'd heard more in the last few months than I cared to remember. Sliding off the bed, I kicked off my shoes and then undid the fly of my grey school trousers before pushing them down.

"The underwear, too."

Jaw ticking, I did as I was told and stepped out of my jocks until I stood in the middle of the room, bollocks naked.

"Wonderful, Johnny," Dr. Quirke said, shifting her glasses higher on her nose. "Now, climb back onto the bed please, and lay on your back."

With my dignity checked at the door, I swallowed a groan and flopped down on the bed.

For a moment, I debated covering my face until it was over, but quickly thought better of it. If they were messing around down there, I needed to see what was happening, dammit.

"Very nice," the good doctor stated and I supposed it wasn't a bad compliment to get, but it was a compliment given to me by a sixty-year-old woman while she was cupping my balls in her glove-covered hands, so I kind of took issue with it. "Both sets of stitches have dissolved and everything seems to be healing beautifully."

*Beautifully?*

I snorted, because how the fuck could I not? Given my current circumstances, it was either laugh or fucking cry. I had an old lady feeling my ball sac, and another two equally ancient female nurses standing over me, smiling at me in encouragement. One of them was actually giving me a thumbs up.

Jesus.

*I was in the bleeding twilight zone.*

When the doctor instructed me to roll onto my side and pull my legs up, I did close my eyes, knowing full well what was coming, and also knowing that there was a good chance I'd never find my dignity again.

"Everything is looking positive," Dr. Quirke said when I was fully dressed and sitting in the chair opposite her. "But I have to ask—" Pulling off her glasses, she twirled them around aimlessly. "Why would you risk yourself like you did, Johnny?"

I shrugged, feeling uncomfortable. "I don't know." I'd been afraid of losing my spot – of being dismissed. I'd seen it happen to countless players since joining The Academy at fifteen. I knew what happened to the boys that didn't quite cut it and I saw what happened to the lads that *did* make it but were cut due to injury. It sucked and I worked my arse off to never be one of those. It was why I had tried to play injured. I was desperate to impress, to stay relevant and on the top of their minds. The thought of some younger, uninjured, fresh-groined fucker coming in and stealing my spot was something that kept me up late at night. "I didn't think," I finally replied. "I just did it."

"Well," she sighed, "I'm recommending another seven days of using one crutch, rather than two, and refrain from driving for at least another week."

"And training?" I asked, knowing it was a long shot. "What's the deal?"

"Hmm." Dropping her gaze to the notes on her desk, Dr. Quirke flicked through a few pages, clicking her tongue every few minutes. "The physiotherapy sessions you've been attending," she mused, studying one specific page in my file. "You've had a full week's worth, yes? How have they been going?"

"Unproductive," I bit out, jaw tensing. "I can do more, I'm *ready* for more, but they're not pushing me."

"And you've been swimming every other day?" she continued, ignoring my response. "In the hydrotherapy pool?"

"Yes," I replied, drumming my fingers against the armrest. "But I need *more*."

"You need to take your recovery slowly," she corrected. "Slow and steady wins the race." Picking up a pen, she scribbled something down on my notes. "Pain relief?"

"Unnecessary," I ground out. "I'm fine."

"I see," she replied even though she clearly didn't see a damn thing. "And you've been doing your stretches and home exercises? You've been following the guidelines?"

Frustrated, I blew out a harsh breath and tried a different approach. "Listen, doc, I'm going to level with you here. I have an important international campaign in the summer – one I *need* to be fit for. I'm doing everything you're asking of me. I've done the physio. I've done the resting. I've done the bleeding everything, so I just need you to cut me some slack. I'm fit, I'm strong—" resting my elbows on the table, I leaned forward and implored her with my eyes to take pity on me "—and I can't wait another *month* to get back out on the pitch."

"You do realize how tremendously strenuous the surgery you've had has been on your lower body?" she asked, blinking back at me through her black rimmed glasses. "Your body needs time to recover. Your muscles and tendons need time—"

"Then give me another two weeks and let me back out," I interrupted. "I can do that. I can wait another fortnight, but you've got to help me out here. I *need* to get back on the pitch, Doc—"

"Johnny, you're not listening," the doctor cut in, tone sharp. "You're recovering from two surgeries, in two separate areas of your anatomy. You need to have *patience*."

"I don't have the *time* to have patience," I shot back, jaw clenched. "What part of that doesn't anyone get?"

"I understand that you're keen to get back to playing, but you need to take caution—"

"He knows, Doctor," my father, who was sitting on a chair in the corner of the room, called out. "Patience is a virtue." Dragging his gaze from a stack of paperwork he was sifting through, he turned his gaze on me. "Isn't that right, Johnny?"

I glared at my father, using my eyes to communicate how little I cared about virtues. I was in a pissy mood with him and in no form for his early morning banter. He knew this and was still goading me. *Lovely.*

"Keep up with the program," Dr. Quirke said, smiling knowingly at me. "And you'll be back on the pitch in no time."

"That's reassuring," I growled. "Because I have *no* time."

"Four more weeks," she mused. "That's nothing in the grand scheme of things."

"Nothing except my future," I grumbled, feeling thoroughly defeated.

"Well, I think we're about done here." Clasping her hands together, she gave me a bright smile. "I'll see you next week for your follow-up appointment."

"Looking *forward* to it," I drawled sarcastically before turning to Dad. "Can we go now?"

"Thank you again for seeing us earlier than normal, doctor," Dad added, tucking his paperwork into his briefcase. "It's his first day back after Easter and he's hell-bent on getting to school." Dad's tone was laced with humor. "Apparently, his mother raised an overachiever."

"That's no problem, Mr. Kavanagh," she replied, smiling knowingly. "And Johnny's always a pleasure, but I'm sure he has some pressing engagements to attend to at school."

"I'm sure he has," Dad agreed with a smirk.

*Jesus Christ . . .*

Standing stiffly, I moved for the door, just about done with the whole bleeding lot of them, when the doctor called out, "Oh, before I forget – ejaculation should be fine now, Jonathan."

*The fuck?*

I swung around and gaped at her. "Come again?"

The doctor smirked at me – she actually fucking smirked at me – before clearing her throat several times.

Was she laughing at me?

She *looked* like she wanted to.

"The pain you were experiencing shouldn't be an issue anymore," she said instead, giving me a reassuring smile. "You're good to go."

"Uh . . ." I scratched my head, feeling unsure of how to deal with the curveball of humiliation I had just been thrown. "That's, uh . . . thanks?"

"Do you hear that, son?" Dad laughed, slapping a hand on my shoulder. "The doctor says you can pull on your balls again."

Fuck.

My.

Life.

"Do you have everything you need?" Dad asked, less than an hour later, when he pulled the car as close to the front entrance of Tommen as physically possible. "Your books? Your phone? Your wallet? Your—"

"My balls?" I offered sarcastically. "Jesus, Da, I expected this overbearing shite from Ma, but you?" I shook my head and unfastened my seatbelt. "It's getting old real fast."

"I'm overbearing for taking you to your checkup and driving you to school?" His tone was laced with humor. "Wow, that's a new one."

"No, *she's* overbearing," I shot back. "*You're* just plain whipped for going along with her."

"She's my wife," he mused. "Your mother can whip me in whatever way she wants—"

"Just *stop*!" I strangled out, horrified. "You know full well what I'm talking about," I snapped, shoving the car door open. "I want my life back. Do you hear me? I want you and Ma to get off my back and give me some fucking breathing space."

Dad grinned. "Ah, to be young and hormonal again."

"I don't know why you're laughing," I hissed. "I'm being serious here."

"This is about Shannon Lynch," Dad said, sobering his features. "Because your mother and I agree that it's better for you to steer clear of her family."

Of course it was about Shannon Lynch. Everything in my life seemed to be centered around the girl lately. I couldn't get her out of my head, and I couldn't see her because my parents had gotten the fucked-up idea in their heads that they could tell me what to do.

Aside from a few measly text messages sent from my mother's phone when her back was turned, and several more unanswered calls, I hadn't spoken to Shannon since last week, seven days to be exact, and I was going out of my mind.

I felt like a bastard just leaving her there and not coming back, but I couldn't exactly walk the fifteen miles from my house to hers. I couldn't drive either, and I had lost my Gibsie privileges for making him take me over there in the first place.

In other words, I had been stuck in my house for the past week, losing my goddamn mind and drowning in concern. The only time I'd been out of the house was for physio and swimming, but that hadn't been productive because I couldn't concentrate on anything other than the girl I'd left behind.

"Because you're making decisions for me that aren't your place to make," I argued, dragging myself back to the present.

"We never said you couldn't see the girl," he said calmly. "You're just not allowed to see her over there."

"It's a joke," I spat, feeling as furious now as I did last week when they sat me down to *lay down the law.* "Her mother might be a headache, but you and Ma are a close second."

"We're trying to protect our son," he stated calmly. "We have *your* best interests at heart, and your best interests involve keeping a wide berth of that family." Smirking, he added, "I'm also trying to keep your mother out of a prison cell."

I grimaced at the memory of that horrific fucking turn of events in the Lynch's front garden last week and how Mam had come *this* close to battering Mrs. Lynch. Shannon's mother had thrown around some shitty threats and called me a few choice names. That was all it had taken for Mam to morph into Floyd bleeding Mayweather.

"You know how Mam gets when it comes to you," Dad added. "She's a firecracker, son. Trust me."

"Yeah, well, I don't need anyone to protect me," I grumbled.

"I think you do."

"You're wrong."

"Maybe I am," he offered, driving me crazy with his devil's advocate approach to every fucking conversation. "But the risk is worth the reward in this circumstance."

The risk, in this instance, was my outrage. "And the reward is?"

"You staying out of trouble."

*Jesus Christ* . . .

Pissed off, I climbed out of the car and grabbed my school bag. "I can make my own decisions." Tossing my bag over my shoulder, I retrieved my crutch. "And I will."

# Back to Tommen

## SHANNON

Over a week had passed since I last saw Johnny.

I honestly didn't blame him for not coming back to my house because even if, by some divine miracle, he still wanted to see me, I doubted his parents would allow him. Mr. and Mrs. Kavanagh had to hate me now. If my son was hanging around a girl whose parents were crazy, I would hate me, too. I would want my son to stay as far away from *me* as humanly possible.

For the first day, I reread the four messages he had sent me until the battery in his phone went dead. I couldn't charge it because none of us had a compatible phone charger, so I just sat there, thinking about his words until I was blue in the face.

I'M NOT GOING ANYWHERE. AND I MEANT IT. I PROMISE. X

JUST TEXT ME WHEN YOU WAKE UP, LET ME KNOW YOU'RE OKAY. X

I MISS YOU. x

CAN YOU CALL ME? CAN I CALL YOU? ARE YOU FREE TO TALK? X

It was at the exact moment that the phone started ringing that it died in my hands. The tsunami of devastation that had spread through my chest as I stared at the blank screen and willed it to come back to life was potent.

*It* hadn't turned back on and *I* hadn't heard another word from Johnny since.

That was six days ago.

Joey was back at home though, making me feel a little less alone in the house. He even came with me to my hospital checkup, much to Darren's dismay. The boys were happier – well, more content at least. I presumed they felt the same as I did; safer with Joey around. He had stayed, which was both a blessing and a curse because the tension emanating from him was almost too much to bear. To be fair, I was emanating some mighty fine tension of my own, all of it directed towards my mother, who I hadn't spoken a single word to since the night Joey helped her to bed.

I couldn't stand to look at her, if I was being honest. I had so much hatred and frustration festering inside of me that I didn't trust my mouth when I was around her; therefore, I avoided her like the plague for everyone's sake.

"Are you ready for this?" Joey asked as he leaned against my bedroom doorframe in his BCS uniform, watching me battle with the lid on a tube of foundation. "Shan?"

Today was the first day back to school after Easter break. I glanced down at my Tommen uniform and shivered, feeling the familiar swell of anxiety creep across my skin, souring my stomach.

"No." Sighing, I tossed the tube on my bed and then sank down beside it. "I am so unbelievably *not* ready for this."

Joey watched me carefully for a long beat before exhaling heavily. "Yeah, I know the feeling."

"I'm scared," I admitted. "About what they'll say." I gestured to my face and the poor attempt I'd made to conceal the crusty scar that was still healing over from where Dad had split my cheek against the kitchen table. "About this." I chewed on my lip, hesitating, before blurting, "And about *Dad*." My voice was small. "They'll all know, Joe."

"Shan—" Shaking his head, Joey walked over to my bed and sank down beside me. "They won't say anything." Leaning forward, he rested his elbows on his knees and blew out a harsh breath. "Your face has pretty much healed up and what hasn't healed, you've covered with that war paint."

"War paint?" I arched a brow. "It's called makeup, Joe." Expensive makeup. "Claire gave it to me."

"War paint, makeup . . . Whatever. It's all the fucking same to me," he shot back with an unapologetic shrug. "Your principal knows about what happened, right?"

I nodded, knowing Darren and Mam had met with Mr. Twomey over the break.

"Then you'll be fine," he added, tone reassuring. "I promise."

"I don't know what to say if anyone asks me about Dad," I confessed. "What if a teacher asks me?" I shook my head, feeling panicked. I felt poisoned. Like I was tainted. Going back to school, knowing that there were people that knew about what had happened was a terrifying concept. It was common knowledge around Ballylaggin, and I was freaking out. "I have no clue how to handle this."

"You handle this with the truth," Joey shot back sternly. "Or you just tell them to fuck off and mind their business if you don't want to talk about it, but you don't lie anymore, Shan. You got that? You don't cover for that piece of shit a minute longer because you've done *nothing* wrong." Straightening his spine, he added, "And if any one of those fuckers opens their mouth and gives you shit, I'll come down there and sort it."

"The truth's hard," I admitted quietly.

My brother nodded stiffly. "Especially when you've been programmed to forget it."

I thought about his words for a moment. "Hey, Joe?"

"Yeah, Shan?"

"What are you going to say if someone asks you?"

"I'm going to tell them to fuck off and mind their business."

I sighed. "I wish I could do that."

"Do what?"

"Be brave," I whispered, feeling wistful.

"You already are." He turned to look at me then, green eyes full of pain. "So fucking brave."

"Don't feel like it," I mumbled with a shaky breath. "I just feel like running."

"Do you want to?" His tone was hopeful and a little desperate. "We could get on a bus right now and just go."

My heart skipped a beat in my chest and I had to fight down the surge of unease rising up inside of me. "When you say go . . . " I kept my eyes on his, gauging his reaction. "You mean for the day, right?"

Joey didn't reply right away. Instead, he just sat there, staring back at me.

"Joe?" I whispered, heart racing hard now. "That's what you meant, right?"

He forced a smile that didn't quite meet his eyes – I hadn't seen one of those in a very long time. "Of course."

"Don't leave me," I strangled out, clutching his school jumper in my hand. "You can't go away again."

"I'm here, aren't I?" he replied, tone strained.

"What about Aoife?" I asked, clinging to the one thing I knew could keep him close. "What's happening there?" *She's a reason to stay . . .*

"We're fine."

"And Shane Holland and his friends?" My heart buckled wildly. "You're not going to—"

"No," he said, tone harder now. "I'm not."

*I don't believe you . . .*

"Joey, your girlfriend's waiting outside in her car for you," Darren's voice filled my ears and I looked up to find him standing in the doorway, shrugging on a jacket. "You better get a move on or you'll make her late, too."

Without saying another word, Joey stood up and stalked out of my room, roughly brushing Darren aside as he went.

"Good morning to you, too," Darren grumbled.

"I'll see ya later, Shan," Joey called back as he disappeared inside his bedroom, returning a moment later with his schoolbag slung over his shoulder and his helmet and hurley in his hand. "Chin up, kid."

"Joey," Darren began to say, "can we not do the wounded boy act today and just be civilized—"

"Eat shit," Joey sneered, holding his middle finger up as he thundered down the staircase.

"Lovely," Darren muttered, rubbing his jaw. "He's pleasant in the mornings."

"Depends on the company," I reminded him, tone petulant. "He was *pleasant* to me."

"Jesus, not you, too," Darren grumbled. "I can't handle *two* hormone-ridden teenagers this early in the morning."

*Then go back to your life.* "Where's Mam?" I asked instead.

"Work. Now, are you ready?" he asked. "The boys are waiting in the car."

"You don't have to drive me," I stated, eyeing the set of car keys dangling from Darren's fingers. "I can get the bus."

"Come on, Shannon," he groaned. "Cut me some slack here. It's my first day on the school run."

"I'm just saying that I could get the bus, like I usually do."

"Yeah, well, sue me for not wanting my sister standing around a bus stop at six o clock in the morning when the drunks are lurking around," he replied. "I'll be driving you to and from school from now on."

"Because of Johnny?" I pushed, jutting my chin out defiantly. "Because you and Mam don't want me catching spins off him?"

"No, Shannon, because our father is still out there and if he's on a bender, you're the first person he'll go looking for," Darren snapped, and I flinched.

"Thanks for the reminder."

"I'm sorry," he said, tone calmer now. "I'm not trying to upset you, but I need you to be *aware*, and I need you to *remember*."

"Yeah, well, just so *you're* aware; I've never had a problem with any of the drunks at the bus stop." I swiped my schoolbag off the floor and gingerly slipped it over my shoulder before brushing past him. "Just the drunks in this house."

"Jesus," Darren groaned, trailing after me, "I'm drowning in mood swings."

# Boom, Boom, Fucking, Boom, Buddy

## JOHNNY

"Look, it's Mister Boombastic himself," Hughie Biggs called out when I rounded the courtyard and found the lads standing around the front entrance of the main building.

"How's the Vengaboy?" Patrick Feely offered, clapping me on the back. "Congrats on the marriage – you're a dark horse."

"I'll say," Hughie laughed. "Any babies yet, lad? Sail any boats?"

Arching a brow, I turned to Gibsie who was leaning against the wall. He had a cigarette hidden under his sleeve which I thought was pretty fucking pointless given the smoke that was wafting around him. "You *told* them?"

"I told everyone," Gibsie shot back with an unapologetic grin. He slid his free hand under his school jumper and began to slap his hand against his chest. "Boom, boom, fucking boom, buddy!"

*Jesus . . .*

"Is she here yet?" Ignoring their ribbing, I kept my eyes on Gibsie. "Have you seen her?"

Feely frowned. "Who?"

"Shannon Lynch," Hughie filled in, sounding amused. "I'm guessing."

"Are you with her now?"

I turned to look at Patrick. "*What*?"

"Shannon," he repeated. "Are you with her now?"

"Well, he was with her in Dublin," Gibsie piped up. "And at his house last weekend."

"I heard about what happened," Hughie said, eyes laced with sympathy.

Yeah, I bet he had. The people in this town were un-fucking-believable for gossiping.

"Is she okay?" he pressed.

*I don't know because I haven't seen her in a week,* I wanted to roar, but held it back. "She's grand."

"He hasn't seen her since Mammy K went to town on her mother," Gibsie laughed.

Feely's brows shot up. "They had a fight?"

"She went for her," Gibsie chuckled. "Kav had to drag her away."

"Christ." Hughie blew out a breath, sounding impressed. "Go Mammy K."

"You're a dirty rat," I growled, narrowing my eyes at my best friend. "After all the shite I keep under wrap for you."

"Calm down, you big vagina," Gibsie laughed. "She'll be here, so just calm your tits." He exhaled a puff of smoke and rolled the butt of his cigarette between his fingers. His brows furrowed and he gave me a peculiar look. "You're acting all . . . " he paused to wave a hand in front of himself before saying, "needy."

I gaped at him. "*Needy?*"

"Needy *and* clingy," Gibsie confirmed solemnly. "You might want to tone it down a tad."

"Cheers for the advice, Gibs," I bit out. "I'll be sure to take it."

"You're welcome," he shot back. "And speaking of appreciation; thank your dad again for me for getting me off the hook with Twomey." Sighing, he added, "It was bad enough last week, I would have been miserable at home without you for another one."

I rolled my eyes. "I'm glad you're not suspended, too, lad."

"Am I allowed home?" he asked. "Can you have me back yet?"

Feely arched a brow. "You've been separated?"

"Temporarily," Gibsie replied, sounding defensive. "It won't last."

Feely chuckled. "What did ye do?"

"The usual." Gibsie shrugged and waved a hand around aimlessly. "Broke the rules, stole a girl, got in some shit."

Feely shook his head. "I don't know about you two. I honestly don't."

"I didn't steal her," I corrected, temper rising. "She came willingly."

"Shannon?"

"Who else?" Gibsie snickered.

"Well, it's good to see you back on your feet, Cap," Hughie said, wisely veering the subject away from Shannon before I had an aneurism. "But you need to get your ass back to training as soon as possible. Barrettsfield RFC hammered Ballylaggin into the ground at the weekend."

And just like that my bad mood worsened. "Barrettsfield?" My voice was laced with disgust, not masking my horror. "Jesus, lad, they're second division."

"He doesn't need to worry about it," Gibsie interjected, tone serious for once in his life. "It's just a game, lads."

"What can I say," Hughie sighed, ignoring Gibsie's words. "We were lacking in the backline and down a captain."

Guilt filled my body. "Final score?"

Hughie grimaced before saying, "48–26."

"Jesus!" Anxiety churned inside of me. "How was your kicking form?"

"16 points," he replied. "Two conversions and four penalties."

"Fair play, lad." I slapped his shoulder. "You kept them in it."

Hughie smiled. "I tried."

"How did the checkup go?" Feely asked then, holding the door open for me.

"Yeah." Gibsie grinned and took another deep drag of his cigarette before exhaling a cloud of smoke. "Did the good doctor give you your green card?"

"Nope." Too pissed off to give him a lecture on his lungs, I stepped inside. "As predicted."

"Bad luck, lad," Feely said as both he and Hughie followed me into the school.

"Ah, it's not all doom and gloom." Taking one last drag of his smoke, Gibsie tossed the butt away and fell into step beside us. "At least you're down to the one crutch."

"Go me," I bit out, ignoring every smile, wave, and 'Hey, Kav,' and 'How's it going, Johnny' as I stalked through the hallway on my way to my locker.

"Just give yourself time," Feely replied calmly. "Everything will work out."

"Exactly," Hughie added, patting my shoulder. "Rome wasn't built in a day."

"Yeah, well, Rome needs to hurry the fuck up, lads," I muttered, leaning heavily on the crutch in my left hand. "Because I'm a little short on time."

"You still have two months, Cap."

"I have forty-six days," I corrected, agitated. "And counting."

"At least they're letting you work out again," Hughie offered, tone optimistic.

"Upper body only," I muttered. "That'll be handy when I need to run a fucking drill, won't it?"

"Jesus, you're a moody bastard," Gibsie quipped. "There's no pleasing you."

"Well, lad, if you spent your morning with three old dolls feeling you up while your da was in the room, you wouldn't exactly be shitting rainbows."

Gibsie scoffed. "If I had three women feeling me up this morning, I can guarantee you that I *would* be shitting rainbows."

Hughie and Feely laughed.

"Trust me, you wouldn't," I grumbled.

Gibs arched a brow. "When you say old . . . "

"I mean geriatric old," I barked, stopping in the middle of the hall to glare at him. "*Mrs. Lovell* old."

Gibsie paled. "Lad."

Encouraged by the sympathy in their eyes, I continued with my sorrowful rant. "Think up the best possible sexy nurse fantasy you have."

He grinned. "Got it."

I nodded in approval. "Now swap that nurse with your granny."

All three of my friends groaned in sympathy. "*Fuck*."

"Yeah," I confirmed grimly, walking again. "Fuck is right."

"Did you at least get your cum card?" Gibsie asked then, and not quietly, when we reached the fifth-year locker area. "Surely, you got the green light for—"

"You had to do it, didn't you?" Hughie sighed, resting against the locker next to mine. "You always have to go that little bit too far, Gibs."

"I'm worried," Gibsie shot back huffily. "I'm being a *concerned* friend."

"You're being a freak," Feely offered dryly.

"I got the cum card, Gibs," I decided to say, knowing that if I didn't tell the eejit, he wouldn't give me a minute's peace. "It's all good."

"You did?" His eyes danced with excitement. "Then what the fuck are you doing at school, Johnny?"

"Exactly that," I shot back. "Because I *have* school."

He arched a brow. "I'm still waiting for an actual reason, lad."

"Because I could hardly tell my da to take me home so I can fuck myself," I sneered sarcastically. "Get a handle of yourself."

Gibsie stared blankly back at me. "I see no problem with that."

"Don't encourage him," I snapped, glaring at Hughie and Feely who were snickering.

"You're the one who needs to get a *handle* of yourself," Gibsie countered, still staring at me in disbelief. "With both hands."

*Give me strength . . .*

Jaw ticking, I turned my attention back to my locker and yanked the metal door open, only to gag when I was hit by a god-awful smell.

All four of us jerked away from the locker simultaneously.

"Jesus," Hughie choked out.

"Uh, lad," Feely groaned. "That's bad."

"You dirty bastard," Gibsie strangled out, his words muffled, as he covered his mouth with his hand. "Jesus Christ, Johnny." Glaring at my locker like it was his mortal enemy, he hissed, "Ever heard of a rubbish bin?"

"I forgot it was in there," I laughed, retrieving the plastic container that was now growing fur. "Didn't exactly have time to clear out my locker for the holidays." Holding it as far away from my body as possible, I walked over to the waste bin and tossed it in before turning back to the lads. Grinning sheepishly, I asked, "What do you think it once was?"

"Chicken," all three lads groaned in unison.

"Hey, Johnny," the bane of my existence's voice peppered through the air then, as irritating and unwelcome as always, and taking with it any semblance of humor. Now, I was the one to shudder in pure, unadulterated repulsion as I watched Bella Wilkinson swagger towards me, all hips and tits and pain in my hole. "How are you feeling?"

"Keep walking," I instructed coldly, hackles rising. Dick move or not, I made a beeline for the lads, finding sanctuary – and safety – in numbers. "I have nothing to say to you."

"Come on, Johnny, I just want to—"

"I'm not doing this with you again," I grumbled, interrupting her. "We've had this talk a million fucking times. It's done with – we're done with – so just *walk away*."

"So, what, I can't even talk to you?" she shot back, looking wounded. "I can't ask how you're feeling?"

"I'm fine," I deadpanned. "Thanks for asking. Now leave me alone."

Her breath hitched in her throat. "Johnny . . ."

"You heard the man," Gibsie ordered, good mood forgotten, as he pointed a finger towards the hallway. "Just keep on walking."

"Fuck you, Gibsie," Bella growled before turning her gaze on me. Batting her blue eyes, she smiled up at me, expression hopeful. "I know things ended badly between us, but I was so worried about you."

"I'm sure you were," Hughie mused. "And I bet Cormac really eased the worrying for you."

"Just stop." Exhausted from months of back and forth with the girl, I scrubbed my face wearily and said, "I don't want to fight with you. I'm done, okay? So, please just walk *away*."

Bella cast a scathing look towards Hughie before looking back to me. "I was just hoping that we could talk for five minutes—"

"And I was hoping to win the lotto at the weekend," Gibsie interjected and then frowned. "But it didn't work out that way because I forgot to buy a Quick Pick.

Feely snorted. "You're under eighteen. Who's going to serve you?"

Gibsie waggled his brow. "I have connections."

Feely rolled his eyes. "Dee?"

Gibsie winked. "Maybe."

"What's your point here, Gibsie?" Bella demanded, glowering at my best friend.

"My point is fuck off, Bella," Gibsie told her. "Fuck *right* off, if you want me to get technical. Far, far away to the land of *Johnny doesn't want to be with you so get a life.*"

"You can't talk to me like that," she challenged, shaking now.

Gibsie arched a brow. "And why not?"

"Because!" she spat, flustered. "Because—"

"Because I have a dick and you have a pussy?" he offered knowingly. "Oh, please. I'm a twenty-first century guy. I support equal rights for everyone, which includes the right for me, a dick owner, to tell a stalk-erish female, such as yourself, to *fuck off*!"

"That was impressive," Hughie mused.

"I'm an impressive guy," Gibs shot back with a smirk.

"Jesus," I muttered, cringing when tears filled her eyes.

"Eight months, Johnny," she sobbed, looking up at me. "And it's like this?"

Biting my knuckles, I resisted the urge to scream. "Listen," I finally said, striving for patience, "this is pointless. I don't have anything to say to you, and you have nothing I want to hear. I'm not interested. I wasn't even interested when I was *supposed* to be interested. So just . . . *please*! I am begging you to just leave me alone, Bella. *Please.*"

"Really?"

"Yes!"

"And that's what you want? For me to just walk away?"

*Dear god . . .* "Yes!"

"Fine!" she screamed, crocodile tears miraculously gone now as she glared up at me. "You want me out of your life, Johnny Kavanagh? Fine. Consider me gone!"

I released a huge sigh and sagged in relief. "*Thank you.*" Obviously, I didn't give Bella the reaction she wanted because she narrowed her eyes and kicked my crutch out of my hand, causing me to stagger backwards. "Thanks for that, too," I bit out, catching a hold of Feely to balance myself.

"I hope you're crippled," she spat. "I hope The Academy drops your ass and you never play rugby again!" Sneering, she added, "In fact, I hope I never see your face again."

*Lovely.*

"Unlikely," Feely said dryly. "Aside from stating the obvious—"

"That you go to school with him," Gibsie filled in, stating the bleeding obvious.

"Yes, Gibs," Feely sighed. "Aside from school, I'm sure you'll see him again in the summer." Shrugging, he added, "You know, when he's on the telly, playing for his country, and you're sitting at home, watching from your couch."

"With Cormac," Hughie added mildly.

"Ah, yes," Gibsie mused. "How is Judas Iscari-cunt?"

"The four of you can all go to hell!" she screamed before turning on her heels and storming away. "Assholes."

"We'll see you there, Devil Pussy!" Gibsie called after her as he bent down and retrieved my crutch and leaned it against the locker. "We'll see you there."

"Jesus," Robbie Mac whistled, stepping aside for Bella as she barreled past him, Pierce, and half the team. "What's her hurry?"

"She needs to get home before the sun comes up," Gibsie said loudly. "You know how vampires tend to burst into ash at the first sign of daylight."

"Fuck you, Gerard Gibson!" Bella screamed over her shoulder.

"Not on your life, *princess*," Gibsie roared after her. "I wouldn't touch you with McGarry's dick!"

"Stop," I groaned, holding a hand up towards Gibs. "Just let it go, lad."

"You're a bad bastard," Feely chuckled. "That was savage, Gibs."

Gibsie shrugged. "Sometimes you have to be a bad bastard when you're dealing with a bad bitch."

Robbie, Pierce, and the lads from the team surrounded us then, each taking turns slapping me on the back and welcoming me back and asking questions I would never in my wildest dreams give them genuine answers to.

"Lads, let Cap's misfortune be a warning to us all of the dangers that lurk behind a decent pair of tits," Gibsie announced. "When in doubt, rub one out."

His comments drew a laugh from everyone – myself included.

"You're a lucky boy," Pierce agreed with a shudder.

"Dangerous pussy," Robbie offered.

"I'll fucking say," I muttered, rubbing my temples.

"And you guys gave me shit for getting with Katie in second year," Hughie mused, sounding awfully fucking smug, as he pushed off the lockers and puffed his chest. "Steady and sensible doesn't look so bad now, does it?"

"After that outburst, *you're* not looking so bad," Gibsie offered.

Hughie grinned, while the rest of us sighed heavily.

*Don't take the bait, Hughie . . .*

*You're walking yourself into it . . .*

"Are you saying that you want my dick, Gibs?" Hughie teased.

"I'm saying I want your sister's pussy," Gibsie shot back, waggling his brows.

*There it is . . .*

"Around my cock," Gibsie continued.

"Gibs," I warned.

"On my face."

"Gibsie!" Feely groaned.

"All over me."

The smile on Hughie's face morphed into a furious scowl. "Take it back."

"No."

"Take it *back*, asshole."

"No."

"Just take it fucking back!"

"Just accept it," Gibsie laughed, bouncing back on his feet when Hughie took a swing at him. "It's going to happen, *brother-in-law*."

"Over my dead body," Hughie snarled, lunging. "She's too good for you—"

"Don't be an eejit, Gibs," I snapped, grabbing hold of Hughie's jumper and dragging him back to me. "Ignore him, Hugh. He's only messing with you."

"He's not messing." Furious, Hughie glowered at Gibs. "He's been obsessed with her since junior fucking infants!"

"Tell him you're messing," I growled. "Tell him, Gibs."

"I'm really not," Gibsie laughed. "And it's not just her pussy I want – although, that's high on the list. I want the whole lot of her, lad, and she wants me back." He grinned devilishly. "*Badly*."

"My sister doesn't *want* you," Hughie sneered. "Claire can't stand you. She only puts up with you because you're friends with me."

"She wasn't saying that last night," he replied, completely unfazed. "When I was—"

"Filter, Gibs!" I barked. "Jesus Christ, lad! *Filter*."

"You better keep your filthy cock on your own side of the road," Hughie hissed, jabbing a finger in Gibsie's direction. "Sister-fucker."

"Not yet," Gibsie snickered, thoroughly enjoying Hughie's discomfort. "But I'll take that title soon enough."

"I'm going to kill ya—"

"Pack it in, the pair of ye!" I snapped, keeping a hold of Hughie's jumper as I gave my best friend a withering look. "And use your bleeding brain before you speak, Gibs. Not everything you think in that fucked-up head of yours needs to be verbalized."

"I'm joking – I'm joking," Gibsie laughed when Hughie broke free of my hold and tackled him to the floor. Rolling onto his back, he held his hands up, still laughing. "I haven't touched her."

"You fucking better not have," Hughie snarled, bitch slapping him. "There's a code that you don't break! You don't mess around with your friends' sisters!"

"I thought that rule was about our mothers," Gibsie shot back, laughing too hard to defend himself. "Isn't that right, Kav?"

"Watch it," I warned, glaring at him.

"It's the clothes," Feely sighed wistfully.

"And the hair," Pierce agreed.

"She's the best cook," Gibs offered.

"And she always smells fantastic," Robbie interjected.

"And that body—"

"That's my mother, ye sick bastards!" I snapped, bristling. "You don't hear me talking about any of yer mams like that!"

"Because none of *our* mothers look like *your* mother," Gibsie snickered. "Mammy K." He sighed dramatically. "Mmm."

"Jesus, yeah." Hughie paused, mid-strangling. "To be fair, Cap, your mother is a pure rid—"

"Finish that sentence and I'll shove my crutch up the highest part of your hole." Turning to Gibsie, I said, "You know what? Go ahead and fuck all of their sisters, Gibs. In fact, go fuck yourselves while you're at it."

"I don't want their sisters – no offense, lads. I'm sure they're all lovely girls," Gibsie snickered. "I only want *his* sister."

"See!" Hughie barked before turning his focus back to Gibsie. "I was only messing about your mother. This prick is serious about my sister!"

"I think you're looking at this all wrong, lad," Gibsie continued to goad while Hughie resumed his throttling. "I'm loyal. I'm beautiful. I'm told I give five-star oral. I'm a solid bet."

"You're a solid whore is what you are!" Hughie snarled. "Don't forget I've known you your whole life, asshole. Which means, I know all about where your cock has been!"

"I was just biding my time, and practice makes perfect," Gibsie laughed and then groaned when Hughie's fist connected with his jaw. "Lad, not the face. Your sister likes me pretty."

Hughie's face turned a deep shade of purple. "She's innocent and good and fucking pure, dammit, so you just keep your goddamn hands off!"

"Ah, Johnny?" Feely muttered, tapping my shoulder. "We have company."

Tearing my eyes off the two eejits rolling around on the ground, I glanced over Robbie and Pierce's heads just in time to catch a glimpse of Shannon as she hurried away.

From *me*?

Oh, hell fucking no.

Shoving my way past the lads, I stalked after her, feeling the burn shoot up my thighs as I moved, but too worked up to slow my pace or turn back for my crutch.

"Shannon?" My heart slammed against my chest bone so fucking hard that I thought it would leave a bruise, as I called after her, "Shannon *like the river*, come back here!"

# Are You With Me?

## SHANNON

When Darren pulled into the carpark at Tommen a little after 8:45am, I felt like a creepy stalker as I wordlessly sought out the familiar Audi A3 only to come up empty. My heart plummeted into my stomach and I felt myself shrinking into the seat, wishing for nothing more than to just vanish into thin air and float away.

"What do you think Tadhg would like for his birthday?" Darren asked as he drove around in circles, looking for a parking spot. "It's this coming Friday and I have no idea what to get him."

"I don't know." Numb, I stared out my window and felt my anxiety grow with every Tommen student that filed into the main building. "Ask Tadhg."

"I'm asking you," he replied quietly.

"Football boots," I mumbled, feeling too sick to pay attention. "It's not like he'll be expecting anything." My stomach was rolling; my palms clammy. It almost felt like someone was holding an ice cube to the back of my neck.

"Good idea."

*Breathe, Shannon.*

*Just keep breathing . . .*

"Do you want me to walk in with you?" Darren asked when he finally found a parking spot in the maze. Killing the engine, he unfastened his seat belt and turned to look at me. "Because I will, no problem."

My head snapped back to him and my eyes widened in horror. "Do you remember secondary school?"

"I'm not that old," he quipped.

"Then you would know that the *last* thing anyone wants is their big brother walking them into school," I strangled out. "Like, ever."

He smiled.

I eyed him warily. "What?"

"You called me your big brother."

"Yeah, well." I sighed and leaned my head back. "That's what you are."

"It was just nice to hear you say it."

His words hung heavily in the air, like deadweight around my neck. I couldn't do this with him. Not this morning. Not when I was *this* close to begging him to turn the car around and take me home.

"I should go," I whispered, feeling resigned, eyes still glued to the swarm of students all piling into various buildings.

*You can do this.*

*You can absolutely do this!*

"I'll be here at four," Darren said when I pushed the car door open and stepped into the rain. "I'll try and get a parking spot close to this one, okay?"

Nodding, I grabbed my bag. "Thanks for the spin."

"Shannon?"

"Yeah?"

"Good luck."

*I'm going to need it.*

Swinging the car door shut, I slipped my bag onto my shoulders and made my way towards the courtyard, body rigid and mind reeling. The closer I got to the main building, the harder it was to keep my breathing regulated and even. I was anxious, and with every step I took, I slipped closer to a full-blown panic attack.

Mentally chanting tiny affirmations to myself, I put my head down, ignored all the stares and whispers, and hurried inside. I felt off-centered and disoriented and not even the heat wafting from the radiators inside the main building could thaw the ice in my veins as I hurried down the hallway, desperately trying to scope out Claire and Lizzie.

"Hi, Shan," a familiar voice called out from behind me.

I spun around to find Shelly, one of the girls in my class, waving at me from the bathroom doorway. The smile on her face quickly slipped when her eyes landed on mine. "Oh god," she whisper-hissed, pointing at my face. "It's really true, isn't it?"

"Probably," I mumbled, feeling anxious.

"I just thought . . . I mean, when I heard the girls talking about it in the bathroom, I just presumed—" She snapped her mouth shut and just stared at me for a long moment. "Damn, girl," she finally breathed. "I'm so sorry."

"Do you know where Claire is?" I asked, voice small. "Or Lizzie?"

"Office with Mr. Twomey. He called them both in when they arrived. They've been in there for ages." Shelly grimaced. "It's probably about you."

"Oh." I stood there for several moments, debating what to say to that before deciding there was nothing *to say* and hurrying away.

I planned on escaping to the third-year common room and hiding there until first class commenced, but my feet had other plans. My pulse raced as I wandered off the beaten track, traveling down corridors I never used, to the fifth-year wing of the school.

I heard her before I saw her. "Get the fuck out of my way, whore!"

Shoving me roughly out of her way, Bella barreled down the hallway, coming as close to running as I'd ever seen a girl in six-inch heels move.

Staggering sideways from the impact, I braced the wall with my hand, breathing hard, and stared after her.

"This is all your fault!" she tossed out over her shoulder before disappearing down another corridor. "You ruined my life."

In some sick and extremely unhealthy way, I almost felt *better*, like a weight had been lifted off my shoulders. Temporarily, at least. Because I *knew* this altercation was coming. I *knew* she was going to do something to me.

Girls like Bella Wilkinson were all the same. They were bitter and angry at the world, and could never let a single thing go. The *thing* in Bella's case was Johnny, and the look she'd given me on the bus that day had assured me that I was in the firing line.

*You've survived far worse than a mean girl,* a small voice in the back of my head reminded me. *In three years' time, she'll be a blip on your radar.*

It was with this knowledge that I steeled my spine and made my way down to the fifth-year wing. I had a whole speech thought up, one that fell out of my head the moment I locked eyes on *him*, leaning against his locker, with his arms folded across his chest, surrounded by a small army of fellow students. Beside him, resting against the lockers, was one lone crutch. I instantly recognized four of the boys with him as Gibsie, Patrick Feely, Pierce O'Neill, and Hughie Biggs. Others, I recognized from the bus. His teammates, I noted.

They were all laughing at something Gibsie was saying. Johnny's smile was a full, double-dimpled one and I could only imagine what Gibsie had said to draw that reaction out of him as he waved his hands around animatedly in usual Gibsie fashion.

His dark hair was styled in that deliciously disheveled look I was fairly sure – no, I *knew* – he woke up in the morning with, and his eyes were dancing with amusement.

Gibsie and Hughie began to play fight then, with Hughie tackling Gibsie to the floor and rolling around, while the others looked on and laughed.

Riveted to the spot, I watched him interact, taking in how carefree he looked with his teammates and friends, and it made me sad.

*He never looks like that with you because you don't make him happy. You never could. All you are is a complication,* a niggling voice of doubt conjured up in my mind. *Get used to watching him from a distance, Shannon, because he's going away soon. He's going to be a star. Look at him, he already shines so bright, it's blinding . . .*

With my bravery abandoning me in a shaky breath, I swiftly turned on my heels, hell-bent on getting away – on putting some much-needed space between my heart and the boy who owned it.

It was too much; my feelings, the crowds, this school, my life . . .

"Shannon?"

*Keep going, it might not be him.*

"Shannon *like the river,* come back here!"

*Busted.*

Freezing in the middle of the corridor with my back to him, I debated my options: pretend I hadn't heard him the first time, or just keep running? The coward in me favored option two, but I forced myself to just *stay*, breathe, and think this through.

*You don't want to run away from Johnny,* I silently commanded myself, *this is silly. You're not scared of him.*

"Were you going to ignore me?" His voice was closer now, achingly closer, and when I felt his fingers brush against my shoulder blade, an involuntary shiver rolled through me. "Hmm?"

Inhaling a deep, steadying breath, I turned around and slapped on the brightest smile I could muster. "Hi, Johnny."

Johnny's face was set in a deep frown, blue eyes full of confusion as they swept over me. God, he was beautiful. It was hard to focus when my eyes kept drifting to his mouth – to his lips I knew on an intimate basis.

"Hi, Shannon," he replied, not smiling.

"H-how are you?" I asked, nervous.

"Fine. How are you feeling?"

"I'm okay . . . " My smile slipped as I took in his thunderous expression. "What's wrong?"

"You were running," Johnny replied, looking hurt. "From me."

"Oh, no, I was just . . . I needed to . . . I mean, yeah, I thought I should—" Exhaling a ragged breath, I let my shoulders sag. "Yeah."

His eyes softened. "Yeah, as in you *were* or you weren't?"

"I'm uh . . . " I grimaced, feeling acutely exposed in this moment. He was putting me on the spot in that direct way of his. "I'm not really sure."

A faint smile ghosted his full lips. "You're not sure of what?"

"Whether you wanted me to come over to you just there? I mean, I didn't know if you wanted to see me . . . or talk? After what happened with my mam, and I just, I wasn't sure if you wanted to talk to me anymore." I blew out a shaky breath, self-loathing strong as I slipped and stumbled over my words. "I didn't know what you wanted." Exhaling heavily, I dropped my head. "I *don't* know," I amended quietly, my voice barely more than a whisper. "What you want."

"Ask me."

Forcing down the urge to run and hide, I forced my chin up and looked at him. "Huh?"

"If you want to know what I want, then ask me," Johnny repeated, closing the space between us. "All you have to do is *ask* me." His hand came down, gently cupping my elbow. "And I'll tell you."

I felt dizzy when I croaked out, "What do you want, Johnny?"

"For a start, I want you to look me in the eyes when you talk to me," Johnny replied, blue eyes burning holes so deeply inside of me, I doubted they could ever be repaired. "Second, I want you to stop worrying about things you can't control. Like Darren and your ma."

"But you didn't come back," I blurted out and then reddened before quickly backpedaling. My heart was racing wildly, my body shaking with a mixture of anxiety and excitement. "I'm sorry. I didn't mean that you *had* to come back or anything like that, and I wasn't expecting you to just drop everything for me. I know you're busy and you have a lot of rehab sessions—"

"I didn't come back because I couldn't, Shannon, not because I was told not to by your ma and not because I didn't want to see you," Johnny explained, sounding pained. "I didn't come back because I physically *couldn't* get to you. I still can't drive, and my ma wouldn't let me out of her sight. They even took Gibsie off me, for Christ's sake. But I wanted to." He exhaled a shaky breath. "I *really* fucking wanted to see you."

It felt like a huge weight had been lifted from my shoulders. For the last week, I hadn't slept, had barely eaten anything, and all because I was literally drowning in my feelings and my uncertainty. The unknown was a terrifying thing for me. Not knowing where I stood with Johnny was even worse. "Oh."

"I tried to call you," he added gruffly. "I texted you every day."

"Your battery died," I explained, feeling lightheaded. "I couldn't charge it."

"Dead battery." Johnny sighed in what looked like relief. "Makes sense."

"Does she hate me?" I asked then, feeling a little faint. "Your mother?"

"No, Shan, she doesn't hate you," he replied, voice torn. "I don't think there's a person on this planet who could hate you."

"But?"

He grimaced. "My ma's just . . . "

"She's just what?" My pulse quickened as I waited in fear for what he would say next.

"Worried," he finally replied. "My parents don't want me going over to your place. They think it's a bad idea."

My heart sank.

*Oh god, you're a bad idea.*

*His parents think you're a bad idea for him, Shannon.*

I worried my bottom lip, biting down so hard I was surprised not to taste blood. "I'm sorry." Feeling at a loss, I clasped my hands together, a nervous trait, and sighed. "For all of it."

Johnny reached up and tucked my hair behind my ear. "Can you do me a favor?"

Nodding, I stopped myself from leaning my cheek into his touch. "Of course."

"Can you not climb back inside that shell of yours every time we're not together for a few days?"

I swallowed deeply, eyes locked on his. "My shell?"

"Your shell," he confirmed. "Don't do that to me, Shannon – don't block me out. Don't give me *you* last weekend and then take it away again. I'm the same me from that night in my house – I'm the same me from every other time we've been together. So, don't put a wall up between us, not when you've already let me climb over it."

"I'm . . . I didn't realize I was doing that," I admitted.

"You're doing it now," he confirmed gruffly. "You do it all the time."

"I . . . " Shaking my head, I shrugged helplessly. "Sorry?"

"Don't say sorry," he replied. "Just start trusting me, okay?"

"I do trust you, Johnny," I strangled out, nodding eagerly, desperate for him to know that. "But they're probably right," I added, feeling a crippling wave of uncertainty flood me. "Your parents, I mean." Blowing out a breath, I touched my forehead with my hand and mumbled, "About it being a bad idea."

"They're wrong," Johnny corrected, sounding so confident and sure in this moment that it was comforting to hear. "I'm right."

"Right about what?"

"I'm right about you."

*Oh god.*

"But I *am* a bad idea for you, Johnny," I replied shakily, needing him to hear me, giving him the out that, if he had sense, he would take. "I'm a lot of trouble."

"I like your trouble," he countered, stepping closer.

"My life is *complicated*."

"I want your complications."

My breath escaped me in a rush. "You do?"

He nodded slowly. "You asked me what I wanted? There's a lot of things, but in a nutshell, I just want you." Shrugging, he added, "And I'm kind of hoping that you're going to say that you want me, too?" He laughed nervously. "Or else I've just made a complete spanner of myself in the middle of the school hall—"

"I do back," I blurted out and then cringed. "You, as well." Shaking my head, I blew out a breath and tried again. "I want you, too."

"Yeah?" He beamed, shoulders sagging in relief. "Thank fuck for that."

"And I missed you," I strangled out the words, forcing them out of my head and into his, because, at the very least, I needed him to know that I missed him. "Terribly," I added, offering up another piece of trust to him. "Like so much."

"Yeah." Tightening his hold on my elbow, Johnny tugged me closer until I was flush against him. "How much?"

"Like a crazy fucking amount," I whispered.

"A crazy fucking amount?" Smirking, he titled his head to one side. "That sounds dangerous."

"It is." I nodded eagerly. "Very."

Grinning, Johnny dipped his face, closing the space between us. "I think I'll take my chances," he whispered, and then brushed his lips against mine.

Once, featherlight, twice, a little firmer, and then . . . *oh god.*

His tongue swept into my mouth, stroking against mine, and my breath hitched, my eyelids fluttering closed.

My hands shot out of their own accord, fingers knotting in his navy school jumper, as I kissed him back with everything I had in me. Whatever I had in this moment, I gave it all up to him, both unable and unwilling to hold back the feelings bursting out of me that were all aimed solely at him.

I knew people could see us, we were standing in the middle of the corridor with his teammates less than ten feet away, but I just didn't care anymore. I could hear the bell sounding for class, I could hear voices around us, people calling his name and wolf-whistling, but I couldn't find the willpower required to tear myself away. I couldn't find it in my heart to *worry.*

Johnny kept one hand on my elbow, holding me roughly against his chest, while his free hand tangled in my hair, holding me in place, letting me know with every thrust of his tongue that he really did like my trouble.

*Oh god . . .*

The bell sounded again and then we were cloaked in a sudden silence.

Trembling, I clung to him, struggling to handle the heat rising up inside of me. The pressure in my chest was almost too much and I gasped into his mouth, needing more and needing him to stop all in one breath. Because I couldn't contain the feeling erupting inside of me. I couldn't stop my heart from rail-roading off-course and charging straight for him.

"Wait, wait, wait—" Breaking the kiss, Johnny stared down at me, breathing hard. "You're my girlfriend now, right?"

Feeling slightly dazed, I craned my neck and stared up at him. "Huh?"

"My girlfriend," he repeated, looking nervous. "Are you?"

"Uh, I . . . I—"

"Because I've never done this before." He glanced around the empty corridor before turning his attention back to me. "And I need to know where I stand with you."

"Oh." I shrugged helplessly. "Neither have I."

"Shite, yeah, sorry." He blew out another nervous breath, looking achingly vulnerable. "So, are you?"

Was he asking me to *confirm* I was his girlfriend or was he asking me to *be* his girlfriend? Or was he asking me if I *thought* I was? Oh god, I didn't know and my mind was reeling, my heart too cautious to make the assumption for fear I was reading this whole thing wrong.

"I don't know," I finally replied, heart racing wildly. "Am I?"

Johnny touched my cheek, his knuckles grazing over my skin with a featherlight touch. "I really fucking hope so."

"Yeah?" A deep sense of relief washed through me and I whispered, "Me too."

"And I'm yours." Grinning, his hand slipped from my elbow to my ass, giving me a little squeeze, before stepping back and releasing me. "Just so you know where *you* stand."

My heart slammed so hard against my chest that I felt a little faint. "Oh-okay."

He then proceeded to tug his shirt out from the waistband to conceal the very impressive bulge in his grey school trousers. "I'm supposed to be in double accounting with Doyle, and I have no fucking clue how I'm going to concentrate on spreadsheets," he explained with a grimace. "What are you late for?"

"I'm, ah . . ." Shaking my head, I tried to clear my thoughts but my gaze kept returning to his blatant erection. "I'm supposed to be in Maths."

When he caught me staring, Johnny shrugged sheepishly. "It's uh, yeah, *that's* probably going to happen a lot when I'm with you," he explained, with a small shake of his head. "But just know that I'm not getting any notions, okay? Just ignore it and it'll go away."

*What if I don't want to ignore it?*

"Okay," I agreed, tone breathy. "I understand."

Feeling like my world had once again shifted beneath me, I watched as Johnny walked stiffly back to his locker, slung his schoolbag over his shoulder and then grabbed his crutch before returning to me.

"Shouldn't you be leaning on that?" I asked when he slung an arm around my shoulder and led me back towards the third-year wing, aimlessly twisting the metal stick around in his hand like a baton twirler.

"It slows me down," he admitted, drawing me closer to his side.

"For good reason," I replied quietly, stopping outside my designated classroom. "Because you're *supposed* to slow down, Johnny."

"So, this is what having a girlfriend's going to be like?" he teased, but thankfully set his crutch down. "You bossing me around the place and telling me what to do?"

"No." I blushed. "I'm just saying that you were given a crutch for a good reason."

"Yeah, I know." Sighing, he released his hold on me and turned to face me. "So, listen, I wanted to ask you about how things were going at home, but I got all caught up in the moment."

At the mention of home, I felt the tension build back up inside of me. "My dad's still gone," I said quietly. "If that's what you meant."

"No sight of him?"

I shrugged. "Not by the Gardaí."

"Shite." Johnny expelled a frustrated growl. "It's been more than two weeks. How the hell have they not found him by now?"

"It's okay." I shrugged, feeling myself grow more rigid at the thought of my father. "I'm not expecting any miracles."

"No, *it's* not okay," he shot back in a passionate tone. "But *you* will be."

"Yeah" Shivering, I stepped into his embrace, pressing my forehead to his chest. "Maybe I will."

"Can we do something after school today?" he asked then, nuzzling my hair with his cheek. "Can you come home with me?"

*God, I wish.* "No."

"No?" He stared down at me. "If this is because you think my folks don't want you at the house then you're wrong, Shan."

"Darren's picking me up," I reluctantly told him. "Apparently, he'll be driving me to and from school from here on out."

Growling, he dropped a hand on my lower back and pulled me closer. "I fucking hate this."

Closing my eyes, I just sagged against him, body coiled tight with tension. "I'm sorry."

"Don't say sorry," he said, smoothing a hand down my back. "It'll be okay. I'm getting stronger. I've been doing all my physio and shite. Once I get my car back next week, and I'm back on the road, it'll be easier." He growled when he said, "I'll be breathing down their necks like their worst fucking nightmare."

"I'm sorry about how they spoke to you," I blurted out. "It was so wrong."

"Shan." He sighed. "Don't even worry about it."

"But I *am* worried about it."

"I know you're scared, but I'm not, and I'm not worried, either," he replied gruffly. "I don't care if your entire family doesn't like me. *Let* them. I'm only interested in *you* liking me because I only care about *you*."

"Joey likes you," I croaked out.

Johnny smirked. "Yeah?"

I nodded. "And he doesn't like *anyone*."

"Good to know I have big brother's approval," Johnny chuckled. "Oh yeah, I almost forgot—" Shoving a hand into his pocket, he dragged out a pricey-looking mobile phone, and aside from being pink in color, it was identical to his black one. "Do you have my phone?" he asked, tapping on the screen of the pink one in his hands.

"Oh—" Slipping my hand under my jumper, I removed his dead phone from the breast pocket of my shirt and held it out to him. "Yeah, sorry . . . uh, thank you again for letting me use it."

Johnny took his phone and slid it into his pocket, before placing the pink phone in my hand.

I stared blankly at the device. "What's this?"

"It's yours," he replied. Slipping his schoolbag off his shoulder, he pulled a charger out of the front pocket and then proceeded to slide it into my bag.

"Wh-what are you doing?"

"It's yours," he repeated, blue eyes locked on mine. "It's got a built-in MP3 and I loaded it up with a ton of songs for you. It's topped up with credit and I put mine, Claire, Joey, and Gibsie's numbers in, but you're going to have to add the rest of your contacts yourself."

My mouth fell open as I gaped at him. "You bought me a phone?"

"You needed a phone, and I missed your birthday." He shrugged, like it wasn't the gigantic deal it was, and said, "Made sense."

"You gave me dinner for my birthday," I whispered, embarrassed.

"I gave you fucking Cheerios," he grumbled, looking annoyed with himself.

"And a toasted sandwich," I hurried to add.

"Don't remind me," he groaned.

"When did you buy it?"

"The other day, after physio," he replied, watching me warily. "Are you mad at me for it?"

"No, I'm not mad," I strangled out, feeling lightheaded. "But I can't accept it." I dropped my gaze to the phone that I knew full well had to have cost at least a couple of hundred euro. "It's too much." I blew out a shaky breath. "Too expensive."

"It's *yours*," he said. "So just put it in your pocket and don't try and send me home with a pink phone." Smirking, he added, "Gibs will never let me hear the end of it."

"But you didn't have to do this for me—"

"I'm going to do a lot of things for you, Shannon." Taking the phone from my hand, Johnny reached into my jumper and slid the phone into my shirt pocket. His fingers grazed my chest and I shivered. "And I'm going to buy you a lot of stuff." He took a step back, never taking his eyes off me, and shrugged unapologetically. "Fair warning."

"But I don't *need* presents." I pressed a hand to my forehead, feeling flustered and stressed as the weight of the phone in my pocket hung heavily on my conscience. "I'm not one of those girls who's out for what they can get from you, Johnny. I'm not Bella," I added, imploring him with my eyes to believe me. *I just need you.*

"I know that, Shannon," he replied, frowning. "Christ, don't even think like that."

"I can't give you anything back," I choked out, telling him the same thing I told him last week, praying he would hear me. "I have *nothing* to give you in return."

"You can give me a call."

"A call?"

He smirked. "And you can text me."

"Be serious," I begged.

"I am." He stepped closer. "I am so fucking serious about you."

*Oh god . . .*

"I need to be able to talk to you." Dropping a hand to my hip, he tugged me closer. "To know you're okay." Exhaling shakily, he flexed his fingers, making me burn with unfamiliar need. "I can't be at home not knowing what's happening in your life." His eyes darkened when he said, "In your house."

"Johnny . . . "

"I can't handle it, Shannon," he whispered. "You have no idea how fucked up in the head it makes me, not knowing if he's back or whether or not you're safe. Every time I think about you in that house, I go into a blind panic. I *literally* drive myself insane thinking all the worst-case scenarios until I see you again."

"But I'm okay now," I hurried to soothe. "I am."

"Maybe," he replied quietly. "But I still need the link."

"Of a phone," I filled in.

"Yeah." He shifted from foot to foot, looking uncomfortable. "I suppose now's a good time to tell you that I get a little obsessed with the things I love, huh?"

*There was that word again.*

"It's okay," I strangled out.

"But it's not," he countered gruffly. "Because it was bad enough before, when I was fighting it, but now I'm just ... " He blew out a pained sigh. "I just want to be with you." He shrugged almost helplessly. "All the fucking time."

"That might change," I breathed, shaking from the impact of his words.

"I wouldn't hold your breath," he replied.

*Don't worry, I'm not.*

"Once I get my car back, we can spend more time together, outside of school, and maybe I won't be so fucking paranoid," he continued. "You can come over to my place and kick my ass on the PlayStation, or we can go to Biddies. Whatever you want."

"I really don't think your parents will want me going over to your house," I confessed, biting down on my lip hard. "I know you think otherwise, but I honestly can't see them wanting you to hang around with me." I sighed. "And I don't blame them, Johnny."

"I'm not hanging around with you, Shannon. I'm *with* you," he shot back gruffly. "And I promise that my parents have no problem with you."

*Yeah right ...*

"I'm serious, Shan," he added, tipping my chin up to meet his eyes. "They really like you."

I didn't believe that, not one word, but I refrained from telling him. Instead, I mumbled a halfhearted, "They're good people."

"*You're* good people," Johnny shot back, blue eyes scorching me. "You, Shannon, you're *good,* and my parents and everyone else knows that. Especially me. So don't be letting that head of yours tell you any different."

A shiver rolled through me. "God, Johnny, I just wish we could—"

"Come on, Shaggy!" Gibsie's voice perforated through the air, startling me and causing me to jerk away. Seconds later, he appeared from the lower staircase, bounding up the steps like an over-excited Labrador. "Oh – hey, Little Shannon."

"Hi, Gibs," I replied shyly before looking up at Johnny. "*Shaggy*?"

Johnny sighed wearily. "Don't ask."

"Oh . . . " I frowned. "Okay?"

"You're looking well, girl," Gibsie acknowledged with a friendly smile before swiftly swiping Johnny's bag off his shoulder and hoisting it onto his own. "Hate to cut the reunion short, but your boy here needs to get his ass to class." His eyes were dancing with excitement when he said, "Lad, you won't fucking believe it, but Miss Moore took my suggestion!"

Johnny stared at Gibsie for a long beat before awareness dawned on him and his jaw fell open. "You're joking."

"I'm so fucking serious right now." Gibsie literally bounced on his feet. "I asked for it months ago and I just presumed they overlooked me for that shitty past-pupil talk before Christmas, but I was wrong. They *listened* to me, lad. It's all set up and everything! I swear this is the best day!"

"They seriously brought them in for the senior talk?" Johnny pushed.

Gibsie nodded eagerly. "You're welcome."

"Jesus," Johnny groaned. "The school's going to shite."

"What suggestion?" I heard myself ask.

Johnny glanced nervously at me. "Ah, you're really better off not knowing."

"Three of them, lad," Gibsie added, clearly delighted with himself. "Three, Johnny! Fucking three!"

"Three what?" I asked, curious.

"Nurses," Johnny muttered, rubbing his jaw.

My brows furrowed. "Nurses?"

Johnny opened his mouth to reply, but Gibsie got in there first. "Not just any nurses. Sex nurses." Winking he added, "And they look *nothing* like the ones touching your balls this morning."

My eyes widened. "Huh?"

"Christ, it's not what it sounds like." Johnny's bewildered expression mirrored mine. "And they're not sex nurses, ya bollox," he added, flustered. Running a hand through his hair, he narrowed his eyes and said, "They're regular nurses who just happen to work at the sexual health clinic."

"I *know*," Gibsie replied joyously. "Better again."

Johnny arched a brow. "Do you even know what the sexual health clinic is used *for*?"

"I know they're handing out *free* condoms, lollipops, and bottles of lube," Gibsie said gleefully. "That's all I need to know." Slapping Johnny on the shoulder, he hurried back towards the staircase, calling out, "Come on – I've emptied my schoolbag. We're going to save a fucking fortune today."

I glanced up at Johnny, who was staring after Gibsie with a mildly horrified expression etched on his face. "What do you think it's like in his head?"

"A happy place?" I offered with a weak shrug.

"Hmm." Frowning, Johnny turned back to me. "Listen, do you want to just blow off the rest of—"

"Come on, Johnny!" Gibsie roared at the top of his lungs. "You're missing the presentation, dammit!"

"Jesus." Grimacing, Johnny leaned down and pressed a kiss to my cheek. "I better go and . . . *rein* him in."

"Of course." I nodded, cheeks reddening as I watched him chase after his friend. "Bye, Johnny."

"Bye, Shannon," he called over his shoulder as he battled with the staircase. "I'll see ya at lunch, okay?"

"Yeah," I blew out a breath, "I'll see you then."

"I'm not, by the way," he called out, pausing mid-step on the staircase to swing around. "So don't worry."

"You're not what?"

"Filling my schoolbag."

I opened my mouth to say something, but I only ended up letting my jaw hang open.

Chuckling softly to himself, Johnny disappeared down the steps, leaving me standing there, catching flies with my mouth.

I must have stood there, still as a statue, staring after him for a solid five minutes, because when I finally snapped out of it, my body felt stiff, my legs like jelly.

Reluctantly, I turned on my heels, gripped the straps of my schoolbag, and forced myself to walk to class.

# Wrap It Up

## JOHNNY

"Nice of you to join us, lads," Coach Mulcahy barked when Gibsie and I stumbled into the jam-packed classroom filled with both fifth- and sixth-year students. "You're only fifteen minutes late." Leaning against the desk at the front of the room, he folded his arms and gave us a no-nonsense nod. "Find a seat wherever you can and be quick about it. Our visitors want to get the presentation underway."

"Hey there," Gibsie purred, winking at the three seriously attractive women standing next to Coach. "I just want to let you lovely ladies know that I'm seventeen, I'm single, and I'm one-hundred percent willing to be a guinea pig for any *hands-on* demonstration—"

"Get away from the ladies, Gibsie," Coach snapped, ignoring the loud snickering around us. "Go to the back of the classroom – and *not* with Kavanagh, Biggs, or Feely. Go sit with someone else."

Shaking my head, I spotted an empty desk five rows back on the left, and moved for it, ignoring the curious stares as I went. Fucking eejits. *You'd swear they never saw a crutch in their lives.*

"I talk to everyone, sir," Gibsie shot back with a chuckle. "And the back row is full." Waggling his brows, he added, "Looks like I'm going to have to sit up front with you."

"Like hell you are." Eyeing the back row of desks, Coach pointed a finger, "Bella, move up to the fifth row with Kavanagh. Gibsie, take her seat."

*No . . .*

*Why, God, why?*

"Fine," Gibsie sulked. "But I'm taking these," he added, grabbing a box of tissues off the desk as he stalked to the back of the classroom and proceeded to wipe down the chair before slumping down. "Can't be too careful these days."

"Are you alright there, Kavanagh?" Coach Mulcahy asked as I tried to maneuver my way down the narrow rows of desks, ignoring the glowering girl sitting at my fucking desk. "Do you need a cushion to sit on?"

"No, sir," I bit out as I gingerly lowered myself onto my seat, careful not to brush against *her*. "My arse is grand."

"Are you sure?" Coach asked, watching me warily. "Do you need a hand?"

Loud snickering came from Hughie and Feely who were perched at the back of the class. Two seats over from them, Gibsie was doubled over his desk laughing.

Twisting around, I not so discreetly gave him the finger.

Gibsie returned the gesture by shoving his hand under his desk and pretending to wank himself – toppling a stack of books off the desk with his over-enthusiastic performance.

*Lovely.*

*Just fucking lovely.*

"Or a mouth?" a familiar voice sneered in my ear.

Disgusted, I turned to glare at Bella. "What did you say to me?"

She rolled her eyes. "It was a joke, Johnny."

"You think because you're a girl it's okay to say shite like that to me?" I hissed.

"Relax," she spat, drumming her long nails on the desk. "I was just making con—"

"Conversation," I deadpanned. "Yeah, I got that." *Fucking double standards.* "Well, here's me making conversation; don't fucking talk to me."

"You're an asshole," Bella growled, purposefully poking me with her elbow. I presumed she meant to hurt me, but it was just plain irritating. "So, what's going on with you and the Lynch girl?"

Clenching my jaw, I leaned back in my chair and folded my arms across my chest, dutifully ignoring her.

*Don't feed the crazy.*

*Don't feed the crazy.*

"Answer me," she whispered-hissed.

*Give me strength . . .*

"You might as well answer me because I'm going to keep—"

"She's my girlfriend," I spat, losing my cool. "Now stop fucking talking to me."

Bella's expression fell. "Your girlfriend?"

I nodded stiffly and turned my attention back to the nurse listing off types of STDs on the projector machine at the top of the class.

"You've lost your mind," Bella growled. "What are you going to do with a girlfriend? You're leaving in a couple of months."

*You don't fight with girls.*

*You don't fight with girls.*

"Ah, now I get it," she mused. "You feel sorry for her."

That got my attention and I snapped my head around to glare at her. "Excuse me?"

"Shannon," Bella replied with a smirk. "She's all fucked up, with a broken home and a bad daddy, and you're a sucker for a sob story," she added, "Just look at Gib—"

"Don't even go there," I warned, hands balling into fists.

"You feel bad about it so you're keeping this charade up," she continued. "I knew there had to be something more to this. It made *no* sense for you to look sideways at the likes of her—"

"Someone swap seats with me!" I roared, causing the nurse who was addressing the class to jump and everyone else to turn and look at me. "Am I a piece of art?" I snapped, standing up stiffly. "Stop fucking looking at me and start moving seats. Now!"

"Kavanagh!" Coach said, looking confused. "What's wrong?"

"Either move her away from me, or find me another seat," I hissed through clenched teeth. "Because I'm going to lose my shit."

Coach obviously took me seriously because he didn't hesitate when he said, "Bella, move seats with Gibsie."

"Woo-hoo," Gibsie hooted from the back of the room.

"Why do I have to move?" Bella growled. "He's the one with the problem."

"Because I told you to," Coach shot back tersely. "Now move!"

"Preferential treatment because he's your star boy," Bella sneered as she shoved her chair back and stood. "Enjoy your pity relationship," she hissed in my ear as she roughly shoved her chair into my leg. "Cripple."

"Move along," Coach warned. "Now, Bella."

Biting back a growl as a wave of pain shot up my leg, I remained stoically silent as she stepped around me, not trusting myself not to explode on her.

"You heard the man," Gibsie sneered, leaning against the desk. "Move along, Devil Pussy."

"Fuck off, Gibsie," she snarled as she stalked to the back of the class.

"You alright, lad?" Slapping a hand on my shoulder, Gibsie slipped around me and sank down on the inside seat. "Did she hurt you?"

"Nah, I'm grand." Sinking back down, I stretched my legs out and breathed easily for the first time since walking into class. "She's just batshit."

"That she is," he mused. "Now listen, I have a plan—" Settling his elbows on the desk, he clasped his hands together, and looked attentively to the front of the classroom. "When they come around with the free-bies, I'll hold the bag open and you just pour the whole tub in, okay?"

"You're an eejit," I chuckled.

"I'm serious," he shot back, keeping his eyes trained on the large container of condoms on the desk.

I studied his face. "Jesus, you *are* serious."

"They're mine," he replied, grinning devilishly. "And I'm taking them all."

"You have no bleeding tact," I growled, eyeing my best friend from across the lunch table. The sexual health talk that Gibsie unintentionally orchestrated rolled into the three classes – and small break – due to the fact that some big, blond eejit wouldn't stop asking questions. I had French and History straight after and I swear my blood sugar levels had dipped from the lack of food. "You say I'm the tactless one, but you?"

Dropping my gaze to the plastic container in front of me, I stabbed the chicken breast with my fork and tore into it. "You are in a league of your own, lad."

His brows shot up. "*Me*?"

"Yes, you," I shot back, nodding to his overflowing bag of *supplies* that he had emptied onto the table the minute we sat down for lunch. I swallowed every morsel of meat and veg in my lunchbox before continuing, "What are you planning to do with all of those? Make water balloons? Because you're not going to use them all. It's physiologically *impossible*."

"*Physiological*?" he scoffed. "You need to get your head out of those books, lad," or at least that's what I thought he said. It was kind of hard to work out what he was saying with half a dozen lollipops hanging out of his mouth.

"How many are you planning on wearing at once?" I shot back, unscrewing the cap on my water bottle. "Half a dozen? Because there's no other reason to fill your bag to the fucking brim, Gibs." Shaking my head, I pressed my bottle to my lips and drained the contents in four long gulps. "They'll be out of date in a year and then what?"

"Say what you want, but I'm being practical," he replied, slurping loudly on his lollipops as he perused his freebies proudly. "And sensible." Sifting through what had to be a minimum of eighty different-colored condom wrappers, he compiled a neat pile to the left of his sandwich. "One of us has to be."

"*One of us has to be*?" I narrowed my eyes. "Are you serious? You honestly think you're the sensible one in this relationship?"

"Well, where are *your* condoms, Johnny?"

I narrowed my eyes. "I'm not having sex, so I don't need any."

"Sure." He, in turn, rolled his eyes to the heavens. "Famous last words, lad."

"You look like a gobshite," I stated. "Pack it away, will ya?"

"Why?"

"Because everyone can see you."

"And I care because?" he shot back, unfazed. "Fuck them all."

Grinning, he waggled his brows. "You're just afraid your *girlfriend* is going to see." Snickering, he shook his head and continued to make small piles. "Lad, I can't believe you signed yourself off." He sighed dramatically. "I guess it's down to me and Feely now – since you and Hugh both fucked yourselves over."

*Dear Jesus, please give me strength to deal with his crazy today . . .*

Leaning back in my chair, I gripped my water bottle and practiced the art of not strangling my best friend to death. "You need to put that shite away," I bit out when I felt calm enough to speak again. I glanced around the room, looking for Shannon and coming up empty. "I'm serious, Gibs."

"It's all foreign," he mused, inspecting the label. "I can't read the instructions."

"What's to explain?" I shot back. "Roll it on your dick when you're ready and roll it off when you're done. I'd say the whole process is fairly self-explanatory, lad."

"Well, this pile's for you," he offered. "Since you were too pussy to get your own."

"I already told you that I *don't* need any condoms," I bit out, aggravated. *I don't need the temptation.* "And if I do, I'll get them, because, believe it or not, Gibs, I am more than capable of getting shite for myself. I've been keeping myself out of trouble for years now."

"True." He shrugged, unfazed. "But that was before you went and got yourself shacked up."

Yeah, it was safe to say I bulldozed this morning, but I had no regrets. For the first time in months, I felt like I had some clarity over my feelings. Like something in my life was falling into place.

Did I push her too hard too fast? Probably. Should I have taken it slower? More than likely.

Either way, I wasn't about to take it back.

"It's not like that with her," I snapped, dragging myself from my thoughts. "So just put them away before she comes in here and you freak her out."

"No, it's not like that with Shannon," he agreed. "It's a lot *worse* and a lot more dangerous because you went and caught yourself some big, fat feelings, didn't ya, lover boy? And I'm telling you now that this valiant act won't mean shit when you find yourself caught in the moment, bollocks naked, and drowning in tight, virgin pussy. Just ask every poor bastard our age with a baby on his hip or on a food run in Dunnes Stores for *cravings*." Pushing a pile of condoms towards me like he was hustling poker chips, he added, "I'm only looking out for you. So here – big boy ones for you."

"I can't deal with you today, Gibs," I growled, throwing my hands up in sheer fucking despair. "I honestly can't."

"Take them."

"No."

"Take them."

"No."

"Yes."

"Did they adjust your medication?"

"Not lately, now take them."

"Jesus, Gibs—"

"Take the condoms or I'll make a scene."

"Fine!" Grabbing two fistfuls of foil packets, I shoved them into my pockets and glared at him. "Happy now?"

He grinned widely. "You will be – when you're not caught out in a *moment*."

"Fine, thank you, Gibs, for keeping my dick protected. Now, will you put it away?" I practically begged.

Nodding, he started to sweep everything back into his bag and I sagged in relief. Because the very last thing I needed was Shannon walking in while we were trading Trojans like Pokémon cards.

"So," he mused, tone slightly more serious now. "How are you feeling?"

I flexed my jaw. "Fine."

"You're in pain, aren't ya?" His eyes landed on mine, full of concern. "Lad, if you need to go home, that's okay."

"I'm just stiff, Gibs," I muttered. "Everything's locking up on me."

Fisting a handful of condoms, he said, "We should go for a swim after school."

"Yeah." I nodded. "I know."

"But you won't?" Smirking, he dropped the wrappers back down and leaned forward. "Because you have other plans?" He waggled his brows. "*Shannon* plans?"

"I don't know, lad." Exhaling heavily, I leaned forward and dropped my elbows on the table. "It's all fucked up."

"Already?" His brows shot up. "Christ, Johnny, you made short work of that, lad."

"Not Shannon," I muttered, feeling my body grow hot with temper. "But her family *hates* me." Dropping my head in my hands, I bit back a growl. "It's so messy, Gibs."

"Messy?"

"Messy," I confirmed grimly, glancing back up at him. "You saw the way her brother reacted to me last week? Well, I'm telling you that was *nothing* compared to how her ma was with me."

"Joey the hurler doesn't have a problem with you," he offered. "Well, no more than the rest of the world."

"One out of seven, lad," I mumbled. "I'm on a winner, aren't I?"

"I don't get it," he mused, catching his jaw. "I honestly don't."

"Yeah, well, you and me both, lad."

"Maybe they find you threatening?"

"If I was a threat, they'd be scared," I countered. "They're not scared, lad. They're just out for blood – *my* blood." My shoulders sagged in defeat. "I can't catch a bleeding break."

"It'll balance out eventually," he told me. "Life has its own built-in weighing scales." He shrugged. "It can't be all bad all of the time, the same as it can't be all good. Something's got to give."

"Yeah?" I grimaced. "I hope you're right, lad."

"You're ridiculous," Hughie said then, as he and Feely joined us at the table, bringing an abrupt end to our conversation. Slapping a tinfoil-covered sandwich down on the table, Hughie sank down on his usual chair to my right and roughly scraped the legs forward, never taking his eyes off Gibsie. "Put that shit away before Katie comes over."

Gibsie stared at Hughie and then me before sighing dramatically. "I don't know where I went wrong with the two of you." Packing away the last of his supplies, Gibsie tossed his school bag on the floor and huffed loudly. "I really don't."

"Let it go, Hugh," Feely, who had positioned himself next to Gibsie, said with a sigh. "It was a joke."

"About my *sister*," Hughie bit out, glowering.

Morbidly curious, I turned to look at Hughie's face and, oh shit, he was still peppering over this morning.

"You're still pissed off with me?" Gibsie accused, sounding amused. "That was hours ago, lad."

"Damn straight I'm still pissed with you," Hughie seethed.

"Hey, Johnny," Katie Horgan, Hughie's tiny, red-haired girlfriend said as she slipped around the back of my chair.

"Alright, Katie," I replied, offering her a nod.

"Hope you're feeling better," she added, giving my shoulder a small squeeze before moving straight for her fella.

"You're overreacting," Gibsie said, smiling at Hughie. "First about your sister and now the condoms." Sighing, he added, "You'd swear you never saw a pair of tits the way you're carrying on."

"If you want to see a pair of tits, Gibs—" Pausing mid-rant, Hughie murmured, "Hey, babe," to his girlfriend. Dragging Katie down on his lap, he pressed a quick kiss to her cheek before turning his glare back on Gibsie, "you need only look in the mirror."

"What's wrong?" Katie asked, curling an arm around Hughie's neck. "Babe?"

"Him." Wrapping an arm around her waist, Hughie drew her closer to his chest, and pointed across the table at Gibsie. "That little fucker."

"Lad." Gibsie threw his head back and laughed, much to Hughie's dismay. "I'm two inches taller than you." Shoving his chair back, he pulled his jumper and shirt up, revealing his bare chest, and grinned. "And are these the tits you're talking about?" he taunted, flexing his pecks. "Fine pair, aren't they?"

"You're an eejit," I muttered wearily.

"An eejit with great tits, apparently," he shot back with a wink.

"I can't believe you pierced your nipples," Katie chuckled, covering her mouth with her hand. "What if they get ripped off in a match?"

"Don't look at *his* nipples, baby," Hughie huffed. "Look at my fucking nipples."

Deciding to eject myself from the storm brewing around me, I leaned back in my chair, zoned out of their conversation, and waited for Shannon.

Checking my watch for the fiftieth time in the last fifteen minutes, I felt a pang of agitation surge through me.

Where was she?

We only had an hour for big lunch and I wanted to spend those sixty minutes with her, because let's face it, it was the only time I was going to get with her.

Glancing around again, I spotted two blonde heads in the reflection of the glass floor-to-ceiling window. Twisting around in my seat, my eyes landed on Claire and Lizzie just beyond the archway of the hall. They were clearly arguing with one another and standing in between them, several inches closer to the ground, was Shannon.

My heart slammed against my chest bone and I took a moment to just soak in the sight of her. She was tugging on their sleeves, pulling them away from the archway, looking all flustered and wide-eyed. As soon as she slipped out of view, my brain kicked into gear and my feet started moving.

# The Rugby Table

## SHANNON

"Shannon?" Lizzie Young's voice filled my ears as I sat on the closed-lid toilet, inside one of the stalls in the girls changing rooms in the PE hall with my uneaten sandwich on my lap. "Are you in here?"

I'd skipped Maths this morning. In fact, I'd skipped all six classes before big lunch. I'd gotten all the way to the classroom door this morning, I'd even put my hand on the door-handle, but I just couldn't make myself go inside and face everyone.

I just *couldn't* do it.

At first, I had debated just leaving school entirely and going home, but when I got to the main entrance gates, I had an unmerciful panic attack, with my father's face at the fore point of my anguish. Spinning on my heels, I had hurried out of the rain, into the PE hall and hadn't left since.

"Hey," a voice said from somewhere above me then, causing me to almost jump out of my own skin.

"Oh my god!" Glancing up, my eyes landed on Lizzie, who was leaning over the top of the cubicle partition with a mildly amused expression on her face. "Lizzie, you almost gave me a heart attack."

She arched a finely plucked brow. "Cozy down there?"

"Shan!" Claire's face popped up from the other side of the cubicle partition. "What are you doing in here?"

"Hiding," I admitted, red-faced.

"From what?"

"School," I offered with a weary sigh, as I stood up and unlocked the door. "The people in it." Stepping out of the cubicle, I walked over to the sinks, leaned against one of the cold, porcelain basins, and sighed. "Life."

"Well, that's a shitty thing to do," Lizzie shot back. Hopping down from the toilet bowl she had been balancing on, she wiped her hands on her school skirt and stalked towards me. Her dark-blonde hair was pulled back in a severe bun, and her lips were painted a scarlet-red color, making her look even more beautiful than normal. "We were worried to death about you," she added, before pulling me into a hug. "You little dope."

"It's true," Claire offered, scrambling down from the toilet bowl she had been standing on. "Not the dope part," she added, coming to join us in a hug. "That was mean and unnecessary, Lizzie – we've talked about this. But the worried-to-death part." She nodded. "We were definitely halfway there."

"Sorry, guys," I whispered, feeling swamped by my friends. Both girls were tall, both were blonde, and both were looking at me like I had the answers to all their questions, and maybe I did, but that didn't mean I could ever tell them. "I just . . . I needed—"

"A minute?" Lizzie offered with a knowing smile. "Yeah, I think you're owed a few of those."

"Am I in trouble for skipping my classes?"

"No." Claire shook her head firmly. "Mr. Twomey's just worried about you. He sent us to look for you, actually. We've literally been out of class all day, roaming the school for you."

"And it's a big school," Lizzie offered dryly. "And you're a tiny person."

"I was just in here," I confessed, feeling terrible now.

"Yeah, the P.E. hall?" Lizzie laughed softly. "Was honestly the last place either of us expected you to be."

"He called us to the office first thing, too," Claire added. "They all want to help, Shan."

"I don't want to talk to him or any of the teachers," I strangled out. "I told Darren to tell them that I didn't want to talk." I shook my head, feeling a little faint at the thought. "I don't want to talk to anyone."

"I know," Claire soothed. "And you don't have to."

"That's why he called us in," Lizzie offered calmly.

"Yeah." Claire nodded. "He wanted to make sure that we were looking out for you."

"Like he even had to ask," Lizzie scoffed.

"Come on," Claire said as she grabbed my schoolbag off the slippery tiles and slung it over her shoulder. "We're going to lunch."

"And then we're going to class," Lizzie added as she pushed me out of the bathroom. "Together."

"I'm scared," I blurted out, feeling that familiar pang of panic claw its way up my throat as we walked out of the hall and down the steep steps.

"We know," Claire replied, wrapping an arm around me as we headed through the courtyard. "But it's going to be okay."

"Yes, it is," Lizzie agreed, folding a loose lock of her blonde hair behind her ear. "Because you're not alone in this."

"I'm sorry, guys," I muttered, feeling terrible. "I'm a pain in the ass."

"Yeah, but you're *our* pain in the ass," Lizzie countered. "And we happen to be sort of fond of you."

"Thanks," I chuckled. "I think?"

"By the way," Lizzie paused mid-step to look at me. "Do you want to talk about what happened?"

"No," I croaked out.

"You're sure?"

"I just ... just be normal with me, Liz," I pleaded quietly. "That's all I need."

"Fair enough." Lizzie nodded and continued towards the main building. "Just know that we're here."

"Speaking of normal," Claire injected, thankfully changing the subject. "Are you going to be normal in here?" she asked Lizzie. Yanking open the glass door, she gestured to us to file in. "No arguments, okay?" We walked inside and Claire hurried in after us. "No bitching at Gerard or any of the boys."

Lizzie shrugged noncommittally, striding off in the direction of the lunch hall. "If Thor and his gang steer clear of our table, we won't have a problem."

"Hey – my brother's in that friendship group," Claire huffed.

"You know what they say, Claire – if you lie with dogs, you get fleas."

"Then you must be riddled with them," Claire shot back. "Since all you seem to be doing lately is lying *under* Pierce O'Neill." Lizzie's cheeks turned pink and Claire arched a perfectly shaped brow. "Nothing to say? Uh-huh. That's what I thought."

"Guys, don't fight," I puffed out as I hurried to keep up with their long strides, only to freeze on the mortal spot when we reached the archway. My heart jackknifed in my chest when my eyes landed on Johnny.

He was sitting at his usual spot at the end of the banquet-like table with his back to me. He had his feet propped up on a chair and his arms folded behind his head. His hair was all mussed up, looking like he'd spent the morning dragging his hands through it.

Several of the girls sitting at nearby tables were all staring at him with the same hungry expression I'd seen him provoke from girls in the hallways.

*The same hungry expression he provoked from me . . .*

He wasn't paying an ounce of attention to the girls, or anyone else for that matter. He was staring straight ahead, attention glued to the table I usually sat at with the girls.

"Uh," I cleared my throat, feeling nervous. "I have something to tell you." Catching ahold of their sleeves, I tugged the girls away from the archway, feeling my heart race at a million miles an hour as my gaze soaked him in. "It's about Johnny," I added, tearing my gaze away from him. "And me."

"Oh god." Lizzie narrowed her eyes. "What did you do with Captain Fantastic?"

"Yes?" Claire's eyes widened in excitement. "What did you do?"

"I . . . " I could feel my cheeks turning red. "Well, see, he's my . . . and I'm his . . . " Flustered, I broke off and pressed a hand to my forehead. "He asked me to be his girlfriend and I said yes."

"Shut the front door!" Claire squealed, clapping and bouncing excitedly. "Oh my god! Oh my god!"

I gave her a weak smile. "Yeah."

"You're his girlfriend?" Lizzie frowned in confusion. "But he doesn't do the whole girlfriend thing."

"Well, he does now," Claire hooted, still bouncing like a playful kitten. "I swear, this is the best day!"

"You know, I don't even know why I'm surprised," Lizzie grumbled. "This has been brewing for months."

"It really has," Claire replied, still grinning as she nodded in agreement. "Months and months."

"It literally just happened today," I told them.

"Yeah, sure, because Johnny Kavanagh blows a head gasket for every girl in this school," Lizzie shot back sarcastically. "I knew that day before Easter break, when you ran out of school and he went all batshit in the courtyard, that something was going on between you. Hell, even before that, he was always watching you like a creeper."

"They were *kissing*," Claire chimed in. "In his bedroom."

"Claire!" I hissed.

"And in Dublin."

I narrowed my eyes. "Thanks for that."

"Well, you were," she laughed. "Because he looooves you."

"Stop it." I blushed bright red.

"Are you sure this is what you want?" Lizzie asked then, watching me carefully. "You really want this, Shan?"

"I'm sure that I want him," I admitted with a wistful sigh. "Badly."

"Ah, god. I just . . . I can't. I am so happy right now." Wiggling around like a bunny on speed, Claire swept me up in a hug that was so tight, my lungs burned in protest.

"Oh god," Lizzie groaned. "I suppose you could do worse than Johnny." She cast a sideways glance towards Claire. "At least he's better than the other one."

"Claire . . . " Spluttering, I pushed at her shoulders, flinching when a sharp jolt of pain ricocheted through my ribcage. "Loosen . . . up . . . "

"Oops, sorry!" Releasing me immediately, she took a step back and grinned sheepishly. "The feels had me a little carried away there."

"The feels?" Lizzie arched a brow. "Girl, you are too much sunshine for one person."

"And you are too much grey cloud," Claire quipped. Turning to me, she cooed, "And Shan, here, is our pretty, little silver lining."

Shaking her head, Lizzie, turned her attention back to me. "Okay, Shan, I'm only going to say this once, and then you can do whatever you want."

Claire rolled her eyes. "Here we go."

"Take your *time*," Lizzie said, tone serious. "There's no rush, okay? If you want to be with him, then that's great. If he makes you happy, then fuck it, I'm all for it, but don't feel like you have to do anything you're not ready for. He's older than you and has a hell of a lot more experience with the world, so just take it at *your* own pace, not Johnny's, and if he pressures you, even a little bit, then you kick his stupid rugby ass to the curb because—"

"Because?" a familiar voice asked from behind me.

Startled and excited, I spun around and came face to chest with Johnny.

He was, once again, crutch-less, but he was minus his school jumper this time. His red tie was just about hanging in there, tied loosely in a halfhearted knot against his white school shirt – a shirt that he filled to the point of stretching the material.

A trickle of fear shot up my spine as I took in the sight of his muscular arms – his muscular *everything*.

God, the boy really was *all there*.

"Alright, girls," Johnny acknowledged gruffly, and then he turned his heated gaze on me. "Hi, Shannon."

"Hi, Johnny," I breathed, heart racing wildly. Flustered, I balled my hands into fists at my sides, not confident enough to touch him first.

*Don't retract, Shannon.*

*Be brave.*

*Do something!*

Smiling brightly, I asked, "How are you?"

*Ugh, better than nothing.*

A small smile ghosted his lips. "I'm good."

"I'm good, thanks," I blurted out and then immediately cringed when I realized he hadn't asked. "I mean—"

"Come here," he chuckled, grabbing my hand and pulling me flush to his chest. "I missed you," he whispered, before lowering his face to mine.

I felt his hands come around my waist and then his lips were on mine. Holding onto his arms, I leaned up on my tiptoes and kissed him back, feeling at a serious height disadvantage and struggling to reach him.

Smiling against my lips, Johnny stooped down to hook an arm around my back and then I was ... oh god, I was being lifted off my feet as he drew himself back up to his full height.

Snaking my arms around his neck, I melted into the kiss, feeling every ounce of tension drain away as my body grew lax and pliant against his.

"I missed you back," I breathed against his lips.

He smiled against my lips. "Good to know."

It was a soft, tender kiss that was over before it started, but it felt achingly intimate and left my whole body tingling.

"If you ditch your brother and come home with me instead, we can do that without an audience," Johnny told me, tone laced with amusement, as he set me back down on my feet.

"Huh?"

He inclined his head towards Claire and Lizzie, who were both watching us, openmouthed.

"Well," Lizzie said, composing herself first, "you just went right on in there, didn't you?"

"Aww," Claire gushed, clutching her chest with both hands. "I love them together." She feign-swooned before adding, "It's like a Great Dane and a Chihuahua trying to mate, but they somehow make it work."

"Jesus," Lizzie grumbled, swatting her arm. "You are so bloody tactless, Claire."

"He picked her up, Liz," Claire squealed, as Lizzie dragged her away. "Did you see that?"

"Yeah, I saw it, now let's go, whore." Keeping her hands on Claire's shoulders, Lizzie pushed her in the direction of the office. "We need to tell Mr. Twomey that we found her."

"But, Liz, he actually picked her up to *kiss* her!"

"Yeah, Claire, I know. I have eyes, too. Stop being such a weirdo."

Mortified, I stared after the girls until they had vanished into the lunch hall, and then I groaned loudly before burying my face in Johnny's chest. "I'm so embarrassed."

"Found you?" Johnny tipped my chin up and stared down at me in confusion. "Did you *need* to be found?"

"I, uh . . . kind of skipped class."

His brows furrowed. "All day?"

"Yeah, I . . . uh, couldn't face it," I admitted quietly, taking a step back to regain my composure.

"Do you think you can face it now?"

I shrugged. "I sort of have to, don't I?"

"*Having* to be ready and *being* ready are two very different things," he offered softly. "Have you been to the office? To talk to Twomey."

"No." I exhaled heavily and rubbed my temples. "But I know that I'm going to have to do it eventually."

"Listen, I know you don't want to, but if you just get it over with, it'll be one less thing to worry about."

"I just don't know what to say if they ask me about it," I confessed, feeling unarmed and exposed. "I'm not *used* to talking about it."

"Do you want me to come with you?" Johnny blew my mind by asking. "We could go now? Get it over and done with."

My eyes widened. "You would do that?"

"Of course," he replied gruffly.

"Would you be allowed in there with me?"

"I'd like to see him stop me," he shot back, and then with a grin added, "And if he asks you about anything you don't want to talk about, I'll take a leaf out of my da's book and jump in with a 'my client reserves the right to not answer that question'."

Smiling, I wrapped my hands around my waist and nodded. "Okay, I'll do it after lunch."

"Yeah?" His eyes burned with tenderness. "Well shite, I'm kind of persuasive when I want to be."

*You have no idea just how much.*

"Is that okay?" I heard myself ask, unsure. "Can you come with me then? I mean, it won't mess with your classes—"

"I'll be there," he cut me off by saying. "Don't even worry about it."

"But I just—"

"*Stop* worrying." Taking my hand in his, he entwined our fingers, and tugged me towards the archway. "I've got your back."

Oh god.

My heart.

Inhaling a steadying breath, I steeled my spine and walked into the lunch hall room with Johnny, holding onto his hand for dear life, and praying for a little invisibility, even though I knew it was no use. If I wanted to go undiscovered, I was holding the hand of the wrong boy. I wasn't letting go of him, though, not for all the tea in China.

Whatever this was, I knew I would hold on with both hands for as long as I could because the prospect of dealing with everything in my life and *not* having him to look forward to was incomprehensible now. It was all so fresh and new and unknown. Usually, I was terrified of the unknown, but with him, I had a burning curiosity. I was excited – terrified to my core but excited.

Silence greeted us the moment we stepped inside, and what felt like a thousand pairs of curious eyes landed on us, causing my body to seize up with dread.

Meanwhile, Johnny looked completely unfazed. Seriously, he either didn't see them staring or he didn't care because his posture remained relaxed, his smile still firmly etched on his face, as he led us over to his table.

"Johnny," I strangled out, tightening my hold on his hand. "Everyone is looking at us."

"Let them look," he replied, giving my fingers a reassuring squeeze. "They'll get bored eventually."

*Will you?*

The words were at the tip of my tongue, but I swallowed them down, deciding on battling the social demon for now.

I could worry myself to sleep with the insecure demon tonight.

Out of the corner of my eye, I noticed Bella watching from her perch at the top end of the rugby table, where she was sitting on Cormac Ryan's lap. The minute our eyes locked, she narrowed hers in a menacing glare and I instantly felt the weight of her fury; it was sharp, potent, and directed entirely towards me.

Dropping my gaze to my shoes, I debated letting go of Johnny's hand, but stopped myself.

*No,* I mentally chastised myself, *you're not afraid of her.*

*Who are you fooling?* another voice taunted. *You're* terrified *of her.*

"Push up," Johnny ordered when we reached the table, distracting me from my frantic thoughts. Feeling flighty, I locked my muscles into place, forcing my feet to stay firmly on the ground and watched as a line of lads, starting with Hughie Biggs, all obligingly scooted up a seat in the row.

"Listen up," Johnny said then, drawing the attention of his friends. "This is Shannon – my girlfriend. She's going to be sitting here from now on, so get used to seeing her around the place." He moved to sit down, but quickly stopped himself and straightened back up. "Oh, and fuck with her and I'll bury you all—" He cast a meaningful look around the table before adding, "Are we clear?"

*Oh my god!*

"Yeah, lad, no bother."

"We already know, Cap."

"Heard it all before, Kav."

"Good." Surprising me, Johnny took the seat that Hughie and his girlfriend had vacated, and pulled out his usual chair at the end of the row for me. "Just wanted to clear that up." He patted the seat beside him then and I practically flopped into it, wanting nothing more than to hide under the table.

If Tommen was a jungle and the students here were animals, then this table was the lion's den. I was a stray gazelle, surrounded by the most dangerous of apex predators, all watching me with curiosity. Luckily for me, I was a gazelle that the king of this particular jungle, and leader of the pack, had taken a shining to. I wouldn't be eaten up. Not today, at least.

*I hoped.*

Johnny's arm came around me then, cocooning me in a blanket of comfort that common sense told me was unsafe and temporary. "Just relax, okay?" he whispered, leaning so close to me that his lips brushed my ear. "You're safe with me."

Shivering from the contact, I nodded and suppressed the urge to bury myself inside this boy and never come back up for air. Because I was falling too hard, depending too much, and growing entirely too attached to him. Red flags were shooting up all around me, and still, I remained exactly where I was – exactly where I *wanted* to be. With him.

Setting my hands on my lap beneath the table, I tucked my chin downwards and cracked my knuckles. To my immense relief, when I looked up again, the only person still staring at me was Gibsie, who was sitting exactly opposite me at the ginormous table, and grinning like the cat that got the cream. "Hey, Little Shannon."

"Hi, Gibsie," I squeezed out, forcing myself to keep eye contact. "H-how are you?"

"All good in the hood." Pulling a lollipop out of his mouth, he twirled it around aimlessly, as his mischievous eyes danced between me and Johnny. "I can see you're doing good, too."

I blushed and Johnny snapped his head towards him. "Rein it in, Gibs," he instructed in a warning tone. "Whatever you're thinking about saying? Don't say it."

"I wasn't going to say anything," Gibsie laughed good-naturedly. "I was making friendly conversation with your *girlfriend.*"

"Hmm." Johnny arched a brow, eyes locked on Gibsie. "Keep it that way."

"How's your brother?" Gibsie asked then, turning his attention back to me. "Is he doing better?"

"Uh, yeah," I mumbled, tucking my hair behind my ears. "Well, he's home and he went back to school today." *I hope.* "So, he's doing a lot better."

Gibsie smiled warmly at me. "Good."

Claire and Lizzie arrived at the table then, making me sag in visible relief.

Lizzie stalked right past the boys with her nose cocked in the air, smacking the back of Gibsie's head as she passed, not stopping until she was halfway up the table and dragging out an empty chair beside her on again/off again boyfriend, Pierce.

"Hey – what was that in aid of?" Gibsie called after her.

"Because you're a dickhead," Lizzie shot back.

"And you're a viper," Gibsie muttered under his breath, rubbing the back of his head. "Jesus."

Claire slumped into the chair beside Gibsie then, much to Hughie's dismay as he glared, red-faced, at the pair of them.

"Hey, Claire-bear," Gibsie said, smiling again. "How's it going?"

"Hey, Gerard," she sighed, sounding sad and looking nothing like the bundle of energy she'd been a few minutes ago. Rolling up her sleeves, she placed her elbows on the table and dropped her head in her hands. "I'm so sad."

"Why?" Gibsie stiffened. "What happened?" His eyes narrowed. "Was someone at you?"

"Dee happened," she grumbled. "*Again.*"

Gibsie's mouth fell open and Johnny muttered something unintelligible under his breath before shifting closer to me.

"Dee?" I scrunched my brows together. "The school secretary?"

"That's the one," Claire replied and then huffed out a pained breath. "I swear that woman hates me for no reason, Shan."

Gibsie choked on his lollipop and several of the lads sitting around the table snickered. Meanwhile, Johnny stared dutifully out the window, looking anywhere but at Claire, while Hughie glowered darkly at Gibsie.

Leaning over the table, I gently touched her wrist to get her attention. "What did she do?"

"I have a hockey match in Thurles tomorrow," she replied, brown eyes full of sadness. "Somehow, my forms have vanished and now Mr. Twomey is saying that I can't go." Pouting, she folded her arms across her chest and added, "Dee told him that I never handed them into the office when I was supposed to, which is a complete lie, because I specifically remember handing them *to her* the Tuesday before we went on Easter break."

"Why would she do that?" I asked.

"Yeah," Hughie bit out through clenched teeth. "I wonder why she would do that."

"Lolly?" Gibsie offered then, pulling a lollipop stick from his mouth and holding it out to her.

Claire stared at it for a moment before shrugging, swiping it out of his hand, and then popping it into her mouth. "Sherbet?" She arched a brow. "You hate sherbet."

"Got it for you," he shot back with a wink. "I know it's your favorite."

"Don't put that in your mouth," Hughie practically spat. "You don't know where he's been, Claire."

"Hmm." Claire shrugged again, like it was a normal thing to be swapping lollipop saliva with him. "It's good."

"Jesus Christ," Hughie hissed in despair. "I don't know why I bother."

"Anyway, I can't play tomorrow," Claire continued to say around the pop she was sucking on. "Which is a complete disaster since Jenny Kelleher is out injured and Saoirse Doyle is still in France with her parents. It was a really important game for Tommen." She sighed heavily, pulled the lolly out of her mouth, and handed it back to Gibsie. "Here – I'm done."

"Yeah, me, too," Gibsie muttered as he shoved the lollipop back in his mouth and jerked to his feet. "I have to go do something."

"Yeah, you do," Hughie spat. "Sort it."

"Huh?" Frowning, Claire stared after him. "Gerard, where are you going? What about your lunch?"

"I just need to ah . . . " He let his words trail off as he pointed towards the archway and then proceeded to dart out of the room.

Johnny, who was watching their interaction, shook his head in clear dismay before scrubbing his face with his hand.

"What's going on?" I whispered, turning my face into his neck. The smell of his cologne wafted into my nose and I shivered. He always smelled so good. "Where's he going?" I asked, pulling back so I could concentrate.

With a heavy sigh, Johnny dropped a hand to my thigh and squeezed. "Trust me, Shan," he said in a low tone, leaning close to my ear. "When it comes to Gibs, you're really better off not knowing."

That was the second time today that he had spoken those words, and for the second time today, I thought he might be right.

# Misunderstandings

## SHANNON

After lunch, I went to the office to speak with principal Twomey and my year head, Miss Nyhan.

True to his word, Johnny came with me. Of course, Mr. Twomey didn't want him there and tried to shoo him out of the office, but Johnny didn't budge. It was quite comical to see our 5'8, aging principal, with his balding hairline and paunchy, middle-age spread belly, *shoo* a 6'3 rugby player. What was even funnier was Johnny's WTF expression when Mr. Twomey patted on his chest. Well, I was sure he was pushing on Johnny's chest, not patting it, but he had that little of an effect on Johnny that it kind of reminded me of a blue-bottle fly buzzing around a bear.

When Mr. Twomey conceded and gestured for us both to sit down, Johnny took the seat beside me, and while he didn't hold my hand, just having him sit beside me gave me this weird form of courage.

I couldn't explain it, but I felt braver when I was with him. Or maybe I just felt safer? It was strange considering I never felt more off-balance than I did when I was with him, but it was a good type of off-balance – an excited, sick to my stomach, about to keel over at any moment but don't stop touching me because my heart's going to burst in my chest and I need to feel you everywhere or I'll explode, kind of off-balance.

I answered all of the standard, mandatory questions doled out to me by Mr. Twomey and Miss Nyhan, accepted all the *I'm so sorry this happened to you* and *don't be afraid to talk to us* small talk and then I went on my way, forcing myself to sit through my last three classes.

Surprisingly, I coped very well with the stares and hushed whispers from my classmates and the sympathetic gazes from my teachers. I guess it helped that Lizzie had melded herself to my side and was emanating some pretty serious *fuck with me and I'll cut your heart out* vibes.

When the final bell rang at 4pm, signaling the end of our school day, I was feeling warily optimistic.

Like maybe I *could* do this after all.

Like maybe I could actually get my life back on track.

"Do you want to come over to my place?" Claire asked, leaning against my desk, watching as I piled my books back into my schoolbag after our last class. Aside from Miss Moore, who was sitting at her desk, we were the last two people in the classroom, with everyone running for the hills the moment the bell sounded, including Lizzie, who had dashed off to meet Pierce, muttering something about a personal crisis. "Even for an hour?"

"I'd love to," I replied, zipping my bag closed before standing up. "But Darren's probably waiting outside for me already." Grabbing my chair, I hoisted it onto the table, and turned to face her. "I'm being monitored."

"Ugh." Claire scrunched her nose up in distaste. "Your family is beyond messed up."

"Yep." Hoisting my bag onto my back, I gave her a solemn nod. "Couldn't agree more."

"Do you want to just come anyway?" she asked as we walked out of the classroom and into the hallway. "Like ditch Darren?" Grinning mischievously, she fell into step alongside me as we headed for the main entrance. "Gerard has the car and I know he'd give us both a spin back to my house."

"What was going on with him at break?" I asked, curious. Tightening my grasp on my shoulder straps, I walked briskly to keep up. "He just ran out at lunch and never came back."

"I don't know, Shan, and sometimes I think I'm better off that way." Sighing, she added, "Something tells me that if I knew, it would be painful."

"*Claire.*" I looked at her sad expression. "Are you okay?"

She nodded and offered me a watery smile. "I'm fine."

"Why don't you just tell him how you feel?" I asked gently. "It's obvious that he feels the same way."

"He doesn't," she mumbled. "It's all about the chase for him. If I give in now, he'll get bored."

I pondered her words for a moment before saying, "He might surprise you?"

"And I might disappoint him," she mumbled.

I stopped walking. "What do you mean?"

She turned back to face me but didn't respond.

I studied her pained expression and blew out a breath. "Claire, you couldn't disappoint anyone if you tried."

"Yeah."

"I mean it," I pushed. "And least of all Gibsie. He *adores* you. It's as plain as the nose on his face that he's mad about you."

"Because he *can't* have me," she muttered. "Because I'm the one girl who hasn't given in to him."

"I don't think that's it," I replied slowly. "Not in the slightest."

"Listen, this isn't a new thing, Shan. You know that. Gerard and I have been like this since as far back as my memory goes. He's always '*wanted me*' and I've always played it down—" Her words broke off and she groaned, like talking about this physically pained her. "Because I don't believe him."

"You don't?"

"No, I don't." Her brown eyes burned with vulnerability as she spoke, "I know Gerard Gibson better than anyone on this planet – hell, I know him better than he knows himself – and trust me when I tell you that boy can't pay attention to anything for longer than a *day*. I've seen it – the way he is with girls. He'll give a girl everything for one day and then he's onto the next one. I don't even think he can help it. I know he doesn't do it on purpose." Her cheeks flushed bright pink. "But I can't be just another *day* to him – just another *girl*. I don't want to pour my heart out to him, only for him to turn right around and realize that the chase was more fun than the catch." Shrugging helplessly, she added, "I think it would break me."

"Have you talked to Lizzie about this?" I asked. "What did she say?"

"I haven't told anyone," she whispered. "Just you."

My heart cracked. "Oh my god, *Claire* . . . "

"It's fine," she hurried to say, slapping on a bright smile. "I'm fine." Breaking into a brisk walk that had me jogging to keep up, Claire yanked open the glass door of the main building and ushered me out first. "Everything is fine."

*It clearly wasn't.*

"I'll come over," I blurted out breathlessly, struggling to keep up with her long strides as she trudged through the courtyard. "If you think it'll be okay with your parents?"

"You will?" Her whole expression brightened. "Of course! My parents love you."

I nodded and continued to waddle/run. "Okay, just let me tell Darren – and slow down. I'm not a racehorse."

"Sorry," she giggled, slowing her pace to what I considered a brisk walk. "Thank you for doing this."

"No problem," I replied, swallowing back a groan at the thought of facing Darren. "Anytime."

When we reached the carpark and my eyes landed on Darren's blue Volvo, I missed my step and stumbled a little. I stumbled even further when I noticed the silver Ford Focus parked three spots up – not to mention the four boys leaning against the side of said Focus, with their heads down, deep in conversation.

Righting myself before I face-planted the gravel, I straightened my shoulders, took a deep breath, and walked over to the Volvo. The smile my brother was wearing slowly slipped when he registered that I was moving towards the driver side of the car rather than the passenger side.

"What are you doing?" Darren asked, winding down the window when I tapped on it. "Climb in – I've got to get the boys home for training."

Glancing into the back seat, I smiled at my three little brothers. "Hey, guys." Ollie and Sean smiled back at me, but Tadhg ignored me, keeping his glowering stare fixed on the back of Darren's head.

"What's going on?" Darren asked, dragging my attention back to him.

"I'm going to go to Claire's house for an hour," I said, forcing back the words *if that's okay*. He was my brother. I didn't need his permission. *I didn't*. "I'll be home later, okay?"

"Shannon, we talked about this." Darren's expression darkened. "You need to come home straight after school."

"No." I shook my head and tightened my grasp on the shoulder straps of my schoolbag. "You and Mam talked about this. I never agreed to stay inside twenty-four-seven."

"She's going to have a coronary if you don't come home," he bit out. "You know the way she gets. I can't handle her like that, so I need you to come home and *help* me."

"I don't care," I shot back, and surprisingly, I meant it. I didn't care. Not anymore. "I'm going to spend some time with my friend like a normal teenager and then I'll come home."

"We're not dealing with normal circumstances," he ground out, jaw clenched.

*Didn't I know it ...* "You can say whatever you want, but I'm still going with Claire."

He narrowed his eyes. "Get in the car."

I held my ground. "No."

"Get. In. The. Car. Shannon."

Anxiety flared to life inside of me. "No."

Unfastening his seatbelt, Darren shoved the car door open and climbed out. "Get in the fucking car." Gripping the door with white knuckles, he hissed, "Now, Shannon."

"Back off, buddy," Claire warned, coming to stand beside me. "I have a weapon—" She pointed over Darren's shoulder. "He's right over there and I'm not afraid to call him."

"I'm not going to *hurt* her," Darren shot back, looking appalled. "I just need her to get in the car and come home."

"There's no problem, Darren," Claire shot back. "Shannon's going to come over to my house. We're going to eat some junk, watch TV, and then my mom or Hughie will drop her home. No harm done."

"I'm supposed to bring you home," Darren stated, ignoring Claire. "You can go over to your friend's house some other day, when I've spoken to her parents first." Shaking his head, he placed a hand on my shoulder and steered me towards the passenger side of the car. "Just cut me some slack here and get in the car—"

"No," I choked out, digging my heels into the concrete. "I'm not going home."

"Shannon—" Exhaling a heavy sigh, Darren placed both hands on my shoulders and looked down at me. "It's not safe for you to be out."

"She doesn't want to go with you!" Claire screamed at the top of her lungs. "She said *no!*"

Stunned, I looked back at my friend, wondering why she had suddenly raised her voice. Darren hadn't hurt me – not physically, at least. But when I spotted Johnny, Gibsie, Hughie, and Feely all watching us with thunderous expressions on their faces, I quickly realized why.

She was calling for reinforcements.

*Oh god . . .*

"Don't do it," Gibsie was shouting. "Don't fucking do it, Cap—"

"Hey – what the fuck do you think you're doing?" Johnny demanded as he shoved past his friends, limp forgotten. "Get your fucking hands off her!" he roared. "*Now.*"

"I can't catch a break today." Releasing a pained groan, Gibsie tipped his head back, not bothering to try and stop the potential carnage. "Have at it, bulldozer – and don't forget your crutch."

"Don't give him *that*," Feely snapped, snatching the metal stick out of Gibsie's hand before Johnny could. "It's a weapon."

"Have you seen the size of him?" Hughie offered with a despondent sigh. "*He's* the fucking weapon."

"Jesus Christ," Darren grumbled, spinning around to look at the boys. "Stay out of it, Kavanagh."

"If you want to keep your arm, I would listen to him," Gibsie called out as he intercepted Johnny before he reached us. Slamming both hands against Johnny's chest, he tried to push him away from the car. "Because he's a little testy right now, and I'm not wholeheartedly invested in keeping you alive if he breaks free." Shrugging, he added, "Just saying . . ."

"It's okay!" Jumping into action for once in my life, I slipped under his arm and backed away. "He wasn't doing anything."

"He was *touching* you," Johnny snarled, glaring at my brother with an expression that was borderline feral. "He was trying to *put* you in the car."

"And she said no!" Claire poked the bear by adding. "A million times."

"I wasn't *hurting* her," Darren sneered. "I'm not that guy."

"He's not," I was quick to defend. "He wouldn't do that to me."

"I don't believe you, Shannon," Johnny shot back, livid. "You lied to me before." He narrowed his eyes on my brother. "And I don't believe *him*."

"Are you accusing me of abusing my sister?" Darren asked, voice deathly cold. "Because you've got it all wrong."

"Kind of like how your mother got it all wrong when she accused me of being a rapist?" Johnny shot back without missing a beat. "Difference is, I *saw* you put your hands on her, Darren." Narrowing his eyes, he spat, "So if I were you, I'd climb back into that car and get the fuck out of here before I do something we'll all regret."

Darren stared hard at Johnny for several long, palpable moments before throwing his hands up. "You know what, Shannon?" he said, laughing humorlessly. "Mam might be fucked in the head, but she's dead on the money about him being like our old man." Stalking around to the driver's side of the car, he opened his door. "But hey – you do whatever the hell you want."

With that, he climbed in and slammed the door shut. Revving the engine, Darren pulled out of the parking spot and tore off without so much as a backwards glance. I watched the three small faces staring out the back window of the car until it faded out of sight.

"Well," Gibsie said in a cheerful tone, breaking the frigid silence, "that escalated quickly."

"Yeah," I breathed.

*Understatement of the century.*

# Take My Advice, Or Not

## JOHNNY

I'd bulldozed.

I didn't need Gibsie or anyone to tell me what I already knew. Shannon was stone-cold silent the entire drive to Claire's house, keeping a full seat of space between us, letting me know in no uncertain terms that I had, indeed, fucked up. Furious with myself, I didn't say a word when I watched her walk into Claire's house, terrified of making a bad situation worse.

Even now, as I heaved my body up and down on the chin-up bar fitted in Gibsie's en suite bathroom doorway, I couldn't relax. I couldn't breathe easy, because I knew in my heart I had made things a million times worse for her. Shannon was only across the street, but it could have been a million miles away for all the good it would do me. I was so fucking mad at myself, I could taste it.

"I should go over there," I announced for the fiftieth time in the space of two hours, and for the fiftieth time, Gibsie responded with, "No, you shouldn't."

He was sprawled out on his bedroom floor with a pen and ruler in hand, surrounded by half a dozen textbooks, and frowning in deep concentration as he used that weird yellow paper that helped him to focus and make sense of his own writing.

"What's that word?" he asked, holding up his History textbook to me. "Renown?"

Locking my arms into place, I squinted at the text on the page before saying, "No, lad, that's renaissance."

"Renaissance," he repeated, churning the word around. "What a stupid fucking word."

I shrugged and continued pulling my body up, feeding off the pain in my muscles as they burned in protest.

"Can I ask you a question?"

"I already told you that I'd give you my History notes, lad," I replied. "You don't have to ask again."

"No, it's not about school," he said. "It's about rugby."

"Oh?" I frowned, interest piqued. "What about it?"

"What do you think my chances are of getting one of those Academy contracts?"

I paused mid chin-up with my arms locked tight and studied his face. "You serious, lad?" He *looked* serious. "You're not messing?"

"I'm not going to go down the college route, Johnny – I can barely handle school as it is." He shrugged. "Mam's been on my case about what I want to do after school, and I like rugby." Sighing, he added, "If I don't make a plan, I'm going to end up in the bakery with her."

"You're good at rugby," I agreed. "You know The Academy were interested in you a couple of years back."

He sighed. "Yeah, I know, and I fucked it."

"You're still only in fifth year," I reminded him. "You have another year to turn it around."

"You think I can?" he asked, grey eyes locked on mine.

"I think you have the potential to do anything you set your mind to," I told him. "You've got the talent and that's ten percent of what it takes."

"And the rest?"

"Determination, dedication, and consistency," I replied. "The 30/30/30 effect."

"I might need a hand with that," he muttered.

"What do you need from me?"

"To pull me into line," he admitted. "I think I can do it, Johnny."

"I know you can," I replied. "I've always said that."

"I know, but I didn't want it before."

"And you do now?"

"I'm wasting my life," he said. "I'm letting all the opportunities slip through my fingers."

"Yeah, well, I've been saying that for years, too."

"So, what do I need to do?"

"Quit smoking, cut back on the drink, and meet me at my house at half five tomorrow."

"That's a bit late in the evening to start—"

"Who said anything about evening?" I arched a brow. "5:30am, Gibs. The early bird catches the worm."

"Oh shit," he groaned. "You're going to kill me, aren't ya?"

I shrugged. "If you're serious, and you want it, then you'll get your ass out of that bed."

"Lock your legs," Gibsie said then, turning his attention back to his book.

"I can't," I bit out, breathing hard. "It's too sore."

"Well, if you went home and rubbed one out, you'd feel better," he shot back, not missing a beat. "And you'd be able to close your legs."

"What would you have done, Gibs?" I asked, ignoring his dig. "If you were me back there?"

"Given what you know about her family?"

"Yeah," I grunted, breathless.

"Exactly the same thing," he replied, confirming that I wasn't alone in my madness. "But I would have stemmed the threats of violence." He tossed his pen down and sat up. "That's her brother, lad."

I arched a brow and gave him a *don't bullshit me* look.

"Fair enough," he chuckled before admitting, "I would have killed him."

I nodded stiffly. "Thank you."

"But I'm not saying that's the right thing," he added, climbing to his feet.

"Do you think she's still pissed?" I asked, gaze flickering to his bedroom window. "Am I in trouble?"

"You're always in trouble," he mused. "It's like your thing."

"You know what I mean," I grumbled.

"I don't know," he replied, tone light. "I've never had a girlfriend. I have no fucking clue of what the relationship etiquette in this situation should be." Grinning, he added, "I usually solve my problems with my tongue."

"Gibs—"

"I'm serious," he added. "Mad at me? Have a lick out. Hurt your feelings? Let me eat you out." He shrugged. "It's all I know, lad."

"Is that what you did today?" I narrowed my eyes. "Used your tongue to sort Claire's shit?"

He stared blankly back at me.

I groaned. "Tell me you didn't."

"I'm not telling you anything," he shot back. "Let's just concentrate on *your* fuck ups for today."

*Fair point.*

"One day," I groaned, dropping my head. "One bleeding day and I made a hash of it."

"Yep." He laughed. "It's a new record for you."

"Fuck it—" Lowering myself back down, I rolled out my shoulders, groaning in relief when my muscles clicked and popped back into place. "I'm going over there."

"Good," he agreed. "About time."

My mouth fell open. "But you said I shouldn't—"

"Hey—" Gibsie held his hands up and grinned. "I'm the last person you should be taking advice from." Shrugging, he added, "I'm following your lead, lad."

"Jesus, we're fucked," I muttered.

"That we are, buddy. That we are," he replied, slapping my back. "But seriously, you really should know better than to take my advice to heart since I've clearly dug myself into a hole I can't get the fuck back out of."

"What's going on there, lad?" I asked, frowning. "Does Dee have something on you?"

"Nah." He shook his head. "Nothing I can't handle."

"You sure?"

"Absolutely."

A trickle of unease ran down my spine. "Gibs, if you're in trouble, you can talk to me."

"Appreciate the concern, but you're the one whose girlfriend is on the other side of the street, Johnny," he chuckled. "And besides, I have a plan."

I narrowed my eyes. "What kind of plan?"

"On how to keep my dick in my pants," he told me.

"What – and out of the school secretary?"

"Yep." He nodded. "I'm injured now. Out of action for the next six to eight weeks." He gave me two enthusiastic thumbs up. "She can't touch me anymore."

"You're injured? Where? How? What the . . . " I shook my head and gaped at him. "You're going to have to elaborate a little more for me here, lad, because if you're using a picture of my cock and pretending it's yours—" He dropped his pants and I sucked in a sharp breath. "Holy shite!" Gaping in horror, my hand automatically moved to cup my own dick. "What the fuck were you thinking?"

"I was thinking I need a way to keep my dick out of the school secretary," he shot back, holding his dick in his hand.

"When did you do this to yourself?" I demanded, outraged.

"During the Easter holidays," he replied. "I told you I was bored."

I balked. "So you went out and got your dick pierced?"

He shrugged. "It's actually kind of genius if you think about it."

"Gibs, you voluntarily allowed someone to stick a needle through your penis," I deadpanned, gaping at the piercing on the underside of his shaft. "That's not genius, lad, that's lunacy."

"It's not so bad," he said in an upbeat tone, stroking the crown of his dick. "It's almost healed, and it's looks a lot better when I'm hard—"

"Don't you dare pull on your dick in front of me!" I warned him. "What the hell is wrong with you? I don't want to see you hard!"

"You wanted to know my plan," he huffed, tucking himself back into his jocks. "So, I showed you my frenum piercing."

Shaking my head, I hissed, *Frenum?*

"Yeah." He nodded eagerly. "Like a Jacob's ladder without the ladder."

"What ... how ... " I gaped at him. "Are you planning on *adding* to it?"

"No," he replied. "Not for a while, at least."

"You're fucking insane," I choked out. "Deranged, even. And you've scarred me for life."

"I've scarred *you* for life? Yeah. *Sure*," he scoffed. "I showed you a piece of body art, lad. You showed me your gangrened ball sac."

"For the last time, I didn't have fucking gangrene," I snapped. "I had a torn adductor."

"Whatever you say, lad." Laughing, Gibsie sauntered out of his room with me trailing after him, still visually traumatized. "But those were the most discolored balls I've ever seen in my life."

"I hate you," I grumbled, hobbling down the staircase after him. "I hope you know that."

"And I love you, too," he snickered.

"Is it sore?" I asked, still grimacing at the thought.

"Nah. It's just heavier. It's taking a bit of getting used to."

"Ah, shite ... "

"Boys, have a bit of respect," Gibsie's mother ordered when we thundered into the sitting room to say goodbye to her. "The Angelus is on."

Grimacing, Gibsie and I both blessed ourselves and mumbled off the prayers imbedded inside of us since birth as the familiar church bell rang loudly on the television. Sadhbh Allen was a religious woman, and for one solid minute, there would be no talking in the Gibson household while we waited, head-bowed, for the signal of the 6:01 news to come on.

"Now," Mrs. Allen said, muting the television when the news came on. Walking towards us with her giant, white Persian cat in her arms, she smiled brightly. "How was school?"

"Fine," we both replied in unison.

"Johnny." She flashed me a warm smile. "How are you feeling since Dublin, pet?"

"I'm grand, thanks," I replied, offering a smile. I stepped forward to give Brian a rub while Gibsie lunged away from the cat. "I'm getting back on track."

"Your poor mother must have been beside herself with worry."

"Yeah." Grimacing, I gently scratched Brian under the chin. "You could say that."

"Where's Fa?" Gibsie asked, using the pet name for his stepfather, Keith Allen. He'd been in Gibsie's life since the age of eight. It was short for father – a term of endearment and sign of respect to the man who had helped raise him. A man who wasn't quite his father, but much more than just Keith. Fa was the middle line and Gibsie had called Keith that for as long as I'd known him. "I thought he'd be back by now?"

"He's still on the building site, pet. There was a delay with a delivery, but he'll be home tonight." Mrs. Allen stepped closer to Gibsie and he comically dived backwards.

"Keep that beast away from me," he strangled out, eyeing Brian warily. "I don't trust him, Mam."

"Ah, he's harmless," Mrs. Allen laughed. "You wouldn't hurt a fly, would you, Brian?"

"No, the flies are grand because his issue is with *me*," Gibsie grumbled. "Isn't it, Brian?" The cat hissed and Gibsie leapt behind me. "You're going to have to do something about his behavior," he warned his mother. "I don't feel safe in my home anymore."

"Anyways, I better get going," I announced, clearing my throat. I was fond of Gibsie's mother and always enjoyed watching Gibsie's cat tear strips out of him, but knowing Shannon was directly across the street was making me anxious. "Thanks for having me, Mrs. Allen."

"Anytime, Johnny," his mother replied, waving me off. "Don't be a stranger."

"I'm going with him, Mam," Gibsie told her as he hurried after me, narrowly avoiding a swipe of the paw from their cat. "I'll be home later."

"Of course, you are," she called after us. "Behave yourself, Bubba."

"Keep your head," Gibsie instructed when we stepped outside and he closed the door behind him. "Just *talk* to her – don't go in all guns blazing like you did earlier."

"I *will* keep my head," I grumbled.

"I mean it," he shot back. "No talking shit about her brother."

"I don't do that," I snapped, flustered. "But I swear to god, lad, if I have to look at her with one more bruise, I'm the one who's going to be in Cork prison, not her da. He'll be in a fucking graveyard with his son beside him if either of them puts their hands on her again."

# Ladder In My Tights

## SHANNON

"There's movement on the western front," Claire announced from her perch on the windowsill in her bedroom. "The front door's opening – slowly. Nope, it's closing again. Oh wait, it's opening again. Make a decision, dammit! Oh wait, I can see one teenage male – no, make that two. They're both together – no surprises there. B2 is locking the front door. He's saying something to B1 – and they're both pushing each other. Looks like they're arguing . . . oh, oh, they're walking towards his car now . . . no, no, they've changed course. They're crossing the road. Getting closer, closer, closer—"

"Claire!" I choked out, panicking.

"Shh—" she held a hand up and pointed to her bedroom door. "Just wait for it."

*Ding-dong.*

She grinned. "Looks like they've come to play with the teddies."

"*Bananas in Pajamas* references?" I laughed, unable to stop myself. "Really?"

"Hey—" She shrugged, grinning. "If the shoe fits."

"What do I do?" I asked, worrying my lip. Everything had gone to hell in the carpark at school, and Johnny hadn't spoken a single word to me the entire drive to Claire's house. When Gibsie pulled into his driveway, I had walked across the road with Claire to her house and Johnny had stayed with Gibsie. I didn't know what to do or make of it. I had no experience in dealing with this sort of thing. "Do you think he's mad?"

"No," Claire replied, rolling her eyes. "I think he thinks *you're* mad." She tilted her head to one-side, studying me carefully. "Are you mad?"

I shrugged. "I don't know what I am."

"It's okay if you are. We all sort of railroaded you with Darren earlier."

Scrunching her nose up, Claire flicked at a piece of fluff on her pajama shorts before adding, "But he put his hands on you, and that's kind of a red flag deal to us."

"Darren wouldn't hurt me," I heard myself say for the millionth time in the space of a few hours. "Not like that. He's just ... he's worried about Mam and the kids ... and my dad." *Because he's still out there.*

"Yeah, I know." Letting her feet fall from the windowsill to the floor, Claire stood up and stretched her arms over her head. Her pale curls, held back from her face with a clip, flowed down her back like vibrant, golden sunshine. She was just so beautiful, with her long legs and toned curves, that it made me feel like a little boy alongside her. "I know he wouldn't '*hurt you*' hurt you, and I'm so sorry for making a scene," she added, tone guilty. "But you have to see where we were coming from. You kept everything inside for so long, buried so many secrets about what was going on at home, that it's hard to trust you."

I flinched from her words and Claire's eyes widened. "I don't mean it in a bad way," she hurried to soothe. "I trust you one million percent with all my secrets and everything, I swear. I'm just saying that when it comes to your family, we're all a little wary."

"I get it." Shifting on her bed so that I was sitting cross-legged and facing her, I let out a defeated sigh. "It's just a mess."

"With Darren?" she asked, eyes warm and laced with sympathy. "Or in general?"

"All of the above," I admitted. "I don't think Darren's coping with being back home." Guilt churned inside of me. "You saw just how well Joey's 'coping' with life, Tadhg has morphed into a walking hormone, Sean can barely string a word together – and he's wetting the bed every night. Mam is being ... well, she's just the definition of a mess, and Dad is ... " Cringing, I added, "The only one that seems to be coping is Ollie, and he's *nine*."

"Sorry, Shan." She gave me a sympathetic look. "That sucks."

"Yeah," I sighed. "And I know I should make an effort with Darren, but it's so *hard*. He just ... he was gone, you know? For *years*. I didn't even know where he was, and now, all of a sudden, he's back, and in charge, and falling into line with her—" My voice broke off and I gnawed anxiously on my fingernails. "I don't know how to process it all. So much has happened and I feel like . . . "

"You feel like what, Shan?"

"Like I'm being smothered," I offered quietly.

"By me?" she asked.

"No." I shook my head. "Never you."

"I'm always here for you." Hurrying over to where I was sitting on her bed, Claire flung herself down on me, knocking me onto my back. "You're my best friend," she whispered, hugging me tightly. "And I know I'm not supposed to squeeze you, but I can't help it because—" Her voice cracked and she dropped her face to rest against my shoulder before whispering, "Because when I got that call from Gerard and found out what happened to you, I was so afraid that I would never see you again." Sniffling, she clutched me tighter. "I felt so responsible."

"I'm still here," I croaked out, holding her tightly, drowning in the smell of her strawberry shampoo as her hair splayed over my face. "And you were never responsible."

"Wasn't I?" she muttered. "I knew something was happening to you and I did nothing about it."

"You were exactly the kind of friend I needed," I told her. "I wouldn't have gotten through any of it without you, so don't ever feel bad for being what I needed."

"I'm always going to feel bad, Shan," she replied. "I don't think that's going to go away in a hurry."

"God, you need a haircut," I spluttered, spitting out a mouthful of blonde curls.

"Huh?"

"Your hair, Claire," I strangled out, batting at my mouth as a mountain of curls swamped me. "It's in my mouth." I pushed at her shoulders. "You're turning into Rapunzel."

"Says the girl with hair down to her arse," she giggled, climbing off me. "My hair's thick and there's a lot of it—" She paused to pull me up, "But you're the one with the length."

"Because it's the only thing about me that *grows*," I joked, settling down to sit cross-legged, facing her. Reaching behind my head, I pulled out my hair tie and tossed my brown hair over my left shoulder. "It's all I have," I added as I began to braid my hair into submission. "So don't judge—"

"I have something that grows," a familiar male voice piped up. "It's growing right now."

"You're supposed to knock, remember?" Claire said, glancing over her shoulder at Gibsie who was standing in her bedroom. "You know the rules."

Hovering in the doorway behind him was Johnny, shifting from foot to foot, looking incredibly uncomfortable.

His gaze locked on mine and he offered me a small smile.

I smiled back.

Relief flooded his features and he blew out a breath.

"I know you're talking right now, babe," Gibsie said, drawing my attention back to him. "And I'm trying really hard to pay attention, but it's kind of impossible when all I'm seeing is you and another girl on your bed, braiding hair, with your sexy ass hanging out of those shorts." Grinning, he added, "Quick, do something else."

"Something like this," Claire replied sweetly, before grabbing a pillow and flinging it at him.

"Fucking perfect," Gibsie choked out, catching the pillow mid-air. "Add in pillow fights and it's like free porn."

"You're a perv."

"A perv who sorted that hockey thing for you."

"You did?" Claire's eyes widened. "How?"

Gibsie shrugged. "I have my ways." Titling his head to one side, he studied her back and asked, "Holy shit – are you wearing a thong?"

"Gerard," Claire sighed.

"Is it red?" He squinted his eyes and then groaned. "It's fucking red, isn't it?"

Rolling her eyes, Claire climbed off the bed and padded over to where he was standing. "You're an idiot," she chided, slapping his arm. "Come on, you can help me clean the kitchen before Mam gets home from work. It'll give these two some time to talk." Smiling brightly at Johnny, she added, "Come on in, Johnny."

"Uh, yeah." Shoving his hands into his pockets, Johnny stepped into her room. "Thanks."

"I'll come anywhere you want if you just show me that thong," Gibsie pleaded, dropping his hands to her waist. "I'll clean all the pots. I'll do anything. Just one peek. That's all I'm asking."

"You'll come anyway," she huffed, catching ahold of his school tie and dragging him out of her room.

"You've got that right," he agreed, trailing after her like a puppy dog on a lead. "Is your bra red, too?"

"I'm not wearing one."

"Oh, Jesus."

Gibsie pulled the door closed, leaving me and Johnny alone in Claire's bubblegum-pink bedroom.

"There's ah . . . that's a lot of pink." Shifting awkwardly, he dragged one hand out of his pocket and waved his hand around aimlessly. "Never seen so many teddy bears and dolls in my life."

"She doesn't play with them anymore," I explained, stifling a laugh at the sight of his confused expression. "She just collects them." Feeling at a loss, I grabbed the huge, white polar bear from the top of her bed and held it out to him. "Gibsie bought this one for her thirteenth birthday and demanded she name it after him," I said. "She compromised and called it Gerry."

"I remember." Johnny sighed and ran a hand through his hair. "Bleeding thing cost him eighty quid. He was cutting grass for the entire summer to pay for it."

My eyes widened. "Eighty euro for a teddy bear?"

Johnny shrugged. "That's the one she wanted."

"Oh," I whispered, not knowing what else to say.

"Are we okay?" he asked then, remaining exactly where he was. "You and me?"

I nodded. "I think so."

Johnny blew out a harsh breath and moved towards me. "I know I fucked up, okay?" he blurted, not stopping until he was sitting on the edge of Claire's bed, eyes locked on mine. "I overreacted. But I just saw him with his hands on you and I *panicked*." He shook his head and reached for my hand. "I fucking saw red, Shan. I couldn't think clearly and jumped to conclusions."

"I get it," I whispered, shifting closer to him. "I'm not mad at you."

"But I've just made things worse for you." He groaned, pulling my hand onto his lap, and looked at me, expression forlorn. "I fucked it, baby."

*Baby?*

*Oh god.*

"And now you're going to have to go home and deal with more of their shite," he continued to say, sounding pained. "All because I couldn't get a handle of myself—"

"Johnny?" I squeezed out, heart skittering around wildly.

He exhaled a sigh and looked at me with a wary expression like he was trying to gauge my emotions. "Yeah, Shan?"

"I love you." I had no idea why I felt the need to tell him that, but the words seemed to clamber up my throat every time I laid eyes on him.

The blue in his eyes blazed with heat. "I love you, too."

"Yeah?"

"Yeah."

I don't know who moved first after that . . . there was a blur of flailing limbs, but when I lunged for Johnny, he was already halfway down on me. Our lips crashed together at the same time I collapsed onto my back, with his big body landing heavily on top of me.

Frazzled, I tightened my hold on his neck and let my legs fall apart, causing him to settle between them roughly.

The contact caused us both to moan loudly.

Knotting my fingers in his hair, I wrapped my legs around his waist and kissed him back with a need that bordered on insanity. Squeezing my thighs, I rocked my hips upward and pulled down hard on his hair, wanting nothing more than to immerse myself in this boy. Plunging my tongue into his mouth, I kissed him hard, unable to get close enough. Johnny rewarded the move with a deep, rumbling growl of approval. The sound was so *sexy*.

I could feel him, hard as steel between my legs, rubbing and grinding against my most private of areas and I moaned, shifting closer, wanting more than anything for him to just press *harder*.

"Christ." His hands roamed all over my body. "You feel so good." His hand slipped under the hem of my shirt, fingers grazing my side. "Taste so fucking perfect."

His hands were everywhere; on my legs, on my hips, in my hair. He touched me everywhere *except* where I needed him to and that only seemed to make me more frantic – more desperate for *him*.

I was behaving like a deranged maniac but I just couldn't contain myself a second longer. I could feel the aching want I had for him deep in my bones, driving me on, encouraging me to push for more. Heat pooled inside of me; a deep, unsettling, throbbing ache.

His tongue and fingers only seemed to intensify that throbbing sensation until I was literally *pulsing* down there. My heart was beating at a hundred miles an hour, the passion and driving need making my movements reckless and clumsy, as my body instinctively chased after an unfamiliar feeling that only his body could provide.

I was a virgin, but that didn't mean I was clueless about sex. I read enough books, watched enough movies, and listened to enough stories to know all about the male body and orgasms. And even though I'd never felt one before, I was well aware that the tingling jolts of pleasure rippling through me every time Johnny thrust his hips against me, were a small promise of pleasure.

*Oh my god, I might come*, the sudden thought sparked to life inside of my mind, causing me to moan into his mouth and buck my hips in encouragement, *I think he's going to make me come*.

Reveling in the feeling of being pinned beneath him, and clouded by lust, I slipped a hand between our bodies and touched the front of his school trousers, shivering when my hand came into contact with his erection.

"Don't, baby," Johnny groaned into my mouth, pulling my hand away and pinning it above my head. "Or I'll lose it."

"Are you sore?" I breathed, panting against his lips. "Does it hurt?"

"You're killing me, Shan," Johnny groaned and buried his face in my neck. "Fuck, baby." Nipping and suckling my flesh, he kissed a trail from my collarbone to my lips before thrusting his tongue into my mouth once more.

I couldn't take it.

I honestly couldn't.

Desperate for more, I slid my hands under his school shirt and clawed at the taut, rippling skin beneath. My fingers on his stomach did something to Johnny, because he pressed me deeper into the mattress, moving harder against me. The hand he was using to pin mine traveled to my leg.

Cupping the fleshy part of my thigh, he hitched my leg up higher and rocked his hips into me. His fingers dug into my skin so hard that I felt my tights rip, but I didn't care. He could rip them to shreds and I wouldn't stop him. Moving higher, I felt his fingertips trace the edge of my knickers. He hesitated and I felt like crying. Frustrated, I hooked my fingers into his waistband and tugged hard. That was all the encouragement he needed; his hand slipped behind me to palm my ass, squeezing and pulling me closer to him as he continued to rub against me.

Somewhere in the back of my mind, I knew it was entirely inappropriate to be rolling around on my best friend's bed with my boyfriend, but my brain could only hone in on the word *boyfriend*. Everything else was inconsequential in this moment because Johnny was my boyfriend, and my boyfriend had me on my back, making my body shake and tremble. It was the only male touch I'd ever welcomed. He was big and masculine and was using all of his strength to make me feel *good*.

In this moment, I didn't care about my family or my bullies, I didn't fear the unknown and I wasn't worrying; all I could think about was the desperate need I had inside to just *link* with him in every way possible.

The sound of foil crackling broke through my lust-filled thoughts and I jerked when something sharp stabbed my thigh. "What's that?" I asked, sounding breathless as I tore my lips from his. I rolled my hips and felt the sting again. "Ouch."

"Are you okay?" Concern flickered in Johnny's eyes, drowning out the desire, and he quickly pulled back to kneel between my legs. "Shit, did I hurt you?"

"No, it wasn't you—" Patting the mattress, my hand stumbled on several sharp-edged packets. "It was this," I breathed, raising one of the little square packets up for inspection. My body flooded with heat when I registered what I was holding. "Uh, this must have fallen out of your pocket," I mumbled, glancing down at the pile of condoms on either side of my waist. "*They* must have fallen out of your pocket," I corrected, counting sixteen condoms – seventeen including the one I was holding.

Johnny stared down at the condom in my hand, blinked several times, and then shot off the bed faster than I'd ever seen him move on a pitch. "Jesus Christ," he strangled out, running a hand through his hair. "It's not what it looks like, I swear." Muttering a string of curse words, he began to pace the floor. "Fucking Gibsie," he bit out, jaw clenched. "He's going to ruin my life."

"Gibsie?"

"They're his," Johnny choked out. "Not mine."

"Oh." Pulling myself up on my elbows, I watched him stalk around the room like a madman. "Okay."

"I'm just holding onto them for him," he hurried to add, still pacing. "I did *not* bring those over here for any other reason than I forgot they were in my pockets."

"It's fine."

"For fuck's sake," he groaned, stopping to cup the back of his head. "I wouldn't . . . I mean I'm not . . . I didn't expect to have sex with you."

"You didn't?"

"*What*?" He gaped at me. "No, Shannon, of course I didn't."

"Oh." I glanced down at the condoms before looking back at him. "Why?"

"Because I—" His mouth fell open and it took him a few moments to recover. "Wait – *what*?"

"Uh, nothing," I mumbled, embarrassed. "It doesn't matter."

"You want to have sex?" he pressed, watching me warily. "Is that what you're saying?"

"I don't know." Nervous, I stood on the other side of the bed, with my back to the window, watching him back with equal wariness. "I mean, I'll do it if you want to?"

"Is that a trick – what the – are you – fuck!" Holding a hand up, Johnny placed his other hand on the top of his head and took several deep, steadying breaths. He looked like he was about to explode as he rolled his lips between his teeth and eyeballed me. "Just give me a minute."

I nodded. "Okay."

"I'm not having sex with you," he finally said when words found him again. His voice was torn, his expression pained. "We're not having sex, Shannon," he reiterated, voice strained. "It's not happening."

*Oh god.*

"I'm sorry." Flustered and mortified beyond belief, I quickly pushed my skirt back down. "It was a stupid . . . I don't even know what I was thinking – I mean, of course you don't want to – ugh, just forget it—"

"I *want* to," he quickly corrected. "Believe me, I want to. I promise. But I just *can't*."

"Oh." My gaze flicked to the tent he was pitching in his grey school trousers. "Because you're still sore?"

"No, baby," he choked out, throwing a hand up. "Because you're not ready."

"But I said I'd do it if you wanted to," I whispered.

"*Exactly*," Johnny groaned loudly. "You said if *I* wanted to – not because *you* wanted to." Shaking his head, he walked over to the bed and sank down. "It's way too soon."

"But when you were with Bella you were having—" I snapped my mouth shut and hovered by the window, watching him. "Never mind."

"Jesus," Johnny muttered, dropping his head in his hands. "Is that what you think I want?" When I didn't respond, he straightened up and looked at me. "Come here." He patted the mattress beside him. "Come sit with me for a bit."

I watched him carefully for a moment before letting my shoulders sag in defeat and walking over to sit down.

"Talk to me," he said quietly. "Tell me what's going on inside that head of yours."

"I just . . ." I stopped short and tensed up, unable to get the words out.

"You just what, Shannon?"

"Nothing."

"*Talk* to me."

"I just want you to want *me* in all the ways you wanted *her*," I blurted out and then flamed in embarrassment.

"No." Johnny shook his head. "You don't want that."

"But I really do," I admitted glumly.

"So, you just want me to *want* to fuck you?" he demanded, tone heated. "You want me to *only* want sex from you? To fuck you and spend the entire time wondering how fast I can get away from you?" He stared hard at me, daring me to tell him yes. "Or wonder how long is socially acceptable to stick around after pulling out of you? Five minutes? Half an hour? Do I have to kiss and cuddle you or can I leave and wash the smell of you off my body? Because that's how it was with her." He ran a hand through his hair and growled. "There were no feelings involved. It was sex and nothing else."

"No, I don't want that," I admitted quietly. "I just want to be what you *want*."

"You *are*," he urged, tone heated. "I don't want what I had with Bella. I want what I have with *you*."

"You promise?"

"I fucking promise, Shannon!" Leaning forward, Johnny rested his elbows on his thighs and exhaled heavily. "Listen to me; Bella was a mistake." He grimaced as he spoke her name. "I think I knew she was a mistake even when I was fucking – uh, making the mistake," he quickly amended, casting a guilty look in my direction. "I was disconnected and I wanted to *feel* something for a little while." He sighed again. "I could see my friends and the lads on the team with girlfriends and all that shite. Like Hughie and Katie? Christ, even Gibs and Claire. And I don't know, Shan, they all seemed so carefree, so fucking reckless about it, that I was jealous." He looked at me when he said, "It gets lonely when you're traveling on one path and all of your friends are on another path together, and I guess I just craved some sort of connection with something or someone other than rugby. But it never happened for me." Straightening back up, he rested a hand on the mattress and turned to face me. "I just *couldn't*, you know? I've never been able to connect with anyone like that." He shrugged helplessly, eyes locked on mine. "Until one day, I looked up from my life and there you were. All blue eyes and full of secrets." He cleared his throat several times before saying, "And I've never felt more connected."

"Johnny . . ."

"No, hear me out, Shan," he hurried to say, resting a hand on mine. "I can only tell you what I know," he added, tone hoarse, eyes heated. "And that's from the very first day you walked into my life, you *changed* me. That very first time I saw you? You sparked to life something inside of me." Releasing a heavy sigh, he shrugged, eyes locked on mine. "And I haven't been the same since."

My heart galloped wildly in my chest. "Really?"

He nodded slowly as a small smile crept across his face. "Boom."

I blew out a shaky breath. "Boom."

"So, to answer all those fucked-up thoughts in your pretty head, I *don't* want Bella or anything even remotely like what I had with her," he continued. "I want what *we* have together. I want our friendship. I want your company. I want our conversations. I just want *time* with you. And I'm not in any rush. I don't want you to feel like you don't know where this is going, or when I'm kissing you that I'm looking for more than you're ready to give. I won't do that to you. I won't take what you can't give, and I *won't* push, okay?" He ran a hand through his hair and sighed. "Sex isn't even important. It's just one fucking part of it – a part that can wait for as long you want."

He was right.

Oh god, he was totally right.

Mortification swamped me.

"I don't think I'm ready, Johnny," I whispered, cheeks flaming.

"I know," he replied, smirking. "And that's *okay*."

There wasn't an ounce of hesitation in his voice, and I clung to his certainty. "Okay," I croaked out, shifting closer.

"You make me happy," he whispered. "I want to stick with that. I want to stick with *you*."

"Johnny . . . " my voice trailed off as I contemplated the importance of what he'd just said. "You make me happy, too."

"And I think I owe you another pair of tights." He poked at the huge ladder in my tights and shrugged sheepishly. "Sorry."

I smiled. "It doesn't matter."

Smiling, he lifted his arm and I slid into the space. "I like where we are, Shan." His words curled around my heart like a comfort blanket. "We'll get there when we get there," he added after a contented pause of silence. "I'm not in any hurry." I felt his lips brush the top of my head. "Not with you."

# Thank You, Jesus

## JOHNNY

I was a saint.

No joke.

I was fairly sure I deserved a medal for the self-restraint I displayed in Claire's bedroom earlier. I doubted there was another lad my age with feelings for a girl like the ones I had for Shannon – for a girl who *looked* like Shannon – that could have stopped that from progressing.

Hours later and I was still coming to terms with the best and worst thing I had ever done. Because I wanted inside that girl more than my next breath and having her dangle her virginity in front of my nose like a fucking Grand Slam medal was the worst kind of temptation. But I did the *right* thing, dammit. I stopped it. I put what *she* needed before what *I* wanted, and that knowledge put me somewhat at peace. So afterwards, when I had smoothed things over and we went downstairs, I drank hot chocolate with her friend, I made the small talk, I provided the reassurance I knew she needed from me, and I reined in Gibsie as best as I could, and I did all this with the worst case of blue balls known to man.

When Sinead Biggs came in from work a little after nine and gave me and Gibs our marching orders, I could have wept with joy. As messed up as it sounded, I was *relieved* the woman had showed up and kicked us out, because I needed a timeout.

I needed to go home, and fast, because I couldn't *take it* anymore.

It had been over five fucking months, and pain or not, I was going to come.

*Even if it killed me, dammit.*

I could hardly speak a word the entire drive back to my house. The anticipation was killing me and I was racked with nerves. Fear, excitement, and lust were the dominant emotions rushing through my body, driven forward by the memory of Shannon on her back, with me between her legs.

Thankfully, Gibsie was brooding silently in the driver's seat and didn't turn off the engine when he pulled up outside my house. Instead, he offered a half-hearted, "I'll pick you up in the morning, lad," before returning to staring out the windscreen.

I had no clue what was wrong with him – I presumed he was sulking over being thrown out by Claire's mother – but right now I couldn't worry about it because I was going to fuck myself, dammit, and his problems weren't my top priority.

When I stepped inside my house, I had a feeling Jesus Christ himself was looking down on me because my mother was on a work call, barking orders into a headset while she paced the kitchen floor with a folder in her hand. I swear to God, I could have dropped to my knees and broke out in prayer at the sight. When she tried to make eye contact with me, I quickly hurried upstairs, using the crutch more for her sake than mine.

Temporarily evicting Sookie from my room, I swung the door shut and started ripping off my clothes. Why I felt the need to strip down bollocks naked, I would never understand, but I was burning the hell up and needed the reprieve.

Feeling a fucked-up concoction of excitement and fear rush through my body, I sat, still as a statue on the edge of my bed, and stared down at my fully erect dick.

*Here it goes . . .*

With my entire body coiled tight with tension, I dropped a hand and held my breath, waiting for the pain I was so damn used to feeling – the one I associated with my dick.

*One stroke . . .*

*Two strokes . . .*

*Three tentative strokes . . .*

When the pain didn't come, I released the breath I'd been holding in, flopped onto my back, and stared up at the ceiling. "Thank you, Jesus."

Closing my eyes, I drummed up every depraved image I had of Shannon and went to town on myself.

# Flashing Lights and New Information

## SHANNON

My body was coiled tight with tension the entire drive back to my house. The familiar feeling of dread had resumed its post of strangling the good out of my day. All thoughts of Johnny had retreated back into the box in my mind inside which I kept him safe, as I numbed out all emotions and switched into survival mode. It was like locking sunshine in an old, cobwebbed chest, not trusting the darkness around me not to taint it.

Like a sixth sense buried deep down inside of me, I knew there was trouble before I saw it. I could feel my body temperature dipping to the point of arctic, with my blood turning to ice in my veins. Every muscle in my body locked tight with fearful anticipation.

I wasn't naïve enough to try and assure myself that everything was fine this time. The sight of my house lit up like a Christmas tree, with every window flooding yellow orbs of light, and the line of cars parked next to the usually deserted footpath outside, not to mention the blue and yellow Garda car, was sign enough that my silent affirmations would indeed be fruitless ones.

"Shannon, pet," Mrs. Biggs said in a concerned tone when she pulled up outside of my house. "Is everything okay?"

"It's probably fine," I croaked out, quickly unfastening my seatbelt, as the jagged claws of panic tore at my gut. "Thanks for the spin, Mrs. Biggs," I added, reaching for the door handle.

"Wait – would you like me to come with you?" Claire's mother asked, tone laced with tenderness, as she placed a hand on my shoulder. "I can park up, honey, and walk you in—"

"No, no, it's fine," I mumbled, shoving the passenger door open, and thanking my lucky stars that Claire had stayed at her house rather than come for the drive. "But I better go inside now."

Mrs. Biggs, who looked so much like Claire, worried her lip for a long moment, clearly anxious.

*Not as much as I am ...*

"Will you call Claire later on?" she finally asked, eyeing me with wariness. "Just to check in?"

I nodded, offered her a small smile, and then hurried out.

*Deep breaths,* I chanted to myself the entire walk from the footpath to my front door. *Whatever's happened, you can handle it.*

*Just keep breathing, Shannon.*

When I reached the front door, a horrible wave of déjà vu wafted through me, and for a moment, I just stood there, my fingers curled around the door handle, and my entire body was out of control.

*He's in there,* my brain hissed, *Run away, Shannon. Get away now!*

My choices were taken away from me when the door swung inwards and my eyes landed on Joey. I drank in the sight of his blood-free face for a moment before a huge shudder racked through me.

"Shh," he whispered when I opened my mouth to speak. Instead of ushering me inside, Joey stepped out and pulled the door shut behind him. "I need to talk to you."

"What's going on, Joe?" I strangled out, panicking.

"It's okay." Catching ahold of my arm, he gently tugged me into the side garden and out of view of the windows and doors. "But we need to talk."

"Talk?" I frowned up at him. "About what?" Flustered, I waved a hand towards the cars parked outside the house. "What's going on? Why are the Guards here, Joe? Why is Patricia's car here?"

"Come here—" Dragging me through the overgrown grass, we slipped into the small gap of space between the garden shed and wall, to the old den we had spent many a night hiding out in. It was nothing to look at; just a few feet of trodden down grass at the back of the shed, secured by the unused oil tank, but the gap to get back here was too narrow for our father to squeeze through. We used to keep blankets, torches, and a small tin of biscuits out here when we were little, but it had been a long time since either of us had come back here. "He handed himself in, Shan." Joey glanced behind us and blew out a shaky breath. "The Guards have him."

"Dad?" I squeezed out, though I wasn't sure if I spoke the word or mouthed it. My heart was racing at a hundred miles an hour, forcing the air from my lungs in a breathy rush. "Are you serious?"

Joey nodded and I felt my body grow weak.

Weaker, and weaker, and weaker, until I was moving towards the ground in slow motion.

"I've got you." Joey's arms came around me. "It's okay." Lowering us both onto the wet grass, he crouched down beside me with his hands on my shoulders. "Shh, you're safe."

Motionless, I leaned against the concrete wall at my back, feeling the damp seep through my school skirt, but unable to move a muscle, as my brain switched into overdrive.

*They had him?*

*He handed himself in?*

*My father?*

"I'm going to be sick—" the words were barely out of my mouth before I twisted sideways and heaved the contents of my stomach onto the grass.

"Good girl." Grabbing a fistful of my hair, Joey pulled it back from my face and patted my back. "Get it out. You'll feel better."

No, I wouldn't.

I was never going to feel better again because this was all *wrong*.

Stomach heaving, I wretched and gawked until I was empty, with nothing left inside of me to give.

"Why?" I croaked out when words finally found me. Chest heaving, I wiped my mouth with the back of my hand and sagged in defeat. "Handed himself in?" I shook my head, rejecting the notion. No, he had to have this all wrong. "He wouldn't do that, Joe." Our father would *never* voluntarily hand himself in for anything. "This isn't real."

"I know," Joey agreed, speaking in a low, hushed tone. "I don't believe it, either." He ran a hand through his hair in frustration. "Something's wrong."

"What else do you know?"

"Nothing," he replied. "I literally just walked in the door from work before you and found them all in the kitchen." He gestured to the greasy overalls he was wearing and shrugged helplessly. "The Guards, Patricia, and a couple of other women I have never seen before all in there with Mam and Darren."

"What are they saying?"

"I don't know, Shan." He shook his head and added, "They wouldn't let me stay – they fucking kicked me out of the kitchen, but I heard one of the Guards say that Dad handed himself in before they shut the door in my face. Then I heard the car pull up, so I came straight out to give you the heads up."

My stomach twisted up in knots. "Well, thanks for the heads up."

"I don't understand what's happening here," he said, ignoring my thank you. "He has to have been to a solicitor or something. Gotten some advice . . . " He let out an aggravated growl. "It makes *no* sense for him to just walk into the station and turn himself in."

"Maybe he felt guilty?" I offered weakly, knowing it was a stupid notion.

"You need to possess a conscience to feel guilt," Joey shot back. "He lacks one of those."

Very true.

"It's bullshit," a familiar voice said, causing both of us to turn as a shadowy figure approached in the darkness. "They're in there, talking about our lives, making decisions for *us*, and we're not allowed to hear it."

"Tadhg," I strangled out, pressing a hand to my heart when he popped out from the small gap, his face illuminated by the street light across the road from our house.

"Where are Ollie and Sean?" was Joey's only question.

"Bed – they're both asleep," Tadhg replied before walking over to where we were crouched and taking a seat on the grass beside us. Resting his back against the wall alongside me, he hooked his arms around his knees and muttered, "But Sean pissed the bed again."

Joey sighed wearily. "I better go—"

"I sorted it," Tadhg cut in. "It's done."

My heart broke.

*Babies taking care of babies.*

"And Ollie's having more nightmares. He keeps waking up crying, saying that he's going to come back in the middle of the night and get us," Tadhg added, tone hard. "I can't get a fucking wink of sleep with the cry-baby."

"Tadhg," I said wearily. "Please don't curse."

"Why?" he snapped, glaring at me. "What are you going to do about it?"

"Because you're eleven and too young to be cursing," I replied sadly. "And I'm not going to do anything about it. It just shouldn't be happening."

"Fuck you, Shannon," he sneered. "I'll be twelve on Friday, and there's a lot of things in my life that shouldn't be *happening.*"

"Pack it in," Joey commanded in an authoritative tone, locking eyes on our little brother. "You want to be pissed with Mam and Dad – with the whole damn world? Then go right ahead. Feel it. It's real and it's justified. You *should* be raging. It's *not* fair. But don't even think about taking it out on her, me, or those two kids upstairs, because we didn't do shit to you, kid. We didn't do a damn thing to deserve this life, the same as you, so remember that before you come out here, aiming your pain at us."

Tadhg stared hard at Joey for a long moment before shuddering violently. "I don't want him to come back," he finally said, voice cracking. Springing onto his knees, he lunged at Joey. "I don't want this," he cried, wrapping his arms around Joey's neck. "I want it to be gone. I just want it to be over!"

"I know, kid," Joey choked out, holding him tightly. "I know."

"And you left me," he sobbed, crying harder. "You can't leave me. I need you to *stay* with me."

"I'm here," Joey whispered, shuddering now, eyes full of anguish and locked on mine. "I'm right here."

"And so am I," I strangled out, wrapping my arms around my brothers. "We're a team, guys," I added, pouring as much enthusiasm as I could into my voice for my little brother's benefit. "We'll get through this."

"Exactly," Joey agreed, voice strained. "We're going to make it."

"Together?" Tadhg sniffled.

I locked eyes on Joey and mouthed, "*Together?*"

"Sure, kid." Joey clenched his eyes shut. "Together."

We sat there like that, on the soaked grass with rain drizzling down on us, until the sound of loud voices disturbed the silence.

"Thanks for coming to speak to us," Darren's muffled voice filled my ears and all three of us stiffened in unison. "I appreciate the update."

Tadhg moved to stand up, but Joey and I both grabbed his pajama top and dragged him back down.

"Don't move," Joey instructed quietly.

Tadhg frowned. "But they're—"

"Just *listen*," Joey urged.

*He had a lot to learn yet.*

"No problem, Mr. Lynch," a male voice that I presumed belonged to one of the Gardas replied. "I'm just sorry it wasn't the news you were hoping for."

My heart sank.

Actually, no, it didn't sink.

It remained exactly where it was; in the pit of my stomach.

Because, just like Joey and Tadhg, I knew that nothing good was happening.

When it came to our father, nothing *good* ever happened.

"Your mother should find some comfort in the fact that he's accepting his responsibilities," the Garda continued to say. "At least it's progress."

"Not quite the progress I expected," Darren replied, tone a little harder than normal. "Or my sister and brothers, for that matter."

"Yes, well, it's out of our hands," a female voice interjected in a neutral

320 • KEEPING 13

tone. "The law is the law, and unfortunately, we don't get to make it. We're only here to uphold it."

"The law is a fucking joke," both Joey and Tadhg muttered at the exact same time.

"Jinx," Tadhg whispered with a small smile tugging his lips.

Joey rolled his eyes and locked an arm around Tadhg. Dragging him onto his lap, he rubbed his knuckles against Tadhg's head. "There – touched wood."

"Shh," I warned them and strained to hear more.

"Look, we won't take up anymore of your time," the male Garda said. "Goodnight, Mr. Lynch."

"Yeah, goodnight," Darren replied. "Thank you."

The sound of an engine roared to life a few moments later and then slowly faded away in the distance.

"I'm going inside—" Tadhg began to say, standing up again, only to be pulled back down by our brother once more. "I want answers, guys!"

"Just stay put," Joey instructed calmly. "They're not done."

Huffing out a breath, Tadhg crossed his arms over his chest and pouted.

Joey shook his head. "You've got a lot to learn, kid."

We waited until Patricia and the other women emerged from the house, got into their cars and drove away, before Joey stood up. "Okay," he announced, inclining his head toward the house. "*Now* we go get answers."

Tadhg steamrolled ahead of us, making it into the kitchen before Joey and I had our feet through the front door, screeching, "What the hell is going on?"

"Listen, let me handle it," Joey said in a low tone, giving my shoulder a small squeeze before walking into the kitchen ahead of me.

Standing in the doorway, my eyes went straight to my mother, who was sitting at her usual perch at the table, with an ashtray in front of her and a cigarette balancing between her frail fingers. *No surprises there.* She had her standard cup of coffee set in front of her – the one doused in vodka or whatever choice of liquid medicine for the night. She was weeping quietly into one hand while she sucked on her cigarettes. *Again, no surprises.*

There was a small stack of white envelopes on the table beside her. One of the envelopes had been opened and the piece of paper lay on the table beside the ashtray.

"What's going on?" Tadhg was demanding as he stood in the middle of the kitchen, glaring at our oldest brother and completely ignoring our mother. "I want to know!"

"Be quiet, Tadhg," Darren snapped. "I'm trying to think—" He paced the floor, clenching a white envelope tightly in his fist. "I can't think!"

"Tell me what's happening and you can go back to thinking," Tadhg spat, not missing a beat.

Hovering in the doorway, I watched Joey stroll straight past Darren without a word and snatch the piece of paper off the table.

My heart felt like it had stopped in my chest as I watched him read, brows furrowing deeper and deeper, until he clenched his eyes shut altogether. Rigid, he balled the piece of paper up and flung it at the wall. "Fuck!"

"That's not helping," Darren admonished quietly.

"No, you know what's not helping?" Joey shot back. "You, Darren. You're not fucking helping!"

"Do you think I want this?" Darren hissed, glowering at Joey. "You're fucking crazy if you think I wanted *this.*"

"Oh god." Mam sobbed loudly. "I can't take this."

"Just shut up with the crying!" Tadhg barked, pulling on his hair in frustration. "We're all sick to death of listening to you whining!"

"Cop on, Tadhg," Darren barked. "Don't speak to her like that."

"Don't tell him what to do," Joey was quick to jump in and defend. "The kid's right. We're all sick of listening to her, you included. He's just got the balls to say it."

"What's going on?" I asked, remaining exactly where I was, with the front door to my back and the option to bolt available if necessary.

"Tell them what's going on, Darren," Joey sneered menacingly. "Go ahead and tell Shan and Tadhg the good news. Or better yet—" Pausing, Joey stalked over to the table and grabbed the stack of envelopes. Sifting through them, he tossed two back down on the table before stalking towards us. "Let them read it." Thrusting an envelope into Tadhg's hands, Joey walked over and handed me the one with *Shannon* scrawled on the front, before shoving the last envelope he was holding into the pocket of his blue overalls. "Makes for a good read, lads," he added, tone laced with sarcasm. "Best fucking fiction I've ever read, isn't that right, Mam?"

I didn't dare open the letter in my hands, not when my brain had recognized the messy scrawl as my father's handwriting.

"He wrote us all our very own letter," Joey sneered, tone dripping with venom and sarcasm. "Lucky us."

Darren shook his head. "Joey . . ."

"Is he dead?" I strangled out, heart thudding violently. "Is that it?" I held the letter up. "Did he k—" my breath hitched in my throat and I had to force out the rest of it, "Kill himself?"

"No such luck," Joey hissed. "He's as fresh as a daisy, living it up in Brickley House."

"Brickley House?"

"It's a treatment center on the other side of the city," Darren explained. "Dad signed himself in two weeks ago, Shannon. The day after you went into the hospital. That's where he's been – why nobody could find him."

I closed my eyes for a moment, trying to wrangle in my emotions and digest what I was hearing, but when I spoke again, all I could come out with was, "*What*?"

"What does that mean?" Tadhg choked out, paling. When no one responded, he screamed, "What's happening?"

"It means he's a clever son of a bitch with friends in high places and access to some slick legal advice," Joey sneered, planting his hands on his hips. "It means he won't see a day behind bars – like I predicted. Like I told you fucking all!"

"No," Darren quickly jumped in. "He'll still have to go to court."

"Why isn't he in prison *now*?" I strangled out, feeling my body shake from head to toe. Swinging my gaze to Darren, I whispered, "That's what you said, Darren. You told me as soon as they found Dad, he would be arrested." A harsh sob tore from my throat and I instinctively clutched my side, remembering all too well what had happened in this kitchen the last time our father had been here. My body seized up with panic. "That's what you said," I strangled out, feeling close to collapsing. "You *promised*."

Darren flinched. "I know what I said—"

"He's *cooperating*," Joey interjected, tone furious.

"What do you mean?" Tadhg asked.

"Admitting himself into Brickley House was enough to show the judge that he is showing remorse for his actions and willing to seek help for his addictions," Darren explained. "It means the judge consented to his bail on the grounds that he completes a thirty-day treatment plan, complies with the no-contact order in place, and shows up to court in November."

"November?" My eyes widened in fear. "But that's months away."

"Which means he'll be a free man in a couple of weeks," Joey added, clapping his hands together. "Well fucking done." Turning his fury on Mam, he said, "You can stop crying now. He'll be back to you soon."

"No, he won't," Darren snapped. "He'll go down for what he did."

"Don't bullshit them, Darren!" Joey roared, completely losing his cool. "Don't fucking lie to them." Turning to face us, he said, "He's going to do his thirty days, come out a changed man, full of remorse and regret, show up to court in a nice suit one of his prick friends sorted him out with, and the judge is going to praise him for his efforts – his clean, sober living. And then we'll get the 'everyone deserves a second chance' spiel before they send him on his way with a slap on the wrist."

"Joey!" Darren snapped. "That's enough."

"A few months will pass, the social workers will phase us out – because, let's face it, lads, there's a line of fuckups just like us to deal with," Joey continued, ignoring Darren. "As long as we're all fed, clothed, relatively unscathed, and keeping up at school, we'll fade off their radar. They'll forget about us – just like before. "

"I said that's enough!" Darren roared. "You're scaring them!"

"And then he'll slither back into her bed like nothing ever happened," Joey added, narrowing his green eyes at Darren. "*That's* what's going to happen, and you're all fools if you believe otherwise."

"I hate you!" Tadhg screamed, throwing his unopened letter at Mam and then bolting from the room, pushing me aside as he ran. The sound of his footsteps thundering on the staircase filled the strained silence that had settled around us in the aftermath of his retreat.

I continued to watch my brothers and mother with wariness, all the while wishing I could feel something inside. Everything was numb and cold and my life felt frozen in time. There was nothing there. I was just *empty*.

*All my faith, my hope, my future . . . poof.*

"I'm going out," Joey finally declared. Rubbing his face with his hand, he exhaled a pained groan. "I need to *not* be here right now."

"Where are you going?" Darren demanded. "Joey, it's almost half eleven at night—"

"None of your goddamn business," Joey spat as he stalked out of the kitchen, carefully avoiding brushing up against me as he went – or making eye contact.

"Joey," I called after him, voice breaking. "Please don't go—"

The front door slammed shut and I was left alone with Mam and Darren.

"It's going to be okay," Darren said, turning to face me. "I promise."

"Don't make promises you can't keep, Darren," I shot back, trembling.

"He's right," Mam sniffled, turning to look at me. "Because I won't let him come back here."

"Don't say anything at all," I whispered, and without saying another word, I turned on my heels and walked up to my room, with my father's letter in hand, wishing I had appreciated the last two weeks of sleep I'd had, because I knew in my heart, I wouldn't be sleeping easy again.

*He'll be back,* was all I could think of as I climbed under the covers and curled up in the smallest ball I could. *He's coming home – just you wait and see.*

*Somebody is going to die in this house.*

*Sooner or later . . .*

I didn't close an eye that night.

# Tissues and Ejaculation Issues

## JOHNNY

"Are you dead?"

Gibsie's voice perforated the best sleep I'd had in years and reluctantly I blinked awake.

"Huh?" I asked, voice raspy and thick from sleep. "The fuck?" Pulling myself up on my elbow, I glanced around, spotting my best friend in the doorway of my room. "What are you doing?"

"I told you last night that I'd pick you up for school," he replied, giving me a curious look. "What's wrong with you?"

"Nothing." Yawning loudly, I ran a hand through my hair. "You woke me up."

"You're always up by now," he stated, eyeballing me. "Are you sick?"

"Do I look sick?" I shot back, pissed as hell that he'd woken me up from the first decent, pain-free sleep I'd had in months. "What time is it?"

"Half past five," he replied, frowning. "And no, you don't look sick, but you definitely look *different*." Rolling up the sleeves of his navy, school jumper, he approached my bed, watching me with suspicion in his eyes. "Peaceful," he noted. "And relaxed." His eyes widened then. "You came, didn't you?"

"Lad, it's too early for you." Dropping back down on the mattress, I grabbed a pillow, tucked it against my chest, and rolled onto my side with every intention of going back to sleep. "Give me a couple of hours. We don't have to be at school until ten past nine."

"But I'm ready to train," he pushed. "You said you'd help me. I need a life goal."

"And I will," I groaned, snuggling deeper into my pillow. "Just . . . let me sleep today, okay?"

"Imagining that pillow's your girlfriend?" Gibsie asked. "*Little Shannon*?"

"Fuck off, Gibs," I grumbled, closing my eyes. "I'm tired."

"Yeah, you're tired from pulling your balls," he shot back. "That's why you won't get up and train me."

"Go without me this morning," I mumbled. "I'll go with tomorrow . . . I promise."

"Fuck that," he pressed. "I'm never up this early—"

"Shh," I coaxed, keeping my eyes closed. "Sleep."

"Jonathan."

"Gerard."

"You fucked yourself into a state of exhaustion, didn't ya?" he accused. "Jesus!"

"I'm not talking about this with you."

"Did you use the bottle of lube I got you?"

"Fuck off and let me sleep."

"Was it sensitive?"

"Gibs!"

"Did you chaff?"

"Jesus—" I blinked my eyes open and stared at the wall opposite me, counting to ten in my head, and striving for patience. "Just go *away*."

"Don't be fucking coy with me," he scoffed as he flopped down on my bed beside me. "We have no secrets."

"Well, maybe we need some," I snapped, rolling onto my back to glare at him. "Jesus."

"I'm not going to stop until you tell me so you might as well just get it over with." Folding his arms behind his head, Gibsie exhaled a loud sigh before adding, "I'm very invested in seeing this through to the end, Johnny."

I stared at him for a long beat before a shit-eating grin spread across my face.

Noticing my smirk, Gibsie's eyes widened. "Holy shit." He grinned, eyes alight with excitement. "For real?"

"It works," I clarified with a sigh of contentment.

"How was it?" he asked then, looking like he was genuinely delighted for me. "Same as before? Better? Worse?"

"It was satisfying," I told him. "But fair warning – you're lying on the wet patch, lad."

"Jesus Christ, Johnny!" Gibsie hissed as he catapulted off the mattress. "Ever hear of a posh wank? I gave you a fucking heap of rubbers."

"I'm not posh," I snickered. "And I just got it working again. I'm not suffocating the poor bastard."

"Look at my ass!" Gibsie howled, and I had to press the pillow I was holding to my face to bury my laughter. "Look at what you did to me!" he screamed, pointing to the tissue clinging to the back of his trousers. "Take it off," he instructed. "Take your fucking sperm off my ass right this instant!"

"No," I choked out through fits of laughter.

"You came on my fucking ass!" he roared. "Your cum is touching my body."

"Stop or I'm going to bust my stitches from laughing at ya!"

"Get up," he demanded, outraged. "Get off your hole and help me!"

"I can't," I strangled out through fits of laughter. "I'm weak."

"Yeah, you're weak," Gibsie snarled as he began to strip off his uniform. "Because you shot half your fucking body weight onto the bloody mattress." Tearing his jumper and shirt off, he kicked off his shoes and shoved his school trousers down his hips before stepping out of them. "You sick bastard," he growled as he picked up his pants and flung them at me. "You're such a . . . a . . . a wanker!"

I laughed because in all honesty, what else could I do?

"I feel like it's on me," he groaned, "Is it on me?" Gagging, he twisted around from side to side, trying to get a better view of his back. "I feel like it's touching my skin!" Glaring at me, he spat. "I feel fucking *violated*, Johnny!"

"It's not touching you," I strangled out, hardly able to draw a breath at this stage, as I threw his pants back at him. "You're grand, I promise—"

"Wash my uniform," he demanded, jumping out of the way. "Drag yourself and your big, swollen dick out of bed and wash my fucking clothes!" Narrowing his eyes, he hissed, "I don't care if you have to crawl on your hands and knees down the fucking stairs, but you better take my clothes down there and wash them! Or else I'm taking your fucking uniform and you can wear your own cum!"

"I've cleaned up more of your bodily fluids than I care to remember," I shot back, smirking.

"I think your actual living sperm on my ass trumps my puke on your sheets, fucker!" he roared, shuddering from head to toe.

"Sperm dies off once it's released, Gibs."

"Not for *seventy-two hours*," he shot back with a shudder. "I was listening to the sex nurses yesterday."

"They weren't sex nurses," I offered, still laughing. "And at least you can't get pregnant."

"Pregnant?" he seethed, voice rising in outrage. "I am fucking pregnant! I'm pregnant with *despair*, Johnny! I have a belly full of fucking disgust right now."

"Boys?" Mam's voice filled the air. "What's the matter – oh, Gerard, why are you in your underpants?"

"Your son," Gibsie paused to point an accusing finger at me before continuing, "ejaculated on me."

"He did?" Mam asked with a hopeful expression on her face.

"Yes, he did!" Gibsie groaned, shuddering from head to toe.

"I didn't fucking ejaculate on you," I shot back, torn between laughing and fucking crying. "I ejaculated and you *sat* on it."

"Same difference," he barked, furious. "Same fucking results, Johnny!"

"Oh, love, I'm so happy it's working for you again," Mam said, sagging in relief. "But you shouldn't be interfering with yourself when your friends are over."

"*What*?" I gaped at her. "Are these words actually coming out of your mouth?"

"It's all over my uniform, Mammy K," Gibsie told her. "He ruined me."

330 • KEEPING 13

"I know, Gerard, love," she coaxed, patting the big bastard on the cheek. "Go and get yourself in the shower and I'll wash your uniform for you. It'll be good as new."

"I'm hungry, too," he added, giving her the puppy-dog eyes.

"I'll put a fry on for you, pet," she replied. "Now, go on in and get yourself washed up."

Shuddering, Gibsie nodded and stalked into the en suite, discreetly giving me the finger as he went.

"Now," Mam said with a weary sigh as she bent down and retrieved Gibsie's uniform off the floor, "I know I might be behind with the times, and this isn't something I ever imagined having to say to you, Johnny, but please don't be ejaculating on Gerard."

"I *didn't*," I strangled out, mortified. "Why *would* I?"

Mam shook her head and mumbled something about, "Who knows with teenagers today."

"Ma," I snapped, flustered. "I had a wank. He sat on the tissue and threw a tantrum. I didn't ejaculate on him."

"And Jesus wept," Mam whimpered, pressing a hand to her forehead, "I could have had a daughter. I could have *understood* a daughter . . ."

"Well, you got me," I huffed, flopping back down on the mattress. "Dick and all."

"Jonathan!"

"Whatever, Ma, you should be glad," I tossed out, dignity long gone. "I might actually be able to give you grandchildren one day."

"Not with Gerard, you won't."

My jaw fell open. "I'm not gay!"

"It would be fine if you were," she offered.

"Thanks, I agree, but I'm still not gay," I shot back. "I have a girlfriend."

I could have kicked my own ass for letting that admission slip out.

Mam froze. "Shannon?"

*Fuck it, in for a penny . . .* "Yeah, Shannon's my girlfriend," I replied, sitting up. "We're together now, and before you even start, just know that nothing you or Da say about her is going to make a blind bit of difference to me."

"I wasn't going to say *anything* about Shannon," Mam replied after a long pause. "I think she's a lovely girl, love." Her brows were furrowed, brown eyes locked on mine, as she watched me carefully. "But her family—"

"I don't want to hear it," I cut her off by saying. "I'm not going out with her family, Ma, I'm going out with her."

"And what about what her mother said?" Mam whispered, paling. "She's only sixteen, Johnny."

"Look at me." I gestured to the bed and then the pile of clothes in her arms. "What do you think I was doing in here?"

"I don't know . . ." Mam worried her lip. "I don't want you to—"

"Grow up?" I offered. "Bit late for that, Ma. I'll be eighteen next month."

"Is it serious?"

"I'm serious about her," I replied, not missing a beat.

"How serious?"

"Serious enough that I love her," I offered, meeting my mother's eyes with steel in my veins. "Serious enough that I'm not going to be scared off."

"Are you . . ." Her voice broke off and she swallowed down a whimper before adding, "taking your time?"

"We're not doing anything," I told her. "I'm not stupid, okay? So, don't worry."

Mam sighed in relief, her small shoulders sagging. "I do like her, Johnny," she added. "I think she's a smashing girl – and good for you. I think she's a *wonderful* influence on you, love, but I just . . . " She sighed again. "You're *my* baby, and I don't want you getting caught up in something that might affect your future." She gave me a knowing look. "I don't want you to make any mistakes."

"I've got my head on straight, Ma," I told her. "I know where I'm going and I know what I need to do to get there. I won't screw myself over."

"Well, then . . . " Releasing another heavy sigh, Mam slapped on a big smile. "You should bring her over for dinner soon."

I blinked rapidly. "I thought you said—"

"I said you weren't allowed over there, but Shannon is always welcome in *this* house," Mam said. "Under supervision."

"I, uh—" Scratching my chest, I watched my mother carefully before shaking my head. "Yeah, I'll do that."

"Lovely." Mam smiled brightly. "And you should invite that brother of hers over, too. Smashing boy, but he seems so lonely. You and Gerard could make a little effort with him – maybe you could take him to the gym sometime?"

"Uh, yeah . . . okay?" *Joey Lynch is as likely to drop a barbell on me as he is to spot me, but you're taking this well so I'll go with it . . .* "I'll do that."

"Good boy. Now, bring your sheets downstairs when you're coming down for breakfast," she added before pottering off with Gibsie's uniform bundled up in her arms. "And next time, be tidier about it. Over the toilet bowl works for your father – less mess."

Fuck. My. Life.

# Breaching Walls and Beaches

## JOHNNY

"You could have really screwed me with the condoms, lad, and I've forgiven you, so get off your high horse and let it go," I reminded Gibsie when he pulled into the carpark at Tommen. He'd spent the entire drive from my house to school bitching about his uniform and I had spent the entire drive reminding him of the many, *many* times down through the years that he'd been a pain in my ass. "You're lucky Shannon didn't freak out on me because this conversation would be taking place in a different location," I added as I shoved the car door open and climbed out. "Like a hospital. Or over your grave."

"Well, I'll never forgive you for this morning," he huffed, rounding the car and falling into step beside me. "You *came* on me, Johnny."

"I'll come on you a lot fucking worse if you don't give it a bleeding rest," I snapped.

Huffing loudly, he grabbed the front of his jumper and dragged it to his nose. "What does your mother wash the clothes with?" he asked, inhaling deeply. "Smells like heaven."

"No idea, lad. The woman puts a ton of different crap into the machine for a load." Shrugging, I added, "Think it's the blue bottle that makes the clothes smell like that."

"Hmm," he mused, expression thoughtful. "Do you think if I brought a—"

"No, Gibs," I cut him off with a weary sigh as we rounded the courtyard. "She's not washing your clothes for you, so don't go there."

"Fair enough, I was only asking – oh shit!" Fisting the back of my jumper, Gibsie yanked me to an abrupt stop and then dragged me back to where he was standing, poker straight and glowering.

"What the hell, lad?" I barked, flinching when pain shot up my legs from the unexpected twist in direction.

"Look," he spat, inclining his head towards the front building. "That little shit."

Confused, I followed his train of vision until my eyes landed on Claire. She was standing outside the glass doors of the main building, talking to who I vaguely recognized as the lad Gibsie had roughed up at the school disco last year. Squinting my eyes, I asked, "Is that—"

"Jamie Kelleher?" he offered flatly. "Yeah."

"And we hate him again because . . . "

"Because he's a prick," Gibsie hissed, glowering. "He wants her."

"He's the ex-boyfriend?" I asked, narrowing my eyes to get a better look at him. "The two-week relationship?"

"Two weeks too many," Gibsie bit out, vibrating with tension. "I hate him – he tried to get her to touch his fucking cock, lad. At the disco." Growling, he hissed, "What the fuck is she playing at talking to him again?"

"No clue," I replied. "She's probably just being friendly."

"Well, she shouldn't," he snapped.

"Gibs, come on, lad, you need to simmer down."

"Fuck off," he shot back. "Easy for you to say."

Jamie obviously said something funny then because Claire threw her head back and laughed. He stepped closer, smiling down at her, and she placed a hand on his arm.

"That's fucking it!" Gibsie hissed. "I'm going to kill him—"

"No, you're not," I instructed, returning the favor of fisting his jumper and dragging him back to me. "You're not going to do anything because you don't have the right."

"I don't have the *right*?" Gibsie spluttered, livid. "What are you *talking* about?"

"Exactly what I said – you don't have the right," I confirmed, keeping ahold of his jumper. "You're not with her, lad, so back down now before you do something stupid that'll evoke girl-tears and drama."

"He'll be the one crying when I get ahold of him," he hissed, jaw ticking. "He's a creep, Johnny. He's not *good* enough for *her.*"

"Maybe," I agreed calmly. "But you'll be the eejit in Twomey's office if you go over there all guns blazing."

"Then I'm going home," he sneered, roughly shaking my hand off. "Fuck this."

"Gibs!" I called after him. "Come on, don't be thick."

"I'm not watching that," he roared over his shoulder as he stalked off towards the carpark. "I'm not fucking watching it again."

*Give me strength . . .*

"You know, all you have to do is ask the girl out," I said as I hobble/jogged after him. "She'll say yes."

"I know," he snarled, sounding even more furious.

"Well, if you know, then why haven't you done it already?" I asked, frustrated.

"Because!"

"Because?" I pushed, resisting the urge to jump on his back and wrestle him to the ground. "You like her, she likes you." I threw my hands up. "What's the problem?"

When we reached his car, Gibsie spun around to face me, chest rising and falling quickly, car keys clenched in his white-knuckled fist. "Do you know what the statistics for relationships formed during childhood lasting are?"

Exhaling breathlessly, I shook my head. "*What?*"

"They're low, Johnny," he hissed. "Very fucking low. The odds of being with your childhood sweetheart twenty years from now are less than fifteen percent."

I gaped at him. "Again, *what?*"

"I'm not prepared to be another statistic," he choked out, sounding deadly serious. "Not with her. So, I'll do what I have to do, I'll bide my time, but I won't tie her down. Not until she's ready. Not until we've both lived a bit of life first." He dropped his head and released a pained groan. "But I won't watch *that.*" He growled again. "Never a-fucking-gain."

"Well, shit." I frowned. "I don't know whether that sounds sensible or insane?"

"It's probably both," he confirmed grimly.

*Probably . . .*

Eyeing him curiously, I said, "You actually believe that?" When he didn't respond, I continued, "That's what's wrong with you? Why you've been driving yourself crazy over that girl for as long as I've known you? You're afraid it won't last?" I tilted my head to one-side. "You're scared?"

"I'm not scared," he bit out. "I just know better."

"Because of your parents?" I asked warily, half expecting a slap in the jaw for the question. From what I gathered, his parents' divorce was a shitstorm of epic proportions that erupted right around the time of his Holy Communion. Gibs had spoken about it to me a grand total of one time in almost seven years of friendship. It was the unspoken law of the land in our circle to never talk about his parents' divorce – and never *ever* bring up his father and Bethany – but I was going there again today because he was clearly messed in the head over it. "Because that's what happened to them? You think that'll happen to you and Claire?"

"Fuck you," Gibsie huffed. "I'm not projecting. I'm protecting."

Oh, he was definitely doing both.

"Hey, I'm not judging you, lad," I replied, holding my hands up. "But I am going to tell you that I think your thought process is all kinds of messed up."

His jaw ticked, but he didn't respond.

"Fuck statistics," I urged. "If you want to be with her, then just *be* with her."

"Says the fella who ran away from a tiny, little girl for months," he shot back tersely. "And you have the gall to call me scared – pussy."

I let his comment fly over my head, concentrating on the issue at hand, because I had no defense. I *did* run away from a tiny, little girl for months – I ran like I was fearing for my bleeding life – but I wasn't running anymore. "So, you're telling me that you'll be fine with her going out with some gobshite like Jamie again?" I pushed him by asking.

"You'll be perfectly okay with that?" I shrugged. "Because that's what it sounds like."

"You know I won't," he strangled out. "It nearly killed me last time."

I cringed in sympathy. "At least you got to box the head off him when it all went to shite."

"Yeah." A small smile tipped at his lips. "That was satisfying."

"I bet," I agreed, taking the opportunity to snatch his keys out of his hand so he couldn't bolt, and then shoving them into my pocket. "Now, are you going to let that little, skinny fucker get the better of you?"

"Fuck no," he growled, running a hand through his blond hair.

"Damn straight, you're not," I replied enthusiastically. "So, pull your finger out of your hole and go over there."

"You know what, Kav?" Needing no other encouragement, Gibs rolled up his sleeves. "That's exactly what I'm going to do."

"Not to fight," I reminded him, stepping in front of him when he tried to charge past me. "To *charm*."

He frowned, looking stumped. "Charm?"

"Charm," I confirmed, nodding. "Believe it or not, you have it in buckets, lad. Go back over there and charm her away from him."

"Charm," he repeated slowly, mulling over the word. His silver eyes flicked to mine and he nodded. "I can do that."

"You've got this," I replied, squeezing his shoulders. "Now go fuck that little weasel over."

Leaning against the bonnet of the car, I watched Gibsie stalk away, muttering the words, "Charm not harm," over and over to himself as he went.

Shaking my head, I hoisted my bag back onto my shoulder before setting off towards the school to find Shannon. I left my crutch in the backseat of Gibsie's car because I couldn't stand another day of walking around with the bleeding thing. Besides, I didn't need it anymore. I was hardly limping now, and with any luck, Coach Mulcahy would spot me all mobile and willing and cut me a deal, because I sure as hell needed someone to take pity on me.

My step faltered when I spotted Shannon leaning against the railing at the bottom of the P.E. hall. She was wrapped up in her winter coat, with a wooly hat perched on her head and a scarf wrapped around her neck, as rain drizzled down on her. To be honest, I almost didn't recognize her through the layers of clothing. She noticed me, though, and raised a hand, smiling softly.

Instantly, I veered off course, striding towards her, with my heart slamming in my chest.

*Something's wrong,* my brain hissed when I drew closer and saw the dark circles under her eyes. *Something bad.*

*Keep the head.*

*Don't bulldoze!*

"Hi, Shannon," I said when I was close enough for her to hear me. Frowning, I added, "Were you waiting out here for me?"

"Hi, Johnny," she replied in a small voice. "Yeah, I . . . uh, was hoping to see you before class." She chewed on her lip, watching me warily before saying, "Can we talk for a sec?"

"Yeah," Stopping just short of her, I gave her my full attention. "Of course."

She smiled up at me and then her entire expression caved. Without another word, she let her schoolbag fall off her shoulders and walked straight into my arms.

"What's wrong?" My heart slammed violently against my ribcage as I wrapped my arms around her and held her to my chest. She was so small, so fucking tiny, that all I wanted to do was pick her up and take her home with me, where I could keep her safe, where no one could make her cry again. "What happened?" *What did they do to you?*

"They, uh, they found my dad," she said, voice muffled, as she buried her face in my chest. "I found out last night."

"They did?" Thank you, Jesus. I tightened my arms around her. "Where was he?"

"Brickley House," she mumbled.

I frowned. "The rehab place?"

"Yeah." Nodding, she sniffled and glanced up at me, eyes wide and full of tears. "But, uh, he's not going to prison, Johnny."

What the actual fuck.

*Breathe, Kav, breathe.*

*Don't lose the head.*

"How do you know?" I managed to get out, squeezing her so tight I was fairly certain I was hurting her. I couldn't seem to loosen my hold, though, and she wasn't complaining as she held onto me just as tightly. "Are you sure?"

"I'm sure," she whispered. "He only has to complete a thirty-day treatment plan in Brickley House and then he's allowed out again, and his c-court date isn't until November. So, he'll be—" Clenching her eyes shut, she leaned her cheek against my chest and exhaled a broken sob. "God, Joey was right."

"Joey?"

She nodded stiffly, her whole body rigid. "He said this would happen. Joey told us that he wouldn't go to prison, but Darren seemed so convinced that I just—" She exhaled a gut-wrenching sob. "I let myself get my hopes up for a little while, thinking that maybe it really *was* over." Sniffling, she added, "But it's not over, and Joey left again last night – didn't come home until five in the morning. It's not over and it's all going bad again."

"Where'd Joey go?"

"Nowhere good," she choked out.

Shite.

"Why didn't you call me?" I croaked out, voice thick and gruff. "I would have come over."

"I did try," she whispered, "but your phone was off."

"I left it charging overnight," I admitted, feeling like the worse piece of shit on the planet. "Forgot to turn it on until this morning."

"It's okay."

*No, it isn't.* "It won't happen again," I told her. "Next time you call me, I'll answer."

"I'm so scared, Johnny," she squeezed out.

"Don't be scared," I hurried to say – to fucking console. "I won't let anything happen to you." My voice was shaking, matching my entire body, as emotions racked through me. "I swear, I won't let him hurt you ever again."

She didn't acknowledge what I'd said.

Because she didn't believe me.

My heart cracked clean open in my chest.

"I don't want to feel this way anymore," she told me, wiping her cheek with the back of her hand. "I don't want this version of life – I don't want to be this version of *me*."

"I love this version of you," I told her, unsure of what else there was to say. I couldn't tell her not to feel the way she did. All I could do was reassure her. "I love all your versions."

"I'm just so tired," she whispered, ignoring my words, drowning us both in her pain. "I'm tired of being scared. I'm tired of not knowing. I'm tired of being fucked up in the head!"

"Jesus, Shan," I groaned, dropping my chin to rest on her head. "You are *not* fucked up in the head." I tightened my arms around her. "Do you hear me? This is not you. This is them. They're the fucked-up ones."

"I hate it," she choked out.

"Yeah." I exhaled shakily. "Me, too."

The way she held me, clung to me like I was her lifeline, well, that evoked emotions inside of me I wasn't sure I was old enough to feel. And I didn't mean sex. It was deeper. A chord of connection channeling deep inside of me and connecting to her. I hoped she never left me, because I was never going to get over this girl.

"Tell me what to do?" I begged, holding her tight and growing more frantic with every desperate shiver and sob that tore from her body. "Tell me what you need and I'll give it to you." I pressed a kiss to her hair, wanting nothing more than to take this away for her. "Just *tell* me what you need from me."

"I just want to go," she sniffled. "I want to leave and never come back."

"You won't do that, though." Panicking, I tipped her chin up, forcing her to look at me. "You won't leave me, right?"

"I'm not g-good for you," she hiccupped. "You're going to r-realize that."

"Bullshit." Cupping her face in my hands, I leaned closer, pressing my forehead to hers. "That's bullshit, Shannon," I repeated, tone gruff, keeping my eyes locked on hers. "I don't want you to say that again, okay?"

Sniffling, she nodded and tightened her hold on my waist. "Okay."

A fierce surge of protectiveness roared to life inside of me, and every instinct I had demanded I do just that; protect her. Do something. *Do anything* . . .

I cast a quick glance around us, debating my next move before throwing in the towel. "Come on," I said, taking her hand in mine. "Let's go." Remembering I still had Gibsie's keys in my pocket, I led her towards the silver Focus. Shannon walked wordlessly beside me, not asking questions. *She was just following me.* It was such a raw display of her blatant vulnerability and it terrified me. I could have been taking her anywhere, but when I unlocked the car, she just climbed into the passenger seat without a word or question.

Silently reeling, I closed her door and rounded the car before taking my perch in the driver's seat. Buckling up, I adjusted the seat back as far as it would go, and placed my feet on the pedals. Gingerly, I pushed down on the pedals, testing out the pressure in my legs.

*Not bad.*

Twisting the key in the ignition, I revved the engine, flicked on the wipers, and slowly backed out of the parking spot Gibsie had hastily rolled into this morning.

"Are we going to get arrested?" Shannon asked, breaking the silence, as we traveled down the long, wooded laneway. "For taking his car?"

"No, Shan, we won't get arrested," I chuckled, pulling to a stop at the main entrance. Flicking on my indicator, I leaned over the wheel and checked the road. "I'll shoot him a text later and let him know."

"Oh." Nodding, she clasped her hands together on her lap. "Okay."

Pulling onto the main road, I dropped my hand to the gearstick and shifted into third and then fourth before finally settling on fifth as the speedometer rose right along with my sense of freedom.

Feeling like I was in control for the first time in weeks, I put my foot down and pushed Gibsie's Focus as hard as it could go, all the while wishing we were in my Audi.

Unlike before, Shannon didn't complain about my driving. Instead, she rolled down the window and rested her cheek against the door, smiling softly when the wind blasted against her face.

We couldn't go back to Shannon's house because, aside from the fact that I was banned from stepping foot on the property, I was likely to cause serious physical harm to that brother of hers, and we couldn't go back to my place because if I rolled into the driveway behind the wheel of a car, my mother was likely to cause serious physical harm to *me*.

One of the best parts of living on the south coast of Ireland was that you were never far from water, so I detoured onto the coastal road, abandoning Ballylaggin altogether. It was half nine in the morning, and with the exception of the odd dog-walker, we should get some peace and quiet.

"Aren't you going to ask me where we're going?" I asked, casting a quick sideways glance her way before refocusing on the narrow, potholed road ahead of me.

"No," she replied softly.

"No?" I cocked a brow. "Why not?"

She opened her eyes and turned to look at me. "Because I trust you."

*Well shite.*

Reaching over, I took her right hand in mine and pulled it onto my lap.

Several hours later, Shannon and I were on what had to be our hundredth lap of the beach, and I was trying not to think about my stomach too much. I had eaten my entire supply of lunch for the day not long after parking up this morning – protein shakes and all – and I was still *starving*. I was putting my hunger down to the sea air, because I sure as hell wasn't burning up enough energy to be craving meat, unless trying to keep my head on straight with Shannon in close proximity constituted as strenuous activity. My heart certainly thought so, as it did the rounds in my chest, leaping around like a fucking jack-hammer. Or maybe it was the nerves making me hungry? Hell, I'd never been a nervous eater, but Jesus, this girl did strange things to my internal system.

Falling into step beside Shannon, I forced my legs to move, concentrating on putting one foot in front of the other and just moving. She didn't make any comment on my pace or how fucking pathetic I looked as I shuffled awkwardly alongside her, freeing out my stiff muscles.

Every once and a while, I would test the waters by holding myself slightly back from her, or inconspicuously stepping a few feet out of touching distance, pretending to look at something that wasn't there, while I held my breath and waited to see what her next move would be. She skittishly closed the space every single time, moving closer and closer until she was sidled back up to my side. I did that at least four times just to make sure that this was where she wanted to be – with me – because it scared me sometimes, not knowing what was going on inside that head of hers.

Every now and then, *she* would stop for a couple of minutes to check a shell on the sand, or pretend to adjust her tights, but I knew that was bullshit. She was giving me pitstops. She was stopping so I could rest.

It was lashing rain down on us, but it didn't seem to bother Shannon. She seemed perfectly content to be here with me.

She was talking again, too; answering every stupid question my brain could think up as we wandered, side by side, over the rocks and wet sand. The more random and pointless my questions were, the more Shannon relaxed, so I asked her everything; from her preference between Nike and Adidas, to her views on the big bang theory, until she was laughing and talking freely. I hashed up every fucked-up thought and memory I could to keep that smile on her face, never once bringing her father into the conversation. She didn't want to talk about her family, and to be honest, neither did I.

I wanted to give her a good day to make up for the bad ones, or at the very least, make her day a little better.

"Are you okay?" Shannon asked as she stood at the bottom of a rock, waiting on the sand for me to climb down to her. Her face was flushed from windburn, matching mine, and she was bouncing the rugby ball we'd found in the boot of Gibsie's car this morning between her hands.

"All good." Every inch of my body was burning up and I knew all the climbing was wreaking havoc on my injury, but I replied with a muffled, "Just give me a sec," as I resisted the urge to sit on my arse and shimmy down like a fucking girl.

"You can do it, Johnny," she encouraged, smiling brightly. "You've got this."

I really wasn't sure if I *had this* or not, but I moved my legs all the same and prayed for the strength I needed to keep myself upright as I hobbled down the rocks at a snail's pace, feeling every ache and burn in my muscles, until I was standing in front of her with my feet planted firmly in the sand.

"Are you ready?" she asked, sounding a little breathless as a playful smile tipped at her lips.

"Yeah." I nodded, feeling the burn on my skin from having her eyes on me. "Go for it."

She held the ball out for me to take, but when I reached for it, she backed up a few feet.

A small smile curled at my lips and I tilted my head, studying her mischievous expression. "Oh, so it's going to be like that?"

Shannon laughed loudly – she actually fucking *laughed* – and nodded. "Come and get it, Mister Rugby."

Shaking my head, I trudged after her, my movements stiff and awkward, but she didn't seem to notice, or she didn't care. She was smiling encouragingly and nodding at me to follow her as she bounced a few feet out of my grasp every time I got close enough to snatch the ball.

She looked fucking adorable as she ran several yards up the beach with the rugby ball in her small hands. Her wooly hat and scarf swamped her face and that mountain of dark hair was blowing around her, with wet clumps sticking to her rosy cheeks. Rain was dripping from her coat, her school skirt was drenched through and clinging to her bare legs, and I swear, I had never seen anything so fucking beautiful.

*Freedom suited her.*

"Shannon, I can't," I called after her when she ran too far ahead of me for the millionth time. "I'm too stiff." *And embarrassed . . .*

"No, you're not," she encouraged, breathless and beaming back at me. "You're just out of practice." Turning around so that she was walking backwards, facing me, she said, "It's just us, Johnny – just you and me. And you *can* do this," she repeated, looking more confident in this moment than I had ever seen her. "I promise."

"Yeah?"

"Yes." She skipped ahead of me with my ball in her hands and my heart in her ass pocket. Christ, she had me hook, line, and sinker, as I trailed after her like she was holding a fishing rod with a line that was attached to something deep inside of me.

Forcing down my anxiety, I did as she asked; I lowered my defenses and moved my legs.

"Well, well, well," Shannon taunted from further up the beach a little while later. Bouncing the ball in her hands, she gleamed at me. "Looks like I win *again*."

"I think the power is getting to your head," I shot back, grinning. "Give me that ball."

"Never," she laughed. "It's mine. You gave it to me, and I'm not giving it back."

*Like my fucking heart?*

"Throw it," I encouraged.

Her eyes widened. "Huh?"

"The ball," I called back. "Throw it and I'll pass it back to you."

She eyed me warily. "You promise?"

"Yes, Shannon." I rolled my eyes. "I promise I'll give you back the bleeding ball."

"Okay." Like a toddler throwing a ball, Shannon held it between her legs, and with her brows set in deep concentration, she tossed it into the air – and about ten feet in the wrong direction.

"I didn't realize I was playing with one of the minis," I laughed, as I went to retrieve it. "Remind me to get you one of those child slides when I take you bowling."

"Hey – I'm all you've got, thirteen," Shannon called back, grinning. "So don't mock me."

She *was* all I had right now – the only person I could trust not to judge me for not being on form.

I couldn't do this with the lads.

I would be too embarrassed.

But it was different with Shannon.

Everything was different when it came to her.

# I'll Keep You Safe

## SHANNON

"Do you think it will ever stop raining?" I mused, staring out the windscreen at the heavy downpour.

It had been consistently raining all day, which wasn't anything new for Ireland, but considering it was April, I'd been half hoping to see the sun soon.

The wind was howling outside the car; whipping against the windows with a thunderous whoosh. Shivering, I turned in my seat to look at the boy lazing in the driver's seat next to me.

Johnny had his seat reclined at an almost horizontal angle and was sprawled out like a lion, using one hand to scroll through Gibsie's iPod while he used his other to hold mine. His dark hair was plastered to his head, and his school shirt was so wet, it looked like a second layer of skin as it clung to his huge body. He'd long since shed his drenched coat and jumper, tossing them in the backseat along with mine, deciding we would dry off faster without so many layers.

He had the engine running again, something he did every half an hour or so to keep the windows from fogging up and warm up the car. The heater was on full blast, blowing delicious hot air against my damp skin, and the last haunting rift of Jim McCann's "Grace" was humming softly from the stereo.

"It's been a long winter," Johnny agreed, flicking through songs before settling on Coldplay's "Yellow". "Hey – look at the name of this playlist." Snickering, he turned the screen of Gibsie's iPod towards me. "The lad's off his rocker."

"*Fuck me, suck me, self-destruct with me*," I mused, reading the playlist name on the screen. "Sounds very . . ."

"Gibsie?" Johnny offered with a shake of his head. "Yeah, that'll be him alright."

"At least he's original," I offered. "I don't think I've ever met anyone like him before."

"That's because the world can only handle one Gerard Gibson," Johnny said with a chuckle. His hand moved to his thigh, almost absent-mindedly, to rub where I knew he was sore.

"Is it painful?" Tightening my hold on the blanket he had found in the boot for me, I asked, "Are you feeling okay?"

"No, Shan." Tossing the iPod on top of the dashboard, Johnny gave me his full attention. "I actually feel great." An indulgent smile tugged at his lips, causing the dimples in his cheeks to deepen. "Better than I have in months."

"Really?" I beamed back at him. "So, I'm a good coach?"

Smirking, he raised my hand to his mouth and brushed his lips over my knuckles. "You're one of a kind." Giving my fingers a gentle squeeze, he placed our joined hands back on his lap.

Repressing a full-body shiver, I turned back to stare out the window, sighing in contentment, as I watched the waves rising, foaming, and crashing against the cliffs.

*Today* . . .

God, today had been the *best* day.

When I woke up this morning, I was sure I would never smile again. Knowing that my father had a little over two weeks left in treatment before he was a free man had crippled something inside of me. It had doused the tiny flicker of hope I had been clinging to these past few weeks, as I'd adjusted to life without him. The letter he had written me was still unopened and tucked into the side pocket of my schoolbag. I wasn't sure if I would ever read it, but I knew that I didn't want to right now. I was so furious with myself for letting my guard down, for allowing myself to contemplate the possibility of a life without him in it.

When I arrived at school this morning, I hadn't planned on seeking Johnny out. It just sort of *happened*. Without my brain's permission, my feet had led me straight to him. When he opened that car door, I didn't need to ask any questions before climbing inside, because I knew I would go anywhere with him. Whether he knew it or not, he had offered me a temporary lifeline and I had grabbed it with both hands.

And now we were here, at the beach, having stolen his best friend's car to skip school and escape our hometown. We spent the day doing absolutely nothing and that meant absolutely *everything* to me.

"Are you going to be in trouble?" I asked. "When your parents find out you skipped?" Evening was trickling in now, bringing with it a darkening sky and the stinging bite of the cold, night air. A prickling chill danced across my bare legs and I knew we would have to go soon. The thought was depressing, but I pushed it back, refusing to taint the best day of my life.

Johnny shrugged nonchalantly. "I'm always in trouble for something."

My lips tipped up. "Me, too."

"We're some pair, huh?" he chuckled.

"Yeah." Unsure of how to word my next sentence, I thought long and hard before giving up entirely on being tactful and just coming right out with it. "What happens in June?" It was the question that had been driving me insane ever since Joey told me about his career. It was the question that made me feel close to catatonic mode every time I thought of him leaving. "With the rugby," I whispered, biting down on my bottom lip as I turned to look at him, chewing so hard that I could taste blood on my tongue. "What happens when you go away?"

Johnny was quiet for the longest time as his gaze flickered between my face and the steering wheel. Finally, he turned back to look at me. "That's a long way off, Shan," he admitted honestly, blue eyes locked on mine. "And I don't even know if I'll make the squad—"

"You're going to make it," I cut in quietly. There wasn't an ounce of hesitation in my voice. "I'm sure of it."

He stared hard at me for the longest moment before tearing his gaze away and focusing on the roof of the car. "I wish I was so sure."

"Well, I'll be sure enough for the both of us," I replied, squeezing his hand. "It's going to happen." *You're going to leave.* "You're going to shine."

He shook his head, brows furrowed. "I want it so fucking bad." Exhaling a pained sigh, he ran a hand through his rain-soaked hair and growled. "Since as far back as I can remember, that's all I've wanted to do, you know?"

"It's going to happen for you," I said, trying to offer him a smidgen of the support he gave me daily.

"I fucked myself over fairly significantly," he muttered. "I didn't listen. I over-trained. I almost killed myself. If I make it—" he paused to look at me, "it'll be a miracle."

"No," I corrected. "*When* you make it, it'll be years of hard work that paid off."

"You think I can do it?"

I nodded. "I know you can."

He blew out a frustrated breath. "I just . . . want to *be* someone, you know? It doesn't take any effort to be ordinary," he shared, his words coming fast and laced with the Dublin accent. "I don't want to be ordinary, Shannon. I want to be extraordinary. I want to *excel*. But all of it – the training and the fucking grafting – it means *nothing* if I don't make it back on the pitch soon." He dropped his gaze to stare at our joined hands and muttered, "It will have all been for nothing."

"What can I do?" I squeezed out, desperate to help him. "Can I help?"

Johnny smirked. "Oh, like coach me again?"

"If you want?" I shrugged helplessly. "I just want to help you."

"You can stay with me," he replied, tone low, blue eyes achingly vulnerable. "Even if I don't get the call."

My chest burned so hard for him it was physically painful.

"Oh, Johnny—" Unable to stop myself, I hitched my skirt up so I could clamber across the console. Climbing onto his lap, I placed a knee on either side of his body before gently lowering myself down, careful not to hurt him. I was met with a wall of thick, unrelenting muscle. There was nothing soft about this boy. With the exception of his face, he was hard all over.

Johnny sat straight up; his hands automatically moving to my hips, tugging me closer. "What are you doing?" he whispered, watching me through hooded eyes. He swallowed deeply, his Adam's apple bobbing in his throat, as his hands drifted to my bare thighs, fingers flexing into my skin every time he drew in another breath. The heat from his hands caused a delicious shiver of warmth to roll through me as he trailed soft circles over my bare flesh with his calloused fingertips. "Shan?"

"I'm here for Johnny *the boy*," I told him, cupping his face with my trembling hands. "Not Johnny *the rugby player*." Exhaling a shaky breath, I leaned closer and pressed a kiss to the corner of his mouth before pulling back to look in his eyes. "I'll stay for both, but I'm only in love with one."

He shuddered and closed his eyes. "You mean it." It wasn't a question. "You really don't care about it."

I shook my head slowly, forcing myself to keep his gaze. "It's not what I see when I look at you – it's not what I have *ever* seen. I only want it for *you* because *you* want it for you," I added, voice hoarse. "But I'm here either way – rugby or no rugby . . . if you want me to be?"

"Christ, Shan, you're killing me," Johnny groaned, tugging on my hips so that we were chest to chest. My heart fluttered wildly; the feel of his chest rising and falling against mine too much to take. "If I make it, it won't change a thing for us." Exhaling a low growl, he buried his face in the curve of my neck and inhaled deeply. "It won't change *me*," he added, voice muffled, as his fingers trailed up and down my ribcage. "Or how I feel about you."

"Really?" I breathed, moving my hands to rest on his broad shoulders. "You promise you won't forget me when you're a big star?"

Lifting his face to mine, he nodded slowly and whispered, "I promise."

Unable to bear the aching need inside of my body a second longer, I snaked my hands into Johnny's hair and dragged his face to mine. He came willingly and our lips crashed together, setting alight a burning trail of heat between my legs. With a low growl of approval, he clamped his hands around my thighs and thrust his tongue between my parted lips, taking the air from my lungs and setting my whole body on *fire*.

I could feel his erection straining against the fabric of his school trousers, pressing hard against me. Desperate for more contact, I arched my back and rocked my hips against his. "You're so perfect," Johnny growled, lips brushing against mine as he spoke. "Your skin is so fucking smooth." Nuzzling my neck, he pressed a trail of hot, wet kisses up my neck, his tongue sweeping out to taste me, as his hands roamed over my legs. "I've wanted you for so long." Moaning, I sagged against him, rocking my hips and arching my neck into his face, shivering and shaking all over. "Fuck!"

I gripped his hair and tugged him closer, nails clawing and retracting like a kitten, as the need inside of me blossomed and burned. God, I loved his hair. It was cut tight around the sides and back, leaving a messy pile of unruly, disheveled, brown hair on top. It was usually styled in some fantastic way, but now that it was wet and I'd run my fingers through it half a dozen times, it looked even better.

Claiming my lips again, Johnny fell back on his seat and pulled me down with him. My school skirt rose up to pool at my stomach as we rocked and rubbed our bodies together in a frenzied sort of unison, but I didn't care. Not one bit. All I cared about in this moment was keeping him with me.

I didn't know what the future held for me and I wanted to make the most of every moment I got to spend with him. In two months, he would be gone. In two weeks, I could be gone. The tangent fear of the unknown was what catapulted me into action. If my dad came back . . . *No!*

*Don't think about it, Shannon.*

*Just be here in the moment with him.*

*Just absorb him.*

His lips were soft, his smell addictive, and the feel of his body rubbing against mine in all the right spots was making me feel incredibly reckless. I felt like I was at the point where I didn't know where I began and he ended.

My heart was beating so hard I was sure he could feel it as we pressed our bodies together. With my heart racing wildly in my chest and anxiety threatening to overwhelm me, I reached for the buttons of his shirt.

"Wait, wait, wait—" Breathless, Johnny craned his head back to look at me. His eyes were so dark there was hardly a hint of blue. Snatching my hand up, he held it to his chest and said, "What are you doing?"

*I don't know.*

*I have no idea.*

"Please just let me," I whispered, shocked at my own forwardness, but not taking it back.

"Shan—" His voice broke off and he groaned. "We talked about this . . . "

"I know," I agreed, breathing hard and fast. "But I just . . . I want to see."

"Just see?" He was breathing hard, his heart racing almost violently against his chest, as he drew in short breaths. "That's what you want?"

Nodding, I sat up and placed my hands on his stomach. "I just want to see." With trembling hands, I reached for my shirt and fingered the buttons nervously. "Do *you* want to see?" Feeling skittish, I unbuttoned the top three buttons of my shirt. "I'll show you, too—"

"Of course, I want to *see*," Johnny groaned, snatching my hand away from my shirt. "But if I see, I'll take," he strangled out, jaw clenched tightly. "And I can't be taking, baby, so please don't fucking show me."

"I don't mind," I breathed, heart racing violently. "I want you to see."

"Fuck!" Inhaling several calming breaths through his nose, Johnny released my hands and dropped his hands to my thighs. "Go ahead." With a stiff nod, he added, "Take what you need."

Releasing a ragged breath, I moved to unbutton his shirt, only to fumble over the first button.

Johnny remained perfectly still beneath me, with his blazing hot eyes burning holes in mine, and his chest rising and falling against my fingertips.

Steeling my resolve, I inhaled a deep breath, shook my hands out, and tried again, not stopping until I had his shirt open and pushed aside.

"You're so . . . " My words broke off and I exhaled heavily, eyes glued to his ripped stomach. I had full permission to touch, to graze my fingertips over the hard plains of his abdominal muscles. And there were muscles *everywhere*. He was built like rock. I trailed my fingers down his stomach, watching with fascination as his muscles contracted under my touch.

"I'm so what, Shan?" Johnny asked, voice thick and gruff, as he lay sprawled beneath me on the reclined seat, with his hands clamped on my thighs. His hips were thrusting upwards in a slow, taunting rhythm, as he watched me watch him. "Hmm?" His fingertips traced the edge of my knickers, slipping under the cotton waistband to trail soft circles over my hipbones. "What am I?"

My gaze drifted to his pecs, and then to the trail of dark hair from his belly button that disappeared beneath the waistband of his pants. Muscles and skin. Flesh and heat. That was all I could see. All I could *feel*. He was so big. So *everything*. "Beautiful," I finally breathed, my gaze flicking back to his. "You're so beautiful."

"You're making this hard for me, Shan." Sliding his tongue over his bottom lip, he hooked his fingers into the waistband of my knickers and dragged me down on his chest. "I need you to *not* look at me like that." Burying his face in my hair, he suckled on my neck, drawing a breathy gasp from my throat. "I'm trying to be good here."

"I'm sorry," I breathed, arching against him. I was aching for him in parts of my body I had never known existed before he explored, discovered, and claimed. "I just want . . . " I wasn't sure what I wanted. All I knew was this boy made everything better, he stopped the tornado of thoughts whirling around in my head, and I needed him to keep doing that.

Maybe I was addicted to him, and maybe it wasn't healthy, my feelings for him certainly bordered on obsessive, but he was encouraging me with every flex of his hips and every thrust of his tongue, showing me that he wanted this just as badly as I did.

If I was doing this all wrong, then Johnny never complained. Instead, he groaned and moaned into my mouth in approval.

He started to touch me, slowly at first, and then more confidently, brushing the pads of this thumbs over my bare skin. When I felt his hands slide under my knickers, a jolt of excitement shot through me, making my movements more frantic and clumsy. "Is this okay?" He palmed my ass and squeezed tightly. "Do you want me to stop?"

"Don't stop." I was painfully aware of the sheer size of him. I was so small in his arms. I was breakable to this boy and it was a troubling thought. He could destroy me in more ways than one. The thing was, I didn't care what he did to my body so long as he left my heart intact. He could have and take whatever he wanted from me, I would gladly give it all to him, so long as I had a promise in blood that he would never hurt me so badly I wouldn't repair. Because I knew I wouldn't bounce back from this. From *him*. Curling my arms around his neck, I pressed my lips to his and choked out, "Don't ever stop."

Breathing hard, he sat straight up and roughly dragged me closer, causing us both to groan when our bodies aligned in the best possible way. "I love you," he whispered. "And I want you – *badly*. But I just . . . I don't want to do anything to fuck this up," he added, tone deep and gravelly. "I can't mess this up, Shan. I need this." Exhaling a ragged breath, he pressed his forehead to mine. "I meant it when I said I needed you for keeps."

"You remember saying that?"

He nodded slowly. "I remember."

The air left my lungs in a sudden rush. "Good."

"I'm going to keep you," he whispered and his hot breath fanned my face. "If that's okay?"

"That's definitely okay," I breathed, pressing my hand to his cheek. "I want you to keep me."

He smiled, dimples deepening. "Thank fuck for that."

Pressing a kiss to the curve of his swollen lips, I whispered, "I'll keep you, too."

"Jesus." Shuddering, he dropped his head in the curve of my neck and groaned. "This is how I'm going to die," was his muffled response and it caused me to laugh. "Think it's funny?" he teased, lifting his head up to grin at me. "I'll be taking you with me."

*God, I really hope you do . . .*

"But for now, I better take you home," he said with a resigned sigh. "Or else your ma will have the Guards out looking for us."

"Oh." My heart plummeted into my stomach and my hold on his neck tightened. "Okay."

"It's going to be okay," he coaxed, blue eyes locked on mine. "Whatever happens with your da, *you're* going to be okay."

No, I wasn't, but I forced a smile for his sake. "I know."

"Because you're not on your own anymore," he whispered, wrapping me up in his arms so tightly that I didn't care that I couldn't breathe. I wanted the world to stop and let us both off because this, right here, was where I wanted to be – where I wanted to *stay*. "You have friends," he continued to whisper. "And you have me."

His words gave me more comfort than I knew what to do with. He was big and strong and dangerously powerful. Given the chance, he could do some serious physical damage to my body. And still, I wasn't fearful. I wasn't *wary*. I didn't have a hint of fear in my body.

"I'm on your team," he added huskily. "Do you get that? I'm totally with you, Shannon Lynch. One call, that's all you need to make, and I'll come. I won't let you down, and I won't leave you alone in this. I promise."

"It's just weird for me because I've never had someone in my corner before." Shivering, I added, "Not someone like you."

"I'm not in your corner, Shannon," Johnny replied in a gruff tone. "I'm standing right beside you."

*Oh god.*

His words hit me deep.

Burying my face in his chest, I curled myself into the smallest ball I could and prayed for time to stand still just for a little while. "I bet you wish you had a normal girlfriend."

"Normal is boring," he replied. "And besides, I could say the same thing to you." He shrugged. "I'm hardly a normal boyfriend."

"I'm just saying that it would be easier for you if—"

"Well, I don't want easy, I want *you*," he cut me off by saying. "Just the way you are."

My breath hitched in my throat. "Really?"

"Really," he confirmed, not missing a beat. "Every part and every piece."

I grimaced. "Even the broken parts?"

He winked. "Especially the broken parts."

I paused then, listening to the song playing on the stereo, before a small laugh tore from my throat.

Johnny smirked. "Something funny?"

"'Proud Mary'?" I questioned, gesturing to the stereo. "How does he go from 'Grace', to 'Yellow', to 'Proud Mary'?"

"I know." Chuckling, he switched off the stereo and dropped back down on his back. "I think it's a fair representation of what goes on in his head." He sighed and stroked my waist. "His head's spinning constantly."

"Can I show you something?" I asked then, as I climbed off his lap and slipped back into the passenger seat. "It's . . . " Letting my words trail off, I reached into my schoolbag at my feet and withdrew the folded-up envelope.

"What's that?" Johnny asked with a frown as he re-buttoned his shirt. "Shan?"

"It's, uh . . . " Holding it in my trembling hands, I unfolded it and looked at the scraggly handwriting before blowing out a sharp breath. "From my dad," I added before thrusting the envelope into his hands.

His brows furrowed as his eyes flicked between the envelope and me. "He wrote you a letter?"

I nodded. "He left one for all of us, but I can't read mine."

He frowned again, deeper this time. "Do you want . . . me to read it?"

"I don't think I want to know," I strangled out, feeling flighty. "I just . . . maybe if you read it, just to check?"

Johnny didn't hesitate. His fingers ripped open the envelope, and with a steady hand, he held the piece of paper to his face, concentrating intently on whatever my father had written.

I watched as his shoulders stiffened and his cheeks reddened. "Is it bad?" I squeezed out. "Is he mad at me?"

"He said he's *sorry*," he bit out through clenched teeth. "That he was sick, he's seen the error of his ways, and he's trying to make things right." Jaw ticking, he rolled his shoulders like he was trying to control himself before adding, "He said that he hopes in time that you can find it in your heart to forgive him, and you can all be a family again."

My heart sank. "Oh."

"Yeah." Looking furious, Johnny refolded the letter and held it out for me.

I shook my head. "I don't want that back."

"You sure?"

"Positive," I strangled out. "Get rid of it."

Nodding stiffly, Johnny reached into the glove box and withdrew a lighter. Torching the letter, he rolled down his window and tossed it out, letting the wind sweep it away.

"Thank you," I whispered, relieved to have that piece of *him* gone from me. "He's lying," I blurted out, feeling panicked. "You know that, right?"

Johnny nodded. "I know, baby."

"He doesn't mean any of that," I heard myself say, desperate to make him understand. "This is a trick – this is something he's been told to do." I shook my head, feeling distraught and frustrated. "He's not sorry, Johnny—" My voice cracked. "He's *never* sorry."

"I'm not going to let him hurt you, Shannon." He was sitting poker straight in his seat, eyes trained on the windscreen, and gripping the steering wheel with such force that his knuckles had turned white. "I promise."

I sighed heavily. "Don't make promises you can't keep."

He turned to look at me. "Have I let you down yet?"

I shook my head. "N-no."

He nodded stiffly, eyes blazing with heat. "Then believe me when I say that I won't let him hurt you again," he repeated, reiterating every single word slowly. "Never again." He fastened his seatbelt and I did the same. "All I need you to do is keep talking to me," he added, starting the engine. "Just keep letting me in." He turned to look at me. "And I'll keep you safe."

"Okay," I breathed, watching him cautiously as he drove us away from the beach. "I will."

# Pushing Back

## SHANNON

"Shan, do you want to keep this?" Darren asked the following Saturday afternoon, as he balanced on a ladder, holding a scraggly-looking teddy bear out to me. "Or will we toss it?"

"Toss it," I told him, taking the bear and shoving it into one of the overstuffed black bin bags in the landing.

"You used to love that thing," he mused, sounding a little sad, as I tied a knot on the now full bag and tore another one off the roll. "You took it everywhere with you."

"I liked a lot of things, Darren," I agreed, opening the new bag up. "But I grew up."

"You used to like me," he muttered quietly.

"And I'd like you again if you didn't keep me stuck in this house," I snapped, flustered. "It's Saturday."

"I know," he agreed with a sigh. "But I need your help cleaning out the attic. We need more space and if we clear it out, I can move up there and give Joey back his room."

"This is a joke," I muttered under my breath. "Our entire family is a joke."

"Is this about him?" Darren asked. "Is this tantrum because you're not allowed to go out with him?"

*Yes.* I hadn't seen Johnny since school yesterday and I was growing agitated. All week, I'd only been able to spend lunch time with him, and I was quickly learning that wasn't enough. Nothing ever seemed to be enough when it came to him. "No," I snapped, dragging my thoughts back to the present. "It's because I am sick to death of being a prisoner in this house." Sighing heavily, I added, "I feel like I am shackled to the walls, Darren. I can't stand it anymore."

"Well, skipping school to hang out with him isn't going to do you any favors," my brother responded. "You were lucky I answered the call from your principal and not Mam," he added. "I covered for you, remember? Told him you were sick when you were off gallivanting around the countryside with him." When I didn't respond, because quite frankly, I didn't have any excuses, Darren sighed. "Come on, Shannon. It's your junior cert year. You know you need to put your head down and study for those exams in June. And he shouldn't be your crutch. It's not healthy to get so attached to that lad – tempting as he is."

"He's not my crutch," I strangled out. "He's my boyfriend, and it's okay to want to spend some time with him."

"*Some* time," Darren agreed. "Not *all* of your time."

"I don't," I bit out. "I only get to see him at lunch."

"Well, boyfriend or not, you need to help out with packing these bags, because I can't clean it all on my own," Darren replied in a dismissive tone. "Do something productive with your day, instead of wasting it pining after some young fella."

"Do you know how I've spent every single Saturday for the last six years?" I asked, and then quickly continued before he had a chance to respond. "*Cleaning*, Darren. That's how I've spent my Saturdays. Cleaning up after everyone in this house."

Darren sighed heavily. "Shan, come on."

"No." Feeling bitter, I blew out a breath and planted my hands on my hips. "This isn't fair. You promised things would be different when I came home from the hospital, but it's not. Nothing changed. She's still in there—" I pointed to the closed bedroom door behind his back. "Hiding away from her responsibilities, while I'm still out here, cleaning up after everyone, and Joey is still dragging the boys along to their training and matches. The only difference now is that I have company." I gave him a meaningful look to let him know that *he* was the company. "That's the only difference I can see here, Darren."

"Really? Because I see things a bit differently," he growled, climbing down from the ladder. "For a start, he's not here. Second, the fridge and cupboards are full. Third, none of you are walking around the place covered in bruises—"

"He's still here, Darren," I shot back shakily. "He's just after taking on another form."

"What are you trying to say, Shannon?" he asked coldly. "Hmm?" Looking furious, he crossed his arms over his chest and glared at me. "Are you calling me our father?"

I shrugged, feeling guilty for what I had insinuated but unwilling to back down.

Darren laughed humorlessly. "You know what? Do whatever you want. Go out and get yourself pregnant for all I care. I'm done trying to smooth things over with you and the boys. In fact, I don't know why I fucking bothered in the first place."

I remained silent as he stalked past me and thundered down the staircase, and it wasn't until the sound of the front door slamming filled my ears, that I exhaled the breath I had been holding in.

Furious with myself and life in general, I continued to bag up the old toys, clothes, and general bric-a-brac from the attic until the landing floor was cleared. I neatly piled all of the bags at the top of the stairs and then I did something that surprised me. I walked into my bedroom, grabbed my coat off the back of the door, and shrugged it on.

Clambering down the staircase with my heart in my mouth, I hurried through the hallway, falling over strewn toys and bits of Lego on my way. I was suffocating in this house. I was drowning in my own life. I needed to get out. I needed something. I just needed . . . *to open the door.*

Flinging the front door open, I barreled outside. Not stopping, I broke into a run, pushing my body to its limits, whizzing past the familiar line of houses, then taking a sharp turn to the right and legging it down the dark lane. With no destination in mind, I pulled the hood of my coat up and kept going, desperately seeking that addictive taste of freedom I longed for with each passing day.

Three hours and a spare change of dry clothes later, and I was curled up on Claire's bed, with a mug of hot chocolate balancing between my hands, and the end credits of *Dirty Dancing* playing on her television.

"I love him," Claire sigh/swooned from her perch beside me. "I swear, I will never get over that man for as long as I live."

"I thought you loved Johnny Depp," Lizzie quipped from where she was lounging at the foot of the bed, flicking through a magazine. "Make your mind up, girl."

"I love them both," Claire sighed. "But Patrick was my first love, and you know how the sweet flame of first love burns forever."

Lizzie rolled her eyes to the heavens, looking thoroughly unimpressed. "I don't know how we've made it through eleven years of friendship."

"I missed this." I sighed in contentment and took a sip from my mug. "I missed you guys."

"We missed you, too," Lizzie replied. "I had to suffer the adventures of Thor and his cat on my own the last time I came over."

"Leave Gerard alone," Claire grumbled. "So he likes his cat. Big deal."

"He *walks* his cat." Lizzie rolled onto her side to gape at Claire. "With a glittery, jewel-encrusted collar and lead." Narrowing her eyes, she said, "Please don't tell me you think that's normal."

Claire shrugged. "I think it's cute."

"Of course, you do – you think everything that big eejit does is cute," she shot back with a shake of her head. "What about you, Shan? What do you make of *Gerard*?"

"I, uh . . . " I looked at both girls before grinning sheepishly. "I think he's great," I laughed. "I like his cat, too."

Claire beamed and Lizzie groaned.

"Shannon has to like him," Lizzie muttered. "He's her *boyfriend's* other half. Speaking of which, how is Captain Fantastic?"

"He's good," I replied, blushing beetroot red.

"*He's good*," both girls chimed in mockingly.

"Oh my god!" Claire squeaked. "I just thought of something." Springing to her feet, she padded over to the television and switched it off before swinging around to face us. "I love two *Johnnys* and Shannon loves another one!" Shimmying around with excitement, her eyes danced with mischief as she said, "If that's not fate, then I don't know what is."

"You know what, Claire?" Lizzie mused. "I take back everything I have ever said about you and Thor being a bad idea. I think you should totally go for it with him. You're a match made in heaven."

"I know, right?" Claire shot back with a smirk.

"Ugh." Shuddering, Lizzie flicked the page of her magazine. "I can only imagine the children that would be created from that union – curly-blonde unicorn-babies."

"I do love unicorns," Claire offered.

"Uh-huh," Lizzie drawled. "See, you're halfway there already."

"How do you know if you're going to have an or . . . " I let my words trail off as I took in the sight of both girls gaping at me. "Uh, never mind."

"Finish it," Claire squealed, bouncing up and down. "An orrrrr . . . "

"Gasm," I whispered, feeling my face burn.

"You had an *orgasm*?" Claire's eyes bulged. "Shut the front door!"

"Whoa," Lizzie muttered, looking begrudgingly impressed. "He's fucking smooth."

"Did you see his willy?" Claire demanded. "Oh my god, was it big? It's big, right? Ugh, I bet he's huge and you're so tiny . . . " Swallowing deeply, Claire waved a hand around in front of her face in dismay. "Oh god, I bet it hurt, didn't it? How are you still in one piece?"

"Calm down, miss I'm afraid of the D," Lizzie shot back before turning her gaze on me. "Did you have sex with him?" Unlike earlier, she looked intrigued by the conversation now. "Oh my god, did he make you come your first time? Because that's impressive."

"What?" I shook my head. "No, no, I haven't . . . I mean *we* haven't . . . "

"Did he go down on you?" Lizzie asked instead. "Use his fingers?"

"No," I choked out. "He just kissed me."

Both girls looked disappointed with my response.

"Just kissed you," Lizzie replied flatly. "Wow. He sounds exciting."

"Don't be a bitch, Liz," Claire chimed in. "We're not all fast movers." Smiling brightly, she nodded to me. "Keep going, Shan. Tell us about your kiss orgasm."

Flustered, I began to explain how I felt the other day when Johnny and I were on her bed, and again when we were in his car, dutifully ignoring the eye-rolls from Lizzie as I spoke. I sat with him at lunch every day this week, and while we had kissed many times before and after school, they were nothing like those other times. When I was finished explaining, I looked to my friends for advice. "Is that normal?"

"It sounds like you were close," Lizzie offered, interested once again. "And it also sounds like he's a beast."

I blushed and Claire snickered. "A beast."

"Imagine what he could do with those clothes off," Lizzie mused, smiling now. She was so pretty when she smiled. It was a rare thing nowadays, but when she smiled, it was wonderful. "I think you should ditch the clothes for your next dry humping session," she added. "And then report back to us."

"Yes." Claire nodded eagerly. "So Lizzie can give you some more of her experienced wisdom, while I listen in because I'm nosey."

"I'm not a whore, Claire," Lizzie grumbled. "Jesus."

"I know that," Claire hurried to assure. "But you've been with Pierce like a million times." Shrugging, she added, "We want to know about it."

"You don't have to tell us, Liz," I mumbled.

"Yes, she does." Claire shushed me before waggling her brows at Lizzie. "Tell us what you know, sensei."

"You don't even have a boyfriend," Lizzie laughed.

"So?" Claire shot back, grinning. "I have an excellent imagination and an insatiable thirst for knowledge."

"Fine, fine." Hauling herself into a sitting position, Lizzie shook her head and smirked. "Do you remember that Shakira music video – the one Claire tormented us into learning the moves of back in sixth class?"

"Vividly," I replied, cringing at the memory.

"That was the best song," Claire replied, eyes bright and full of that relentless optimism.

"Well, when you're on top, it's kind of like that." Her cheeks turned pink. "You just sort of grind and rock your hips and rotate."

"Whoa," Claire breathed. "I don't know if I'd like that." Scrunching her nose up, she said, "I think I'd like to be on the bottom."

"You'd be surprised what you find you like," was all Lizzie replied.

I sighed heavily. "Johnny said he doesn't want to have sex with me."

"What?" Both girls gaped at me.

"He said he doesn't want to have sex with me," I repeated, mortified.

"Who doesn't want to have sex with you?" Claire's older brother Hughie stopped in the hallway and arched a brow. His eyes widened then. "Holy shit! You're talking about Cap?"

"No," I blurted out, horrified. "I mean, I don't ... I didn't—"

"Dammit, Claire," Lizzie snapped. "I told you to close your door when you came up with the hot chocolates."

"I didn't expect perverts to be lurking around," Claire growled, narrowing her eyes at her brother. "Go away, creep."

"You're all too young for that kind of talk," Hughie stated, casting a meaningful look towards his sister. "Especially *you*."

"Oh my god, we're sixteen!" Claire laughed. "And that's rich coming from the boy whose headboard is positioned directly against my bedroom wall." Walking over to her dresser, Claire began to bang her palm down on the dresser in a hard rhythm. "Oh, yeah, baby, give it to me," she mimicked in a male voice. "Oh, Katie, I love what you do with your tongue—"

"Claire," Hughie hissed in warning. "Pack it in."

Unperturbed, Claire continued to mimic his voice, speeding up the banging. "Yes, baby. Now, now, I gotta pull out or I'm gonna cooooo—"

Hughie slammed the bedroom door shut just as Claire screamed, "Come!" and all three of us erupted in laughter.

"Fuck off," Hughie roared as the sound of his bedroom door slamming filled our ears.

"What is it with brothers thinking they know everything?" Claire snickered, flopping down on the bed. "Eejits."

I nodded. "You can say that again."

"I think you should text him," Lizzie chuckled. "Johnny," she added when we both looked at her in confusion. "Text him with that disgustingly pink phone he bought you," she encouraged. "And see if he wants to . . . *hang out?*"

"Oh yeah, that's good." Claire waggled her brows. "*Hang out.*"

Excitement thrummed inside of me. "I don't know." Pulling my phone out of my jeans pocket, I glanced at the screen and then back at my friends. "I'm not even supposed to be over here, guys."

"You've had a shitty week," Lizzie shot back. "One filled with *way* more drama than any of us could handle. I think you should text your boyfriend and spend Saturday night hanging out together."

"She's making all the sense today, Shan," Claire agreed with a grin. "You're already out, which means you're already in trouble." Shrugging, she added. "Might as well make it worth it."

"What if he's busy?" I whispered, biting down on my lip.

"He's not," Claire chimed in. "He's at the gym with Gerard."

"How do you know?"

"Because that's where they were when he called me earlier," Claire replied. "And that's where they'll be until the place closes."

I gaped. "All day?"

Claire rolled her eyes. "He's your boyfriend, Shan. You should know that he spends every hour of his waking day working out." She flexed her bicep and kissed it before adding, "Chasing those gains."

"You're so dumb," Lizzie chuckled.

"It's true," Claire laughed.

"Text him," they both said in unison.

Inhaling a deep breath, I opened my messages and began to tap out a text message.

"Ask him what he's doing tonight," Lizzie said.

"Oooh, see if he wants to go on a date?" Claire added. "Oh, oh, you can get dressed here."

"I've sent it," I breathed, dropping my phone down on the bed.

Snatching up my phone, Lizzie read through my messages before narrowing her eyes at me. "*Hi Johnny*," she deadpanned. "That's what you sent?"

I shrugged and clasped my hands together. "That's okay, right?"

"If you're four," Lizzie grumbled. "No kiss at the end?"

I shrugged, feeling at a loss. "Is that bad?"

"Not if you're texting your brother," Claire offered with a sympathetic smile.

"Oh my god, switch it off," I groaned, feeling sick. "Turn the phone off."
*Ping.*

"Ah, he texted you back," Claire squealed, snatching the phone out of Lizzie's hand and climbing off the bed.

"Hi baby," she began to read, only to stop and clutch her chest. "Oh sweet Jesus, he called her *baby*!" Flopping back down on the bed, she added, "And he gave her two kisses at the end." She sighed in contentment. "I think *I* just had an orgasm."

"Give me that," Lizzie grumbled, swiping the phone back from Claire. "Hi baby, how are you doing? Can I call you later tonight? Kiss, kiss."

My heart galloped wildly. "Tell him that he can call me," I said as I watched Lizzie type back a message. "Did you tell him he can?" I asked when she set down the phone on her thigh. "Liz?"

Lizzie opened her mouth to respond but the phone pinged again before she could respond. Glancing down at the screen, she grinned deviously.

"Oh my god." A shiver of unease rolled through me. "What did you do?"

"I told him that instead of calling you tonight, he could pick you up from here." She winked before adding, "He'll be here at eight, so you better get ready."

"Wait!" Pressing my fingers to my temples, I forced myself to breathe slowly and not panic. "Just . . . give me a minute." I inhaled several deep, calming breaths before asking, "Is this a date?"

Claire nodded her head vigorously. Meanwhile, Lizzie looked at me like I was a brand-new species of human. "I don't understand you, Shan," she sighed. "He's your boyfriend. You spend half of lunch every day with his tongue down your throat. You're meeting up with him on a Saturday night. *Of course,* it's a date."

"Should I . . . get him something?" I asked, feeling my heart rate spike.

"No," Lizzie shot back, appalled. "Why would you?"

"I don't know!" I flailed anxiously. "I'm just panicking, okay? What if he takes me somewhere? I don't have any money."

"It doesn't matter."

"It does," I choked out. "It matters to me."

"You could make him a mixtape?" Claire offered then. "Or a mix-CD for his car – if you wanted to give him something."

"That's a good idea," Lizzie mused. "What are you going to put on it?"

"I don't know." Leaning back against the pillows, I sighed. "Maybe it's a bad idea?"

"No." Walking over to her desk, Claire grabbed her laptop. It's a great idea," she assured me, inserting a disc into the slot on the side of her laptop. "Now do it."

"Do boys even like that sort of thing?" I asked, fingers hovering over the keys. "Aoife's always making mix-CDs for Joey and he never listens to them."

"Well, Gerard makes them for me and I love them," Claire replied. "Give him your thoughts, Shan. Find your feelings in songs and reveal them to him."

"Is that what you do?" Lizzie asked flatly.

"All the time," Claire groaned. "And I know he listens to them." Sighing, she added, "He just chooses not to *hear* them."

"Oh, dear god," Lizzie muttered. "That boy's a donkey."

"But Johnny's not like that. He'll listen, Shan. He *always* hears you. Oh here, take this—" Tossing a permanent black marker at me, Claire smiled. "Write something down on the disc once you're done, so he doesn't mistake it for one of Gerard's creations."

"You are so tiny, it's sickening," Lizzie groaned an hour later. "If I didn't eat a bite of food for the next year and a half, I still wouldn't be your size."

*That would be the hunger,* I begrudgingly thought. *Be glad you've never felt those kinds of pains.* "Do I look bad?" I croaked out, feeling nervous, as I glanced down at my outfit. "Am I okay?"

"No." She sighed and steered me towards the full-length mirror in the Biggs's family bathroom. "You look amazing and perfect and I'm disgustingly jealous of you right now."

"Ta-da," Claire squeaked, waving around a foundation brush in her hand. "You look like a . . . like a . . . sexy bitch!"

Eyes locked on the mirror in front of me, I took in my appearance and blew out a shaky breath. "Whoa."

"I know," Claire agreed knowingly. "Hot stuff."

"I'm going to freeze," I whispered, taking in the sight of the halter-neck red dress Claire had practically wrestled me into. She told me it was a dress, but I knew she was lying because I specifically remembered admiring the same red halter-neck last month – when she wore it with j*eans.* To be fair, it *was* a dress on me, reaching mid-thigh. On the upside, it was snug and not hanging off my body like most things I wore.

"The jacket will keep you warm," Lizzie corrected, flicking the black, leather jacket I was wearing.

"And the skirt is for easier access," Claire snickered. "Just joking. Hey – what size shoe are you?"

"I'm a three," I replied, watching myself warily in the mirror. My lips were blood red to match my dress and my eyes were smoky. My hair was tousled up in a purposefully-messy high ponytail that still reached my elbow in length.

"God, how unfair is that?" Lizzie grumbled. "I would kill to have small feet."

"Mam's a four. Hmm. Gimme a sec," Claire mumbled before darting out of the bathroom. She returned a few minutes later with a pair of black heels. "Perfect."

I eyed the six-inch heels with caution. "I'm not sure that's a good idea."

"It's a *great* idea," she coaxed and then dropped to her knees and shoved the shoes on my feet before I had a chance to object. "Good god, you're like a Bratz Doll with those big, popping eyes and all that hair," she said excitedly, standing up to take in my appearance. "You're so cute it hurts."

"Well, she's not a doll, Claire," Lizzie reminded her. "She's a person and she looks – stop it!" Slapping the hairbrush Claire was inching towards me away, Lizzie smiled. "You look gorgeous, Shan."

"Are you sure I shouldn't wear a bra?" I asked, feeling self-conscious.

"No," Claire huffed. "You should absolutely *not* wear a bra! It will ruin the whole outfit."

"Shan, if I could get away with not wearing a bra, then I would be roaming free 24/7," Lizzie said, squeezing my shoulder.

"Me, too," Claire offered supportively. "Flaunt those itty-bitty-titties, girl."

"Don't you think that's a bit short?" Hughie quizzed, cocking a brow as he leaned in the doorway of the bathroom. Frowning, he added, "I feel like I need to take off my jumper and put it on you."

"Shut up, Hugh!" Claire growled. "Leave her alone."

"Fair enough." Holding his hands up in defeat, he said, "Now clear out of the bathroom, will ye? I need to get ready. I'm picking up Katie in half an hour."

"*Katie* . . ." Claire mocked, fluttering her eyelashes. "Make sure you wash your willy for Katie."

"There is something very wrong with you," Hughie replied, scowling at his sister. "Mam and Dad brought the wrong baby home from the hospital." Turning to me, he added, "By the way, Johnny's parked outside."

My eyes widened. "H-he is?"

"Yay – let's go!" Clapping, Claire butted Hughie out of the way with her hip. "I'm so excited."

"Calm down," Lizzie grumbled. "You're not going."

"I'm a vicarious spirit," Claire replied. "I live for this stuff."

# Date Night

## JOHNNY

After scrubbing myself half raw in what had to be the fastest shower known to mankind, I tore my wardrobe apart trying to find something other than a jersey and hoodie to wear. Jesus Christ, my heart hadn't stopped racing since I received that text from Shannon earlier this evening.

> S: You can pick me up instead. I'm at Claire's house. I'll be waiting for you. Xx

I had no fucking idea what was happening here, and I cared even less, because the concept of spending time with my girlfriend outside of school had my head in a spin. All week, I had to make do with seeing her in the halls and a few scanty minutes at lunch, but now? Now I got to have her to myself for a night. Thanking Jesus that today was the day my mother had decided to relinquish the keys of my car back to me, I whizzed around my bedroom with a toothbrush hanging out of my mouth and paste dripping down my chin, trying to find something respectable to wear.

*Was this a date?*

*Did she want me to take her out?*

*Should I?*

*What the fuck was I going to do?*

*What about a condom?*

*Should I?*

*No!*

*Stop it!*

*Don't even tempt yourself.*

*Fuck . . .*

"You look very handsome," Mam announced when I walked into the kitchen five minutes later to grab my keys and wallet.

"Indeed." Gibsie, who was perched on a stool at the island, snickered loudly. "Very handsome, Jonathan."

I shot him a look that said *don't you fucking dare open your mouth*, regretting not dropping him straight home after the gym. I should have, but I'd been so thrown off-kilter that I took the big eejit home with me. I also told him about my plans, which was a rookie mistake, one I only made because, again, I had been thrown by that text. To be fair, I felt like I owed him an explanation for almost decapitating him at the gym earlier when I'd stopped spotting him to text Shannon back.

Gibsie smirked and gestured that his lips were sealed.

That would be a first.

"I look the same as always, Ma," I grumbled, knowing I needed to get in and out of this room before the woman gave me the mothering version of the Spanish Inquisition. "I'll be home late tonight," I added in as breezy a tone as I could muster, slipping my wallet and keys into my back pocket. "So, don't be panicking, okay?" *Or blowing up my bleeding phone.*

"Is that a new shirt?" Mam, ignoring my statement, asked as her gaze traveled over my body.

*Ugh.*

*Too fucking late . . .*

"No." Self-conscious, I pulled at the black fabric currently welded to my chest and shrugged. "It was in my wardrobe."

Mam smirked. "And new aftershave?"

"It's the bottle I got at Christmas." I shifted uncomfortably. "Why?"

"Oh, no reason, love," she replied with a knowing smirk. "Did you get your hair cut today?"

"Yes," I bit out impatiently, feeling on full display. "I stopped off at the barbers after the gym and got a haircut."

Her eyes sparkled with mischief. "Did you gel it, too?"

"Jesus Christ, Ma," I muttered, patting my hair. "So what if I did?"

"You've made such an effort with your appearance," she mused, arching a brow. "You must be going somewhere special tonight."

"With *someone* very special," Gibsie, the fucking turncoat, threw petrol on the fire by adding.

"You got a haircut, too," I reminded him.

"True, but I'm not the one with a date."

I glared at Gibsie.

He raised his hands and grinned sheepishly.

"Oh, love, take off your pants," Mam said then, dragging my attention back to her. "There's a crease down the front of your jeans." Hopping down from her stool, she moved for the ironing board. "Whip them off and I'll run the iron over them."

"What?" I gaped at her. "It's grand, Ma. I have to go."

"Jeans off," she ordered sharply, plugging in the iron. "No child of mine is going outside the front door in creased clothes."

"Jesus Christ." Muttering out a string of curse words, I kicked off my boots and dropped my jeans. "I need to go," I muttered, as I stepped out of my jeans and handed them to her. "Like, right now, Ma."

"You look good," Gibsie stated, tone serious, as he eyed the scar trailing down my thigh. The other one was thankfully concealed by my jocks. "It's really clearing up."

"Thanks?" I replied, giving him a WTF look as I shifted from foot to foot, waiting for my jeans. "Can you hurry it up, Ma?" I begged. "I need to go."

"Are you taking Shannon to the pictures, love?" Mam asked, smiling knowingly.

"It's called the cinema, Ma," I growled, rubbing a hand over my jaw. "No one – and I mean no bleeding one – calls it the pictures anymore."

"I do," Mam chirped back happily. "So, is that where you're taking her?"

"I don't know yet," I muttered. "I was going to let her decide."

"Ah, that's lovely, that is." Turning to Gibs, Mam smiled. "Isn't that lovely, Gerard?"

"It sure is." Gibsie snickered.

"You should be taking that young one to the pictures," Mam added. "What's her name – the Biggs girl."

Gibsie reddened and I smirked.

*Ha fucking ha.*

"Claire," he said, clearing his throat.

"Ah, yes, Hughie's sister." Mam smiled to herself as she ran the iron over my jeans. "You've been chasing after that girl since the day Johnny brought you home here, looking like a little blond, chubby cherub."

I snorted, and it was Gibsie's turn to glare at me.

"You were such a gorgeous little boy." Setting the iron down, Mam picked up my jeans and shook them out, inspecting her work, before thankfully handing them back to me. "Do you remember the summer back in primary school when you all camped out in the acre? You fell into that bush of nettles trying to lift her over the electric fencer because she was afraid of the neighbor's bull?" Mam laughed softly to herself. "You were all stung and nettled but you still managed to get her out of that field."

"Oh yeah," Gibsie chuckled, scratching his chin. "I forgot about that."

"I said it to Sadhbh and Sinead back then that they would have to keep an eye on the pair of you," Mam mused. "You were supposed to be Hughie's friend, but you and that young one were always inseparable. Joined at the hip with that little girl, you were."

"Well, thanks for the walk down memory lane, Ma," I said impatiently as I yanked my jeans back on and slipped on my boots. "But we have to go." Placing my hands on Gibsie's shoulders, I steered him towards the back door. "Night."

"Johnny, be good," Mam called after me.

"That's a song," I called over my shoulder.

"And a warning," she shot back. "Keep it in your pants."

*Jesus.*

Fifteen minutes later, I had dropped Gibsie off and was parked outside the Biggs house with sweaty palms and a solid semi in my jeans. Jesus Christ, the anticipation of just *seeing* Shannon was driving me half demented. Excitement and nervousness thrummed in my veins, making me feel all fucked up but that's what she brought out in me. Closing my eyes, I breathed deep and slow for several moments, wrangling my emotions into submission before attempting to get out.

When I felt slightly calmer, I climbed out and walked up the driveway, fighting an internal battle on what the fuck I was supposed to do when I reached the front door. Did I knock? Did I just walk in like I usually did? Jesus, I didn't know. I had no fucking clue what I was doing.

Thankfully, the front door opened inwards when I was halfway up the garden path and Shannon was physically shoved outside by two blondes before the door slammed shut behind her.

*Holy fuck.*

My feet faltered as my eyes drank her in. She was wearing a tiny, red dress, with a black, leather jacket, and matching black heels that made her legs look like they went on for days. Her hair was pulled back in a ponytail and flowing down her right shoulder, and her face? Jesus Christ, her lips . . . her eyes . . . fuck, I was in so much trouble.

Clasping a carrier bag in front of her, she smiled shyly. "Hi, Johnny."

Giving my head a little shake, I closed the space between us and pressed a kiss to her cheek. "Hi, Shannon," I said gruffly. "You look beautiful."

"How was the gym?" she asked, smiling up at me. "Were you careful?"

I could hardly make out a word of what she had just said because my entire focus was trained on her swollen lips that were puffy and red and making me think the most depraved thoughts.

*Get it together, asshole.*

"Yeah," I choked out and then roughly cleared my throat. "It was good." Taking her hand in mine, I led her down the path to my car. "You look so fucking beautiful." *You said that already, lad.* "Seriously, you're gorgeous." *Shut up, Johnny.*

"Uh, thanks." Under the street lamps, I could see the blush on her cheeks. "It's the clothes and makeup."

"It's the girl," I corrected, giving her hand a squeeze.

Shannon ducked her face and I bit the inside of my cheek.

"Hey – you got your car back?" she said then, eyes wide. "That's great."

"Yeah." Nodding, I opened the passenger door and gestured for her to get in. "I just got it back this morning." Shannon climbed in and I closed her door before rounding the car. "So, how'd you get out?" I asked, sinking into the driver's seat. "With Darren on patrol?"

Shannon grimaced as she fastened her seatbelt. "We had a fight and he stormed off. Mam was in bed so I sort of just . . . walked out." She shrugged. "He hasn't called since so I guess he hasn't gone home yet, either."

Fucking asshole.

"Well, I'm glad you're out," I told her, fastening my own belt. "And I'm thrilled that you texted me."

She smiled shyly. "You are?"

"Of course."

"Oh, here—" Reaching into the carrier bag, she withdrew a CD case and thrust it into my hands. "I made this for you."

"Uh, okay?" I stared down at the CD case. "Thanks?"

"You're welcome. It's a mixtape," she explained, face burning red. "Or a mix-CD."

I stared down at her handwriting on the case.

*Shannon's songs for Johnny.*

Fuck me.

"You look really nice," Shannon said, cheeks so hot I swear I could feel the heat radiating off them, as she gestured to my clothes. "And you smell great."

"Uh, thanks." I shifted in my seat, feeling a huge swell of relief.

"I love your haircut," she added, reaching over to trail her fingers through it. "You kept the length on top." She hesitated and moved to pull her hand back but then settled it on my cheek. "You're beautiful."

A shiver rolled through me, her words hitting me deep, and I leaned across the seat. *Jesus.* "Come here." Tangling a hand in her hair, I pulled her face to mine, knowing that I was about to be plastered in lipstick but not giving a shite either way.

The moment my lips fused with hers, I was done for. Every coherent thought, plan, and notion I had for tonight went clean out the window when I felt her tongue sweep out to duel with mine. Shannon moaned into my mouth and the vibration against my lips caused the semi I'd been sporting to shoot to full mast. I heard the sound of a seatbelt clicking and then she was right there, scrambling over the seats to straddle my lap.

*Jesus Christ, this girl was going to ruin me.*

My hands moved of their own accord, clamping down on her hips to hold her still as I pushed against her, driving myself to the point of pain with the need I had to just bury myself inside this girl and never come back up for air.

"Johnny?" she gasped, breathing hard against my lips. "What do you want to do tonight?"

Jesus, that was such a loaded question with endless possibilities. She didn't need to be giving me any notions. I needed basic instructions right now because I was in unknown territory and *she* was all I wanted to do.

"I don't know." Striving for self-control, I leaned back to look at her. "I was waiting to see what you wanted to do."

"I just want to be with you," she replied simply, placing her small hands on my chest and setting my body on *fire*. "I don't care if we sit in this car all night."

"Do you want to go to the cinema?" I offered, knowing that staying in the car all night was a dangerous idea – tempting, but very dangerous. "Or we could go to Biddies for a game of pool? Or Spizzico for dinner?" I shrugged, feeling flustered. "Whatever you want."

"I . . . " She glanced down at my chest before tipping her chin back up, eyes locked on mine. "I don't want to go anywhere?"

*Was that a question?* "You don't want to?" I asked, uncertain. "Do you want to go home?"

379 • CHLOE WALSH

"No." Shannon shook her head. "Not . . . " Her words broke off and she ducked her face again.

"Not what, baby?" I asked. "If you don't tell me, I won't know."

"I just want to be alone with you," she whispered, looking up at me through hooded eyes. "You know?"

I *knew*.

But I also knew that it was a terrible idea.

"You want to go to my house?" I asked, feeling my body ache with the pressure it was taking to take this slowly. I knew I needed to, but Christ, she wasn't making it easy for me. "My room?"

She nodded. "If you do?"

Fuck.

# I'm Coming!

## SHANNON

The moment Johnny drove through the opened gates of his property, he killed the lights of the car, leaving us completely in the dark. Excited and nervous, I kept my eyes trained on his face, and my hand on top of his as he changed gears, slowing to a complete halt halfway up the long, narrow laneway.

Cutting the engine, he turned to look at me. "I'm going to take you up to my room, but we're going to have to sneak in through the front, okay?"

Nodding eagerly, I whispered, "Okay."

"That's not because you're not welcome," he hurried to add. "It's because my ma won't let us have a minute's peace otherwise." Unbuckling his belt, he pushed the driver's door open and climbed out, gently closing his door before rounding the car. "You ready?" he asked, reaching for my hand when I stepped out and closing the car door behind me.

"Yeah," I replied, keeping my voice low. It was raining hard again and the cold droplets were pelting against my bare skin, causing a shiver to roll through me.

"Bonnie and Cupcake should be in their run for the night," he explained as we crept up the pitch-dark laneway. "It's around the back of the house, so we should be good."

"What about Sookie?"

"Sookie won't bark at me," he replied confidently.

"How will she know it's you?"

"She'll just know." Sliding his keys into his hand when we reached the driveway, Johnny literally dragged me across the gravel to lean against the house. "You okay?"

"Should we be doing this?" I asked, breathing hard.

"Honestly? Probably not, but we're going to do it anyway."

"Okay." I nodded. "We are?"

"I don't know." Johnny hesitated. "Are we?"

"Uh, I think so?"

"Fuck it—" Shaking his head, he kissed me hard and then dragged me towards the front door. Releasing my hand, he held a finger to his lips, and then turned the key in the door, cringing when the door creaked open. "Go on," he mouthed, inclining his head towards the hallway.

Kicking off my high heels I bent down and snatched them up before hurrying inside. Johnny quietly closed the door after us and for a few moments we both stood in the entry hall, with our eyes locked on each other.

After a minute or so of complete silence, a slow smile crept across his face and I grinned back at him.

"Bingo," he purred, before hooking an arm around my waist and pulling me flush against him.

Feeling heady with lust and adrenalin, and smothering a squeal, I wrapped my arms around his neck, shoes and all, and pulled his face down to mine.

Our kiss was warm, clumsy, and overloaded with an overwhelming need for *more*. Johnny made this deep, gravelly sound in his throat, and then we were moving, stumbling blindly down the hallway.

"You're back early, love. Did your car break down?" Mrs. Kavanagh's voice cut through my lust-filled thoughts and I jerked away from Johnny like I had been scalded.

Mortified, I turned to stare at his mother who was sitting on the bottom step of their impressive staircase. She had a washing basket set on the floor at her feet as she paired socks. Sprawled out beside the basket was Johnny's old, black Labrador. The moment Sookie spotted Johnny, she clambered unsteadily to her feet and bounded towards him.

"Jesus," Johnny muttered under his breath as he pushed both hands through his hair before dropping a hand to pet his dog. "I didn't see you there, Ma."

"That's alright, Johnny, I saw you," Mrs. Kavanagh replied with a smirk. "Great effort, though." Turning her attention to me, she smiled warmly. "Hello, Shannon. It's lovely to see you again."

"Hi, Mrs. Kavanagh," I strangled out, mortified beyond belief. "H-how are you?"

"I'm grand, love." Setting a pair of socks she had paired into the basket, she stood up and dusted down the back of her jeans, smile still firmly in place. "You look stunning tonight."

"Uh, thanks?" Heat crept across my skin. *Should I apologize for being here? Was she mad? Should I apologize again for my mother's behavior? Should I just go?* "So do you," I wheezed out, feeling slightly sick now. *What the hell should I do?*

Making the decision for us, Johnny reclaimed my hand and pulled me towards the staircase. "We're going to go watch a film," he announced, watching his mother with what looked like great caution, as we passed her.

"Oh?" his mother replied, arching a brow. "Nothing good playing at the pictures?"

"I have one in my room that we wanted to watch," Johnny shot back, half-dragging me up the staircase after him. "So, yeah. That's what we're going to do."

"What film?"

"Jesus Christ, Ma, a film!" Johnny groaned, halting at the top of the staircase to look down at his mother. "What does it matter?"

"*Love Actually*," I blurted out the first title that popped into my head. Johnny nodded eagerly. "That's right."

"Gibsie lent it to us," I added to my lies, realizing that I was a far better liar when put under pressure from an authoritative figure than he was. *Years of practice.* "He said it's his favorite, and he was going on all week at school that we needed to see it."

"Exactly." Giving my hand a small squeeze, he pulled me up the last two steps to join him. "And Shannon's never watched it."

"Why don't you bring the DVD down and we can all watch it in the living room together?" his mother called after us.

"*What?*" Johnny gaped. "Ma, *no!*"

They stared hard at each other for a long beat before Mrs. Kavanagh released a heavy sigh and nodded. "Fine, go ahead and watch your film, but keep your door open," she said in a low, warning tone of voice. "Wide open, Jonathan."

Without another word, we strode off down the hallway towards his room. Slipping inside, Johnny closed the door behind us and deftly turned the lock before leaning against it. "I am so sorry about her," he muttered, pinching the bridge of his nose. "She's . . ."

"Only looking out for you," I whispered. "It's okay."

"She's smothering me," he corrected, shoulders sagging in defeat. "I can't move anymore and she's watching me like a hawk."

"I don't think she wants me here, Johnny," I confessed, chewing on my lip nervously. "Maybe I should go?"

"What?" He shook his head and stifled a groan. "No, Shan, that's not it." Striding towards me, he captured my hand and walked us over to his bed. "My mother really likes you. I promise. She's just . . ." Sinking down on his bed, Johnny released a heavy sigh. "It has nothing to do with you being here and everything to do with you being up here alone with me." Shrugging, he looked up at me and said, "She's just afraid of something happening between us."

I sat down beside him. "Happening?"

"Sex," he replied gruffly, shifting his body to face me.

My breath hitched. "Oh." Swallowing deeply, I nodded. "Okay."

"But that's not what's happening here," he hurried to say, even though he leaned closer.

"Okay," I breathed, heart hammering in my chest.

"We don't have to do anything," he added, voice thick and gruff, eyes locked on mine. "We can watch a film, if you want?"

"No." I shuffled closer. "I don't want to do that."

"Are you sure?" His eyes darkened. "We could play PlayStation?"

"Johnny?"

"Yeah, Shan?"

I leaned forward and pressed a kiss to the corner of his mouth, pulling back slowly to gauge his reaction.

"Shan." He was watching me with a dark expression. "Shan . . . "

Feeling brave, I did it again.

A beat passed.

His pupils grew darker.

My heart hammered harder.

"Ah, fuck it," he growled and smashed his lips to mine.

Wrapping my arms around his neck, I scrambled up the bed, taking him with me. Falling onto my back, Johnny's lips never left mine as his weight came down hard on me, pressing my body deep into his luxurious mattress. Unwilling to detach my body from his, I wrapped my legs around his waist.

"We shouldn't do this," he whispered over and over against my lips, but he wasn't stopping and I knew I never would, as I attacked his lips with a desperate hunger of my own. The way he kissed me, like my lips and mouth were the only thing that mattered to him in that moment . . . It was addictive and intoxicating.

Sliding my hands from his neck to his chest, I ripped at the buttons of his black shirt, desperate to feel the heat of his bare skin pressed against me.

"Shan," he groaned into my mouth, hips thrusting against me. "What are you doing, baby?"

"Please," I begged, clumsily snapping the buttons open until the fabric parted like the Red Sea. "Just . . . take it *off*."

"Fuck . . . " Breaking our kiss, Johnny sank back on his knees and made short work of his shirt, dragging it off his body. I took that as my opportunity to remove my jacket. Tossing it aside to join his shirt on his bedroom floor, I flopped back down, with my dress pooled at my waist, begging him with my eyes to just *keep going*. Hormones invaded my mind, kicking my common sense out the window and taking hold of the steering wheel of my brain, letting me know that my virginity was in serious danger of evaporating tonight.

Kneeling between my legs, wearing only his jeans and with his hair sticking up in forty different directions from our antics, Johnny looked down at me all fluffed out on his pillows and exhaled a sharp breath. "I'm keeping you, Shannon Lynch."

"Really?" I breathed, staring up at his swollen lips and wanting just one more taste.

"Really," he confirmed, eyes locked on mine. Shrugging almost helplessly, he offered me a crooked grin, giving me a tiny glimpse of vulnerability and making me fall deeper for him. I was stumbling further into the black abyss of the unknown with this boy, with no safety net to break my fall. Pressing the brakes wouldn't make a blind bit of difference because my heart was in the driver's seat and powering ahead without thought for consequences.

"Are you sure you don't want to play GTA?" Johnny offered then, tone thick and gruff. He playfully walked his fingers up my bare thigh, skimming the edge of my knickers. "I might beat you this time." Just when I thought he was going to move his fingers higher, when everything inside of me was *screaming* at him to move his fingers higher, he pulled his hand back to rest on my thigh again. "What do you say? Hmm? Do you want a rematch, Shannon *like the river*?"

I shook my head, my breathing hard and uneven. "No."

"No?" He arched a brow, smirk still firmly in place. "Then what do you want from me?"

Finding a bravery I only seemed to have when he was with me, I pulled myself up on my elbows and whispered, "I want you to finish what you started."

The blue in his eyes darkened, and the smile he was wearing turned almost feral, as he grabbed my thighs and dragged my body closer to his. "I always finish what I start." Resting his weight on one elbow, he hovered above my body, with his lips so close to mine that I could feel his breath. "But we're not going there." He pressed a drugging kiss to my lips before burying his face in my neck. "Not yet." Nuzzling my neck, he pressed a trail of hot, wet kisses up my neck, his tongue sweeping

386 • KEEPING 13

out to taste me, to claim me with leisurely swipes that I felt in every nerve ending in my body. Nestling between my legs, he didn't make any further move, he just continued to kiss me with hot swiping flicks of his tongue, destroying me with his weight alone.

"Really?" I practically cried as my fingers dug into the hard ridges of his waist. "You're sure?"

Groaning, Johnny nodded. "I'm sure." His hand moved from my hair to my hip, shifting our bodies into the perfect alignment, and the move caused a moan to tear from my throat. He responded to my small gasp of surprised pleasure with a low growl of approval of his own. "But I can do other things for you." He brushed his lips against mine almost lovingly before pulling back to gauge my reaction. "If you want me to?"

My pulse skyrocketed and I blew out a ragged breath, nodding up at him.

His eyes blazed with heat as he lowered his lips to mine. "I promise I'll make you feel good," he whispered between kisses. "Just tell me if you don't want it, or if I'm moving too fast and I'll stop, okay?"

"Don't stop," I strangled out, hands shooting out to clutch his shoulders. "Please."

Johnny chuckled softly. "I haven't started yet."

"I don't care," I breathed. "Don't ever stop."

Rearing back on his knees once more, Johnny stared down at me. Breathing hard and fast, I remained on my back, overloaded with adrenalin and lust, as I watched him watch me for the longest time. The anticipation of the unknown was making me feel faint and all I wanted to do was drag him back down on top of me, but I stopped myself, knowing that I had no clue of how to progress from here, just that I desperately wanted to.

"You're so fucking beautiful," he whispered, with a small shake of his head. "Jesus." Trailing a finger over my cheek, he leaned down and kissed me. His hand trailed down my neck, moving lower and lower until his thumb brushed over my nipple. "I love you," he whispered, and then he was cupping my breast in his hand, gently stroking his thumb over the fabric of my dress as my nipple hardened to the point of being painful. "Is this okay?" he asked against my lips as he continued to touch me.

"Johnny—" Shivering violently, I arched into his touch, kissing him almost frantically. "So much okay."

His hand moved lower, fingers grazing over my hipbone, before his hand settled on the front of my knickers. "What about this?" Stroking his nose against mine, he slipped his hand inside my underwear and cupped me *there*. "Is this okay?"

My body jerked beneath him, hips bucking, and I nodded like a mad person. "Don't stop."

Exhaling a ragged breath, he slipped his tongue into my mouth at the same time he slid one finger inside me.

Careful not to moan too loudly and alert his mam as to what we were getting up to in his bedroom, I let my legs fall open, welcoming his touch, as I plastered my lips to his, clinging to his broad shoulders for all I was worth as I shuddered beneath him.

"I want you," he growled into my mouth, as he worked his finger inside me, moving slowly, in and out, deep and drugging. "More than I've ever wanted anyone in my entire life." Kissing me hard, he pulled out only to push a second finger inside me. "Fuck, you're so wet, baby." Trembling, I clung to him, bucking my hips excitedly. "So fucking tight . . . shite, is this okay?"

"It's okay, Johnny, it's okay," I practically screamed as I dragged his lips back to mine, bucking my body in encouragement. "Just stop asking stupid questions and keep going!"

Chuckling against my lips, Johnny crooked his fingers, doing something inside of my body that was entirely unfamiliar but *oh* so *welcome*. I felt a tightening sensation in my core as a blast of white-hot heat crept up my body. It was a feeling that I wanted to chase down, some basic, primal instinct inside of me demanding I do so.

Bucking my hips, I moved against his hand, hunting down that feeling. His lips came down on mine, muffling my cries, as he moved his fingers faster inside of me, taking me further, pushing my body to the point of no return.

Helpless to sensation, I clutched his broad shoulders and clung to him, trusting him with everything I had inside of me. When his tongue entered my mouth, sweeping over mine with the same rhythm as his fingers, I couldn't hold on, or else, I just couldn't hold back. Whatever it was, it felt like I was crashing over a cliff. I couldn't explain it but my body went lax and I jolted violently beneath him as what I could only describe as ripples of ecstasy shot through my body.

"Jesus," I cried out, tearing my lips from his as my entire body jerked violently. "What's happening – oh my god!"

"Shh," he coaxed, kissing my neck. "Just ride it out." He suckled on my neck. "Enjoy it."

"Uh." Clenching my eyes shut, I allowed myself to absorb what I was feeling. "*Okay . . .*"

"You like that, Shan?" he whispered in my ear, pumping his fingers in and out, prolonging the seizure-induced pleasure, wrecking me. "Coming on my fingers?" He kissed me again, harder this time. "Because I fucking love it."

*Oh my god . . .*

When I finally stopped shaking, Johnny slid his fingers out of me, and I thought he was going to roll off me, but he didn't. Instead, he grabbed my hips and settled between my legs once again, rocking his hips against me, causing another blast of tingling shockwaves to erupt inside of me. I could feel his erection pressing against me; so hard it was terrifying. The friction from his jeans as he ground his body against mine was too much. Crying out, I slipped my hands into the waistband of his jeans and pulled him closer, wanting with everything I had to just fall into this boy and never come back out again.

Johnny grabbed my hands and dragged them above my head, holding both of hands down on the pillow above my head with one of his. His free hand moved to my hip as he continued to grind against me, lips fused together, his tongue massaging mine with almost wild, uncontrolled, lust-filled thrusts. Gasping against his lips, I hooked my legs around his waist, moving with him instinctively with every thrust of his hips.

*Bang, bang, bang . . .*

"Johnny!" Mrs. Kavanagh's voice came from the other side of the door as another loud knock sounded. "I thought I told you to keep this door open."

My eyes sprang open in horror and I froze. "Oh my god."

"Jesus Christ," Johnny groaned, breaking the kiss with a panting breath. Roughly clearing his throat, he called out, "We're watching the bleeding film, Ma!"

"Well, now I'm up here, you can open the door and let me see you," his mother called back.

"Give me a minute!" Rolling off me, Johnny flopped onto his stomach and muttered a string of curses into the duvet before climbing off the bed. "I'm sorry about her," he grumbled as he watched me scramble off the bed and readjust my clothes.

"It's fine," I choked out, feeling mortified as I pushed down my dress and straightened my ponytail. "Don't worry about it."

"Hey – you okay?" he asked, watching me with concern. "Shan?"

"I'm just . . ." I looked around his room and shrugged helplessly. "I don't know how to act now." Clasping my hands together, I gestured to his bed and sighed. "I'm . . . embarrassed."

Johnny smirked and closed the space between us. "Was it okay?" he asked, voice low and husky, as he smoothed a hand over my hair and tipped my chin up. "What I did . . . did you like it?"

I nodded, cheeks reddening. "Yeah."

"Then don't be shy with me," he whispered, stroking my chin with his thumb. "And don't be embarrassed, either. I love you, okay?"

"I love you, too," I whispered, burying my face in his chest.

"The door, Jonathan!" Mrs. Kavanagh barked, knocking repeatedly on the other side of the door. "Now!"

"*All right*," Johnny roared back. "Jesus Christ, I'm coming, Ma!"

"That's what I'm afraid of," his mother shot back. "Now open up."

# Slamming Doors

## JOHNNY

Yeah, I was in trouble. The girl sitting in the passenger seat of my car was proof of that.

Shannon's phone was blowing up – had been for the past twenty minutes. I knew I was going to get the blame for keeping her out tonight, I knew I was going to get threatened, I knew a million other disastrous things would be waiting for me once I pulled onto her street, but I couldn't find it in me to worry. Screw worrying, I was fucking *delighted* with myself.

My uneventful Saturday had somehow morphed into Saturday night with my girlfriend on her back, and my fingers inside her. Jesus Christ, the sounds she made when she came around me would haunt me.

I didn't want to give her back, but I also didn't want to make her suffer the third degree from my mother. I went too far tonight. I knew it, but I couldn't regret it, because she was just . . . mind-blowing. Honest to god, I was in so far with her that I knew I would drown. They might as well lock me up now, because I was done for.

Shannon's knees were bopping restlessly as she stared out the windscreen of the car, watching the other cars whizz past us. I wanted to put her at ease, but I had no way of doing that. It wasn't like I was going to be invited inside for tea and biscuits when I walked her to the door. *More like threats and handcuffs.*

"I hope Joey's home," Shannon said, dragging me from my thoughts.

"Hmm?"

"Joey," she repeated, cracking her knuckles. "I really hope he's at home."

Reaching over, I took one of her hands in mine and gave it a reassuring squeeze. She was trembling and it was making me feel murderous.

"He'll be there," I told her, praying like hell that I was right. For reasons I would never fully understand, Shannon was close to Joey. In her mindset, he was as good as a god. I didn't ask too much about it because I was scared of the answers. Some of the things she had told me about her childhood terrified me. I didn't want to hear about what they had endured because I didn't trust my reactions. It was the worst feeling in the world, feeling helpless, and I didn't cope well with helplessness. Thinking about how that was *exactly* how Shannon had felt for most of her life made my chest constrict.

The minute I pulled up outside the house of fucking horrors and cut the engine, the sound of screaming filled my ears. Jesus, what was wrong with their neighbors? I could hear the carnage from the garden wall.

"Uh . . ." Swallowing deeply, Shannon tucked her hair behind her ears and moved to unfasten her seatbelt. "Thanks for a great evening." She gave me a bright smile and reached for the carrier bag she had placed in my car earlier. "I had the best time, Johnny."

"Whoa, stop—" I reached over and closed the car door she had opened. "Don't do that."

"Don't do what?"

"Pretend we're both deaf and can't hear what's going on inside that house."

Shannon sagged in her seat. "I don't know what to say." She pressed a hand to her forehead. "It's nothing out of the usual for us." Sighing heavily, she added, "It's probably because of me." She glanced over at the house and then down at her lap. "Because I went out."

*Yeah, fuck that.*

Unfastening my seatbelt, I climbed out of the car and walked around to her side. "What are you doing?" Shannon asked, looking all panicked, as she scrambled out of the car with her bag fisted tightly in her small hand. "Johnny?"

"I'm walking you to your door," I told her, trying to keep the anger out of my voice. "And I'm making sure you're okay."

"I'm okay," she hurried to say.

"And I want to make sure you stay that way," I told her as I took her hand in mine. "So, let's go."

Shannon was a bundle of nerves as we walked to her house. By the time we reached the front door, she was visibly shaking. "Thanks for staying," she said in a small voice before pushing the door inwards.

"Anytime," I replied gruffly, but my response was swallowed up by the loud shouting that greeted us.

"Where the hell were you?" Darren demanded, stalking from the kitchen towards us. His eyes shifted from Shannon to me and his feet faltered.

Leaning against the doorframe, I folded my arms across my chest and stared back at him.

*Yeah, I'm here, fucker.*

"I went to Claire's," Shannon explained, stepping inside and dropping her carrier bag on the floor. "Why are you all shouting?"

"Shannon!" her mother strangled out, rushing from the kitchen. "Why did you do that?"

"Do what?" Shannon replied, tone harder than I was used to hearing. "I went for a walk to my friend's house. There's no law against it, Mam."

Pride roared to life inside of me.

*Go on, baby. Don't let them push you around.*

"And where does he fit into this walk?" her mother demanded, slurring her words a little. "And those clothes?"

I arched a brow and studied her closer. Bleary eyed, swaying from side to side, and slurring her words. *Christ, she was hammered.* I squinted my eyes, taking her measure. *Or is she high?*

"Are you drunk?" Shannon asked, voicing my thoughts aloud.

"No," her mother strangled out. "I'm after my tablets."

*High*, I mentally confirmed. *High as a kite on Valium or some other sedative by the looks of it.*

"Where are your kids?" The words were out of my mouth before I had a chance to filter them. Three pairs of eyes landed on my face, and being the absolute glutton for punishment that I was, I decided to go with it. "Tadhg, Ollie, and Sean."

"*My* children are in bed," Mrs. Lynch hissed, glaring daggers at me. "Which is exactly where Shannon should be."

"Shannon's not a child," I replied, forcing myself to speak and not roar at this woman like I so badly wanted to. I had a feeling she didn't work on the same frequency as the rest of us and shouting was the only way to get through to her, but I refrained. "She's going on seventeen. She is her own person, with her own friends, and her own mind, and *you* need to step back and stop trying to smother her in your fucked-up attempt to make up for not protecting her when she actually needed you to."

"Excuse me?" Mrs. Lynch choked out, clutching her chest.

"You heard me," I told her. "You were shouting and roaring so loud, we could hear you from the street. You have the gall to throw shit at her while you're off your face on tablets with three small children upstairs?" I shook my head. "You're a disgrace."

"Back the fuck off, Johnny!" Darren snarled. "You have no idea what you're talking about."

"I know a lot more than you think," I sneered. "And you're all quick to judge me, when not one of you is in the position to throw stones."

"Johnny," Shannon croaked out, eyes wide. "It's okay."

"It's not okay, Shan," I said gruffly. "It needed to be said."

"Get off my property, or I'll have you done for trespassing." Shannon's mother warned before bursting into tears and running back into the kitchen. I felt a smidgen of guilt rush through me, but not enough to take back what I had said. The truth had a bitch of a sting to it sometimes.

"You heard her," Darren said coldly, glaring at me. "And don't come back around here, Johnny."

"Darren," Shannon strangled out. "Don't say that."

Another Lynch popped up then, but this one came from behind me. "Kav," Joey acknowledged in a friendly enough tone as he strolled up the overgrown path in a pair of mechanic overalls, face covered in grease, and a plastic lunchbox dangling from his hand. He slapped a hand on my shoulder as he passed by. "Causing more shit?"

"The usual amount," I replied evenly.

"I bet," he mused. "Alright, Shan." Ruffling her ponytail, he roughly shoved Darren out of his way. "You coming in or are you just going to stand there leaving the cold out?"

"It's the heat out," I muttered.

"Maybe in your house," he shot back, not missing a beat, before disappearing into the kitchen.

"He's not coming in here," I heard his mother scream from the kitchen. "Tell him to leave!"

"Christ, could you give it five minutes before you start the crying." A cupboard door slammed and Joey's voice filled my ears again. "I'm tired, I'm hungry, and I *just* got off work."

"Go home," Darren said before closing the door in my face.

The door swung back open seconds later and Shannon popped her head out. "I'm so sorry," she whispered, eyes laced with pain. "I love you—"

"Shannon, get in here!"

"Bye, Johnny."

And then the door slammed shut in my face again.

# Crisis Averted. Everyone Breathe

## SHANNON

"Why did you do that?" I demanded, furious, as I glared at Mam and Darren. "He was just dropping me home."

"Look at the cut of you," Mam choked out. "Going out dressed like that."

"There's nothing wrong with what I'm wearing," I shot back defiantly.

Mam's face reddened. "You look like a—"

"Whore?" I offered. "Thanks, *Dad*."

Mam flinched and dropped her head in her hands.

I rolled my eyes, too furious to deal with her waterworks right now. "You were both horrible," I hissed, focusing on Darren. "You just shut the door in his face!"

"Can you blame me?" Darren growled. "You heard how he spoke to Mam."

"He was telling the truth," I spat, blinking back the traitorous tears that were pooling in my eyes. "And you know it!"

"And you wonder why this family has a bad reputation," Joey mused around bites of a ham sandwich. "Shan's right." He took a swig from his can of Coke. "That was rude as fuck."

"Our family has a bad reputation because *you* can't keep yourself out of trouble, so don't you start giving me shit," Darren shot back angrily. "I know you were suspended from school again yesterday for fighting. Your principal *called* me, Joey. What was it this time? Some lad said something you didn't like so you go ahead and puck the head off him?"

Joey shrugged, unaffected. "Something like that."

"If you don't steady up and learn to control that temper, you're going to end up getting yourself locked up," Darren warned. "Mark my words."

"I thought this was about Kavanagh?" Joey replied, scratching his jaw. "How did this suddenly get turned on me?"

"It's not about Johnny," I hissed, keeping my furious gaze locked on Darren. "It's about how you're trying to control *my* life."

"He's still outside, you know," Joey added.

My heart leapt in my chest. "He is?"

"Stay where you are, Shannon," Darren warned before stalking into the hallway and swinging the door open. Muttering a string of curses under his breath, he slammed the door shut and returned with a thunderous expression. "He's still there."

"Like I said," Joey replied, taking another bite of his sandwich. "Go on out to him, Shan," he added mid-chew. "Don't mind the two of them."

"Don't even think about it, Shannon," Mam screeched. "I don't want you going anywhere near that boy."

"Jesus Christ," Joey growled, tossing his half-eaten sandwich down on the counter. "You're making a big fucking deal out of nothing. Just let her go outside and talk to him, let him do all his checkups to see she's not being hurt or whatever the fuck he does that calms his nerves, and then she'll come back inside. No harm done."

"No harm done?" Mam choked out. "*Plenty* harm could be done, Joey."

"Give her a bit of credit," my brother hissed in a disgusted tone. "She's not you."

Mam wailed and Joey rolled his eyes.

"Intelligence doesn't play a role in this," Darren bit out. "*Hormones* play the only role in this."

"Well then, I happen to possess the perfect antidote to *hormones*." Joey slipped his hand into his pocket and withdrew his wallet. Flipping it open, he retrieved a condom and waved it around. "I know *you've* never seen one of these," he added, sneering at our mother. "And I doubt they're even holding fucking hands, but just in case – here, Shan, hold the tip when you roll it on." He tossed me the condom and winked.

"Now." Picking his sandwich back up, Joey took a big bite and chewed. "Crisis averted. Everyone breathe."

"What the fuck is wrong with you, Joey?" Darren growled, snatching the condom out of my hands and shoving it into his pocket. "She's sixteen years old."

"I'm aware," Joey agreed, taking another swig from his Coke.

"He's too old for her," Mam wailed.

"No, he's not," Joey scoffed. "He's seventeen, not seventy. Relax, woman."

"Yes, he damn well is too old," Mam countered shakily.

"Well, that's your opinion," Joey shot back.

"It's the truth," Mam strangled out. "And you shouldn't be encouraging her."

"Listen," Joey snapped, wiping his buttery fingers on his overalls. "I know you're both *new* at this, but here's a helpful parenting tip: you either swallow your pride and let her be with him, or this whole thing blows up in your face. I think it's pretty clear by now that he's not going anywhere, so you might as well get on board with it." Shrugging, he added, "Shannon has a boyfriend. Big deal. She's not a baby anymore, and it's about time you two stop treating her like one."

"That's ridiculous."

"No, what's ridiculous is you going along with that woman's fucked-up thought process and trying to keep Shan in this house after everything that happened," Joey countered. "If you keep it up – if you force them apart – he *will* lose his shit. Draw a battle line with that fucker and he will go to war with you." Turning to Mam, he added, "And if I was you, I'd lay off throwing threats around because you have a hell of a lot more to lose out of this – and a lot more skeletons to be exposed – if his daddy decides to have *you* done for slander."

Mam had her head in her hands and Darren had his back to me, but Joey was facing me and when he noticed me edging closer to the kitchen door, he smirked and winked.

"What are you—" Darren's voice trailed off and he spun around, catching me red-handed. "Don't even think about it," he warned.

Tearing through the hallway, I yanked the front door open.

"Shannon, I'm not messing around here—"

I didn't stop to listen to him. Instead, I hurried out the front door, breaking into an excited run when my eyes landed on Johnny leaning against the side of his car, scowling at my house like it personally offended him. His eyes found mine and relief flooded his features. "Are you okay?"

Nodding, I barreled barefoot through the garden and rounded the footpath at top speed, not stopping until I was flush against him. "You didn't go home," I said, panting, as I looked up at him. "You didn't leave."

"I couldn't," Johnny replied thickly. His hands dropped to my hips, pulling me closer. "I needed to know you were safe."

My heart burst open in my chest, and I felt like I was drowning in feelings. "I'm safe."

"You sure?" He looked so vulnerable when he said, "Because I think I'm going to need a promise."

*Oh god . . .*

Reaching up, I snaked a hand in his hair and pulled his face down to mine. "Would you settle for a kiss goodnight?"

"Only if you promise you'll still be here in the morning," he replied, brushing his lips against mine. "So, do you promise?"

I blew out a ragged breath. "I'll be here."

"If you need me, you call me," he whispered, tucking a strand of hair behind my ear and then cupping my cheek. "Doesn't matter what time it is. Just pick up that phone, and I'll come, okay?"

Unable to stop myself, I leaned my cheek into his touch. "Okay."

"I'll call you tomorrow," he added gruffly, trailing his thumb over my cheek. "And I'll pick you up for school on Monday."

"No, no, no. You don't have to do that for me," I hurried to say. "I can get a—"

"I want to pick you up," he interrupted. "If you want me to?"

I nodded weakly. "I want you." *To. Add the to, Shannon.* "To," I croaked out. "I mean, I want you to pick me up."

"I want you, too," he said with a smirk. "In every way."

My body grew hot and achy. "I, uh . . . I—"

Johnny didn't wait for me to respond before pressing his lips to mine, firmer this time. Deeper.

Holding onto his arms, I kissed him back with everything I had, desperately trying to show him how much he meant to me.

"If that's what you call hand-holding then I'd really like to know what you call the other shit," I heard Darren say from somewhere nearby.

"Maybe they're gone beyond hand-holding," I heard Joey muse. "I can't always be right."

# Better Safe Than Sorry

## JOHNNY

"What do you mean you're not *telling* me?" Gibsie demanded, letting the ball spin from his hands. It was Sunday evening and we were down the pitch, attempting to throw a ball around. Well, *I* was attempting to throw the ball. Gibs was doing his best Inspector bleeding Gadget impression, trying to milk information about my night with Shannon.

"Exactly what I said." Ignoring the burn in my lower half, I extended my arms and jumped to catch his piss-poor throw. "I'm not fucking telling you."

"We can talk about it," Gibsie called back, arms out to catch the ball. "You're allowed to tell your best friend."

"I'm not talking about her."

"Holding things in isn't good for a person."

"What do you want me to say?" I snapped, flinging the ball back at him.

"I want you—" words breaking off, he caught the ball with a loud *ooof,* and then tossed it on the grass before continuing, "to tell me what you got up to in your room." He waggled his brows. "When you snuck Little Shannon in there."

"Jesus." Giving up on having a normal conversation, I grabbed my water bottle off the grass and headed for the carpark. "I'm calling it a day."

"Already?"

"I'm tired."

"Because you were up late bumping uglies with your girlfriend?" Gibsie teased, falling into step beside me. "Ah, yes, that can take it out of a fella." Bumping shoulders with me, he said, "So, what are we talking here? Full-on penetration or just some heavy petting? Or the *slip and slide?* The old *rub and bump.* The 'just a little more'. The 'we'll stop here, except we never do'?" His eyes lit up. "Holy shit, did you go bareback?"

"What are you *talking* about?"

"Sex," he replied simply.

"We didn't have sex," I muttered, pulling my keys out of my pocket. "It's not like that."

"Not *like* that?" Gibsie shot back, disbelieving. "Don't piss down my back and tell me it's raining."

"Gibs," I snapped, flustered. "It's not, okay? I'm not doing that with her." Pressing the button on my key fob, I unlocked my car and moved for the driver's side. "It's too soon."

"Did Shannon say that?"

"I said that," I growled, yanking the door open and climbing in. "Me, Gibs. *I'm* saying it's too soon."

"But you were tempted, weren't ya?" he asked, dropping into the passenger seat beside me. "No one's that much of a saint."

I debated turning on the stereo to drown out his voice. That's what I *should* have done. Instead, I heard myself say, "I wanted to." Sighing heavily, I added, "Badly."

"But?"

"But she's not ready," I strangled out, furious with myself for talking about this. "And *I'm* not bleeding ready."

"Lad, you've had sex before," Gibsie replied, frowning. "I know it's been a while, but you weren't reborn a virgin when you came out of surgery."

"It's different with her."

"How?"

"Feelings, Gibs," I bit out. "Huge fucking feelings."

"Ugh." He shuddered. "Sounds awful."

"It's all *more* with her," I explained, knees bopping restlessly. Drumming my fingers against the steering wheel, I thought about what I wanted to say, tried to find a tactful way to phrase it, then said to hell with it and came right out with, "I'm losing control over my life. She walked in and tossed everything on its ass. I'm literally scrambling, trying to put everything back together and piece out a new plan. I don't know how to handle her, and I'm scared of pushing her too far, too fast, and fucking it all up. I think *she* thinks I don't want her that way, which is fucking insanity because you've seen her. Jesus, who *wouldn't* want her? But that's the problem. I don't just *want* her. I want to *keep* her. And what if I hurt her? She's so small, Gibs. And she's only sixteen. And her ma's threatening me. I feel like if I put one foot wrong here, it's over, and I'm so fucking scared of screwing this up, Gibs. I don't want to wreck it. I can barely breathe when I'm around her. Everything goes all hazy and *feelings* . . . fucking feelings just *flood* me!" I blew out a breath, feeling relieved to have it off my chest. "I'm completely fucked, aren't I?"

"I think so," Gibsie agreed.

"Yeah." I sighed. "I think so, too."

"Your mind is a scary place to be," he mused, scratching his chin. "Can you not overthink everything?" He tilted his head to one side, studying my face with a peculiar expression etched on his own. "Seriously, can't you just turn that big sponge of a brain off and just relax?"

"No." I shrugged helplessly. "This is how I'm wired."

"Well, then—" he tapped his temple "—there's a lot to be said for having a simple mind."

"You *are* simple," I muttered dejectedly. "And I'm simple for listening to you."

"Do you still have those condoms?" he asked then.

I glared at him. "Did you not hear a word of what I just said?"

"I heard you," he replied calmly. "Now answer the question."

"No," I muttered, shoulders sagging. "I panicked when they fell out on top of her in Claire's room so I just threw them in her bin."

"What a waste," Gibsie whimpered, biting on his fist. "Ugh – right, so you need to go to the chemist. Pronto."

I gaped at him. "But I just told you—"

"I know what you told me—" he cut me off with a wave of his hand

"—and I'm telling *you* that the road to fatherhood is paved with good intentions."

"It's 'the road to hell is paved with good intentions', Gibs."

"Considering pussy is one of the leading factors in a man's admission to hell, I'd say both statements are fairly on point, lad."

"*What*?"

"Just buy a packet of condoms. Put one in your wallet. Even if you don't use it, it's there."

"I don't want to tempt myself."

"And *that's* your first mistake," he told me. "It's not the condom in your wallet that will lead you into temptation. It'll be the naked girl sprawled out beneath you." Waggling his brows, he added, "The one that floods you with all the *feelings*," in a teasing tone.

Jesus, he was making sense.

How the hell was he making sense?

"Better safe than sorry, lad," he added with a shrug.

"You're right," I choked out.

He winked. "I know."

"Would you step back, Gibs," I growled, bristling with tension, as I stood in the condom aisle at the chemist. He was hovering so close to my back that I could feel his chin resting on my shoulder. "You're breathing down my bleeding neck!"

"Why do they do that?" he asked, unperturbed. Stepping around me, he reached down and picked up a rectangular, pink box from the bottom shelf. "Why would they put pregnancy tests next to condoms?"

"No clue." I shrugged. "But they do it everywhere."

"Well, it doesn't exactly scream out that they have confidence in their product, does it?" he continued, waving the test around aimlessly. "It's like 'hey, wrap up your dick, buy some lube, hell, even throw in a cock ring for a bit of craic, and have a great fucking time, but just in case it fails, you know where to come back to confirm the end of your life.'" He rolled his eyes. "I think it's a terrible marketing idea."

"It's not a marketing idea, lad," I muttered wearily. "It's for convenience."

"And here's more of it," he grumbled, grabbing a box of ovulation test strips off the top shelf. "Are we preventing babies, confirming babies, or planning babies?" His voice rose with his outrage. "Which is it? All three? What the fuck, Johnny?"

"*We* are preventing babies," I growled, snatching up a twelve pack of extra-safe condoms. "The rest of that shite isn't for us, so put the tests down and walk away, ya bollox!"

"I should make a suggestion," he huffed, "on how *not* to traumatize their male customers."

"You do that, Gibs," I replied wearily, condoms in hand. Heading for the front of the store, I side-stepped a woman with a litter of young children swarming her legs. "I'm sure they'll listen."

"I hope so," Gibsie grumbled, falling into step alongside me.

"Hello, Jonathan," the woman said. "Hello, Gerard."

I swung back to face her and inwardly groaned when recognition dawned on me.

*Jesus Christ, why me?*

"How's it going, Miss," I muttered, discreetly moving the box of condoms behind my back.

"Yeah, hey, Miss Moore," Gibsie purred in that tone of voice he used for flirting, causing me to repress a shudder. *He had a fucking thing for the older women.* "You're looking your usual lovely self."

"Well, thank you, Gerard," our guidance counsellor replied. "Fancy meeting you two boys in the chemist on a Sunday evening." She smiled up at us. "I presumed you'd both be running around a field somewhere with a soccer ball."

"A rugby ball," I correctly quietly. "And we were. We just had to—"

"We're on a condom run," Gibsie blurted out – much to my horror. And then he went a step further and gestured to her five small kids. "Something your husband obviously doesn't buy very often."

"*Lad*," I hissed, mortified. "I'm sorry about him, Miss," I hurried to say, feeling my face burn. "He doesn't have a filter."

"I'm well aware," Miss Moore replied, thankfully smiling. "Well, I'll let you two go about your business, and I'll see you both at school tomorrow."

"Yeah, see you at school." Cringing, I grabbed the back of Gibsie's neck, stepped around a couple of identical red-haired girls, and hauled him towards the checkout. "Come on, you fucker," I hissed in his ear. "Before you do any more damage."

"Oh, and boys?" Miss Moore called after us.

"Yeah?"

"If you ever need someone to talk to . . . " Frowning, she gestured to the pregnancy test Gibs was still holding before continuing, "my door is always open."

"Uh, that's okay." I laughed nervously and elbowed Gibsie in the ribs. "We're good."

"The fuck, lad?" Gibsie groaned, rubbing his side.

"Put it down," I hissed, still smiling like a maniac at our teacher.

"Oh, we're not pregnant," Gibsie laughed, awareness finally dawning on him. With a carefree shrug, he tossed the test into a basket of makeup samples beside him. "Oh shit, I'm sorry—" Digging it back out, he held it out to our teacher. "Did you want them?"

*Ugh.*

"Jesus Christ." Rubbing my jaw with my hand, I turned around and walked away, stalking up to the checkout with only one goal in sight; pay and get as far away from that lunatic as possible.

"Good afternoon," the middle-aged pharmacist chirped when I dropped the condoms on the counter in front of her.

"Yeah," I muttered, cringing when I heard Gibsie talking animatedly to Miss Moore from a few feet behind me. "Can I get a bag please?"

"Are you sure you need a bag?" she asked, ringing the condoms through her till. "It's an extra fifteen cents."

"I'll pay," I ground out. "Just give me the bag please."

"Okie-dokie," she replied, handing me a plastic carrier bag. "That'll be €13.14 please."

"Thanks." Pulling out my wallet, I handed her a twenty and swiped up the box.

"What's wrong?" she asked after about a minute and a half of a struggle.

"Nothing."

I couldn't open the plastic bag.

*I couldn't fucking open it!*

My hands were sweating, fucking perspiring, which was ridiculous because I had bought condoms before – frequently. Granted, it had been a while since I made the necessary rubber run, but still . . .

*Six long fucking months.*

Oh Jesus, I hoped this wasn't going to be a new thing for me.

Was I losing my touch?

I couldn't find the fucking opening of a plastic bag.

Fuck.

Was this going to happen to me with everything?

"Do you want a hand with that?" she asked for the third bleeding time.

"I can do it myself, lady," I snapped, flustered, and more than likely frightening the poor pharmacist. "I *can* do it," I repeated in a calmer voice. "I'm just out of practice."

"Out of practice *shopping*?" she asked, frowning.

"With a lot of bleeding things," I muttered under my breath before finally opening the bag. "See!" I grinned, victorious, as I held the twelve pack in one hand and the tricky fucking carrier bag open with the other. "I *can* do this."

"Yes, you can," the pharmacist replied, giving me an encouraging thumbs up.

*Jesus . . .*

# Bust Ups and Push Ups

## SHANNON

In a world where everything was changing at the speed of light, I could depend on one thing to remain the same, and that was Lizzie and Gibsie's blatant dislike of each other. Every day during lunch for the almost two weeks that we had been back to school, they had tossed snarky comments and remarks back and forth at each other. Some cruel. Some funny. Some downright disgusting.

I couldn't understand what the problem was between them, and even though Lizzie was one of my best friends, I had to admit that she was the orchestrator of every argument. She seemed to find a problem with everything Gibsie did. He was either breathing too heavy, or chewing too loudly, or taking up too much of the table. It didn't matter what Gibsie did or didn't do; Lizzie *always* found fault with him.

By lunchtime on Thursday, the tension bubbling up between them had reached a breaking point, and I was seriously beginning to rethink our sitting arrangements, wondering if we would be better off sitting at our old table. At least they would be far apart from one another. The only thing that kept me at the rugby table was the boy whose arm was slung over my shoulder.

I couldn't look at Johnny too often; it just wasn't good for my poor heart. I tried to just breathe and be normal, focus on anything other than him, because I knew that if I thought too much about how good it felt having his big body pressed to mine, or how he made me shiver when he leaned close to whisper something in my ear, and how he absentmindedly stroked my arm with his thumb as he laughed and joked with his friends, I would burst into flames.

Johnny's father was back in Dublin and his mother was with him, they wouldn't be home until late tonight, so he had invited me to go over to his house after school today. I wanted to go, more than anything, but I was a nervous wreck thinking about the storm I knew I would face when I got home tonight. They were already furious with me for taking spins to and from school with him, so I knew I would be returning to a battle, heightened by the fact that my father was due to be discharged from Brickley House any day now. I tried not to think about my father too much, knowing that thoughts of him evoked crippling panic attacks. Instead, I focused on the positives in my life. I focused on my friends and my brothers, but mostly, I focused on Johnny. My mother's wrath or the fear of my father wouldn't stop me from going to the Kavanagh's house, though. To be honest, I wasn't sure anything could. I was desperate to spend time alone with him. He made me feel safe, and wanted, and I was sticking to that feeling like glue.

"Are you seriously that stupid?" Lizzie's high-pitched snarl cut through my thoughts, causing me to almost leap out of my skin.

"You okay?" Johnny asked, turning to look at me.

"Yeah," I choked out, resisting the urge to press my hand to my chest. "I just wasn't expecting that."

"Ignore them," he whispered, resuming his thumb tracing on my shoulder.

"Are you being for real?" Lizzie continued to hiss, glaring daggers at Gibsie, who was sitting across from me. "Or is this just another stupid joke to you?"

"Relax," Gibsie huffed, folding his arms across his chest. "I was only asking a question."

"Well, ask good questions," Lizzie countered and then shoveled a forkful of salad into her mouth. "Not stupid ones that only make you appear even stupider than you already are."

"Stupider is not a word," Gibsie scoffed, and then quickly looked to Johnny for back up. "Right, Cap?"

"It's a comparative adjective, lad," Johnny replied, shifting uncomfortably.

Gibsie gave him a blank stare.

Johnny blew out a breath. "It's a word, Gibs."

"How is *stupider* a word?" he demanded. "That just sounds stupid."

Johnny shrugged. "I didn't make the rules."

"Maybe it was put in the dictionary to describe you," Lizzie offered dryly. "As in; Gerard Gibson is stupider than any person I have ever met."

"That's it—" Shoving his chair back, Gibsie jerked to his feet. "I'm calling Father McCarthy to intervene on your behalf. You need an exorcism and Jesus."

"And you need institutionalizing," Lizzie shot back, nostrils flaring. "Idiot."

"The whole fucking world isn't your punching bag," Gibsie roared back, furious. "I don't know who told you different, but they gave you some bad advice."

"Gerard—" Claire, who was sitting beside him, began to interject, but Gibsie wasn't having it.

"No, Claire, I'm done with taking her shit," he growled, picking up his schoolbag. "You are a mean girl, Lizzie Young, and it astounds me that you managed to snag two decent girls to be friends with you."

"Astounds you?" Lizzie countered in a sarcastic tone. "Wow. Big word, Gibs. Can you spell that, too?"

"You know what?" Tossing his bag over his shoulder, he gave her look of pure disgust. "Fuck you, Lizzie." Having said that, Gibsie stalked out of the lunch hall, red-faced and fuming.

"Are you happy with yourself?" Johnny asked, glaring at Lizzie. "Did that make you feel good? Belittling him like that?"

"He's a big boy," Lizzie shot back defensively. "He can take it."

"He's dyslexic!" Johnny snapped. "And you just made him feel about two feet tall in front of half the school."

Surprise flashed in Lizzie's eyes and her cheeks reddened. "I didn't know that."

"Well, now you know!" Pressing a quick kiss to my cheek, Johnny shoved his chair back and said, "I'll see ya later, Shan," before hurrying off in the direction Gibsie had gone.

"Did you have to do that to him?" Claire hissed. "That was cruel."

"He does it back to me," Lizzie defended, still red-faced. "And I didn't know he was dyslexic."

"It shouldn't matter," Claire snapped. "That was a horrible thing to say to anyone." She rose from her chair, adding, "And there's a lot that you don't know about him so don't be so quick to judge!"

"I didn't know," Lizzie muttered, turning to me when Claire was gone.

"I believe you," I told her. And I did. "But . . ."

"But?"

"I know you and Gibsie don't get along, and that's okay, but just . . . just stay away from each other and don't be so mean," I blurted out. "I think you really hurt his feelings."

"Yeah, well, no more than his actions hurt others," Lizzie hissed, as she became the fourth person to stalk away from the table.

"Well, that escalated quickly," Hughie stated calmly.

I blew out a shaky breath. "I'll say." Pushing my chair back, I stood up and grabbed my schoolbag. "I'll see you later, guys."

"Bye, Shan," they all chorused as I hurried away from the table, feeling too shy to sit there without Claire, Lizzie, or Johnny.

Slipping my bag onto both shoulders, I clutched the straps and maneuvered through the crowded hallway in the direction of the bathroom, only to halt in my tracks when my eyes landed on Bella standing outside the bathroom door.

"Slut," she hissed, narrowing her eyes at me.

Sidestepping a group of boys, I ignored her and hurried away from the bathroom, choosing the sanctuary of the third-year common room instead. Slipping inside, I sagged in relief when I found it empty. Dropping my bag on the floor by the table, I walked over to the kitchenette and flicked on the kettle. A loud sniffle from the armchair startled me and I swung around.

"Lizzie?" My brows shot up in surprise when I spotted her slumped in the chair. Abandoning the kettle, I made a beeline for her. "Are you okay?"

"I'm fine," she whispered, wiping her cheeks with the back of her hand. *She clearly wasn't.*

Sinking into the chair opposite her, I rested my elbows on my knees and offered her a small smile. "Do you want to talk?"

She shook her head. "No."

"I . . . " Hesitating, I reached over and took her hand in mine. "Are you sure?"

"I'll be okay, Shan," she strangled out, dropping her head so I couldn't see her cry. "Honestly, I'll be fine."

"I know," I agreed, giving her hand a small squeeze. "But it's okay if you're not fine right now."

"I'm just so angry all the time," she confessed, keeping her head down. "It won't stop."

Careful not to push her for more than she was willing to give, I remained silent and continued to hold her hand. I knew why she was angry with the world and I didn't blame her. "It's coming up soon, right?" I finally found the courage to ask. "Your sister's anniversary?"

Snatching her hand away, she slumped in her chair and nodded stiffly. "The end of the month."

I blew out a shaky breath. "It's hard."

"There's no justice in the world," she bit out.

"No," I agreed sadly. "There isn't."

"I fucking hate this school, Shannon," she hissed. "I hate that team and everything they represent."

My heart sank. "Gibsie reminds you of him?"

Lizzie flinched. "I can't help it. Every time I look at him, I see *him*."

"They're not the same person, Liz," I offered quietly. "Gibsie isn't Mark."

"Whatever, Shan," she said wearily. "I don't want to talk about it."

"Okay." Clasping my hands together, I studied her closed-off expression. "Are you and Pierce at least okay?"

"No," she strangled out, as her eyes filled with tears once again. "It's all a mess."

"Why?"

"Because I can't get *past* it," she sniffled. "I can't see beyond it, and I can't get over it. I'm stuck and I keep driving him *away*." Releasing a furious growl, she wiped her eyes and jerked to her feet. "It doesn't even matter. He can fuck off if he wants to. I'm not holding him down and making him stay. If he wants to be done then we're done."

"Lizzie—"

"I don't want to talk anymore," she cut me off by saying. "I *can't*."

"Okay." Rising to my feet, I slapped on a bright smile. "We won't talk."

She sagged in relief. "Thank you."

"What time are your parents going to be home?" I asked breathlessly.

"Not until later tonight," Johnny grunted and I watched as a bead of sweat trickled down his brow. "Will we go again?"

"Yeah." I blew out a breath. "Are you sure it's okay that I'm here?"

"Hundred percent." He shifted beneath me, hands moving into position. "Is this good for you?"

Shivering, I nodded. "It's good."

"Poker straight," he instructed. "Don't bend."

"I won't," I replied, only to laugh when his fingers touched a particularly ticklish part of my thigh.

"Come on, baby," he grunted, breathless beneath me, arms locked tight like vices on my body.

I could hear the smile in his voice, but I knew this was important so I didn't push for playful. "I'm sorry, I'm sorry," I giggled, smothering my laugh. Inhaling a sobering breath, I locked my body into position and said, "Okay, muscle man, go for it."

"One, two, three—" His words broke off and I was lifted into the air, held there for a moment, and then lowered back down. The movement was effortless as he repeated it over and over.

"You okay?" he asked, voice raspy and a little breathless, as he continued to pump my body up and down.

"All good," I assured him, holding myself perfectly still.

"I'm going to go faster," he warned me, tightening his hold on my body. "Tell me if it's too much for you."

"I can handle it," I promised, feeling a little off-centered and dizzy.

"The fuck?" Gibsie's voice perforated through the grunting and heavy breathing.

Startled, I swung my gaze to where he was standing a few feet from us with a huge grin on his face.

"Do you mind?" Johnny grunted, not breaking his rhythm. "We're in the middle of something here."

"I've heard of fellas using household items as makeshift weights," Gibsie mused, scratching his jaw, as his gaze trailed over us. "But using Little Shannon as a barbell? This is a new thing for you, Johnny."

"His parents aren't here and they locked the garage," I called out by way of explanation, feeling my face flame with embarrassment. "We were just improvising."

"So you have a free house and you're weight training?" Gibsie replied in an amused tone. "And people say I'm weird." Pushing off the doorframe, he stepped into the room. "Be careful. You're not out of the woods yet, Cap."

"Upper body," Johnny muttered, jaw locked tight in concentration, as he continued to lift me up and down.

"Yeah," I hurried to explain. "See, we're not touching anything below the waist, and that's allowed."

Gibsie's brows shot up and his smile deepened. "Is that so?"

Johnny let out what sounded like a pained growl.

I tried to nod, but it was impossible considering he was still lifting me up and down.

"Fuck, I feel like I should put some *mood* music on," Gibsie said then, causing us both to look at him.

My brows furrowed. "Huh?"

"Oh, not for you," he explained. "For me. I'm getting hard watching this."

"Jesus Christ Gibs," Johnny barked, lowering me onto his chest so that I was sprawled across him. "The hell is wrong with you?"

"I don't know," he groaned, diving into the armchair. "I'm feeling very confused right now. But please, continue. I want to see how this plays out."

"I'm going to, uh . . . go to the bathroom," I squeezed out, as I twisted around onto my hands and knees.

The move wasn't my best idea, considering it left me straddling Johnny. But in his defense, he looked as uncomfortable as I felt. His hands moved to my thighs of their own accord as he pulled himself into a sitting position. "I'm getting you counseling," he said to Gibsie as his hands remained clamped on my thighs. "Seriously, lad. You're getting out of hand."

"Can I go?" I blurted out, tapping his hands to get him to release me. "I really need to pee."

Gibsie snickered and Johnny gave my legs a squeeze before letting go. "Take your time," he told me, keeping his eyes locked on Gibsie. "I need a word with my buddy here."

Springing unsteadily to my feet, I hurried for the door, only to hesitate and turn back around. "Hey, Gibs?"

"Yeah, Little Shannon?" he replied, smiling warmly at me.

"Why do you do that?" I asked, my mind straying.

"Do what?"

"Call me *Little Shannon*?"

"Because you're little?" he laughed. "And you're Shannon." Grinning, he shrugged. "Little Shannon."

*Fair enough.* "Well, I just wanted to ask if you were okay?" Shifting uncomfortably, I clasped my hands together. "After what happened at lunch today?"

"It's all good," he told me, smile still in place. "No worries."

"Okay." Shrugging helplessly, I added, "but for the record, I think you're really smart."

His brows shot up. "Me?"

"You," I confirmed quietly before slipping out of the room.

# Fired Up

## JOHNNY

"Lad, I think I love your girlfriend," Gibsie stated when Shannon whizzed out of the sitting room. "That's weird, right?"

"What's weird is you *telling* me that you love my girlfriend," I replied, climbing to my feet. "That's dangerous."

"You know I don't mean it like that," he chuckled, holding his hands up. "I'm just saying that she's a really decent girl and I like her." Scratching his jaw, he looked at me thoughtfully for a long moment before adding, "You did a good job."

"Yeah, she is." Frowning, I reached for my bottle of water off the coffee table. "And thanks ... I think?"

"I'm still trying to work out how you went from Bella to Shannon." Shrugging, he added, "They're like night and day, lad."

*Don't remind me.* Unscrewing the cap of my bottle, I drained the contents before asking, "So, are you really okay after earlier?"

"Yeah, I'm grand," he grumbled, dropping the mask. "I just don't get what that girl's problem is with me, lad."

"Did you ever offend her?" I asked, feeling as clueless about it as he did. "Call her a name or something?"

"Me being *alive* offends her, Johnny," he countered with a huff. "So, I'd say yes, I offend her by waking up every morning."

"I don't get what her problem is either, lad," I offered with a shrug. "I'm thinking she has some serious issues."

"We all have issues," he countered. "Not all of us go around taking those issues out on other people."

"True."

"I'm done taking her shit," he added. "I mean it. I don't care if she's Claire's friend. I'm not giving her a free pass anymore."

"Never thought you should have given her a free pass anyway – regardless of who she's friends with," I told him. "You teach people how to treat you by setting boundaries, lad. If you let someone walk all over you, they're going to think it's okay."

"I just felt sorry for her over all that stuff that went on with her sister a few years back," he muttered. "But there's only so many times I can let it slide."

"Lizzie has a sister?" I frowned. "I didn't know that." Curious, I asked, "What went on with her sister?"

Gibsie blinked rapidly. "You don't know?"

"No." I narrowed my eyes. "What don't I know?"

"I'm not supposed to say anything about it," he muttered. "I'm literally sworn to secrecy."

"Come on, lad, it's me. Who am I going to tell?"

"Look, it happened before you moved down here," he said. "And that's all I'm saying."

"Gibs—"

"Trust me, you don't want to know anything about it," he hurried to say. "I promise."

I thought about it for a moment, weighed up how much shit I had going on in my own life, weighed up the drama I was dealing with when it came to Shannon's family, and decided Gibsie was right. I didn't care enough to poke around in Lizzie Young's life. I had my own issues to handle and she was my girlfriend's ill-tempered friend who I could barely tolerate but did so for Shannon's sake. "You're right," I agreed. "I don't want to know."

Gibsie nodded in approval. "Good." His brows furrowed for a brief moment before smoothing out again as a smile crept across his face. "So, you and Shannon were working out, huh?"

"Yes," I replied, eyeing him warily, not knowing what he was about to come out with, but knowing whatever it was wouldn't be good. "What's wrong with that?"

"Nothing," he mused. "Other than the obvious."

"Which is?"

"You have a free house with Shannon inside it, and instead of making good use of it, you're throwing her around like a bag of sand."

"You know why," I bit out. "I'm taking my time."

"Hmm." He tilted his head to one side "Did they break your instincts when they operated? You know, like when they neuter a dog and he doesn't pick up the scent anymore? Because the Johnny I remember wouldn't waste such a rare opportunity."

"I wasn't neutered, you insensitive prick," I snapped, outraged. "And my sperm swims just fine. They checked!" *Twice.*

"Then there's something wrong with you," Gibsie shot back, not missing a beat. "Because that girl is insanely sexy and you're thinking about rugby."

"Hey," I warned, bristling. "Don't call my girlfriend sexy."

"Why not?" he taunted. "Don't *you* think she's sexy?"

"Of course I think she's sexy," I spat. "I think she's a lot of fucking sexy."

Gibsie waggled his brows. "Is that so?"

"Yeah, that is so – but that's not the point." Flustered, I shook my head and pointed at him. "*You* don't say that she's sexy." I narrowed my eyes. "*You* keep your beady little eyes off her."

"Well, it's the truth," he laughed. "And I'm not blind, lad."

"You *look* at her?" I demanded, appalled. "At *my* Shannon?"

"*Your Shannon*," he snickered. "Yeah, I do, and it's not just me. We all look at her – and apparently *looking* at her is all you do, too."

"Are you fucking with me right now?" I demanded, furious.

"Nope."

"Who's we?"

Gibsie shrugged. "Me, Feely, Hugh, Danny Mac, Luke, Pierce, Donal—"

"Well, stop looking at her that way!" I roared, livid. "Jesus Christ!"

"I'm just saying, she's gorgeous and we all have eyes," he snickered. "But that doesn't mean I'm imagining myself naked on top of—"

"If you finish that sentence, I will rip your head off," I seethed. "Fair warning."

"Are you getting mad, Johnny?" he chuckled, arching a brow. "Hmm? Are you getting all fired up, lad?"

"What does it look like?" I snarled, not bothering to deny it.

"Perfect." Springing out of the chair, Gibsie grinned. "Now that we've established that testosterone still pumps in your blood, go do something productive with your girlfriend." He sauntered over to the door. "And none of that hand-holding bullshit," he added. "You're not twelve, Johnny, and neither is she."

"Get the hell out of here," I bit out, jaw clenched.

"Oh, and if you're still in the air about full penetration, then I highly recommend going down the mouth-to-pussy resuscitation route."

"Jesus Christ, Gibs!"

"It's a scenic view and very rewarding." He winked. "It's a win-win, lad."

"Go home." I pointed at the door. "Right this instant or you'll be the one needing resuscitating."

"Aye-aye, Cap," Gibsie shot back with a salute before darting from the room.

"Yeah, you better run, fucker!" I roared after him, chest heaving. "Because when I'm back to a hundred percent, I'm going to strangle—"

"Are you okay?" Shannon asked, appearing in the doorway, looking flushed and uncertain.

"No," I bit out, chest heaving with a mixture of anger and lust as my eyes roamed over her body, drinking in the sight of her. She was so fucking beautiful, standing there in the black leggings, fluffy socks, and an oversized white t-shirt she'd changed into after school. Her hair was pulled back from her face in a high ponytail, her face was void of makeup – and bruises – and I'd never seen anything so fucking perfect.

I was destroyed.

I'd fucked up phenomenally and I couldn't get out. I was all in – heart, head, body, balls ... *every* part of me was wholeheartedly *in* with this girl. It felt like she had been in my life forever. Like I'd never known anything other than Shannon. She was my first love, and she was scary as fuck to me. Being with her was an obsession that threatened to consume me daily. I had to work my ass off to keep my head in check, but remembering to keep my feet on the ground and my head out of the clouds was easier said than done when I had a girl that knocked me on my ass with one glance. She wrapped me up in childish, illogical, irrational knots, with a new one attaching itself to my heart with every day that passed. I was completely losing control and that was a problem for me, and my feelings for her were a serious issue because they were too strong to rein in, too much to take, and too reeking of permanence. In other words, I was royally fucking screwed.

"I'm not okay," I strangled out, running a hand through my hair in frustration.

"Wh-what's wrong?" she whispered, looking up at me with wide eyes. "Are you sore?"

"No, it's not—" I stopped myself and released a pained growl. Her eyes burned holes in me so deep that I had to look away before completely losing myself in the girl. It was too much. *She* was too fucking much.

"What is it?" she asked, cautiously moving towards me. "Johnny, what's wrong?" Her small hand curled around my arm, her touch tentative, the feel of her skin on mine setting my body on fire. "You can talk to me," she added in a small voice, and the smell of her perfume flooded my senses. *God help me.* "You can tell me anything."

"What do you want from me, Shannon?" I croaked out, feeling incredibly vulnerable, as I stared down at the only girl I had ever loved. I needed her to tell me what to do. She needed to set the pace because I was weak around her, and I needed more than I feared she was ready to give. Gibsie had fucked with my head, and now my mind was stuck in fucking beast mode. I wanted her so damn badly, I couldn't think straight. Knowing that we were all alone only made it a million times more intense.

"What do you mean?" she asked, looking fearful.

"From me," I replied, heart racing. "From this?" I shrugged, feeling helpless. "From our relationship. What do you want from *me*?"

"Honestly?"

I nodded. "Always."

"Everything," she whispered, looking into my eyes. "Especially the broken parts."

Aw, shite.

She gave my words back to me, and I was done for.

*Completely fucking done for.*

I knew it the moment my lips crashed down on hers. I knew when I hoisted her up and felt her legs wrap around my waist like a vice. And I especially knew it as I carried her upstairs to my bedroom, spurred on by her moans of encouragement as she kissed me back just as fiercely. When I kicked my bedroom door open, I didn't feel any pain. It was drowned out by the desperate urge I had to feel skin on skin with her. My knees hit the base of the bed, sending us toppling onto the mattress.

"Shite," I growled, trying to pull myself up on my elbows so I didn't smother her. "Did I hurt you?"

"Don't talk," Shannon begged, wrapping herself around me like ivy, and dragging my body back down on hers. "Don't stop."

I didn't think I could stop if I wanted to, which I definitely *didn't*.

"Are you sure?" I forced myself to ask anyway. My heart was racing so hard I was sure she could feel it. "We can stop—"

My words were cut off when she dragged my face down to hers and kissed me hard. "Or maybe not," I breathed, falling deeper into our kiss – deeper into *her*. I loved it when she clutched my neck with her small hands, like a kitten extracting and then detracting her claws, leaving marks on me for days with her nails.

Shannon's hands moved to my t-shirt and she yanked on the hem. Smiling against her lips, I rested my weight on one hand and used my free hand to reach over my shoulder. Catching ahold of the fabric of my t-shirt, I tugged it over my head, tearing my lips off her for the millisecond it took to toss my shirt away before returning to her. And then her hands were on me, tugging and pulling on my bare skin, nails digging into my flesh, as she rocked her body against mine almost fervently.

Hard as I'd ever been, I thrust myself against her, groaning every time I was met with her bucking hips meeting me halfway. Her skin was hot and flushed, her body trembling beneath mine, as she drove me half-demented with need.

"Johnny?" Shannon strangled out, pressing her hands against my chest. "Can you get off me for a sec?"

"Shite." I sprang back faster than a moving bullet. "Did I go too far?" I asked, panting, as I knelt between her legs. "Do you want to stop?"

"No." Shaking her head, Shannon sat up and reached for the hem of her shirt. "I don't want to stop."

My heart hammered violently and my dick strained against its constraints. "Shan, you don't have to—"

She whipped her shirt over her head and my eyes instantly drifted to her chest. Adam's apple bobbing in my throat, I watched as she reached behind her back and unhooked her bra. Achingly slowly, she slid her hands out of the straps and discarded her bra on the floor. "Hi," she whispered, letting her hands fall to her sides, revealing her breasts.

"Hi." I swallowed deeply, desperately trying to keep eye contact with her and not let my gaze wander to her perfect fucking tits. Jesus, they were so perky, with little rose-bud nipples all puckered and straining. "You're so beautiful," I told her, giving up the fight and taking my fill of the sight of her. "I don't even know what to say." The fresh-looking scar between her side and right breast caught my attention and I froze, feeling like I'd been doused in cold water.

"What?" Shannon asked, sensing my withdrawal. "What's wrong?"

Battling down a tsunami of anger, I reached out and brushed my fingertips over the scar. "Is it sore?"

"Not anymore." She shook her head. "I don't even feel it now."

Well, I felt it; deeper and harder than I thought possible. I couldn't take my eyes off it. That's how they saved her. How the doctors helped her breathe when that bastard almost beat the life out of her. "Johnny, don't think about it," Shannon croaked out. "Don't look at me and see my dad."

"I'm not," I strangled out, struggling to rein in my emotions.

"You are," she countered shakily. "I can see it in your eyes."

"I'm not doing it on purpose," I admitted, shoulders sagging. "It's just hard for me to know what he did to you, and know that he's getting out any day now, and I can't fix it for you."

"I'm not asking you to fix me," she whispered, shivering. "I'm asking you to be with me."

"I am," I told her.

"Without feeling sorry for me," she added, lip wobbling. "Or looking at me like I'm broken."

"Shannon, that's not what I'm doing," I hurried to say, but it was too late; she was already off the bed and reaching for her shirt.

"It doesn't matter," she squeezed out.

Shite . . .

"Hey, hey, hey—" Springing off the bed after her, I intercepted her shirt before she could. "Just hear me out first, and then you can put your shirt back on," I said, tone thick and gruff. "Please?"

Shivering, she covered her chest with her hands and nodded.

Sagging in relief, I continued, "I'm in love with you—"

"Johnny—"

"No, no, please just listen," I coaxed before ploughing ahead. "I'm in *love* with you, Shannon. I'm completely fucking hooked on you, so when you're hurt, it affects me. It *hurts* me. I can't pretend that it doesn't." She shuddered and stepped closer to me. "But that doesn't mean that I'm with you because I feel *sorry* for you—" I hooked an arm around her bare back and tugged her all the way until she was flush against me, "It just means that I'm going to get upset when you're upset, and that when someone hurts you, I'm going to want to cause some serious harm to them in return. I'm all in, Shannon. Scars and all. Fucked-up father and all. One hundred and fifty percent." Brushing her ponytail over her shoulder, I gently tugged at the end, forcing her to look at me. "I feel everything for you," I admitted, feeling my own body shake from the pressure building in my chest, caused every time this girl put her eyes on me. "And I'm saying all of this while you're standing here, looking like the sexiest thing I've ever seen in real life, praying that you don't run out on me, because I have a raging hard-on for you and it's going to take me a few minutes to calm myself down before I can chase after you."

Her breath hitched. "You think I'm sexy?"

"Look at me, Shannon—" Stepping back, I gestured to the obvious bulge in my sweats, trying to keep the outrage out of my voice. "Look at what you do to me. Do you not get that? You are so damn sexy, I can't even tell you how much."

Shannon blushed. "Really?"

"Really," I confirmed, pulling her back to me. "Really fucking really, Shan."

"If I had one of those, it would be sticking up, too," she blurted out, cheeks pink. "For you, I mean. Because I feel the same way about you."

"Uh, *thanks*?" I chuckled, shaking my head. "That's not a visual I'd like to think about *ever*, but I appreciate the sentiment, baby."

"Say something else," she said in a breathy voice. "Please?"

"Like what?"

"I don't know." She shrugged and let her hands fall to her sides, cheeks reddening. "Maybe something that's not about my tube scar?"

Awareness dawned on me and I bit back a groan. Christ, I was slow on the uptake. My girlfriend was standing here, naked from the waist up, and I'd made her feel insecure.

"I can do that." Keeping an arm hooked around her, I steered her backwards to my bed and lowered her onto the mattress. "You drive me crazy," I purred, climbing onto the bed to hover between her legs. "You're fucking sexy." Dropping a kiss to her mouth, I trailed my lips over the curve of her jaw, peppering kisses down her neck until I reached her breasts. "And you have the nicest tits I've ever seen."

A shiver rolled through Shannon's body as she fisted the duvet beneath her. "They're small."

"They're perfect," I corrected huskily, swiping my tongue out to trace her nipple. "*You're* perfect."

"Johnny—" Shannon's breath caught in her throat and she arched her back, pushing herself against me.

"You like that?" I coaxed, kissing and suckling on her nipple. "Hmm?"

"Don't stop." Shaking beneath me, she knotted her small hand in my hair and tugged. "It's ... oh god—"

"So, am I forgiven?" I coaxed, switching my attention to her other breast. "For staring at your scar and not your tits like I should have?"

"Yes ..." Shannon nodded vigorously. "All ... mmm ... for ... ugh ... given ..."

I trailed a path of kisses from her breasts to her ribs and then her bellybutton, licking and nipping as I went, until I reached the waistband of her leggings.

*Stop now,* I mentally commanded myself, *that's far enough for one day, fucker.*

With more self-control than I knew I possessed, I took a de-tour with my tongue and backtracked all the way up her body until my lips found hers.

"Why'd you stop?" Shannon panted against my lips, as she wrapped her arms around my neck.

*Jesus ...*

"Because ..." I let my words trail off, concentrating on her swollen lips and the addicting taste of her. "I like how we are." I kissed her again, softer this time. "I don't want to be put on a timer."

"A timer?"

"Yeah, Shan." I nodded and pressed a kiss to her nose. "I don't want to rush this with you. I want us to take our time – make the important moments worth it." Sitting up, I took her with me, pulling her onto my lap. "I want you, okay?" I hooked an arm around her back, tucking her flush against me. "Badly. Don't ever doubt that." Smoothing her hair over her shoulder again, I kissed her softly. "I just don't want to look back in five years' time and know that I fucked up the important parts because I couldn't be patient."

A small smile crept across Shannon's face.

"What?" I mirrored her smile. "What's so funny?"

"You said in five years' time," she whispered, curling her arms around my neck.

"I already told you, I need you for keeps," I replied gruffly. "There's no expiration date between us."

"Whoa." Shannon released a shaky breath and beamed at me. "You say the best things, Johnny Kavanagh."

I grinned back at her. "Want to hear something else?"

She nodded eagerly.

"I have an idea."

Shannon tilted her head to one-side, studying me with wary eyes. "What kind of idea?"

I laughed. "Come on—" Setting her down, I passed her t-shirt back to her before reaching for my own. "I'm going to show you."

"What the hell." Slipping her shirt over her head, she stood up and smiled at me. "I've got nothing to lose."

I did.

*Her.*

"This is not a good idea," Shannon announced half an hour later, as she sat in the driver's seat of my car in the yard, staring at the steering wheel in front of her like it was a poisonous snake about to strike. "This is really, really *not good*, Johnny."

I stifled a laugh and fastened my seat belt. God only knew what notion had struck me to make this seem like a good idea, but we were here now, and I was going with it. Besides, I knew she could do this. She just needed some confidence. "You can do this."

"No." Throwing her hands up, she flailed helplessly. "I can't."

"Yes, you can," I encouraged. "I've talked you through it. You know the gears, baby, and we're in a big, empty yard with nobody around. You've got this."

"No. No. Honestly, I don't! I don't have this!" Her eyes widened when she turned to gape at me. "I don't even have a license. Not even a tractor license. I'm sixteen, Johnny, and this is an expensive car. Oh god, I'm going to kill us both!"

"No, you're not," I coaxed. "You're going to smash this."

"Yeah," Shannon strangled out. "Into a *tree*, Johnny!"

Smirking, I leaned over the console, slipped the car out of gear, and then turned the key in the ignition. "Let's go."

"Oh my god, help me!" Shannon screamed, whimpering when the engine roared to life beneath us. "This is so bad." She grabbed the wheel, looking all wide-eyed and panicked. "What if I crash?"

"Don't crash," I shot back. "Now put your foot on the clutch and I'll change the gears for you."

"Don't let me die," she begged, as I slipped the car into first.

"I won't," I laughed. "Don't close your eyes, baby—" Reaching over, I pulled her hand away from her face. "Look straight ahead."

"I am, Johnny," she wailed. "I *am* going to die!"

"No, Shan, you're going to *live*," I laughed. "Now slowly release the clutch and tap down nice and gently on the accelerator—"

"I broke it!" She wailed when the car stalled. "I'm so sorry."

"You didn't break anything," I replied, slipping the car out of gear and leaning over to turn the key in the ignition. "We'll start over." The engine roared to life once more and I repeated the same instructions, shifting the gears for her. "Good job!" I praised when she didn't stall and the car started to crawl. "That's it, Shan. You're doing it, baby."

"I'm not sure about this, Johnny," she muttered, sitting so close to the wheel that her nose was kissing the windscreen, as the car chugged along. "This is nothing like GTA."

An hour later, and I knew I had awoken the beast I'd met in my bedroom a few months ago. "I'm doing it!" Shannon exclaimed, eyes bright with excitement, as she whizzed around the back of the house, using my driveway like it was her own personal racetrack.

"Slow down," I begged as she took the corner of my house with more speed than was necessary. "Please god, Shannon, just slow it down."

"What's wrong, tough boy?" she teased. "Are you *scared*?"

*Fucking terrified . . .*

"Oh my god – did you see that?" she squealed in delight. "Did you see me slip into fifth by myself?"

"I saw," I strangled out, gripping the *Oh Jesus* handle for all I was worth. "Can we be done now?"

"Please just one more time?" she begged as she headed for the laneway for the hundredth time. "I promise I'll be done then."

"Last time," I choked out, clenching my eyes shut only to think better of it. "Watch out for the—" my words broke off and I held my breath as Shannon swerved. "Pothole," I finished, exhaling a shaky breath.

"This is exactly like GTA," she laughed.

"Except there's no restart button," I groaned. "So please don't kill us."

"It's like you said," she giggled, pushing the pedal to the metal. "I've got this."

# Takeout and Updates

## SHANNON

We were sitting on the couch in Johnny's sitting room after my impromptu driving lesson, with our school books sprawled out, having just finished our homework, and I couldn't wipe the smile off my face. I'd had the best evening with him, and now I knew how to drive. *Me.* I could actually drive a real car. I had no idea what spurred him to take me out in his car earlier, but I wasn't regretting it. I felt so free behind the wheel, and having that much power was such a thrilling rush.

Feeling content, I absorbed the heat wafting from the open fire as I listened to Johnny place a food order. "Yeah, can I get a portion of cheesy bread with that orange dip and a large pizza with no mushrooms and extra pineapple?" Johnny looked over at me and made a gagging motion before saying, "Yeah, I'm sure, lad, pile on the pineapple."

"Hey—" Stretching out, I poked him with my toe and whispered, "Don't judge me, mister *I only eat chicken.*"

"The world is judging you," he mouthed back as he snatched my foot and placed it on his thigh. "Actually, do you have skinless chicken?" I stifled a laugh. "You do?" Peeling the sock partially off, he trailed his fingertips over my ankle. "How's that cooked? It's fried?" His brows furrowed and he tapped his fingers against my ankle, looking genuinely conflicted, before blowing out a breath. "Fuck it, give me a dinner box with an extra breast and leave the skin on it – oh, and throw in a bottle of Coke." He looked over at me and winked. "Yeah, she needs the *real brand*." He hung up the phone and grinned. "Looks like the diet's out the window."

"You can always start again on Monday," I snickered.

"Are you saying I need to diet?" he teased, pulling me onto his lap. "Huh?" His lips moved to my neck and I sighed in contentment.

"You're so pretty," I whispered, biting down on my lip as I sagged against him. "You don't need to diet."

He paused mid-kiss and pulled back to stare at me. "Did you just call me *pretty*?"

"Yes." I smiled. "What's wrong with calling you pretty?"

"Everything," he replied, looking appalled. "Shan, you can't call me *pretty*."

"But you *are* pretty," I teased. "You have pretty eyes, and pretty hair, and a pretty smile."

Johnny gaped at me. "I'm offended."

I laughed at his horrified expression. "You *are* a pretty boy."

"Nope—" Shaking his head, he tossed me onto my back and then dove on top of me, "No, I'm not having that." Slipping his hands under my shirt, he tickled my ribs. "Take it back!"

"Ahhhh, stop!" I screamed through fits of laughter as I squirmed beneath him. "I can't – I'm ticklish!"

"I know," he laughed, continuing to torture me. "Now take it back, or I'm going in for the kill."

"I take it back!" I squealed, twisting and turning. "You're not pretty – ahhhhh, Johnny, I can't – you're sexy! You're sexy, okay? Ah, ah, mercy. I scream mercy!"

"I show no mercy," he snickered, slipping his head under the hem of my shirt and upping his efforts. "Your leg kicks out when I tickle you here," he chuckled, tickling my rib. "That's so weird."

"I'm going to get you back for this," I warned him, hardly able to breathe from laughing so hard, as I wiggled and bucked beneath him. "You just wait and see—"

The sound of tires screeching on the gravel outside cut through the air and Johnny's head popped back out from under my t-shirt. "Jaysus," he mused, hair sticking up in forty different directions. "That has to be some kind of record on delivering."

"It can't be the pizza." I arched myself up to look out the window, but because it was dark outside, I could only make out a set of headlamps.

"Oh my god, what if it's your mam?" I spluttered and then proceeded to scramble off his lap at top speed. Knowing my luck, that's exactly who it was. "I should go." Grabbing my schoolbag, I started throwing all of my books back in, while I multitasked by toeing on my runners in the process. "You should take me home."

"Shan, relax," he chuckled, climbing to his feet. "It's not my ma, and if it is, you don't need to go."

*Bang, bang, bang . . .*

"See?" Johnny coaxed, moving for the door. "My mother wouldn't knock." My shoulders sagged in relief and I loosened my grip on my schoolbag. "Just wait here," he added before slipping out of the room.

A few seconds later, a familiar voice boomed through the house. "Where's my sister?"

*Darren?*

"She's here."

"Tell her to come outside. She needs to come home with me now."

*Oh god . . .*

"Come in."

"What?"

"I'm not telling her what to do, so come in if you want to talk to her."

Less than a minute later, Johnny strolled back into the sitting room with Darren trailing stiffly behind him. "Your brother's here, Shan," he said, keeping his eyes trained on mine as he walked over and stood beside me.

"What's wrong?" I asked, instantly on edge. "Wh-why are you here?"

"I should ask you the same thing," Darren replied, but he didn't sound angry. *Just tired.* "You were supposed to come straight home after school." His gaze drifted to the school books laying open on the coffee table and surprise flickered in his eyes before he shook his head, features somber once again. "It's almost eight o' clock, Shannon."

"I was coming home," I told him. "We were just going to eat dinner first."

"We need to talk," he replied. "It's important."

Panic flared inside of me. "What's wrong?" I asked, because something had to be wrong for him to obtain Johnny's address and drive all the way out here. He wasn't even fighting with me. This was bad. Something terrible was going to come out of his mouth. I could *feel* it. "Darren?" My voice was shaky, matching the rest of me. "What's going on?"

My brother's gaze flicked from me to Johnny and then back to me before he blew out a harsh breath. "It's Dad."

I stiffened, feeling every muscle in my body lock tight with tension, while I waited for Darren to confirm what I knew in my heart was coming.

"He was released from Brickley House today, Shannon," Darren announced, voice thick with emotion. "He's back in Ballylaggin."

The air left my lungs in strangled rush, and in its place came a flood of hurt, pain, fear, and paranoia. It would never end. This would never be over. Joey was right. He was always right. Dad would come back, and when he did, he was going to make me pay . . .

A large hand slipped into mine then; warm, strong, and short-wiring my panicked thoughts. Trembling, I glanced down at our joined hands and then up at Johnny. He was standing right beside me – big and strong, and so close that I could feel the heat radiating off his body. His presence in this moment was deeply comforting. "What does this mean?" he asked the question I couldn't get out of my throat. "For your family?" He roughly cleared his throat. "For Shannon?"

"No offense, Johnny, but it's a private matter," Darren replied, giving him a sharp look.

"No offense, *Darren*, but I don't give a shite," Johnny shot back, not missing a beat. "Whether you like it or not, I'm her fella, and if she's in danger then I want to know about it." Bristling, he added, "I can help."

"I don't need your help," Darren replied in a weary tone. "But I do need you to come home," he added, turning his attention to me. "Mam's a nervous wreck and we all need to talk about where we go from here as a family."

"Is Joey at home?" I asked, watching him carefully.

Darren sighed heavily. "I don't know where he is."

"What do you mean you don't know?" I strangled out. "Where is he, Darren?"

"Tadhg didn't take the news about Dad too well and stormed out," he muttered, pinching the bridge of his nose. "Joey's out trying to find him." Running a hand through his dark hair, he expelled another pained breath before gesturing to the books on the coffee table. "Can you pack up what's yours so we can go? I've left Sean, Ollie, and Mam at home."

"I don't think she should go home," Johnny was quick to say.

Darren gave him a sharp look. "Excuse me?"

"I said that I don't think she should go home," Johnny repeated calmly. "She can stay here with me. Your da doesn't know where my house is."

"She's coming home," Darren replied tightly. "Now."

"I don't see why she has to—" Johnny began to argue, but Darren cut him off.

"You need to back off," my brother warned. "Seriously."

"It's okay," I reluctantly said, wanting to do anything else in the world than go back to Elk's Terrace, but knowing I had no choice. "I'll go." Shoulders slumped, I released Johnny's hand and grabbed the last of my stuff off the table. Tears filled my eyes, making it impossible to see the opening of my pencil case as I tried to shove all of my pens and ruler inside. "Just give me a minute."

"I'll wait for you in the car."

I nodded stiffly, keeping my back to him as I packed up my stuff. "Okay."

The sitting room door clicked shut and then Johnny was beside me. "Talk to me."

I shook my head and tossed the pencil case down on the coffee table. Shaking, I pushed my hands through my hair, taking deep, slow breaths, desperately trying to keep my emotions under control. "I . . . " Snapping my mouth shut, I stepped around him and walked to the window. "I . . . " I shook my head again, dragging in a sharp breath.

"Shannon, come on," he urged, following me. "Give me your words."

"I think—" Pausing, I dropped my head and clutched the sill, "I'm going to cry."

"That's okay," Johnny told me, standing so close behind me that I could feel his thigh against mine. "It's okay to cry."

"I don't want to do that in front of you again." Exhaling a ragged breath, I clenched my eyes shut and strangled out, "I don't want you to see me fall apart all the time."

"Well, you don't have a choice," he replied, turning me around and pulling me into his arms. "Because I'm not leaving you."

Shaking my head, I kept my eyes closed and whispered, "Johnny, I can't—"

"I'm not going anywhere," he said, tightening his hold on me.

I tried again. "You can't—"

"I'm not going *anywhere*, Shannon."

"You don't need to—"

"I'm with *you*. All of you. Every part. Good and bad. I'm staying. So, don't hide this part from me."

I remained rigid for the longest moment. It didn't faze him because he didn't let go. He just held me there, refusing to let me go, refusing to leave me alone.

And when I caved? When I finally crumbled? It was into him. I broke down. I absolutely lost it right there in Johnny's sitting room.

I didn't want to have a conversation.

I just wanted to *cry*.

Johnny seemed to sense it because he didn't ask me any questions. He didn't say a word. Instead, he kept his arms wrapped around my body, holding me close, as my life fell down around me.

# Help Her

## JOHNNY

I couldn't sleep. My brain was on high alert and every muscle in my body was locked tight with tension. Every time I closed my eyes and tried to fall asleep, I was bombarded with mental images of Shannon lying in that hospital bed, beaten and bloodied.

Her father was out.

He was walking around a free man.

In fucking Ballylaggin of all places.

Furious, I turned onto my side and tried to empty my mind, but it didn't happen for me. Feeling at a loss, I threw the covers off my body, cringing when Sookie groaned in her sleep. "Sorry, baby," I whispered, padding across the room in the darkness.

Slipping out of my room, I flicked on the light in the landing and made the trek to the opposite end of the house. It had to have been at least nine years since I last slipped inside my parents' bedroom in the middle of the night, but that's where I found myself – at one in the bleeding morning.

"Da?" I whispered, nudging his shoulder as I towered over him, feeling like a creep. "Da?"

"Johnny?" His voice was raspy and thick from sleep. "What's wrong?"

"I need to talk to you," I whispered, eyeing my mother's sleeping form, and praying that she stayed asleep. "It's important."

"Go back to sleep, son," he grumbled, rolling back onto his side and tightening his hold on my mother. "The sky's not falling, I promise."

I rolled my eyes at that last part. Fucking Chicken Licken. "Da, I really need to talk to you."

Raising himself up on his elbow, he peered up at me with a sleepy expression. "Really?"

I nodded. "Really."

Yawning loudly, he threw the covers off himself and stood up. "Alright, son, put the kettle on."

"I will," I hissed, covering my eyes, "when you put some clothes on."

Three hours and two pots of coffee later, we were still in the kitchen. My father was hunched over the counter in his jocks, nursing a cup of coffee, while I paced the floor like someone jacked up on coke. "There has to be another way around it," I hissed, scratching my bare stomach. "He can't just get to walk around scot-free after everything he put them through."

"Family law is complicated, son," Dad replied. "Every case is different."

"That's not good enough—" Swiping the coffee pot off the counter, I poured myself another cup and downed it in three gulps. "Goddammit!"

"I'm cutting you off," Dad yawned, reaching over and taking the pot away from me. "Or else I'm never getting to bed."

"You should have seen her tonight," I continued, pacing and ranting. "Shannon's face when her brother told her that their father was out." I shook my head. "She was fucking terrified, Da."

"Johnny," Dad sighed. "There's nothing you can do."

"But there's something you can do, right?" I shot back, feeling all jittery and energetic. "Can't you take their case?"

"It doesn't work that way," he replied with another yawn.

"Why?" I demanded. "Why doesn't it work that way?"

Dad exhaled wearily. "I've already explained this to you a dozen times; the DPP made the decision to take it to trial. They have been appointed a solicitor through legal aid, and besides, Mrs. Lynch made it very clear that my services weren't needed – or welcome."

"Then she's a fool." I snarled, upping my pacing. "You're the best."

"I am," he agreed with a sleepy nod. "But her emotions are clouding her judgment."

"She's incompetent is what she is, Da." Stalking over to the window,

I rested my hands on the sill and exhaled a furious growl. "The woman's a liability and my girlfriend isn't safe in that house." I swung around to glare at him. "None of those kids are safe with her – and especially not now that he's sniffing around again."

"They have social workers on the case," Dad explained calmly, as he walked over to the sink and emptied the pot of coffee down the drain. "That means house calls and strict supervision."

"It doesn't mean shite, Da, and you know it," I shot back, frustrated. "She's not safe in that house."

"Then what do you want me to do here, Johnny?" he asked, rinsing out his cup and placing it on the draining board. "All of the Lynch children would have been spoken to after Shannon's accident. They wouldn't have been returned to their mother's care without an investigation and of course, being asked about their mother's treatment of them. Obviously, the caseworkers involved found some merit in Mrs. Lynch's ability to parent them."

"They're all brainwashed," I hissed. "Don't you get it? They're fucking terrified of being sent into foster care and separated, so they lie and cover for their parents because they're under some screwed-up belief that they're safer where they are!"

"What's going on?" Mam asked, standing in the kitchen doorway with her white dressing gown wrapped around her. "It's half past four in the morning. What are you doing up?"

"Your son wanted to have a chat," Dad explained calmly. "Nothing to worry about. Go on back to bed, sweetheart."

Mam arched a brow and gave my father her 'do you seriously think I'm buying that shite?' look before stepping into the kitchen and heading for the kettle. "Is Shannon alright, love?"

I stopped pacing and frowned at my mother. "How did you—"

"Know this late-night chat was about Shannon?" Mam filled in with a knowing smile. "Because I know you." Making herself a coffee, she joined my father at the island. "Now." Taking a sip from her cup, she looked at my father. "Start talking, sweetheart."

With a resigned sigh, my father began to recap what we had spoken about, with me interjecting with the parts he left out.

"And there you have it, Ma," I announced when my father was finished. "The absolute horror that is our justice system!" Swiping her cup of coffee off the counter, I tossed it back and moved for the kettle. "What am I supposed to do now, huh? Go to sleep in my nice, warm bed and wait for a phone call to tell me she's back in the hospital – or worse?" Shaking my head, I poured myself another coffee, splashing water all over the counter in the process. "She deserves a hell of a lot better than the life she's been handed."

"I agree," Mam said in a sad tone of voice. "They all deserve better."

"Then do something, Ma," I pleaded, feeling at a complete loss. "Because I'm going to lose my fucking mind if I have to drop her home from school every day and wait until I get to school the next day to see if she's made it through the night!"

Tears filled my mother's eyes when she asked, "And her brother? Darren?"

Frustrated, I took a swig of my coffee before answering. "He doesn't know anything about them," I bit out. "He's been gone for years. He's all about his mother's best interests and not the kids. Joey doesn't trust him, and neither do I."

Mam and Dad looked at each other then, and I felt like I was being left out of a private discussion that was taking place without words. "What are you thinking?" I asked, anxious. "Can you do something?"

Dad sighed heavily. "What do you want us to do, son?"

"I want you to nail that bastard to the wall," I told him. "I want justice for those kids. I want justice for my girlfriend. It's not enough that he gets to walk away from this when they can't." I turned to my mother. "They're completely fucked up, Ma. He wrecked them!"

Both of my parents were silent for so long that I gave up on them answering me. "Forget it," I growled, tossing my cup in the sink. "I shouldn't have bothered."

Stalking towards the hallway, I halted in my tracks when Mam spoke. "We'll do what we can, Johnny."

I turned to look at them. "What does that mean?"

"It means we'll do what we can to help," Dad explained calmly, resting his hand on top of Mam's. "Now, go upstairs and try and get a couple of hours sleep before school."

Feeling dejected, I headed back upstairs to my room with my shoulders slumped and my stomach in knots. The birds were singing outside when I walked back into my room and sank down on the edge of my bed to stare out the window at the dark sky. Grabbing my phone off my bedside locker, I unlocked it and scrolled through my messages, reading and re-reading every text she had sent me until I had driven myself half demented. "Fuck it," I muttered to myself as I tapped into my phonebook and brought up her contact. I had my finger on the call button when my phone started to vibrate in my hand, signaling an incoming call from Shannon.

Heart racing, I clicked accept and put the phone to my ear. "Shan?"

"Hi, Johnny," came her hushed voice on the other line. "Did I wake you?"

"No, I was awake," I replied, exhaling a shaky breath. "Are you okay?"

"I'm okay," she whispered and I felt my shoulders sag in relief. "I just . . ."

"You just what, Shan?"

"I wanted to hear your voice," she admitted croakily. "Is that weird?"

"Well, if it is, then I'm a weirdo, too." Lying back on my bed, I folded an arm behind my head. "Because I was just about to call you."

She exhaled heavily into the phone. "Really?"

"Really," I confirmed gruffly. "I was thinking about you all night."

"Me, too," she replied. "You, I mean," she hurried to amend. "I was thinking about you all night – not me."

"I know what you meant," I told her, smiling to myself at her cute verbal blunder. "Are you getting up now? It's only—" Craning my neck, I checked the time on my alarm clock before saying, "a quarter to five."

"I thought you might be going to the gym," she whispered. "I was . . . well, I was going to ask you if I could come and just wait in the car?"

A trickle of unease crept up my spine. "What's happening, baby?"

"Nothing."

"Shan . . . "

She blew out a harsh breath. "I'm scared."

I sat straight up. "Do you want me to come and get you now?"

"No, no, no," she hurried to say, tone hushed. "There's nothing wrong. I'm just nervous." She exhaled another shaky breath before saying, "Can you stay on the phone with me? You don't have to talk. I just . . . I feel better when I know you're close."

Closing my eyes, I flopped back down and swallowed a furious growl. "Of course," I managed to say instead, keeping my tone gentle. Settling under my duvet, I whispered, "I'm right here, baby."

# Busted

## SHANNON

My father had been out of treatment for a week, and I was having trouble sleeping. Every time I dozed off at night, I was bombarded with nightmares so frightening that I jerked awake and spent the rest of the night in a panic-induced frenzy, body on high alert, waiting for the sound of the key turning in the lock. It hadn't come yet, but that didn't mean it *wouldn't*. That was the scariest part of it; knowing that our futures balanced on our father obeying the barring order and our mother keeping her resolve. I wasn't naïve enough to hold out much hope for either.

Forcing all thoughts of my father to the back of my mind, I focused on the present. On the boy sitting on the grassy bank of the pitch beside me. Blocking out the rest of the world, I concentrated entirely on my boyfriend.

It was hard for me to comprehend why a guy in Johnny's position, with everything going for him, had so willingly attached his sail to my damaged mast. But he had. And every day that had passed since was made bearable because I had him.

When Joey and Darren were fighting at home, I blocked it out.

When Mam was catatonic at the kitchen table, I breezed straight past.

When the fear of my father coming back threatened to spin me into a panic attack, I distracted myself by texting him a homework question.

I found that I could do those things now, because I knew I had something to look *forward* to. He had become the safe place where I could let down my defenses. I wasn't focusing on my family all the time. I wasn't dwelling on the negative because I had the best version of positive in the form of my boyfriend. This house had become a temporary pitstop for me. It wasn't the cell I spent most of my waking hours trapped inside. It was a means to an end. A place to lay my head at night. Because in the morning when I woke up, I knew *better* was waiting for me.

*So much better.*

I knew that sounded pathetic, but for me, someone who had never had anyone besides Joey, it was bewildering. For the first time in my life, I had someone who was just for *me*. I didn't have to share him with my brothers or my friends. I didn't have to compromise or double check. He was mine. *Just mine.*

I savored every minute I got to spend with him at school, and even then, it was never enough. The kisses weren't enough. The hand-holding wasn't *enough*. The nights I snuck out of the house to drive around in his car with him until the sun came up weren't either. Nothing seemed to be enough when my body and heart continuously screamed out for *more*.

Every morning I woke up for school, it was with hope in my heart, because I *knew* I would get to see him. I knew that once 07:45 rolled around, Johnny Kavanagh would pull up outside my house, after his gym session, and sit on my garden wall, taunting Mam and Darren, until I came outside and climbed into his car. He was like clockwork, so rigid in his routine, and I found it deeply comforting. When Johnny told you that he would be there, he would *be* there. He was never late, and he never cancelled.

Once I climbed in that car with him, the best part of my day would begin. Lunch breaks, stolen kisses between classes, steaming up the windows of his Audi . . . it was *everything* and not nearly enough all at once.

Dragging myself from my thoughts, I turned to look at Johnny. We were sitting on the hilly bank after school, the one he had knocked me down on all those months ago, watching the team train, and I knew he was upset. He'd been quiet all day. I could *feel* it. All the smiles in the world couldn't hide that. *Not from me.* Last week was hard for him, too. Tommen had lost the final against Levitt, and I knew he'd felt that loss deep in his bones as he'd watched on in dismay from the sidelines. Hooking my arm through his, I rested my cheek on his shoulder and whispered, "You're going to make it, Johnny."

"Don't put money on it," he replied quietly, hand moving to his thigh. "I don't think it's going to happen for me, Shan," he added, voice barely more than a whisper, as he adjusted the bandage I knew was strapped to his thigh beneath his school trousers. "Not this summer."

"I do," I countered, sliding my hand down his arm to link with his. "I know it." Entwining our fingers, I gave his hand a reassuring squeeze. "You have your appointment with your doctor tomorrow, right?"

Johnny nodded, shoulders sagging. "But even if she signs me off to play, there's not enough time to pull this back—"

"Johnny, you don't have anything to pull back," I urged. "You're already the *best*." Releasing his hand, I twisted my body sideways so that I was kneeling with my knees touching his thighs, and reclaimed his hand. "You might only have six weeks left to train and prepare – or whatever it is you guys do—" I scrunched my nose up at the thought of him getting smashed up on a pitch before quickly shaking the horrible image out of my head and continuing, "but you've already done all of the hard work. You've already impressed the coaches and you are weeks ahead of schedule on your recovery. You've *earned* this. It's *yours*." Squeezing his hand, I smiled brightly at him. "You're going to get that spot on the team and you are going to *shine*. I know it."

His lips tipped upwards and he arched a brow. "Oh, you know it, do you?"

"Yep." I nodded in confirmation. "I'm very wise."

Chuckling, he stroked my cheek with his thumb. "God, you're so adorable."

"Adorable?" I grimaced. "Sookie's adorable, Johnny. I'm supposed to be—"

"*Be*?" he teased, dipping his face closer to mine. "What are you supposed to be, baby?"

"More than adorable," I breathed, losing focus now that his lips were so close to mine.

"Cute?" he purred, trailing his fingers under the hem of my school skirt. "Pretty?" Smirking, he leaned closer and brushed his nose against mine. "Sexy?"

Nodding, I exhaled a shaky breath. "The last one."

Suddenly, and without an ounce of warning, Johnny kissed me hard and pulled me on top of him. Throwing a leg over either side of his hips, I settled on his lap, our lips never parting as we kissed each other almost violently. His lap wasn't a soft place to sit; the opposite in fact. He was ripped from head to toe and it was a painful test to my willpower to *not* touch. Especially when everything inside of me demanded I do just that. *Touch, and pet, and rub . . .*

Unable to stop myself, I snaked a hand in his hair and tugged. He rewarded my bravery with a small thrust of his hips. His hands were on my hips, coaxing and encouraging. It didn't seem to matter to either of us that we were on school grounds with his teammates a stone's throw away on the pitch.

"You're so fucking sexy." His voice was deep and husky and his words took my breath away. "You drive me crazy, Shannon *like the river*," he whispered against my lips, rocking my hips against his. "I want you so badly I can't think straight anymore."

A delicious shiver rolled down my spine and I sagged against him, the pressure in my chest too much to take, his words taking me further down the dark and terrifying path I was on with him. "Johnny?"

"Yeah, Shan?"

"There's nobody at my house until six." Heart racing, I leaned back to look into his eyes. "Do you want to come over?"

His eyes darkened and his grip on my waist tightened. "Now?"

"Now," I confirmed, breathless.

"Should I have parked further up the street?" Johnny asked between kisses as he stumbled into my bedroom with my body wrapped around his. "In case your mother or Darren come back early?"

Shaking my head, I reached around and slammed my bedroom door shut before turning back to crush my lips against his. "Forget about them," I encouraged, breathing hard, as I squeezed my thighs against his waist. "Turn off your brain."

"Ah fuck," he groaned, walking the small space from my door to my bed. "You're going to get me killed, aren't ya?" His shins hit the base of the bed and then we were falling onto the mattress with Johnny landing heavily on top of me.

Wrestling around on my small single bed, I clambered out from beneath his big body and straddled his hips. Feeling victorious, I took his hands in mine and pinned them above his head, pressing them into the mattress. "Gotcha."

Growling, Johnny bucked his hips sharply, causing me to fall forward on his chest. "Gotcha back," he purred before claiming my lips with his. I could feel my pulse thrumming in my veins as my blood turned to lava and my resolve disintegrated with every stroke of his tongue.

"Listen, I don't want to push you into anything you're not ready to do," he said against my lips. "I have two hands and an excellent imagination – filled with images of you." Holding my face in his hands, he leaned back and stared at me. "I can *wait*."

I stared at him, feeling more in this moment than I had my whole life. I could feel his heart hammering against his chest like a caged bird fluttering wildly, matching the rhythm of mine. Unable to form a coherent sentence, I reached for the hem of my school jumper and whipped it over my head, taking my school tie with it. Johnny's eyes darkened as I moved for my white blouse, clumsily undoing the buttons.

"Don't—" he began to say, but his words twisted into a pained growl when I let my blouse fall from my shoulders. "Jesus," he groaned, his hungry eyes roaming over my body. His tongue swept out, tracing his lower lip, as his stare remained riveted to my body.

My breath came out in a loud, breathy puff when I reached behind my back and unclasped my bra, wishing I had lacy bras like Claire and not plain cotton ones.

"Fuck," Johnny growled, thrusting his hips upwards. His breath hitched in his throat when I slipped my bra off and tossed it on my bedroom floor. I could feel him hardening beneath me and the sensation sent a thrill through me. "You're so beautiful."

Sitting up with me in his lap, Johnny reached a hand behind his head, swiftly yanking his school jumper off before tossing it on my bedroom floor. Knotting his fingers in my hair, he pulled my face to his, kissing me hard and recklessly. Straddling his hips in nothing but my school skirt and knickers, I rocked against him, matching his recklessness with a fevered wildness of my own.

His hands moved from my hair to the front of his shirt to unbutton it, never taking his lips off mine as he worked. I reached behind my back and lowered the zipper of my skirt. Breaking the kiss, I clambered off the bed, trembling from head to toe, and let my skirt fall to the floor, never taking my eyes off his.

Standing in nothing but a pair of white, cotton knickers, I exhaled a shaky breath and whispered, "Hi, Johnny."

"Hi, Shannon," Johnny replied, voice strained, eyes dark and blazing, as he shrugged his shirt and tie off and tossed them on the floor. "Fuck, what are you doing to me, baby?"

My chest rose and fell rapidly when I climbed back onto his lap. "I love you," he said gruffly, brushing his lips against mine. I shivered when his arms came around me, the heat from his skin scorching mine. "So fucking much." His hand moved to my ass, pulling me closer for a long, drug-inducing moment, as he rocked me on his lap, grinding our bodies together. Growling, Johnny deepened our kiss, plunging his tongue into my mouth as he twisted around and knocked me onto my back. "So sexy." He sounded absolutely torn, and a little hopeful, as he settled between my legs. "So goddamn beautiful." His hands roamed all over my bare flesh as he trailed kisses down my neck. "You're all I want."

Moaning in encouragement, I tilted my hips upwards, groaning breathlessly when his body aligned with mine in the most primal of human ways, pressing hard against me.

"I shouldn't be doing this," he whispered, mouth hovering over my breasts. "It's . . ." his voice trailed off as he pulled my nipple into his mouth and sucked.

"Johnny," I panted, knotting my hands in his hair, as he tormented me with delicious swipes of his tongue. "Don't stop."

"Fuck . . . " Releasing my breast, he moved back to my lips and thrust hard against me, so hard that the headboard of my bed banged against the wall. "Shite," he muttered, nestling his face in the crook of my neck. "I should stop," he groaned, but his actions proved opposite as he continued to feel me and kiss me and rock his hips against me.

*Don't stop.*

*I don't care.*

*Just don't stop.*

"Shh." I gripped his hips and tugged him closer, as the need inside of me blossomed and burned. I wanted him to push me deeper into this mattress. I wanted to feel every inch of him on me, in me, all of him inside all of me. I wanted *more*. "It's okay."

"No, no, no . . . " Johnny shook his head and groaned louder, shifting closer, nuzzling deeper. "I'm not thinking clearly—" His hand moved to my hip, jerking me closer and clamping down hard. "Tell me to go."

"No." Heart racing, I arched against him. "Don't go."

"Fuck," he groaned, as his big body shuddered under my touch. He exhaled a harsh breath against my neck that caused my skin to erupt in goosebumps. "It's too soon—"

I trailed my trembling fingertips down his stomach, not stopping until I reached his belt buckle. "I don't care." Sliding my fingers into the waistband of his school trousers, I inhaled a steadying breath and tugged hard. "*Stay*."

His breathing was hard and uneven.

"What are you doing?" he asked, breathing hard, as I fumbled with the buckle of his belt. "Shannon, we can't—"

"Please?" I breathed, freeing his belt buckle and popping the button on his trousers. "I want you."

"I don't have a condom," he groaned in to my mouth, hips thrusting wildly. "I'm sorry."

"Condoms," I moaned, bucking my hips up to meet his thrusts. "In

Joey's room." Raiding Joey's bedroom wasn't uncommon behavior for me, but planning to steal from his condom stash was a different matter entirely. I had no clue what I was thinking if I was being truthful with myself. I just wanted him. *Badly*.

"No—" Breaking our kiss, Johnny shook his head and stared down at me, eyes almost black with desire. "Not like this."

"Don't you want me?" I whispered, feeling my heart sink.

"You know I want you," he panted, pressing his forehead to mine. "I *only* want you."

"Then why—"

"Because I'm not taking your virginity in this house, Shannon!" he growled, jaw clenched. "On an after-school whim, with your brother's fucking condom." He shook his head. "I'm not doing that, baby."

"I don't mind, Johnny," I urged. "Honestly, I don't."

"Well, I mind," he shot back, pulling himself up on his elbows. "I'm not having sex with you and skulking out the door an hour later because your family will be home." Groaning, he pressed a kiss to my lips and climbed off me. "You deserve better, and I'm not doing that to you." Chest heaving, he walked over to my bedroom window and leaned against the sill. "When we sleep together, I want us to *sleep* together." He looked over his shoulder, blue eyes blazing. "All night."

Scrambling into a sitting position, I didn't make a sound, too busy concentrating on trying to control the rapid rise and fall of my chest, as his words speared through my heart.

"I want to make it good for you," he added, turning back to face me. "And I can't do that on a timer."

"Oh," I finally breathed, watching him watch me. "O-okay."

"That doesn't mean that I don't want this." Exhaling heavily, Johnny walked back to the bed and sank down beside me. "Because I do, Shannon," he said gruffly, pulling me onto his lap. Smoothing my hair back, he pressed a soft kiss to my lips. "I just . . . I need to do right by you."

"Okay," I whispered, burying my burning face in the crook of his neck.

"Are you mad at me?" he asked hoarsely, nuzzling my bare shoulder with his nose as he trailed his fingers over my spine.

I shook my head, keeping my face buried in his neck. "No, I'm not mad at you, Johnny."

"No?" He pressed a kiss to my shoulder. "You sure?"

"Positive," I whispered, keeping a death grip on his neck. "I just want to keep you."

He chuckled softly. "You can."

"You promise?" I croaked out, clenching my eyes shut and tightening my hold on his poor neck.

"I promise," he replied gruffly, pressing another kiss to my collarbone. "I'm already yours."

"What are we going to do, Johnny?" I dared to ask the question that had been plaguing me for weeks. "When you get the call up?"

Johnny sighed heavily. "That's an if, not a when, Shannon, and a very big one at that."

"You're going to get the call," I strangled out, chewing on my lip nervously. "What happens when you go?"

"I don't know how that's going to play out," he finally replied.

"It's scary," I admitted in a small voice. "Thinking about you going away soon."

"I know," he told me, voice thick. "It's scary for me, too."

"Really?" I asked shakily.

"Of course! Shannon, I don't want to leave you," he said, tightening his hold on me. "But if I make it onto the squad, it's only for a month of the summer and then I'll be back to you."

I exhaled a ragged breath, panicked at the very thought of spending that long a time away from him. "I know."

"Don't be sad," he coaxed, wrapping me up in his arms. "It might not even happen."

*It was going to happen.*

*Johnny was going to leave.*

*Just like he warned me months ago . . .*

"I love you, Shannon *like the river*," he said then, breaking through my depressing thoughts. "Only you." Leaning back so that I had no choice but to lift my face and look at him, he smirked. "Like a crazy fucking amount."

"I love you, too," I strangled out, voice thick with emotion, giving him back his words. "Like a crazy fucking amount."

Pressing a gentle kiss to my lips, Johnny pulled back and whispered, "I want to make you feel good."

My heart hammered wildly. "You do?"

He nodded slowly, blue eyes locked on mine. "Can I?"

I blew out a ragged breath and nodded weakly. "Yes."

Shifting us around so that I was beneath him with my legs dangling off the side of the bed, he pressed the palm of his hand against my stomach, encouraging me to lie back down. "I want to taste you," he told me as he knelt on my bedroom floor and reached for the edge of my knickers. "Is that okay?"

*Was it?*

*Oh god.*

"Yeah." Nodding eagerly, I sagged back against the duvet, arching my hips upwards as Johnny slid my underwear off and pushed my thighs apart.

My breathing was ragged and uneven as I pulled myself up on my elbows to see him, feeling both embarrassed and curious.

With his hands on my thighs, spreading me open, Johnny dipped his head and trailed his lips up the inside of my thigh before shifting his attention to my other thigh. "You're perfect," he whispered, lips brushing against my most intimate of areas.

I felt his tongue swipe out, touching me, tasting me, and my eyes rolled back in my head. He did it again, and then again and again, until I was a panting, breathless mess, bucking wildly against his face.

"Oh my god—" Writhing on the bed, I reached for his head, digging my nails into his scalp, as he continued to torment me with his lips and tongue and fingers. "Johnny, I'm going to—"

"Shh, Shan," he coaxed, dragging my hips to the edge of the bed and placing my legs over his shoulders. "I'm just getting started." And then his mouth was back, tongue teasing me, fingers plunging in and out, causing my back to arch off the bed.

"Oh shit—" Biting down hard on my fist, I pulled on his hair, too delirious with sensations to control myself. "I can't . . ." My body shook violently as tremors of illicit pleasure shot through me. "Oh god, I need—"

*Bang, bang, bang* . . .

"Shannon?" Darren's voice filled my ears and I wanted to *cry.* "What are you doing in there?"

"Oh fuck!" Johnny's head popped up from between my legs, wide-eyed and flushed. "Your brother."

*No* . . .

"Don't stop," I begged, tugging on his hair. "Johnny, please—"

"Shannon, if you don't answer me, I'm coming in," Darren called out.

"Don't come in!" I screamed at the top of my lungs as Johnny lunged for the door and turned the lock. "I'm getting dressed."

Scrambling for my pajama bottoms under my pillow, I quickly dragged them on, eyes locked on Johnny who was digging through the pile of discarded clothes for his own. He tossed my shirt at me to put back on before grabbing his own.

"He's in there, isn't he?" my brother demanded from the other side of the door as I clumsily buttoned my blouse. "That's his car parked up the street?"

"Shite," Johnny mouthed as he slipped his shirt on. Leaving it unbuttoned, he pulled his jumper on, only to pull it back off when he realized it was my jumper. "I knew I should have moved the car."

"Open the door, Shannon," Darren demanded, banging loudly. "Right now."

"Fuck off," Johnny mouthed, giving my bedroom door the middle finger. "Asshole."

Stifling a giggle, I darted off the bed and pushed open my bedroom window. "You can climb out here."

"I can't jump down," Johnny hissed, gesturing to his crotch. "My dick."

Now, I did laugh – loudly.

Johnny narrowed his eyes. "It's not funny, Shan. I only just got it back *working*."

"He'll kill you if you go out the door," I mouthed back at him.

Johnny rolled his eyes. "I'm shaking." Smirking, he added, "You really do shake all over just before you—"

"Open the damn door, Shannon," Darren roared.

"I'm getting dressed, Darren!" I screamed back at him. "God!" Turning back to Johnny, I mouthed, "What do I do?"

"Open the door," he replied.

I shook my head. "No way."

He nodded. "Yes way."

"Johnny."

"Shannon."

"Shannon Maud Lynch, open the fucking door or I'm going to kick it down!" Darren bellowed.

Johnny arched a brow. "Your middle name is *Maud*?"

Cringing, I nodded. "My parents hate me."

He grimaced in sympathy. "Ouch."

"I'm knocking this door down in five, four, three, two—"

"Okay, okay, I'm coming!" Summoning every ounce of bravery inside of me, I inhaled a steadying breath, walked over to the door and flicked the lock. "Just be cool," I whispered to myself as I cracked the door open just enough to pop my head out. "Hey, Darren, what's up?"

"Send him out," was my brother's terse response. "Now."

"Who?" I asked, playing dumb.

"Your boyfriend."

"My boyfriend?"

Darren's face turned purple. "*Shannon*, pack it in."

"It's alright, Shan," Johnny said as he gently tugged me away from the door before swinging it inwards. "Before you say it, I'm already leaving," he told Darren. "And, no, I won't do it again."

"Not so fast," my brother growled, folding his arms across his chest. "Are you being safe with my sister?"

"I'm not talking about Shannon with you or anyone else," Johnny replied, jaw clenched.

"Oh, you can bet your hotshot ass you're going to talk to me," Darren growled. "I'm her brother."

"Her brother," Johnny agreed, folding his arms across his chest. "Not her fucking keeper."

"Darren," I spluttered. "Stop."

"Don't 'Darren' me," he shot back, glaring at me. "Your blouse is inside out and buttoned all wrong, and you're locked up in your bedroom—" he gestured stiffly to Johnny, "with him looking like every teenage girl's wet dream."

"Oh my god," I choked out, mortified. "Stop talking."

"Are you protecting her?" he continued, directing his question at Johnny. "Are you being safe? Am I going to have to worry about her coming home with a plus one?"

"What I do or don't do with Shannon is none of your bleeding business," Johnny shot back, looking wholly enraged. "So, back the fuck off."

"It's my business if she comes home pregnant—"

"No," Johnny snapped, interrupting him. "It's *my* business if that happens. Not yours, or any other member of your fucked-up family. It's *mine*." Turning back to me, he pressed a kiss to my cheek and said, "Bye, Shannon," before stalking out of my bedroom.

"Bye, Johnny," I croaked out.

"Don't let me catch you in my sister's room again, Kavanagh," Darren called after him.

"Yeah, yeah," Johnny shot back, not missing a beat. "I'll call you later, babe."

"Yeah," I breathed, staring after him as he disappeared down the staircase. "Okay."

"If Mam had caught him in here, this would have ended very differently," Darren grumbled when the front door slammed shut.

Unable to wipe the smile from my face, I walked over to my bed and flopped down with a contented sigh.

"Shannon?" Darren pressed, leaning in my bedroom doorway. "Are you even listening to me?"

"No," I replied softly. "I'm really not."

"Jesus," he muttered to himself. "You're in trouble, girl."

*Didn't I know it . . .*

# Flying Bras

## JOHNNY

"I want a word with you, Jonathan Kavanagh," Mam announced, stalking into my bedroom with a basket of folded laundry in her arms. "Right now."

"Jesus Christ, Ma!" Scrambling for the towel I had discarded when I stepped out of my en suite I wrapped it around my waist and gaped at her. "Did you ever hear of knocking?"

"I'm your mother, Johnny. I housed you in my body for nine months, so no, I don't believe in knocking," she shot back, unfazed. "And stop fidgeting around, will you? There's nothing you have underneath that towel that I haven't washed, wiped, and talcum powered."

*Jesus Christ . . .*

"Now." Setting the basket down on my bed, she turned to stare at me, hands on her hips. "Is there something you want to tell me?"

"Like what?"

"It'll be better for you in the long run if you just confess now," she told me, eyes narrowed.

My mouth fell open.

*Was she serious?*

*What the fuck did I do?*

"Is this about training?" I asked, confused. "Because you heard Dr. Quirke. I'm allowed to attend light sessions starting this week." I had been given the all-clear by not one but *three* different doctors last week. I had been put through fitness evaluations, strength training, pelvic examinations, and a whole heap of other bullshit before they finally deemed me fit enough to return to the pitch.

"No," Mam replied evenly. "Try again."

I frowned. "It's *not* about training?"

"Nope."

My brows shot up. "Are you sure?"

"Positive."

I scratched the back of my head. "Is it about *rugby?*"

"Last chance," Mam said, tapping her foot on the floor. "Make me proud."

"I would if I knew what I'm supposed to say," I choked out, feeling nervous.

"Well then," Mam said in that tone of voice that sent shivers down my spine, "let me give you a little hint." Shoving her hand into the laundry basket, she yanked out a white, cotton bra. "Imagine my surprise when I was hoovering your room yesterday and found *this* under your bed."

*Aw shite . . .*

Dangling Shannon's bra from her fingers, Mam arched a brow. "Care to explain?"

"Would you believe me if I told you that was mine?" I offered weakly.

"It's not your size," Mam growled before taking aim at me with the bra. "In my house!" she wailed, slapping me over the head with Shannon's bra. "And then I went to tidy your bedside locker, and guess what I found in your drawer?" She took another swipe at me with the bra. "A box of condoms!"

"*Unopened* because I didn't do anything—" Diving into damage control mode, I tightened my hold on my towel and ducked around her. "Ma, we didn't have sex, I swear to god!"

"I'm taking the lock off your door," she warned. "I mean it, Johnny. You can't be trusted."

"Fine," I strangled out, backing up as she prowled towards me. "I don't need it, because I'm not doing anything."

"Then why was your girlfriend's bra under your bed?" Mam demanded. "Huh?"

"She got changed in here after school a few weeks back," I lied through my teeth. "She must have forgot to pack it in her bag."

"Is that so?"

"Yes! That is so." Feigning hurt and outrage, I glared at my mother. "Jesus, Ma, I can't believe you'd think so little of me." Huffing out a breath, I added, "I know I'm not perfect, but knowing my own mother thinks that about me really hurts."

Mam narrowed her eyes. "Don't you play mind games with me, *Brains*. I taught you everything you know, you little pup!"

Fuck.

"Look, we haven't had sex," I said evenly, keeping my eyes on Mam, hoping like hell she'd believe me and release her death grip on Shannon's bra. "I promise, Ma. We haven't." I held my breath and waited for her to make her next move.

"I just want you to be safe," Mam finally said with a heavy sigh as she sank down on the edge of my bed. "No, scratch that. I want to go back in time so that you're ten years old again."

"I'm not ten," I replied, edging closer with caution. "I'm eighteen next month."

"Ugh, don't remind me," she wailed, shoulders slumping. "The years are going by too fast."

"It'll be alright, Ma," I assured her, not knowing what else to say. "Don't be getting upset."

"It's all happening now," she continued to weep. "You're back to training this week, and you have a girlfriend. One of these days, I'm going to blink and you'll be gone on me. Off to France with the rugby. And then what?"

"Come on, Ma," I coaxed, sitting down beside her. "I don't even know if I'm going to make the squad this year."

"I know you will," she replied, resting her cheek on my arm. "And I'll be so proud of you."

"Then why are you sad?"

"Because you're my baby." She sighed heavily. "And it's hard to watch you fly from the nest."

"I'm not jumping any nest," I shot back. "I'd die on my own."

"Johnny," Mam admonished in a sad tone, "I'm being serious."

"So am I." Wrapping my arm around her, I gave her shoulder a squeeze. "I'm being deadly serious. I wouldn't make it a week without you."

She smiled. "You think?"

I nodded. "I know."

Mam was quiet for a long moment then, before asking, "Are you excited for today?" Wiping her eyes, she turned to smile up at me. "Your first day back on the pitch?"

"Terrified," I admitted.

Concern flashed in her eyes. "You don't have to go back," she hurried to say. "If you're not ready, I can call your coaches—"

"I am ready," I cut her off by saying. "I'm just worried."

"About what, love?"

"Not being the same," I muttered. *Not being good enough.*

"You know how I feel about the rugby," Mam said. "I've never made any secret of it, but you should know that I support you one hundred and fifty percent. I know you're brilliant, love, and I know you're going places. You're a phenomenal player, and you need to remember that. It's okay to be nervous. You've had a hard few months with your surgery and recovery, but know that there are other boys out there who would *kill* to play like you do on your worst days."

"You really think that?"

"I've been on the sidelines watching you play since you were in the minis in Blackrock," Mam replied. "And I can't count the number of coaches and other parents who have come up to me, telling me that my boy was destined for the green jersey." Smiling, she added, "I've always been proud of you, love, and I've always known you were brilliant."

"You've never said any of that before," I mused, scratching my jaw.

Mam smirked. "Because I'm still holding out hope that you'll take up golf instead."

"I doubt it, Ma." I shrugged sheepishly. "Sorry."

"Well, just keep your brain safe out there," she muttered, standing up. "Don't be letting any of those thugs hit you on the head."

"I'll do my best," I laughed.

"And no more naked Shannon in your room," she added, giving me a scathing look as she tossed the bra on my lap. "For clothes changing or anything else."

# Let's Make Some Bleeding Babies

## SHANNON

Johnny had been back on the pitch a little over a week and my anxiety was still through the roof. He was training full-time again – working his body to maximum capacity. It was terrifying to watch because I had a godawful fear of him injuring himself, but I had to concede that it was different this time. *He* was different. He was talking now and addressing his pain, working with his physios, OTs, doctors, and trainers, and following all the orders laid down.

Panicked and nervous, I sat in the stands of Ballylaggin RFC on Saturday morning, knees bopping, as I looked on with my heart in my mouth. With a disposable cup filled with creamy hot chocolate, I clutched it between my glove-covered fingers and blew into the rim, enjoying the heat of the steam as it rose up and hit my cheeks. It had been hammering down with rain all day, and I was grateful to be sitting under the plastic awning in the stands.

Like always, my attention was riveted to the boy in the number 13 jersey. He had a woven cap on his head with the club logo etched on the front and a long-sleeved, black body warmer on beneath his training jersey. Beneath his black training shorts, I could see the white support bandage strapped to his thigh, and it made me feel a little queasy.

I watched him for the longest time, stretching and sprinting, following orders, and completing drills with effortless ease.

*Let him get this.*

*Please god, let the boy make it.*

*He deserves it.*

*He's earned this.*

"It's a training session, Shan, not a match," Claire chuckled, dragging me from my thoughts. "If you keep clapping every time he catches a ball or completes a lap, the lads on the team are going to give him a roasting."

"Oh." Mortified, I stilled my hands and tucked them under my thighs, knocking my empty paper cup off the bench in the process. "I don't want to embarrass him. I'm just—"

"In love?" She feign-swooned and dropped her head on my shoulder. "I know."

"Proud," I corrected, cheeks flushed. "He's worked so hard to get back out there."

"And look at him go," Claire mused, pointing to where Johnny was whizzing around the pitch like a bullet, outrunning his opposition with relative ease. "He's on fire today."

"Yeah." I sagged in relief when Johnny side-stepped the big, beefy boy charging straight for him, and threw the ball back to Feely who ran straight for the posts. They all smashed against one another – Johnny included – and I groaned into my hands. "God!" Reaching up, I pulled my woolly hat down over my eyes until they had stopped pummeling each other. "I hate this sport."

"You're so cute." Claire laughed softly. "So, how'd you get out of the house?"

I scrunched my nose up at the memory of Mam screaming at the top of her lungs for me to stay inside or my father would find me this morning when Aoife offered to drop me off at Claire's house. If that wasn't bad enough, Mam had followed me into the front garden, crying and wailing in full view of the neighbors. I didn't know what she expected me to do; stay in my bedroom and rock? I didn't feel safe there.

The truth was, I was more likely to see Dad sitting at our kitchen table than at the rugby club. Besides, I wanted to support Johnny. This was huge for him, and I wanted him to know that I was there for him – regardless of what was happening in my home life. Focusing on Johnny kept the panic thrashing around inside of me at bay. Being here gave me the escape I needed. I felt like I had a purpose, like there was a reason to not lie down and cry into my pillow. Like there was a reason to fight *back*.

*You can do this,* I mentally whispered, focusing all of my attention on him, as I eyed him from my perch. *I know you can.*

"Can I tell you a secret?" Claire asked in a low tone, hooking her arm through mine. "But you can't tell anyone."

"Of course," I replied, turning to face her. "And I would never tell."

"Something happened with Gerard."

My eyes widened. "When you say *happened*?"

Claire blushed but didn't elaborate.

I hesitated, unsure whether to push for more or wait for her to tell me in her own time. Finally, I settled on, "Whatever *happened* between you two . . . " I paused, trying to word it right, "did it happen recently?"

"Kind of," she whispered, biting down on her bottom lip.

"Are you . . . *happy* about it?"

She shrugged. "I don't know."

"Do you . . . *regret* it?"

"I think he does," she strangled out.

Frowning, I turned back to the pitch to where Gibsie was stealing glances at Claire. "Whatever it is that you did, I don't think he's regretting it, Claire," I told her, catching Gibsie for the millionth time as he glanced up at where we were sitting. "He's been watching you all morning."

"This is all a big game to him," she grumbled. "And I'm going to lose."

"*What*?" I shook my head. "Claire, come on, don't think like that."

The sound of the coach's piercing whistle cut through the air, signaling the end of training and putting an end to our conversation.

"Don't say anything about it when he comes over," Claire whisperhissed as Gibsie bounded straight for us, caked from head to toe in mud. Seriously, he was so dirty you couldn't make out what color his hair was supposed to be. "Please, Shan."

"I won't," I promised, slapping on a bright smile as he approached. "Hi, Gibs."

"Hey, Little Shannon," he replied before turning his attention to my best friend. "Claire-bear," he purred with a devilish grin. "I have something for you."

Claire's brows rose in surprise. "You do?"

"Uh-huh." Nodding, Gibsie leaned against the barrier that separated the pitch from the stands and crooked his finger. "Come here and I'll show you."

Clambering over her seat, Claire approached him warily. "You better not be planning on – oh my god, Gerard, don't!" she screamed when he dragged her clean over the barrier and tossed her over his shoulder. "Put me down!"

"Are you sure you want to climb down my body?" he laughed, purposefully smearing her with mud as he lowered her to her feet. "I'm such a dirty boy."

"You asshole!" she strangled out through fits of laughter as he dumped a huge sop of muddy grass that was clung to his thigh onto her hair. "It's not funny."

"Then why are you laughing?" he snickered, dodging her fist when she broke free and swung for him.

"I was trying to lure you into a false sense of security," she shot back, charging towards him.

"Hi, Shannon," Johnny's voice filled my ears and I swung my gaze to where he was leaning against the barrier, smirking at me. Instantly, my heart fluttered wildly in my chest.

"Hi, Johnny." Blowing out a shaky breath, I stood up and moved towards him, only to hesitate. "You're not going to do that to me, are you?" I asked, pointing to where Claire and Gibsie were having a full-blown wrestling match on the pitch. "Because I'm not into that."

Johnny laughed softly. "Only if you don't come over here and give me a kiss."

Smiling, I closed the space between us and wrapped my arms around his neck, pressing a kiss to his lips. "Hi."

"Hi." With a tender affection in such stark contrast to his previous behavior on the pitch, Johnny pressed his forehead to mine and nuzzled. It was such a primal, male move that I could do nothing but stand there and reciprocate the dominant petting. Exhaling a heavy breath, he pressed a kiss to my nose, and brushed my cheek with his thumb. "Your cheeks are all rosy."

"And you're all grass," I whispered, plucking a few strands from his hair. "How are you feeling?"

"I feel good, Shan," he replied, eyes bright and full of excitement. "How was I looking out there?"

"Like a big, bright, shining star," I told him proudly. "You were the best one out there by a mile."

Smirking, he leaned forward and kissed my cheek. It was a soft, sweet act of affection and more intimate than if he'd stuck his tongue down my throat. "Come on—" Hooking me under my arms, Johnny helped me over the barrier before reaching for my hand. "I just need to change and we can get out of here."

"I thought you had the gym?" I asked, falling into step beside him. "I was going to go home with Claire."

"I've already been," he explained, hooking an arm around my waist to lift me over a giant puddle of mud.

My brows furrowed. "But it's only half three."

"The early bird catches the worm, Shan," he shot back. "I've been up since five."

*Whoa.*

"And they say chivalry is dead," Johnny said in an amused tone of voice, eyes locked on Gibsie who had won the scuffle with Claire and was currently sitting on top of her, banging his fists against his chest in victory. They were both caked in mud and Claire's lovely white coat was brown to match her now muddy-brown hair. "Gibs, get off her, ya eejit."

"There's nothing chivalrous about him, Johnny," Claire growled before popping Gibsie in the stomach with her fists. "Take that, you big donkey!"

Rolling onto his back in dramatic fashion, Gibsie clutched his stomach and writhed on the grass, laughing his arse off. "*Donkey.*"

Claire took that as her opportunity to counterattack. Ignoring all of the other boys who were wolf-whistling and calling out suggestive comments as they left the pitch, Claire scrambled onto her hands and knees and lunged for Gibsie. "Keep laughing," she growled as she straddled his chest. "But you're going down."

"On you?" he shot back, waggling his brows. "Yes, please."

"Gerard!"

"Claire," he purred. "Ag—"

She slapped a hand over his mouth. "Don't you *dare* finish that sentence," she hissed, leaning close to his face. "And stop licking my hand."

"You . . . ant . . . e . . . oo . . . ick . . . your . . . ussy . . . stead . . . " Gibsie replied, but his response was muffled by the hand Claire had over his mouth. "Mmmmm—"

"Stop!" she giggled, wiggling around when his hands shot up to tickle her sides. "Gerard, I can't—"

"Claire!" Hughie barked, jogging towards us with Feely in tow. "What the hell are you doing?" Narrowing his eyes, he snarled, "Get off my sister, fucker!"

"Oh great, the life and soul of the party is here," Claire groaned, dropping her hand from Gibsie's mouth. "I'm just killing your friend, Hugh, relax."

"And your sister's on top of *me*," Gibsie added with a wolfish grin.

Hughie's face turned a dark shade of purple. "Gibs, I swear to god, if you don't leave her alone, I'm going to hurt you." He took a menacing step towards them. "I'm not kidding around anymore—"

"Okay," Feely interjected calmly as he stepped in front of Hughie. "They're only messing around, lad. Just relax."

"*She's* messing around," Hughie spluttered, eyeballing Gibsie. "*He's* got an ulterior motive."

Johnny groaned beside me. "This is going to end in tears," he announced, rubbing his jaw.

"What?" I frowned up at him. "Claire and Gibs?"

Johnny nodded. "I can see it coming a mile off."

"Calm down, Hughie," Claire huffed, climbing to her feet. "You're making a big deal out of nothing." Purposefully stepping on Gibsie's stomach as she went, she stalked off in the direction of the carpark. "Like always!"

"Gibson! Kavanagh!" their coach roared from across the pitch. "No girlfriends at training! This isn't a fucking discotheque."

"She's my sister, not his girlfriend," Hughie roared back. "Don't insult her intelligence."

"Yet," Gibsie offered with a snicker.

"Ever," Hughie shot back, furious, as he stalked off in the direction of the clubhouse.

"We'll see," Gibsie called after him, earning himself the middle finger from Hughie.

"I'd call that a shitstorm of epic proportions," Feely mused. "Keep it up with his sister, and I predict messy times ahead for you."

"Yeah, well, as long as the conditions are wet, I'll be a happy man," Gibsie offered with a wink.

"Wow," Johnny shook his head. "That was even creepier than usual, lad."

"Yeah, I just heard it there," Gibsie replied, frowning for a brief moment before grinning sheepishly at him. "To be fair, it sounded so much better in my head."

"Maybe some things should stay in your head, Gibs," Johnny offered.

"Come on, ya big eejit," Feely said, holding a hand out for Gibsie who was still sprawled out on the grass. "Let's go before you get yourself in more trouble."

"You know I can't help it, lad," Gibsie laughed as he climbed to his feet and headed off the pitch with Feely. "Trouble follows me."

"Training's over, Kavanagh," the coach barked. "And no girlfriend at training next week!"

Looking a little pissed-off, Johnny scratched the back of his neck and called back, "Alright, coach." Turning back to me, he cupped my elbow in his hand and leaned down. "I just need to change." He brushed his lips against mine. "Then we'll get out of here, okay?"

I blew out a shaky breath and nodded. "Okay."

"I'll be right back," he whispered, giving my ass a quick squeeze before releasing me, smirk firmly intact, never taking his blue eyes off me as he slowly backed away.

I swear I felt the heat of his stare in my bones long after he disappeared from sight.

"Are you sure this is okay?" I asked Johnny when we parked up at the back of his house a half an hour later. He was fresh from a shower, donning clean clothes, and smelling absolutely delicious beside me. "Your parents won't mind me coming over?" I added, warily eyeing the black Range Rover he was parking his Audi next to. "You're positive?"

"Relax, Shan, she's not even here," Johnny replied, cutting the engine. "They booked a night away in Killarney for tonight. They must have taken my father's car."

Excitement bubbled to life inside of me. "They did?"

"We're all alone." Unfastening his seatbelt, he turned to grin at me, dimples deepening in his cheeks. "Whatever will we do?"

With trembling fingers, I unfastened my seatbelt and climbed over the seats, not stopping until I was sitting on his lap. "What about the others?" I whispered, pressing my forehead to his, as I thought about Claire and Gibsie. "They're following us over here from the pitch."

"They can wait," he growled, clamping his hands down on my hips. "I really don't give a fuck."

"So, what do you want to do?" I breathed, feeling him hardening beneath me.

"Just be with you," Johnny replied gruffly, pressing a kiss to the corner of my mouth. "Spend some time on our own."

I sagged against him. "Me, too."

"Do you want to go up to my room?" he asked, lips moving to my neck.

"Yeah." I nodded and tightened my hold on his shoulders. "A lot."

Groaning into my neck, Johnny gave my hips a squeeze and pulled back, eyes blazing with heat. "Let's go."

Excited, I shoved open the driver's door and scrambled out and watched Johnny climb out after me. My heart was pounding in my chest as he caught ahold of my hand and pulled me along after him to unlock the back door.

"You sure about this?" he asked, sounding excited.

Nodding, I reached up and dragged his face down to mine.

"Aw fuck—" His hands dropped to my ass and he hoisted me up. Wrapping my legs around his waist, I held onto his shoulders and kissed him back as we stumbled into the utility, all breathless and laughing.

*"Mmmm."*

We both froze and stared at each other.

*"Mmmm, that's it."*

Our eyes widened in unison.

*"You know how I like it . . . "*

"That little bollox got back here before us," Johnny hissed, as he stalked towards the kitchen door with me still wrapped around him like ivy. "Gibsie," he snarled, swinging the door open. "I swear to Christ if you brought some girl back here – oh fucking god!" He roared spinning around, only to give me a perfect view of his parents. "What are you *doing?*" he choked out, horrified. "Ye freaks!"

Mrs. Kavanagh was sitting on the island counter top and Mr. Kavanagh was standing between her legs.

*Naked.*

"Oh, Johnny, love, you're home early," his mother replied.

"Ma!" Johnny hissed as he set me on my feet. "What are you . . . oh Jesus – what the fuck are you letting him do to you?" Clutching his stomach, he gawked. "I'm going to be sick."

"Hello, Shannon, love."

"Uh, hi?" I strangled out, blushing furiously.

"Cover your ass, Da," Johnny roared. "My girlfriend's in the room!"

"Sorry, Shannon."

"That's okay."

"No, it's not," Johnny corrected. "Nothing about any of this is okay."

Mr. Kavanagh moved to pick up his clothes off the floor and Johnny let out a demented scream. "Don't fucking pull out," he choked out. "I don't want to see it." Johnny covered my eyes with his hand, and pulled me into his chest. "Don't look, Shan. Honestly, baby, keep your eyes closed. I'm scarred for life."

"Relax, Johnny," Mr. Kavanagh replied in an amused tone of voice.

"*Relax*?" Johnny spluttered, dropping his hand from my eyes. "Are you serious right now? I eat my fucking *dinner* on that counter – not anymore, apparently. No, I'm never eating in this bleeding kitchen again." Shaking his head, he pushed his hands through his hair, looking truly appalled. "And you had the audacity to lecture me over a bra. You two are a disgrace." Stalking towards his parents, he swiped their clothes off the floor and thrust them at them. "You're an embarrassment, and I am ashamed of the both of you!"

"You are supposed to be at the gym," Mr. Kavanagh replied calmly, popping his t-shirt over his wife's head. "You always go to the gym on Saturday." He smirked at his son and that only seemed to push him off the ledge.

"And you're supposed to be in *Killarney*," Johnny roared back.

"We're going shortly," his father replied. "We got a little distracted."

"*Distracted*," Johnny sneered. Narrowing his eyes, he pointed a finger at his parents. "Is this the kind of thing you get up to when I'm not around? Riding my mother in the kitchen? Huh? Where else have you been? Jesus Christ, tell me you haven't touched my room!"

"Johnny, love," Mrs. Kavanagh interjected. "Calm down—"

"No, I won't fucking calm down, Ma. I'm *traumatized*!" Shuddering, he ran a hand through his hair and glowered at his parents. "You let him do that to you . . . Jesus, you both just ruined my life!"

"Hey, it's okay," I whispered, slipping my hand into his. "It's, uh, kind of normal?"

"*Normal*?" Johnny spluttered, eyeballing me with unrestrained outrage. "Shan, there is nothing normal about those two . . . two . . . *geriatrics*!"

I laughed into his face. I felt bad, but I honestly couldn't help it.

"This is *funny* for you?" Johnny accused hotly. "You're supposed to be on my side here, baby!"

"I am," I coaxed, holding his hand with both of mine. "I'm always on your side."

"Sex is a beautiful thing, love—"

"Don't you *dare* start that shite with me or I'm leaving," Johnny warned, swinging his glare on his mother. "I'm serious. I'll move out."

"And where will you go?"

"The fucking dog shed would be better than staying here with the two of you," he snarled.

"Don't be so dramatic, Johnny," Mr. Kavanagh laughed. "You're overreacting."

"The garage – I'll convert it," Johnny barked, still going strong. "I'll move my girlfriend in with me and then I'll fuck her for good measure. Loudly. Repeatedly. In fact, we'll both quit school so we can fuck all the damn day long. Because, *apparently,* that's the norm around here!" Furious, he waved a hand in front of himself. "Visualize that, you inconsiderate freaks. Would you like that? And I won't wear a condom. I'll get her pregnant. How about some grandchildren? Sound good? Shannon and I will become another statistic, and you'll have no one to blame but yourselves for traumatizing me!"

"Oh, you're so grounded," Mrs. Kavanagh told him, still smiling, still half naked.

"Did you not hear me?" Johnny demanded. "I'm about to go out to the garage and impregnate Shannon. Think about that."

"You're too smart to be stupid, Jonathan," his father shot back.

"Yeah? Well, we'll see about that." Grabbing my hand, Johnny dragged me down the hallway. "Come on, Shan. Let's go make some bleeding babies."

"The garage is outside, son," Mr. Kavanagh laughed.

"Don't talk to me," Johnny choked out, upping his pace.

"Keep your bedroom door open, Jonathan," Mrs. Kavanagh called after us.

"Fuck off, the pair of ye," he roared, pulling me up the staircase. "And put some clothes on. My friends are on the way over."

"Uh, I don't want to make any babies today, Johnny," I croaked out, hurrying up the steps after him.

"Me either, Shan," he grumbled, leading me down the landing to his bedroom. "And I couldn't if I wanted to because it's *gone*."

Biting down on my lip to stop myself from laughing, I hurried after him. Stalking into his bedroom like a man on a mission, Johnny shuddered and muttered under his breath. "Fuckers," he continued to growl as he paced the floor. Reaching behind his head, he yanked his hoodie over his head and tossed it on the floor. Rolling his shoulders to loosen them out, he continued to pace his bedroom floor, twisting his neck from side to side as he went. He was sewn into his blue t-shirt, his broad chest and shoulders filling out the fabric better than any grown man could. "I'm ruined."

Deciding on leaving him to his ranting, I gingerly stepped around him and walked over to his television, switching it on. Grabbing both controllers off the console, I sank down on one of the beanbags and set up the game.

"I'm not playing," Johnny declared, tone still laced with outrage. "My pride can't take another hit after *that*."

"Come on," I replied, stifling a giggle. "It'll distract you."

"Doubtful." Grumbling to himself, he dropped into the beanbag beside me and pressed a kiss to my cheek. "Very fucking doubtful."

"Lad—" the bedroom door flew inward and Gibsie came barreling into the room, breathless and grinning like a demented puppy dog. "I think your dad was just giving it to your mam in the kitchen." Eyes wide with excitement, he added, "They were getting dressed when we walked inside."

"Oh, Jesus." Groaning, Johnny tossed the controller away and twisted around in what looked like physical pain. Covering his face with his hands, he hissed, "Fuck my life."

"Oh my god! Your dad is so hot, Johnny," Claire gushed, charging into the room after Gibsie. She was freshly changed in what looked like boy's clothes, but at least the mud was gone and her hair was back to its blonde glory. "Did you see him, Shan? What a babe!"

"Let me die, baby," Johnny choked out, dropping his head in my lap. "Seriously, just kill me now."

"Shh." I stifled another laugh as I trailed my fingers through his hair. "You'll be better before you're married twice."

"I'm only doing that once," he huffed, wrapping his arms around my waist. "So I'll never be better."

"Don't feel bad, Johnny," Claire said, plopping down on his bed as if she owned it. "Your parents are both hot, and hot people tend to have hot sex with one another."

"Wow, Claire, thanks so much for the insight," Johnny deadpanned. "I feel a lot better now."

"You're welcome," she chirped, sifting through a stack of magazines and papers on his bedside locker.

"Yeah, don't worry about it, lad," Gibsie snickered, sprawling out on the bed beside Claire. "Your father's a legend."

"Fuck right off," Johnny growled.

"Aww," Claire gushed, holding a newspaper up for me to see. "Look at the two of you."

My gaze landed on the huge two-page spread from several months ago when Tommen won the School Boy's Shield. In the picture, Johnny had his arm wrapped around me and I was grinning like a maniac at the camera. "You should have this on your wall of fame," she stated, giving Johnny a scathing look, as she bounced off the bed with the newspaper in hand. "It's ridiculous that you don't have a photo of your girlfriend in here."

"I'm kind of in the middle of a personal crisis here," Johnny grumbled, nuzzling my stomach with his nose. "I haven't had time to redecorate."

"Well, I can do that for you."

"Claire," I warned, feeling my cheeks grow hot. "It doesn't matter."

"Of course it matters," she replied, carefully tearing the page out.

"You're a babe," she added, standing in front of Johnny's desk, scrutinizing the cork board hanging over it. "Now which one of you is losing their thumbtack?" She made a clicking sound with her tongue before grabbing a picture off the board. "Sorry, B.O.D, you treasure of a man," she mused, pressing a kiss to the photograph in her hand. "But I need your spot."

"Claire—"

"Let her do it," Johnny interrupted. "I meant to hang it up ages ago anyway."

"Do you want to get out of here?" Gibsie asked then. "I'm bored."

"You're always bored," Johnny shot back.

"Because you're boring," Gibsie countered.

"If I'm boring, fuck off home and find someone else to torment," Johnny grumbled.

"I can't," Gibsie mused. "You might be a boring fucker, but I'm awfully fond of you, and I always miss you too much when we're apart."

"Jesus . . . " Grumbling to himself, Johnny rolled onto his back and said, "Fine. What do you want to do, Gibs?"

"I don't know, Johnny," Gibsie replied, smirking. "What do you want to do?"

"I want to go back in time and *not* see my da boning my ma on the bleeding counter," Johnny shot back, lifting himself up on his elbows to glare at his friend. "But since I haven't perfected the art of time traveling, I'm going to go with bleaching my eyeballs instead. Sound like fun?"

"Only if I get the full experience of seeing your mother naked, too," Gibsie shot back. "Although, god himself couldn't make me erase the mental image of your mother—"

"Get out of my room," Johnny snarled, causing Gibsie to roll around on his bed laughing.

"Why don't we go into the city?" Claire offered, as she re-arranged Johnny's entire cork board of pictures and autographs. "We could get a bite to eat first and go to the cinema afterwards?" Dragging the desk chair over to the wall, she climbed onto it and reached for the pictures of the naked women tacked to his bedroom walls. "Oh, and I'm confiscating these, pervert," she told him. "Just letting you know."

"Go for it," Johnny replied, clearly unaffected, as he dropped back down to rest his head on my thighs. "What do you think, Shan?" he asked, looking up at me from his perch on my lap. "Do you want to go?"

"Uh . . . " Embarrassed, I looked around the room aimlessly before leaning close to his ear and whispering, "I don't have any money."

"I have," Johnny whispered back, holding my head in place with his hand. "And I'm paying." Pressing a kiss to my lips, he added, "So don't overthink this."

"Are you sure?" I asked, feeling embarrassed.

"I'm always sure," he replied. "Stop worrying."

"If we're going, you're going to have to disentangle yourself from Little Shannon and drive," Gibsie interjected. "Because I'm not comfortable with the roundabouts yet."

"Yeah." Sighing heavily, Johnny released my face and stood up. "It'll probably be safer if I drive." Reaching for my hand, he pulled me to my feet. "At least we'll get there in one piece."

"I haven't killed you yet, have I?" Gibsie huffed.

Johnny arched a brow. "*Yet* being the appropriate word, lad."

"Now you're just being ungrateful," Gibsie countered. "I drove your ass around for weeks when you broke your dick – and I kept you alive!"

"Thank you so much for driving me and my broken dick around and keeping us both alive, Gerard," Johnny said, rolling his eyes. "How can I ever repay you?"

"You're more than welcome, Jonathan," Gibsie replied with a grin. "And you can repay me by not ejaculating on me again."

"What?" Claire and I both laughed in unison.

Johnny narrowed his eyes. "You're so fucking dead."

"It's a long story, girls," Gibsie snickered, diving for the door. "I'll tell you all about it in the car."

# Mannequins and Movies

## JOHNNY

I was going to kill my best friend, and after enduring seven years of his antics, I was positive there wasn't a jury in the country that would convict me. Not after his latest stunt.

"Get out of the window before the girls come back from the bathroom," I growled for the fifth fucking time. It was no use, though. My words were falling on deaf ears. Gibsie didn't even blink in response as he stood, still as a statue, in the display window of Debenhams department store in Mahon Point shopping center, with his hands on his hips in a Superman pose, his jeans around his ankles, and a scantily clad mannequin's faceless head positioned against his dick.

"There are kids around," I hissed when a lady with two small children cut me a dirty look as she hurried past. "Come on, lad," I pleaded, spotting Shannon and Claire heading in our direction. "Just come out and I'll buy you a combo."

"I want the extra-large combo – *with* Minstrels," he stated before turning to stone once more.

"Fine," I agreed, flustered, waving back at Shannon. "No problem – just get out of window before you get us lifted by security."

Grinning widely, Gibsie pulled up his jeans and climbed out of the window, laughing to himself. "Lad, you're so easy to get a rise out of."

"Just get out of the shop," I growled, repressing the urge to strangle him.

"What are you two doing?" Claire asked, eyeing us suspiciously. "Were you shopping?"

"Maybe," Gibsie teased. "Do you want me to have been shopping?"

"Definitely not," I muttered, making a beeline for my girlfriend, grateful to have her here so I didn't have to sit next to that gobshite for an entire film. "You all set?"

"Yeah." Smiling brightly, Shannon nodded and tucked into my side. "I'm ready when you are."

Slinging an arm over her shoulder, we strolled into the lobby of the cinema complex to queue up for our tickets.

I'd been to the cinema countless times with Gibsie and Claire down through the years, and was more than prepared for the argument that ensued when I asked the dreaded "What are we going to watch?" question. It was the same fight they had before every bleeding film. Like an old married couple, they threw down right there in front of the ticket booth.

"You're wrong, Gerard," Claire growled, folding her arms across her chest. "I'm telling you, we need to go see *The Wedding Date*."

"I'm not listening to you," he shot back, glaring right back at her. "Not after *The Notebook* escapade."

"That was a *great* movie," she choked out, clutching her chest. "You have no taste."

"You cried!" he spat. "For days!"

"So did you!" she shot back. "Louder than me."

"Exactly," Gibsie ground out. "Which is why I'm not listening to you again."

"Yes, you are."

"No, I'm not doing it," he told her. "I'm not, Claire. Not this time."

Tapping her foot, she pouted up at him.

"Don't give me that look," Gibsie warned her. "It's not working this time. It's my turn to pick."

"What about *Sin City*?" I offered.

"No," they both shot back in unison.

"We're seeing *House of Wax*."

"No, we're not!"

"Yes, we are."

"Anyone want to ask what me and Shannon want to watch?" I asked.

"No," they both barked again.

Shannon chuckled into my side. "They're so funny."

"Claire, it's my turn," Gibsie hissed. "You've picked for the last ten fucking years!"

"No, I haven't," she countered. "You made me go see the *Pokémon* movie."

"Because you made me watch *The Spice Girls* movie!" Gibsie shot back, looking appalled. "Do you know how much shit I got off the lads for that? Huh?"

"Okay," Claire coaxed. "Just let me pick tonight and I swear you can choose next time."

Gibsie's eyes bulged. "That's what you said *last* time."

She rolled her eyes. "I didn't mean it last time."

"No," Gibsie growled, standing firm. "We're watching my film tonight, Claire. Mine. *Me*. What *I* pick." He pointed a finger at her. "And you're going to *like* it!"

"Fine," she deadpanned.

"No, no, no," Gibsie growled, frustrated. "Don't say fine. That's a dangerous word when it comes out of your mouth."

"I said it's fine, Gerard," Claire said flatly. "Pick the film. I don't care."

"You're lying," he accused. "It's not fine and you're going to make me suffer."

"Do what you want, Gerard."

"Stop mind-fucking me!"

"Fine."

"Don't say that."

"Fine."

"Fine!" He threw his hands up in the air. "Fucking fine. You win." Turning to the man sitting behind the counter, he said, "Two tickets for *The Wedding Date* please, and a container for her to store my balls in." Sighing wearily, he gestured over his shoulder to me. "And that poor bastard behind me will have the same."

"Yay!" Claire squealed happily and wrapped her arms around his waist. "You're going to love it."

"It's not fair, but whatever," Gibsie muttered as he paid the man and handed Claire the tickets, stepping aside for me to pay and collect mine and Shannon's. "Doesn't ever matter what I want."

"You're the best." Pressing a kiss to his cheek, she stepped back, waving the tickets in the air. "I'll share my popcorn with you."

"Hmm," he grunted, with his nose cocked in the air. "I'm not hungry anymore."

"Oh, come on, you big, cranky baby," she coaxed, grabbing his hand. "You're hungry and you know it. Let's beat the food queue."

Gibsie relented with a huff and let Claire drag him off in the direction of the concession stands. "Fine, but you get the Maltesers and I'll get the Minstrels – that way we have it covered."

"Obviously," she snorted.

"Do you want something to eat?" I asked, turning to look at Shannon. She shrugged and tucked her hair behind her ear. "I don't know."

"You don't know?" I arched a brow. "Are you hungry?"

"Are you getting something?" she answered my question with one of her own.

"I might." I watched her carefully. "Only if you get something."

She blew out a small breath, cheeks reddening. "If you're sure?"

"Is this about money?" I came right out and asked her. "Because I already told you I'm paying."

Looking embarrassed, she glanced down at her feet and then back up at me. "I'll eat some of your popcorn if you're getting some."

Knowing that was all I would get out of her, I nodded and led her to the food court and ordered a large tub of popcorn, a large Coke, and a bottle of water. "Thank you," she whispered as we trailed through the complex after Gibsie and Claire. "I really appreciate it—"

"If you thank me for buying you a bleeding Coke, I'm going to throw a tantrum worse than Gibs." Handing her the drink, I pulled the door of screen one open and gestured for her to go ahead of me. "I mean it, Shan."

"Like the one in the kitchen earlier?" she snickered, hurrying inside. "With your parents?"

"Ugh." I shuddered and followed after her. "Don't remind me."

"It's okay," she teased. "When the lights go out, I'll make you feel better."

"Do you promise?" I muttered under my breath.

"I promise," she whispered, squeezing my ass.

*Jesus . . .*

# His Daughter

## SHANNON

We were leaving the cinema in Mahon Point later that night when it happened – when I saw *him*. Johnny, Gibsie, and Claire were walking alongside me, deep in conversation about the movie we'd just watched, but I couldn't hear a word they were saying over the sound of my pulse hammering violently. My feet faltered, my body stiffened to the point where I couldn't move another step. Blinking rapidly, I tried to rid my mind of the image, pretend I had imagined it, but when I looked again, it was still there. *He* was still there. Sitting in a car, three spots up from Johnny's Audi. *With a woman.*

"Shan?" I felt Johnny squeeze my hand. "You okay?"

I couldn't answer him.

My lips weren't working.

Releasing Johnny's hand, I began to back away, moving like a ghost, praying that he hadn't seen me.

"Shannon?" Johnny called out, tone laced with concern. "Baby?" He was right in front of me now, hands on my cheeks, blue eyes locked on mine. "What's wrong?"

Shaking my head, I opened my mouth to answer him, but all that came out was a puff of air.

"Oh no," Claire whispered, finally seeing what I was seeing. "Shan, it's okay."

"What's okay?" Johnny demanded, looking around the dimly lit carpark. "What the fuck is going on?"

Gibsie shrugged. "No clue, lad."

"It's her *dad*," Claire choked out. "He's over there in that black car."

"I need to go," I finally managed to squeeze out as I continued to stumble away. I was in full-on panic mode and my delayed flight instinct had kicked in. "I need to leave—" Spinning around, I made a run for the shopping center entrance. "I need to go *now*!"

"No, no, Shannon, don't run—" Johnny's arms came around my waist, pulling me against his chest. "I'm right here with you," he whispered in my ear. "I won't let anything happen to you."

"Did he see me?" Sagging weakly in his arms, I clenched my eyes shut as tears dripped down my cheeks. "What if he *saw* me, Johnny?"

"It doesn't matter," he coaxed, turning me around in his arms. "He can't touch you."

"Just take me away," I whispered brokenly, as I buried my face in the fabric of his hoodie. "Please get me out of here."

"I will." I felt Johnny stiffen and then he was pulling me closer if that was even possible, both arms wrapped tightly around my body. "I promise."

My stomach churned violently and I broke free from Johnny's hold, staggering away, clutching my stomach as the familiar taste of bile assaulted my senses.

"Are you going to be sick?" Johnny asked, tone thick and gruff. "Shan—"

Shaking from head to toe, I doubled over on my hands and knees and heaved violently as my stomach emptied itself on the footpath.

"Shh, it's okay," Johnny coaxed, pulling my ponytail out of the danger zone. "Everything's fine, baby." Crouching down beside me, he continued to hold my hair and rub my back. "Just breathe, Shan. Nice and slow . . . Good job. That's it . . . " Digging his car keys out of his pocket, he tossed them towards Gibsie and said, "Bring the car over here, lad."

"I'm sorry," I strangled out as I sank back on my knees and gasped for air.

"Don't be sorry," he said softly. "Are you done?"

I nodded weakly. "Sorry."

"It's okay, Shan," Johnny replied, helping me to my feet. "You're fine, baby."

A car pulled up beside us then – Johnny's Audi, I realized, with Gibsie in the driver's seat and Claire sitting in the back. Leaving the engine running, Gibsie jacked the handbrake and climbed over the seats and into the back to join Claire.

Swinging open the passenger door, Johnny helped me inside and closed the door behind me before stalking off.

"Oh my god," I cried, turning to see him heading towards my father's car. "Johnny, don't!" Pushing the door open, I scrambled out. "Just leave it alone, Johnny!" I choked out, stumbling weakly after him. "Please don't do anything—"

*Bang.*

I watched in a mixture of shock and horror as my boyfriend slammed his palm down on the windscreen of my father's car, hard enough that I was surprised it didn't form a crack.

The impact startled both my father and the woman whose head was in his lap. Both jerked up, wide-eyed and staring.

"Get out of the car," Johnny ordered, pulling on the locked driver's side handle. When my father didn't make a move to oblige, Johnny grabbed the door handle with both hands and began to pull on it violently, causing the car to shake. "Get out of the *fucking* car!" he roared, slamming the side of his fist on the window next to my father's head.

I watched the scene unfold like a car crash, petrified but unable to look away. The woman in the car looked on in horror. I briefly wondered if she knew he was married. *If she knew he was evil . . .*

My father looked enraged as he unlocked the car and shoved the door open. Johnny looked equally incensed, but he took a step back, giving my father the space required to actually obey his command and get out of the car.

I shuffled closer, unsure but needing to get closer to this, needing to go to my boyfriend.

"You," Johnny snarled, chest-heaving, when my father stood up and faced him, "are the worst piece of shite I've ever had the misfortune of coming across – and that is saying something considering I've travelled the fucking world."

They were face to face, foreheads pressing against the other like two raging bulls in a heated showdown. Fear choked me. If my father hit him, what would he do? Would he break up with me? I couldn't control any of this. I felt as weak as my mother – as useless, too.

"Only god fucking knows how you managed to father her," Johnny was roaring. "Because I sure as shit don't understand how something so good could come from something so fucking toxic."

"Who the fuck are you?" my father snarled, red-faced.

"You should know me," Johnny seethed, shoving my father so hard that his back hit the side of the car with a loud bang. "I'm the rugby prick, remember?" Fisting the front of my father's shirt, Johnny reared his head back and bopped my father in the face. Blood sprayed everywhere and I flinched. "I'm your daughter's boyfriend," he continued, shoving my father against the car once more before swinging his fist and connecting with my father's jaw. "And I've been *dying* to meet you."

"Who the hell do you think you are, you little shit?" my father bellowed, spitting out a mouthful of blood. "A spoiled, private school prick, that's who."

"I'll tell you who I am," Johnny snarled, clearly livid, keeping my father pinned to the side of the car. "I'm the one trying to sort through a life's worth of damage you've caused her. You fucked your kids up and you don't even care. You're a fucking disease and you deserve to be put down like the dog you are!"

"Please don't!" Terrified, I hovered near the bonnet of the car, too afraid to move any closer. "Johnny," I continued to sob over and over as tears dripped down my cheeks. "Please just walk *away*."

"Go back to the car, Shannon!" Johnny commanded.

My father turned to look at me. "Shannon—"

Feeling weak, I staggered backwards, shaking my head as if it could somehow stop him from talking to me.

"Don't fucking look at her!" Johnny roared, hitting my father again. "You keep your goddamn eyes off her!"

"Johnny, lad," Gibsie called out as he jogged towards us, "you need to walk away—"

"Back the fuck up, Gibs!" Johnny roared. "I'm not done."

Holding his hands up, Gibsie nodded and stepped back.

"Hit me back, you fucking coward!" Johnny snarled. "You're so quick to put your hands on your girls, fucking try it with me! Come on, big man; hit me. See where it'll get ya!"

"Get out of here before I call the Guards," my father roared. "You jumped-up prick."

"And say what to them?" Johnny laughed in his face. "You can't touch me, you serpent." He shoved him again. "And your little mind games? Whatever it is you do to get inside her head? It won't work on me." He shook his head and sneered. "I'm fucking bulletproof."

"Johnny," I strangled out. "Please just take me home . . ."

Johnny shuddered and a furious growl tore through him. "Here's how this is going to work," he hissed, releasing his grip on my father's shirt. "You're going to get back in your car and drive far away. You're going to uphold the barring order and you're going to leave her alone. You're going to stay far away from your daughter's house and you're going to continue ignoring her, and I'm going to continue fixing the holes you've put in her. And if you ever touch her again, I'll know about it. One fucking bruise, I'll see it, and I'll know who put it there," he snarled, chest heaving. "And then I'll come for you, and when I do, god himself won't save you." He shoved him again. "Are we clear, you poisonous piece of shit?"

My father didn't respond and, for a moment, I was terrified Johnny wouldn't walk away, but he did. Turning stiffly, he walked over to where I was cowering and held out his hand.

Taking a step forward, I braced myself and placed my hand in his, feeling the commitment he was offering me wrap around my body like ivy. His touch calmed something deep down inside of me, soothing the terror enveloping me from being in my father's presence again.

"I knew I was right about you, girl!" Dad sneered, brown eyes narrowed on me. "You're no daughter of mine."

"She *is* your daughter, you sick fuck." Releasing my hand, Johnny spun around and stalked back to where my father was opening the door. "But you're no father to anyone," he snarled, throwing one final, unmerciful punch to his jaw that knocked my father to the ground. "See this piece of shit," Johnny demanded, glaring in the window at the woman screaming in the car. "He abuses women and children, so you should think about running while you still can."

Having said that, Johnny turned around and closed the space between us. "You hit my dad," I croaked out, feeling numb, as he wrapped his arm around my shoulders and steered me towards his car.

"I did," he bit out, tightening his arm around my shoulders.

"A lot," I whispered, knotting my fingers in the side of his hoodie.

"He deserved it."

"He did."

"Are you okay?"

"Are you?"

"I don't know."

"Me either."

Yanking the passenger door open, Johnny bundled me inside before closing the door and rounding the driver's side. Climbing inside, he slammed his door shut and pulled on his seatbelt, jaw clenched, tension emanating from him.

"Good job, lad," Gibsie said, climbing into the back seat behind Johnny and patting his shoulder. "I'm proud of you for walking away."

"I should have *killed* him," Johnny seethed, glaring out the windscreen, gripping the steering wheel with bloodied knuckles. "It's not enough."

"Are you okay, Shan?" Claire asked, leaning forward to wrap her arms around me.

Sniffling, I reached up and clutched her forearm. "Can we just go please?"

Nodding stiffly, Johnny put the car in gear and tore out of the carpark, wheels screeching from the unnecessary speed.

"Should we call the Guards?" Claire asked. "He's not supposed to go near you."

"He didn't go near her," Gibsie replied calmly. "Johnny went near him."

"Okay," Claire mumbled. "No Guards."

"What if he calls them on you?" I strangled out, panicking. Turning to look at Johnny, I whispered, "What about The Academy?"

"He won't do anything, Little Shannon," Gibsie interjected. "He couldn't if he wanted to – and even if he tried, Mr. K would have it sorted in an hour, so don't even worry about it."

"Exactly, and Johnny's still a minor," Claire offered. "He was provoked by emotions. No one would blame him."

"I'm right here," Johnny bit out. "Stop talking over me."

"Sorry, lad," Gibsie replied. "We're just trying to figure this out."

Exhaling heavily, Johnny ran a hand through his hair and glanced sideways at me. "Are you mad at me?"

My breath hitched. "For w-what?"

"For making it worse for you," he admitted gruffly. "I just . . ." Shaking his head, he blew out another frustrated breath. "He was right fucking there, and I saw red. I *couldn't* walk away. I knew I should, but I just . . . couldn't." He gripped the wheel tighter. "Not after what he did to *you*."

"No one's blaming you, Johnny," Claire chimed in. "You did the right thing."

"He deserved everything he got and more, lad," Gibsie added.

"I'm sorry, Shannon," Johnny said in a low tone, ignoring the others. "I'm so fucking sorry, baby."

My hand shot out of its own accord, gripping his forearm he was resting on the gearstick. "I love you so much," I breathed, feeling so much in this moment that I feared my heart might burst. "Don't say sorry."

His shoulders visibly sagged as he turned his hand over and entwined our fingers. "Will you come home with me tonight?" He glanced at me, blue eyes blazing with heat. "Will you stay with me? So I know you're safe?"

"Yeah." I blew out a shaky breath and nodded, knowing there was nowhere else I wanted to be than with him. "I'll stay with you."

My gaze was riveted to the mobile phone flashing silently on the nightstand next to the bed. I didn't dare reach over and answer it. In fact, I mentally envisioned myself climbing out of bed and throwing it out of the window instead. When I sent that text to Joey earlier, letting him know that I was staying at Johnny's, I should have turned my phone off. I knew it was Darren trying to call me, or worse, Mam. I couldn't deal with them right now.

Remaining motionless, I immersed myself in the sensation of my heart thrashing against my ribcage, and the sound of my pulse thrumming wildly, while I desperately tried to remind myself that I was okay.

*For now . . .*

*Only for now, Shannon.*

*He saw you, and you saw that look in his eyes.*

*Be afraid.*

*He's coming back for you.*

*Stop it!*

A shaky breath tore from my chest then, an involuntary reaction to my anxiety, as I contemplated what my future held in store for me. A deep groan came from nearby and I quickly swung my gaze to the boy sleeping on the far side of the enormous bed, sprawled out in his jocks, on top of the covers.

Rolling onto my side, I pressed my cheek into my pillow and just soaked in the sight of him. "Johnny?" I croaked out, feeling anxious and desperate for some sort of comfort I wasn't even sure he could give me. "Are you awake?"

Silence.

Chewing on my lip, I debated my next move.

Should I get up?

Go for a walk?

Try to wake him up?

My thoughts were scattered when I felt a warm hand cover mine. "Hi, Shannon," he whispered, eyes open now and locked on mine.

"Hi, Johnny," I breathed, shivering from the physical contact.

"Can't sleep?"

I shook my head.

"Scared?"

I nodded, unable to speak now.

His hand tightened around mine. "I'll keep you safe."

"Come here," I whispered, holding onto his hand with a death grip. "I need you close."

"You sure?"

I nodded. "Positive."

Releasing my hand, Johnny stood up and pulled back the covers before climbing in beside me.

"Closer," I begged, rolling onto my side. "I need you."

His arm came around me, pulling my back flush against his bare chest before settling his hand against my lower belly. "I'm right here, baby." His breath was hot on my neck, and then his lips were on my skin, pressing soft, hot kisses to my neck and collarbone. "You are not your father's daughter, and there's no orchard in the world far enough from the tree your apple fell from." His arms tightened around me, the heat from his body cocooning me. "He won't break you, because I won't let that happen. Not ever."

"I love you, Johnny Kavanagh," I choked out, clenching my eyes shut as I grabbed his arm and held it to my chest. "Most in the world."

"I love you back, Shannon Lynch," he said quietly in my ear and I felt the connection I had to him in the deepest part of my soul. "Most in the world."

"For keeps?" I breathed.

He kissed my shoulder. "For keeps."

# You Don't Steal Kids, Lad

## JOHNNY

Shannon Lynch changed me.

I knew that sounded like contrite bullshit, but it was the truth.

That day back in January, when I knocked her out with my ball, I'd been so fucking lost and miserable. I hadn't realized just how much until I looked into those midnight-blue eyes and was met with an almost mirror replica of my own secrets and pain. I was hurt and scared for reasons completely different to hers, but something snapped into place for me that day, and I hadn't been the same since.

She happened to me when I least expected her. I didn't want it, wasn't willing to negotiate with the change I knew she would bring. So, I blocked her out. I kept her at arm's length. Until one day, I couldn't do it anymore.

It took me some time to figure out what was happening to me, to understand the feelings thrashing through me, but once I did, once I accepted what I was feeling and set my sights on her, I was all in.

Five months had passed since the day she burst into my life, throwing everything in a spin, and my feelings for her were deeper than ever. I honest to god felt like I was drowning in everything she was. Her pain, her smiles, her horrible fucking family, her playful personality – the one that peeked out when we were alone together. I was completely caught up in her.

I was fairly sure that neither of us had a clue of what we were doing – I certainly didn't – but I knew whatever it was, I had no intention of stopping. She wasn't a test I could study for, or a match I could prepare for with practice and countless hours at the gym. For the first time in my life, I was out of my element, and winging my way through a relationship I wasn't entirely sure how to navigate, but the feelings she evoked from me were addictive. Fuck addictive, I was *obsessed* with my girlfriend. I was in so deep with her that I could hardly *breathe* and, still, I jumped in deeper, pushed down further, wanted more and took it, doing whatever I could to just *be* with her.

Between her family despising me and my rigid training schedule that was back in full swing, spending time on our own together was a problem for me. I was struggling to find a balance between rugby and my girlfriend, and most days, I fluctuated between working in the gym or on the pitch, and wanting to blow off training, get in my car, and go pick her up.

Feeling stronger than ever, I worked myself to the bone, falling back into my 5am gym sessions, and working overtime to make up for precious lost time. I was throwing everything into building myself back up in time, hungry to recapture and retain my position. She never complained about how much I trained or how often I went to the gym. She just *encouraged* me, giving me a steady flow of silent support that was more comforting than anything else, while continuously telling me that she believed in me. *'You can do it, Johnny, I know you can.'* Her words were powerful to me. They affected me more deeply than she realized. Those small affirmations helped me drag my arse out of the bed each morning when my body screamed out in protest.

I tried not to think about what the future held for us – about what would happen when that call came through, because for the first time in my life, I was invested in something other than rugby. I was invested in *her*.

Before I met Shannon, I wouldn't have considered myself to be an impulsive person, but something had re-wired itself in my brain, morphing me into a reckless, unthinking eejit. I knew I messed up with her father a few weeks back, but in fairness, how the hell could I walk away? How could anyone let *him* walk away? Someone needed to make that monster pay.

The sound of my phone ringing cut through my thoughts and I pulled the car over outside Shannon's house before taking it out of my pocket to answer it. Glancing at the screen, I smirked when I saw her name flash on the screen. "Hi, Shan."

"Hi, Johnny," came her soft reply. "How was training?"

"Same as always." Sighing contently, I leaned back in my seat. "I'm outside."

"Oh no," she mumbled. "I'm not there."

"That's okay," I replied, pushing down the surge of disappointment churning inside of me.

"I'm actually at Claire's house," she said down the line. "We're going shopping."

"Shopping?" I smirked to myself and plucked a piece of fluff off my thigh. "You got anything nice in mind to buy?"

"Uh, no, not me," she replied, voice muffled. "But I can come over later tonight, if that's still okay with you? Hughie said he'd drop me to your house if you still want me to come over?"

"You better come over," I teased. "Otherwise, I'm going to have to come scale the side of your house and break you out."

She laughed softly. "Oh, hang on—" The sound of ruffling and muffled whispers filled my ears before Shannon came back to the phone. "Claire wants to know if Gibsie is with you?"

"No, he drove to training today," I replied, glancing down at my watch. "He should be home soon."

"Did you get that?" I heard Shannon say to Claire. "I miss you," she added then, directing this part at me. "A lot."

"I miss you, too, baby."

"You two are disgusting," Claire's voice snickered down the line. "You saw each other at school yesterday."

Something caught my eye in the front window of Shannon's house then, distracting me from the conversation. Arching up, I peered over the wall, watching as the curtains twitched again. "Who's home, Shan?" I asked, curious.

"Huh?"

"At your house?" I asked. "You said Darren was in Belfast this weekend for work?"

"Oh, he is," she replied.

"So there's nobody home?"

"There shouldn't be," she replied.

"Oh." I watched as the curtains twitched around and then a little blond head popped out and then quickly disappeared. "Hmm."

"Why?" she hurried to ask, panic evident in her voice. "Is there something wrong?"

"Nope," I replied, keeping my voice calm as I climbed out of the car. "I'm just heading home now, so I'm going to have to hang up."

"Okay, thanks for calling."

"You called me, Shan," I reminded her as I rounded the garden wall, heading for the house.

"Oh . . . yeah, right. Sorry."

"Don't worry about it." I chuckled to myself, imagining her blushing. "I'll see you later, okay?"

"Bye, Johnny."

"Bye, baby." Hanging up, I slid my phone into my pocket and crouched down in front of the window. Less than a minute later, the net curtain twitched and a pair of big, chocolate-colored eyes locked on mine.

*Sean*, I mentally noted as the toddler stared through the glass at me, face solemn and streaked with dirt.

"Hey," I mouthed, waving at him.

He didn't respond.

He just stood there, staring back at me.

Unsure of what to do, I placed my hand against the windowpane and held my breath. Seconds ticked by, and just when I thought the baby had turned to stone, he pressed his small, chubby hand against the glass, mirroring mine.

Smiling, I slowly stood back up, knowing that I needed to get back in my car and far away from this house, but moving towards the front door anyway. Knocking softly, I waited for a response, forcing down the urge to storm inside and demand to know what the fuck was going on.

Finally, the door opened inwards, and I was faced with the same tiny blond boy from the window. "Hey, Sean," I said in my best coaxing voice. "How are you?"

Another boy, no more than eleven or twelve, rushed towards us then, intercepting the toddler, and sweeping him into his arms. Swinging around, he locked his mistrusting glare on me. "Get out."

"How's it going?" I heard myself say as I retreated a couple of steps. "I'm Johnny."

"Yeah? Well, fuck off, Johnny."

Jaw-ticking, I swallowed down a snarky response and tried again. "You're Tadhg, right?" I hoped like fuck I had the name right. "I'm your sister's boyfriend. And I know your brother Joey, too."

A third boy appeared then, peeking around what I knew was their kitchen doorway. "You're *that* Johnny?" he asked in a small, hopeful voice. "Shannon really likes you."

"Don't talk to him, Ollie," Tadhg said coldly. He turned his hard stare on me and hissed, "Leave."

I wasn't leaving.

I *couldn't*.

"Where's your mother?" I asked.

"Mind your fucking business," Tadhg spat.

*Christ, this kid was almost as feral as Joey.*

"Where's Joey?"

No answer.

"Are you guys home alone?"

With a scathing glare, Tadhg moved to swing the door shut on me.

I reached out and stopped it from closing. "You can tell me where she is," I said calmly. "Or you can tell the Gardaí."

"Joey had to go to a match," the middle one spilled his guts and said. "Mammy was supposed to drop us to Nanny's but she's still in bed, and she won't wake up."

"Jesus fucking Christ, Ollie," Tadhg roared. "What are you trying to do to us?"

"He asked," Ollie replied, lip wobbling.

"And you just *tell* him our business?" Tadhg snapped. "You know better!"

The middle one hung his head and sniffled. "I'm sorry."

"If you call the Guards on us, I'll make you pay," Tadhg hissed, turning to glare up at me. "I'm dangerous."

I bit down on my lip to stop myself from smiling. "I believe you," I told him, keeping my expression somber. "You're a big lad for your age."

"Yeah, I'm twelve," he growled, puffing out his chest. "I could take you."

I nodded solemnly. "Definitely."

"He talks funny," Ollie said then. "Why do you talk funny?"

"That's because he's a *Dub*," Tadhg sneered, giving me a scathing look. "Everyone knows Cork is the real capital of Ireland."

Was he picking a fight with me over my *birthplace*?

*Jesus . . .*

"So, what time's Joey due back from his match?" I asked, trying for nonchalance, as I leaned against the doorframe.

"A few hours," Ollie said, forthcoming. "But if he's working afterwards, then he'll be really, really late."

"Dammit, Ollie." Tadhg shook his head in resignation. "You can't keep anything to yourself."

"I'm just answering his question," Ollie huffed.

"Did you guys have dinner yet?" I asked, smiling at Sean who was staring up at me, wide-eyed. "Are ye hungry?"

"We're fine," Tadhg growled.

"I'm hungry," Ollie piped up. "And we didn't have dinner because we don't know about the cooker."

My heart cracked in my chest, but I masked it with a small laugh. "Yeah, same here," I told them, trying to put them at ease. "I don't know much about cookers, either."

"Joey cooks," Ollie offered. "Shannon, too."

Smiling, I nodded. "Yeah, Shannon's a great cook."

His eyes widened. "Have you tried her spaghetti? It's my favorite."

"Not yet," I replied. "I must ask her to make it for me sometime."

"You should," Ollie agreed. "It's really good."

"Hey, you know what I really like?" I said. "McDonald's." Their eyes widened and I hurried to say, "Do you want to go?"

*What the fuck are you doing, Johnny!*

"With you?" Ollie asked, eyes wide.

*Say no, asshole. Say fucking no!*

"Yeah," I replied.

"Now?" Tadhg piped up, sounding reluctantly excited.

*You're going to jail, Cap . . .*

"Yeah," I choked out. "Why not."

Three hours, one trip to the playground and two food-runs to McDonald's later, and I was bleeding exhausted. Panic-stricken, I pulled onto Gibsie's street, knowing that I needed some backup and some life advice.

"Lads, wait in the car, okay?" I coaxed, glancing back at the three blond heads in the rear of my Audi. Ollie and Sean were stuffing their faces with bags of sweets. Tadhg was slurping down a slushy. Empty Happy Meal boxes were scattered all over the floor of my car and I was praying these kids didn't have allergies because I'd loaded them up on more shite than I dared to think about. "I'm just picking up my buddy."

"Can I drive now?" Tadhg asked, unbuckling his seatbelt and moving to climb through the seats. "We're on a cul-de-sac."

"*No,*" I shot back. "I already told you."

Huffing, he sat back down and took a sip from his straw. "You suck."

*You cheeky little fucker.* "Just wait here," I muttered, climbing out of the car before I strangled my girlfriend's baby brother.

"What did you do?" Gibsie asked, watching me from his front door as I hurried up the garden path towards him. "*Johnny?*"

"I'm in trouble," I strangled out when I reached him. "Big trouble."

"I know," Gibsie replied, eyeing me with suspicion. "I can tell by your face. What the hell did you do?"

"I took them!" I choked out, pointing at my car.

"You took what, Johnny?" Gibsie asked warily.

Swallowing down a groan, I grabbed his arm and dragged him down the path towards my car. "Them," I strangled out, pointing to the three blond boys looking out at us.

"You *took* them," Gibsie deadpanned. "You just went ahead and *took* some kids?"

"You weren't there!" Exhaling a furious growl, I ran my hand through my hair and hissed, "You didn't see what I saw, so don't fucking judge me."

"Don't *judge* you?" Gibsie spluttered, eyes wide. "Lad, you stole some fucking *kids*." His voice rose, turning all pitchy, as he continued to rant. "And you brought them here – to *my* house – making me an accomplice!"

"I didn't *steal* them," I growled. "I took them."

"Steal, take – it's all the same, Johnny," he snapped. "They are not a product of your fucked-up dick therefore you have no business taking them anywhere." He stepped around me and peered through the window. "What's wrong with that one?" he asked, pointing at Sean. "Why is he eating his fingers?"

"I don't know, he doesn't talk," I groaned, flustered. "I don't know what the fuck I should do next."

"Take them back to whatever playground you found them in."

"It's a little more complicated than that," I bit out, grinning and giving the boys two thumbs up. Ollie and Sean waved back at me. Tadhg gave me the middle finger. "We can drop that one back," I muttered under my breath. "Look," I said, turning back to Gibsie, "can we bring them inside?"

"Inside my house?" Gibsie balked. "Yeah, because that doesn't sound at all predatory and fucked-up. Two seventeen-year-old lads bringing three small boys into their house."

"Can we?"

Gibsie gaped at me like I had lost my mind, and the truth was I probably had. But I was in this now and I was rolling with it. "Fuck no!"

"Then what am I supposed to do with them?"

"Take them back."

I shook my head. "I can't do that."

"You don't steal *children*," he hissed. "It's like the fundamental rule of life."

"I wasn't thinking."

"You have issues," Gibsie accused, sounding horrified. "You have serious fucking issues with taking things that aren't yours. You're like a kleptomaniac but with *humans*!"

"I know," I choked out. "I'm going to work on it, but I need you to help me with these ones."

"Why?" he demanded. "What aren't you telling me, Johnny? Christ, I can't help you if you don't tell me what's going on."

"They're *Shannon's* brothers." Turning my back on the car, I whispered, "They were all alone, lad. Their Ma was in bed and they were hungry. I couldn't leave them there." I shrugged helplessly. "How can I take them back to that house?" I pointed back to the car. "That one's only a baby."

"Shit." Gibsie dropped his head and groaned. "Should we call Shannon?"

"No," I snapped, flustered. "She's having a good day for once in her life. I'm not wrecking that with more shite."

"Then we'll take them back to your house," he replied. "Your mam's at home. She'll know what to do with them."

"She's going to kill me," I mumbled dejectedly.

"Yep," Gibs replied, clapping me on the back. "And me with you."

"Whoa!" Tadhg and Ollie chorused when we pulled up outside my house a little while later. "Your house is *huge*."

"None of you are afraid of dogs, right?" I asked as Bonnie, Cupcake, and Sookie bounded around in the back garden.

"Nope," Ollie replied, pushing the door open and running straight for the dogs. "I like the black one," Tadhg stated as he hurried out after his brother.

"Her name's Sookie," I told him, climbing out after them. "She's old so be gentle with her."

"Hey, Sookie," Tadhg called out, running across the grass to where Ollie was rolling around with my mother's two golden retrievers.

"What are we going to do with this one?" Gibsie asked, as he leaned against the side of my car and pointed to Sean who was still sitting in the backseat, chewing on his fingers. "Why does he keep eating himself?"

"He's not eating himself, Gibs," I snapped, feeling oddly defensive of him. "He's just nervous. This is all new to him, so just . . . leave him alone, will ya?"

"Jesus," Gibsie muttered, holding his hands up. "Sorry, *Dad*."

Ignoring my best friend, I walked around to the back door and crouched down. "Hey, buddy," I coaxed, making eye contact with him. "You want to come inside with me?"

Sean stared at me for a long moment before crawling over the seats and slipping his small hand into mine. Uncertain, I looked at his small face and plastered on what I hoped was a reassuring smile. "Good boy." Helping him out of the car, I had to hunch while we walked, so I didn't pull the kid's arm out of its socket.

"You know, if the rugby ever fails, you'd make a mighty fine child-care provider," Gibsie snickered, holding the back door of the house open for me.

"Fuck off," I mouthed as I helped Shannon's youngest brother over the back step, and threw a few *Hail Marys* up for self-preservation purposes. "Ma?" I called out, blessing myself, as I pushed the kitchen door inwards and found my mother sitting at the island with one of her work portfolios laying open. "I have a problem and I need your help."

"Try three problems," Gibs mused. "Three huge fucking problems."

"But don't panic," I hurried to add. "Little ears are listening."

Her gaze went straight to the toddler whose hand I was holding and then to Gibsie before going back to me. "Oh, Johnny, what have you done?" Pushing back her stool, she stood up and walked over to us. "Who owns this child?"

"This is Shannon's baby brother," I explained as calmly as I could, careful not to spook the small child clinging to my hand.

"There's two more where he came from in your garden," Gibsie offered up. "Johnny stole them."

"You stole her *children*?" Mam strangled out, paling.

"Yep, so you might want to call your husband and see if he's familiar with child abduction cases," Gibsie replied for me. "And full disclaimer here: for once, this was *not* my idea."

"This is Sean," I said, eyeballing my mother. Keeping my voice soft and gentle, I crouched down beside him and spoke directly to him. "Sean, this is my mammy. Her name's Edel."

Sean stared up at my mother, shoving his entire fist into his mouth this time.

"He likes to eat his hand," Gibsie offered, like that was important information. "But Johnny reckons it's okay." Shrugging, he added, "Don't know much about kids, myself. All I have at home is a cat."

"Gerard, go down to the office and get my husband for me," Mam whispered. "Hurry now, love."

"Will do," Gibsie replied, before racing down the hallway towards my father's home office.

"Now." Crouching down in front of Sean, Mam smiled brightly. "Hello, Sean, love, how are you?"

Sean watched her carefully, not making a sound.

"Does he speak?" Mam asked gently, casting a quick glance to me.

I shook my head. "Don't think so."

"Johnny?" another small voice called out. "Can I feed your dogs?"

"Yeah, do you have a lead so I can take Sookie for a walk?"

Seconds later, Ollie and Tadhg came barreling into the kitchen, bright-eyed and rosy-cheeked. The minute they locked eyes on my mother, they stiffened and bunched together.

"Lads, this is my ma," I explained. "Edel."

"Hello, boys," Mam said softly, smiling warmly at the brothers.

"Ma, these are Shannon's brothers; Ollie and Tadhg." I made the

499 • CHLOE WALSH

introductions from where I was still crouched next to Sean, who was squeezing my hand tightly in his. "It's okay, buddy," I whispered in his ear. "You're safe."

"Hi, Dellie," Ollie said shyly.

"God, Ollie, he said her name is Edel," Tadhg grumbled. "Not Dellie."

"That's okay," Mam chuckled, rising up. "My god, you're the spitting image of your brother," she added, smiling at Tadhg.

Tadhg watched her carefully. "Which brother?"

"Joey," Mam replied.

His eyes widened. "You know Joey?"

Mam nodded. "I do. He's a lovely boy."

Tadhg frowned. "Are you sure you know *Joey*?"

Mam chuckled again. "So, you like Sookie?"

The hardness in his eyes softened. "She's okay."

"Her voice is funny, too," Ollie announced. "Isn't it, Tadhg? Her voice is stranger than Johnny's."

"She's from *Dublin*," Tadhg groaned, looking embarrassed. "God, Ollie."

"And what about you, Ollie?" Mam turned her smile on the middle one. "Do you like Bonnie and Cupcake?"

"I love them," he told her, beaming. "They're so big. I want a dog. Like so, so much, but we're not allowed to have one because of when my dad got the last—"

"Ollie," Tadhg said in a warning tone. "Quiet."

Ollie snapped his mouth shut and blushed.

"What's this about you kidnapping the Lynch children?" my father chuckled as he strolled into the kitchen, looking amused. However, the moment his eyes landed on the three boys standing next to me, his smile vanished. "Oh, dear."

The moment he stepped into the room, the atmosphere changed and the boys seemed to go on high-alert. Ollie and Tadhg both took a step towards me, with Tadhg shifting Ollie behind him. Sean turned into my chest and wrapped his little arms around my neck, clinging to me.

Tears filled my mother's eyes and she covered her mouth with her hand. "Oh, lord."

"Don't cry, Ma," I mouthed as I carefully wrapped my arms around Sean's tiny body and lifted him up. "You're okay, buddy," I coaxed. Nodding he tucked his face in my neck and cupped my cheek with his drool-covered fingers.

*Men*, I realized. They were fucking terrified of grown men. Gibsie and I weren't as much of a threat to them because we were the same age as Joey, who all these children seemed to adore – Shannon included. Disgust filled my body at a rapid rate, making it hard to function. "Lads," I said, dragging myself back to the present, "this is my da – John." I looked to my mother for help, but she looked just as stumped as I was. "He's a . . . " I scrambled for the words I needed to put these kids at ease. Clearing my throat, I added, "He's a big eejit, lads, but he's completely harmless."

Their eyes widened in shock as if they couldn't believe what I had just said.

"That's right," Mam said, catching on quickly. Taking my father by the hand, she led him over to the island and shoved him down on a stool so he wasn't so intimidating standing at his full 6'2 height. "He's our fool, aren't you, John?" she added, ruffling his hair. "A big, old softie."

"Hi, John," Ollie said, eyeing my father warily, and offering him a small wave. "I'm Ollie."

"Hello, Ollie," Dad replied, smiling at the middle Lynch boy. "It's lovely to meet you."

"Did you hear that, Tadhg," Ollie said, jabbing Tadhg in the ribs. "He talks the same as us."

"Because *he's* from *Cork*," Tadhg muttered, shaking his head. "Obviously."

"Hello, Tadhg," Dad added. "How are you doing?"

"Fine," Tadhg replied warily. "Thanks."

Dad smiled. "So, what did Johnny do, lads?"

"He took us to McDonald's," Ollie blurted out. "Two times."

"Twice," Tadhg corrected with a heavy sigh. "Say *twice*, Ollie."

"And the playground," Ollie continued, unperturbed. "And we met that weird guy over there—" He paused to point at Gibsie. "Well, Tadhg says he's weird. I think so, too, but he's also kind of nice." Grinning, he added, "He gave me a fiver."

"Thanks, kid," Gibsie chuckled. "I think you're kind of nice, too."

"Oh, so you boys aren't hungry?" Mam asked as she opened the fridge. "Not even for some . . ." She let her words trail off as she pulled a huge chocolate cake from the fridge. "Dessert?"

"Whoa," Ollie gasped, moving straight for her, all fears of my father forgotten now that there was cake involved. "We're allowed to have some, Dellie?"

"Edel," Tadhg muttered, pinching the bridge of his nose. "Not Dellie."

"Only the three biggest pieces," Mam replied, making her eyes go all wide with fake excitement. "How does that sound?"

Ollie nodded eagerly. "It was Tadhg's birthday last month and he didn't get a cake. He loves chocolate, don't you, Tadhg?"

"It's okay," Tadhg mumbled, edging closer. "I guess."

"Well, come over here with me and we'll cut it up," Mam announced, tone cheerful, but eyes watering. "And I'll get some ice-cream to go with it."

"Oh my god!" Ollie exclaimed, trailing after my mother. "Your mam is the best, Johnny."

"And you," Mam said as she set the cake down on the counter and lifted Ollie onto a stool, "remind me of your sister." Stroking his hair, she smiled down at him. "And you are just as sweet."

Ollie beamed up at her. "I am?"

Mam nodded. "Yes, you are."

Tadhg snickered, joining Ollie at the island. "You look like Shannon."

"So?" Ollie huffed, keeping his gaze trained on the cake Mam was cutting. "I'm *sweet*."

"You want some cake, Sean?" I asked when his head popped up, eyes trailing his brothers. "I bet it's nice."

"He doesn't talk much," Tadhg explained, eyes widening when my mother placed a huge slice of cake in front of him. "He only says like seven words."

"It's true," Ollie agreed, picking up his slice of cake with his hand and taking a huge bite. "And he hasn't said anything since Daddy hurt Shannon—"

"Ollie," Tadhg groaned, shoulders slumping. "Stop talking."

"It's okay, boys," Mam coaxed, voice shaking a little as she set a plate of cake down in front of Dad. "We don't have to talk about that today."

"Hey," Gibsie interjected then, winking at Tadhg. "Don't you be eating all that cake, fatty. I want some."

Tadhg snorted. "You look like you've had enough cake for a month."

"I'll have you know that it takes hours in the gym to look as good as I do," Gibsie shot back, joining them at the opposite side of the counter, taking the stool next to my father.

"Yeah," Tadhg snickered between bites of his cake – again, using his hands and not the fork beside him, "hours with your head in the fridge."

Gibsie threw his head back and laughed. "You're a cheeky little fucker."

"Gerard," Mam said, giving Gibsie a grateful smile, as she set a plate of cake in front of him. "No bad language."

"Sorry, Mammy K," Gibsie replied with a sheepish grin before stabbing into his cake with relish. "Mmm."

"I'll get the ice-cream," Mam announced then, before hurrying into the utility room, smothering a sob as she went.

"Will we get some?" I asked Sean, who was now physically gravitating towards the food. "Yeah?"

Sean nodded and wiggled in my arms. I took it as a signal to put him down and the minute I did, he scooted towards his brothers, trying and failing to climb up. Both of his brothers ignored him, entirely too focused on their own cake as they scoffed it down. Giving up on getting their attention, he moved around the island, stopping at my father's legs. I watched as he seemed to hesitate before reaching up and tugging on the leg of his pants.

Wordlessly, my father reached down and lifted him onto his lap, not making a big deal of it, as he set his plate of cake in front of Sean. Diving for the cake, Sean started to shove it into his mouth, sitting contently on my father's lap as he ate.

Ollie and Tadhg turned to watch their little brother, both eyeing my father with wary curiosity.

When Mam walked into the kitchen with the tub of ice-cream, she quickly backpedaled out again. Shaking my head, I followed her into the utility to find her sobbing against the freezer. "God love them," she whispered, tears dripping down her cheeks. "Oh, Johnny, those poor babies."

"I know, Ma," I replied, keeping my voice low. "But don't be crying. You'll freak them out."

"It's just terrible," she choked out. "How anyone could do *that* to those babies—"

"Ma, stop." Closing the space between us, I placed my hands on her shoulders and sighed. "Feed them," I encouraged. "Fill them up with ice-cream and all that shite you gave us when we were small. They don't need any more tears."

"You're right." Sniffling, she wiped her cheeks with the back of her hand and forced a smile. "No more tears."

"Edel," Dad said, popping his head around the door with Sean balancing on his hip. "We need to talk."

"I know, John."

"No." He shook his head and gave my mother a meaningful look as Sean pulled on his tie. "We need to talk now, sweetheart."

"This is bullshit," I snarled, pacing my father's study like a deranged lunatic. "I'm not bringing them back there, Da."

"We don't have a choice, Johnny," Dad replied wearily. "We have to return them – preferably before their mother realizes that they're gone."

"That family is in dire need of an intervention," Mam choked out. "I don't know what's wrong with the world, but I can't understand how they're just left in that home with her – or how that man is walking around scot-free."

"Calm down, sweetheart," Dad coaxed, rubbing her arm.

"It's not fair, John," she strangled out. "I can't *bear* it."

"No, it's not fair," Dad agreed. "But you can't be getting yourself worked up over it."

"Look at them, John!" Stalking over to the window, she pointed outside to where Gibsie was rolling around on the lawn with the three boys. "*Look* at them."

"I see them, Edel," Dad replied calmly. "I see everything you're seeing, sweetheart."

"If you see them then how can you possibly expect me to send them *back*?" Mam hissed. "Something has to be done. *Better* has to be done for those children! They're just kids. They don't understand, and they don't deserve this. And Shannon?" Mam's expression caved. "He *saw*, John." She pointed a shaky finger at me. "Our son recognized it from the very beginning. He might not have understood what he was seeing, but he heard the cry for help. He heard *her*. And he unraveled a darkness no child should be exposed to."

"I *know*," Dad replied, giving her a meaningful look. "But right now, we don't have a legal leg to stand on. Do you want your son to be arrested, sweetheart? Because that's exactly what will happen if we don't do this the *right* way."

"Then *when*?" Mam choked out. "*When*, John?"

"When what, Ma?" I asked, watching her carefully.

Mam opened her mouth to respond, but my father got there first.

"Edel." He shook his head in warning. "This isn't a conversation I want us to have in front of our son."

"Do what the right way?" I asked, suspicious. "What's going on here?"

"Don't ask questions," my father said. "I promise, you don't need to know."

"Of course I need to know, Da—"

"No, Johnny, you don't!" he snapped. "You need to trust me and *not* ask questions."

"I can't do it," Mam choked out, dropping her head in her hands. "I can't send them back there."

"Johnny, I need you to text their brother," Dad instructed. "Ask Joey to come over here."

"What?" My brows furrowed. "Now?"

Dad nodded. "Now."

"Why Joey?"

"Because he's over eighteen and the least likely to have you arrested," Dad shot back.

"Fuck," I muttered.

"Yes," Dad offered. "Fuck indeed, son."

"But Da, I don't think they should go back there—"

"Do what I say," Dad ordered. "I've never guided you wrong before, and I don't have plans on starting, so just trust me and text their brother."

Frustrated, I dragged my phone out of my pocket and sighed dejectedly. "What do you want me to say?"

"Tell him the truth," Dad commanded. "Tell him exactly what you told us and ask him to come pick them up."

"No." Mam shook her head. "Please, John—"

"Trust me," Dad bit out. "This is the only way, Edel."

Sniffling, Mam nodded. "Text Joey, love."

Panicked, I pulled my phone out and sent a text to the one person I hoped wouldn't have me arrested.

J: YEAH, SO, STRANGE THING HAPPENED TODAY . . .

JOEY THE HURLER: WHY ARE YOU TEXTING ME?

J: BECAUSE I TOOK YOUR BROTHERS AND THEY'RE AT MY HOUSE.

JOEY THE HURLER: WHY?

J: I DON'T KNOW.

Joey the hurler: Do you plan on giving them back?

J: I guess.

Joey the hurler: You're really fucked up, Kavanagh.

J: I know.

Joey the hurler: I'm on my way.

"Done," I muttered, sliding my phone back into my pocket. "He's on the way."

"Thank you," Dad said with a sigh.

"Don't thank me, Da," I muttered. "Not for doing the wrong thing."

Mam glanced between me and my father before sighing heavily. "You did the right thing, Johnny." Shoulders sagging, she walked over to where I was standing and wrapped her arms around my waist. "Everything will be okay." Pressing a kiss to my shoulder, she added, "I'll put the kettle on," before walking out of the kitchen.

"What's going on, Da?" I demanded, feeling out of the loop. "What aren't you telling me?"

"I don't tell you a lot of things," my father replied evenly. "Parent/child privilege."

"You know what I mean, Da," I snapped. "If you know something to do with Shannon and you're not telling me, I'm going to lose it."

"Nothing about Shannon," Dad told me.

"Then what's going on with you and Mam? What did all of that mean?"

My father sighed. "Johnny, you really don't need to know."

"I *want* to know," I countered hotly.

"But you don't *need* to know," he shot back with an air of finality in his tone. "Because what your mother and I talk about is private."

"Are you fighting?" I asked, at a complete fucking loss. "Over the Lynchs?"

"If we are, then that is also private," Dad shot back, not missing a beat. "Respect that."

Jaw-ticking, I swallowed down a snarky response and nodded stiffly.

"Good man," he said, pulling his car keys out of his pocket. "Now, I need to go and make a few calls and see if I can keep you out of prison – at least until you turn eighteen." He turned and walked for the door only to halt and spin back around. "I forgot to ask you how training went?"

"Fine," I grumbled.

"And Coach Dennehy?" he pushed. "Any word yet?"

*No* ... "Uh, can we talk about it later?" I said instead. "My head's wrecked."

"Of course." Giving me a wink, he said, "Colorful family you've gotten yourself attached to, son."

"Like you can talk," I shot back accusingly, thinking about my mother's side of the fence.

"Don't remind me," Dad muttered. "See you later."

"Yeah." I frowned after him, wondering what the hell he was up to. "I'll see ya."

# Pound Shop Razors

## SHANNON

"We are living our best lives, girls," Claire announced as she dumped the contents of her days' worth of shopping onto her bed and grinned. "Now, it's makeover time."

"No," Lizzie grumbled, flopping down on the bed, looking thoroughly exhausted. "Forget it. I'm not doing anything else for rest of the evening."

"Oh yes you are," Claire chirped. "We're having makeovers and that includes you, grumpy pants."

"Claire," Lizzie snapped. "You dragged us all over the city shopping for seven hours. I am *exhausted*."

"I'm kind of with Lizzie on this." Sinking down on the floor, I pulled off my runners and rubbed my feet. "It's already seven in the evening, and I'm really tired." *And I want to go see Johnny . . .*

"Exactly! I didn't traipse all over Cork City, buying all of this crap just for it to go to waste," Claire growled, tapping her foot. "You're *both* getting makeovers and you're *both* going to love them."

Exhaling a heavy sigh in defeat, I climbed to my feet and nodded. "Fine, I'll do the makeover."

"Yay," Claire squealed, clapping her hands. "Thank you, *Shannon*."

"Turncoat," Lizzie muttered under her breath.

"For that, you're going first," Claire countered, grinning devilishly at Lizzie. "And I'm starting with that unibrow."

"She doesn't have a unibrow," I chuckled, sifting through the pile of goodies on the bed.

"No, I don't have a unibrow, Shan, but *she'll* have a fist to the face if she comes anywhere near me with tweezers," Lizzie shot back.

"Why do we need razors?" I asked, picking up the packet of razors and a can of shaving foam.

"Because we're going gardening, girls," Claire replied breezily. "Down under."

"You come anywhere near my vagina with a razor and I'll stab you," Lizzie warned. "I'm not even joking."

"Fine," Claire countered. "You're such a beast you'd need the whole packet to tame you."

Lizzie rolled her eyes and gave Claire the finger.

"Yeah." I eyed the packet of razors warily. "I'm not sure this is a such good idea."

"It's a terrible idea," Lizzie interjected. "You shouldn't be shaving down there anyway. That's what waxing is for."

"Well, I can't afford waxing," Claire huffed. "I'm not a millionaire, Lizzie."

"So, you're going to mangle yourself with pound shop razors?"

"They cost two euro," Claire countered.

"From the pound shop," Lizzie added sarcastically.

"Why are you trying to ruin this for me?" Claire demanded, glaring at Lizzie. "This is supposed to be a fun, bonding moment."

"Have you ever shaved down there before, Claire?" Lizzie asked.

Claire frowned. "No."

"Well, if you had, you'd know that I'm not trying to ruin anything for you, I'm trying to save you both from friction burn," Lizzie drawled. "But whatever, go right ahead and scalp yourself. Just don't come running to me when you're walking around like a constipated cowboy."

"Well, I think it's a great idea," Claire encouraged.

"Of course, you do," Lizzie mocked. "God, you're so clueless."

"Ignore her, Shan," Claire said, turning her back to Lizzie and giving me a bright smile. "We can do it together."

"I'm not doing that with you," I laughed. "That's strange, Claire."

"I didn't mean doing it sitting side by side in the bathtub," she snickered. "We'll take turns."

"Well, if you two are planning on going all Edward Scissorhands on your fannies for the evening, I'm off home to catch up on my soaps,"

Lizzie announced as she climbed off the bed and strolled towards the door. "Have the first-aid kit on hand, Shan; you're going to need it," she added before sauntering out of the room.

My eyes widened. "First-aid kit?"

Claire rolled her eyes. "She's lying."

"Oh god, I don't know about this," I mumbled, feeling uncertain.

"Come on," Claire coaxed. "Live dangerously."

"Are you sure?"

"Why not?" Grinning devilishly, she shrugged her shoulders. "I'll even go first."

Twenty minutes later, Claire hobbled back into her bedroom, cheeks flushed, legs spread apart. "Bathroom's free, Shan," she bit out as she thrust the can of shaving foam into my hands.

"Oh my god!" I gasped. "Are you okay?"

"All good," she replied with a grimace as she gingerly lowered herself onto the mattress. "It's your turn."

"Claire, I really don't know about this." I eyed her suspiciously and the way she was fanning herself. "You look like you're in pain."

"Shannon, I did this for you!" She narrowed her eyes. "It's *your* turn."

My mouth fell open. "No, you didn't."

"Yes, I did," she accused. "I'm trying to help you. This was my not-so-subtle way of doing it."

"How?" I gaped at her. "How in the name of god is this going to *help* me?"

"With *Johnny*," she explained. "You're going to his house tonight, aren't you?"

"Yeah."

"Exactly!" she replied. "What do I need to shave my pooch for? I don't have a boyfriend."

"Your pooch?" I frowned. "You call it a *pooch*?"

"Pooch, puss – meh, it's all the same," she replied, waving a dismissive hand around. "The point is, I don't need to shave. Nobody is sticking their face in my knickers."

"You *promised* you wouldn't tell anyone," I strangled out, blushing.

"And I didn't," she shot back. "We're *alone*."

I huffed out a breath. "Well, I think you're lying to me."

Claire's eyes widened. "Excuse me?"

"You heard me," I told her. "I think Gibsie is very familiar with *your* knickers."

"Ugh!" She clutched her chest with her hand and gaped at me in horror. "You lie."

"*You* lie," I countered. "And you're using my vagina as a coverup for your night-time antics with the boy across the street."

"I am *not*."

"I don't believe you."

"Come on, Shan," she pleaded then. "You're my best friend. You can't leave me on my own in this."

*Ugh.* "Fine." Grabbing the disposable razors, I skulked into her bathroom. "But if this goes wrong, I'm holding you responsible."

"Good luck," she called after me.

*Learn to say no, Shannon.*

*In future, just say no!*

"I need to tell you something," was the first thing Johnny said when he opened his front door and pulled me into his house. His hair was standing up like he had dragged his fingers through it a million times, making him look gorgeously disheveled. Catching ahold of my hand, he sprinted down the hallway, heading straight for the staircase. "It's so bad, Shan," he strangled out, dragging me up the staircase. "So fucking bad, baby."

"Okay, but I really need to show you something first," I strangled out, wincing in discomfort as he moved at top speed, not stopping until we were inside his bedroom with the door closed behind us. "It's so bad, Johnny," I whimpered, removing my jacket. "Like the worst kind of bad ever."

"Oh, mine's worse, Shan," he muttered, pacing the floor. "Trust me. It's like insanely bad."

"Can you just look at mine first?" I begged, feeling close to a panic attack.

"I stole your brothers, baby!" he blurted out and then froze. "Sorry," he squeezed out. "I love you." Grimacing like he was in physical pain, he added, "Please don't break up with me."

"Huh?" It took me a moment to register what he had said before my mouth fell open. "*What?*"

"I'm so sorry," he groaned, diving onto his bed. "I don't know what came over me," he added, face-planting the mattress. "I don't normally do this shite – that's what Gibsie's for."

"My brothers?" I frowned. "My *baby* brothers?"

Johnny popped his head up and nodded slowly.

"All of them?"

"All of them," he confirmed grimly. "But I gave them back again."

I shook my head, feeling at a loss. "Does my mam know?"

"No – thank Jesus," he muttered. "Joey came and got them before she noticed they were gone."

"Was he mad?"

"No." Johnny frowned. "More amused than mad."

"Wait, wait—" I held a hand up, feeling all confused. "They were supposed to be with Nanny today."

"That's *it*," Johnny agreed, springing off the bed. "That's what they said, but she was in bed, Shan, and they were all on their own." Pacing resumed, he continued to explain, hands flying around as he moved. "I was on the phone with you, and then I saw the baby in the window and he was just looking right at me, and I couldn't fucking walk away. He's so small, and he's got these big puppy eyes. So I *took* him, and then I took the other ones for good measure – the big one has a serious attitude problem, by the way. Anyway, I brought them to McDonald's and the playground – and I'm pretty sure I overfed them – but then Gibsie said it looked like I was a pedophile, and I got all freaked out about that, so I brought them home and gave them to my ma." He blew out a ragged breath, expression guilty. "Are you mad at me?"

"That's a lot of information to process, Johnny," I mumbled, pressing my fingers to my temples.

"I know," he groaned, running his hands through his hair. "Ugh."

"Are you in trouble?"

He paused to frown at me. "Huh?"

"Are you in trouble?" I repeated, panicking. "You're sure she doesn't know you took them?"

"No, I'm not in trouble," he replied, watching me warily. "Joey said they won't say a word about it."

"Oh, thank god," I strangled out, clutching my chest.

"You're not mad at me?" he asked in a cautious tone, edging closer.

"No, I'm not mad." I knew I should take a moment to consider everything he had just told me, or demand to know why my brothers hadn't gone with Nanny, or why my mother was in bed when she was supposed to be watching them, but I honestly couldn't concentrate on anything other than the fire in my pants. "But I really need your help."

Concern flickered in his eyes. "Shite, Shan, what's up?"

"I'm going to have to show you," I choked out, flustered, as I kicked off my runners and unbuttoned my jeans.

"Whoa, whoa, whoa – *stop*," Johnny warned, holding a hand out. "What are you doing?"

I didn't stop.

Dragging in a humiliated breath, I shoved my jeans down and cried out, "Save me."

"What the *fuck* did you do to yourself?" Johnny strangled out, eyes wide.

"I shaved," I choked out.

He gaped at me. "Everything?"

"*Everything*," I sobbed, flailing my hands aimlessly. "There was blood *everywhere*!"

"There *was*?" Johnny croaked out, looking horrified. "Jesus Christ."

"Am I having some sort of sensitive skin reaction?" I asked, kicking out of my jeans, in full panic mode. "There's a lot of nicks, Johnny." I glanced down and whimpered. "*Help me*."

"Baby." He held his hands up. "I have a dick. I am clueless right now."

"But it's bad, right?" I asked, feeling anxious. "It's really bad? It shouldn't look like that, should it? It's burning – like, I'm on *fire*."

"I don't know," he shot back, voice rising several octaves. "How am I supposed to know?"

"Because you've seen more of them than I have," I cried. "So just tell me straight, Johnny. Is it bad?"

"Ah, no. Not really. I mean it's . . . " Johnny frowned and rubbed his jaw with his hand. "It's not *that* bad?"

"Don't lie to me," I warned him.

"Let me get a better look at what we're dealing with here—" I watched in horror as Johnny crouched down to *get a better look* before straightening back to his full height and shaking his head. "Yeah, Shan, it's pretty bad."

"I told you it was!" I wailed, slipping my underwear back into place and groaning loudly when the friction made it worse. "I'm never listening to Claire Biggs again," I added. "Stupid pound shop razors."

"Pound shop razors?" Johnny half-laughed/half-groaned. "You do know there are like salons and beauticians you can go to for shite like that?"

"Yeah, well, I'm shy," I huffed, flopping down on his bed. "How can I just show someone *that*?"

He shot me a disbelieving look.

"You don't count," I snapped, flustered.

"My poor pussy," Johnny said with a sigh as he sank down on the bed beside me. "You're a butcher."

Exhaling a strangled sob, I fell onto my back. "It hurts."

Mirroring my actions, Johnny flopped down on his back beside me. "I know, baby." He placed a hand on my thigh and gave me a reassuring squeeze. "But it will grow back."

"How long do you think that takes?"

He twisted to face me. "Do you want me to shave my balls?"

"What?" I gaped at him. "No!"

"Then stop asking me about something I have no clue about," he shot back.

"I'm sorry." I blushed beetroot red. "I just ... you always know things." Whimpering in sheer distress, I twisted onto my stomach and buried my head in the plush duvet that smelled like that washing detergent his mother always used and *Johnny*. "I'm so embarrassed—" I paused to gasp for air and then wailed, "It burns ... and now it's *ugly*."

"No, it's not." I felt his hand smooth over the back of my knickers. "And I'm hard as rock for you right now."

"I don't know how you could be," I replied with an anguished wail. "It's hideous." Groaning at the realization of what I'd done to my poor body, not to mention the prickling sensation between my legs as my underwear played havoc with my tender flesh, I whispered, "I don't know how I'm going to put my jeans back on." Grimacing, I added, "Or look you in the eye again."

"No pants sounds good to me," he laughed, hands still roaming over my ass. "Come on, Shan, just look at me."

I shook my head. "I can't."

"Yes, you can," he coaxed, trailing his fingers up my sides. "If you don't turn around and look at me, I'm going to tickle you."

Twisting onto my side, I peeked up at him. "Hi."

"So—" Leaning down, he pressed his lips against mine. "Care to explain why you shaved?"

I squirmed in shame. "I don't know."

He waggled his brows. "Big plans?"

"Ugh!" I moved to bury my face back in the duvet, but Johnny captured my lips with his before I could.

"I got an awful roasting from the sun when I was on tour last summer," he said, brushing his nose against mine. "I still have some Aloe Vera in my bathroom." He kissed me again. "It'll help cool it down."

Mortified, I exhaled a shaky breath and nodded. "Thanks."

"You're welcome." Pressing a kiss to the tip of my nose, Johnny climbed off the bed and strolled into his bathroom, returning a moment later with a small bottle of ointment. Unscrewing the cap, he climbed onto the bed and handed it to me before moving for my knickers.

"What are you doing?" I choked out, lifting my hips when he pulled my underwear down my legs. "Johnny?"

"I'm saving you," he replied with a smirk. "Remember the whole *'save me, Johnny, please, save me'* comments?"

"Yeah, but . . . " Taking the bottle from my hands, he poured a dollop of Aloe Vera on his fingers and dropped his hand. "Oh my god," I whimpered in relief when the cool gel numbed out the fire. "That's amazing."

Moving further down the bed, Johnny leaned over my hip and gently blew against my bare skin. My breath hitched in my throat and I had to lock my muscles into place to stop my hips from bucking upwards. Looking up at me through hooded lashes, he continued to blow cold air on my tender flesh. "Enough?" he asked in a gruff tone before pressing a small kiss to my flesh. "Or more?"

Breathing hard, I sat straight up and fisted his t-shirt. "Take it off."

His blue eyes were blazing with heat as he reached over his shoulder and pulled his shirt off.

Exhaling shakily, I raised my arms over my head, never taking my eyes off his. "Now mine."

Without a word, Johnny leaned forward and whipped my shirt over my head with effortless ease before reaching around me to unhook my bra. It was almost frightening how quickly he could unsnap a bra clasp, but as he slid the straps down my shoulders and tossed my bra on his bedroom floor, I couldn't find it in me to care.

Falling onto my back, I dragged him down with me, fingers digging into the hard muscles of his back. Johnny obliged, pressing his weight down on me as I let my legs fall open to welcome him. "You look good in my bed." Clamping his hands on my thighs, he dragged my body closer, groaning loudly when we connected. "On your back," he added, hovering above me, "with me between your legs," before sealing his lips to mine.

Moaning, I closed my eyes and wrapped my arms around his neck, rubbing my body against his. Everything about this boy felt good, and real, and *right*. His lips were everywhere; on my neck, my breasts, my belly . . . I could feel him all over my skin and still it wasn't enough. Bucking restlessly, I cried out when I felt his finger slide inside me, making the ache growing inside of me almost unbearable. Clutching his shoulders, I rocked into his touch, wanting everything he would give me.

"This is a bad idea," Johnny said in a raspy voice before his mouth crashed down on mine, his tongue dueling with mine almost violently. "I should stop," he growled, increasing the speed of his fingers as he thrust inside of me. "Worst fucking idea ever."

"I love your bad ideas," I whispered, reaching for the waistband of his sweatpants. "Don't stop." When he didn't move to stop me like he usually did, I pushed them down his hips. "I want you."

He groaned and plunged his tongue into my mouth, holding himself up on his elbow so I could push them over his erection. "I fucking love you," he whispered, kicking his sweats all the way off. My breath hitched in my throat when I moved my hand over the front of his boxers and felt how thick and long he was. "You're big," I whispered, breathing hard and fast. "Like really, really big."

"Fuck, don't say that," he growled, attacking my neck with hungry kisses. "You'll make me explode."

"But you are," I panted, rocking into his touch as the familiar jolts of pleasure rippled through me. "And I'm going to . . ." Closing my eyes, I rocked against his hand as a wave of bliss consumed my whole body, setting my skin on fire, and causing my muscles to contract and spasm. "Johnny . . ."

"Shh." Pulling my bottom lip between his teeth, he tugged gently before thrusting his tongue inside my mouth, fingers moving at a perfect rhythm as my body slowly grew lax beneath him.

"Don't worry," he whispered, lips moving to suckle on my neck. "I'll keep my dick in my jocks."

"I don't want you to keep it in your jocks."

He stiffened. "What?"

"I want you."

He stilled for a moment then raised himself up on his elbows to look at me. "You're serious?"

"Yeah."

His eyes searched mine, uncertainty flashing across his features, as he slid his fingers out of me and reached for the waistband of his black Calvin Kleins. "Are you sure?"

"I'm sure." I nodded, feeling my heart racing wildly in my chest. "I want all of you."

# Don't Open the Door!

## JOHNNY

What was I doing?

What *the hell* was I doing?

I couldn't think straight. All I could see was Shannon, sprawled out naked on my bed, and every doubt, fear, and concern I knew I *should* be feeling flew clean out the window.

"You're sure?" I asked her again, needing the reassurance. "You're really, really sure?"

Shivering beneath me, she nodded, wide-eyed and flushed. "I'm ready, Johnny."

"But you're sore," I croaked out as my dick strained against my jocks, desperate to get to her. "I don't want to hurt you."

"You won't hurt me," she whispered, reaching up to cup my jaw. "I want this."

*Fuck.*

*Fuck!*

Exhaling shakily, I climbed off her and stood up, knowing that it was way too soon, but resigned to doing it anyway. "You can say no," I told her as I slid my fingers into the waistband of my jocks and pulled them down. "You can *always* say no," I added, stepping out of them and moving back to her. "And I'll hear you, okay?"

Nodding, Shannon pulled herself up on her elbows, attention riveted to my dick that was standing at full mast.

"Yeah ... so, this is my dick," I stated and then mentally kicked the shite out of myself for saying something so fucking stupid. Like I needed to label a cock and balls.

*Jesus Christ.*

"Yep," Shannon blew out a shaky breath and sat all the way up. "That's your dick, alright." I held my breath as she reached out and stroked a finger over the head and of course, my dick jerked and twitched from the contact. "It moved." Her gaze flicked up to meet mine. "By itself."

"You're encouraging it," I choked out, feeling weak at the knees, as I took a step closer. "Touch it and it's going to get all kinds of fucking notions."

She trailed her fingertips over my scars then and exhaled another loud breath. "You're so beautiful, Johnny." Leaning forward, she pressed a kiss to the jagged line on my pelvis before placing another one on the scar much lower. "I love you so much."

*Fuck.* "I love you, too," I bit out through clenched teeth, hands balled into fists at my sides. There were no words to explain the sensations that flooded my body when she put her lips on me. Deciding to sit down before I collapsed, I lowered myself down on the bed and pulled Shannon down so that we were on our sides, facing each other. "We don't have to do anything, okay?" I said, cupping her cheek. "I'm happy just being here with you."

"Johnny?" she whispered, mirroring my movements by cupping my cheek.

My breath caught in my throat. "Yeah, Shan?"

"Shh."

And then she kissed me.

And I *lost* it.

Whatever sliver of self-control I'd been clinging to snapped the instant she decided it would be a good idea to put her lips on mine. Pushing me onto my back, Shannon climbed on top me, never once breaking our kiss, as she slid her hands into my hair, doing that thing with her fingers that drove me fucking mental.

I couldn't take it.

She was too much for me.

Rolling her onto her back, I settled between her legs, kissing her deeply as I stretched a hand out and reached for my bedside locker. Slapping around aimlessly, I accidentally dropped my hand down on the remote to my stereo, causing Athlete's "Wires" to blast loudly from the speakers. "Shite," I growled, reaching for the remote. "I'll turn it off—"

"No, it's okay," Shannon breathed against my lips. "Leave it on."

Groaning into her mouth, I yanked the drawer open and grabbed the box of condoms, all the while throwing a silent prayer to the heavens, thanking Jesus for my fucking fantastic best friend and his forward thinking.

*Good man, Gibs . . .*

Fumbling around one-handed, I managed to tear open the box and pull a condom free. Tossing the box on my bedroom floor, I settled between her legs, hands shaking like an ivy-leaf, matching the rest of me. "You sure, Shan?" I asked, tearing my lips from hers as I ripped open the wrapper and rolled the condom on. "You really want this?"

"I really want you," she whispered, nodding up at me, and I swear my heart seized in my chest. I couldn't take the sight of her laid out on my pillows. She was too much for me.

"I love you so much," I strangled out, voice thick with emotion as I settled between her legs and dropped onto one elbow. "I'll be careful," I added, kissing her deeply as I slowly nudged myself against her. "I promise."

"I trust you," she breathed, hands moving to my hips. "I want this with you."

"It might hurt," I admitted, pressing my forehead to hers, as my heart pounded so hard against my ribcage that I could hear it. "I don't want to hurt you."

"I'm not afraid," she whispered, pulling on my waist and tilting her hips upwards.

I could feel her; so warm and hot and fucking perfect, and Jesus was I scared. I'd never been more frightened of breaking anything in my life as I was in this moment with this girl. She was the virgin, but I was the one shaking enough for the both of us. I felt too much for her. I loved her more than was safe for me.

"I want this," she whispered, curling her arms around my neck and pulling my lips to hers. "I promise," she added before pressing her lips to mine. Her tongue invaded my mouth, stroking mine with that sweet, tentative touch I craved so much.

A deep shudder rolled through me and I clenched my eyes shut before pushing inside her in one steady thrust. Shannon whimpered and I froze, heart racing violently in my chest. "Are you okay?"

Nodding, she clung to my neck and slammed her lips to mine once more. "Keep kissing me," she begged.

Holding my hips still, I continued to kiss her, desperate to soothe the ache I knew she was feeling as her body jerked and stiffened beneath mine. "I love you," I whispered between kisses, over and over again, as emotions I'd never felt in my life all battered through me – all for, because, and directed towards this girl. "I love you so much, Shannon *like the river.*"

I was holding onto my self-control by the skin of my teeth. The prospect of moving inside her was almost too much for me take. She was so tight, so fucking warm. Every time she clenched, clamping down on my dick like a vice grip, my eyes rolled back in my head. The small, needy, little whimpers and moans coming from her mouth as she adjusted to the feel of me inside her were *killing* me.

*Jesus . . .*

"Are you okay?" I whispered, as I battled the overwhelming urge to bury myself to the hilt inside her. Holding my weight up on one elbow, I cupped her cheek with my free hand and stroked her nose with mine, watching her face with lustful eyes. "Shan?" Pressing my forehead to hers, I released a shuddering breath, "Can I move yet?"

"Not . . . yet," she breathed, digging her nails into my shoulder blades as she clung to my body.

"It's okay," I soothed, kissing her lips and then moving to her neck. "You're so beautiful."

"Johnny . . ." her words broke off and she arched her hips upwards, causing me to slide deeper inside her.

I couldn't stop the groan that tore from my throat when she squeezed me harder and my balls tightened.

"I want you," she whispered, slowly thrusting herself upwards. "I want you to move in me."

"You sure?" I croaked out, eyes glued to hers.

"Yeah, it's good now," Shannon breathed, cheeks flushed. "You feel good in me."

Ah fuck.

Exhaling a ragged breath, I leaned down and kissed her as I slowly pulled out, before sinking back inside her, chest heaving with the effort it was taking to not come. "Is that okay?"

Moaning into my mouth, Shannon nodded and rocked her hips against mine as we built up a slow, gentle rhythm. Trailing my hand down her body, I hitched her thigh around my waist, causing us both to moan when the move made everything feel deeper, tighter, more *connected*.

"You feel so good," she whispered, trembling beneath me. Releasing the death grip she had on my neck, she relaxed into the mattress and trailed her hands down my chest and over my sides. "You're so beautiful."

Jesus Christ, she was killing me. "You're the beautiful one," I growled, moving a little faster, as the familiar swell of pleasure began to build. "Fuck," I groaned, claiming her lips once more. "Shannon, I need . . . fuck, I need—"

*Bang, bang, bang . . .*

"Johnny, love, Dad's back with the Chinese. He got you chicken balls."

*No.*

*No.*

*Dear God no!*

"That bleeding music will deafen you."

*Did I lock the door?*

*Did I?*

*I couldn't fucking remember!*

"Johnny," Shannon hissed, eyes wide in horror, as she slapped at my chest. "Your door—"

"Don't open the door!" I roared, abruptly pulling out of Shannon and then panicking when she winced in pain. "Oh shite, Shan, baby, are you okay?"

"The door," Shannon strangled out. "Stop the door."

"Johnny, can you hear me, love?" Mam called out. "I'm coming in."

"No!" I roared over the music. "Just fucking wait a second please!"

"What are we going to do?" Shannon whimpered, flapping like a caged bird on my bed.

"I don't know . . ." Shaking my head, I glanced around, feeling helpless. What a disaster. "Fuck!"

"Johnny, are you coming down for your chicken balls?"

"Give me a bleeding minute, Ma," I called out, as I grabbed the sides of my duvet and wrapped my girlfriend up like a taco before rolling her under my bed. "Stay down, Shan," I told her. "I'll sort this." Stumbling over the remote, I slammed my hand down on the stereo, cutting the music, before moving for the door.

"Johnny!" Shannon whisper-hissed from under my bed.

"What?"

"You're naked."

*Shite.*

Rolling the bloodstained condom off my still fully erect dick, I flung it across the room and lunged for my dresser, pulling out a pair of jocks and quickly slipping them on. Adjusting my raging fucking hard-on, I inhaled a steadying breath and walked over to the door.

"You took an awful long time to answer your door," Mam stated, eyeing me suspiciously.

"Yeah, sorry about that." Flustered and breathing hard, I nodded and feigned a yawn, desperately trying to steady my breathing. "I was sleeping."

"*You* were sleeping?"

I nodded.

"At half past eight in the evening?" Mam arched a disbelieving brow. "With your music blaring?"

I shrugged. "I'm tired."

"I bet you are." She moved to step forward and I quickly intercepted her, blocking her path. "What are you doing?"

"Nothing," I lied, moving my body like a bleeding octopus when she tried to peer around me. "What are *you* doing?"

"Checking for dirty washing," Mam replied. "Let me in."

"I don't have any washing, Ma, and I don't want any Chinese." Smiling at her, I attempted to close my bedroom door, but she held a hand up, stopping me in my tracks.

"What's going on?"

"Nothing."

"Nothing?" she repeated, giving me a *'don't bullshit me'* look before stepping around me and marching right into my room.

I held my breath, while mentally debating if Shannon would break up with me if I hauled ass and ran while I still could because this woman was going to cut my dick off.

"Are you alone?"

"Of course." Biting on my fist, I reluctantly turned and followed her, praying to all that was holy for my mother to just *fuck off*. "I was trying to sleep, Ma."

My gaze flicked to Shannon who was staring up at me from under my bed, eyes bulging. Padding over to the bed, I stood in front of her and watched my mother. She was clearly looking for something. *My girlfriend.*

"So, where's Shannon this evening?" Mam asked, tone laced with suspicion.

"No idea," I replied quickly. *Too fucking quickly.*

"You have no idea?" Mam shot back, tone disbelieving, as she searched my room with her eyes.

"Actually, I think she might be at Claire's," I hurried to amend my blunder. "Yeah." Nodding vigorously, I sank down on my bed and added, "She definitely told me that she was spending the night at Claire's."

Mam arched a brow. "Is that so?"

"Yes, Ma." Trying to be inconspicuous, I dragged the bed sheet off the bed and let it fall over the edge, concealing my girlfriend. "Jesus, what's with the third degree?" A hand wrapped around my ankle then, nails digging into my skin, and I jerked from the contact. "Jesus!"

"Excuse me?" Mam asked, hands on her hips.

"Tired," I choked out, clutching at straws. "Jesus, I'm really tired."

"Hmm." Something caught her eye then, something really fucking bad because her eyes narrowed and her face turned purple. Without a word, Mam walked over to the side of my bed, and I watched in horror as she bent down and retrieved the condom box.

Fuck.

My.

Life.

"*Opened*," Mam growled, as she stalked back to where I was slumped and tossed the box on my lap. "Now, where is the girl to go with the *johnnies*, Johnny?"

I hung my head, knowing that I was thoroughly fucked. "Uh . . . "

"I'm here, Mrs. Kavanagh," Shannon croaked out, peeking out from between my legs. "Sorry?"

"Shannon." Mam blew out a ragged breath. "Come on out from under the bed please."

"I kind of can't, Mrs. Kavanagh," Shannon squeezed out.

"Why not?"

"Because I'm kind of naked?" she choked out, blushing.

"And Jesus wept," Mam wailed, covering her face with her hands. "Both of you put your clothes on and meet me in the kitchen in two minutes," she strangled out before moving to the door, only to hesitate. "And give me those," she snapped as she stalked back to where I was sitting and snatched the box of condoms out of my hands. Swatting the back of my head with the condom box, she hissed, "You little toe-rag!" before marching back out of the room, screaming, "John! Call the parish priest. That child of yours needs confession!"

# I Made You A Promise

## SHANNON

I planned on dying a slow death.

The cause of my untimely demise: mortification.

Never in my life had I been so embarrassed as I was when I stepped through that kitchen doorway and came face to face with both of Johnny's parents just minutes after losing my virginity in what had been the best and then worst moment of my life.

*"I need to talk to you about something."*

*"About what?"*

*"About sex, Shannon, love."*

*"Don't do this to her," Johnny begged from the stool next to mine. "Please, Ma, I'm begging you." He turned to look at me. "Cover your ears, baby . . . "*

Groaning loudly at the memory of Mrs. Kavanagh's voice when she'd sat me down at the island for the *talk,* I pulled my purple duvet over my head and mentally prepared to spend the rest of my life clung to this bed because I could never leave my house again.

Worse, Johnny's mother had insisted on driving me home *alone,* which meant even more one-on-one time to discuss the birds and the bees and how I was not to let her son *corrupt* me in any shape or form. According to Mrs. Kavanagh, all teenage boys were hormone-driven dogs – her son included – and I was not to let *Jonathan* lead me astray.

*Too late for that,* I thought to myself as I curled into the smallest ball I could and sighed. I felt really bad, because even though it had been my idea, Johnny was the one who had taken the brunt of his mother's wrath, all while his father had smirked into his newspaper, nodding and agreeing whenever prompted by his wife. In Mrs. Kavanagh's eyes, he was older and possessed the penis, therefore, he was the one who should have known better. I had no clue what to say or do when she started lecturing us both about how private-parts were private and not for sharing with each other. It was *so* humiliating, and hours later, my face was still on *fire*.

Unlocking my limbs enough to stretch my arm out and grab my phone off the nightstand, I pulled it back under the sanctuary of my duvet and checked the time, only to groan when I saw that it was gone two o' clock in the morning.

*Go to sleep, Shannon,* I mentally coaxed. *Just turn off your brain and stop overthinking.*

Tap, tap, tap . . .

Stiffening, I held perfectly still and listened carefully.

Tap, tap, tap.

Springing up in my bed, I looked around my dark bedroom, illuminated by the street lamp outside, and tried to source the root of the noise.

Tap, tap, tap.

My gaze locked on the window.

Tap, tap, tap.

Throwing off my covers, I scrambled out of bed and inhaled a steadying breath before pulling back the curtains.

My mouth fell open and my heart kickstarted in my chest when my eyes landed on the huge boy balancing on the veranda outside my window.

"Johnny!" I gasped, as I pushed my window open and stared at him in pure shock. "How did you get up here?"

"I climbed up on your wheelie bin," he strangled out as he lunged for the windowsill. "Let me in before I die."

Hurrying to step aside for him, I watched as he climbed through the window, landing on my bedroom floor with a loud thud. "What about your dick?" I croaked out, eyes glued to him.

"Fuck my dick," Johnny grumbled, standing up. "I couldn't leave things like that after my ma – which, by the way, I am so fucking sorry about. I don't even know where to start on fixing that mess." Shaking his head, he closed the space between us and pressed a kiss to my cheek. "Hi, Shannon. You smell fucking great," he said in a hushed tone before quickly delving back into his rant. "I don't know what the hell happened to me back in my room, Shan. I always lock my door—" he paused and quickly tested my door before nodding in approval. "I don't even know how I went from helping you with shaving burn to taking your virginity, but I'm so fucking sorry." He moved to pace my floor but quickly stilled when he realized there was barely enough room to swing a cat. "I wanted it to be good for you and then I – and she – and I just – fucking chicken balls!" Exhaling a huge sigh, he added, "I know I'm not supposed to be here, but I had to keep my promise."

I stared at him in confusion. "What promise?"

"I told you when we slept together, we would sleep together," he said gruffly. "And I know I made a balls of the first part." With a vulnerable look in his eyes, Johnny shrugged and gestured to my tiny bed. "But do you think you can fit me in for the second part?"

Oh God.

This boy.

My heart.

Stepping around him, I climbed onto my bed and pulled back the covers. "Yeah." Nodding, I exhaled a shaky breath and whispered, "Come here."

Stripping down to his boxers in record time, Johnny climbed into bed alongside me, wrapping his big body around mine so that we were chest to back. "I swear, I'm not looking for anything," he whispered, pressing a kiss to my shoulder as he spooned me. "I just need to hold you."

"You didn't make a balls of anything, Johnny," I whispered, nestling my back to his warm chest. "It was great."

He was quiet for a long moment before asking, "Are you sore, Shan?" Tightening his arm around me, he nestled his face in the crook of my neck and sighed. "Did I hurt you?"

"No, you didn't hurt me, and I'm not sore." Shivering, I clutched his forearm, wanting more than anything to just keep him with me for the rest of my life. "I just feel . . ."

"What?" he urged, nuzzling my ear. "What are you feeling?"

"Stretched?" I offered, biting down on my lip. "And a little achy, but not sore."

"We don't have to do it again," he hurried to say. "Not until you're ready."

"I was ready then, Johnny," I told him, unable to stop myself from yawning. "I'm still ready now."

"I've never done that before," he admitted quietly.

"Done what?"

"Taken anyone's virginity." He exhaled a heavy sigh and the vibration from his chest rippled through me. "I was so scared of hurting you, Shan."

"So, I'm your first *first*?" I asked sleepily.

"You're my everything."

*Whoa.*

"Night, Shan," he whispered.

I closed my eyes and grinned. "Night, Johnny."

# Chest Pains

## JOHNNY

"Be at The Academy training grounds Saturday morning at 7a.m. sharp," the head coach of the U20's said down the line on Monday morning. "I've cleared a session with your coaches, and secured a pitch for the morning, so we'll see how it goes."

"I will." Nodding like a deranged lunatic, I paced the floor of the gym, clutching my phone tighter than necessary, excitement and panic flooring me. "I'll be there."

"Bring your gear, Johnny," he added. "But don't get your hopes up. I don't care what your doctors have said, you won't be stepping foot on the pitch for me without my own team doctor's go-ahead. Dr. Malachy will be giving you a full examination, so bring any notes you have with you."

"Understood." I nodded again, heart hammering wildly in my chest. "I have everything from Dr. Quirke – Dr. O'Leary, too. I have all the reports from my physiotherapist and trainers."

"Good," he replied briskly. "Bring everything with you."

"I'm ready, Coach." *I've been ready for weeks.* "I'm good to go."

"I hope you are, kid," my coach replied. "I sincerely do."

"If I am—" Pausing, I grimaced, trying to find the right words to phrase my next question. "If Dr. Malachy gives me the go-ahead, do you think I'll—"

"Let's just get you through this next round of medicals, and we'll talk about the squad then," he cut me off by saying. "You have a lot of conditioning to catch up on. But I will say that Ó Donnell and Gilbert will be traveling down with me. They're interested in you, Johnny. They want to make their own assessments—" He paused for a long moment before adding, "I don't have to explain what an opportunity this is. It's not every day the senior management travel down for a U20 player. .

With Daly and Johnson both out on long-term injury, they're down two centers for the summer tour next month in South Africa. If they're coming to watch you, I need you to take it seriously. If you're not fit, then you need to tell me now, kid. Wasting their time isn't going to bode well in your favor – or mine."

*Shite.*

*Jesus Christ.*

*It's happening.*

*It's fucking happening, Johnny.*

*Keep the head!*

"I understand," I replied, batting Gibsie away as he bounced in front me, mouthing *'what's he saying'*. *"Back off,"* I mouthed at my best friend before turning my back on him and giving the man who held the key to my future my full attention. "And I am fit – one hundred percent. I know what this means, Coach, and I promise, I'm all in."

"Never doubted your commitment for a second, Johnny," Coach replied. "I'll see you on Saturday."

"Yeah, I'll see you then," I breathed. "Thank you again."

"Good luck, kid."

The call ended and I stood there for several moments, both reeling and reveling from the phone call I had been waiting my whole life to receive.

"Well?" Gibsie demanded. "Are you back?"

"I'm back," I confirmed, blowing out a shaky breath. Swinging around to face him, I couldn't wipe the smile from my face. "I'm fucking back, Gibs!"

"Damn fucking straight, you are." A huge smile spread across his face. "You fucking did it, Cap!" Enveloping me in a hug, Gibsie laughed. "Looks like I need to buy a ticket to France this summer because my best friend is going to the fucking U20's!"

"Nothing's confirmed yet," I replied, trying to keep a steady head and not lose the run of myself. "I've got a lot of work to do and only two weeks to do it."

"Pssh," Gibsie countered, waving me off. "You're going to France with the U20's next month and I'm going on the piss in celebration! *Vive la France.*"

"Ó Donnell is coming to see me on Saturday, Gibs," I whispered, feeling my heart race at a hundred miles an hour. "Gilbert, too. They're down a couple of centers for the senior campaign in South Africa."

Gibsie's eyes widened. "Holy shit, Johnny!"

I nodded, feeling a huge wave of emotion wash through me. "I *know.*"

"Does that mean—"

"Don't say it," I strangled out, holding out a hand. "Don't jinx me."

"But that's what it means, right?" Gibsie pushed, eyes alight with pride. "You'll be in France with the U20's for the first half of June and then onto South Africa for the second half—" his voice rose with excitement "—with the *senior fucking team,* Johnny!"

"I might not make it onto either team," I muttered, trying to keep my feet firmly on the ground. It wasn't working, though. My heart rate was spiking and panic was setting in. "They might pass me over."

"For who? Cormac Ryan?" Gibsie scoffed. "You're the fucking *best,* lad."

"I don't know," I hissed, feeling a little weak. "Jesus Christ, I think I'm having chest pains."

"Sit down." Catching ahold of my arm, he led me over to the bench press and pushed me down. "Just put your head down and *breathe.*"

"Jesus, I'm dying," I groaned, pressing my hand to my chest. "Gibs, I think I'm having a heart attack." Shaking my head, I tried to breathe, but my lungs wouldn't fill. "I'm suffocating!"

"You're not dying," he laughed. "This happened when you got accepted into The Academy, remember? You hid in our treehouse crying like a bitch, shouting that you were going into cardiac arrest and begging anyone that looked at you to call an ambulance. Happened when you got the call up for the U18's too. You took to the bed with stroke symptoms. And you didn't die then either, lad."

"This is worse, Gibs," I choked out, clutching my arm. "So much worse."

"Because this is bigger," Gibsie explained calmly. "So much *bigger*." Sitting down beside me, he placed a hand on my back and began to rub. "It's your adrenalin spiking, lad. Just remember that this is a *good* thing. You've worked your ass off for this, Johnny – since you were six years old. You did the surgery in March. You've done all the rehab and hospital bullshit. You've followed every order you've been given and built your body back up. This is your time!"

"What if it's not my time?"

"It is," he assured me.

"But what if—"

"It's your time," he repeated firmly. "This is it, lad. Feel it."

"I'm scared," I strangled out. "I've only been back on the pitch a few weeks, lad. What if I'm not—"

"You *are* ready," he cut me off by saying. "And you're better than good enough." He squeezed my shoulder. "I honestly can't think of another person who deserves this more than you, Kav." Sighing contently, he added, "So enjoy this feeling, lad, because this is the start of huge fucking things for you."

"Yeah." I forced myself to *calm* down and breathe. "Fuck, I need to call Shannon."

"Ah, maybe this is a conversation you should have face to face," Gibsie offered. "Telling your girlfriend that you're more likely than not leaving for the summer isn't really text message news, lad."

"Fuck," I groaned, dropping my head in my hands. "Shite." Shannon's face sparked to life inside of my head, bringing on another set of chest pains. "Oh, Jesus," I choked out, leaning against him for support. "What am I going to do about Shannon?"

"What do you mean?"

"It's a month, Gibs," I bit out, knees bopping. "I'll be gone for a month – longer if I make the seniors."

"I know that," he replied. "You know that, and *she* knows that. So you don't have to do anything except *breathe*."

"I can't leave her for a month—"

"Johnny, get a fucking handle on yourself," Gibsie ordered. "This is the Irish squad. Ireland. As in, our fucking country. It's one month and the opportunity of a lifetime. Don't make me bitch slap you back to common sense."

"You're right," I muttered, breathing deep and slow.

Of course he was right.

*But that didn't make me feel any better.*

Releasing a pained growl, I ran a hand through my hair. "Can we just play this down?" I looked at him. "Can you not say anything about this to anyone?" *Not to her.* "At least until I know for sure?"

"She's going to be happy for you, Johnny," he replied. "Shannon loves you, lad. She's been in your corner since your surgery, willing you to get this shot."

"I know," I muttered. "But I just . . . " *I honestly don't think I can leave her.* I shook the crazy thought from my head. "Just keep it to yourself until I'm one hundred percent sure about what's happening."

"Fair enough, lad." Gibsie sighed. "My lips are sealed."

"Thanks." Shoulders sagging, I rested my elbows on my knees and tapped out a quick text to Shannon, letting her know that I would be leaving the gym soon to pick her up for school.

"But this is good news," Gibsie added before heading off towards the changing rooms. "And for what it's worth; I'm proud of you."

"Thanks." I exhaled a heavy sigh and trailed after him. "I think."

"You know," he confirmed, whipping off his clothes the minute we stepped inside the changing room. It was empty because we were the only two eejits demented enough to be here since 5am on a Monday morning. "This is a good thing, lad. They're going to select you. Shit, I'm fairly sure you would have made the squad back in March when your guts were spilling down your legs."

"I don't know, Gibs." Shaking my head, I walked over to my locker and stripped down. "I feel like it's all coming around too fast."

"Because you're afraid to leave her," he mused. "And you want more time."

I shrugged helplessly. "How *can* I leave her?"

"Because you have to," he reminded me. "Because you're seventeen and this is your future and you're not going to throw it all away." Grabbing a towel out of his gear bag, he headed for the showers. "It's one month, Johnny. Four weeks, lad. That's nothing in the grand scheme of things."

"I know, but it's just ..." I shook my head again and tapped out another text to Shannon before tossing my phone on the bench and grabbing my towel and shampoo. "It's a bleeding mess."

"This is what I've been saying all along," Gibsie called out from behind one of the shower stalls. "Don't get mixed up in anything serious when you're still in school. It's a recipe for disaster, lad. You all think I'm crazy, but I'm telling ya, I'm the smart one."

"Well, I'm thoroughly mixed up in something serious," I grumbled, stalking into the stall next to his. Slamming my hand on the chrome nozzle, I closed my eyes as a spray of scalding water poured down on me. "So, I clearly didn't get the memo."

"That you are, lad," he chuckled. "That you are – oh, spot me some shampoo, will you?" His hand came over the wall separating us. "Please?"

I squirted a dollop of shampoo into my hand before tossing the bottle over to him. "I messed up with Shannon the other night." Lathering my hair, I scrubbed myself down and sighed. "Really bad, lad."

"What did you do?" he asked from the other side of the wall.

"Something stupid."

"Come on," Gibsie coaxed. "Tell me all about it, buddy. Get it off your chest."

"I can't say it," I muttered, grimacing. "I'm too fucking disgusted with myself."

"What did you do?" he laughed. "Fuck her in the car or something?"

I hung my head in shame.

"Your silence is speaking volumes," he teased. "Come on, lad. Whatever it was, it can't be that bad."

"It *was* so bad, Gibs," I strangled out. "I can't even—"

"Whoa—" The shower curtain around me sprang open. "Did you get your hole?" Gibsie stood in front of me, naked and covered in suds. "Well? Did you fuck her?"

"Get out, ya bollox," I snapped, dragging the curtain back into place. "And I didn't get my hole – Jesus, don't say it that way."

"Sorry, I forgot you're a little sensitive about how I word things that involve your little *girlfriend*." Dragging the curtain back, he rolled his eyes and gave me an expectant look. "Did you make *love* to her?"

I grimaced.

"Holy shit." His eyes widened. "You *made* love!"

"I . . ." Snapping my mouth shut, I switched off the water and sighed heavily. "We shouldn't be having this conversation. It's not right."

"Fuck that!" he shot back, looking affronted. "You had sex with your girlfriend and you weren't going to tell *me*! When did this happen?"

"Saturday night," I choked out, feeling heat creep up my neck. "And don't look at me like that."

"Like what?" he huffed.

"Like I betrayed you."

"I *am* betrayed," he growled. "You don't get to keep juicy news like that from me. I should have known about this first thing on Sunday morning."

"Jesus, Gibs—" Stepping around him, I grabbed my towel off the floor and stalked back to the changing area. "You're ridiculous."

"So, you *had* sex with her?" he asked, following after me. "Come on, Johnny. Tell me."

"It wasn't like that," I snapped, flustered.

"Did you penetrate her with your penis?" he demanded. "Because if you did, then that's exactly what it was like."

"Fine, we had sex," I choked out. "Happy now?"

"Lad!" He grinned widely. "I'm so proud of you."

"No—" I pointed an accusing finger at him. "Don't be proud of me for being a reckless eejit."

538 • KEEPING 13

"I am so proud of you, buddy," he countered. "This is the proudest I've ever been of you."

Exhaling wearily, I sank down on the bench next to my locker. "I don't know what happened to me."

"I do," Gibsie snorted as he toweled himself off. "You got naked with a fucking fabulous-looking girl and banged your brains out." Tossing his towel on the bed, he slipped on a pair of jocks and laughed. "No wonder you don't want to go on tour anymore. You got the taste of *more* off Little Shannon, didn't ya?" He waggled his brows. "And now you're starving."

"Gibs," I hissed, cringing. "Don't say it like that."

"Wait—" He eyed me suspiciously. "Did you wrap it up?"

"Yes," I bit out.

"With the condoms I made you buy?"

I nodded.

He grinned. "Did you silently thank me?"

"Listen to me, fucker, I'm older than you," I growled. "I was scoring with girls while you were still waiting for your voice to break."

"I caught up, though, didn't I?" he shot back, unaffected. "And you're welcome."

"I bought you your first box of condoms," I hissed. "So enough of the *you're welcome* comments because I've had your back plenty of times."

"Fair point," he chuckled, clearly amused by my misfortune. "So, how was *it*?"

"A complete disaster," I admitted as I toweled myself off and threw on my school uniform. "It was her first time, Gibs, and my ma walked in on us when I was just getting going."

"Ah Jesus," Gibsie groaned, pressing his hand to his mouth. "Tell me you're joking?"

"I wish I was, lad," I muttered, pulling on my pants.

"Did she kill you?" he asked, wincing in sympathy.

"Worse," I grumbled. "She took Shannon into the kitchen for *the talk*."

"Oh my fucking god," he wailed. "This is just . . . ugh." He shook his head and gaped at me. "Your dick can't catch a break."

"Nope." Pulling on my jumper, I closed my locker and shrugged. "It's cursed."

# She's In Love With The Boy

## SHANNON

"I'm scared, Joe," I strangled out, rocking baby Ollie back and forth in my arms to stop him from sobbing. "What do we do?"

"I don't know, Shan." At ten years old, Joey's voice was still boyish and unbroken. "But we have to do something."

"You do nothing," Darren's emotionless voice came from the bunkbed below us. He had turned fifteen yesterday and his voice sounded like a real grown-up now. "You stay in here and keep your mouth shut."

"We can't leave her down there with him," Joey hissed. "She's just had the baby. If he hits her, he'll kill her!"

"He won't kill her," Darren replied, sounding frustrated. "But he will kill you if you go down there, idiot."

"Mammy," four-year-old Tadhg sobbed, curling into my side. "Mammy."

"Shh, Tadhg," I coaxed. Shifting baby Ollie onto my other thigh, I wrapped my arm around his chubby shoulders. "Mammy's fine."

"She's not fine," Joey choked out. "And he knows it."

"What do you want me to do, Joey?" Darren demanded. "I'm trying to keep you safe!" Rolling off his bunk, he stood up and glared at the four of us. The streetlight flooding through the window illuminated his bruised and battered face. "I tried to stop him and look at me—" His voice broke and he dragged in several deep breaths. "They're having . . . he's trying . . . listen, you don't understand what's going on down there – you're too small to understand – but I do, and I'm telling you to stay in bed."

Releasing a furious growl, Joey sprang down from the top bunk and grabbed his hurley from behind the door. "She's our mother," he hissed, staring up at Darren with narrowed eyes. "And if you won't help her, I'll do it myself!"

"He'll kill you," Darren warned, watching Joey as he unlocked the *bedroom door and slung it open.* "Don't go down there, Joey. You don't understand what's happening—"

"I don't care what's happening," *Joey spat.* "I know it's wrong. And maybe you can listen to her crying, but I can't!" *With that, he stormed out of the room with his hurley in tow. The sound of his footsteps thundering down the stairs had my heart leaping in my chest.*

"Stop him," *I begged as the screaming grew louder and Tadhg cried harder.* "Please, Darren!"

"I can't stop the man," *he strangled out, sinking down on his bunk.* "I tried . . . he's too fucking strong! I can't—"

"Here, Tadhg, hold your baby brother." *Shifting Ollie into Tadhg's arms, I climbed down the ladder and charged for the staircase with Darren shouting,* "Shannon, please don't!" *after me.*

*I knew I shouldn't go down there, but I had to. I couldn't leave Joey on his own. We were the two amigos. We were supposed to stick up for each other.*

*Stumbling down the staircase, I hurried into the kitchen, only to skid over something wet and land hard on my bottom.*

*Glancing down at the pool of red I was sitting in, I shuddered in repulsion and quickly clambered to my feet, wiping my hands on my Barbie nightdress. I didn't like blood. It always made me feel sick.*

"You little bastard," *Dad roared, dragging my attention away from the blood.*

*My gaze automatically locked on my father and fear spiraled inside of me so strong, I felt faint. He was standing in the middle of the kitchen and he was bleeding. Thick, oozy blood was dripping down the side of his face and he looked furious. His jeans were hanging open, something I found very strange. What was he doing with his jeans open?*

"Look at ya," *Dad sneered, glowering at Joey.* "A little fucking mammy's boy!"

"Get the fuck away from my mother," *Joey hissed as he stood in front of our mother and stared back at Dad. He was gripping his bloodied hurley in both hands, stance protective.* "Or the next time, I'll kill ya!"

*Dad laughed cruelly.* "Do you think you're a big, tough man now, boy?"

542 • KEEPING 13

"Do you?" Joey shot back, not missing a beat. "Pushing her around? Making her do that! Does that make you feel like a man?"

"Joey," I strangled out, panicking. "Joe—"

"Go back upstairs, Shan," Joey instructed, tightening his grip on his hurley, never once taking his eyes off Dad. "I've got this." His cheek was swollen and red, but his eyes were blazing with fury, not fear.

I didn't know how he could do this.

How could he be so fearless?

"Mammy," I sobbed when I saw her on her hands and knees behind Joey, clothes torn, face so swollen I could hardly see her eyes. Her jeans were on the floor and her t-shirt was ripped down the front. I could see her private parts. I didn't understand any of this. Why was she naked? Why was there a bottle of baby milk spilled on the floor beside her? "Mammy—"

"Go back to bed, Shannon," Mam sobbed as she scrambled to cover herself up. "I'm okay, baby."

She wasn't okay.

I was only eight years old, but I knew that none of this was okay.

"Leave him alone, Teddy," Mam choked out, curling a hand around Joey's ankle. "He's just a boy."

"He's a fucking mistake," Dad roared. "They're all mistakes— and you're the biggest one of the lot, Marie."

"Then just go," she wept. "Leave us be."

"What did you say to me?" Dad asked, voice deathly cold.

"N-nothing," Mam mumbled.

"Say it again," Dad ordered.

"I didn't say anything," she strangled out. "I'm sorry." Cowering on the floor, she shook violently. "You know I love you."

"That's better," he sneered. "Remember your fucking place, woman."

"You don't need to say sorry to him, Mam," Joey growled, chest heaving from temper. "He's the mistake."

"You little shit." Wiping the blood from his face, Dad stalked towards Joey. "I'm going to put manners on you—" His words broke off when Joey took another swing at him, slamming the hurley into the other side of his face. *"Jesus Christ, boy!"* he howled, clutching the other side of his head. *"You're a lunatic."*

*"If I'm a lunatic then you're the fucking devil,"* Joey hissed, tightening his grasp on his hurley once more. *"Come at me again, old man. I fucking dare ya!"*

*"Joey,"* Mam wept. *"Please just go to bed ... "*

*"Are you serious?"* Joey strangled out. *"He was trying to make you—"*

*"Just go to bed, baby,"* she sobbed. *"You're only making everything worse."*

*"Worse?"* Joey spluttered, looking wounded. *"I'm trying to protect you!"*

*"What the fuck are you looking at?"* Dad demanded, noticing me standing there. *"Did I say you could come down those stairs, girl?"*

Panicked, I shook my head and backed up until I hit the fridge. *"N-no, Daddy."*

*"Then what are you doing down here?"* he slurred, taking a menacing stagger towards me. *"You think you're a hero like that little cunt?"* His hand shot out, gripping my arm. *"You want to take a swing at me, too?"* He shook me roughly, causing my head to snap back. *"Mark my words, Marie, this runt will be as bad as you."*

*"Get your hands off my sister,"* Joey snarled, rushing at Dad.

Unlike before, Dad was ready for him. Keeping one hand wrapped around my arm, he caught Joey by the throat. *"You're a fiery little fucker,"* Dad hissed, squeezing his throat hard enough to make him drop his hurley to pull at Dad's hand. *"Yeah, that's right, boy. You're not strong enough to take me on yet."*

*"Back off."* Darren's voice filled the air, commanding and deep, as he thundered into the kitchen. His eyes went straight to Mam and a shudder rolled through him. *"You're a fucking monster,"* he strangled out.

*"Get out of here, Darren,"* Dad barked. *"You have a match in the morning."*

*"A match?"* Darren shook his head in outrage. *"Let them go."* His hands were balled into fists at his sides and he was shaking violently. *"They're only children."*

*"Then they should be in bed,"* Dad barked. *"Not down here, interfering in my business."*

"Fu . . . ck y . . . ou," Joey strangled out, kicking and lashing at our father. "Ass . . . hole."

"Well shit." Dad laughed and shook his head. "This one—" he inclined his head toward the son whose throat he was clutching "—has more balls than brains."

"Let them go," Darren repeated coldly. "If you want me at that match tomorrow, you better take your hands off those kids."

Dad stared at him for a long moment before releasing Joey and me. "It'll be a good match," he said, doing a complete one-eighty. "We should win," he added. "If you're on form."

Coughing and spluttering, Joey charged for our father again, but Darren blocked his way. "Go to bed."

Tears filled Joey's eyes. "But he just—"

"Take Shannon and go to bed," Darren repeated, giving Joey a hard look. "Now."

Furious, Joey looked to our mother. "Don't do this, Mam," he begged. "Don't brush this under the table."

"Do what he said, Joey," she sniffled, offering him a small smile. "Everything's going to be okay."

"No," Joey choked out, "it won't be." Reaching for my hand, he dragged me to the door. "He's going to leave us, Shannon," he whispered, low enough so that only I could hear him. "He'll be gone soon."

"Daddy?" I asked, hopeful.

"No." Joey shook his head, half-dragging me up the staircase. "Darren."

"Darren won't leave us," I replied, feeling sick at the thought. "He said he'd never leave us."

"I saw it," Joey hissed. "In his eyes. He's going to leave. He doesn't care, Shannon. He's just waiting until he finishes school and then he'll be gone."

I shook my head. "But he can't go . . . "

"Don't worry," he said, stopping outside his bedroom door. "No matter what happens, we'll stick together."

"You promise . . . "

Jerking awake with a start on Monday morning, I kicked the bed covers off my sweat-soaked body and just laid there, still as a statue, waiting for my pounding heart to return to its normal rhythm. The back of my neck was slick with sweat and I could feel the cold beads trickling down my skin. Shivering, I focused on one singular spot on my bedroom ceiling and breathed in and out, deep and slow, until my heart stopped trying to thrash its way out of my ribcage.

Every night since coming home from the hospital, I'd woken up to the exact same nightmare. *Memory,* my brain reminded me. *They're only nightmares if they're not real.*

Why my brain seemed to be stuck on one specific night eight years ago was obvious, and the fear of the unknown had me paralyzed to my mattress most mornings, drenched in a cold sheen of sweat, and burning in my own personal hell.

In the throes of my panic, I came to the conclusion that my brother was psychic. It was either that, or he was a living, breathing lie detector, because everything Joey had ever predicted, good, bad, or indifferent, down through the years, had come to pass. He had this spooky ability to look at a situation, feel out the lies, taste the danger, and then submit his prediction with crushing words and eerie accuracy.

Like Joey predicted, Darren was beginning to crack under the pressure of living under this roof. He was withdrawing from the family life, and was taking more and more extended work trips to Belfast. We hadn't even met his boyfriend, Alex, which only proved to me that he had no intention of blending his real life in Belfast with his temporary one in Cork.

Patricia and her team of social workers had scaled back on their visits. Content with our progress, they popped in once every couple of weeks rather than every other day – like Joey predicted.

And just like Joey predicted, our father was currently walking around Ballylaggin a free man. It had been a couple of weeks since Dad and Johnny's confrontation outside the cinema, and while the piece of paper downstairs in the kitchen assured us that he couldn't come back here, the woman who'd birthed me gave me room for pause.

Everything was changing, my life was in a spin, and the only thing that seemed to be still and calming in the middle of the carnage was the boy whose t-shirt I was wearing. My phone pinged then, right on time, and I practically fell out of bed in my rush to swipe it off the charger. Every time I heard my phone vibrate or saw the screen light up, I was immediately attacked by an onslaught of butterflies in my stomach. My heart fluttered. My palms turned slick from sweat. I was completely enraptured with him. It wasn't good or safe or sensible, but it was exactly how I felt – and I craved the danger. I longed for the text messages and secret meetings. I longed for *him*.

J: Leaving the gym now, baby. Be with you in 30. X

Excitement thrummed in my veins, making it hard to keep my hands steady enough to tap out a text.

S: How did it go? Are you sore? Were you careful? X

I clutched my phone to my chest and waited impatiently. Less than a minute later, my phone sounded.

J: All good. Stop worrying. X

I couldn't help it. I *was* worried. I was *always* worried about him. My phone sounded again.

J: Stop . . . x

Smiling like a dope, I tapped out another text.

S: I can't help it. x

J: YOU CAN GIVE ME A THOROUGH EXAMINATION WHEN I GET THERE. JUST TO PUT YOUR MIND AT EASE. ;)

S: WOW, YOU'RE SO THOUGHTFUL. :P

J: DRIVING NOW. SEE YOU SOON. x

S: OKAY. x

J: SHOW ME YOUR TITS.

I laughed loudly at the message on the screen.

S: NICE TRY, GIBSIE.

J: FUCK! HEY LITTLE SHANNON.

Setting my phone down, I hurried out of my room and dove into the shower before any of my brothers could get in there. Pulling my hair up in a messy bun to keep it dry, I lathered myself up with body wash, and let my mind wander. Like usual, my thoughts automatically drifted to Johnny.

*Always Johnny . . .*

Today was May 9th, the second week of summer, and as the days were growing longer, my feelings were growing predominantly stronger for him. Saturday night changed everything for me. Being with him in that way made it all feel so much *deeper* now. My feelings for him threatened to overthrow all common sense . . .

"Shannon!" Mam's voice filled my ears as she rapped against the bathroom door. "I thought we made it clear that you were to travel with Darren to and from school."

Excitement bubbled up inside of me.

*He's here.*

Switching off the shower, I wrapped a towel around my body and hurried back to my bedroom to get dressed, dutifully ignoring my mother as I went. Slamming my bedroom door shut in her face, I dressed in record time, pulling my hair out of its bun and dragging a hairbrush through it. Sliding my phone into my shirt pocket, I slipped on my shoes, grabbed my schoolbag, and swung my door open once more.

"When I ask you a question, I expect an answer," Mam said, standing in the doorway with her hands on her hips. "What is he doing here?"

"He picks me up for school every morning," I reminded her. "You already know this." *Or at least you would know if you weren't at work or in bed all the time.*

"And you already know that you're supposed to go with Darren," Mam shot back, brows furrowed.

Resisting the urge to roll my eyes at her, I stepped around her and moved for the bannister. While Mam had given up on the Garda threats, Johnny was in no way tolerated or welcome in our home. She didn't acknowledge him or our relationship. She pretended he didn't exist at all, which was fine by me because I was doing the same thing with her.

"Shannon Lynch!"

"Bye," I called back, thundering down the staircase, my smile widening with every step I took that moved me closer to the front door. *To him.*

"You know you're supposed to come with me," Darren began to say as he emerged from the kitchen with a bowl of cereal in his hands. It was a half-hearted effort from him, though. He didn't really care whether I drove with Johnny or not. He was just reciting the usual blah-blah-blah. "It makes no sense for him to drive half an hour out of his way—"

"See ya," I called out, yanking the front door open and rushing outside into the early morning sunshine.

My step faltered when my eyes landed on Johnny sitting on my garden wall, his car keys dangling between his fingers. He wasn't wearing his school jumper – nothing new there – and his shirt was untucked, his tie loose, making him look deliciously disheveled. He was scowling at the front of my house, but the moment he noticed me, a lazy smile crept across his face.

"Shannon *like the river*," he purred, hopping down to his feet. Gesturing to his body, he winked. "I'm here for your inspection."

Grinning, I closed the space between us, forcing myself to walk to him and not run like I so badly wanted to. "Hi, Johnny."

"Hi, Shan," he replied, pressing a kiss to my lips before slinging an arm over my shoulder. "All set?"

Nodding, I slipped my arm around his waist and sighed in contentment as we walked to his car, feeling right for the first time since last night. "Good to go."

"Shannon!" Mam stepped outside, wrapping her dressing gown around her. "Can I have a word?"

Tensing up, I spun around and begged her with my eyes not to say anything. "About what?"

Mam cast a scathing look to Johnny before focusing on me. "In private." She inclined her head towards the front door. "Now."

"I need to go," I replied shakily, knowing full well that if I went back inside, I wouldn't be going to school today. "We can talk later." Except we wouldn't because I had no intention of having this conversation with her. "Bye."

"Shannon," she repeated, this time in a warning tone. "Come inside *now*."

I stiffened. "I am *going* to school. I have three weeks left before the summer holidays and I'm not missing any days, Mam. I have my junior cert coming up."

"Not with him," Mam bit out. "You're not going anywhere with *him*."

"*He* has a name," I shot back, mortified that Johnny was seeing and hearing this. Steeling my spine, I narrowed my eyes at her. "It's Johnny, and he's my boyfriend."

"You have no respect," Mam hissed, turning her anger on Johnny. "You're a horrible boy."

Johnny sighed wearily. "I'm not on your property, Mrs. Lynch."

Keeping his tone politer than she deserved, he added, "I know you don't like me, but I'm not breaking any law here."

"I told you to stay away from my daughter," Mam strangled out, shaking now. "And you won't listen."

"Mam—"

"With all due respect, I have my own ma to tell me what to do," he replied evenly. "I'm here for Shannon, not you, so you can like me or not, but, either way, you might as well get used to seeing me, because I'm not going anywhere."

Mam's face reddened. "If you so much as think about putting—"

"Don't worry, Shannon's Mammy." A blond head popped through the sun roof of the Audi, with a shit-eating grin attached to it. Grinning widely, Gibsie waggled his brows and said, "He'll take good care of your little girl," before disappearing back into the car and cranking the stereo to the max. Popping back up once more, he threw himself into the chorus of Madonna's "Like A Virgin," as he sang at the top of his lungs and made suggestive hand movements, all directed at my mother.

"Jesus Christ," Johnny groaned, shaking his head. "I'm going to kill him."

Mam's mouth fell open as she gaped in horror at Gibsie.

"Gerard!" Claire's blonde head popped up through the sunroof. "You're so tacky."

"You know you're the only virgin I want to touch," he told her with a suggestive waggle of his brows.

"Gerard!"

"Just let me know when you want me to do that – *for the very first time*," he added.

"That would be never," she shot back, blushing. "You big mope!"

He arched a brow, giving her a look that screamed *bullshit*.

I took my mother's momentary distraction by Gibsie as mine and Johnny's opportunity to get away before another blazing row erupted. "Let's go." Grabbing Johnny's hand, I half-dragged him to his car.

Yanking the passenger door open, I practically dove inside, slamming the door behind me.

"Hey girl!" Claire chirped from the backseat. "Sorry about him," she added, pointing to the lower half of Gibsie that wasn't wedged in the sunroof. "I don't know what to say."

"Yeah," Feely, who was sitting in the back, nodded solemnly. "We'd like to give you an explanation for his behavior, but honestly, I don't think there is one."

"The fuck do you think you're playing at, Gibs?" Johnny demanded then. Diving into the driver's seat, he slammed his door shut and revved the engine. "As if the woman doesn't hate me enough—" Tearing away from the house, he reached over and switched off the stereo. "You had to go and push it, and put more bleeding notions in her head!"

*I wish he would put more notions in* your *head, Johnny Kavanagh!*

"I was using my charm," Gibsie laughed, lowering himself back through the sunroof. "Worked, too," he added, sinking down on the backseat between Claire and Feely. "Got her out, didn't it?"

"Oh my god," I choked out through fits of laughter as I fastened my seatbelt. "I can't believe you just did that."

"I know, right?" Gibsie shot back, grinning. "It was getting a little heavy for a Monday morning, and it just felt *right*. Like an urge or something."

"When things feel right in your head, they're usually very fucking wrong," Johnny grumbled, looking pained. "Next time, repress the urge, Gibs."

"Whatever, lad," Gibsie snickered. "I saved you from another mother-in-law tongue lashing and you know it," he added, before falling into a heated debate with Claire about the appropriateness of serenading virgins.

Reaching for my hand, Johnny lifted it to his mouth and dropped a kiss to my knuckles. "So, listen," he said in a low tone, ignoring the noise coming from the backseat. "I wanted to ask you about something."

"Oh?" Excitement thrummed in my veins and I turned in my seat to give him my full attention. "What?"

"Dinner tonight." He cast a quick sideways glance at me before refocusing on the road. "At my place."

Instantly, my anxiety piqued. "I don't know, Johnny," I mumbled, feeling my face grow hot. "I'm not sure if that's a good idea." It was a terrible idea. His mother was kind and warm and loving, but I doubted she wanted me back there after Saturday night. I'd seen the way she'd looked at me when she'd dropped me home; all suspicious and worried. Johnny's words from months back were still floating around in my head.

*"My parents don't want me going over to your place. They think it's a bad idea..."*

It didn't take a genius to read between the lines of that statement and know that *I* was the bad idea.

"It was her idea," Johnny said, knowing where my thoughts had gone.

My brows shot up in surprise. "It was?"

"It's true," Gibsie offered from the back seat. "Mammy K has been tormenting him to bring you home again. I heard them talking on the phone this morning. She has some big news for the two of you."

My eyes widened. "Big news?"

"Gibs!" Johnny barked. "Stop fucking earwigging."

I frowned. "What news?"

"No clue," Johnny muttered, rubbing his jaw.

"I'm in the same car as you, asshole," Gibsie growled. "I can clearly hear your conversation. What do want me to do? Stick my head out the window and bark at the traffic like a dog?"

"I want you to stop listening in on my conversations," Johnny shot back, vein ticking in his neck. "Jesus!"

"Fine." Holding up his hands, he leaned back in his seat. "I'll say no more on the matter."

"Thank you."

"Wait – I'm invited for dinner tonight, too, right?"

"Gibs!"

"Am I?"

553 • CHLOE WALSH

"*No.*"

"Why not?"

"Jesus Christ, Gibs. I swear to god, I will pull this car over and you—"

"Fine!" Gibsie huffed. "I didn't want the roast spuds anyway. My mam's are better."

"Gerard," Claire coaxed, "it's okay. You can have dinner with me."

"Can I eat you?" he asked, sounding playful once more.

"If you're good," she replied, patting his shoulder.

"What?" Gibsie's voice rose so high, it was almost girlish. "I mean—" he roughly cleared his throat several times before adding, "*What?*"

Feely chuckled quietly. "Lost for words, Gibs? That's a first."

"I know, right?" Claire giggled, using her finger to close Gibsie's mouth. "I think I broke him."

"So, will you come tonight?" Johnny asked, drawing my attention back to him. "*Please?* It would mean a lot to me."

"Okay," I whispered, forcing out the word when all I wanted was to say no and hide. "I'll come."

He turned to look at me and beamed. "Really?"

*Oh god, that smile.* "Really," I confirmed, heart racing. "If you're sure?"

"I'm sure," he replied, eyes blazing with heat.

"I know I'm not supposed to talk to you," Gibsie interjected. "But eyes on the road, Cap. I have a very pressing dinner arrangement to get to this evening, with a tantalizing main course up for grabs, and I don't want to be showing up dead to it."

"What – oh, Jesus!" Johnny barked, swerving the wheel and narrowly avoiding the traffic coming in the opposite direction. "I think I ran a red light," he added, cheeks reddening.

"You sure did, bulldozer," Gibsie mused, patting his shoulder.

"What's that thing he's always saying to the lads, Gibs?" Feely added, "Oh yeah; get your head out of the girl and onto the road."

"Funny," Johnny deadpanned. "Very funny."

"What are we doing for your birthday, Johnny?" Claire asked then. "It's only what – three weeks away?"

"We?" Johnny arched a brow. "I didn't know we were '*we*' kind of friends, Claire."

Claire made a pssh noise. "Your girlfriend is my best friend, Johnny Kavanagh, which means I'm going to be at your party. I'm going to be a lot of places you are. Like your car right now. So get on board with it and tell me what you want for your present."

"I'm turning eighteen, not eight." Johnny laughed. "And I'm not having a party, so don't buy me any bleeding presents."

"Oh yes you fucking are having a party," Gibsie countered. "A big one. With cake, cocktail sausages, and a shit ton of tequila."

"Tequila again?" Feely glared at Gibsie. "*Really*?"

"Listen, I'm not going to sit here and apologize for something that happened a million years ago," Gibsie huffed. "I puked on your dog, Feely. It was a genuine mistake. I've done it to Sookie a million times and you don't see her giving me the cold shoulder. And I haven't done it since, so can we please move past it?"

"I don't have a dog – that was my mother you puked on!" Feely snapped, sounding outraged. "And it was last Christmas, not a million years ago, asshole."

"What?" Gibsie frowned. "That's was your mam?"

"Yes, asshole!"

"Ah, lad, I'm so fucking sorry," Gibsie strangled out, slapping a hand across his mouth. "I thought she was a dog."

"Not making it any better, Gibs," Johnny mused, lips twitching.

"I didn't mean that *she* looks like a dog," Gibsie quickly corrected. "But she was so soft and furry—"

"Repress it," Johnny ordered.

Gibsie frowned. "Hey, is that why your parents won't—"

"Won't let you step foot inside the house anymore?" Feely filled in, giving him a dirty look. "Yes, Gibs. That's exactly why."

An uncomfortable silence enveloped us then, one Claire thankfully broke by clearing her throat and saying, "Anyway, moving on from Gerard's less than stellar regurgitation antics, I think we should do something for your eighteenth, Johnny, and if you don't want to have a party, we could go camping."

Johnny's brows furrowed. "Camping?"

"Camping," Claire confirmed, tone laced with excitement. "School will be over by then, the weather should be good, you all have cars, so we could go anywhere we wanted. And best of all, Shan, Lizzie and I don't start our junior cert until the week after your birthday." Grinning, she added, "It's a win-win."

"Babe, you're a genius," Gibsie declared. "I fucking love camping."

"What do you think, Shan?" Johnny asked, casting a sideways glance at me. "Would you go?"

"Does a bear shit in the woods? Of course she'll go!" Gibsie answered for me. "Right, Little Shannon?"

"Don't put words in her mouth," Johnny growled. "She doesn't have to—"

"I'll go," I blurted out, excited.

Johnny's brows shot up. "You will?"

I nodded. "Absolutely."

"But your mam . . ."

"Will say no," I agreed, squeezing his hand. "But it's your eighteenth, and I'm still going."

"Then it's settled," Claire chimed in, clapping her hands together. "We're going camping!"

# Enough!

## SHANNON

"We better go back to class," Johnny groaned, breaking our kiss. It was the end of big lunch and we were hidden behind the school greenhouse where we spent the second half of lunch break together most days. Like usual, I was sitting on the wall surrounding the vegetable garden and, like usual, Johnny was standing between my legs, with his hands clamped on my hips, and his tongue in my mouth.

"We can go straight to my place after school," he offered, pressing another searing kiss to my lips. "Do something before dinner?"

I didn't want dinner unless *he* was on the menu. "What kind of something?" I asked, voice a little breathless, as I traced my fingers down the hard ridges and grooves of his stomach. "What have you got in mind?"

"I don't know," he replied gruffly, hands moving to my ass. "We could play a little GTA? Or talk?" He squeezed tightly and I moaned. "Whatever you want, Shan." Dropping his face to my neck, he suckled hard on my flesh. "Shite, I think I marked you," he muttered, jerking his head back, eyes locked on my neck. Grinning sheepishly, he added, "Sorry."

"Sure you are." He looked about as far from sorry as a person could get. "I believe you."

"How are you feeling?" he asked then. Smiling softly, he grazed my hip with his fingers. "You okay?"

"I'm fine," I whispered, tugging him closer. "Stop worrying."

"I can't help it," he groaned. "I'm always worried about you."

"I wanted what happened, Johnny," I reassured him. "I still do."

His eyes darkened. "Yeah?"

Shivering, I nodded. "Yeah."

"I don't know what I'm going to do with you, Shannon Lynch," he admitted in a husky voice. "You make me lose my head."

"Good," I teased. "I like it when you turn your brain off."

The second bell sounded, letting us know that we had two minutes to get to class, but I remained exactly where I was, gripping his waist with my thighs and mentally begging him to *stay, stay, stay* . . .

One hour of lunch wasn't enough. It was *never* enough time with him, but I reluctantly released him when he mumbled something about a French test.

Johnny helped me off the wall and then secured my hand in his as we made our way back to school. "You nervous about dinner?"

I nodded. "Terrified."

"She won't bring it up," he promised, tracing his thumb over my knuckles. "So don't even worry about that, Shan."

"Will your dad be there, too?" I asked, voice small.

"Yeah," he replied, holding the door open for me to step inside. "He's still trying to make more of an effort and be *present*." He rolled his eyes at the notion. "She's still driving me around the bend, Shan. It's worse than ever. The closer we get to June, the more of a weeping mess she becomes," he added with a shudder. "It's all '*how's your willy, love*,' and '*are your testicles swelling again*' or else she's reading out statistics on head injuries in rugby."

I knew exactly how his mother felt. The closer we got to June, the more *I* became a weeping mess, too. I was just careful to do it when Johnny wasn't around. I didn't have the luxury that most girls my age had. My boyfriend would be leaving soon. I knew phone calls were coming in from the scouts, whether he told me about them or not. I knew we were on borrowed time, moving closer and closer to the good-bye that kept me up at night – to the day he would leave and I would stay.

"So, what do think about what Claire said in the car this morning?" I asked, dragging myself from my depressing thoughts. Pulling him to a stop outside the girls' bathroom, I squeezed his hand and smiled up at him. "The camping trip for your birthday? Are you excited?"

"Only if you're going." Johnny looked down at me and frowned. "I'm not going if you're not."

"I'm *going*, Johnny." Hail, rain, or snow. "I'm not missing your birthday."

"Oh yeah?" He grinned. "Are you going to share a tent with me?"

"That depends," I teased, grinning back at him. "Can you pitch a tent?"

Johnny gave me a knowing smirk and my face flamed in embarrassment.

"Not *that* kind of tent," I quickly amended, blushing.

"You're so cute," he chuckled with a shake of his head. "I'll meet you here after last class, okay? We can head back to my place together."

"No, I'll need to go home first and get changed."

"You look perfect as you are," he argued. "Better than perfect." Grinning, he hooked an arm around my waist and dragged me flush against him. "In fact, you look like dinner."

I sagged against him, feeling my body grow hot and achy. "I still need to go home first and check in on Joey." Pressing my hands against his chest, I took a safe step back before I lost all common sense and did something reckless. "I can ask him to drive me over to your place around eight? You'll be done with training by then, won't you?"

"Oh, shite, yeah." Johnny frowned, like the notion of training had only come to him. "I have training."

"I know," I agreed, smiling. "I can come over afterwards."

"Or we could just blow—"

"You train and I'll come over when you're done," I cut him off by saying. "That's the plan, remember?"

He looked frustrated but he gave me a reluctant nod. "Yeah, you're right."

I grinned. "I know." Taking another step back, I waved him off. "Now go on – and enjoy double French."

With a heavy sigh, Johnny pressed a kiss to my cheek before strolling off down the hall. "Hey Shan?" he called over his shoulder.

"Yeah?"

Smirking, he said, "*Je veux lécher la chatte de ma copine.*"

I frowned. "*What?*"

Johnny grinned devilishly. "I said, *je veux être à l'intérieur de toi.*"

I scrunched my nose up. "You know I'm terrible at French."

"I'm counting on it," he laughed as he sauntered off. "See you tonight, baby."

Grinning like an idiot, I waved him off and rushed into the bathroom. I'd been bursting to pee since the class before big break, but didn't want to waste a minute of my lunch hour with him. However, the moment I stepped inside the bathroom, I regretted it. Not only had I just come face to face with Bella Wilkinson, but she had two of her sixth-year friends with her.

Up until now, I had miraculously managed to avoid being on my own with her, and aside from the daily comments in the corridors and the lunch hall, she hadn't given me any trouble. I had a feeling that was about to change. The look of pure loathing on her face as she prowled towards me only confirmed those feelings.

"Look who it is, girls," Bella mused, looking as devastatingly beautiful as always, as she stood in front of my only exit. "The little whore without her guard dogs."

"Leave it alone, Bella," one of the girls – the one with the brown hair – surprised me by saying.

"She's a bitch, Tash," Bella spat, casting a warning look to her friend. "You know what she cost me."

In full-on flight mode, I turned on my heels and moved for the door, but she intercepted me, blocking my path.

My heart hammered wildly in my chest, bucking and leaping and screaming at me to get away. Instead I just stood there, looking up at the girl I knew hated me. "I need to go," I strangled out, my voice barely more than a panicked whisper. "Let me out," I added, forcing myself to straighten my shoulders.

"We're not done talking," Bella hissed. "We're not even close to being *done.*"

"I don't want to talk to you." My heart was racing so hard, it was making me feel faint. "I just want to go," I added in a shaky tone. "I don't want any trouble."

"You just want to go," Bella mimicked and then laughed. "Well, tough shit, honey, because I have plenty to say to you."

*You fool,* my brain hissed, *you know better than to come in here alone.*

We only had three weeks of school left and then we were done for the summer. Bella would be done with Tommen altogether. I could have avoided her for twenty-one bloody days.

*Dammit, why did I have to walk in here?*

Tilting her head to one-side, Bella smiled cruelly down at me. "How's Daddy, Shannon?"

My body seized up as a concoction of devastation and humiliation flooded me.

"Did you hear about Shannon's father, girls?" Bella continued to taunt. "Her father is an alchy scab on the welfare." Narrowing her eyes, she added, "Apparently, he beat the shit out of her at Easter and put her in the hospital, but I think fair play to the man. He was probably just trying to beat the slapper out of her."

"Bella, stop!" the girl she had called Tash barked. "That's enough."

"It's not enough," Bella snared. "That bitch stole my boyfriend, Tash."

"Well, I'm not being a part of this," the Tash girl said, and with that, she stalked out of the bathroom, shoving Bella out of her way as she went.

The other girl, the blonde one leaning against the sink, didn't say anything at all. She just stood there, glancing anywhere but me, reminding me of so many other girls I'd met down through the years, and making me despise her most of all. I hated girls like her. The ones who knew something was wrong but did nothing to stop it.

*Fight back, Shannon.* Joey's voice flooded my mind. *Don't let those bitches intimidate you!*

"I didn't steal your boyfriend," I shot back, shaking from head to toe. "Because Johnny was never yours."

Bella arched a finely plucked brow. "And you think he's *yours*?"

"Yeah," I replied, shocking myself with my words. "He is."

"Then you should know that he's only with you for one thing," she spat, looking furious. "An easy fucking lay."

"That's all he was with *you* for," I stunned myself by saying. "We're not all like that, Bella."

Her face reddened. "Excuse me?"

"Let me out," I repeated, making a point of staring at the door. "Now."

When she didn't step aside, I moved to go around her, only to stagger backwards and land awkwardly on the floor when she pushed me full force in the chest.

"I said we're not done, bitch." Stalking towards me, Bella swiped my schoolbag off my shoulder. Unzipping it, she poured the contents on top of me. "You're a dirty slut," she hissed, shoving my forehead with her fingers. "You don't belong in this school, so go back to the council estate with the rest of your fucked-up family."

"*. . . You're a useless cunt . . .*"

"*. . . You're the biggest mistake of them all, girl . . .*"

"*. . . Your own mother didn't want you . . .*"

"*. . . You're the poison in this family . . .*"

*Enough.*

*Enough.*

*Enough.*

"Enough!" I screamed, scrambling to my feet. "Don't *touch* me!" Tears were pooling in my eyes, but I blinked them away, feeling more fury in this moment than I had in my whole life. "Don't you ever fucking touch me again!" I continued to scream as I completely took leave of my senses and charged at Bella.

I caught a glance of her surprised expression about two seconds before I lunged at her, releasing sixteen years of pain and mistreatment into my fingertips as I scratched and shoved at her with everything I had in me. She was too big for me, and I knew I didn't have a hope in hell of finishing what she started, but for once in my life, I was fighting back. Something had changed inside of me, I'd felt it the day I woke up in that hospital bed, lucky to be alive, and I refused to take any more. I wasn't going to be pushed around by her or anyone else.

"You fucking bitch," Bella snarled as she knocked me onto the bathroom floor and climb on top of me. "Who do you think you are?" she screamed as she scratched and tore at my hair and face with her nails. "Little fucking scumbag."

Refusing to just lie there and take it like I had a million times before in my old school, I pushed and shoved back at her. "Get off me!" Catching ahold of her hair, I yanked hard, stunning myself with my own strength when a clump of her black hair extensions came away in my hands.

"My hair!" she wailed loudly. "Oh, I'm going to *destroy* you!" Rearing back, she smacked her hand across my face before roughly pinning my hands above my head. "Kelly – get my bag."

"Stop!" I could hardly breathe from the weight of her on top of me, but I continued to thrash and buck and try to break free. "Get off, Bella!"

"Uh, Bella, maybe we should just—"

"Get my fucking bag, Kelly!" she screamed at the top of her lungs. "Now!"

Without another word, the blonde handed Bella's schoolbag to her. "What do you want from it?"

"Lunch, water, and makeup," Bella ordered before hacking up a huge phlegm ball and spitting it on my face. Kelly pulled out a plastic lunch box and Bella said, "Pin her hands down for me."

"But I—"

"Do it!"

Sighing heavily, Kelly knelt down and took over pinning my hands down, while Bella opened her lunch box and began to smear the contents all over my uniform. "Like that, bitch?" Bella hissed, as she opened a tuna sandwich and smudged it against my jumper and skirt. "The smell suits you."

Still straddling me, she grabbed a tube of lipstick from her bag and then roughly cupped my jaw in her hands. "Go on," she mocked, as she smeared the lipstick over my forehead and cheeks. "Cry, little baby. I dare you!"

*I will not cry.*

*I will not cry.*

*Do not give her the satisfaction, Shannon.*

Bucking against her hold, I desperately tried to free myself, but it was no use.

I wasn't strong enough.

"Are you not going to say anything?" Bella taunted as she climbed off me, holding her water bottle in her hands. Turning it upside down, she poured the contents over me. "No, that's right. You're *not* going to say a word, because if you do, I'll fucking ruin you."

*Don't lie there,* Joey's voice hissed inside of my head. *Fight back, even if you can't win.*

A lone tear slid down my cheek.

"Aw, look, the little baby's crying," Bella taunted. "Fucking loser."

*Fight back, Shannon.*

*Come on.*

*You can do this.*

"Fuck you!" I choked out. "Fuck you both."

"Fuck me?" Bella sneered. Pulling her phone out of her skirt pocket, she flipped it open and started to take pictures. When she was done snapping her photos, she slid her phone back into her pocket and cupped my face, digging her nails into my cheeks so hard that I winced from the pain. "*Fuck. You. Bitch.*"

Every ounce of fight went out of me, right along with my fickle faith in humanity. She thought she was hurting me, but she didn't know what pain was. Shivering violently, I remained perfectly still, just waiting for it to be *over.*

"Come on, Kel," Bella said when she had given me the final once-over, clearly admiring her handy work. "Let's leave the bitch here."

"I'm so sorry," the blonde girl named Kelly whispered in my ear before hurrying to her feet and following Bella out of the bathroom.

Numb to the bone, I remained exactly where I was for several minutes, counting the ceiling cubes above me before finally dragging myself to my feet.

Every inch of my body ached, my lungs were burning, but it was my pride that had taken the hardest blow. Humiliated and trembling, I pulled my phone out of my shirt pocket and sobbed in relief when I realized it hadn't been soaked along with the rest of me.

Clutching my phone in my hand, I staggered over to the sink and heaved violently until everything inside of my body was swirling down the drain. Panting, I clutched the basin with my free hand and forced myself to look at my reflection. Tiny trickles of blood tinged my cheeks from where her nails had been, and I wasn't even surprised to see what she had written on my face.

*BJ-13* was scrawled across my forehead to match *Kav's* on my left cheek and *Slut* on my right.

Tearing my gaze from the mirror, I focused on my phone, and with shaky hands, I dialed the number I knew off by heart.

*Please pick up.*

*Please pick up.*

*Please don't be in class and pick up . . .*

"Shan?" his familiar voice came down the line. "What's going on?"

"Joey." Clenching my eyes shut, I shuddered violently. "I n-need you to come g-get me."

# Flying Fists

## JOHNNY

I was used to seeing a lot of strange things go down at Tommen. Hell, I couldn't count the weird encounters I'd had in this place down through the years. But the sight of a lad in a BCS uniform stalking through the school carpark towards me after last class of the day was definitely a new thing for me.

It took me a few moments to register the lad wearing the grey jumper with the public-school crest as Joey Lynch, and a second too long to register that the arm he was rearing back was intended for me. His fist connected with my face so fast that my head snapped sideways.

"What the fuck did you do?" he demanded, looking livid. "If you hurt her, I'm going burn you alive and piss all over your bones."

"What are you talking about?" I roared, spitting out a mouthful of blood. I was about done with this whole family, and while up until the punch to the jaw, I'd actually liked Joey, I had a feeling that was about to change. "I didn't do anything to anyone!"

A huge crowd was forming around us, cheering and hollering like bleeding eejits.

"She's inside that school somewhere crying," Joey snarled. "She called me to come get her." Slamming his hands against my chest, he stalked towards me. "You wouldn't happen to know anything about that now, would you?"

"No, I fucking wouldn't," I snarled, shoving him away from me. He needed to step back and fast because he was pushing my patience out to sea and I was packing about four inches of height and four stone of muscle on him. "Back the fuck up, Lynch."

"Or what?" he sneered, moving for me again. "What are you going to do, Kavanagh?"

"Whoa, whoa, whoa," Hughie commanded as he jumped into the

mix, running through the carpark to step in between us. "Just calm down, lads."

"I am calm!" I roared, clearly *not* calm. "He's the prick who walked over here and hit me in the face."

"Because you hurt my sister," Joey shot back.

"I didn't *hurt* your sister," I snarled. "I would *never* hurt her."

"Well, someone fucking did something!" Joey roared before lunging for me once more.

This time it was Gibsie who intercepted Joey from behind. "Howdy, buddy," he said in a friendly tone, as he wrapped his arms around him and dragged him away from me. "I see we're in the old front-to-back position again."

"Get the fuck off me, Gussie," Joey snapped, wrestling against his hold.

"It's Gibsie," he replied calmly. "And no can do. You can't be going around hitting my center, Joey. He's got some important business to attend to this Saturday, and it would be terribly irresponsible of me to let you go right now."

"Joey!" a female voice called out above the noise of the crowd. Seconds later, a blonde appeared in my line of vision, moving straight for Joey. His girlfriend, I noted. *Aoife.* "What are you doing, Joe?" she puffed out, stepping in front of him. "I thought we said no fighting." Catching ahold of his face, she forced him to look at her. "Ask questions first, remember?"

"I forgot, baby," he muttered, sagging enough that Gibsie released him and took a step back.

"What the hell is happening?" I demanded, feeling a mixture of fury and panic shoot through me.

"Shannon called me," Joey snarled, shaking with temper. "Someone in this stuck-up school did something to her."

"*Did* something to her?" I gaped at him in confusion. "What?" Something happened to Shannon? "What did they do to her?" What the hell? "I was just with her at lunch," I added, feeling a swell of rage build up inside of my body. "What the fuck is going on, Joey?"

"I don't know!" Running a hand through his blond hair, he released a growl and glared at the crowd. "But when I find out which one of you privileged pricks hurt my sister, I'll do time for ye!"

"What's going on here?" the familiar voice of Mr. Twomey cut through the air and the crowd around us quickly dispersed until it was just the five of us and Mr. Twomey remaining in the carpark with cars buzzing past, honking loudly.

"Johnny," he said with a sigh when he noticed me in the middle of what was going on – nothing new there. His gaze flicked to Joey and Aoife and his eyes narrowed. "Are you two aware that you are not permitted on school property if you are not enrolled here?"

"Fuck you," Joey shot back, causing Aoife to groan into her hand.

"Joe!" she hissed, placing a hand on his chest. "He's their principal."

"So?" Joey shrugged, unaffected. "He's not mine." Narrowing his eyes on Mr. Twomey, he spat, "I'm here to pick up my sister since your piece-of-shit school can't control its students and keep her safe."

Mr. Twomey's brows furrowed. "And your sister is?"

"Shannon Lynch." Mr. Twomey paled and Joey lunged for the jugular like he could smell fresh blood. "Yeah, that's right," he sneered. "You know who I'm talking about. You made all sorts of promises to her, didn't ya? About keeping your students safe? What a fucking joke you are!"

"I beg your pardon," Mr. Twomey strangled out. "I have no idea what you're talking—"

"Hi, Joe," a small voice said and we all swung around to find Shannon walking towards us.

Her hair was drenched and clothes destroyed with food. Her face was red and blotchy, like she'd scrubbed herself raw, but when I looked harder, I could see scratches and *words?* Her gaze flicked to me and her expression caved. Tears pooled her eyes as she sniffled. "H-hi, Johnny."

"What the actual fuck?" I demanded, stalking towards her. "What happened to your face, Shannon?"

She shook her head and practically collapsed against me when I reached her. "I want to go home," she sobbed, shaking violently. "I just want to go."

"It's okay – shh, just calm down." Cupping her face in my hands, I squinted my eyes and tried to make out the *lipstick* marks on her face.

*Kav's slut?*

*BJ-13?*

"Who did this to you?" Joey demanded, shoving me out of the way – or at least he attempted to. It didn't work out so well for him because I didn't move an inch. "Shan, what happened?"

"Was it her?" I asked, shaking just as much as she was now. "What am I saying – of course it was *her*."

"Who?" Mr. Twomey strangled out. "Who did this to you, Shannon?"

"Bella fucking Wilkinson," Gibsie sneered. "Who else?"

"I want her out of this school," I snarled, swinging around to glare at him. "She can't get away with this. You know what she's going through. She's supposed to be *safe* at school!"

Mr. Twomey moved towards us. "Shannon, are you saying Miss Wilkinson did this to you?"

"Back the fuck up," Joey warned, taking a protective stance in front of his sister. I didn't know what he thought old Twomey was going to do, but the lad wasn't taking any chances. He was coiled tight with barely restrained feral fury and I had a feeling the only reason he hadn't exploded already was the blonde stroking his arm. "Don't come near my sister," he added, glaring daggers at our principal. "I'm warning you."

Mr. Twomey's mouth fell open and I felt a pang of sympathy for the old man to be thrown in the deep end like he had. God knows, I knew what it felt like. Being at the end of Joey Lynch's wrath wasn't a good feeling.

Out of the corner of my eye, I spotted Bella and Cormac strolling through the courtyard towards the carpark, all smiles.

*Oh, hell fucking no!*

"You!" I roared, side-stepping Shannon. "I want a fucking word with you!"

"Johnny, don't move," Mr. Twomey warned.

"Johnny, don't—" Shannon begged.

"Cap, you're in contract," Hughie shouted.

"Think about Saturday," Gibsie called after me.

"Take the high road," Hughie added.

"Fuck your high road," I snarled, glaring after them. "And fuck them, too."

Cormac paled as I approached. "Alright, Cap?"

"What did I tell you?" I demanded, stalking straight for him. "Huh? What the fuck did I tell you about that bitch?"

"Whoa, Johnny, I have no idea what you're—"

Bang.

Cormac hit the ground like a sack of potatoes before I had a chance to raise a fist.

Confused, I swung around and locked eyes on Joey. "What the—"

"I owed you one," he explained with a shrug as he shook out his wrist. "Besides, I'm already getting arrested."

I gaped at him. "For *what*?"

"For this," he replied before lunging at Cormac.

"Get off him!" Bella screamed as she slapped and punched at Joey's head. "You dirty, little scumbag."

"Hey – don't call my boyfriend a scumbag," Aoife snarled as she barreled towards Bella. "Is this her, Shan?" she demanded. "Did she do this to you?"

"Please, just leave it," Shannon strangled out.

"Who the hell are you?" Bella hissed, glaring at Aoife.

"Oh, I'm your worst nightmare, bitch." Taking her to the ground in one fell swoop. Aoife straddled Bella. "You like terrorizing little girls?" she demanded. "Try someone your own size."

"How's your money fairing out for ya now, rich boy?" Joey sneered, grappling with Cormac on the road. "Being a scumbag has its benefits, doesn't it?"

"Think you can call my boyfriend a scumbag?" Aoife continued as she full-on punched at Bella. *Whoa, there was no palm slapping with this girl.* "Think you can bully his sister, huh? Think you're safe because you're a girl and he can't hit you back?" She reared her fist back and cracked Bella in the mouth. "Well, I can!"

"I'm calling the Gardaí!" Mr. Twomey roared. "Stop it this instant or I'll have every last one of you arrested!"

"Call the Guards and you're down a quarter of the rugby team," Hughie interjected calmly. "And looking at some serious bad press for the school. Look what she did to her." He pointed to Shannon's face. "I thought there was zero tolerance for bullying at Tommen? If so, you better change your policy because that girl's been giving Shannon hell for months." Shrugging, he added, "I'd also love to know what your policy is on stalking, because she's been tormenting Johnny day and night for a year. He's just too damn polite to say so."

"Joey, stop!" Shannon cried, running towards her brother. "Don't—"

"They're not going to do this to you," Joey snarled. "No fucking more, Shannon!"

"It wasn't him," Shannon strangled out as she pulled at her brother's shoulders. "Don't – please. You're going to get in trouble."

"Come here," I coaxed, pulling her away from the fight. "Stay back, Shan."

"Stop him," she begged, clutching my arm. "*Please!*"

"Okay, the party's over," Gibsie announced as he stepped in and dragged Joey off Cormac, giving me the side eye in the process, as if to say *WTF.*

I shrugged unashamedly. I wasn't about to break up shit. They both deserved *everything* they got and more.

"This is all my fault," Shannon choked out, shaking violently. "I shouldn't have called him—"

"No, it's not," I corrected, tucking her into my chest. "It's *her* fault. Not yours."

"Come on, baby," Joey panted breathlessly, as he dragged his girl-friend off Bella. "Come on. She's not worth it. You can't be fighting in—"

"She called you a scumbag," Aoife snarled, trying and failing to break free from her boyfriend's hold. "I'm not having it, Joe!"

"I know, baby," he coaxed, walking backwards with Aoife in his arms. "But I need you to be careful."

"Everyone, follow me to the office! I'm calling your parents," Mr. Twomey barked as he pulled out his phone and gestured for Bella and Cormac to follow him. "*All* of your parents."

"You do that," Joey sneered, watching our principal like he was a defenseless antelope that had been separated from the pack. "Be useful for something."

"Joe!" Aoife croaked out, slipping her hand into his. "You're on a warning."

"I need you to get out of here, Aoife," Joey panted, still watching Mr. Twomey as he scampered off to the office with Bella and Cormac limping after him. "You weren't here and you didn't see shit." Turning to his girlfriend, he said, "You got that?"

"What?" Aoife shook her head, eyes wide. "No, no way. I'm not leaving you—"

"Get in the car and go home, baby," he ordered. "Now." He glared at us. "Nobody's going to mention you."

"But you're going to be—"

"I'll be grand," he whispered, pressing a kiss to her forehead. "Just go, and I'll call you when I can."

# The Office

## SHANNON

Reeling, I sat outside the office on the wooden bench with Johnny, Hughie, and Gibsie. On the bench opposite us sat Bella and Cormac.

"Oh my god!" I couldn't stop the tears that were dripping down my cheeks as I watched the Gardaí take my brother away in handcuffs from the school. "Please don't take him!"

"It's okay, Shan," Joey called over his shoulder as they led him down the corridor. "I'll be grand – don't cry."

It wasn't *okay*.

*Nothing* about any of this was *okay*.

My brother was being arrested and it was all my fault. "I'm sorry, Joe," I strangled out just before he was carted out the main door by the two male Gardaí. "I'm so sorry."

"It's okay," Johnny continued to whisper over and over as he kept his arm around me. "It's going to be fine, Shan."

"I'm such a fuckup," I choked out, crying hard and ugly. "He's going to be in so much trouble."

"You've got that straight," Cormac sneered. "I'll be pressing charges on your scumbag brother."

"Back off," Johnny snarled, tensing beside me. "Or you won't be around to press charges."

"Please don't," I begged, sniffling. Rolling up the sleeves of Johnny's school jumper that I was now wearing, I wiped my cheeks and tried to get a handle of my emotions. It was close to impossible, though. I was so worried about Joey, I could hardly breathe. "My brother's going through a lot," I tried to plead. "Please don't get him in trouble."

"I don't give a shit what he's going through," Cormac snapped. "He broke my *nose*, Shannon."

"Shut the hell up, Ryan," Hughie sighed wearily. "Don't make a bad situation worse."

"He attacked me!" Cormac shot back defensively.

"And she attacked *me*," Bella sobbed.

"Because you attacked her," Johnny snarled, chest heaving, as he pointed to me. "There's only one scumbag around this place, Bella, and that's you!"

"Screw you, Johnny Kavanagh," she spat. "This is all your fault."

"You need to keep your mouth good and shut," Gibsie hissed. "Stupid, fucking girl."

"I'm a victim here," Bella wailed.

"*You're* a victim?" Gibsie shot back, sounding outraged. "Jesus Christ, I hope your parents didn't breed any more of you because you are one septic girl. The world doesn't need another one of your kind prowling around."

"Go away and find some water to drown in, Gibs," Cormac shot back, glaring at Gibsie. "Like the rest of your—"

"Back the fuck off!" both Johnny and Hughie roared in unison.

Meanwhile, Gibsie remained rigid and silent.

"Don't even *think* about going there," Johnny snarled, wholly enraged. "What the hell is wrong with you?"

"He called my girlfriend names—"

"So that justifies you saying *that*?" Johnny seethed. "Don't even think about trying to make excuses, Ryan. That's bleeding despicable."

"From here on out, we're done, Cormac," Hughie added, shaking with temper. "If you're thick enough to knock around with someone like her, then don't even bother looking in my direction. And I mean that on the pitch as well as off it."

"No skin off my nose, Biggs," Cormac sneered. "You're so far up Kav's ass, it doesn't make a difference to me—"

"Who is she?" Bella demanded then, dragging the attention back to her. "The girl who attacked me – what's her name?" Narrowing her eyes, she spat, "I know you all know who she is."

"What girl?" Gibsie replied calmly. "I didn't see a girl, did you, lads?"

"Never saw any girl," Johnny agreed. "But I did see Cormac hit Joey first."

Cormac's eyes widened in disgust. "You *liar*."

Johnny shrugged. "That's what I saw."

"Funny, I saw that, too," Gibsie offered. "He just lunged at you, Johnny – Lynchy was protecting you."

"That's what I saw," Hughie agreed. "And Mr. Twomey was standing behind Johnny. His view was obstructed so he couldn't see who threw the first punch."

"And there are no cameras in the carpark," Gibsie mused. "I guess that makes it your word against ours."

"Five against two," Hughie offered. "Funny that."

"Karma's a beautiful thing," Gibsie agreed with a smirk.

"There was six of you!" Bella hissed. "There was a *girl*."

"Nope," Gibsie replied with a shrug. "You're imagining things."

"You're a pack of liars," Bella hissed, furious.

"You do realize you caused all of this?" Hughie shot back. "Or do you just not care?"

"Leave her alone," Cormac quickly came to her defense. "She's hurt."

"She's a parasite, is what she is," Gibsie sneered. "And you'd do well to get as far away from her as possible because you're not acting like the lad we grew up with."

The sound of whistling grew closer and all six of us turned our heads just as Ronan McGarry, one of the boys from my year, turned the corner of the hallway. When his eyes landed on all of us sitting outside the principal's office, he did a double take. "What are you all doing out—"

"Keep walking, prick face," Johnny warned, bristling beside me. "And keep your bleeding mouth shut."

Ronan glared at Johnny for the longest moment before flicking his gaze to me. "Causing trouble again, Shannon?" A ghost of a malicious smirk teased his lips. "Why am I not surprised?"

"I said go!" Johnny snarled, rising to his feet. "Before I mangle you."

Ronan stumbled backwards so quickly that he dropped his school-bag, causing Gibsie to snicker.

"Ah, lad," he chuckled. "Thanks for that. I needed the laugh."

"Shag off, Gibs," Ronan growled, red-faced, as he grabbed his bag off the floor. "I'm not afraid of him—"

"Get out of here, you little pervert," Johnny's voice boomed loudly and was laced with authority, as he took a menacing step towards Ronan. "Don't think I've forgotten about what you did!"

Ronan backed all the way up the hall he'd just walked down before disappearing around the corner.

"Brilliant." Laughing hysterically, Gibsie slapped his own thigh. "I thought he was going to piss himself—"

The office door opened inwards then, causing them all to fall silent as our parents filed out – well, *their* parents.

First to emerge was Bella and Cormac's mothers. Mrs. Ryan and Cormac walked away without speaking a single word.

To my absolute shock, Mrs. Wilkinson marched over to her daughter and hissed, "Stand up." Pouting and huffing loudly, Bella stood up, dabbing her cut lip with a tissue. "Now, give me your phone."

"Mam—"

"Give. Me. Your. Phone."

Wordlessly, Bella slid her phone out of her pocket and handed it to her mother. Mrs. Wilkinson tapped furiously at the keypad, stiffening when she found what she was looking for. She looked over at me, eyes laced with guilt, and then turned back to her daughter. "Go over there and apologize for what you did to that poor girl."

*Oh god . . .*

My entire body coiled tight with dread.

I didn't want her to apologize to me.

I didn't want her to come anywhere near me ever again.

Bella groaned. "But Mam—"

"Don't push me on this, Isabella!" her mother seethed. "You're lucky

I'm not taking you down to the Garda station and handing you in myself! I've never been so disappointed in you as I am today."

"Her friend hit me," Bella squabbled. "And they know who she is—"

"I'm not surprised," Mrs. Wilkinson snapped, red-faced. "After what you did to that girl, it's a miracle her guardian isn't pressing charges. Now go over there and apologize!"

"Don't even think about it," Johnny cut in when Bella and her mother moved towards us. "Walk your daughter away from my girlfriend and keep her away," he ordered, tightening his arm around me. "Shannon doesn't want her apologies. Your daughter has done enough damage. Sorry means nothing to us. So just walk away and leave her alone."

Mrs. Wilkinson opened her mouth to say something, but then closed it again. She cast a sympathetic glance my way before dragging Bella away.

"Thanks," I whispered, melding myself into his side.

"No problem," he replied gruffly.

Next to emerge was Sinead Biggs, followed swiftly by Gibsie's mother, whose name I learned was Sadhbh.

"Oh boys," Claire's mam sighed as she wrapped her arm around Hughie's waist. "What are we going to do with you?"

"I didn't hit anyone today," Gibsie offered brightly. "I was a good boy."

"*Today* being the appropriate word," his mother replied with a sigh. Ruffling his blond hair, she added, "Come on, Bubba. Let's get you home before you find any more trouble."

"That's the thing, Mam," Gibsie replied as he bounded after her, "trouble finds *me*, not the other way around."

It wasn't until we were on our own that Johnny spoke. "When did it happen?" His voice was low and thick with emotion. Shifting sideways to face me, he choked out, "What did she do to you, baby?"

"It doesn't matter," I mumbled, feeling bone weary. I'd already explained it all to Mr. Twomey and Darren when it was our turn to speak to him in the office earlier.

"I need to know, Shan," Johnny replied. "So please . . . just *tell* me."

Exhaling a tired sigh, I explained what had happened in the bathroom with Bella and her friends, leaving nothing out. Too exhausted to censor myself, I told Johnny everything, right down to the vomiting.

"Why didn't you call me?" he asked when I was finished. "Or come find me. Shan, I would have—"

"Because you had a French test and I didn't want to get you in trouble," I whispered, knees bopping restlessly. "I know The Academy and the scouts are watching your every move right now, and I was afraid you'd get mad and retaliate, so I called Joey because I thought he would come pick me up—" My voice cracked and a huge sob tore from my throat. "I just wanted a spin home. I didn't think he would *do that*."

The door of Mr. Twomey's office opened again and this time, Mr. Kavanagh stepped out with both Darren and Mr. Twomey in tow.

"Again, I am terribly sorry for what happened," Mr. Twomey said, extending his hand to Darren. "Please, rest assured that Tommen adheres to a strict zero-tolerance for bullying policy and this matter will be dealt with immediately." When Darren didn't take his hand, Mr. Twomey's gaze flicked to me and he grimaced. "Shannon, I saw the photographs and I am very sorry."

"So, what are you doing about it?" Johnny asked in a tight tone of voice. "It's all well and good saying you're sorry, but that means nothing if you don't take action. Is Bella being expelled? What about Kelly? She was involved, too. And Tash? She's just as bad for walking away and not stopping them."

"Johnny," Mr. Twomey sighed wearily, "stay out of this."

"No!" Johnny erupted, springing to his feet. "Three of them cornered my girlfriend in the bathroom – two of them held her down and assaulted her. They're all sixth years. They're over eighteen. Shannon's a minor. They should all be done for assault."

"Johnny," I muttered, feeling another wave of shame sweep through me. "Just let it go."

"No, Shan," he shot back. "I'm not letting this go." Glaring at our principal, he hissed, "I want *justice*."

"It's not good enough," Darren shocked me by agreeing with Johnny. "My sister was brutally assaulted by two girls during school – one of whom, I learn, has been bullying her for months. My brother has been arrested for defending her when your teaching staff failed to do so. We're going through hell as it stands, something you are well aware of, and all you can say is that you're *sorry*?" Darren shook his head. "Forgive me for saying this, Mr. Twomey, but what the hell are we doing paying thousands of euros in school fees if you can't do something as basic as guarantee my sister's safety at school?"

"Bella has been suspended for the next three days," Mr. Twomey responded, cheeks flushed. "I will be bringing this incident to the attention of the board of management at our next meeting. We'll decide on the appropriate action to take then."

"Take action by *expelling* her," Johnny seethed, furious. "Screw a three-day suspension. That won't do any good. She shouldn't be let back inside this school after what she did to my girlfriend!"

"My hands are tied," Mr. Twomey replied, looking to Johnny's father for help.

"This is a mess, Seamus," Johnny's father stated calmly. "I sincerely hope the school has sufficient legal representation – and for the Wilkinson family's sake, I suggest you let them know the same. I will, of course, be offering my services to the Lynch family, and will be in touch when my client decides on the course of action *she* wishes to take – be it against Miss Wilkinson alone, or the school for their negligence and failure to safeguard a minor in their care."

Mr. Twomey's mouth fell open in surprise and I was pretty sure that his expression was a mirror image of mine and Darren's faces as we gaped at Johnny's father. "Excuse me?"

"Well, it's very clear, Seamus," Mr. Kavanagh replied in that sickly-sweet voice only people with great power used, "you were so quick to call the Gardaí and press charges on the Lynch boy for his role in the incident, that I find it only fair, and my personal responsibility, to make my services available to their family. However, given the circumstances surrounding both Lynch children, I feel I should advise you that you will have a challenge on your hands to find a judge the length and breadth of this country unsympathetic enough to their plight to convict Joey Lynch – and believe me, I know several of those judges." Adjusting his tie, Mr. Kavanagh smiled. "Have a good day, sir."

Johnny grinned at his father.

Meanwhile, Darren and I both continued to gape in wonder.

"Let's go," Mr. Kavanagh instructed in the cool, calm, and collected tone of his, as he turned to his son. "Your mother needs me to pick up pepper sauce for dinner, and I have to take a trip to the Garda Station before I—"

"Wait, wait, wait," Mr. Twomey strangled out. "Mr. Kavanagh, can you step back into my office please?"

Johnny's father made a big deal of checking his watch and sighing before reluctantly nodding. "I can give you fifteen minutes."

"Yes, yes, thank you." Mr. Twomey sagged in relief and scurried back into his office.

"Shooting fish in a barrel, Da?" Johnny quipped.

Chuckling softly, Mr. Kavanagh winked at his son before following Mr. Twomey. Pausing in the doorway of the office, he turned to Darren and said, "I'll have your brother home by ten tonight."

"Thank you so much." Exhaling heavily, Darren strode over to Mr. Kavanagh and extended his hand. "And I'm very sorry for the way my family—"

"Irrelevant," Johnny's father replied, shaking Darren's hand. "We all need a little mercy sometimes." Flicking his sharp gaze to Johnny, he said, "Bring that pepper sauce home to your mother before you go to training, son." He looked to me then and gave me a soft smile. "I hope one day we will meet under happy circumstances, Shannon." With that, Mr. Kavanagh sauntered into the office, letting the door swing shut behind him.

"He's going to torture him," Johnny chuckled, as he strolled over to where I was sitting and pulled me to my feet. "Don't worry, Shan," he added, wrapping an arm around my waist. "He'll get this sorted."

I blew out a ragged breath. "I can't believe he did that for us."

"Neither can I," Darren muttered, rubbing his jaw.

"I told you my parents love you," Johnny coaxed, taking my hand in his. "Do you believe me now?"

Trembling, I squeezed his hand and sagged against his chest. "I'm sorry."

"Don't even say that," he whispered, wrapping me up in his arms.

"I smell like fish," I warned him. "You'll get it on your clothes, too."

"I don't care," he whispered, dropping a kiss to my hair. "I love fish, I love you, and I still want to eat you for dinner."

"Not as much as chicken," I sniffled.

"I fucking *love* chicken," he agreed with a chuckle. "Everything's okay, Shan." Stepping back, he cupped my face in his hands, and stared down at me. "Do you hear me?"

I shrugged weakly. "I hear you."

"You're going to be okay," he said gruffly, blue eyes locked on mine. "And so is Joey."

"I don't think I'm going to make dinner tonight, Johnny," I squeezed out.

"That's okay," he replied, dropping his hands to rest on my shoulders. "We'll do it another time." Stroking his thumbs over my collarbone, he added, "I'm going to make this right for you."

I sagged against him. "Doesn't matter."

"It matters," he corrected, pulling me back into a hug. "And it's never going to happen to you again."

"I'm just so scared for Joey," I confessed, burying my face in his chest. "I don't want him to be in trouble over me."

"My Da will get it cleared up." He pressed a kiss to the top of my head. "Seriously, if you knew the half of what he's managed to drag Gibs out of down through the years, you wouldn't be worrying. He'll clear it all up, Shan. He'll make it go away."

"Really?" I sniffled. "You're sure?"

"Hundred percent," Johnny replied. "He meant what he said – Joey *will* be home tonight."

Relief washed through me but I was afraid to absorb it. I was *petrified* of getting my hopes up only to have more bad news thrown my way.

"I misjudged you," Darren's voice cut through the air. Stunned, I spun around to find he was looking at Johnny. "I was wrong about you," he added, tone hoarse. "And I owe you an apology."

"Yeah, you were wrong," Johnny said tightly. "I'm not the person your ma makes me out to be." Sighing heavily, he added, "But I don't need an apology."

"Well, you have it all the same," Darren replied wearily.

"And I accept it," Johnny stunned me by saying. He didn't need to accept anything from Darren. He'd been treated terribly by both my brother and my mother. "No hard feelings," Johnny added, giving my brother a clipped nod. "But I'm still not going anywhere."

"Yeah." Darren sighed. "I'm beginning to gather that."

Johnny sniffed. "Just so we're clear."

"We're clear, Kavanagh," Darren replied before turning to me and asking, "Are you coming with me?"

*Am I?*

*Was he giving me an actual choice?*

I frowned. "Huh?"

"Are you coming home now?" Darren repeated slowly. "Or later?"

"I, uh . . ." Shaking my head, I looked at my brother and said, "Now."

"You sure?" Johnny asked, stiffening behind me. "I can take you home."

"You have training," I whispered. "And I need to go home and get cleaned up."

"I don't have to go, Shannon," Johnny told me, tone uncertain, eyes flicking between me and Darren. "I can stay with you."

I wanted to scream *yes*, but I stopped myself. Johnny was on track with his training. He spent most of his days staring longingly at his phone. I knew he was expecting that call from the Irish coaches to come soon, and I couldn't expect him to railroad his life every time something happened to me. This wasn't my first disaster and it wouldn't be my last.

*Besides, when he goes, you're going to have to do this on your own.*
*Because he* is *leaving, Shannon . . .*

"I need to help my brothers." I gave him a watery smile. "I'll call you later."

Johnny didn't look convinced, but he didn't argue with me. Instead, he pressed a kiss to my forehead, nodded stiffly, and stepped back. I felt the absence of his touch in the deepest part of my soul as I walked away with Darren.

# Persuasive Fathers

## JOHNNY

Shannon blamed me for what happened today. I fucking *knew* she did, and the worst part of it was knowing she was right. It *was* my fault. They did that to her because of me. I watched her leave school with her brother earlier, knowing full well that I needed to step in and say something to make it right, but I didn't have the words. I didn't know how to fix this for her.

Jesus Christ, I was so mad I could practically taste it.

I went to training this evening for no other reason than if I had to sit at home alone with my thoughts and feeling useless, I would lose it. It didn't help one bit to curb the fury thrashing around inside of me. I couldn't concentrate worth a damn. Throughout training, my mind was stuck on Shannon. Physio was the same. I couldn't get her out of my head. I had a little over four days to prepare for what would be the most important meeting of my life and, still, I couldn't get my head in the game.

*Fucking Bella.*

I knew I messed up letting her go home with Darren, but short of shoving her in my car and driving away, what could I do? She said she wanted to go with him. It was a lie. Shannon never wanted to go *home*.

Doubt was setting in, unfamiliar and unnerving, and like usual, I began to overthink everything. I had an issue with my brain. It moved too quickly, thought up too much crazy shite, whizzed around too fast. Most of the time, I managed to remain in control with routine and structure, but I was struggling today. That phone call this morning, added with what had happened at school, had thrown my mind into a spin. Everything was up in a heap, my braincells were shot to shite, and I was second-guessing everything.

When I finally parked up at the back of my house a little after nine that night, I was still bursting with energy. No amount of drills, laps, and practice plays had doused the fury blistering inside of me.

Pissed off and anxious, I grabbed my gear bag off the passenger seat and stalked inside, with every intention of hoofing down the contents of whatever Mam had cooking on the stove. However, my appetite evaporated and my feet faltered when I stepped into the kitchen and saw *Joey* slumped at the island with his head in his hands. Mam was sitting on the stool opposite him.

Pausing in the doorway, I watched as she pushed a cup towards him. He didn't take it.

"I think it does matter, Joey," Mam told him in that tone of voice she used when she was coaxing something out of us when we were kids. *We* being me and Gibsie, because he was the closest thing I had to a brother. "And I think you matter, too."

"You're wrong," Joey replied in a voice so low I had to strain to hear him. He glared at the coffee cup in front of him, jaw clenched, expression mistrusting and wary. "So just *give up.*"

"Joey," Mam said gently. "You've been traveling down a very long road, love. Maybe it's time to rest those feet and let someone else carry the load for you?"

Silence.

"Let me help you."

More silence.

"Let me save you, Joey."

"You can't," he strangled out, cracking his knuckles anxiously. "There's nothing left to save, Mrs. Kavanagh. So please just *stop.*"

Clearing my throat, I dropped my gear bag at the door and walked in. "You're out."

"Yep," Joey muttered, not bothering to lift his head.

"Oh, love, you're home." Mam offered me a smile, but it was laced with concern. "How was training?"

I gaped at her. Shit, this was bad. She *never* asked about training. "Grand," I replied warily. "What's going on?"

"Are you hungry, Johnny?" Mam asked, ignoring my question as she moved for the stove. "I made roast beef with pepper sauce."

Shaking my head, I walked over to the island and pulled up a stool. "Jesus," I muttered, taking in the swelling under Joey's right eye. "Cormac got you good."

"Yeah, and I got you good," he shot back, gesturing to my busted lip. "Sorry about that." Grimacing, he added, "Poor communication skills."

I shrugged it off. "So, what's happening now?"

"I'm in a bit of shit, Kav," Joey deadpanned. "That's what's happening now."

"Yeah, I gathered that much." Resting my elbows on the marble countertop, I leaned forward and studied his guarded expression. "Are you being charged?"

"He's not going to be charged with anything," Mam answered for Joey, tone confident. "Your father has made sure of that."

My brows shot up. "You're off the hook?"

Joey shrugged, looking at a complete loss. "Apparently." He gave me this strange look then and I swear I could see terror in his eyes before the shutters clamped back down and he looked away. "According to your parents."

"Where's your ma?" I asked then, bracing myself for the backlash I knew would come with a question like that. "Did she go down to the station for you?"

Joey shot me a look that said *what the fuck do you think, asshole*, and in that moment, I felt a surge of sympathy flood my chest. "She's working," he explained tightly. "Couldn't get through to her phone."

"That was Principal Twomey," Dad announced, breezing into the kitchen with his phone in his hand. "The school board held an emergency meeting tonight."

I stiffened. "And?"

"And Bella will not be returning to Tommen to finish out the school year," Dad replied.

Joey blew out a harsh breath. "Thank Christ for that."

"She will be allowed to sit her leaving cert in one of the local schools, but she will not be welcome back at Tommen. Her locker has been cleared out, her phone has been confiscated, and all photos she took of Shannon have been erased," Dad explained, sliding his phone into his pocket. "Natasha O Sullivan and Kelly Dunne have both been given a week's suspension for their roles in the incident – though, due to Shannon's statements, and following a lot of discussion, it has been decided by the board that both girls will return to Tommen after their suspension, and *will* be permitted to sit their exams there."

"That's bullshit!" Joey and I both hissed in unison and then turned to frown at each other.

"Pick your battles, boys," Dad replied. "This is a good result." Mam handed Dad a cup of coffee and he kissed her cheek before turning his attention back to us. "Take emotion out of the equation and look at the result for what it is: a win."

"And Cormac?" I said, locking eyes with my father. "How'd you manage to pull that off? He was hell-bent on pressing charges earlier."

Dad winked. "With a great deal of persuasion."

"Well, shite." I blew out a breath, impressed. "Remind me never to go against you."

"It's not all good news," Dad warned, turning his steely-blue gaze on Joey. "You have been expelled from Ballylaggin Community College. Apparently, you were on your final warning following seven suspensions this year alone and countless others tracing all the way back to your first week of first year." Dad pulled at his tie, loosening it. "I did what I could, Joey, but they're not budging. Committing an act of violence against another school while wearing your BCS uniform is against their policy and punishable by immediate expulsion."

Joey shrugged wearily. "It's okay."

"*Okay*?" I gaped at him. "But you're supposed to sit your leaving cert next month?"

"Doesn't matter," he muttered.

"Yeah, it does," I shot back. "It does fucking matter."

"I wasn't going anywhere anyway," he replied. "So it's all the same to me."

"What the hell, Joey?" I snapped. "This is important." Turning to my father, I asked, "Is there anything you can do for him?"

Dad sighed. "My hands are tied, son. Joey here has a record for violence that makes Gibsie look like a saint. They're unwilling to negotiate having him return to school – not even to sit his exams."

"What about Tommen?" Mam interjected.

"Tommen is private, sweetheart," Dad replied.

"Another public school then?" I offered.

"Not in the area," Dad replied. "Nothing public, at least."

"Then the city?"

"No school will touch me with a ten-foot barge pole," Joey said flatly. "Your dad's right, Kavanagh. My record is shocking, no one's going to want me, and it doesn't matter anyway, because I don't care. So don't waste your breath talking about it."

I looked to my father who confirmed this with a small nod.

"Jesus," I muttered, dropping my head in my hands. "What a disaster."

"Can I use your bathroom, please?" Joey asked as he rose from the stool and looked at my mother.

"Of course, you can, Joey," Mam replied, tone thick. "You don't have to ask, love."

Nodding stiffly, he walked towards the hallway door, only to hesitate in the doorway. "Thank you," he said in a low voice, glancing over his shoulder. "For everything."

"No problem, Joey," Dad replied. "Remember what we said. The offer's on the table and it has no expiration date."

Nodding stiffly, Joey muttered, "I'll think about it," before disappearing down the hallway. The sound of the front door slamming reverberated through the house a few seconds later.

"Don't," Dad warned, stopping Mam who was moving for the door. "Just let him be, Edel."

"Who's going to take care of him?" Mam demanded, swinging around to glare at my father. Her eyes were full of unshed tears and her voice was thick with emotion. "Well? His own mother couldn't be arsed to show up to the Garda Station to check on him, John, and his father's a psychopath." Her shoulders sagged and she sighed heavily. "There's something very special about that boy, but he's lost, and if somebody doesn't step up and do something, he'll never find his way back."

"I hear you, sweetheart, I really do. But he's legally an adult."

"He's a *child*, John," Mam strangled out, sounding fiercely protective. "He's a broken, little boy, trapped in a grown man's body, and he needs *us*."

"Edel, I know—"

"They're not a pick and mix," Mam continued to rant, not giving my father a chance to speak. "You don't get to pick and choose your favorites and leave the rest in the box. There's five of them, and broken, bent, or out of shape, I want them *all*!"

"The Lynchs?" Awareness hit me smack in the chest and my jaw fell open. "You're taking them?"

"I'm taking them," Mam confirmed with a determined gleam in her eye. "All of them."

"Jesus," Dad muttered, running a hand through his hair in clear exasperation, "I don't know how I've survived living in a house with two bulldozers."

"Great food and even greater sex, that's how," Mam shot back, not missing a beat.

Dad smirked. "That's true."

"Hold the fuck up," I strangled out. "Someone please explain to me what the hell is happening here."

"Language," Mam scolded.

"If you knew the half of what was going in my head right now, you wouldn't be giving out to me for saying the word fuck," I growled. "Someone start talking."

"Do you remember when we lived in Dublin?" Dad began. "The little girl who lived with us for eighteen months?"

I gaped at him. "*No*. What little girl?"

"He was only a toddler, John," Mam explained, sinking down on the stool next to Dad. "He wouldn't remember Rayna."

"Who?" I gaped at them. "Who the hell is Rayna?" I narrowed my eyes. "Did you two smoke something with Joey?"

"We fostered a child in Dublin," Mam explained. "Her name was Rayna. She was a year older than you, and you were mad about her."

"I find that hard to believe considering I have no fucking clue who you're talking about," I muttered under my breath.

"If you start listening to me instead of your own voice, then maybe you'll start understanding," Mam snapped.

Huffing out a breath, I gestured for her to carry on.

"We had Rayna from the age of two until just before her fourth birthday," Dad jumped in and said. "We classed her as your sister," he added. "There was no difference – not to us."

"What happened to her?"

"She was returned to her birth parents," my father replied and Mam sniffled. "It was very hard for your mother," he added, wrapping an arm around Mam. "So, we made the decision not to foster any more children. It was too hard for us – handing Rayna back after spending so much time with her."

"We considered her our daughter," Mam whispered. "Just the same as we consider you our son."

"Just the same as you consider me your *son*?" *What the hell?* I scratched the back of my head, trying to take this all in. "Are you trying to tell me that I'm adopted?"

Dad threw his head back and laughed. "No, Johnny, you're one hundred percent the fruit of my loins."

"And my eggs," Mam offered with a smirk.

"You just cost a small fortune to cook up in a lab," he added, still laughing to himself.

"Worth every penny." Mam winked. "Our little test tube baby."

*What the . . .* "That's a fucking horrendous thing to tell me," I choked out, outraged. "You make it sound like they cooked me up in a microwave and sold me down a backstreet alley!" They both laughed like my humble embryo beginnings was a big joke to them. "You know what?" I huffed out a breath. "I reckon I *was* adopted."

"The point we're trying to make, Johnny," Dad said, struggling to sober his features as he smothered his laugh, "is that we have experience working with the foster care system."

"And we want to foster Shannon and her brothers," Mam came right out and told me. "We've been approved." Grabbing an envelope off the counter, she thrust it at me. "It just came through this morning."

"Tact, baby," Dad groaned, dropping his head in his hand. "In sensitive situations, you need to use a little more tact."

"You want to foster Shannon?" I asked, quite frankly stunned.

"Yes," Mam replied, not missing a beat. "And Ollie, Sean, Tadhg, and Joey."

"Wh—" I shook my head, trying to figure this out. "When did you plan this?"

"March," Mam replied.

"No," Dad coaxed. "We discussed it in March."

"We applied in March," Mam corrected. "The day after I found Shannon and Joey in our house."

"And you didn't tell me?" I demanded. "Why wouldn't you *tell* me?"

"We didn't want to get your hopes up. It's a long process, and we weren't sure if we would be approved, given our stage in life and our careers," Dad explained.

"You're forty-six and forty-nine," I shot back. "You're hardly over the hill."

"We also didn't want you to tell Shannon," Dad added.

"Why *wouldn't* I tell Shannon?" I asked, gaping at him.

"Because this is sensitive," Dad replied. "There's a process we have to follow, son. We can't just barge into their home and take them—" He paused and gave me a thoughtful look. "Well, *we* can't," he affirmed, gesturing to himself and Mam.

Cheeks reddening, I shrugged. "I have no regrets."

"And so you shouldn't, love," Mam agreed, reaching across the counter to pat my hand. "I would've done the exact same thing in your position."

"Jesus, Edel," Dad muttered. "At least give me a fighting chance to put the lad on the right track."

"Well, I would," she huffed. "It's that simple, love."

Shaking his head, Dad turned his attention back to me. "We have everything in order, son," he said. "But we won't make a move unless you're one hundred percent on board with this."

"When you say make a move?" I eyed him warily. "What are you planning?"

"There's a severe case of negligence in that home," Dad replied. "It's blatant child abuse, and your mother's not willing to turn a blind eye to it – and neither am I. So, if I have to play dirty in order prove it and get those children out of that environment, then that's exactly what I'll do."

"Shite," I muttered. "You're serious."

"Deadly," Mam agreed. "They are victims of trauma. Those children need a family. They need *healthy* guardians, and a stable environment where their needs are met without the fear of backlash or emotional abuse. They need to be given the opportunity to just be *children*. Their mother can't do that for them, and the system can't promise to keep them all together, but *we can*."

"But like I said, this is your decision, too," Dad interjected. "We won't do anything without your blessing."

"You don't need my blessing," I choked out, voice thick with emotion. "I want her – and I'm not talking about sex or any of that teenage shite you're thinking, Ma," I hurried to add. "I want *her*. I need her safe."

Mam sighed sadly. "I know, Johnny, love—"

"No, you don't," I said hoarsely. "I love that girl. Like I *really* fucking *love* her, and I can't cope with knowing she's in that house right now. I lose sleep worrying about her." Blowing out a shaky breath, I said, "I got a call off Dennehy today. They're coming down to see me this Saturday. I'll more than likely know by the end of the week if I'm in or not—"

"What?" Mam blurted, eyes wide. "Oh my god."

"That's fantastic news, Johnny." Dad beamed. "I'm so proud you—"

"No, it's not. It's not fantastic news, Da. It's terrifying," I choked out, frustrated. "For *months* I've been worrying myself to death over how I'm supposed to leave her if I get the call up," I admitted gruffly. "And now that it's right around the corner, less than a bleeding month away, I know that I can't do it."

Dad frowned. "What are you saying, Johnny?"

"I'm saying I can't leave her in that house, Da. Not with that woman, and not with him sniffing around. I *can't* walk away, not for an entire month, not knowing whether she's safe or not, so if there's a chance I can get her out of that place, then I'll take it." I looked at my parents. "Save her." Swallowing deeply, I added, "Save them all."

Mam's eyes blazed with heat when she said, "We will, love."

"I can't *not* tell Shannon about this," I warned my parents. "We don't keep secrets from each other."

"We're not expecting you to keep anything from Shannon, son," Dad replied. "We both know you're a hopeless liar."

"The cat would be out of the bag in an hour," Mam agreed, smiling at my father.

I glared at them. "I'm not that bad."

They both smirked back at me.

"I'm *not*," I defended. "I can lie just fine."

"Badly," Mam mused.

"You're an open book, Johnny," Dad agreed with a chuckle. "And that's a good way to be."

"No, no, no, I pulled the wool over your eyes plenty of times with my adductor," I argued. "And my doctors, trainers, and half of The Academy." Mam's eyes narrowed and I knew I'd shot myself in the foot. "Yeah, that was a bad example," I muttered sheepishly. *You bleeding eejit.* "Forget I said anything."

"The only one you were lying to in that situation was yourself, son," Dad shot back. "And the only one you were hurting with that lie was also yourself."

Shoulders sagging, I nodded in defeat. "Yeah, I know."

"I wanted to have Shannon over for dinner this evening so we could talk to her," Mam said, thankfully steering the conversation away from my less than stellar discretions. "We wanted to ask her how she would feel about the possibility of coming to live with us."

I didn't know about Shannon, but I knew how I felt: fucking *ecstatic*.

"But this will be a slow process," Dad said, always the voice of reason in our house. "Don't lose the run of yourselves here, guys. It's not going to happen overnight, and they might not *want* to be with us. There's a lot of legal hoops we'll have to jump through before we come close to crossing that bridge, so keep the head." He gave Mam a knowing look. "And don't bulldoze."

# Go To Sleep

## SHANNON

When my mother came in from work earlier and Darren and I explained what had happened at school, she collapsed in a heap on the floor, crying and wailing. After a few minutes of watching my brother trying to console her, I just stepped around them both and went up to my room.

I couldn't handle her anymore, I realized. The patience I used to be able to call on was depleting at a rapid rate, and every time she cried, I just wanted to scream. I knew that was bad and it made me a terrible person, but I couldn't help it. I could barely tolerate being in the same room as my mother anymore.

Patricia arrived to the house a little after six o' clock, and by then Darren had managed to get Mam to pull herself together. She'd asked all her questions, filled in all her notes, clicked her tongue, snapped her heels, and left shortly after.

Numb, I had returned to my room, clutching my phone and praying for mercy for my brother. Aoife had texted me at least thirty times throughout the evening, asking for updates, and every time I'd replied with a 'nothing yet' a little piece of me died. When ten o' clock came and went, the anxiety I had been feeling all evening skyrocketed to the point where I couldn't move a muscle.

*Mr. Kavanagh said ten o' clock.*

It was almost eleven now, and I was still sitting on my bed, watching the clock tick by, waiting for him to come home.

The sound of a key turning in the lock filled my ears and I sprang off my bed. Pulling out my phone, I typed out a quick text to Aoife.

S: He's back.

A: Oh thank god . . . I'm on my way.

Tossing my phone down on my bed, I moved at top speed through the landing and down the staircase. The moment my eyes landed on Joey closing the front door behind him, a huge swell of relief washed over me. Riddled with emotion, I stumbled down the last three steps and threw my arms around him. "You're back!" I pressed my cheek to his back and exhaled a ragged breath. "Thank god."

"It's okay, Shan," he mumbled, words slightly slurred. Patting the hand that I had wrapped around him, he kept his head down as he slipped around me and moved for the kitchen. "It's all good."

"Wait—" Catching ahold of his hand, I pulled him back. "Look at me."

He didn't.

Fear trickled down my spine.

"Joey." I pulled harder on his hand. "Look at me."

Reluctantly, he did as I asked and my heart sank.

"Joe." Tightening my hold on his hand, I stared up at his bloodshot eyes in despair. "*Why?*"

"Just get off my back, Shan," Joey grumbled, yanking his hand away to run through his hair. "I'm fine." Shaking his head, he turned and stalked into the kitchen, ignoring Mam and Darren who were sitting at the table.

"Joey!" Mam sucked in a sharp breath. "Oh, thank god."

"Mother," he drawled sarcastically. "You're keeping well?"

Darren jumped to his feet and closed the space between them, dragging our brother into a fierce hug. Joey remained rigid the entire time, hands balled into fists at his sides, not hugging him back. Pulling back, Darren frowned. "What's wrong with you? Why are you shaking?" Cupping his cheek with one hand, Darren inspected his eyes before releasing a growl. "For fuck's sake, Joey!" Furious, he roughly shoved him away and paced the floor. "What the hell is the matter with you?"

"What's wrong?" Mam croaked out.

"What's *wrong*?" Darren spun around to glare at her. "What's wrong is your son is back on drugs!"

Mam's eyes widened. "W-what?"

Shaking his head, Joey moved to the fridge, pulling out his usual can of Coke and the packet of cooked ham for his sandwich, dutifully ignoring Darren and Mam as he went.

"Is this true?" Mam demanded, springing to her feet. "Joey?"

"I'm not back on drugs," Joey grumbled.

"Yeah, because you were never *off* them to begin with, were you?" Darren demanded.

Joey rolled his eyes. "You're all overreacting."

"You're high," Darren spat. "*Again.*"

"And you're an asshole," Joey countered. "Again."

"What are you *doing*, Joey?" Mam hissed, stalking towards him. Grabbing the can of Coke out of his hand, she slammed it down on the counter and shook her head. "Why would you put that stuff in your body again?"

"You're one to talk," he shot back, laughing humorlessly. "Drowning yourself in Prozac and Valium."

"*Prescribed* to me by a doctor," Mam choked out. "Not the thugs from the terrace."

"Okay, Mam." He rolled his eyes again. "Whatever you say."

"Is it Shane Holland?" Mam growled. "Is he sniffing around again?"

"Jesus Christ, what do you care?" Joey hissed. "Everyone get off my fucking back."

"No, I won't get off your back," Darren barked. "You're back on drugs, you've been expelled from school, you're off the hurling team—" His words broke off and he threw his hands up. "You are ruining your life!"

"I don't have a life!" Joey roared, dropping the packet of ham he was trying to open. "I've never had a life."

"Well, life or not, if you keep this up, you're going to turn into him," Darren snarled. "You're going to end up becoming the one thing you hate most in the world."

"Darren, shut up!" Swallowing the lump in my throat, I rushed over to him. "Joey, shh, it's okay." I was watching his downward spiral and felt more helpless than I had when our father roamed the house. "Don't listen to him, okay? It's not true. You're going to be okay—"

"Stop fucking saying that, Shannon!" he strangled out, red-faced. "Nothing's okay. *Nothing*!" Running his hands through his hair in frustration, he choked out another humorless laugh. "You know, I sat in that cell for hours, thinking *how* did this happen to me—" his voice broke and he dragged in a trembling breath before continuing. "How did I end up the way I am – all fucked up in the head? But then I called you," he added, lip wobbling, as he locked eyes on Mam. "I called you to come help me and you *didn't* pick up." A lone tear trickled down his cheek. "And then I knew. I said to myself, *that's why*. That's how I turned out like this." Sniffling, he locked eyes on Mam. "Because you *broke* me!"

Mam choked out a sob. "That's not true." Shaking her head, she hissed, "Take it back."

"You fucked my head up worse than he *ever* did," Joey roared into her face. "He hurt me, but you *wrecked* me. He used his fists, but you?" Joey tapped his finger against his temple. "You got in my *head*. You *broke* my mind. I don't work right anymore and it's because your voice is stuck in my head. The sound of you crying and begging me to help you is all I can hear. Every time I close my eyes, you're there. In my head. Crying for me. Begging me. Screaming '*Save me, Joey. Save me*'. But I couldn't ever save you, Mam. I couldn't save you because you didn't *want* me to! You *wanted* him to be here! You *wanted* all of this to happen—"

Mam's hand shot out so fast that Joey didn't have a chance to react before her palm smacked against his cheek loudly. "Don't you dare blame me!" she strangled out. "I did everything I could for you and your brothers and sister."

"You did everything you could for *him*," Joey hissed. "You can't lie to me, remember? I see right through you—"

Mam slapped him again, harder this time, so hard in fact, that Joey's face turned sideways from the contact.

"Mam!" Darren choked out. "What are you *doing*? Don't slap him."

I froze, barely breathing, waiting in fearful anticipation.

*Walk away, Joe,* I willed him in my mind. *Just walk away.*

"And *I'm* the one turning into him?" Joey asked in a deathly quiet tone of voice. "I'm not living like this anymore." Shaking his head, he stormed out of the kitchen, taking the staircase three steps at a time. "I'm done!"

"Joey, stop . . . wait – *wait*!" Scrambling after him, I chased after him only to pause in the doorway of his bedroom when I saw him throwing clothes into a gear bag. "What are you doing?"

"I can't stay here," was all he replied, his voice barely more than a broken whisper as he pulled out drawers and grabbed random items of clothing from them. Tears were dripping down his cheeks as he filled the bag. "I'm sorry." Clenching his eyes shut, he shuddered and continued to pack. "I'm going to explode if I stay in this house."

"You mean for the night?" I croaked out, shaking. "You'll go to Aoife's and come back tomorrow, right?"

He didn't answer me.

"Joey, please—"

"I'm *sorry*," he strangled out, tossing a few pairs of socks on top of the bag before zipping it closed. "I've tried, but I *can't* do this!"

"Joey, please!" Desperate to stop him, I grabbed his sleeve and pulled him to a stop. "What about me?"

"What about *me*?" he roared back in my face, green eyes filled with tears. A huge sob tore through him and his voice cracked. "What about *me*, Shannon?" Tossing his bag over his shoulder, he sniffled and wiped his eyes roughly with the back of his hand, before shoving past me. "What about *me*?"

"I love you!" I cried hoarsely. "*I do.* I love you so much, Joe." Tears clouded my vision and I roughly batted them away. "I *care* about you. You're important to *me*. We can figure this out," I sobbed, knotting my hand in his hoodie and dragging him back to me. "We can get through this together. You don't need to do—"

"Listen." Inhaling a steady breath, he clenched his eyes shut and I watched as tears fell from his lashes. "I need you to take care of *yourself*, okay? I need you to do that for me." Clutching the back of my head, he stepped forward and pressed a kiss to my forehead. "Don't depend on her, or Darren, or anyone else, because in the end, the world will let you down. *They* will all let you down."

"And you?" I choked out, tears flowing freely down my cheeks now. "Does that include you?"

"Especially me," he strangled out before brushing past me and moving for the stairs.

"Where's he going?" Tadhg's voice filled my ears and I swung around to see him and Ollie standing in their bedroom doorway. "Is he leaving us?"

"Forever?" Ollie whispered, eyes shining with tears. "But he can't go."

Wiping my eyes, I ran for the staircase, desperate to stop my brother from leaving. "Joey, don't go!"

"Joey, think about this," Darren was saying when I reached the bottom step. He had his back to the front door, blocking Joey's path. "Don't rush out. Just sleep on it, and we can talk about it in the morning when you have a clear head."

"I can't do this, Darren," Joey choked out. "Get out of the way."

"Joey, no – talk to me."

"Get out of my way, Darren," Joey repeated, shaking all over. "Now."

Devastated, I looked around aimlessly and spotted Mam in the kitchen. She was sitting on her chair with a cigarette in hand. "Do something," I begged from the hallway. "Mam, say something. *Please.* Stop him!"

She looked straight through me like I wasn't even there.

"Joey, don't go," Ollie begged, running down the stairs. "Please."

"You swore," Tadhg cried harshly. "You fucking promised you wouldn't leave us!"

"O-ee," Sean wailed as he shimmied down the steps on his bottom. "O-ee!"

A huge shudder rolled through Joey and he dropped his head. "I'm so sorry."

"*Stay*, Joey," Darren whispered. "I can't do this without you."

Tipping his head back up, he looked at Darren. "You're going to have to." Brushing him out of the way, he pulled the door open. "Don't let them down."

The minute the door slammed shut behind Joey, our little brothers began to scream and wail so loudly that I couldn't hear what Darren was saying as he tried console and coax them back upstairs.

Stricken down with panic, I ran for the door, refusing to let this happen – refusing to watch him leave. Yanking the door open, I ran outside only to stumble over my own legs when my eyes landed on Aoife. Her car was parked across the drive of our house and she was in her pajamas, leaning against the driver's door of her car, blocking Joey's way.

"You were going to leave without telling me?" she demanded hoarsely as her long blonde hair blew around her face. "I'm not even worth a fucking goodbye?"

Joey looked broken as he stood in front of her, his gear bag shouldered on his back, and his head down.

"Look at me!" she screamed. "Goddammit, Joey Lynch, you better look at me!"

"Aoife, please," he whispered, shaking his head. "Just let me *go*."

"I can't," she cried, sniffling. "I *won't*!"

"I have *nothing* to give you!" he roared brokenly. "I'm not good for you. Why can't you get that into your head?"

"I don't care about stuff, Joey," she strangled out as she wrapped her arms around his waist and clung to him. "I only want you."

"I'm done, Aoife." Shaking his head, he held his hands up. "I'm done dragging you down with me."

"Please . . . "

"I can't." Sniffling, he moved her hands away from his body. "I'm so sorry," he whispered, stepping around her.

"Don't go," she screamed after him. "*Please.* Please don't go. Joey! *Joey!* I love you!"

"I know," he choked out, not looking back, as he walked away. "And it's not *good* for you to love me."

"Joey, I need you—"

"No, you don't. You need to let me go, Aoife," he roared. "That's what you need to do."

"What about the—"

"Just go home and don't come back here. Do yourself a favor and forget about me!"

I watched in horror as Aoife's legs gave out beneath her. Collapsing on the ground with a thud, she shoved her hands in her hair and screamed. "Come back!"

Numb to the bone, I hurried over to kneel beside her. "I'm sorry." Wrapping my arms around her shoulders, I hugged her tightly. "I'm so sorry."

She turned her face into my neck and cried hard and ugly, shaking so badly that I was afraid she was going to have a seizure. "Make him come back," she begged, wrapping her arms around her stomach. "Please! I need him."

*Me too* . . . "Shh." Pushing her hair back off her face, I held her tightly, whispering, "It's okay," over and over in her ear.

But I was a liar.

Because as my brother disappeared from sight, I knew nothing would ever be *okay* again.

"I'm going to go look for him," Darren said quietly, and I hadn't even realized he had come outside. With his car keys in hand, he rounded the garden wall and walked over to his Volvo. "You should go inside, Shan." He pulled open the driver's door before adding, "And you should go home, Aoife."

"Please find him, Darren," I choked out.

"I will," he replied, before climbing into his car and closing the door. Sniffling, Aoife slowly pulled herself to her feet. I watched as she dusted down the back of her fluffy, yellow pajama bottoms in rigid, robotic movements. "I'm going to go now," she said in a hollow tone of voice. "Goodbye, Shannon."

"Bye, Aoife."

Without another word, she climbed into her old, battered Opal Corsa and drove away.

I waited for Darren to pull away from the house in his Volvo before I dropped my head in my hands, right there on the ground, and let myself cry. I cried hard and ugly, unable to contain myself a second longer.

I cried for my broken home, for my fucked-up family, for my little brothers, but mostly I cried for Joey, for self-destructing and detonating the one good thing he had in his life.

A little while later, I heard a car engine in the distance, coming closer, bright lights lighting up the dark street. When it parked up outside the house, I couldn't stop the spark of hope from springing to life inside of me.

Sniffling, I wiped my cheeks with my hands and stood up. "Joey?" I called out, straining to see who was behind the tinted windows. "Is that you?"

The driver's door opened and he stepped out, all blond hair and smiles.

Except it wasn't Joey's blond hair, and it wasn't his smile.

*No . . .*

"Hello, Shannon."

The air escaped my lungs in a pained whoosh and I sagged, feeling my heart stop dead in my chest before restarting with a violent thud. "N-no." Shaking my head, I staggered backwards only to lose my footing and land on the ground in a heap. "You're n-not supposed to b-be here."

Dad stepped into the garden and walked towards me. "I live here, remember?"

Fear exploded in my chest, paralyzing my limbs and locking me into place.

"Come on." Stopping in front of me, he glanced down at me, eyes bloodshot, body swaying, and smiled. "Give me your hand," he said, holding his out to me. "You should be in bed." The smell of whiskey hit my senses like a tidal wave, bringing with it a tsunami of pain and memories. "I'll help you to bed."

*He's back to finish you off.*

*You should have kept your mouth shut.*

*Get away now, Shannon!*

Jumping into action, I pulled myself onto my hands and knees and half-crawled, half-stumbled towards the front door, with my heart pounding so hard it hurt. "Help!" I screamed, slamming my hand down on the door handle and falling into the front hall on my hands and knees. "Mam!" I shouted, gasping for air as my skin crawled with the familiar feeling of dread. "Mammy!"

"What?" Mam came barreling out of the kitchen, only to halt in her tracks when she saw who was standing in the doorway behind me. "Oh my god." She pressed a hand to her chest and staggered backwards.

"Hello, Marie."

"Mam." Shaking violently, I scrambled across the floor on my hands and knees and clung to her leg. "Mam!"

"Teddy," Mam croaked out, shaking as much as I was. "You're not allowed to be here."

He held his hands up. "I only want to talk to you." He took another step inside the house, swaying on his feet a little as he moved. "I'm not going to hurt you anymore, darling."

*He's lying.*

I shook my head. "Mam, no, don't listen!"

"You need to go," Mam gasped, backing up and taking me with her. "You need to leave now."

"Marie," he said in that coaxing voice of his, slurring his words. "We're a family." He closed the door behind him and turned the lock. "We need to be together."

"No." Mam shook her head. "No, no, you need to go now."

"Are the children in bed?" he asked, ignoring her pleas, as he slipped the house key into his pocket. "That's good." He took another step towards us. "It's best they stay asleep."

"Teddy . . ." Mam's voice cracked. "Please don't—"

"It's okay, Marie," Dad coaxed. "We'll all be together again."

*This is bad, Shannon.*

*This is really bad.*

*You need to get out.*

*Go.*

*Run . . .*

Letting go of my mother's leg, I lunged for the staircase with every inch of my body locked tight in fearful anticipation.

"Good girl, Shannon, I'm not going to hurt you," Dad slurred. "Go on up to bed now and close your eyes. Everything will be better in the morning."

Choosing to escape rather than stick around and wait for him to change his mind, I stumbled up the staircase as fast as my legs could carry me.

"What's going on?" Tadhg demanded, peeking out from his bedroom. "Shan—"

"Lock your doors," I choked out. "He's back."

Tadhg's eyes widened in fear. "Wh-what?"

"Lock your fucking door, Tadhg!" I screamed. "This isn't a joke."

He ran back into his room and bolted the door.

Breathing hard, I ran into my own bedroom and slammed the door shut. Flicking the lock, I looked around wildly as panic clawed at my gut. With my survival instincts kicking in, I lunged for my dresser and pushed with all my might until it was blocking the door. Still frantic, I dragged my bedside locker over, too.

His voice was there.

I could hear it.

I could hear *her.*

They weren't screaming or shouting.

They were *talking.*

Why were they *talking*?

Flailing around, I tried to catch my breath, but it wasn't coming easy to me. Diving for my bed, I slipped under the covers and roughly pulled the duvet over my head. Something clattered on the floor then and I stiffened.

*My phone.*

Trembling, I shoved the duvet off and swiped it off the floor. I didn't even think about what I was doing as I dialed. It was like I was moving on instinct. Pressing call, I put the phone to my ear and held my breath.

"Gibs," Johnny's sleepy voice came down the line, bringing with it a tsunami of relief. "If this isn't an emergency, I'm going to wring your bleeding neck."

"H-hi, Johnny."

"Shannon?" His voice was softer now. "Are you okay?"

I shook my head and jerked to my feet, unable to sit still. "No."

"What's wrong?" Concern filled his voice. "What's happening?"

I couldn't speak.

I couldn't say it out loud.

"Talk to me, Shan," he coaxed. "Hmm?"

"He's here," I choked out. "He's downstairs and I'm scared."

"What do you mean?"

"My dad," I strangled out. "He's in the house, Johnny."

"Can you get out?" he demanded.

"No." I shook my head and bit back a sob. "He's in the kitchen. I can't go back down there."

"I'm on my way," he replied without hesitation. "I'm leaving right now."

"I'm sorry," I whispered, sinking back down on my bed.

"Don't say sorry," he told me. "Are you safe? Are you in your room?"

"Yeah." I nodded. "My door's locked."

"I'm in my car now, Shan," he said. "I'll be as fast as I can."

"They're not shouting," I strangled out. "Why aren't they shouting?"

"I don't know, baby," he growled. "But I'm coming."

"Something's wrong," I bit out. "He's *different* tonight. I don't know what's happening, Johnny, but something's very wrong. I can feel it in my bones."

"I'm going to get you out of there," he vowed. "I promise. I'm going to take you out of that fucking hole and you're never going back."

"Johnny, I'm really scared."

"I know," he coaxed. "I know, baby, but I'm coming." He sighed heavily. "Shannon, I love you."

"I love you, too, Johnny," I whispered, ending the call. I knew it was selfish to call him in the middle of the night and drag him from his bed, but I honestly couldn't take another second of this. I felt like I was close to the edge of something that I wasn't sure I could come back from.

*I was afraid of dying in this house.*

I held my breath, not daring to breathe too loudly, listening to the deathly calm sound of my father's voice.

Why wasn't he shouting?

Why wasn't *she* shouting?

Oh god, I couldn't do this anymore.

I couldn't be in this house.

I needed an *out*.

I counted down the thirty-three minutes I knew it took to get from his house to mine, and when he didn't arrive at the projected time, the panic inside of me flourished into a monster-sized knot of fear, gripping at my lungs, and making it hard to breathe.

Restless, I ran my hands through my hair at least a dozen times before giving up and fixing it into a braid down my right shoulder.

Footsteps on the staircase filled my ears and I flinched.

*Hurry up.*

*Please hurry up.*

Slipping on my runners, I leaned against my bedroom window with bated breath and stared out onto the street.

The more time that passed, and the louder the noise downstairs grew, the more of a paranoid wreck I became.

By the time the familiar headlights pulled onto the street, my breathing was audibly uneven.

A knock sounded on the other side of the door and my body instinctively seized with dread. "Are you in bed, Shannon?" my father's voice called out from the other side of the door.

My eyes were wild and panicked as I glanced from my door to the window. "Yes," I managed to strangle out, though it was hard to breathe from the panic consuming me.

"Good girl," he called back and the sound of something spilling on the floor outside my door filled my ears. "Go to sleep now, Shannon." The stench of alcohol wafted under my bedroom door and terror clawed at my chest. "Your brothers are all sleeping, too," he added. "Just close your eyes and it'll all be better in the morning."

"Okay," I croaked out, trembling from head to toe, as I pushed open my bedroom window and climbed onto the ledge. "G-goodnight, Dad."

# Get Them Out

## JOHNNY

Jerking awake, I remained perfectly still and listened for the noise I was certain had woken me. A few seconds later and the familiar vibrating sound filled my ears. Shifting around, I felt for my phone, grabbing it out from under my pillow. Bleary-eyed and half asleep, I clicked the accept button and put it to my ear. "Gibs, if this isn't an emergency, I'm going to wring your bleeding neck."

"H-hi, Johnny."

At the sound of Shannon's voice, I was instantly alert. "Shannon?" Pulling myself up on my elbows, I ran a hand through my hair and tried to blink awake. Twisting sideways, I glanced at the alarm clock on my nightstand. 01:23 it read. "Are you okay?"

"No," her voice was so hushed it was barely audible.

"What's wrong?" I demanded. "What's happening?" The sound of sniffling coming from the other end of the line had me throwing off my covers. "Talk to me, Shan," I coaxed, voice still thick from sleep, as I rummaged around in the darkness for my clothes. "Hmm?"

"He's here," she choked out, voice laced with fear. "He's downstairs and I'm scared."

"What do you mean?"

"My dad," she strangled out. "He's in the house, Johnny."

*Fuck.* "Can you get out?"

"No. He's in the kitchen. I can't go back down there."

*Shite.* "I'm on my way," I replied, snatching my keys off my desk and moving for the door. "I'm leaving right now."

"I'm sorry."

"Don't say sorry." Thundering down the staircase, I darted through the hallway. "Are you safe?" Skidding across the kitchen, I bolted through the utility room and out the back door. "Are you in your room?" *Please tell me you're in your room . . .*

"Yeah, my door's locked."

*Thank Jesus.* "I'm in my car now, Shan," I said as I unlocked my car and climbed inside. Balancing my phone between my ear and my shoulder, I turned the key in the ignition and tore off, sending gravel spraying everywhere. "I'll be as fast as I can."

"They're not shouting," she told me and the terror I could hear in her voice was crippling. "Why aren't they shouting?"

"I don't know, baby," I choked out. "But I'm coming."

"Something's wrong," she said in a small voice. "He's *different* tonight. I don't know what's happening, Johnny, but something's very wrong. I can feel it in my bones."

"I'm going to get you out of there," I hissed, struggling to rein in my fury. "I promise. I'm going to take you out of that fucking hole and you're never going back."

"Johnny, I'm really scared," she sobbed.

"I know." Using one hand to steer, I dragged my seatbelt across my chest with the other and snapped it into place. "I know, baby, but I'm coming." Gripping the wheel, I had the biggest urge to tell her that I loved her. A voice inside of my head was screaming *do it now because you might not get another chance.* "Shannon, I love you."

"I love you, too, Johnny," she whispered and then the line went dead.

"Fuck!" Slamming my hand down on the steering wheel, I drove like a deranged lunatic all the way to her house.

When I pulled up outside Shannon's house half an hour later and climbed out of my car, I couldn't stop my hands from shaking. Wholly enraged, I stalked up the overgrown garden path with every intention of kicking the fucking door down to get my girlfriend out of that house.

"Johnny?" Shannon's voice filled my ears and I backtracked, my gaze landing on her bedroom window on the second level of the house.

*Jesus Christ.*

"Whoa, whoa, whoa—" I held my hands up, pulse racing. "Don't come out there, baby," I warned her, watching with my heart in my mouth as she climbed onto the windowsill and lowered herself onto the shitty veranda. I knew it was shitty because I'd almost cracked my neck climbing up there. Shannon was dressed in a pair of navy pajama shorts and vest and had a worn pair of runners on her tiny feet. No hoodie. No jacket. Nothing. "Just climb back in," I coaxed, panicking at the sight of her up there. "And I'll come inside and get you."

"I *can't*." She shook her head and continued to shimmy on her ass to the edge of the veranda. "He locked the door."

"Throw me down your keys," I called back. "Don't climb down here—"

"No, no, no, you don't understand," she whispered. "He's acting really strange, Johnny, and I don't want him to know I'm leaving. Just catch me, okay?"

*Ah fuck.*

"Shannon, you're going to hurt yourself," I strangled out, in full-blown panic mode now. "You can't climb down from there, baby. You're too small."

"Don't go near the door, Johnny," she begged when I moved to do just that. "Please! Just . . . just break my fall, okay?"

Furious, I bit down a snarl and walked to the edge of the path, feeling thankful as hell that I was almost 6'4. "Okay." Reaching up, I held my hands out to her, praying she had the dexterity to not trip up and break her bleeding neck. "Nice and slow."

She nudged herself to the edge of the veranda and I panicked. "Don't jump," I warned her. "Just drop your legs down, and I'll grab them."

Thankfully, Shannon listened to me and gingerly lowered her legs. "Good job." Catching ahold of her legs, I wrapped an arm around them and held my free hand up for her to take. "I've got you," I promised. "Trust me—"

I didn't get a chance to finish my sentence, because Shannon quite literally flung herself down to me.

Catching her easily, I hooked an arm around her back and lowered her to her feet. "Don't you ever do that to me again," I choked out, breathing hard from the almost heart-attack she'd given me. "You could have killed yourself."

"Sorry," she whispered, burying her face in my chest. "Thanks for coming."

"Where's Joey?" I asked as I led her to my car.

"He's gone, Johnny," she sobbed. "He left."

"And Darren?"

"He went to find Joey," she sniffled, sinking into the passenger seat. "It's all gone to hell."

"Is your mother in there with him?"

She nodded. "I couldn't do anything. He just . . . he just showed up and she was standing there. I was afraid so I ran and left her with him."

"Good," I told her, drowning in the relief that she'd had the good sense to run.

"No, no, it's not," she argued weakly, sounding confused. "It's not good at all." Shaking her head, she pressed her fingers to her temples and exhaled a ragged breath. "He came upstairs to make sure I was asleep and he was being nice." She looked up at me, wide-eyed and terrified. "I don't understand what's happening here."

"Where are the boys?"

"In their rooms." She dropped her head in her hands and sobbed. "I panicked. I should have brought them in my room with me, but I . . . I couldn't think straight."

*Jesus Christ.* "Okay." Trying to keep my voice calm, I pulled my phone out of my pocket. "I'll call the Guards. He's not allowed to be here. They'll arrest him—"

"Wh-what? Johnny no, no, no—" Shaking her head, Shannon lunged for my phone. "If you call them, they'll take us away right now," she choked out, panicking. "I'll be sent away." Tears streamed down her cheeks. "I won't see you again."

"No, you won't," I tried to coax. "Nobody's going to take you anywhere—"

"You don't understand," she sobbed. "You don't know how it works, but I do."

I stood there, feeling at a complete fucking loss. What the hell was I supposed to do? I couldn't just walk away from this. "Shannon," I tried again. "I won't let anyone take you. My parents said that they'll—"

"You don't get it," she sniffled, cutting me off. "If the Guards come, they'll call Patricia and the social workers." A huge sob racked through her frail body. "We'll be removed from the house, and you won't be able to stop that. No one will."

"You can't live like this, baby," I choked out, feeling the anger rattle through me. "It has to stop."

"I know," she sobbed. "I just don't know how to stop it."

Releasing a low growl, I ran my hands through my hair and looked back to the house. "Listen, just stay in the car, lock all of the doors, and wait for me."

"Johnny—"

"Just stay here," I said, trying to keep my tone gentle. "I need to get the boys. I can't leave them in there with him, okay?"

"No!" Springing out of the car, she clutched my t-shirt. "He wants us all in bed. If he sees you, he'll know I called you – he'll know I'm not in bed – and I don't know what he'll do." She shook her head vehemently, fingers knotting tightly in my t-shirt. "He's calm now, but if you go in there, he could hurt them. He could hurt *you*! You don't know what he's capable of, Johnny. You don't!"

Red flags were shooting up all around me. "I won't let him see me," I told her, keeping my voice steady. "I'll sneak in, get the boys, and I won't get caught. I promise. But I can't leave them inside that house, Shannon."

She looked torn, watching me with a pleading expression. "Then I'll come with you—"

"No, you won't," I practically hissed, guiding her back into the passenger seat, my heart hammering at the thought of her going any-where near that man. "Just stay in the car, baby," I ordered, slamming the door shut before she had a chance to respond, and hurrying back to the house.

My hands were shaking when I grabbed the wheelie bin and quietly dragged it over to the veranda. I hated heights, but not as badly as I hated this bleeding house. Climbing on top of the bin, I hoisted myself up onto the veranda, trying not to think about what I was doing, and praying Shannon had the good sense to stay in the car. Grabbing the window ledge, I hauled myself through her bedroom window, careful not to make a noise. The overwhelming stench of whiskey was the first thing that hit my senses as I quickly moved the furniture she had piled against the door.

*Drunk bastard.*

Every instinct inside of me demanded that I go downstairs and rip his fucking head off, but my brain was louder, screaming at me to get these kids out of this house, and take Shannon away from here.

*Don't lose it,* I mentally chanted as I worked to clear my path, *be smart.*

*You can't protect her if you're in a prison cell, Johnny.*

*Keep your goddamn head.*

*They've been through enough.*

*Get them out of here!*

Heart hammering in my chest, I unlocked her bedroom door and slowly pulled it inwards, wincing when it creaked. The silence in the house was eerie and the hushed voices drifting up from the kitchen had me on edge. Shannon was right. Something was very wrong about this picture. Stepping over a puddle of god knows what, I crept into the landing only to freeze in terror when my eyes landed on Sean who was toddling down the steps on his bottom.

On complete impulse, driven forward by my gut instinct that was screaming danger, I whispered his name, "Sean."

He paused on the turn of the staircase and looked up at me, wide-eyed and fearful, and I swear to god, my heart cracked clean open in my chest.

Smiling as brightly as I could, I waved and gestured for him to come back up to me. Horrified didn't begin to cover the feeling that engulfed me when I watched a wet stain spread across the crotch of his Bob the Builder pajama pants as he obediently toddled back up the stairs towards me. Come to look at it, he was wet all over.

*Jesus Christ . . .*

When he stepped back onto the landing, he just stared up at me, hair drenched, clutching a raggedy looking teddy bear, looking all wide-eyed and broken as he sucked on three tiny fingers.

"Hey, Sean," I whispered, crouching down to his level and almost spluttering when the smell of whiskey hit me. "Do you remember me?" I asked him, eyes watering from the stench. "I'm Johnny."

He looked up at me with those big, lonesome eyes and nodded slowly.

"Do you want to come for spin with me again?" I asked, desperate to get him the hell out of this hellhole. "Does that sound like fun?"

Silent as a ghost, he nodded again.

"Good boy – I'm going to pick you up, okay?" I coaxed, slowly stretching my hands out to him. "I'm not going to hurt you. I'm a nice friend, remember? I've got that fast car and a shit ton of sweets for you—" I slowly lifted him into my arms like he was a bomb that could detonate at any minute. *Jesus, he was soaking through.* "Good job, buddy," I coaxed when he didn't resist me. "I'm going to take you to your sister now, okay?"

"O-ee."

I froze, stunned to hear him speak for the first time. "Hmm, Sean?" I whispered, heart in my mouth. "What did you say?"

"O-ee gone," he whispered, touching my face with his slobbery fingers. "O-ee."

"I know, buddy, but he'll be back soon." Shifting him onto my hip, I moved from door to door, checking each room for the boys. "I'm going to get you some help. I'll take you back to my house where there's no mean shouting – and you can have a bath. A big bubble bath with ducks and everything. We'll get that dirty booze off you."

"Daddy bad," he whispered, stroking my jaw with his chubby fingers.

"I know, buddy," I bit out. "But I won't do that to you."

615 • CHLOE WALSH

"Daddy ow," he whispered. "Ow, ow, Daddy."

*Keep the head, Kav.*

*Don't lose it while you're holding a toddler.*

"You like Bob the Builder?" I asked, distracting us both from the very real fact that I was about to commit kidnapping. *Again.* "Me, too. I love Bob. Bob's the bleeding best—"

"Fuck off!" a familiar voice spat from behind the locked door at the end of the hallway when I tried the handle. "I've got a knife."

"Tadhg," I whispered. "It's okay. Open the door."

"Who's there?"

"Johnny," I told them. "Don't be scared, lads. I'm going to get you out of here."

"I want to go," Ollie said from behind the door.

"Shut up, Ollie," Tadhg hissed. "We don't know for sure if it's him."

"It *is* him," Ollie choked out. "He's got the funny voice, Tadhg."

"It is me," I coaxed, striving for patience when all I wanted to do was kick down the door and drag them out of here. "I'm here to get you out, boys, but I need you to be as quiet as you can. Can you do that? Just whisper and don't make any noise."

I waited a solid minute and a half before a click sounded and the bedroom door cracked open just enough for two blond heads to pop out. "How come you're here?" Tadhg whispered, watching me with mistrustful eyes.

"Shannon called me," I replied calmly. "I know he's down in the kitchen with your ma, and I'm here to get you guys out."

"Can I come?" Ollie asked, looking at me with a hopeful expression.

"Of course," I strangled out, voice thick with emotion. "I'm here for all of you."

"Ollie!" Tadhg whisper-hissed. "What about Mam?"

"I don't care," Ollie cried as he pushed back the door and slipped into the landing. "I don't want to be here."

"What about my mam?" Tadhg asked, eyeing me warily as if he was weighing up his options. "Can she come, too?"

"If she wants," I forced myself to say. "But I have to get you out without your da seeing us first, okay? Then I'll come back for her," I added, trying to find a way to sway him out of that room. "I'll take you to my place and then I promise, I'll come back and get your ma."

His nostrils flared. "Really?"

I nodded. "Really."

He studied me carefully for a moment. "Will your mam be there?"

"Yes," I replied evenly, sagging in relief as he loosened his grip on the door.

"Will she give us ice-cream again?"

"Definitely."

He glanced back to his room and released a sigh before turning back to face me. "Okay."

"Okay." I sighed in relief and gestured for them to follow me into Shannon's room. "Listen, the door's locked downstairs, so we're going to have to climb out the window."

My heart was racing so hard, I was afraid the toddler in my arms could feel it. In fact, I was sure he could because Sean pressed his small hand to my chest and whispered, "Bang, bang."

"We can't climb out the window," Ollie said in a hushed tone, when I leaned out with Sean in my arms. "You'll drop him. And I'm scared."

"It's okay," I bit out, knowing there was no safe way to get three small boys out of a two-story window without killing them. "We'll figure something else out."

"How are we going to get out?" Tadhg asked, sounding panicked. "Are we stuck?"

"We are stuck," Ollie wept. "Daddy's downstairs and he's going to kill us if he sees you." Sniffling, he added, "He said we were all supposed to go to sleep, and we're not asleep!"

"Something's wrong, Johnny," Tadhg strangled out. "We're in trouble, aren't we?"

"No, no, we're not," I assured him, heart racing. "I promise, I'll get you guys out of here. Your da's not going to see us. Everything's going to be fine." Searching the tiny bedroom with my eyes, I said, "We just need to find Shannon's house keys."

"She keeps them in her coat," Ollie choked out, visibly shaking now. "She always hangs it on the bannister downstairs."

Nodding, I desperately tried to rein in my emotions as I shifted Sean onto my other hip and held a hand out for Ollie. He came willingly, wrapping his arms around my waist with a death grip. "Don't be scared," I whispered, trying to console him. "We're going to creep downstairs as quiet as we can, okay?" Looking to Tadhg, I said, "Hold Ollie's hand and stay right behind me."

"What if he sees us?" they both asked.

"He won't," I whispered, making yet another promise I wasn't sure I could keep as I moved for the staircase with Sean clung to me like a baby monkey. "Don't make a sound," I whispered. Barefoot and in their pajamas, Tadhg and Ollie both nodded and trailed after me without a word.

As I crept down the wooden staircase that was slippery and wet, I felt the worst pang of remorse in my heart for the way these kids had to live. When I was nine, I'd been playing with Pokémon and building forts. When I was twelve, my biggest concern was scoring a try. I couldn't comprehend what these boys must be feeling.

"Good job," I whispered into Sean's ear. The further we descended down the stairs, the harder he shook in my arms. "We're nearly there." Never in my life had I been so glad to see a khaki coat as I was when my eyes locked on Shannon's one resting on the bannister. Slipping off the wet bottom step, I managed to right myself before toppling over. Regaining my balance, I slid my hand into the pocket of Shannon's coat and almost wept in relief when my fingers closed around her key chain. Glancing back to Tadhg and Ollie who were standing on the bottom step, I gave them what I hoped was a reassuring smile. Both boys sagged in relief when I waved the keys in front of them.

"It doesn't have to be this way," I heard Shannon's mother weep and I froze, heart jackknifing in my chest. Swinging my gaze to Tadhg and Ollie's terrorized faces, I held a finger to my lips. "You know I love you," she continued, voice low and hushed. "We can sort this out, Teddy, but not if you—"

"Marie, Marie, Marie," their father slurred. "It's the only way."

A small whimper tore from Sean's throat and I tucked his face into my chest, praying to all that was holy to help me get these kids out. "Shh," I mouthed, rocking him in my arms. "Shh."

"Not for them," their mother sobbed. "For us maybe, but not them, Teddy."

"They are us," he replied in an eerie tone of voice. "They're all us."

"Please," she continued to sob quietly. "I love you, Teddy. Don't do this. I love you."

"This is the only way," he replied calmly. "Now have a drink with me. It'll take the edge off it."

Holding a hand up when Tadhg started to move towards me, I glanced around the hallway, wondering how in the hell I was going to get these kids to the door without their parents seeing us. The kitchen door was wide open and they would have a perfect view of the front door.

Forcing myself to breathe slowly, I kept my back to the wall behind me and edged closer to the door, gesturing for Ollie and Tadhg to follow me slowly. That bleeding staircase was like a deathtrap. Ollie slid clean off the bottom step and lunged for me. Wrapping his arms around my waist, he clung to me tighter than Sean was. "Shh," I whispered when he hiccupped a tiny sob. "Shh, buddy."

Trembling from head to toe, Tadhg skated across the floor to my other side, burying his face in my side, and my heart cracked clean open. I knew this kid was prideful. He was badass for twelve. To see him fall apart like this was sobering.

Smoothing a hand over his blond head, I carefully moved for the door with the three of them literally hanging off me, wary of the water on the floor, and never once taking my eyes off the kitchen doorway as I moved.

When I reached the front door, my eyes landed on their father slumped in a chair at the kitchen table, with his back to the door. Several empty bottles of whiskey and vodka were lined out on the table in front of him, and I knew if he turned around right now, I was going to kill him. I'd made the decision the minute I heard his creepy voice and I was oddly at peace with it. If he put a hand on these children, I was going to bury the man.

Focusing on keeping my hand steady, I slid the lone key into the lock and slow turned it back, wincing when it clicked.

A loud cough from the kitchen muffled the noise and I jerked my head back to see Shannon's mother staring right back at me.

Holy shit.

My heart stopped in my chest and for a few terrifying moments, I waited to see what she would do.

She nodded.

I hesitated.

She nodded again.

Keeping my eyes glued to her, I slowly pushed the handle down and swung the door inwards. She coughed loudly again, drowning out the creak from the hinges as I pushed Tadhg and Ollie through the small crack in the doorway.

With Sean in my hands, I turned my back to leave, but quickly swung back to face her, hovering anxiously in the doorway.

"Go," she mouthed, looking me right in the eyes. "Go now."

"What about you?" I found myself mouthing back, feeling torn and conflicted.

"I'll have a drink with you," Mrs. Lynch said in a calm tone, eyes glued to mine. "A goodbye drink."

"Good girl," her husband slurred, shoulders slumped.

"I'll close that door first," she added. "We don't want to wake them."

"That's right," he replied, nodding his head. "It's better if they sleep through it."

Standing up, Mrs. Lynch walked calmly to the kitchen door, face void of all emotion, eyes locked on mine. "Get them out," she mouthed slowly. "Take them away from here."

Stunned and confused, I hovered at the front door with her baby in my arms. "Come with me," I mouthed, urging her to just *run*. "Come on."

She shook her head. "No."

"*Why?*"

"Just go."

"I *can't*."

"Go *now*!"

"I'll come back for you." Feeling at a complete loss, I exhaled a ragged breath. "I promise."

"Don't come back." She shook her head. "Just save my children." Her gaze flicked to Sean who had his face buried in my neck and a lone tear trickled down her cheek. "Tell them I'm sorry," she mouthed and then she closed the kitchen door.

Silently reeling and still clutching her youngest child in my arms, I slipped out of the house, quietly closed the door behind me, and ran for my car.

# Ah Shite

## SHANNON

Numb to the bone, I sat in the passenger seat of Johnny's Audi, with his hand resting on mine on top of the gearstick, and my three little brothers in the backseat. The boys were barefoot, in their pajamas, and Johnny had the heater on full blast to keep them warm.

"What about this one, lads?" he asked, cranking up the volume of The Offspring's "Why Don't You Get A Job". He'd been playing every explicit song he could find on Gibsie's mix-CD since we left Elk Terrace. The more cursing and foul language in the song, the more my brothers' sobs and sniffles turned to laughter. Johnny was trying to distract them and it was working. Singing at the top of his lungs, he bobbed his head like a madman, encouraging the boys to curse and sing along with him.

By the time Eminem's "Just Lose It" came on, and Johnny threw himself into an enthusiastic rap, even Sean was giggling. His tear-streaked cheeks were stretched in a wide smile as he stared in wonder at my boyfriend.

"You should stick with the rugby," Tadhg snickered from the back-seat. "You're a terrible rapper, lad."

"*You're a terrible rapper, lad,*" Johnny mimicked a Cork accent, making his voice rise several octaves. "At least I don't sound like I'm singing when I'm talking."

"No," Tadhg chuckled. "Because you can't sing for shit."

"Tadhg." I sighed heavily. "Don't be cursing."

"*He* said we could," Tadhg argued, pointing at the back of Johnny's head.

"That's 'cause he's got that funny voice," Ollie laughed. "He says shite instead of shit."

"Ollie," I scolded. "Don't say that."

"But he *does*," Ollie defended. "Say shite, Johnny. Show her."

"Don't, Johnny," I warned.

"Shite," Sean blurted out from the back seat, pronouncing the word crystal clear.

Ollie and Tadhg howled laughing.

"Ah, shite," Johnny muttered, giving me a sheepish look.

"Shite," Sean repeated, clapping his hands together. "Shite."

"Of course," I groaned. "He would pick *that* up."

"It's a one night only free-pass, lads," Johnny announced. "And you might want to mind your P's and Q's around the grown-ups."

"What about Mam?" Tadhg asked then.

Smooth like honey and not missing a beat, Johnny said, "I talked to your ma before I left. She said you're all allowed stay at my place tonight."

Ollie's eyes widened. "She did?"

Johnny nodded and I didn't miss the tremor in his hand – the one he discreetly tried to shake out. *He was lying.* "It's all good, lads," he added, driving through the open gates of his property. "Consider it an adventure."

"I like adventures," Ollie offered.

As we approached Johnny's house, every light in the place was on, making the building look even more impressive than during the daytime. Desperate to keep my mind as empty as possible, I counted and then recounted the eighteen windows at the front of his house, and then I wondered how many times a month Mrs. Kavanagh had the window cleaners out to the house. They were always streak-free and sparkling clean.

The moment Johnny cut the engine of his car, the front door swung inwards and his mother came running outside in her dressing gown, wide-eyed and frantic looking. "Where did you go?" she demanded, hand pressed to her chest. "I've been calling you!"

"Ah, shite," Johnny muttered, unfastening his seatbelt. "Just wait here for a sec – I'll go calm her down." Climbing out of the car, he hurried over to his mother, patting her on the back when she threw her arms around him. "I'm alright, Ma. I'm grand – I left my phone in the car."

"I didn't know what was happening," she strangled out, clutching her son. "I heard tires screeching and checked your room and you were gone." Shaking her head, she reached up and cupped his face in her hands. "You can't do that to me, Johnny." Turning back to the house, she cried out, "John, he's okay. Call Sadhbh back, love. Tell her to let Gerard know he can stop looking. He's home."

Reaching across the seats, I pressed the button on Johnny's door to wind up the windows, not wanting my brothers to hear what was being said.

"Why's Dellie crying?" Ollie whispered, leaning between the seats to watch the commotion.

"Because she was worried about Johnny," I explained, feeling my throat tighten at the sight. "He's her son."

"What was she worried about?" he asked, turning his brown eyes on me. "Is he in trouble or something?"

"No, Ollie, but it's the middle of the night, and she was probably scared for him."

"Because it's so late?"

I gave him a watery smile. "Exactly."

Ollie glanced back to where Mrs. Kavanagh was still clutching her son in a death grip before blowing out a breath. Mr. Kavanagh had joined them and was cupping the back of Johnny's head as they spoke over his wife's head.

"Whoa," Ollie whispered. "His mammy and daddy really love him, huh?"

"Mam loves us, too," I croaked out, feeling the need to reassure my baby brother. "Don't ever doubt that."

Tadhg made a noise from the backseat and muttered something unintelligible under his breath – something that sounded awfully like '*yeah, in your fucking dreams*'.

"Sean, are you cold?" I asked, trying to keep the tremor out of my voice.

Shivering, my youngest brother nodded.

"He stinks," Tadhg noted with a huff. "He's pissed himself again."

"And he smells like Daddy," Ollie added, scrunching his nose up. "It's not a good smell, Shan."

"Come up here to me, Sean," I coaxed, holding my hands out to him. "I'll keep you warm."

"Hang on," Tadhg grumbled when Sean tried to get up with his seatbelt still on. "I have to free you first, silly goose."

"Shite," Sean whispered, waiting for Tadhg to free him.

"That's right," Tadhg snickered, unbuckling his belt.

"Don't encourage him to use bad language," I warned my brothers as I helped Sean through the seats and cuddled him to my chest. "He's only three."

Ollie and Tadhg shrugged in response before busying themselves with opening every compartment and pressing every button they could find in the back of Johnny's car.

"O-ee," Sean croaked out, shivering violently, as he wrapped his small arms around my neck. "O-ee gone."

"No," I whispered, gently rocking him in my arms. "He'll be back."

My heart was hammering wildly in my chest, my fingertips numb and tingling as I forced myself to remain calm. I was embarrassed, terrified, and ashamed. Ridiculous as it sounded, I didn't want Johnny to see this part of my life, but he was seeing it all now; the ugly reality that was my family. My reasons for why I was the way I was. All of my issues . . . they all began and ended with that man I called my father.

I kept my eyes on the Kavanaghs, knowing the exact moment Johnny explained what had happened tonight because Mrs. Kavanagh covered her mouth with her hands and buried her face in her husband's chest. His father's gaze flickered to the car and I could see the concern in his eyes. They spoke for several more minutes in hushed voices, while I sat, still as a statue, feeling like I was on trial, before Johnny jogged back towards us. His mother moved to follow him, but Mr. Kavanagh walked her back into the house. Rounding the car, Johnny opened my door and smiled down at me. "Come on, Shan. Let's go inside."

*Oh, thank god.*

I blew out a ragged breath. "Are they sure?"

He nodded and reached for Sean. "Come on, big man." Lifting my baby brother into his arms, Johnny held a hand out for me. "Let's get you all warmed up." Glancing to Ollie and Tadhg, he said, "Come on, lads, my ma's getting the ice-cream out for ye."

"Score," Tadhg cheered as he shoved his door open and barreled out of the car, running into the house ahead of Ollie who was calling out, "Wait for me, Tadhg," as he chased after him.

Trembling from head to toe, I climbed out of the car, feeling cold to the bone, and looked up at my boyfriend. "Thank you," I croaked out, teeth chattering, as my heart thudded a rhythm of adoration for the boy standing in front of me. "For everything."

"I'd do anything for you, Shannon *like the river*," Johnny replied gruffly, pulling me into his side. "Anything."

I believed him, but I wished he didn't have to.

# The Sharp Knife of Awareness

## JOHNNY

I was surprised at how I could remain so calm when I was having a nervous breakdown on the inside. When I told my parents what had happened, Dad instructed me to act normal with Shannon and her brothers while he went inside with Mam to call the Gardaí. The realization of what I'd done was hitting me hard, and the smell of alcohol wafting off the tiny child in my arms was bringing with it terrible fucking thoughts. I knew I had to go back for their mother. I'd promised her I would. Every instinct in my body was screaming at me to go back to that house right now, but for once in my life, I was trying to do what my father had asked by keeping my head and letting the Gardaí deal with it.

With Sean in one arm and Shannon tucked under the other, I led them into the sitting room, where Dad was re-lighting the fire. It humbled me to see how incredibly resilient these kids were. They'd just been through something that would rattle a grown man – myself included – and yet here they were; just accepting the hand they'd been dealt, bouncing back up and getting on with it. Just like I'd seen their sister do on countless occasions. Jesus, they were the ultimate survivors.

"Whoa," Ollie, who had run down from the kitchen with a bowl of ice-cream in hand, gasped and skidded to a halt in the middle of the sitting room. "That's like a cinema." He pointed to the flat screen mounted to the wall over the fireplace and nudged his brother. "Look at the size of it."

"I have eyes," Tadhg shot back, too interested in the bowl of ice-cream he was scarfing down. "And what do you expect? They're loaded."

"Are we allowed to say that?" Ollie asked, looking up at his brother. "Call them rich?"

Tadhg shrugged. "It's true, isn't it?"

"No, you're not allowed to say that," Shannon choked out, looking mortified, as she walked over to her brothers and glared at them. "Now have some manners and thank Mrs. Kavanagh for the ice-cream."

"Thanks, Dellie," Ollie chimed.

"Yeah," Tadhg mumbled, flushing a little as he looked up at my mother. "Thanks for this, Edel."

"You're more than welcome, boys," Mam replied, voice hoarse as she walked into the sitting room. "And, Shannon, love, call me Edel."

"Sorry, Mrs. Kavanagh," Shannon mumbled, flustered. "I mean – Edel."

"Alright, boys," my father said, waving the remote control of the television in his hand. "What are we watching? We have all the channels."

"Score!" Tadhg cheered and dove for the couch. "Can I pick?"

"No, no, me," Ollie begged, racing after Tadhg. "Please, John. Me, me—"

"*Me, me,*" Tadhg mimicked, gleaming in victory when Dad handed him the remote. "Thanks, John." Turning to Ollie, he smirked. "Sit down, kid. You'll get your turn when you're up against Sean."

Huffing out a sigh, Ollie sank down on the couch beside him and shoved a spoon of ice-cream into his mouth. "It's no fair being younger."

"Yeah, well, that's how it feels for me with Shannon and Joey," Tadhg shot back, unaffected. "Deal with it."

"And Darren," Ollie offered. "He's the oldest."

Tadhg snorted. "He doesn't count."

Ollie turned to look at his brother. "Does Joey still count?"

Tadhg nodded stiffly. "For now."

"Okay." Nodding in acceptance, Ollie turned to watch the television as Tadhg channel surfed with my father.

"Are you alright, Shannon, love?" Mam asked in a low tone, eyes glued to my girlfriend's scratched-up face.

Shannon blushed and nodded. "I'm fine, thanks." Tucking her hair behind her ear, she moved to walk back to me, but quickly stopped herself short and stiffened, looking uncertain. "I'm just, ah . . ." Glancing around at her brothers, she exhaled a ragged breath. "I'm really very sorry for bringing my trouble to your door again, Mrs. Kavanagh." Shoulders sagging, she whispered, "I just didn't know what else to do."

"Oh, pet, come here to me—" Mam walked straight over to her and pulled her into her arms. My mother wasn't a tall woman at 5'4, but she still dwarfed Shannon who was barely 5'0. "You're going to be okay," I heard Mam whisper in her ear as Shannon remained rigid. "I'm going to take care of all of you."

Shuddering, Shannon slowly relaxed and hugged my mother back. "I'm so sorry."

"Don't be sorry, love. You did everything right tonight." Pressing a kiss to Shannon's head, Mam pushed her hair off her face, cupped her small face between her hands, and smiled down at her. "You and your brothers are going to stay with us for the night. We'll get everything straightened up in the morning, okay?"

Shannon nodded weakly. "Thank you so much for your help."

"I'm very proud of you for calling," Mam continued to say. "I know you must have been scared, and it was very brave of you to make that phone call when you knew what might happen."

"Do you think my mam is okay?" Shannon whispered, her gaze flicking nervously to the boys and then back to Mam before landing on me. "I shouldn't have left her there."

"I'm sure she's fine, love. Why don't you sit down with your brothers and Johnny can go and put the tea on for me?" Mam suggested, steering the conversation away from her mother. "And *I'll*—" walking over to me, Mam tickled Sean's toes and grinned up at his lonesome face "—give this gorgeous boy a wash?" Smiling at Sean, she stroked his cheek. "Hmm? What do you say, Seany baby? Will we get you all cleaned up?"

"Good idea, Sean," Shannon encouraged, voice thick with emotion. "But I don't have any clothes for him." Blushing furiously, she whispered, "And he still, uh . . . he tends to have accidents when he's nervous."

"Not to worry," Mam replied, still smiling at Sean. "There's plenty of boxes of Johnny's old clothes in the attic."

"What do you say, bud?" I asked Sean. "Are you going to go for a nice bath and wash that stinky booze off ya?"

Sean looked up at me for a long moment before nodding and leaning his body towards my mother.

"Oh, you're such a good boy," Mam coaxed, cuddling him close to her chest as she trailed out of the sitting room. "Oh, and you give the best hugs."

My father's phone began to ring then. "Two minutes, lads," he said, standing up from where he'd been sitting between Ollie and Tadhg, refereeing their battle of the remote. "I'll just take this." As he walked past me, he inclined his head for me to follow him.

"I'll be two minutes," I whispered, kissing Shannon's forehead. "Okay?"

Shivering, she wrapped her arms around herself and nodded. "O-okay."

I walked over to the door only to hesitate and turn back. "Shan?"

She looked up at me with a lost expression. "Yeah, Johnny?"

"I love you."

Relief flashed in her big, blue eyes and she smiled back at me.

"*I love you*," Tadhg mimicked from the couch. Not taking his eyes off the television, he made loud kissing noises before snorting loudly. "Lad, you are so whipped."

"Ugh," Ollie snickered. "I bet he kisses her with tongues, too."

"That's our sister, you little creep," Tadhg grumbled. "I don't want to be thinking about Shannon's tongue in Johnny's mouth."

"Is that how it works?" Ollie asked, sounding appalled. "They put their *tongues* in each other's *mouths*?"

"*Yeah*."

Ollie frowned. "For *what*?"

"They probably do a lot worse than that, Ol," Tadhg muttered. "It's disgusting but whatever."

"They do?" Ollie's eyes widened. "Like what?"

"Uh, you should probably stop asking questions now," Tadhg muttered, nudging Ollie in the ribs.

"Yes, you should definitely stop asking questions, Ollie," Shannon strangled out, red-faced, as she hurried over to her brothers and sank down on the couch between them. "Tadhg, don't tell him anything else."

"I can't believe you let him stick his tongue in your mouth," Ollie accused, gaping at his sister. "What is wrong with you?"

"I don't do that," Shannon snapped, flustered. "He's joking, right, Tadhg?"

"She does," Tadhg countered. "I saw them cracking on outside the house."

"Tadhg!"

"They were steaming up the windows of his car," Tadhg snickered. "Oh – and she snuck him in her bedroom on Saturday night, too. He was there all night long."

"What? I didn't know Johnny had a sleepover," Ollie replied, sounding puzzled. "You never said."

"That's because she was too busy," Tadhg chuckled. "She was all, *oh, Johnny, yes! Please!*"

"I was not," Shannon spluttered. "You little liar."

"*Kiss me, touch me, hold me, love me,*" Tadhg mocked in a girlish voice. "*Mwah, mwah, mwah. Yes, I love your rugby balls—*"

"Tadhg!"

"Yuck," Ollie groaned. "That's disgusting."

"Shannon does it with Johnny, Joey does it with Aoife, Darren does it with Alex," Tadhg continued, not missing a beat. "And you'll do it when you're older with someone you fancy, Ol."

"I will *not*," Ollie spluttered, looking horrified. "I don't even like my own tongue in my mouth."

"Yeah." Tadhg snorted. "Sure."

"Do you do it?" Ollie asked.

"I'm starting secondary school in September," Tadhg replied nonchalantly. "What do you think?"

"So?" Shannon replied, eyeing her brother suspiciously. "What does starting secondary school have to do with kissing?"

"Just that I know what I'm talking about," Tadhg told her. "And that's all I'm saying on the matter."

"Johnny—" my father's voice filled my ears and I tore my gaze off Shannon and her brothers before hurrying into the hallway after him.

"What's going on?" I asked, watching him warily as he nodded and answered whoever was on the phone to him with one-word responses. "Da?"

"Come here," he mouthed, gesturing for me to follow him.

A nervous tremor rolled down my spine as I trailed after him, not stopping until we were in the kitchen with the door closed behind us.

"Thanks a million for calling me, Billy," Dad said into the phone. "I will – yes . . . yes, I know, man. I understand. Thanks. Yeah, I'll see you there." Hanging up, he looked at me and sighed heavily. "Johnny—" his voice cracked. Shaking his head, he placed the phone on the kitchen island and exhaled a pained breath before saying, "Sit down, son."

And I *knew.*

I knew right there in that very moment that something terrible was going to come of his mouth.

"Da," I bit out, shaking like an ivy-leaf. "What's going on?"

"Johnny—" Releasing another pained sigh, my father walked over and steered me to a stool. "I need you to sit down, son."

Fuck.

Feeling weak, I sank down on a stool at the island and dropped my head in my hands. "Just tell me," I strangled out, clenching my eyes shut. "Just say it. Please."

"That was Billy Collins on the phone," Dad explained, taking the stool opposite mine. "Do you remember Billy? I went to school with him? We were great friends. He's been over here a few times with his wife for dinner—"

"I know he's the superintendent at the station, Da," I choked out, knowing exactly who my father was talking about. His Garda buddy. "What did he say?"

Dad nodded stiffly. "He's sending a car over here. They'll be with us shortly." Dad glanced down at his phone which was lighting up again. "I called Darren, too. He's on the way."

"Are they taking them back?" I growled, flicking my gaze up to meet his. "Are you seriously going to let them take those kids back to that fucking house?"

"No, Johnny," Dad replied calmly. "That's not what's—"

"She's not going anywhere," I hissed, feeling anxious and wildly protective. "I don't give a shite what you, Darren, or any bleeding Guards say. You're not taking Shannon back there. I'm keeping her here with me!"

"Nobody is taking anyone back there," Dad coaxed. "I promise, son, so just calm down."

"Then why are the Guards coming here?" I demanded.

"They need to take your statements," Dad replied softly.

"Statements for *what*?" I gaped at him. "Am I in trouble for taking them? Because their ma told me to—" My words broke off and I dragged in several deep breaths before continuing. "She told me to go, Da," I hissed, shuddering at the memory of Mrs. Lynch's haunted eyes looking into mine. "She said *take them*!"

Tears filled my father's eyes and I blanched. "Oh fuck, it's bad, isn't it?" I choked out, jerking off the stool. "What's happening here?" Trembling, I backed away from the island, knowing in my heart something bad was going on. "Did he hurt her?" Pain speared through me at the thought. "Is that it? Is she in the hospital?"

"Johnny, just breathe—"

"I don't understand what's happening here!" I roared, feeling my heart hammer violently against my ribcage. "Just tell me what's going on, Da!"

"There was a fire at the Lynch house."

"*What*?" My heart stopped dead in my chest. "No, no, no." I shook my head, rejecting the words coming out of his mouth. "I was there less than two hours ago, Da. There was no fire!"

"There *was* a fire, Johnny," Dad told me. "When you showed up here with the children and I called Billy, he was already at the scene of a fire in Elk Terrace. By the time the emergency services arrived, the house was up in flames."

"*What?*" my voice rose with my panic. "I don't ... how ... what?"

"Johnny, pet, you need to sit down."

"It's a half an hour from their house to ours," I spat. "How does a house burn down in half a fucking hour, Da?"

"A house burns down that quickly if it's lit intentionally," Dad replied gruffly. "The house was doused in flammables, Johnny, and all the windows and doors were locked. They didn't have a chance of getting out." Shivering, he added, "Billy called me back just there to let me know that two bodies were pulled out." Sighing heavily, he added, "Given all the information you told me that I relayed to him, he's confident that the fire was set mere minutes after you took the children – and the bodies are—"

"Don't say it—" Holding my head in my hands, I staggered backwards, knocking up against the sink. "No, Da. Jesus Christ, don't tell me *that*—"

"Johnny, shh – it's okay, son." Pushing his stool back, my father walked towards me. "Come here—"

"She's dead?" I whispered, feeling tears drip down my cheeks. "But I told her I'd go back for her," I choked out, shaking my head. "Jesus Christ, I should have made her come with me!"

My father's arms came around me. "Shh," he whispered, holding me up when my body felt weak to the bone. "It's okay. I've got you."

"I left her there, Da," I strangled out, clutching my father. "I left her in that house!"

"Do you know what you did tonight?" he asked, tightening his hold on me. "You saved four children."

"No." I clenched my eyes shut and buried my face in his neck. "Don't say it like that—"

"They would have burned to death inside that house if you hadn't been the crazy, reckless, brilliant man you are," he continued to say. "They wouldn't have had a chance in hell of getting out of there, son. Sean was doused in alcohol. You saved them all, Johnny. They were in their beds, son. They were terrified of him. There was no way those kids would have left their rooms if you hadn't gone in there to get them." Dad shuddered before adding, "And what you said about slipping on the staircase and the landing and hallway when you were inside the house? That was alcohol and petrol, Johnny. One spark of a flame and it was all over for those children – the entire place would have ignited with all of you in there – but *you* kept your head and *you* got them out."

"No, no, no," I strangled out, terrified. "I didn't know what I was doing."

"You trusted your instincts," he corrected. "You might not have understood what was happening, son, but you *knew* they needed to get out. Because of you, there are four children alive and breathing in this house tonight."

"Do they know yet?" I whispered, clenching my eyes shut tightly.

"No," Dad replied.

"Fuck," I croaked out. "How am I going to tell Shannon?"

"Tell me what?" Shannon's voice filled my ears and I flinched.

"Shan," I choked out, pushing away from my father and finding her hovering in the kitchen doorway, looking small and terrified. "You okay?"

"What's wrong?" she croaked out, eyes wide and full of fear. "Why are you crying?"

"I'm not crying, baby." Sniffling, I wiped my eyes and moved to go to her, needing to hold her in my arms and just stop the world for a minute. My head was spinning, my heart was reeling, and I couldn't take it all in. Closing the space between us, I pulled her into my arms and squeezed her body tighter than I knew I should. "I love you," I whispered, holding her close. "Jesus Christ, Shan, I'm so fucking sorry."

"Why are you sorry?" she choked out, clinging to my waist. "What's going on?"

"I tried, Shan," I strangled out, tightening my hold on her. "I really did."

"Johnny, what's happening?" she asked, voice cracking.

"Shannon!" Darren's voice filled my ears and I turned just as he burst through the utility room door, tears streaming down his cheeks. "Are you all okay?" His bloodshot eyes were wild and panicked as he staggered into the kitchen. "Where are the boys?"

"Darren?" Shannon cried, breaking out of my hold. "What's happening here?"

"Shan—" A gut-wrenching sob tore from his throat. "I can't—"

"The boys are all here and they're all safe," Dad replied, moving to catch Darren just as his legs gave out beneath him. "That's it – you're okay." Lowering them both to the floor, my father pulled him into his arms. "I've got you."

"Mam," he cried, burying his face in my father's neck. "My mam!"

"I know," Dad whispered, cupping the back of his neck. "Shh, I know, lad. I know."

"What's wrong with Mam?" Shannon choked out, trembling violently. "Wh-what did he d-do?"

"She's dead!" Darren cried. "He fucking killed her!"

"No!" Shaking her head, Shannon backed away like her brother's words had scalded her. "No, no, no, you're telling lies."

"He *killed* my mother," Darren choked out, clutching my father. "Fucking bastard—"

"Stop saying that!" Shannon screamed, pulling on her hair. "She's not dead, Darren. She's at home – I *saw* her!" Clutching her head in her hands, she glared at her brother and hissed, "She's fine." Tears streamed down her cheeks as she looked up at me. "Tell him, Johnny!" she begged, lunging for me. "Tell him he's wrong!" Grabbing my hand, she tugged aimlessly. "J-just t-tell h-him—"

"There was a fire at your house, Shan," I strangled out, feeling my body shake with the effort it was taking not to lose it.

"A fire?" Her eyes were wide and full of tears. "No, Johnny, no!"

"There *was* a fire, baby," I croaked out, heart racing. "And your ma . . . she, ah—" my words broke off and I cleared my throat before forcing the words, "she and your da didn't make it," out of my mouth.

"No." It was one word but I knew the sound would haunt me until my dying day as she stared up at me, those big, blue eyes begging me to tell her different. I wanted to – more than anything – but there was no escaping this. Her parents were dead.

"I'm so sorry," I whispered, moving for her. "Shan, I'm so—"

"No!" she repeated, backing up until her back hit the wall behind her. "No!" Covering her face with her hands, she slid down the wall. "Mammy, no, no, no! Not my mam . . . not my mam."

A tear slid down my cheek as I watched her, feeling more helpless than I ever had in my life. Crouching down beside her, I placed a hand on her knee. "Shan—"

"No," she strangled out, shaking my hand off. "No, no, no."

Exhaling brokenly, I tried again. "Shan—"

"I said no!" she sobbed, wrapping her arms around her legs. "No . . ." Burying her face in her knees, she rocked back and forth. "Oh god, they're both gone."

"I know." Feeling at a complete loss, I edged closer and nuzzled her shoulder with my cheek, desperate to give her comfort. "I'm so sorry."

"Joey," Shannon sobbed. "Joey . . . Oh, god, where's Joey?"

"It's okay, Shannon," my father replied, tone coaxing. "We'll find him, pet."

"He doesn't know," she wailed. "He's gone!" She tugged roughly on her hair. "He's just gone—"

"Don't," I choked out, taking her hands in mine. "Don't do that to yourself, baby." I couldn't take another second of watching her like this. "Please."

"Don't touch me!" Trembling, Shannon yanked her hands away from mine, chest heaving. "D-don't do it, okay?"

"Okay." Holding my hands up, I watched her watch me, feeling my heart crack clean open in my chest. "I won't do anything you don't want me to."

I remained exactly where I was, keeping my hands to myself, as I waited for her to take what she needed from me.

Eventually, she did.

With a huge sob, Shannon scrambled onto my lap and threw her arms around my neck, clinging to me in a way I knew I would never fully deserve. "Don't leave me—" Tightening her arms around my neck, she buried her face in my chest and whispered, "Please don't go . . ."

Exhaling a broken sigh, I wrapped her up in my arms and held her to me. "I won't." Tightening my hold on her frail body, I rocked her gently. "I'm right here." Exhaling a ragged breath, I ducked my face and dropped a kiss to her hair. "I promise."

I wanted to stand in front of this girl and shield her from all the horror she was exposed to. It wasn't right, dammit, and I felt like I was drowning in the unfairness of her life. If I could lay her cuts and bruises over my skin, I would.

A loud knock came from the back door then, followed by a male voice. "John, is it okay if we come in?"

"We're in here, Billy," Dad called out, still holding Darren. "Come on in."

Two uniformed Gardaí walked into our kitchen then, followed by my father's friend, Superintendent Billy Collins. The moment they removed their hats and said, "I'm so sorry for your loss," the worst, most heartbreaking sob tore from Darren's throat and Shannon sagged weakly against me.

Holding her tightly, I slowly rocked her in my arms, whispering everything and anything I could think of in her ear so she didn't have to hear what the Guards were saying to my father and Darren. She was hysterical, gasping for air, and crying harder than I'd ever heard her cry before. My heart was shattering into a million pieces, my mind reeling, but I stayed right there with her, unable to separate my emotions from hers.

When Dad, Darren, and the Gardaí went down to the sitting room to where Mam was with the younger boys to break the news, and the screaming started, I held her even tighter. Right there on the floor of my kitchen, I cradled her in my arms, feeling every one of her sobs and cries in the deepest part of my soul. "Shh, little darling . . ."

"You're s-singing." Sniffling, she clung to my chest. "'Here Comes the Sun'."

I *was* singing.

I was doing whatever I could to make this better for her.

"That's m-my Granda Murphy's s-song," she hiccupped. "You remember me t-telling you t-that?"

"Yeah." I remembered her telling me about her grandfather singing this song to her when she was frightened and it was all I could do in this moment. "Should I stop?"

"N-no." Shannon shook her head. "D-don't stop."

Trembling, I continued to rock her in my arms and softy hum the words of the song in her ear, while I waited for the doctor I knew had been called.

# Here Comes the Sun

## SHANNON

At first, I was numb, completely and utterly numb, as my mind tried to digest the words, the images, the unknown. Then, a tingling sensation swept through my body, attacking every nerve ending inside of me, making every limb tremble violently. But it was the pain that was the most unbearable. It came last, and drowned me in jagged, crushing, life-altering torment. My heart couldn't take the pressure and I was certain it would stop beating. It didn't and that surprised me. I was surprised to be still alive having had my heart cut clean open. I wasn't stabbed in the back. I was stabbed in the front, in the chest, right through the middle. And unlike a blade, the damage felt like buckshot, splaying and splicing me in countless areas and so many irreparable ways. How it was still beating was truly beyond me.

I couldn't think about him without a surging attack of grief and anger washing over me, drowning me in my bitterness.

I wasn't sure if I was still screaming because I couldn't hear my own voice anymore. Someone had come into the house and hurt me. Poked me with something sharp. At least, that's what it felt like. The person stabbing me told me that it was okay, that I was such a brave girl, and this would make me feel better. I didn't listen to that voice. Instead, I concentrated on the deep timbre of *his* voice as he sang the words of The Beatles' "Here Comes The Sun" in my ear over and over. Sagging against Johnny, I closed my eyes, feeling woozy, and tried to breathe through it – as I tried to find a way to survive the godawful hemorrhaging of my heart, and the annihilation it had taken at the hands of my father. My sanity had certainly slipped. Delirious and grief-stricken, my mind continued to whizz around and haunt me with the truth.

They were dead.

They were both dead.

"Mammy," I slurred brokenly, not even recognizing my own voice now. "My mam—"

"You're my little darling," Johnny whispered. His large hand cupped the back of my head as he held me to his chest, slowly rocking our bodies. "My little darling is safe with me."

The familiar smell of his bedroom was all around me then, but that didn't make sense. How were we in his bedroom? I was just in *my* bedroom? Everything was dark and I couldn't figure any of this out. "Shh," Johnny whispered, laying me down on something soft and warm. "I'm right here."

Trembling, I clung to his body, feeling the floor dip beneath me. Or maybe it was a mattress. I couldn't be sure of anything anymore. Shivering in his arms, I closed my eyes and breathed him in. "Mammy."

"Shh," he whispered over and over, holding me so close to his chest that I could feel his heart banging against my cheek. "Just close your eyes." I felt his lips against my hair. "I'll be here watching over you."

"You're always doing that," I slurred, feeling drowsy and numb. Everything was slipping away from me. I couldn't keep ahold of my thoughts. I felt like I was falling away. Like a warm and enticing darkness was trying to cloak me. "My mind is going on me."

"Let it go," he whispered. "You don't need it tonight."

Nestling closer, I held onto him, feeling numb and bone weary. "I might be dying."

"You're not dying." His arms tightened around me. "You're just sleepy."

"Joey ..." I tried to blink, but my eyes wouldn't open back up. "Joey's ... all gone ..."

"I'll find him," Johnny whispered. "I'll bring him back for you."

"You ... promise?" I croaked out, feeling a thick wave of exhaustion sweep through me.

"I promise" were the last words I heard Johnny say before I stopped clinging on and let the darkness take me away.

# I See Fire

## JOHNNY

"You don't have to come with me, son," Dad said for the tenth time as we drove through Ballylaggin town. "I can turn around and take you home."

"I'm coming." I couldn't stay at home. I needed out of that house and away from the screaming. The doctor had arrived a while ago and given Shannon some sort of injection to sedate her. She was sleeping now, curled up in a small ball and passed out cold on my bed. I held her while the doctor took care of her, unable to let her go, until she finally gave in and let sleep take her. Mam was still in the sitting room with Darren and the younger boys. They were still weeping and sobbing their hearts out. It was too much to take and I felt like I was smothering in their grief. "I need to not be there right now," I admitted, knees bopping restlessly. I couldn't do shit in that house, but I could help my father get Joey. Billy had called to let Dad know that Joey had shown up at the house and was understandably hysterical. He'd managed to barge his way past the authorities and make a break for the house before the firemen dragged him back out. The Guards couldn't make any hand of him and didn't want to arrest or restrain him. They were looking for a next of kin, someone to help him and take him away from the area, but all the Lynchs had was an eighty-something-year-old great-grandmother – and us.

"It's going to be daunting," Dad said as he turned up the familiar hill to Shannon's house. "The fire's not out yet – and they might not have moved the bodies. Are you sure you can handle it?"

"I'll be fine."

He glanced sideways at me. "Johnny, are you sure?"

I nodded stiffly. "I need to do this, Da."

Flames, smoke, and fire were all I could see, all I could smell when my father pulled onto the street. Reality came crashing down on me as I took in the sight of Shannon's house burning. Jesus Christ, I'd been in that house just a couple of hours ago.

*Those kids . . .*

*Shannon . . .*

A shudder rolled through me.

*They could have all been burnt to death.*

"Da," I choked out, eyes locked on the ambulance and fire engines. "I had the chance to save her and I didn't . . ."

"No," my father replied, cutting me off as he parked the car and turned to face me. "You saved her children."

"But she was *right* there," I strangled out, shaking. "Right in front of me." I dropped my head in my hands. "And now they don't have anyone."

"They still have us," Dad corrected, unfastening his seatbelt. "And I still have you." Reaching over, he grabbed my neck and forced me to look at him. "You could have died in that house tonight," he whispered. "I could have lost my boy—" He pressed his forehead to mine and exhaled a ragged breath. "I'd throw the whole world away to keep you – them included – and I'm not sorry for it."

"I'm fine, Da," I choked out. "I'm okay—"

"Then don't do this to yourself," he ordered, smoothing my hair back. "You did everything *right*. You are a *good* man. You saved her *children*."

"I feel so responsible," I confessed.

"*Don't*," he replied, steely-blue eyes locked on mine. "This is *not* on you. This is the work of a madman."

"How could he do that?" I croaked out. "I don't understand . . ."

"Neither do I, son," Dad replied. "And I don't want to." Pressing a kiss to my brow, he leaned back and looked me straight in the eye. "I need to go and get Joey now," he said calmly. "You can stay in the car, Johnny. You don't need to come with me—"

Commotion surrounding a group of Gardaí caught my attention, and we both turned to see Joey thrashing around like a maniac, throwing off a blanket they were trying to place over his shoulders. He was frantic and screaming as he tried to push and barge his way into the house. He was all on his own. The last Lynch, standing all alone. "My brothers and sister!" he was screaming, as he pushed against the Gardaí holding him back. "Let me the fuck in!"

"There's no one else inside."

"You're wrong!" he roared. "My brothers and sister are upstairs! They're inside that house. You have to let me get them. I left them! I left them in there with her!"

"Ah shit," Dad muttered, as he climbed out of his Mercedes and jogged towards the house. "Joey? It's alright, lad."

"I left them in there!" he continued to scream. "Get your fucking hands off me, you dirty pig—"

"Ah, shite." Unfastening my seatbelt, I shoved the car door open and rushed for the house. Ducking under the tape, I moved straight for my girlfriend's brother, slipping past the authorities trying to stop me. "Joe, it's okay—"

"Kav," he strangled out, noticing me. "I fucking left them in there." Tears were dripping down his soot-stained cheeks as he broke free from a Garda's hold and ran straight for me. "You have to help me get them out," he panted, eyes wild, and clothes covered in soot and smoke stains. "I walked out – I got pissed and left – but I couldn't do it. I couldn't leave them, so I came back, but the house was – and my mother . . . fuck, Shannon . . . Tadhg! Nobody's listening to me—"

"I have them, Joey," I snapped at him, desperate to get him to *hear* me. "I got them out."

"You *have* them—" His voice cracked. "You got them *out*?"

I nodded, shaking. "Ollie, Tadhg, Sean, and Shannon."

"Shit . . . Darren." Panic filled his eyes and he bolted towards the house once more. "My brother's still in there—"

"No, he's at my house, too," I choked out, dragging him back to me. "They're all there. I swear to god, lad, all of your brothers and Shannon are at my place right now." Wrapping my arms around him, I held him back as I whispered, "They're safe."

644 • KEEPING 13644 • KEEPING 13

A ragged breath tore from his throat and he sagged against me.

"You both need to get out of here," a fireman barked. "It's not safe."

"We're going," I strangled out, backing away with Joey in my arms. "Come on, lad—" My breath caught in my throat when my gaze landed on the body bags being wheeled into the back of an ambulance. I spun us both around, desperately trying to block the image out of both my head and his. "You don't need to watch this."

"This is my fault," he whispered.

"No." Shaking my head, I hauled him back under the tape and moved straight for my father's car. "It's not." Flicking my gaze up to meet Dad's, I gestured for him to climb in. "This is his fault, Joey. Not yours."

"I was high," he choked out. "I lost my head and walked out on them."

"And if you stayed, you'd have been passed out in your bed," I barked. "Darren wouldn't have been out trying to find you, Shannon wouldn't have been awake to call me, and you all would have burned to death in your sleep!"

"Jesus Christ," he hissed, stiffening in my arms. "My mother—"

"This is *not* on you," I practically snarled in his ear as I hauled him into the backseat of my father's car and climbed in beside him. "So don't you dare let that bastard get in your head!"

Sinking down on the seat, Joey tipped his head back and closed his eyes, still as a statue and silent as a ghost.

"You didn't do this," I repeated, leaning over to fasten his seatbelt. "He did this."

"Joey," Dad said from the driver's seat as he started the engine and pulled away from the house. "You're going to come home with us now, okay?"

He started to shake violently, but didn't respond. Keeping his eyes clenched shut, Joey placed his hands on his knees to steady himself.

"We're going to take care of you," Dad continued, keeping his voice calm and steady. "And that's not me asking you, son – that's me telling you."

"I should have been here," he whispered, trembling. "It's my job to keep them safe."

"They *are* safe." Reaching over, I slung an arm around his shoulders. "And so are you."

"No." He shook his head and I watched as a tear trickled down his cheek. "It was my job to keep *her* safe."

"They're going to hate me," Joey hissed, backing away from the sitting room door when we finally managed to coax him from the car into the house. "I can't do it. They're going to blame me—"

He spun around to leave, but my father clamped his hands down on his shoulders, forcing him to keep eye contact with him. "Nobody could hate you," Dad coaxed, keeping ahold of Joey for fear he would run. It was a very big possibility with this guy. He was a flight risk. "And no one is blaming you for anything."

"Get off—" Breaking free from my father's hold, he heaved violently. "I don't want you to touch me."

"It's okay," Dad replied calmly. "You're safe."

"I fucked it all," he strangled out, gripping his hair with his hands. "I fucked it all."

"Then we'll fix it," Dad replied. "I can help you, Joey, but you need to let me."

"I don't need your help," he choked out. "I just need—" He glanced around wildly, looking cornered and frightened. Backing up a couple of steps, he ran a hand through his sooty hair and asked, "Where's Shan?" Shaking, he looked around once more, clearly agitated and frightened. "Where's my sister?"

"She's upstairs sleeping," I told him, trying to keep my voice steady. "In my room. You can go up to her if you want, lad," I coaxed, edging closer to him with my hands up. "Whatever you want to do—"

"Don't touch me," he spat, batting at my father's hand when he reached for him. Looking startled, he shook his head and hissed, "Just . . . just stay back."

"Joey, it's okay," I coaxed, closing the space between us. "You're okay—"

"Don't fucking touch me!" he hissed again, shoving at my chest. "I don't want—"

The sitting room door swung open before he had a chance to finish his sentence and my mother appeared in the doorway. "Oh, Joey, love," Mam sobbed, moving straight for him. Not stopping until her hands were cupping his cheeks, my mother looked up at him. "Oh, my poor sweetheart," she soothed, pulling his head down to rest on her shoulder. "Come here to me."

Holding my breath, I watched him warily, praying that he didn't do anything in this moment to make me have to hurt him. If he lashed out at my mother, grief-stricken or not, I would lose my bleeding mind.

Exhaling a ragged breath, he slumped against her, arms shooting out to clutch her tightly. "What am I going to do?"

"I'm here," Mam whispered in his ear as she stroked his hair and rubbed his back. "Shh, I'm right here for you, Joey, love."

"You came back," Ollie sobbed as he came running out of the sitting room. "Tadhg! Joey's here." Mam stepped aside just as Ollie threw himself at his brother. "I knew you'd come back," he cried. "I told them all."

"O-ee," Sean wailed, toddling into the hallway with his hands out. "O-ee!"

Sinking to his knees on the hallway tiles, Joey scooped his baby brother into his arms. "I'm sorry, Seany-boo." Sniffling, he hooked an arm around Ollie and held both boys to his chest. "I'm so sorry, Ol."

"Mammy's in heaven," Ollie cried. "The Guards said Daddy took her away."

Sniffing, Joey nodded and pulled them closer. "It's okay."

Mam buried her face in my father's chest, sobbing quietly. "Shh," Dad whispered, wrapping an arm around her. "It's okay, baby."

"But she's gone," Ollie wept. "Gone to heaven without us."

"Mammy," Sean cried. "Mammy gone."

"She's not gone, guys," Joey whispered, sniffling. "She's just an angel now instead."

"An angel?" Ollie sniffled, looking up at Joey. "With wings?"

"Yeah. Big, beautiful wings," he choked out, wiping his cheek against his shoulder. "A special angel just for you."

"Daddy?" Sean asked, looking wary. "Ow, ow."

"Daddy's all gone," Joey promised. "No more ow, Sean."

"Mammy's an angel?" Ollie whispered, sounding almost reverent. "Wow."

"Yeah, and she's watching you right now," Joey continued to speak in a low, hushed voice to his brothers. "She doesn't want to see you crying. That would m-make her sad. You need to be h-happy—" his voice broke off and he dragged in several sharp breaths before continuing, "Think happy thoughts, okay?"

"You left." Tadhg's sharp voice came from the sitting room doorway. Tears dripped down his cheeks as he stared at Joey, jaw jutting out. "You fucking *left* us!"

"Leave him alone," Ollie defended, sniffling. "He's back now."

"O-ee, no go," Sean croaked out. "O-ee stay with Sean."

"I know," Joey choked out, voice trembling, as he stared back at his brother. "I'm sorry."

"I hate you!" A small sob of pain tore from Tadhg's throat, and then he was running, barreling against Joey, folding himself up in his big brother's arms. "I fucking hate you," Tadhg sobbed as he clung to Joey. "I hate you so much."

"I know." Clenching his eyes shut, Joey held all three boys against him. "Me, too."

"You found him," Darren said, voice thick with emotion and relief, as he stood in the doorway where Tadhg had just been, eyes locked on my father. "Thank you." Staggering forward, he hesitated for the briefest moment before couching down beside his brothers. "Hey, Joe."

"Hey, Dar," Joey whispered, green eyes glued to his brother.

"You okay?"

Joey shook his head and his face contorted in pain.

"Look at me—" Cupping his face in his hands, Darren pressed his forehead to Joey's and exhaled a ragged breath. "You did more for her than anyone else."

Joey clenched his eyes shut. "I didn't do enough—"

"You did," Darren corrected, voice hoarse and raspy. "You are the reason they survived as long as they did. Not me or anyone else. Just you."

Tears trickled down his cheeks. "No, I should have been there—"

"*You*," he repeated. "You couldn't have done anything more."

Silently, Mam and Dad ushered Tadhg, Ollie, and Sean back into the sitting room, giving Darren and Joey some privacy.

"I left them," Joey strangled out, dropping his head on Darren's shoulder. "I did that to them. Me. I walked *away*."

"You didn't leave anyone," Darren whispered, smoothing his hand over his brother's head. "You just took a time-out."

"I'm in trouble, Darren," he squeezed out through sobs. "I've got a problem and I can't stop."

"I know," Darren soothed, holding onto him. "We'll get you some help, Joe. I promise."

"He did it," Joey choked out, crying hard now. "He finally finished her off—" His voice cracked and he heaved a huge sob. "Jesus Christ, he burned her alive . . . "

The sound of a car engine came from outside and I spun around and moved shakily for the door. I couldn't be in here. I couldn't listen to their pain another second. Yanking the front door open, I practically ran out into the night, staggering away from the house in my bid to get some clarity.

When my eyes landed on the silver Ford Focus parking up outside, and the familiar blond head climbing out, I felt my body give out beneath me.

"I've got you, Johnny," Gibsie said, wrapping his arms around me just before I collapsed in a heap. "I'm right here, lad," he whispered, lowering us both to the gravel. "Let it out."

So, I did.

"You saved their lives, Johnny," Gibsie stated when I'd managed to compose myself enough to tell him what had happened. We were sitting, side by side, in our old, battered treehouse down the back field from my house, looking out as the sun rose over the mountains. "All of them."

"You should have seen the baby, lad. He was soaked in whiskey." Shuddering, I hooked my arms around my knees and swallowed down a scream. "At the time, I didn't even think about it – I just thought that drunk bastard spilled his drink on him or something." I shook my head, feeling lost and bewildered. "It didn't click in my mind, Gibs."

"Why would it?" he replied, mirroring my actions. "Who does something like that?"

"Him," I muttered, still reeling.

Gibsie sighed heavily. "Are they all in your house now?"

"Yeah, they're inside with my folks. I just . . . I had to get out and get some breathing space." I shrugged helplessly. "It's too upsetting."

"You did good, Johnny," he replied quietly.

"She was *right there*," I choked out, eyes filling with tears. "Looking right in my eyes. I told her I would come back for her." I clenched my eyes shut and shuddered at the memory. "She looked resigned, Gibs. Like she *knew*."

"She probably did know, lad," he told me. "And you must have given that lady some serious peace. Seeing her kids getting out? Knowing that they would be safe? You gave that to her, lad. She couldn't go anywhere. She knew that. The whole place was rigged to blow. If she had tried to leave with you and he lit that match, you'd have all burned to death before you had a chance to blink– you and Sean included."

"Why would he do that?" I hissed, shivering at the realization of how close to death I'd come. "Why would anybody do *that,* Gibs?

"I don't know, Johnny," he replied.

"It doesn't make any sense," I strangled out.

"No," he agreed with a heavy sigh. "It doesn't."

"I'm so freaked out," I confessed, biting down on my lip. "I keep thinking, what if he turned around when we were in the hall?" I shivered again. "What the hell would have happened to those kids—"

"But that didn't happen because you got them out," Gibsie reminded me. "You're all safe, lad."

"She got them out, too." I turned to face him. "She helped me, lad, and I know that sounds fucked up, but she did. It was like she was . . . *willing* me to get them out of the house." I shuddered. "And once I did? She just turned around and went back to him. She . . . *sacrificed* herself for those kids. For me . . . "

"Shit," he whispered.

"Yeah." I nodded. "Shite."

We sat in silence for several minutes before Gibsie finally rose from his feet and moved for the ladder. "I better make tracks," he said. "My mam will be in meltdown mode."

"Gibs?"

"Yeah, lad?"

"Don't go home yet, okay?"

He paused on the ladder, hands clasping the wooden frame, and I watched as a multitude of emotions flashed across his features. Finally, he climbed back up and reclaimed the space beside me. "You know, if you wanted to watch the sun come up with me, you only had to say, lad," he mused, nudging my shoulder with his.

"Yeah," I choked out a hollow laugh. "That's what it is."

# Rebuilding

## JOHNNY

"What are you doing up there, lad?" Gibsie asked on Friday afternoon when he found me down the field at the back of the house. It had been four days since the fire, since Shannon and her brothers' world had collapsed and I'd never felt more helpless in my life. The sun was splitting the stones and I'd been out here since dawn broke and the crying restarted. Sick to death of social workers and the Gardaí, not to mention family friends and relatives, I kept my distance from the house. Nothing I said or did seemed to be helping matters anyway, so I decided to remove myself from the situation. Not far enough that I couldn't come back if she needed me, but enough to give her some space with her family.

Besides, people had been calling to the house all day, every day since it happened, and if I had to hear the *'you're a hero, young man'* spiel one more time, I was going to lose my shit. I was no hero; I loved my girlfriend and I did what any other lad in my position would have done.

"You're afraid of heights, Johnny," Gibsie reminded me, like it was something I could easily forget. "And you're up pretty high there, buddy."

"I'm revamping our old treehouse," I replied as I dangled from a branch of the old oak, with a hammer and nails in hand. "And I'm not afraid of heights," I bit out. "I'm warily cautious of anything that poses the threat of me plummeting to my death."

"Makes sense." With his hands on his hips, Gibsie stared up at me, expression thoughtful. "So, why are we revamping the fort?"

"Because I need to do something," I explained. "And I can't do anything in the house."

"You been to training today?"

"Nope."

"The gym?"

"Nope."

He signed heavily. "Johnny . . ."

"I need to do this, Gibs," I choked out, voice thick with emotion. I felt useless and it didn't bode well with me. I couldn't fix this for her and I couldn't change what had happened. "I need to fix *something*."

"Then we'll fix it," Gibsie replied simply. "I'll call the lads."

Within an hour, Hughie and Feely had arrived on one of Feely's father's tractors and trailers, drawing old boards and planks of timber. "Hope you don't mind, Cap, but my mam's after pulling up with Claire and Lizzie," Hughie puffed as he hauled a tractor tire off the back of the trailer and rolled it over to the trunk of the tree. "They're gone inside."

"Pity about Lizzie the viper," Gibsie grumbled, throwing some old boards off to the side. "I hope she's in good spirits."

I shrugged, not breaking my stride, as I ripped the flooring off the old treehouse and tossed the boards down to Gibsie. "Can't hurt."

After that, we all worked in silence. I didn't think any of us wanted to be inside right now. I couldn't leave her, but I couldn't fix this, and the guilt I was feeling was drowning me. It was insurmountable and I was close to my breaking point. Throughout the afternoon and evening, Mam popped in and out with trays of sandwiches and flasks of tea, but none of us broke stride long enough to make small talk.

"When's the funeral?" Feely asked after a couple of hours of working together in companionable silence.

"After twelve o' clock mass on Monday," I replied, feeling my chest squeeze tight at the thought. "They only got the bodies back this morning – with the post mortems they had to perform and all that shite."

"So, the rosary is tomorrow night, and the removal is on Sunday?"

I nodded stiffly. "It's a closed funeral – obviously, it will be closed coffins, too."

Feely sighed heavily. "Shit, lad."

"Yeah." Wiping my brow with my forearm, I exhaled a heavy sigh. "Throw me up a bottle of water, will ya?" Locking my legs around the limb I was balancing on, I whipped off my t-shirt and tossed it away. "I'm bleeding melting up here."

"You're not the only one sweating your tits off," Feely grumbled, throwing a bottle up to me. "I'm as a red as a lobster."

I peered down at his bare shoulders and winced. "Ah, lad. You should put some cream on your shoulders."

"I did," he growled. "We don't all tan like you, Cap."

I glanced down at myself and shrugged. "I'm not that tanned."

"*Yet*," Feely countered. "Give it a week of this weather and you'll look like you the spent the fecking summer in Oz."

"Ah now, don't be jealous, Pa. You have a grand farmer's tan," Gibsie offered. "Your arms are lovely."

"I *am* a farmer," Feely growled. "But thanks, Gibs. I appreciate the sentiment. Your arms are lovely, too."

"I'm lovely all over," Gibsie corrected, gesturing to his tanned chest. "I'm sallow skinned," he added with a wink. "The sun loves me."

"Good for you," Feely shot back huffily.

"Someone needs to tell your mother to bring the Child of Prague statue back inside, Pa," Hughie puffed. 'Tis hot enough and you won't be doing hay until June."

"She's superstitious," Feely said with a noncommittal shrug. "And they're at silage this week, so she won't be taking him out of the field for a while."

"Great," Hughie groaned. "We'll just swelter so."

"You guys are so fucking weird," I chuckled. "You seriously believe putting a little, holy statue out in a field brings the good weather?"

"You're damn straight we do, city boy," Gibsie shot back. "It's one-hundred percent effective. Same as when my nanny lights a candle for me before exams. It's bulletproof."

I rolled my eyes. "Culchies."

"Hey – what about Joey?" Hughie asked then. Covering his eyes from the sun, he looked up at me and asked, "What's happening there?"

I leaned down and grabbed another board off Gibsie before dragging it

654 • KEEPING 13

up and laying it down on the beams of the treehouse. "The treatment place are sending some guys down to escort him after the service on Monday."

"Jesus," Hughie muttered, rubbing his jaw. "What the hell was he thinking getting mixed up with drugs?"

"He was probably thinking his dad was a psycho prick who spent the best of his life beating the living shit out of him and he wanted an escape," Gibsie snapped, pulling his t-shirt out of the back of his jeans and using it to wipe his brow. "None of us know what he went through, Hugh, we haven't been in his shoes, so don't judge him."

"I'm not judging him," Hughie replied, holding his hands up. "I'm just sorry for him – for all of them. I remember when Shannon first started hanging around with Claire. He was so fucking prickly and protective of her. I could never figure it out. We didn't go to the same primary school or anything, but we were the same age and I couldn't understand why he cared so much about his little sister. I couldn't fucking stand Claire when we were small, but Joey? He kept Shannon with him everywhere he went. Now I know why."

"How long will he be gone?" Feely asked.

"The summer," I replied, feeling numb to the bone as I hammered the board down. "It's a ninety-day program, but it depends on how he copes. It might take longer. It might take less." Shrugging, I added, "He wants to do it."

"That's good," Gibsie agreed, tone steady, as he passed me up another board to hammer down. "He's only eighteen. He's got as good a chance as any of beating it."

"And the rest of them?" Feely asked. "What happens to Shannon and the younger ones?"

"They're staying here," I said. "Da pushed for an emergency hearing. Himself and Ma were approved temporary guardianship."

"And Darren was okay with that?" Gibsie asked, looking confused.

"Apparently, he supported it," I said wearily. "He's still staying here."

"But he won't stay forever, right?" Gibsie asked. "He'll go back to Belfast eventually?"

"Who fucking knows anymore, lad." I shrugged, feeling stupid for not having the answers. "My folks said he can stay for as long as he wants."

"And Shannon?" Feely asked. "How's she doing?"

My shoulders sagged in defeat. "She's a mess."

"Where is she now?"

"Last I saw, she was with Joey," I mumbled. "They were holed up in one of the spare bedrooms together. They don't leave each other's side." I shook my head. "They're like magnets."

"What about the others?"

"I don't know if Sean understands what's happening, but Ollie and Tadhg are as good as you can expect given the fact that their father just burnt himself and their mother alive," I came right out and told them.

Feely flinched. "Jesus."

"I don't even know what to say, lad," Hughie choked out. "I'm so sorry."

"Yeah? Well, me too." Turning my attention back to the treehouse, I hammered the last floor board into place. "I should have dragged her out of that house with me when I had the chance." Furious with myself and the whole damn world, I tossed the last of the nails down, and then I flung my hammer for good measure. "Her blood is on my hands. Those kids have no mother because I left her in that house. With *him*. I looked her in the eyes and I walked away. I left her to burn. It's on *me*."

"No, it fucking is not!" Gibsie snapped, climbing up the old rickety ladder to join me in the newly floored treehouse. "We've been through this – that kid was a walking explosion, Johnny! The entire house was rigged to go up in flames the minute that psycho freak sparked that match," he continued to rant. "You saved four lives, lad. Four *innocent* lives – five, including yourself. Don't punish yourself, because *you* did more for that family than anyone else."

"I just feel so responsible," I choked out.

"Oh, you will be responsible," Gibsie shot back, eyes narrowed. "For me throwing you off this fucking tree if I ever hear that shit come out of your mouth again."

"I just—"

"You are *not* responsible!"

"But I—"

"Hughie, get me the hammer," Gibsie ordered. "I'm going to beat some sense into his big, stupid brain!"

"It's how I feel, lad," I snapped.

"Then your feelings are all fucked up!" Gibsie countered. "So, stop it!"

"Stop it?"

"Yes. Stop it," Gibsie growled. "Stop feeling like that. It's dumb. It's pointless. You're making yourself miserable. You're a fucking hero and if you don't cop on and get a fucking handle on yourself, you're going to be a dead hero because I'll kill you, Johnny. You know I'll do it!"

"Uh, that's probably not the best threat given the circumstances, Gibs," Hughie interjected.

"I know what it's like, Johnny," Gibsie barked. "I've been there, so I can tell you to stop. I have the right and the experience to tell you to get a fucking grip. You did what you could and you did a damn good job. Now *enough*. Stop torturing yourself. Dwelling won't change what happened to her. All it's going to change is what happens to *you* – present and future tenses."

I stared across the treehouse at him for a long moment before a reluctant smile pulled at my lips. "You'd be a fucking terrible counsellor, Gibs."

"You're smiling, aren't ya?" he shot back, giving me a lopsided grin.

"Very true," Feely mused from the ground, hammer in hand. "Do you need this?"

"That depends," Gibsie replied, keeping his eyes locked on mine. "Am I going to have to hammer some sense into you, Johnny?"

I shook my head in defeat. "No, you already did that, lad."

"Good." Gibsie nodded in approval. "And here's another thing that's going to happen—" Swinging down from a branch, he landed on his feet and stretched before turning back to look up at me. "We're going to finish this treehouse. We're going to make it the best fucking revamp imaginable and put a smile back on those boys' faces. And then we're going to train, because *you* are going to be ready for those Irish coaches tomorrow morning."

"Gibs." I shook my head. "I can't go now—"

"You are fucking going, Johnny Kavanagh," he said, cutting me off, "if I have to strap you to my back and take you there myself! This is your future, and you're not throwing it away. No goddamn way in hell am I letting that happen."

"Jesus," I muttered, rubbing my jaw. "When did you get so bossy?"

Gibsie shrugged. "Sometimes Robin has to take the lead."

"Robin?" Hughie laughed. "Did you seriously just refer to yourself as Robin?"

"So, Cap's Batman and you're Robin?" Feely mused. "Hmm. Makes sense."

"You're so fucked in the head," Hughie snickered.

"Could be worse," Gibsie shot back with a grin. "We could be like you two."

"Oh yeah?" Hughie taunted. "And how's that?"

"Yeah," Gibsie agreed, smirking. "Bebop and Rocksteady."

"I'm not Bebop *or* Rocksteady!" Hughie huffed, looking offended. "If I'm anything, I'm Robin!"

"Uh-huh." Gibsie snickered. "And you say I'm fucked in the head? Yeah, *okay*, Bebop."

"That makes no sense," Hughie argued. "They're from two completely different cartoons."

"Exactly," Gibsie drawled. "Just like we're on two completely different levels." Grinning, he held his hand over his head and said, "I'm up here with your sister, and you're—" he dropped his hand to his waist, "all the way down here . . ."

"Feely, give me the hammer," Hughie snarled as he stalked towards Gibsie. "I'm going bury this fucker, once and for all."

# I See You

## SHANNON

"Nanny is downstairs with Darren," I whispered, sitting on the edge of his bed, stroking his clammy forehead. "Do you want to go down and see her?"

He didn't respond. Instead, he just continued to tremble and clutch the pillow he had pressed to his stomach. At least he wasn't vomiting anymore. To be honest, I didn't think there was anything left inside of him to throw up. His eyes were vacant, hollow, green orbs in his head. Nothing seemed to be happening.

"Joe?"

Silence.

"Please talk to me," I begged, brushing his blond hair out of his eyes.

Nothing.

A tear dripped down his cheek and I reached over to swipe it away. "I love you." Leaning over, I pressed my cheek to his. "So much."

Unresponsive, he continued to lay on his side, facing the window and staring out at nothing in particular. The doctors had come and gone several times in the past few days since the fire. According to them, my brother was going through withdrawals. He'd admitted to Mrs. Kavanagh and Darren that he had been using serious drugs for months and months before I ended up in the hospital. I hadn't known. I hadn't picked up on the signs. He was also in shock, and I was terrified to leave his side in case he ran away again. Looking at him right now, I wasn't sure he had the energy to lift himself out of the bed, but I could never be sure with Joey. He was as unpredictable as an Irish summer.

They were taking him away soon. Once the funeral was over, he was going into a special hospital to make him better. Somewhere they could treat his addictions and his mental health. I didn't understand why he had to leave, and I didn't want him to go, but he had signed the paperwork himself just before he stopped talking. He *wanted* to leave, and I was terrified of Monday coming, because I honestly didn't know how I was going to survive all of this without him.

A soft knock came from the other side of the bedroom Joey was staying in and Mrs. Kavanagh's head popped through the crack in the door. "Hello, Shannon, love," she said, smiling warmly at me. "You have two visitors here to see you."

My breath hitched in my throat and I stiffened. I couldn't handle any more social workers or Guards. I was too tired. "I don't—"

"Claire and Lizzie," Mrs. Kavanagh hurried to explain. "They're downstairs in the sitting room, pet."

"I, uh . . . " I hesitated, not wanting to leave my brother. "Maybe . . . I shouldn't leave him on his—"

"And I have a visitor for you, too, Joey," Mrs. Kavanagh announced in a gentle tone. She pushed the door all the way open to reveal Aoife standing beside her. "Go on in, love."

I panicked at the sight of his girlfriend, knowing that the last time Joey spoke, he warned us to *not* let her in. He made Darren promise to keep her away. He didn't want her here. He didn't want her to *see*.

Joey remained completely motionless, still clutching the pillow, still staring out the window, as Aoife walked into the room. "You can't hide from me," she told him as she moved straight for him. "And you can't give up, either."

I watched him carefully, praying for some sort of reaction and then feeling a spike of relief shoot through me when he jerked at the sound of her voice.

Standing up, I hovered close to the bed, unwilling to leave him, eyes glued to Aoife as she sat down on the side of the bed he was facing. "My Joey," she whispered, cupping his cheek in her hand. "My baby."

A shudder rolled through him and he tightened his hold on the pillow, feet twitching sporadically.

Leaning her face close to his, she gently nuzzled him with her nose. "Come on back to me," she coaxed, whispering in his ear as she smoothed her hand over his hair and then his cheek and jaw. "Because I'm not giving you up."

He shook harder, limbs spasming, as a pained groan tore from his throat.

My eyes widened in shock. It was the first noise he had made in days.

"I know," Aoife continued to whisper as she touched him and petted him like he was a small child. "You're in there, aren't you? Hmm?" She pressed a kiss to the corner of his mouth. "I see you, Joey Lynch." She stroked her nose against his and whispered, "You can't hide from me."

His hand shot out then, moving straight to her stomach.

"That's it," she encouraged, pulling his head onto her lap and cradling him there. "Come on back to me, baby."

Another pained noise tore from his throat and he buried his face in her stomach, shaking violently.

"It's okay," she whispered, leaning over his broad shoulders to hold him close. "You can't scare me away." Her blonde hair pillowed around them as she whispered, "You're mine, remember?"

"Come on, Shannon, pet," Mrs. Kavanagh cleared her throat and said and I tore my eyes off my brother to look at her. She smiled sadly. "Let's give Joey and Aoife some time on their own."

Reluctantly, I complied and followed Mrs. Kavanagh out of the room, watching as she closed the bedroom door behind us. Nervous and unsure, I trailed after her, feet faltering when we reached the top of the staircase and I heard all the different voices coming from downstairs. "I don't know," I blurted out, stalling.

"Hmm?" Mrs. Kavanagh turned back to look at me. "What did you say, pet?"

"I'm not sure," I strangled out, clutching the banister. I inclined my head to the stairs and shifted around uneasily. "There's a lot of people down there."

Mrs. Kavanagh's eyes filled with sympathy. "Oh, my little pet." She closed the space between us and pulled me into her arms. "You're safe with us."

"Do I have to go down there?" I whispered, shaking. "I'm scared."

"What are you scared of, Shannon?" she coaxed. "Hmm? Nothing's going to hurt you again, darling."

"Reality," I admitted. "Facing everyone."

"Reality can be daunting," she agreed, taking my hand in hers. "And facing it can be worse, but you're a strong girl." Smiling at me, she added, "And you can do this, Shannon Lynch. I know you can."

I blew out a shaky breath. "Really?"

Smiling, she nodded. "Really."

Exhaling a ragged breath, I released my grip of the bannister and walked down the stairs, clinging to her hand for all I was worth, knowing that this woman must have fallen clean out of heaven above because she wanted to help us. To *keep* us. *All of us.* I didn't understand her, I probably never would, but I knew I never wanted to leave this house. She was good and kind, and she made me feel *safe.*

"Is Johnny around?" I asked when I reached the bottom step, forcing myself to ask the question and feeling my heart beat rapidly from the pressure it was under.

"He's around, love," Mrs. Kavanagh replied. "He's down the back field with the boys."

I hadn't seen much of Johnny since that night. Everything was happening so quickly and I was so afraid of leaving Joey alone that I hadn't spent any time with him. I was feeling his absence in the deepest part of me, which was ridiculous considering I was staying at his house.

"Should I call him?" Mrs. Kavanagh asked, dragging my thoughts back to the present. "He'll come straight back to the house, Shannon. I know he'd love to spend some time with you—"

"Oh, no, no," I hurried to say, releasing my hold on her hand. "It's okay, please don't bother him." Swallowing deeply, I forced a smile. "He's with his friends."

"Are you sure?" she asked, eyeing me with concern. "I know you wouldn't be bothering him in the slightest."

*No.* "I'm sure," I croaked out, clasping my hands together. "I'll, uh, I'll go say hi to the girls now, if that's okay?"

"Of course." Taking a step back, she waved me towards the sitting room. "You don't need to ask anyone's permission."

"Thank you," I told her in a voice thick with emotion. Spinning around before I lost it, I forced myself to breathe slowly as I made my way down the fancy hallway and slipped inside the sitting room.

My bravery, resolve, and grip on my emotions floated away from my grasp the moment I laid eyes on my two best friends.

"Shan," Claire cried, jerking up from the couch.

"Oh, Shan," Lizzie choked out, joining her.

"I'm so sorry about your parents," Claire whispered.

"Me, too," Lizzie whispered. "Are you okay?"

My face contorted in pain and I shook my head before rushing towards them.

"We're here," they both whispered, throwing their arms around me. "We're not leaving you."

The floodgates inside of my heart opened and I just let it all out, pouring every ounce of pain and heartache out of my system before it crippled me to the point of no return.

# Hammers and Her

## JOHNNY

We were putting the finishing touches to the treehouse when Ollie's voice echoed up from the ground. "Whoa," he gasped, staring up at the four of us with a look of awe on his face. "That's the biggest treehouse I've ever seen!" He shook his head. "In my whole entire life."

"You like it?" I called back to him, leaning over the railing we'd added to the edge. "Pretty nice, huh?"

"Which one is he?" Feely whispered.

"Ollie," I replied quietly.

"He's my favorite," Gibsie announced.

"Hey, Ollie," Feely said, waving down at him.

"Yeah, hey, lad," Hughie added, popping up.

"Hi." He waved at the lads as his gaze trailed over the treehouse. "It's so cool, Johnny!" A huge smile spread across his face. "What are you guys doing up there?"

"We're having a secret meeting," Gibsie piped up. "Over-seventeens only, kid."

Ollie's face fell and I shook my head before turning to glare at Gibsie who was balmed-out on his back in the treehouse, smoking his brains out. "You bleeding eejit." Turning back to Ollie, I smiled down at him and said, "Don't mind him, Ollie. We made this for you and your brothers."

"You did?" His eyes widened. "Really?"

I nodded. "Yeah, so go and get Tadhg."

"Whoa!" Spinning on his heels, Ollie darted back through the field towards the house, screaming, "Tadhg!" at the top of his lungs. "You gotta come see this!"

"I don't want to give it up," Gibsie groaned, exhaling a cloud of smoke. "I love this treehouse."

"You are the biggest child I've ever met that never grew up," Feely muttered.

"But it's so nice," Gibsie huffed. "And now we have to hand it over."

"I'm sure they'll let you visit," I shot back, rolling my eyes. "Now put that cigarette out before they come back."

Less than three minutes later, Tadhg and Ollie came running through the field back to us.

"Holy shit!" Tadhg choked out when he reached the tree. His puffy eyes were wide in astonishment. "You guys seriously built this?"

"I told you," Ollie said proudly. "They made it for us."

"You did?" Tadhg frowned. "Why?"

"Because we were feeling generous," Gibsie drawled, climbing down the ladder. "And I expect free access whenever I want."

"It must be sturdy," Tadhg mused, casting a sideways glance at Gibsie. "To hold your weight."

"I'm not fat!" Gibsie huffed. "I'm a flanker! I'm supposed to be stocky. I'm all muscle. I'll show ya—"

"Jesus," I muttered, climbing down after him. "Keep your clothes on, Gibsie."

"Flanker," Tadhg snickered, darting up the ladder once Feely and Hughie had climbed down. "More like wanker."

"Oh now, he's *my* favorite," Hughie laughed.

"I'm going to lose my shit with that kid," Gibsie grumbled as he chased Tadhg back up the ladder. "You're twelve," he panted, climbing into the treehouse. "You're supposed to be a sweet child, not a little monster."

"If I was sweet, you might try and eat me," Tadhg shot back. "And you've clearly eaten enough."

"For the last time, I am not fat," Gibsie growled. "I'm big boned – there's a huge difference."

"Huge," Tadhg snickered, clearly enjoying the banter. "You've got that right."

"I can't deal with this kid," Gibsie growled.

"It's okay, Gibsie," Ollie said, joining them in the treehouse. "I don't think you're fat."

"Thank you, Ollie," Gibsie sniffed. "It's nice to know there's one nice kid around the place."

"That's 'cause I'm sweet," Ollie replied innocently. "Dellie says so."

"Will you lads be alright out here by yourselves if we head inside for a bit?" I called up to them.

"Oh, I'm never coming down," Ollie shouted back. "So I'm super okay."

"Hey, Johnny?" Tadhg called out, poking his head over the railing.

"Yeah?"

"Uh, thanks." His cheeks reddened. "For this."

"You're welcome."

"And, uh, for the other part, too," he croaked out, brown eyes trained on mine. "The coming to get us part."

"Yeah." I swallowed deeply and nodded. "No problem."

"Tadhg, look," Ollie squealed and Tadhg disappeared from sight. "It's a tennis scope."

"A what?"

"A tennis scope."

"Telescope," I heard Tadhg sigh. "Gibsie, give him a turn, will ya? He's only nine."

"Come on, Gibs," I chuckled, scratching the back of my head. "I'll make you a sandwich."

"Fine, but I want it toasted *and* a packet of crisps," Gibsie grumbled. "Oh, hold up – we forgot our tools."

"I swear he's stuck in his seven-year-old mind," Hughie mused.

"You're probably right," Feely agreed. "He hasn't changed much since we made our Communion."

"Timber—"

*Bang.*

"Ah, Jesus Christ!" I roared out, clutching the back of my head as pain ricocheted through my scalp. Glancing around me, I spotted the hammer on the grass and blanched. "What the fuck, Gibs?" I snarled, glaring up at the big bastard who was peeking over the railing. "*Timber*? What's that supposed to mean?"

"It's a code," Gibsie called back sheepishly.

"A code?" I demanded. "Code for what? Trying to split my head open?"

"Timber is a valid warning word to get out of the way, Johnny," he countered. "You're the academic. You should know this."

"So is fore," I spat. "Fore is a code."

Gibsie shrugged. "Fore's a golfing reference."

"I'm more of a golfer than a fucking woodcutter," I hissed, still clutching my head. "Jesus!"

"I was throwing a hammer, not a golf club," he defended, climbing down the ladder to join us. "Ah, balls, lad," he muttered, heading straight for me. "Your head's all gooey and bleeding."

"No shit, Sherlock," I snapped. "Because you threw a bleeding *hammer* at me."

"Technically, I threw a hammer *on* you, not at you – and I did call timber," he reminded me as he poked at my scalp. "It's not my fault you can't read signals – I think you might need a stitch or seven."

"Just give me your t-shirt," I growled. "And you're banned from the treehouse and handling tools. Do you hear me? No more."

"Are you okay, Johnny?" Ollie called out, sounding worried.

Ah shite.

*I couldn't even kill him in peace.*

"I'm grand, lads." Snatching Gibsie's t-shirt out of his hands, I pressed it to my head and forced a smile when all I wanted to do was throttle my best friend. "Make sure you both come back to the house before it gets too dark," I added, before turning my back on the treehouse and mouthing, "*You better run, bitch,*" to Gibsie who was already legging it in the direction of the house.

"Don't hurt him too much, Cap," Feely called out as I broke into a run after Gibsie.

"Don't listen to him, Cap," Hughie chuckled. "Torture him."

"Look – it's like a Hippo trying to outrun a Cheetah," I heard Tadhg and Ollie laugh, and even though I was mad as hell and had blood dripping down the back of my neck, I had to admit, it was a lovely sound.

"Gerard, you don't throw hammers at Johnny," Mam repeated for the tenth time when we walked back into the kitchen, having just returned from the out-of-hours doctor for a quick stitch-and-go.

"Fine," Gibsie huffed, folding his arms across his chest. "But you remind him right back of what he's not supposed to do to me."

"Oh, lord, save me from the stupidity of teenage boys." Setting her handbag down on the island, Mam ushered us both onto the stools and sighed heavily. "Johnny, you don't smother Gerard with your bloodied t-shirt and trip him up – you know he gets squeamish around bodily fluids."

"*My* bloodied t-shirt," Gibsie corrected, narrowing his eyes at me. "It was my bloodied t-shirt to match *my* broken chin."

"You didn't break your chin," I scoffed. "You grazed it."

His mouth fell open. "I have a gaping hole in my *face*!"

"Yeah." I glared back at him. "To match the gaping hole in my *head*!"

"I have *four* stitches," he growled, pointing to his bandaged chin.

I pointed to my bandaged head. "I have *six*!"

"The point is, you shouldn't be giving each other stitches," Mam snapped. "You're both going on eighteen years of age. You're getting a bit old in the tooth for this carrying on."

"Oh, Jesus," Dad said when he walked into the kitchen with Sean on his hip. "What did you two do now?"

"We had a small miscommunication," Gibsie replied, elbowing me in the ribs. "A little crossing of wires."

"Yeah," I agreed, elbowing him back. "But it's balanced out now." My gaze landed on Sean in his brand-new Bob the Builder pajama set and I winked at him. "How's my big man?"

He grinned back at me. "Onny." Wriggling down from my father's arms, he scooted across the kitchen, heading straight for me with his little hands up. "Ow-ow, Onny."

"Yeah." I nodded and bent down to pick him up. "That's right, but I'm okay." Setting him down on the counter in front of me, I poked his belly and snickered when he howled laughing. "You've got a big belly," I chuckled, poking him again and grinning like a dope when he squealed in delight. "Is this Santa's belly? Hmm? Give me that belly—"

"You really like this one, don't you?" Gibsie mused, watching as I lowered my head for Sean to investigate my bandage. "You're going soft, Kav."

"Look at him," I defended, pointing at my girlfriend's baby brother. I'd spent a lot of time with this kid since they all moved in. Sean always seemed the happiest to see me, and he was too bleeding heartbreaking to ignore. I knew it wasn't right to favor children, and I'd never admit it aloud, but if I had my pick of the bunch, it would be this one every single time. And maybe Ollie. Screw it, I liked them all, but this one? He was something else. "Look at those big eyes," I ordered, pointing at Sean's big, chocolate-button eyes. "He's like a puppy. How could you not love that face?"

"He's a person, not a puppy," Gibsie laughed.

"He's my puppy, aren't you, buddy?"

Sean nodded happily. "Onny." He smashed my cheeks in his hands. "My Onny."

"Your Onny?" Gibsie teased. "No, no, I don't think so." Draping an arm over my shoulders, he said, "This is my Onny."

Sean's face reddened. "My Onny." Clutching my face in his tiny hands, he pulled me closer. "My Onny."

"Christ, lad, you're like the baby whisperer," Gibsie chuckled, sounding impressed. "He was barely communicating the last time I saw him, and now he's all over you." Frowning, he asked, "Is it just the J's he has trouble with? Is it a speech impediment or something?"

"He doesn't have any trouble," I replied in a baby voice, pulling a face at Sean. "You're just taking your time, aren't ya, buddy?"

Sean nodded happily and I knew he didn't have a notion of what I was talking about, but he was so fucking cute that he made me laugh anyway.

"See that bold boy, Sean?" I teased, pointing to Gibsie. "We're going to get him, aren't we? What do we say when we chase people?"

"Oof." Narrowing his eyes at Gibsie, he lunged forward and barked, "Oof."

"Oh my god!" Clutching his stomach, Gibsie fell off the stool from laughing. "You did not teach the baby to bark!"

"Onny oof," Sean barked. "Onny shite oof."

"Johnny!" Mam gasped. "You did not teach the baby to curse."

"Ah, shite," I groaned.

"Ah, shite, Onny," Sean mimicked, rubbing my head. "Ah, shite."

"And that's enough play time with Johnny," Dad chuckled, sweeping Sean up in his arms once more. "Come on, little man." Grabbing a beaker of milk off the countertop, Dad strolled back down the hallway. "Let's have a story before bed."

"Don't read him that book," I called after him.

"Oh, don't worry, love," Mam coaxed. "I burned that book years ago for you."

"You're not still freaked out over that book, are you?" Gibsie snickered. "It's been *years*."

"I'm okay," I growled. "But he's only small."

"Johnny, lad, no one else thinks the way you do," he chuckled. "We don't all overanalyze everything like you do. It's a storybook about a chicken."

"It was legitimately terrifying," I defended. "I couldn't sleep for weeks."

"You couldn't sleep because you couldn't turn that brain of yours off," he shot back. "You're still the exact same now."

"He's right," Mam chimed in. "You're a bit of a worrier, love."

"Yeah," I muttered, deciding not to bother arguing when they were spot on. "Fair point."

"Well, I'm thinking I should hit the road and let you get some sleep before the big day," Gibsie said, giving me a meaningful look. "Do I need to come and pick you up in the morning and drag your ass over there, or are you going to be a big boy and drive yourself?"

"I'll drive," I told him. "Thanks anyway, lad."

"Oh, sweet Jesus, the trials," Mam gasped, slapping a hand over her mouth. "I completely forgot."

"It's alright, Mammy K," Gibsie said. "I've got your boy's back." He gave me a scathing look. "Be up or I'm coming for you."

"I'll be there," I replied, voice thick and gruff. "I'll see this through."

"Damn straight you will," Gibsie replied, nodding. "Call me as soon as you're done." Turning to my mother, he pressed a kiss to her cheek before swiping a sandwich off the tray she was holding and sauntering out the back door. "Tootles."

"Johnny," Mam whispered when the back door closed behind him. "I am so sorry, love." Hurrying over to me, she pulled out the stool Gibsie had vacated and sat down next to me. "I don't know how I forgot about the coaches coming down tomorrow."

"Ma, it's okay," I muttered. "It's not a big deal."

"It's a huge deal," she corrected, placing her hand on my arm. "You've worked so hard to come back from injury. Your whole life . . . oh, Johnny, baby, I'm so sorry."

"You've had a lot on your mind," I reassured her. "And a lot of kids to be minding. It's just another trial. Don't even worry about it."

"But you're my son," she choked out. "I should have been supporting you, and helping you prepare for this."

"Ma, we have six people staying in this house that just lost their home and both of their parents," I told her. "I'm not going to begrudge loaning them mine."

"Oh, pet." Mam smiled sadly. "I just want you to know that you're still my number one."

"I know." I smirked. "And you should know that I don't need that kind of reassurance." I patted her hand. "I know who I am, and I know who I belong to." I shrugged. "I'm not worried, Ma, so don't worry about me."

"Do you want me to come with you in the morning?" she offered, squeezing my hand. "I can wait in the car, or sit in the stands—"

"Show up to training with my mother?" I shook my head and laughed. "Come on, Ma, what are you trying to do to me? The coaches would never let me live it down."

"What about Dad then?" she offered, tone hopeful.

"No." I shook my head. "No Da. No you, and no Gibsie. I'll go by myself."

"Oh, Johnny, are you sure?"

"Hundred percent."

"Fair enough," she sighed. "But I'll be thinking about you the entire time – and I'll light a candle for you, pet."

"Try not to worry about it," I replied. "It's just another day."

"How about I do the worrying for the both of us?" she offered, smiling. "You just concentrate on blowing their socks off."

"Yeah." I pushed down my nerves and forced a smile. "I'll do that."

"Oh, you will," she replied. "You always do, love."

"How's Shannon?" I asked then, forcing the question out of my mouth, the one I was both desperate to ask and terrified to know the answer to. "Did she come out of her room today?"

"She came downstairs for a little while to visit with Claire and Lizzie." Mam sighed heavily. "But she went back up to Joey shortly after. Aoife's still up there, too. I told her that she can stay as long as she wants. She seems to be making more progress with him than anyone else."

I nodded, slowly digesting everything. "And Darren?"

"He's dropping their Nanny home," Mam explained. "She's such a lovely lady, Johnny. My heart goes out to the poor crater. Marie was her granddaughter, you know. She raised her from a small child."

"Is she eating yet?" I asked, unable to concentrate on anything other than my girlfriend. "Did she have anything today?"

"Yes, she had some soup with the girls," Mam replied.

"Thank Christ," I choked out, shoulders sagging in relief. "She's after losing a lot of weight, Ma."

"She'll be okay, Johnny, love," Mam coaxed. "She just needs some time to take it all on board. It's a lot to process."

I knew that, but it wasn't easy watching her from a distance.

Mam chewed on her lip before saying, "I think it's more that she's scared to let Joey out of her sight for fear he runs than anything else."

"It's okay, Ma," I muttered.

"I don't want you feeling like you're being left out," Mam hurried to console. "She's not mad at you, pet. She's just grieving."

"I know."

"Are you *sure* you know?"

*No.* "Yeah." Pushing back my stool, I stood up and stretched my arms over my head. "I'm going hit the sack. Try and turn my brain off for an hour." I pressed a kiss to her head before heading for the hallway "Night, Ma."

"Goodnight, Johnny, love," she called after me.

Closing the kitchen door behind me, I trailed down the hall and took the stairs three at a time, listening to the sound of voices coming from all directions. Tadhg and Ollie were back from the treehouse and I could hear them banging around in one of the spare bedrooms. It was so unusual to hear anything other than my own thoughts in this place that I took a moment to just stand on the landing and listen to the brothers arguing over sweets before making my way down to my room, forcing my legs to walk past the room I knew *she* was in.

Slipping inside my room, I closed the door and pressed my forehead against the frame. Leaving the light off, I forced myself to breathe deep and slow. My mind was reeling, my thoughts a jumbled mess, as I tried to focus on what was coming in the morning – what I knew I had to show up to both physically and mentally. Problem was, my mind was stuck on the girl in the room down the hall. The one I couldn't fix. The one who owned me. What was I thinking going tomorrow? It wasn't like I could leave now. How could I leave her? Jesus Christ, I felt like I was going to explode . . .

"Hi, Johnny."

Startled at the sound of Shannon's voice, I spun around to find her sitting on the edge of my bed in the darkness. The moonlight pouring in from my bedroom window illuminated her pale face as she looked up at me with the loneliest expression I'd ever seen. "Hi, Shannon," I replied, quickly clearing my throat when the words came out all thick and gruff. Wary, I remained exactly where I was, unsure of what she wanted me to do. "How are you feeling?"

Her long hair was loose and resting over one shoulder, and she was dressed in a pajama set from one of the countless bags of new clothes that were filling up the spare room. The lads' mothers had been dropping things over to the house for days now, and I knew from one glance at the pink, glittery string top and matching shorts she was wearing, that Claire had a hand in purchasing it.

"I, uh . . . " She glanced down at her clasped hands and blew out a shaky breath before retraining her gaze on my face. "Oh god, Johnny, your head," she choked out. Her voice was panicked, her eyes wide. "What happened?"

"Well, it all started back in the Spring of 1988, when Gerard Gibson entered the world. Ten years later, he was thrown into my life and it all went to shite from there," I chuckled and then mentally kicked my own ass for cracking jokes. "Sorry."

"It's okay," she whispered, tugging on the hem of her vest nervously. "I miss you."

My heart cracked in my chest and my legs were moving before my brain had a chance to catch up. "I'm right here, Shan." Sitting down beside her, I resisted the urge to pull her onto my lap, settling on placing a hand on her bare knee instead. "I never left, babe. I was just trying to give you some space."

"I don't want any more space," she whispered, shifting closer. "I just want you."

"You have me," I croaked out, feeling my heart thump rapidly. "Always."

"You saved my life, Johnny." Shivering, she leaned her cheek against my arm and exhaled a ragged breath. "You saved my brothers' lives."

"Yeah, well, you saved mine a long time ago," I replied gruffly. "I was only returning the favor."

She shook her head, body rigid. "No, I didn't—"

"Yeah, you did." Wrapping my arm around her thin shoulders, I tucked her frail body under my arm. "You woke me up, Shan. Made me see things differently. Gave me a life outside of rugby. Something to look forward to." Shrugging, I leaned down and kissed her hair. "You've done a lot for me right back, so don't be thinking otherwise."

"Your parents want to foster us," she confessed, looking up at me all wide-eyed and guilt-ridden. "Me and my brothers."

"I know, Shan," I replied softly.

"Your mother told us that she wants to keep us – *all* of us," she squeezed out. "Even Joey."

"Yeah?" My heart fluttered in my chest as I tried to take her measure. "And how do you feel about that?"

"I want to stay," she admitted quietly. "With your family."

I mentally heaved a sigh of relief. "That's a good thing then, right?" I coaxed. "That you want this?"

"I just feel so bad about it," she strangled out. "All of this . . . " Her shoulders sagged and she ducked her head. "We're all here in your space, and none of this is fair on you—"

"I want you here," I interrupted her by saying. "I want you in my space, Shannon." Twisting sideways, I tipped her chin up, forcing her to meet my gaze. "There's nowhere else I want you to be than right here with me and my family, okay?"

"But it's not fair on you," she whispered, eyes full of unshed tears. "All of my brothers and my problems." Shivering, she leaned her cheek into my hand and sighed. "I don't want you to end up hating me."

"Hating you?" I shook my head. "Shannon, I *love* you. I'm fucking desperate to keep you here."

"But my brothers—"

"I want them to stay, too," I hurried to tell her. "I love little Sean – and Ollie? Christ, I even like Tadhg. He's a mouthy little fucker, but I understand him. And Joe? He just needs some help. Shite, even Darren's growing on me." Wiping a tear from her cheek with my thumb, I leaned closer. "I want all of you to stay with my family."

"But we're a lot of trouble," she whispered, sniffling.

"I like your trouble," I told her. "I want your trouble, and your complications, and everything else that comes with you." Leaning closer, I stroked my nose against hers. "I want you."

"What if you change your mind?" she asked, pressing her forehead to mine. "What then?"

"I won't change my mind."

"But what if—"

"I already told you that I'm a not a fleeting guy," I said gruffly. "I'm not that person, Shannon. I won't change my mind about you." Smiling, I pressed a kiss to her lips and leaned back to look her in the eye. "I'm here forever."

"Really?"

I nodded slowly. "Hundred percent."

"I just . . ." Swallowing deeply, she released a torn breath. "I just don't know what I'm going to do now." Tears spilled down her cheeks. "I'm never going to see her again," she sniffled. "I never got to tell her goodbye, or say sorry for all of the mean things I said to her—"

"You don't have anything to apologize for," I told her, forcing myself to keep my emotions in check. "You didn't then and still don't. She made a lot of mistakes with you, Shannon. She knew that, baby. She didn't need to hear you say sorry."

"I'm still mad at her," Shannon confessed. "I love her and I hate her and I want to scream at the unfairness of it all." A small sob tore through her and I couldn't resist pulling her onto my lap a second longer. "I just . . ." Sniffling, she buried her face in my neck and held onto my shoulders. "I want to go back to when we were little and *beg* her to love herself more than she feared him. To just love *us* more than she loved *him* . . ."

"She loved you," I said, trembling now. "She did, Shannon."

"I don't know—"

"Well, I know," I told her, tightening my hold on her. "You think I got those kids out of the house? Well, I couldn't have done that without your ma. She *helped* me, Shannon."

"What do you mean?"

"When I was trying to get the door open," I explained hoarsely, my body racked with grief and guilt. "My hand was shaking so fucking bad, and the kids were crying. I was sure your da was going turn around and see me there. But then your ma started coughing, making enough noise to muffle their sobs, making enough of a distraction for me to open that door and get them out."

"Wh-what?"

"Yeah." I forced myself to continue. "Your mother did a lot of fucked-up shit, baby, and I'm not excusing any of it, but that night, when it came down to the wire, she looked me dead in the eyes and told me to *save her children*. That was the only thing on her mind at the end. Making sure *you* and your brothers were out of that house."

Shannon's breath hitched in her throat. "You s-spoke to h-her?"

Guilt-ridden, I looked my girlfriend in the eyes and nodded. "He was sitting with his back to the kitchen door, and there were empty bottles spread all over the table. I just didn't know what they were at the time – or else, I blocked it out." Shaking the horrific image from my head, I focused on Shannon's face as I spoke. "But your ma saw me, and she nodded her head. I didn't know what to do . . . I thought for sure she was going to scream at me, but she didn't. She looked at me and nodded. She was telling me to *go*. And then she walked over to the door, and I—" I cut myself off, struggling to verbalize the night that was haunting me.

"Keep going," Shannon begged, silently crying. "*Please?*"

"We couldn't talk," I choked out, "so we were mouthing words to each other, and she said '*go, go now*—'" Shuddering, I wiped my cheek against my shoulder and forced myself to keep going. "'*Get them out*,' she kept saying to me. '*Take them away from here*.'"

"Oh god ..." Shannon's hands tightened on my shoulders. "D-don't stop."

"I told her I'd come back for her," I admitted brokenly. "I said '*I promise*' and she s-said '*don't come back*—" My voice cracked and I had to inhale a shuddering breath before I could finish. "I couldn't understand it. I didn't know why she wouldn't come with me. I begged her to just *come* with me. I would have protected her. I swear, I would have. I thought she was afraid of him hitting her. I didn't know he was going to do *that*, but she must have known because she told me to save her children. Those were her exact words – *save my children*." Sniffling, I croaked out, "And she told me to t-tell all of you t-that s-she was s-sorry." A sob tore through me and I desperately tried to wrangle my emotions into check. "And then she just ... she c-closed the kitchen door and I walked *away* ... " I clenched my eyes shut, trying to stop my own tears. "I left her there, in that house with him, and I'm so fucking sorry, Shannon!"

"Johnny—"

"I'm sorry—" Shaking my head, I buried my face in her neck and whispered the words, "I'm so sorry," over and over until I felt like I couldn't breathe. She was crying right along with me and I knew I would never fully get over the decision I made that night. "If I could go back I would," I promised her. "I'd change it all—"

"Look at me," Shannon sobbed and I shook my head. I was too ashamed. "Johnny Kavanagh, look at my face." When I didn't comply, she cupped my face in her small hands and forced me to look at her.

"I'm sorry," I whispered, feeling tears trickle down both cheeks. "So sorry—"

My words broke off when her lips crashed hard against mine. Shuddering into her touch, I kissed her back, feeling the dampness of her tears mix with mine.

"You don't say sorry," Shannon croaked out, dragging her lips away from mine. "You don't apologize to anyone because you *didn't* do this. You are *good*. You *saved* me. So many times. So, you don't put *that* on you. Not ever." Sniffling, she wiped my cheeks with her thumbs and blew out a shaky breath. "Are we clear?"

"Yeah." I nodded, drowning in her words. She didn't *blame* me. She wasn't mad at me. She didn't *hate* me. "We're clear."

"I love you," Shannon whispered, still holding my face in her hands. "For keeps."

Exhaling a ragged breath, I kissed her swollen lips. "Most in the world."

"Can I stay in here with you tonight?" she asked then. "I just . . . I want to be close to you."

"Yeah." My voice was thick and gruff. My heart was hammering at the speed of light. "You can stay with me."

I waited for her climb off my lap and slip under the covers before dragging off my clothes and climbing in beside her. "Your skin is always so hot," she whispered when I draped an arm around her and tucked her into my chest. "It's nice." Shifting around so that my other arm was under her head, she nuzzled her cheek against my arm and inhaled a deep breath. "You smell like home."

Shivering, I curled my body around hers and pressed a kiss to the curve of her jaw. "You *are* home."

When I left the house this morning, I'd left Shannon sleeping in my bed. Hours later, I could still feel *her* on my skin. I was washed, dressed in clean training gear, and far away from the girl, and I could still *feel* her on me.

*"You can do this, Johnny,"* her voice filled my mind. *"You're going to shine."*

Feeling sick to my stomach, I sat on the bench in the changing room of The Academy training grounds, having passed every medical examination that had been thrown my way this morning, and concentrated on keeping my heartbeat even. Anxiety was gnawing at my gut, adrenalin pumping through my veins at a furious rate, making my knees bop restlessly.

Shaking my hands out, I inhaled a steadying breath and retied the laces on my football boots before moving my attention to the strapping on my thigh. Blocking out everything around me, I emptied my mind and strapped my body until I was satisfied with the level of support. Standing up, I tested my limbs, twisting from side to side, making sure I was good to go.

They were waiting for me.

Right outside.

This was it.

*You can do this,* I mentally chanted to myself. *You were born to do this.*

A loud knock sounded on the other side of the changing room door, followed by my coach's voice, "Let's go, Kavanagh."

"On the way," I called back, unable to suppress the shudder that rolled through my body as my nerves tangled with my excitement.

Closing my eyes, I blessed myself and threw a silent prayer up to the man upstairs.

*Please, God, don't let me fuck this up . . .*

My phone pinged then, alerting me to a text message. Scrambling for my phone, I quickly unlocked the screen and clicked into the message.

S: You've got this, Johnny Kavanagh. Go show them what you're made of and shine. I'm proud of you. I love you. (A crazy fucking amount.) xx

Fuck me.

# Lightning Crashes

## SHANNON

Sitting in the front row pew in St. Patrick's Church on a beautiful summer's day in May, with my brothers on either side of me, I felt a mask slip into place as countless faces stepped in front of me, shaking my hand, telling me how sorry they were for our loss. I wasn't sure which loss they were talking about; our mother, who had been murdered, or our father, who had murdered her.

All five of my brothers looked smart in the identical black suits, crisp white shirts, and black ties Mrs. Kavanagh had delivered to the house before the rosary on Saturday. She had bought me a knee-length black dress and cardigan to wear, with small black heels. In the midst of my turmoil and my world crashing down around me, all that kept popping into my head was that my dress *fit*. It was the strangest, most inconsequential detail, but it kept swirling around and around in my mind.

My eyes were glued to my parents' coffins laying side by side in front of the alter.

His coffin was on the right.

Our mother was on the left, closest to us.

Like the steps of the stairs, my brothers and I were lined up according to our age, with Darren sitting at the edge of the pew, Joey to his left, followed by me, and then Tadhg, Ollie, and finally Sean.

Darren was thanking everyone that sympathized with us, like the head of the family did during these ordeals, while Joey sat rigid, eyes glued to our mother's coffin in a trance-like state, ignoring everyone who shook his limp hand. Ollie was crying softly into his tissue, while Tadhg scowled at anyone who tried to pat his head. Sean was looking around at the Stations of the Cross hanging on the walls, and the beautiful, stained-glass windows all around us.

Sean didn't seem to understand what was happening and his lack of awareness gave me immense comfort. He had a fighting chance to survive this. The couple sitting behind my brothers gave me hope for all of their futures. John Sr. had his head bent between Ollie and Tadhg, whispering something in their ears that was amusing enough to draw a smile from Tadhg and a sniffling thumbs up from Ollie, while Edel had positioned herself on the kneeler behind Sean, quietly entertaining him and explaining all the different pictures and statues.

Beside Mr. and Mrs. Kavanagh sat my mother's sister Alice, her husband, Michael, and my eighty-one-year-old maternal great-grandmother, Nanny Murphy.

That was it.

That was all the family my mother had to show for thirty-eight years on this earth.

I knew mine and my brothers' friends and their families were filling up the pews behind us. I'd seen them all earlier when they had come up to sympathize, and it gave me the strength to not look at the other side of the church, to where *his* family were sitting, weeping and wailing loudly. None of us knew our father's side of the family, and I had no plans to start now.

Every time one of his family members sobbed too loudly, I felt Joey stiffen beside me. Darren noticed too because he reached down and placed a hand on Joey's knee to stop him from shaking. Hooking my arm through Joey's, I held onto him for all I was worth, terrified of what he might do if they didn't *stop*. The Lynch side had caused terrible trouble over the funeral arrangements as it stood, making a big deal of the family plot, and demanding that they both be laid to rest together. Darren had hit the roof, insisting on cremating our mother before he allowed her to be placed with him, before Mr. Kavanagh stepped in with his wallet and organized for my mother to be buried in her own fresh plot. My parents would share a service and a cemetery, but at least she could finally rest in peace.

"We're nearly there," I whispered in Joey's ear when one of our father's sisters wailed particularly loudly as the priest sprinkled holy water on our parents' coffins. "Another little bit and we're done."

Joey nodded stiffly, never once taking his eyes off the photograph of Mam that was sitting on top of her coffin.

Trembling, I leaned back in my seat, seeking the comfort of the hand hooked under the back of my seat and stroking my side. I knew in my heart that the only reason I was managing to hold it together was the boy who was sitting in the pew directly behind mine. Every instinct inside of me was demanding I climb over the pew and seek comfort in my boyfriend's arms, but I held firm, staying strong for my brothers.

When the mass ended and my father's family stood up to shoulder his coffin out of the church with the second priest on the alter, I reached down and gripped Johnny's hand tightly, needing the connection to build up enough courage to hold my ground. All six of us remained seated and turned our heads away, refusing to watch as our mother's killer was shouldered away by his friends and relatives.

The emotions I was desperately trying to wrangle in got the better of me and a pained sob tore from my throat, but then I felt *him* right behind me. I heard the words, "You can do this," in my ear as his lips brushed against my earlobe. Nuzzling my cheek with his nose, he whispered, "I promise."

Shuddering, I nodded and pressed his hand to my chest, clutching it so tightly that it had to be uncomfortable for him – he clearly had to kneel behind me in order to give me so much of his arm – but I couldn't physically let him go. Not when I'd already lost so much today.

Finally, when *he* was gone, and it was our mother's turn to be shouldered from the church, I watched Darren and Joey rise to their feet. Everyone was crying behind us, sobbing loudly as my mother's two eldest children carefully removed her picture from her coffin and handed it to Father McCarthy, before folding the pall and returning that to him, too. But then Darren and Joey just stood there, staring at our mother's coffin, looking completely lost, with tears dripping down their cheeks.

Exhaling a shaky breath, I let go of Johnny's hand and stood up. Keeping my back straight, I walked up to my brothers and whispered, "What's wrong?"

"We need six people to carry her," Darren whispered back. "I didn't think—" He shook his head and sniffled. "I don't know what to do . . . "

Everyone in the jam-packed church was staring at us. Some in confusion. Most in pity.

"Johnny?" Darren called out in a hoarse voice, turning his attention to my boyfriend, who was sitting next to Aoife in the second row, and pulling faces at Sean.

Snapping his attention to us, Johnny straightened up, looking like he'd been caught red-handed doing something he wasn't supposed to. "Yeah?"

"Will you shoulder our mother with us?"

Clearly taken aback, Johnny sank back in his seat. "Are you sure?" His uncertain blue eyes flicked from me to Joey before settling on Darren. "You want *me*?"

"There would be four white coffins up here if you hadn't done what you did," Darren replied, gesturing to our brothers and me. "We want you, and she would want you, too."

Emotions flooded Johnny's eyes and he quickly rose to his feet. He didn't have his jacket on, just his white shirt and tie, as he stumbled out of the pew and walked up to stand beside me at the side of my mother's coffin.

Our aunt's husband walked over to us then, shaking hands with Darren just before Alex, who'd driven down from Belfast on Saturday, joined us in front of the alter. "I'll stand with you, baby," he whispered in his ear. Ignoring the priest who was giving them a peculiar look, my brother's beautiful boyfriend leaned in and kissed Darren right on the lips. "Always."

Darren sniffled and gripped Alex's hand. "We just need one more."

"Gussie," Joey said shakily, pointing to Gibsie, who was sitting in the third row with our friends. "I need a favor, lad."

"Say no more, buddy." Gibsie rose from his pew and walked straight up to Joey. "Gussie's here," he said, patting him on the shoulder.

Trembling, I returned to Tadhg and Ollie, clasping their hands tightly in mine as the undertakers carefully raised her coffin onto their shoulders and then quickly reorganized the boys by height before giving them the go-ahead.

Father McCarthy walked down the aisle and everyone got to their feet. With their arms banded around each other, Darren and Joey shouldered our mother's coffin from the front, with Alex and Michael in the middle, and Johnny and Gibsie at the back.

Sobbing quietly, I slowly trailed after the coffin as they slowly walked my mother out of the church and into the glorious sunshine in the adjoining cemetery. "Sean," I mumbled to Tadhg when we stepped outside. "Oh, god, we forgot Sean."

Glancing around me, I looked through the crowds, frantically searching for my baby brother, only to find him a few feet behind me swinging happily between Johnny's parents, blissfully unaware of that fact that we were about to lay his mother to rest. My eyes landed on Aoife then and her golden hair as it blew around her face in the light summer breeze. She wasn't looking at me. Her entire focus was on my brother as she watched him like he was a precious jewel that could vanish at any moment.

"Mammy," Ollie sobbed, burying his face in my side.

"Shh. It's okay." I tore my gaze from Aoife and wrapped my arm around his small shoulders, holding him to my side, keeping Tadhg's hand firmly in my other hand. I continued to walk us after the coffin, keeping my eyes trained on Johnny's white shirt – the only white shirt in a sea of dark jackets.

When we reached the freshly dug grave in the far corner of the grave-yard, I watched numbly as they shifted my mother onto the boards next to the plot. Wordlessly, Joey and Darren returned to stand beside us as Father McCarthy continued to pray over my mother's grave.

Johnny was standing so close behind me that I could smell his aftershave and feel the light movement of his shirt against my back as he breathed in and out.

Slow and steady.

In and out.

*Thump, thump, thump.*

I allowed myself to lean against him, taking all the comfort he was offering me, allowing him to be my strength in this moment.

When Father McCarthy finished the final part of the service, I watched as Patrick Feely stepped up to the microphone the priest had been using and gently strummed on the guitar strapped to his chest. Father McCarthy had asked if there was a song we would like to be played during the service, and Johnny had mentioned to Darren that his friend played the guitar and would be honored to play for us. With the help of Feely, Darren had picked some lovely songs for the ceremony but it was Joey who had chosen the song to be played when Mam was being lowered into the ground. He was adamant that it had to be that specific song.

When Feely began to sing the words of Live's "Lightning Crashes", his voice so beautiful and haunting, the lyrics so cutting and deep, I lost the battle with my emotions. Knowing that Joey had chosen this song for Mam made it almost unbearable to hear. The pain in my heart was too much to handle.

"I can't—" Crying hard and ugly, I spun around and buried my face in Johnny's chest, unable to watch Joey and Darren slowly lower her into the ground. "I can't do it!"

"I've got you, baby," Johnny whispered, wrapping me up in his arms. "I'm right here."

"No! The worms – it's too dark! Stop! Mammy – Mammy, no!" Ollie started to scream so loudly that I jerked away from Johnny with the intention of cuddling him, but he pushed his way through the crowd and ran straight for Mr. Kavanagh. Crouching down, Johnny's father lifted Ollie into his arms and quickly walked him away from the grave and back towards the gates to where Mrs. Kavanagh was standing with Sean.

My brothers carefully lowered her into the ground and then blessed themselves.

Sobbing hard, Darren walked straight over to Alex.

Like he had when she was alive, Joey remained right by our mother's side, staring into the hole in the ground that would be her final resting place. A lone tear drop fell from his cheek and I watched it as it disappeared into the grave with her.

Patrick finished his song, and the crowds of mourners slowly scattered away until just a few of our close friends remained.

Sniffling, Tadhg walked over to where Joey was standing and placed his hand in his. Never taking his eyes off the grave, Joey draped an arm around our little brother and pulled him into his chest. "You have to go, Joe," Tadhg told him. "Those guys are waiting down at the gates with John and Edel to take you to the hospital."

"I'm, uh . . ." Clearing his throat, Joey patted Tadhg's head. "You go on with Darren. I just need some time."

"But you have to go now—"

"Come on, Tadhg," Darren cut him off gently as he led him away from Joey. "Give him a minute." Squeezing Joey's shoulder, he whispered, "I'll be up to see you as soon as you're allowed visitors."

"Come back, okay?" Sniffling, Tadhg wrapped his arms around Joey's waist. "Get better and come back to us, you fucker."

"Yeah." Joey nodded weakly. "That's the plan, kid."

"He's going to get better," Darren told them. "You are. You can do this, Joey Lynch. You're the strongest, most headstrong person I've ever known in my life."

"Just take him, Darren—" Exhaling a ragged breath, Joey dropped his head. "I can't do this with them here."

Without another word, Darren led a crying Tadhg away from the grave.

"Joe," I croaked out, tears dripping down my cheeks, as I clung to my boyfriend. "I don't want you to—"

"Don't say it, Shan," he begged, tearing his gaze off the grave to look at me. "If you say those words, I won't be able to. And I *really* need to do this—" His voice cracked and he dragged in a sharp breath before turning his bloodshot gaze on Johnny. "Kavanagh, can you do me a favor and look after—"

"Consider it done, lad," Johnny replied gruffly, tightening his hold on me. "No worries."

Aoife, who had been standing to the side, silently observing everything, stepped forward then. Without a word, she walked right up to my mother's grave, dropped a single red rose inside, and turned around to face my brother.

"I told you not to come," he told her, trembling.

"And I told you to save your breath," she replied, tipping her chin up to face him.

"You shouldn't be here," he strangled out, shaking his head. "You know it's not good—"

"I don't care," she cut him off by saying. "Now put your arms around me and hold me like you're not going to see me for another three months."

"Jesus—" Shuddering, Joey pulled her close and rested his forehead against hers. "You don't wait, do you hear me?" Sniffling, he cupped her cheeks in his trembling hands and looked into her eyes. "You live your life, okay?"

"You shut up, Joey Lynch," she sobbed, gripping his sides. "I love you."

"You shut up, Aoife Molloy," he shot back gruffly and pressed a kiss to her brow. "I love you, too."

"I'll be here when you get out," she told him.

"*Don't* be here," he strangled out. "Be somewhere better."

"I don't take orders from you," she squeezed out. "You should know that by now."

"Because you're crazy stupid," he whispered. "You're wasting your life on me. You know this. Everyone keeps telling you, but you won't listen—"

"Because it's my life to waste," she shot back defiantly. "Now, you get your sexy ass better and come home to me." Reaching a hand behind him, she pinched his ass for emphasis. "Because I'm going to need you healthy, okay?"

"Aoife, I'm a bad bet—"

"*Okay?*"

He heaved a heavy sigh and nodded. "Yeah, okay."

"Now, give me a kiss and tell me you love me," she instructed, lip wobbling. "And make it a good one."

"Come on, Shan," Johnny said, distracting me from Joey and Aoife as he wrapped his arm around my shoulder. "Let's leave them be."

"Yeah, okay." Shivering, I leaned into his side as we walked away from the graveside. "Thanks for today," I told him, slipping a hand around his waist. "For everything."

"Shan, you were so amazing these last few days," Johnny replied gruffly. "I don't know where that strength comes from, but it's so humbling." He shook his head and blew out a breath. "I don't even have the words to tell you how fucking incredible you are, Shannon Lynch."

"I'm not an incredible anything, Johnny," I croaked out. "I'm just trying to keep my head above water and not drown."

"You won't drown – you're a survivor," he told me.

"I'm not a good swimmer," I admitted.

"Then I'll throw you a lifejacket and swim out to get you," he shot back, tucking me into his side. "Because I'm an excellent swimmer."

"You talking about your swimmers on a day like today?" Gibsie quipped when we joined him and the rest of our family and friends at the gates of the cemetery. "Christ, Johnny, you sure do pick your moments, lad."

"Oh, shut up, you big eejit," Lizzie grumbled, slapping the back of his head. "You need to pick *your* moments."

"It's called looking on the bright side," Gibsie shot back, glaring at her. "And that's called assault."

Lizzie rolled her eyes. "Whatever. Don't talk to me."

"Fine," Gibsie countered. "Don't touch me."

"No problem," Lizzie muttered. "I need hand sanitizer anyway."

"Yeah," Gibsie bit out. "For your tongue."

"Can you two pack it in for one bleeding day?" Johnny hissed, bristling. "Christ, look at where you are." He inclined his head to where my younger brothers were standing with his parents, watching their interaction with curious eyes. "Just call a truce for an hour," he added, smoothing a hand up and down my arm. "We don't need any more fighting."

"Yeah," Lizzie said, cheeks reddening. "Of course."

"Ignore them, chickie," Claire said, stepping forward to wrap her arms around me. "You did such a good job today. I'm so proud of you."

"Thanks, Claire." Shivering, I hugged her back tightly before taking a step back and smiling weakly. "Thank you all for coming." I looked up at Feely who was standing between Hughie and Gibsie and said, "Thank you so much for doing that for my family." Clasping my hands together, I nodded to the guitar case at his feet and smiled. "You have a very beautiful voice."

His cheeks turned bright pink. "I was honored to be asked."

"He's our dark horse, this fella," Gibsie interjected good-naturedly, slapping a hand on Feely's shoulder. "Pa's full of surprises."

"John, did you have to give him chocolate buttons?" Mrs. Kavanagh groaned loudly and it caught my attention. "It's twenty-four degrees outside and he's wearing a custom Ralph Lauren." Kneeling down in front of Sean, she pulled a tissue out of her designer handbag and dabbed at my baby brother's chocolate-covered face and fingers. "What did he give you, Seany, hmm?"

"He wanted a snack." Mr. Kavanagh chuckled, not sounding one bit sorry. "And you're worse for putting a six-hundred-euro suit on a toddler, baby." Slipping his hand into his tailored suit pants pocket, he pulled out a handful of mini bags of chocolate buttons and passed them around to Tadhg and Ollie, who were grinning in delight.

"Don't be jealous," Johnny warned Gibsie who was scowling at my brothers. "You're on a diet – *and* you're a grown-ass man."

"Don't worry, my old flower," Mr. Kavanagh said before tossing a packet to Gibsie. "I've got some for you, too."

"Score," Gibsie snickered as he ripped open the packet and hoofed them down in one mouthful.

"I don't know about you, Gibs," Feely said with a pained sigh. "I really don't."

"Take the boys back to the car, will you, love? I need to have a word with Joey before we go," Mrs. Kavanagh said as she straightened up and smoothed down her dress. "You're all more than welcome back to the house for some lunch."

"Thank you."

"Yeah, thanks a million, Mrs. Kavanagh."

"Sound as a pound, Mammy K," Gibsie chimed in. "I'll be there with bells on."

"And don't you dare give those boys anymore treats before their lunch, John." Smirking at her husband, Mrs. Kavanagh leaned up on her tiptoes and pressed a kiss to his clean-shaven cheek before saying, "Or you won't be getting *your* treat."

"Jesus Christ," Johnny strangled out, scrubbing a hand down his face. "Come on, Shan—" Gagging, he grabbed my hand, and moved for the gate. "Let's get out of here before we both start anxious puking."

# Picnics and Piercings

## JOHNNY

It was a sweltering summer's day, and under any other circumstances, I would have been stripped down to my jocks someplace close to a beach or a river, but my girlfriend had just buried both of her parents, so I sucked it up and settled for removing my tie and undoing the top three buttons of my dress shirt instead.

Eight of us were sprawled out in the back field of my house, still clad in our funeral clothes, watching as Tadhg, Ollie, and Sean played in the treehouse. All of the grown-ups were back at the house, serving food and chatting general shite. It was too much for Shannon – I'd known it the moment we stepped through the door and she had been confronted with a fresh horde of sympathizers – so we had escaped outside with our friends and a mountain of food tucked under our arms.

Stretched out on the flat of my back in the grass, I curled a strand of her hair around my finger and inhaled deeply, breathing her scent into my chest and then sighing in contentment.

"I could stay here forever," she whispered, voicing my thoughts aloud, from where she was nestled in the crook of my arm, baking in the summer sunshine. Tangling her fingers with mine, she nuzzled her cheek against my chest. "Just right here in this moment."

"Hmm." Nodding in agreement, I gave her fingers a reassuring squeeze. "Me, too."

"Well, I can't take it anymore," Gibsie announced with a huff. "I'm really sorry, Little Shannon," he added as he sat up and started ripping at the buttons of his shirt. "I know I'm supposed to be respectful and considerate of your feelings and shit – and I really am trying to be good here – but if I don't get out of these clothes soon, you're all going to be burying *me*!" Yanking off his shirt, he tossed it on top of Claire, who was sprawled out beside him, before moving for the buckle of his belt. "My balls are sweating so bad, I'm going to chafe my gooch!"

I opened my mouth to give him a lecture about discussing his bollocks around my girlfriend, but the sound of her laughter had me holding my tongue. "What's a gooch?"

"Oh my god, you did not just ask him that, Shan," Lizzie grumbled from where she was making a daisy chain.

"Ew," Katie groaned, joining her daisy chain to Lizzie's one. "I hate that word."

"Me, too," Lizzie agreed. "It's beyond disturbing."

"What?" Shannon shrugged. "I don't know what that is."

"Me either," Claire offered, holding her hand up.

"Well then," Gibsie chuckled, rising to his feet, "it's about time I gave you girls an education on the male form, isn't it?"

"If you take your jocks off in front of my sister and my girlfriend, you won't have a gooch left," Hughie snarled, glaring at Gibsie who had his suit pants and shoes kicked off and was reaching for the waistband of his white boxers.

"Or a heartbeat," I warned, pulling myself up on my elbows to glare at him. "Don't even think about it, fucker."

"Put your pants back on," Feely said calmly. "There are kids up that tree."

"I'm not putting my pants back on," Gibsie shot back, looking outraged. "For the benefit of innocent eyes, I'll agree to leave my jocks on, but that's my best offer. It's too damn hot."

"Look at his boobies," Ollie laughed from the treehouse. Pointing a finger at Gibsie, he said, "He's got earrings on them."

"Stop earwigging, Ollie," Shannon called back.

"And look! He's got a tattoo on his—"

"Ollie," Shannon snapped. "Go and play."

"Fine," Ollie huffed before disappearing back into the treehouse.

"Boobies," Hughie snickered. "I love that kid."

"Hey, Katie," Gibsie purred in retaliation, waggling his brows at

Hughie's girlfriend. Flexing his pecs, he asked, "What do *you* think of my boobies?"

"I prefer Hughie's boobies," Katie shot back with a smirk. "They're so much perkier."

"Nice try, fucker," Hughie snickered, pulling himself up from his lying position to smack a kiss to his girlfriend's cheek.

Huffing out a breath, Gibsie turned to Claire and grinned devilishly. "The gooch is the area of skin between a man's balls and his a—"

"Shut the fuck up, lad," I hissed, tossing a bottle of water at him.

"His asshole," Gibsie finished, completely unaffected by the bottle that had just smacked off the side of his head. "Or anus, if you want to get technical."

"Shut the front door!" Claire gasped, clambering into a sitting position. Her eyes were wide in wonder and glued to the front of Gibsie's jocks. "And you never told me that before?"

"I can show you," he offered in a flirtatious tone. "Come behind that tree with me and I'll give you a thorough lesson in the male anatomy—"

"Wait a damn minute!" Hughie growled, attention riveted to the same place his sister was staring. Springing straight up, he pointed to Gibsie's jocks and hissed, "When did you get *that*?"

"I have no idea what you're talking about," Gibsie whistled, feigning innocence.

Looking mildly horrified, Hughie tilted his head to one side, clearly inspecting his junk. "Show us."

"You said I'm not allowed take my jocks off," Gibsie sniffed, folding his arms across his chest. "You threatened my gooch."

"Holy shit," Feely choked out a laugh. "You didn't!"

"He fucking did," Hughie muttered, paling a little.

"Ah, lad," Feely groaned, rolling onto his side. "You are troubled."

"You don't seem surprised, Cap," Hughie noted, eyeing me suspiciously. "Why are you not surprised?"

"What did he do?" Shannon asked me.

"Uh . . ." Sitting up, I resisted the urge to tuck her face into my chest and cover her ears. "You don't want to know."

"The genius pierced his penis," Lizzie deadpanned. "Look at it – I can see it popping out through his jocks. It's practically waving hello."

"Don't look at it," I barked. "None of you look at it." Turning to Gibsie, I hissed, "You put it away."

"I can't believe you got a Prince Albert piercing," Lizzie said, rolling her eyes. "That's so tacky."

"He didn't," Claire was quick to defend. "He got a Jacob's Ladder, and it's not tacky. It's very nice."

"And how the hell would you know?" Hughie demanded, glaring at his sister. "What have you been up to? Hmm?" He narrowed his eyes. "Were you looking at his ladder?" Claire's cheeks reddened and Hughie turned his glare on Gibsie. "Did you corrupt my sister?"

"No . . ." Claire replied, cheeks burning red now. "I . . . uh, just spotted it."

"*You spotted it*," Hughie repeated, his tone laced with disbelief. "And where did you happen to *spot* his pierced *dick*, Claire?"

"Johnny got the call up!" Gibsie blurted out, throwing me right under the bus. "Johnny got the call up. Johnny got the call up. Focus on that!"

"What?" Hughie's eyes widened and his head snapped towards me. "You got the call up?"

"You did?" Feely demanded, eyes wide in astonishment. "*When?*"

Shannon stiffened beside me and I mentally envisioned myself standing up and beating the ever-living shite out of my best friend. "Thanks, *friend*," I bit out, glowering at Gibsie.

"Yes!" Claire squealed, nodding eagerly. "Please god, focus on *that*."

"And not what I did to your sister," Gibsie agreed.

"What the fuck did you do to my sister?" Hughie demanded. "If you put that metal rod near her, I'm going cut it off—"

"Johnny got called up for the senior team, too," Gibsie blurted, driving over me with his double decker bus once again in his pathetic attempt to cover his tracks. "U20's *and* senior." *Keep fucking mowing me down, why don't you . . .* "He got two call ups!"

"Holy Jesus, you did it, Cap!" Stumbling to his feet, Hughie clutched his chest and gaped in wonder. "You actually fucking *did* it!"

"The senior team? Oh Christ, I'm going to throw up," Feely announced, breathing hard through his nose. "I'm so proud and so scared for you right now that I can't feel my feet."

"I'm only a reserve for the senior team," I said, feeling incredibly uncomfortable.

"And *starting* outside center for the U20's," Gibsie reminded me. "I guess the number 13 isn't so unlucky for you, is it, Cap?"

"It's not that big of a deal," I said, eyeing my girlfriend warily. Yeah, I was on the cusp of being rewarded for everything I had worked for. I had spent the past twelve years in beast mode, working to achieve the elusive career that was now knocking on my door. All the sacrifices I made in my life; skipping parties, controlling my food intake like a robot, and training until my body hit its breaking point. Being a boring bastard, pumping it out in the gym on Saturday evenings and Sunday mornings instead of hanging out with my friends? It had all been for this exact moment. To get to this point. To be recognized for who I was and what I was capable of achieving. To be taken into the coach's office last Saturday and be told that I *was* good enough. That I *had* made it. And instead of feeling fulfilled, I felt *empty*. Because somewhere along the way, without my brain or heart's permission, my dreams and goals for my future had shifted. I didn't even notice the shift happening. I didn't feel the full force of my apprehension until this exact moment in time as I was hit with the sudden realization that I didn't want any of this without *her.* The contract looming over my head, the one I was guaranteed with my home province in Dublin if I performed during the summer games, meant absolutely nothing if it took *me* away from *her.* Because she would be here, and I would be leaving. And how the fuck could I leave her after everything?

Getting onto the U20's squad had been my plan for so long, and I was starving for my shot. I'd earned it. I *wanted* it. Jesus, of course I wanted it. More than almost anything in the world. Just *not* more than her.

I was feeling thoroughly conflicted, and with the prospect of traveling with the senior team for the summer tour, combined with the death of Shannon's parents and upheaval of her life, I was completely torn apart.

I knew what I needed to do for *me*, but it wasn't the same as what I needed to do for *us*. If I left, it meant walking away from her during a time when she needed me most. She had her junior cert exams coming up, and her brother was in rehab. Her fucking world had fallen down around her and I was contemplating chasing a rugby ball around a pitch half a world away.

For days, I'd wrestled with telling Shannon about the squad, struggling with forming the words to explain it, before deciding to put all talk of rugby on the back burner until after the funeral. Now that the cat was out of the bag, courtesy of my eejit best friend, Shannon was just *staring* at me with an expression I couldn't fathom.

Silently raging with Gibsie for opening his mouth, today of all damn days, I quickly hurried on. "I'm not even sure if I'm going yet, and it's another few weeks away, so can we not talk about it? At least until we get school out of the way? We still have this week and next week to go. And final exams—"

"*No*," both Hughie and Feely shot back in outrage.

"All of the dreaming and scheming, the early mornings and the countless grind and hustle?" Hughie shook his head and stared at me like he didn't recognize my face anymore. "You're finally going to show the world what you're made of, Cap."

"This is a huge deal, Johnny," Feely added. "Like colossally huge."

"It's really not," I muttered, playing it down, as I ran a hand through my hair in sheer exasperation. "So, can we all just calm down?"

"Actually, it's probably the biggest deal of your life to date," Lizzie decided to join the fold by saying. "Just saying."

"Could you not *just say*," I snapped, flustered. "Jesus, today is not the day to talk about this."

697 • CHLOE WALSH

"Congratulations," Shannon choked out, tears trickling down her cheeks. "You did it."

Was she happy? Was she sad? I didn't know. I had no fucking clue. All I could think of was her heartbroken face as she watched her mother being lowered into the ground only a few short hours ago. I wanted to tell her I wouldn't go – that I'd stay right here with her. And I truly would if she wanted me too . . . but a part of me was *desperate* for this opportunity. I was disgusted with myself for feeling this way, but I couldn't change it. "Shan, don't cry, baby. It's not a definite yet. I haven't made any dec—"

"You *did it*!" she cried and then threw her arms around me. "You made it, Johnny!" Scrambling onto my lap, she wrapped her arms and legs around me and squealed. "Oh my god, I'm so proud of you."

My brows shot up in surprise. "You are?"

"Of course," she sniffled, pulling back to smile at me. "You fought for this, Johnny." Stroking my cheeks, she leaned in and pressed a kiss to my lips. "You've earned this."

"But you're crying," I choked out, voice thick with emotion.

"Because I'm so happy for you," she half-sobbed/half-laughed. "You're being rewarded for all of your hard work." Sniffling, she cupped my face in her small hands and pressed her forehead to mine. "This is your time." With her big, blue eyes locked on mine, she urged, "Take this. It's yours," before pressing a hard kiss to my lips. "Take it and *shine*."

"I'm scared," I whispered in her ear, not giving two damn shites that our friends were lurking around, eavesdropping. I needed to get this off my chest before I exploded. "I'm scared to take this and lose *you*."

"I'm yours, too," she promised. "You can have both."

"I've been fighting for this my whole life, Shannon," I strangled out, feeling my chest constrict so tight that I struggled to breathe. "This isn't a whim to me."

She nodded. "I know."

"I *have* to do it," I confessed, begging her with my eyes to forgive me. "I have to see it *through*."

She smiled. "I *know*."

"Then why does it feel all *wrong*?" I choked out.

"It's not wrong, Johnny," she whispered. "It's *right* and that's what's scary."

"I won't do it," I blurted out, panicking and backpedaling. "If you have doubts, tell me now, and I'll stay. If you don't want me to go, then I won't. Just tell me what to do and I'll do it—"

"I *want* this for you," Shannon cut me off by saying. "I want you to chase your dreams and show the world how *amazing* you are."

"But I'll be gone for a month," I croaked out, heart hammering violently in my chest. "Maybe even a month and a half. Could be more. That's a long time, Shan."

"And I'll *be* here when you come home. If it's in a month, or a month and a half, or two months, or four—" sniffling, she gave me a bright smile, "I'll be right here waiting for you."

"You're hurting my ladder," Gibsie said in a sad tone of voice.

"What?" Shannon and I both asked in unison as we turned to look at him.

"My ladder," Gibsie explained with a lonesome sigh. "You made it shrink with all this talk of Johnny leaving." Sinking down on the grass beside Claire, he huffed out a breath. "Now, I'm fucking depressed."

"Oh, come on. He'll come back to you, too." Hooking her arm through his, Claire leaned her cheek against Gibsie's shoulder. "And you can't be too sad, Gerard – we're having babies together this summer, remember?"

"Yeah, I know," he sighed heavily as he rested his chin on her head. "But I'm still not sure we're ready for that kind of responsibility, babe. I mean, I'm only seventeen."

"Well, ready or not, the babies are coming," Claire replied, patting his knee. "And it's your fault for letting him in."

"What the actual fuck?" Lizzie and Hughie both demanded at the same time.

"Brian," Gibsie explained in a glum tone. "Turns out he had an undescended testicle and wasn't shooting blanks like we thought."

"And that explains why you're having babies this summer how exactly?" Katie choked out, eyes-wide.

"He had sex with Cherub," Gibsie wailed. "We caught them at it in Claire's room back during Easter break. And now she's *pregnant*."

"Our cat *Cherub*?" Hughie demanded. "Brian got her pregnant?"

"We've had our suspicions for a while, but the vet confirmed it last Wednesday," Gibsie groaned. "We saw them and everything, didn't we, babe?"

"Uh-huh – on an ultrasound monitor," Claire agreed. "She's having *six* kittens."

"Did you know a cat's pregnancy can last anything from 56 to 67 days?" Gibsie asked.

"No," the rest of us replied.

"Well, she could give birth anytime from the middle of next month onwards," Claire told us. "Isn't that exciting?"

"It's going to cost me a small fortune," Gibsie sighed. "And my mam says that they're *my* responsibility because I brought him into her bedroom, and I should have known better, but I didn't fucking know better because I was under the assumption that he was walking around with a permanent condom on his cat dick. But no, he lied to me – lied to the vets, too. He had a sperm-filled ball all along!"

"And she's not the only cat on the street he knocked up, either," Claire added. "Apparently, Mrs. Lovell's grey tabby had a litter of snow-white kittens last Tuesday. They had long hair and *everything*."

"What can I say other than he's a whore?" Gibsie confirmed with a grim nod. "He's an abusive, one-bollocked bastard on a mission to impregnate every pussy he gets his claws into – but I'm only standing over Cherub," he added with a huff. "That's it. I'll father them. I'll do the night feeds with you, Claire. I'll be there at the birth. But that's it. Yours are the only babies I'm claiming. I know *nothing* whatsoever about Mrs. Lovell's tabby or any other woman's pregnant pussy. That's my story and I'm sticking to it."

"You two are made for each other," Katie chuckled. "It's so adorable."

"Don't tell them that, babe," Hughie growled. "You'll give them ideas."

"But they're having *babies* together," Katie pointed out. "They're already committed."

"Okay, topic changer before I throw my lunch up," Lizzie interjected, feigning a gag. "What are we going to do about transition year?"

"What do you mean?" Shannon asked, wiping her cheeks with the back of her hand.

"They spoke about it at school last week," Lizzie explained. "They're introducing the leap year option."

"Are you fucking serious?" I demanded, feeling a sudden pang of outrage. "I *begged* them to let me skip fourth year, but Twomey was adamant that they weren't going to offer the gap year program at Tommen."

"Well, he clearly changed his mind because it's being offered to us," Lizzie told me. "We have the option to skip fourth year and move straight into fifth year after the summer." She looked at Shannon and Claire. "And I'm taking it, guys."

Claire frowned. "You are?"

"And endure one less year of bullshit? *Of course* I'm taking it," Lizzie shot back. "I'd leave right now if I had my way."

"Good choice," Feely interjected quietly, giving her a small nod.

Lizzie blushed. "I know."

"Well, I don't know what I'm doing yet," Claire announced. "I haven't even thought about it."

"You should skip," Gibsie encouraged, waggling his brows at her. "Then you're one year closer to me."

"And what good would that do me?" Claire teased.

"It'll put us ahead of schedule," he replied, not missing a beat. "It's a good omen. I can feel it in my balls."

Claire rolled her eyes. "You and your weirdness."

"And his gooch," Katie offered with a snicker.

"Always the gooch," Gibsie agreed with laugh.

"Jesus," Hughie groaned. "Enough of the gooch already—"

"Should we even be talking like this?" Feely asked then, casting a guilty look in Shannon's direction. "You know, given the circumstances—"

"Please don't stop," Shannon hurried to say. "Just keep being normal with me." Shrugging shyly, she settled into a sitting position between my legs, facing the others, and whispered, "It helps."

"You want normal?" Gibsie asked, giving her a wolfish grin. "I can do that."

"He can't," Lizzie interjected. "It's physiologically impossible for him to act like a normal human."

"Oh, and there she is; the viper," Gibsie countered in a sarcastic drawl. "Fair play, girl. You kept that poisonous tongue of yours under control for over an hour."

"Eat shit," Lizzie growled.

"I'd eat shit before I'd eat you," he shot back.

"I'm *devastated*," Lizzie fake gasped. "Watch me wipe my tears," she added, using her middle finger to wipe her cheek.

"Are you two ever going to get along?" Claire groaned. "Even for one day?"

"Nope," they both replied at the same time before glowering at each other.

Shannon leaned against my chest and sighed softly. "Tears, rugby, and those two fighting? This is our normal."

"Yeah." Wrapping my arms around her, I kissed her shoulder. "I guess it is."

# Recovery

## SHANNON

"How did it go, Shannon, love?" Mrs. Kavanagh asked when I walked into the kitchen two weeks after the funeral and set my schoolbag down on the counter beside her.

It was the smell that always hit me first when I walked into this house. It was hard to describe, but it was like I could smell the *warmth*, which was ridiculous because you couldn't smell someone's kindness. But this woman? She radiated goodness. And the food . . . God, I couldn't keep up with the sheer amount of delicious meals and snacks on hand all day long. "Well, I'm finished third year," I told her, dragging my thoughts back to the present. "I did it."

She beamed at me. "Yes, you did."

"But I'm going to fail those exams," I croaked out, glancing at Sean, who was sitting at his own tiny table by the window, concentrating on the latest *masterpiece* he was painting – to join the dozen others hanging on the fridge and walls. Sookie was snoring at his feet with a streak of green paint on her head. "My junior cert? I won't pass it." I swallowed deeply and turned back to Johnny's mother. "I just . . . I don't want you to get your hopes up on me." I shrugged, feeling helpless. "I'm not smart like what you're used to—"

"What did I tell you about those exams?" she replied, setting a steamer filled with potatoes down on the sink and walking straight over to me. "It doesn't matter what marks you get." Cupping my face in her hands, she smiled down at me. "We won't even have to open the results when they come because they don't matter, pet. A score on a piece of paper tells me nothing, but *you* rising back up and returning to school to finish out the year and sit in that classroom tells *everything* about the wonderful, strong girl you are. And you make me prouder than any exam results could." She gave me a quick squeeze before saying, "Now, sit down and let me feed you. We'll put meat on those bones yet."

Smothering a laugh, I complied and sat down at the island, eyes widening when she set the biggest plate of bacon and cabbage I'd ever seen down in front of me. "Uh, thank you," I strangled out, wondering how in god's name I was going to eat a tenth of what was on my plate. She wasn't joking about the putting weight on my bones comment, either. I'd gained six pounds in the past month from Mrs. Kavanagh's cooking alone.

"You're more than welcome, pet," she replied, setting a plate of spuds down on the counter. "Now, where's that son of mine?"

"At The Academy." Picking up my knife and fork, I started to cut my bacon into tiny pieces. "He dropped me home first, but the coaches are pushing him pretty hard to get him prepped before he leaves for the tour. He said he'll be home before nine, but you know how it is with those trainers."

"Oh Jesus," Mrs. Kavanagh muttered. "I hate that bleeding game."

"Yeah." I knew what that felt like. Refusing to dwell on the very real fact that my boyfriend would be leaving in seven days, I shoveled a forkful of meat and veg into my mouth, chewing and swallowing before asking, "Where are the boys?"

"Doing their homework in the treehouse," Mrs. Kavanagh replied with a feigned sigh. "I swear, they'd live in that thing if they got their way."

"It's the first time they've ever had space that was entirely theirs," I explained with a small smile. "It's a huge novelty to them to have a place to go where no grown-ups can fit. It makes them feel safe."

"Do *you* feel safe?" Mrs. Kavanagh asked, taking a seat at the island. "Are you happy here, Shannon, love?"

Nodding eagerly, I swallowed a mouthful of food before responding. "Oh yes, and I'm so grateful to you, Mrs. Kavanagh – you *and* Mr. Kavanagh for taking us all in—"

"It's John and Edel," she corrected with a smile. "No more of that Mr. and Mrs. Kavanagh talk, do you hear me?"

"Yes, Mrs. Kavanagh – I mean, Edel," I amended, blushing. "Thank you."

"I went to see Joey this morning," she told me then. "He's looking good, love."

My eyes widened. "Did he say anything about me coming to visit?"

"He needs some more time, Shannon, pet." She smiled sadly. "He'll come around."

"Yeah." My heart sank. Joey wouldn't see me. He wouldn't see any of us – Aoife, included – since checking himself into that treatment center. I knew he needed to be there for reasons that stemmed far deeper than his addictions, but it wasn't easy not talking to him every day. "Okay."

"But he's going to be okay," she assured me. "And so are you."

"Darren called again today," I said then, cringing at the memory of my oldest brother's frantic phone call sessions. "Four times today."

Mrs. Kavanagh smiled. "He called the house, too."

"Yeah?" I arched a brow. "How many times?"

"Five," Mrs. Kavanagh chuckled.

"He needs to relax," I sighed. "A million phone calls every day isn't good for anyone."

"He's just adjusting to the change," she said, still smiling. "It's hard for him being all the way up in Belfast and not seeing you guys every day. He'll settle down eventually. He's worried about you because he loves you. He cares."

"I know," I mumbled, and I did. I had some clarity now, something I didn't have in the past. I could see my brother in a different light. I knew Darren loved us, and he showed us just how much by doing the right thing and letting us go to the Kavanaghs. He and Alex couldn't raise the boys on their own; they both had careers and were too young to make that kind of commitment, and he admitted that.

"And your aunty Alice phoned," Mrs. Kavanagh added. "Your Nanny is settling in down in Beara. She wanted us to know that Nanny is fine, and you and Joey aren't to worry about her."

"Is she really fine?" I croaked out, thinking about how frail my great-grandmother looked the last day I saw her – the day after my parents' funeral, when she climbed into a car filled with all of her possessions, and left for her new home in Beara with her granddaughter. "Are you sure?"

"She's old, she's tired, and she's grieving, Shannon," Mrs. Kavanagh replied gently. "It's time for her to unwind now. Have a bit of peace and quiet in her life. Your aunt is taking good care of her."

"My Onny," Sean announced then, holding a picture of two green circles up in his hands. "Sean and my Onny."

"Wow!" Mrs. Kavanagh gushed as she stood up to inspect Sean's picture. "This one is the best you've done."

Sean beamed up at her. "My Onny."

"Yes, love," Mrs. Kavanagh chuckled, taking the picture from Sean's sticky fingers and hanging it up on the fridge. "He's your Johnny."

Understatement of the century. Sean was obsessed with Johnny. Seriously, he followed him around everywhere, watching his every move. In the beginning, I was worried because I didn't want Johnny to feel uncomfortable. I felt bad enough that we were in his personal space without my baby brother clinging to him like a monkey, but Johnny didn't seem to mind in the slightest. In fact, he always made time for Sean. Every evening when he got home from the gym or training, he would sit on the couch with Sean and listen patiently as he babbled on about his day. Most of what Sean said made zero sense, but Johnny always listened to him anyway, responding with enthusiastic words of encouragement and smiles. Yeah, it was safe to say that my baby brother had attached himself to my boyfriend, and I was terrified of how he would react when Johnny left for France next week.

"Sean, love, will you go down to the office and get John?" Mrs. Kavanagh said then. "And tell him his dinner's ready?"

Nodding eagerly, Sean bounded out of the kitchen with Sookie hot on his heels.

"Good boy," Mrs. Kavanagh called after him before turning her smiling face back to me. "Now that we have a minute alone, I wanted to talk to you about something."

Instantly, I began to panic. "Uh, okay?" Setting my fork and knife down, I tucked my hair behind my ears and tried not to fidget. "Wh-what about?" *Don't send us away. Please god, don't send us away . . .*

"Relax, pet, there's nothing wrong," Mrs. Kavanagh coaxed, taking the stool opposite mine. I blew out a ragged breath and felt my shoulders sag in relief. "I just wanted to have a little girls' chat."

"Okay." I gave her my full attention, feeling more gratitude for this woman than I knew what to do with. "Of course."

"So, the camping trip for Johnny's birthday is next Wednesday," she said, brown eyes warm and focused on mine.

"Um, yeah," I replied, nodding.

"And you'll all be sharing tents," she continued. "Boys and girls . . . You and Johnny."

I blushed as awareness dawned on me. Suddenly, I knew *exactly* where she was going with this. "I'll be sleeping in Claire's tent," I lied, feeling heat creep up my neck. "It won't be a problem."

"I love you for trying to put me at ease," Mrs. Kavanagh replied, smirking. "But I'd be a foolish woman to believe you."

I reddened.

"I'm not mad at you, Shannon, love," she hurried to soothe. "I've actually been in a situation very similar to yours." Smiling, she reached over and took my hand. "I lived with John's family for years before we married."

My mouth fell open. "You did?"

"I did," she confirmed. "I ran away from home when I was a little younger than you are now. John's mother took me in. She put a roof over my head, fed and clothed me, and she gave me access to an education that sparked a successful career in fashion." She gave my fingers a gentle squeeze before saying, "She gave me the second chance I desperately needed. She saw something in me, something I didn't even see in myself at the time, and she nourished it. She was a wonderful woman, and when she was dying, I never hesitated about moving back to Cork to take care of her," Mrs. Kavanagh continued. "Johnny was *furious* to leave Dublin and the city life behind him, but I knew I had to come back here. I wanted my son to grow up in the same place his father had. To be around the kind of goodness that just naturally seemed to ooze from his grandmother. I wanted to nourish those roots." Smiling, she added, "That's why we stayed in Cork, and because my son grew into the man he is today, I know I made the right decision."

"Whoa," I breathed, feeling a swell of emotions surge through my chest. "She sounds like an incredible person." *Just like you.*

"She was," Mrs. Kavanagh agreed, smiling fondly. "But what I loved her most for was the day she sat me down in her kitchen and gave me the most *uncomfortable* talk I'd ever sat through in my life." Mrs. Kavanagh smirked. "Kind of like the talk I'm about to have with you now."

*Oh god.*

"I know you love my son," she continued. "And I know he loves you very deeply in return. Therefore, I'd be a foolish woman to put my head in the sand and pretend that you're not both experiencing urges."

"Urges?" I croaked out, mortified. *Oh my god!*

"Urges," Mrs. Kavanagh confirmed. "Like the kind of urges I found you both giving into last month?"

*Oh no.*

*Please god no . . .*

"Johnny's a good boy, Shannon," she continued. "He truly is, but he loses his head around you."

Embarrassed, I clasped my hands together and swallowed down a whimper. "I'm sorry?" I finally offered, not knowing what else to say. "For taking his head?"

"I want you to know that John and I both think you are a wonderful influence on our son," she added, smiling. "I've seen Johnny come out of himself more and more since you came into his life. He's playful again. Behaving like an actual teenage boy. I was worried that was gone for him, but you bring the boy out of him – but you also bring the reckless out of him." Sighing, she added, "I'm not a silly woman, Shannon, love. I understand what's happening here, and living in close quarters like this . . . well, I need to make sure that you're protecting yourself."

"Oh my god," I choked out, close to tears from the shame.

"I've had this very same conversation with Jonathan a dozen times, but I know he's lying to me about your physical relationship."

I blinked rapidly. "Uh . . . "

"And I know that if I ask you the same questions, you'll lie, too," she added. "I love my son, Shannon, more than words can express, but if he gets you into trouble, I will kill him. You're in my care, love. I'm responsible for you, and I love you, and while I can supervise your relationship while you're at home, I need to be prepared for what happens when I'm *not* around. Like this camping trip, for example."

"Uh . . . " I really didn't know what to say other than, "Uh . . . "

With another warm smile, she asked, "Did your mother ever talk to you about birth control?"

"Um, no." Blushing, I re-tucked my hair behind my ear and sighed. "She wasn't much of a contraception woman." It was a terrible joke, and I hung my head in shame. "No, she didn't," I whispered. "We didn't have that kind of relationship."

"So, you're not on anything?

I shook my head, not meeting her gaze.

"How would you feel about us making an appointment with the GP?"

I peeked up at her. "What do you think?"

"I think I'm damned if I do and I'm damned if I don't," she said with a wry smile. "If I take you, it's almost like I'm approving, which I most certainly am *not* – at least not until you're twenty-five, minimum – and if I don't and something happens, I'll have failed you both. So, I'm thinking I'll go with the first option and to hell what anyone thinks of it."

"Are you mad at me?"

She laughed softly. "No, Shannon."

I blew out a shaky breath. "You won't kick me out?"

"*Never*," she vowed, squeezing my hand. "This is your forever home – you *and* your brothers – and you're going nowhere, okay? I'm just preventing something from happening – like the death of my son if he so much as contemplates putting his private parts near yours and making me a grandmother before I turn fifty."

I wasn't sure if I wanted to cry, run, or throw my arms around this woman. "Okay." Swallowing deeply, I nodded. "I'd like that – the, uh, appointment," I quickly amended. "With the birth doctor." I shook my head, flustered. "I mean the GP."

Mrs. Kavanagh smiled. "Good girl."

I smiled weakly. "Thanks."

"But this is not a free pass," she added, tone sterner now. "My house rules still stand. No sharing bedrooms. No closed doors when you're hanging out together, and *no* Jonathan creeping into your bedroom at night, and absolutely no private parts touching—"

"Bacon and cabbage? Thank you, Jesus!" Johnny's voice filled the kitchen and I spun around to watch him toss a gear bag on the floor and saunter into the room, looking freshly showered and devastatingly beautiful. It was actually painful to look at him in the summer time in those damn loose-fitting vests he wore – the ones that showcased every protruding muscle on his sculpted chest and arms. I could see his brown nipple when he turned sideways and I discreetly clamped my thighs together.

"I'm bleeding starving, Ma." Grinning, he walked straight for us, smoothing a hand down my back before reaching for my plate. "You done with that, Shan?" I opened my mouth to tell him yes, but he was already inhaling what was left on my plate. "Fucking delicious," he mumbled between bites, giving his mother a wink. "My stomach loves you."

"Language, Jonathan," his mother scolded, although she had a ghost of a smile on her lips. "How many times do I have to tell you?"

"Keep feeding me like this, and I'll do anything you want," was his mumbled response. Walking to the stove with my now-empty plate, he started to pile another heaping of bacon and cabbage for himself. "Any spuds going, Ma?"

"On the counter," Mrs. Kavanagh mused, rolling her eyes at him.

Nodding in approval, Johnny sauntered back to the island and sank down on the stool next to mine. "Where's my small man?" he asked, pausing to press a kiss to my cheek before reaching across the counter and loading five potatoes onto his plate. "What? I need the carbs," he said with a wink when I arched my brow at him.

"Sean's down in the office with your father," Mrs. Kavanagh explained, watching her son carefully as he shoveled food into his mouth with a gusto. "Shannon and I were having a chat about sex, weren't we, love?"

Johnny coughed so loudly that I was sure he'd swallowed his food down the wrong pipe. "Sex," he finally replied, clearing his throat several times.

"Yes, and the camping trip," his mother replied. "And birth control methods."

"Sex and the camping trip," I blurted out anxiously, the words pouring out of my mouth like vomit. "And no grandchildren!"

He coughed louder this time, his face turning slightly purple. "Christ," he finally choked out, eyes trained on his plate. "That's a lot of information to take in on a Friday evening."

"And we went over the house rules again," Mrs. Kavanagh added, keeping a watchful eye on her son's face. "You remember those, don't you, love?"

"I remember Da asking me to do something," Johnny announced, shoving back his stool. Grabbing his plate, he bolted for the kitchen door, calling out, "What's that, Da?" before legging out of the kitchen. "Yeah, I'll be right there."

"She's putting you on the pill?" were the first words that came out of Johnny's mouth when he slipped into my bedroom later that night.

"Shh," I whispered, hurrying to close my bedroom door behind him. "Ollie's right across the hall and he's still on lookout patrol – and I don't have a lock on my door."

"That little turncoat," Johnny muttered, rubbing his jaw. He was wearing a pair of red boxers and his hair was sticking up like always. "I offered him a tenner to turn a blind eye."

"And your mother offered him twenty every time he reported you near my bedroom door," I reminded him. "He's almost up to the price of that new Lego set he wants, so he's out for your blood."

"That's bleeding lovely, isn't it?" Johnny grumbled, padding over to my bed. "First, Tadhg takes my dog as his bed buddy, and now Ollie's taking my backup."

"Oh, so I'm your backup now?" I folded my arms across my chest, watching as he dove onto my bed and rested his hands on his stomach. "Wow, Sookie must be a great spooner."

"You're my queen," he purred, slapping his thighs. "So, come here and let me worship ya."

Giggling, I flicked off the light and raced over to my bed. Climbing onto his lap, I smothered a squeal when he slipped his hands under the hem of my nightie. "You're so full of it," I snickered, leaning down to brush my lips against his.

"So, what's all this about birth control?" he asked against my lips.

"Your mam asked me if I wanted to go on something," I told him, pulling back to gauge his reaction. "She offered to make me an appointment with the GP."

"Oh." His hands moved under my nightie to grip my waist. "And what did you say?"

I trailed my fingers down his abs and smiled. "I said yes."

His eyes blazed with heat. "Yeah?"

"But you're still not allowed in here," I whispered, biting down on my lip to stop myself from moaning when Johnny bucked his hips upwards and I felt all of *him* growing against me.

"No?" His voice was husky, his tone flirtatious. "Are you going to tell on me, Shan?" He pulled me down hard against his waist as he thrust upwards. "Hmm?" He hooked his fingers into the waistband of my knickers and tugged. "Are you going to rat me out for being in your bed?" Releasing the elastic so that it snapped back against my flesh, he palmed my ass. "Are you going to do me wrong, baby?"

Breathless, I shook my head. "Never."

He smirked. "Christ, you're so fucking sexy."

*Oh god.* "Johnny . . ."

"And your skin is so smooth—" Reaching for the hem of my nightie, he sat up and slowly dragged it over my head. "Tell me if you don't want this," he whispered, his bare chest brushing against mine. "And we'll stop."

"D-do you remember that night in your room?" I asked, heart racing violently in my chest. "Before your mother came in?"

Johnny nodded slowly.

"That's what I want," I whispered when words found me again. "That's what I need from you."

"Are you sure?" he asked in a raspy tone of voice.

I nodded. "Hundred percent." We hadn't slept together since that first time, and knowing he was leaving soon made the pressure in my chest too much to take. "I want to be with you before you leave," I told him, surprising myself with my bravery. Pulling back, I looked him in the eyes and said, "I want us to be *together* before you go away. In every possible way."

"Shannon, I'm coming back to you," Johnny replied, eyes burning with heat. "There's no rush."

"I know," I replied.

"And I don't want to pressure you," he added. "Not after everything you've been through—"

"I *need* this connection with you, Johnny," I told him. "I do. I need it."

"Yeah." He blew out a shaky breath. "I need that with you, too, Shan."

My heart fluttered. "Really?"

"Fucking always." He rolled me onto my back and teased my mouth with his. "Are you going to ruin me, Shannon *like the river*?" He pressed a hot kiss to my lips. "Hmm?" His lips trailed to my neck and then my bare breast. Flicking his tongue over my nipple, he asked. "Are you going to break me?"

"No." My spine jack-knifed off the mattress when he spread kisses up the inside of my thighs. His lips were soft, his jaw scratchy and ticklish against the apex of my thighs, causing every muscle south of my bellybutton to contract. Exhaling a ragged breath, I buried my fingers in his hair and moaned. "I would never break you."

"Then you better plan on keeping me," he warned, settling between my legs. "Because I'm all fucking yours." Hooking his fingers into the waistband of my knickers, he slid them off before settling my legs on his shoulders. "Keep your eyes on that door," he ordered before dipping his head between my legs.

"Oh my god." Closing my eyes, I rocked into his touch, fingers knotting in his hair. "Johnny . . . "

"Shh," he coaxed, teasing me with his fingers and tongue. "Keep your eyes on that door and don't make a sound."

"Oh, Jesus," I cried out, heart fluttering wildly in my chest. "Okay, okay . . . " Moaning into my hand, I pulled on his hair, hips bucking frantically against his face. "Oh . . . I'm . . . Johnny, I—"

"You're not watching out," he growled, raising himself up on his elbows, and breaking the contact. "You need to keep your eyes on that bleeding door, Shan. She's like a fucking sniffer hound – and that brother of yours is worse! Keep moaning my name and I'm a dead man."

"I don't care," I practically hissed, flopping back on the pillow. "It doesn't even matter. Just keep going . . . please!"

"Believe me, it matters." Pressing a kiss to the curve of my thigh, he grumbled, "And you will care if she kills me."

"Fine—" Nodding frantically, I forced myself to strangle out the words, "Eyes . . . door . . . got it."

"Thank you," Johnny replied before getting back down to business.

"Johnny!" I cried out, eyes rolling back in my head. "What are you . . . oh my god, *yes*—"

"Fuck, you're going to get me killed," he groaned. With an impatient growl, he removed my legs from his shoulders and reached forward to hook me under my arms. "If I'm going out tonight—" he paused to lift me up and toss me further up the bed, "Then I'm going out inside you." Lowering himself back down on top of me, he kissed my lips, smothering my moans with skillful thrusts of his tongue.

Reaching down, I pushed at the waistband of his boxers, desperate to feel skin on skin. "Take them off," I begged against his lips. "Please."

"I will," he coaxed. "Just *relax*."

I *couldn't*. I was desperate to have him. To just *be* with him again. Everything felt so frantic. *I* was frantic. "Please?"

"Fuck, please don't say it like that," he choked out as he climbed off me. He dragged a foil wrapper out of the side of his jocks and tossed it onto the bed before stripping off. "Keep begging me, and you're going to make me explode before I even touch you."

"Sorry." Trembling, I scurried under the covers and watched in fascination as he ripped the condom wrapper open and quickly rolled it on. "I just . . . yeah." Nodding, I flopped onto my back and whispered, "Yeah."

"Yeah?" Pulling back the covers, Johnny climbed in beside me. "Are you sure?"

Unable to bear another moment of not touching him, I cupped Johnny's neck in my hand and drew his face to mine, lips sealing together in a kiss that I never wanted to end. He moved over me, and then on me, slowly nudging my thighs apart with his. I let my legs fall open, fingers digging into his sides as I felt him settle against me. He was breathing hard, his chest rising and falling in quick succession as he pushed himself inside of my body with an aching gentleness.

His forehead touched against mine in a move so comforting and tender that I felt the bite of tears sting my eyes as my emotions threatened to rip through me. "Shite," he groaned in an oddly helpless tone, sounding pained, as he held himself above me, taking his weight on one elbow, while using his free hand to cup and stroke my cheek. "Are you sore?" Stilling inside of me, he whispered, "Am I hurting you?"

I was overwhelmed, drowning in sensations that were both searing me and setting me on fire, but he wasn't hurting me in the way he thought he was. Biting down on my lip, I shook my head and pulled his face down to mine. "No," I breathed against his lips as I wrapped my arms around his neck. "You're perfect."

His eyes searched mine, uncertainty flashing across his features, as he pressed deeper inside of me, burning a scorching trail of delicious destruction with every thrust of his hips. "Are you sure?"

My hands were wrapped so tightly around his neck, I was sure I was cutting off circulation somewhere, but I couldn't release him. I physically *couldn't* let him go. I was frightened of the unknown, unsure of the future, and desperately in love with him. The only true thing I knew in this moment was that I *trusted* this boy. I trusted him with every inch of my body, and with my eyes, I willed him to never break my heart. "I'm sure of you," I whispered. "Move in me."

A shudder rolled through his body and then he was moving in and out, deep and slow, hips rocking in an addictive rhythm as his lips never left mine. Clutching him like a lifeline, I locked my legs around his waist and trusted my body's instincts, rolling my hips upwards with every downwards thrust of his. "Tell me again," I begged, arching my back upwards, fingernails digging into the sun-tanned flesh of his bare back. "Please—" Biting down on my lip to stop myself from crying out, I absorbed the feel of him, of his weight pressing my body deeper into the mattress, of the inexplicable sensations he brought to life inside of me, as he thrust inside me over and over. "Johnny . . . tell me again."

"I love you, Shannon *like the river*," he whispered, and the heat of his breath on my flesh caused a shiver of pleasure to roll through me. "And I'm coming home to you." He was breathing hard, his heart racing almost violently in his chest as he drew in short breaths. "I promise."

A momentary flash of relief coursed through me, but it was quickly overtaken by the pleasure thrumming through my veins as my body drowned in love.

# Birthday Boy

## JOHNNY

Someone singing *happy birthday to you, happy birthday to you, happy birthday, old purple balls, happy birthday to you,* broke through the best fucking dream I was having that involved a naked Shannon, with her mouth around my dick. The sound of a door slamming loudly tore through my happy thoughts, and then I was buried beneath an insufferable weight, as her pretty face disappeared from my mind's eye.

Jerking awake with a start, I scrambled to push the covers I was smothering under away from my face. "My best friend is all grown up!" the voice continued to say. "The big one-eight! You can legally buy me drink and smokes whenever I want now. It's like it's your birthday, but I'm the one reaping the benefits."

"Get off me, you big bastard!" I snarled when I finally managed to free myself from the sheets I was tangled up in. Shooting straight up in my bed, I snaked an arm out and shoved Gibsie off the bed before throwing back the covers, panic-stricken at the thought of the pancake he might have made of my girlfriend if he managed to land on her, but she wasn't there.

Confused, I searched my mattress, but no naked Shannon.

"That's a lovely way to treat me," Gibsie huffed from where I had knocked him onto the floor. "Charming."

"What time is it?"

"You just threw me off your bed when I came all the way over here to wish you a happy birthday," he grumbled, climbing to his feet. "You should apologize for manhandling me, Johnny, not ask me for the time—"

"What fucking time is it, Gibs?" I snapped, rolling out of bed to search the mattress.

"It's only half-six," he huffed. "Jesus, you're supposed to be peppy on your birth – oh for the love of god! Would you put that oversized *beast* away!"

"If you don't want to see my cock, *knock* before you walk into my room," I shot back as I stalked, bollocks naked, into my bathroom and slammed the door behind me. In a hushed voice, I said, "Shan, you in here?"

"Over here," she whispered back.

Grinning, I pulled back the shower curtain and cocked a brow. "I *knew* I didn't dream you up."

"Uh, nope, not a dream." Blushing, she dragged the shower curtain back around her body and squirmed. "Happy eighteenth birthday."

"Best birthday yet," I purred, pushed back the curtain once more to step into the tub. "You in my bed—" Pausing, I grabbed her thighs and hoisted her into my arms. Pressing her against the wall of my shower, I smirked. "With your mouth around my—"

"Are you talking to yourself again?" Gibsie shouted from the other side of the door. "Should I be worried? Are you having another panic attack? Is it because of the tour or your birthday? Because you're only turning eighteen, lad, not eighty, and the tour will be grand. Just breathe. Nice and slow. Will I get your mam—"

"No! Jesus Christ, don't get my ma," I strangled out, burying my face in her neck. "I'm not having a panic attack, lad."

"You're not?"

I snapped my head back up. "No!"

"Then what are you doing?"

"I'm taking a shite," I shot back, causing Shannon to giggle. "Shh," I mouthed, rubbing myself against her. "Go downstairs and wait for me, Gibs," I called out. "I'll be like fifteen minutes—" My eyes roamed over her naked body and my dick strained. *Fuck.* "Maybe twenty."

"Yeah, I see pink knickers on your floor, so I know exactly what kind of shit you're taking, you lucky bastard," he called back. "Hey, Little Shannon."

Shannon's eyes widened. "Uh, hey, Gibsie."

"Nice floral bra, Shan," he added. "I love the colors – hold on a second! Are you a *B cup* now?"

"Get the fuck out of here," I roared. "And don't touch her bra!"

"I'm just saying that a full cup size is a big jump in one month," Gibsie replied. "Fair play, girl. You're blossoming—"

"I'm going to rip your gooch off and feed it to you, ya bleeding pervert," I snarled, setting Shannon down so I could climb out of the tub. Swinging the bathroom door open, I stalked towards him. "And how the fuck would you know what size bra *my* girlfriend wears?"

"Because I have eyes," he laughed and then flung Shannon's bra at me before diving across the bed to get away. "You know when people say they're a great judge of character? Well, I'm a great judge of tit size—"

"I hope you enjoyed your last meal, Gerard," I snarled, leaping onto my bed, stark naked. "Because you're going to die today."

"You keep that *beast* away from me!" he choked out, making the sign of the cross with this index fingers. "The power of Christ compels you!"

"What are you doing?" Ollie's voice filled my ears and I dropped to the mattress quicker than a cat.

"Alright, bud?" I strangled out, covering myself with my blankets.

"Why are you naked, Johnny?" he asked, standing in my doorway in his Spiderman pajamas. "Where are your pajamas?"

"I was having a shower," I lied through my teeth and told him, scrambling to cover myself up. "Gibsie broke in and stole my towel, so I'm giving out to him."

"Yeah." Laughing nervously, Gibsie shrugged. "We're always playing jokes on each other."

"That's not funny," Ollie said with a scowl. "He could get the double die-monia if he doesn't dry his hair."

"The double die-what-e-a?" Gibsie snickered.

"The double die-monia, " Ollie repeated. "Mammy told us it nearly whipped our Nanny once." His brows furrowed. "I'm not sure what that means, but she got it 'cause she wasn't drying her hair, and it's supposed to be like *super* bad. They put you in a hospital and everything!"

"He means double pneumonia," I corrected, stifling a groan. "I'm all good, Ol. Don't worry. It's the summertime. I won't get sick."

"Yeah, well, it's still not funny," he huffed. Turning to Gibsie, he added, "How would you feel if someone took your towel?"

"Fair point, kid," Gibsie replied, stifling a laugh. "I promise I won't take Johnny's towel again."

"Well, give it back to him now," Ollie insisted, not budging from the doorway. "Come on," he urged. "Do the right thing, and say you're sorry."

"I'm so sorry, Johnny," Gibsie choked out, holding a hand in front of his mouth. "And I would love to give you back your towel, but I seem to have misplaced it."

"Don't worry, Johnny," Ollie said with a huff. "I'll get you a new one." He moved for my bathroom quicker than I had a chance to register what was happening.

"No, no, no—" I called out, but it was too late. He had the door wide open, revealing Shannon standing there – thankfully wrapped in a bath towel.

"Ollie, get out," Shannon hissed, slamming the door shut once more. "Oh my god!"

"Dellie!" Ollie shouted at the top of his lungs. "I caught them again!"

"Please, please, stop shouting," I begged. "Don't tell her—"

"I want my money," Ollie shot back. "And you know the rules, mister rule-breaker." Narrowing his eyes at me, he said, "You're not allowed to play with my sister on your own." He folded his arms across his chest. "And you've got no clothes on. Dellie says that's a big no-no."

"But it's my birthday," I strangled out, not against emotional blackmail given the current circumstances and prospective consequences. "And I'll give you fifty quid if you don't tell Dellie."

He tilted his head to one-side, studying me carefully. "One-hundred."

"What?" I gaped at him. "But it's my birthday!"

"That's why it's one-hundred," Ollie replied. "Otherwise, I'd need a trillion."

I narrowed my eyes right back at him. "What do you need a hundred quid for?"

"For my Legos," he replied. "And my business."

"Oh yeah?" I arched a brow. "And what business is that?"

"My spy business," he told me. "And you're my number one target." He squinted his eyes at me. "I'm watching you all the time."

*Jesus Christ* ... Shaking my head, I pointed to my jeans. "Get my wallet."

"Woo-hoo!" Grinning from ear to ear, Ollie dragged my wallet out of my discarded jeans and handed it to me. "That's a good choice, Johnny."

"You better keep quiet about this," I warned him as I handed over two fifties. "Or else I'm going to declare war on your treehouse."

"You wouldn't dare," he gasped.

"Oh, I would," I shot back with a nod. "Gibs and I will make an even bigger treehouse, and then we'll bomb yours with water balloons until you surrender, and then we'll hijack it like pirates."

"Oh, I'm so fucking down for that," Gibsie declared in an excited tone. "I have an excellent aim."

"Fine, I won't tell on you," Ollie huffed, snatching the cash out of my hand and then holding it up to the light to check its authenticity. "But this is a one-time deal. If I catch you near my sister again, you're fair game, Johnny Kavanagh."

"Deal," I agreed. "Now, out you go."

With a stiff nod, Ollie stalked out of my room only to pause in the doorway and run back to my bed. "Oh – and happy birthday," he said, giving me a quick hug. "I love you." With that, he scampered out of my room with my cash in his hands.

"That kid is slick," Gibsie said in a tone laced with admiration for the young hustler. "Little Lynch has more of Joey *the hurler* in him than I thought."

"Yeah? Well, little Lynch just walked out of here with our beer fund for the camping trip today," I grumbled as I reached for my discarded boxers and slipped them on.

"That little *shit*," Gibsie growled, not looking so fucking admiring now. "For that, I *am* going to water-balloon and hijack his treehouse."

"No, you're not, lad," I said wearily. "You're going to go downstairs and wait for me in the kitchen."

"Fine," Gibsie huffed, heading for my door. "But one of these days, we're going to take the fort back. "We're going to take it *all* back," he added before closing my bedroom door behind him.

"Coast is clear, Shan," I called out. "We're off the hook."

"Oh my god!" Shannon burst out of my bathroom, red-faced and flailing. "I am so *embarrassed*."

"It's okay," I coaxed, patting the mattress next to me. "Come here—"

"No way!" Shannon strangled out, grabbing her clothes off my bedroom floor. "He'll be back. That bribe only stands for as long as it takes him to put that cash in his money box. He's ruthless, Johnny. I give him five minutes, tops."

"Will you give me a kiss, at least," I grumbled when she rushed to my door.

"I'll kiss you later in our tent," she called out, blowing a kiss at me before legging it down the hallway. "Love you!"

"Yeah," I muttered, flopping back onto my mattress. "Love you back."

# Camping and Carnage

## SHANNON

"Cork, Claire?" Hughie deadpanned, leaning against the side of his car. "Of all the places in the country we could have gone camping, you chose *Cork*?"

Winking, Johnny gave me a knowing smirk and continued to haul bags out of the boot of his brand-spanking new Audi A4 – courtesy of his parents – and pass them to Feely. Hughie had been complaining about our camping destination ever since we left the Kavanagh's house three hours ago, and I was grateful that I got to ride shotgun in Johnny's car with him and Feely, and not with the others. Katie was in a mood, Gibsie looked mutinous, and Lizzie was her usual raging-self. Hughie and Claire had been fighting since they walked through the door this morning. The only person who seemed to be himself right now was Feely, and I could never take his measure anyway because he was always so quiet. Something was going on – something that had nothing to do with where we were staying tonight – and it was depressing, because today was Johnny's birthday. He was leaving on Friday. We had two days left together and our friends were fighting.

"It's a lovely place," Claire said with a heavy sigh. "It has a river and it's surrounded by a woodland." Grabbing a selection of green, white, and gold colored rugby ball shaped balloons out of the back of Johnny's car, she shrugged. "It's absolutely beautiful here, and I promise we'll have fun." Reaching into the back seat, she pulled out two huge red-colored balloons, shaped as the numbers *one* and *eight*. "Just try to be positive."

"Well, I think it's great, Claire," Johnny interjected in a calm tone. "I really appreciate all the effort you went to, so thanks a million."

"You're welcome, Johnny," Claire replied, sounding relieved.

"I agree," I offered. "This is the most beautiful place I've ever been in my life."

723 • CHLOE WALSH

"You've only been out of Cork once," Lizzie drawled. "For the Dublin match."

"Twice," I mumbled, red-faced. "I went to Kerry once when I was small."

"But you've still only been in three places, Shan—"

"For now," Johnny shot back, giving Lizzie a warning look.

"But this is still *Cork*, Cap," Hughie grumbled.

"*West* Cork," Gibsie corrected, and there was a hint of warning in his voice as he took a defensive stance in front of Claire. "And fuck right off with your pessimistic attitude," he added, tucking a slab of Heineken under his arm. "At least your sister had the imagination to think this whole trip up. We'd be sitting in Biddies, downing pints and warding off clingers if it wasn't for her." Turning to Claire, he said, "Don't you mind him, babe. You did a great job." With his free hand, he tugged on her ponytail, forcing her to look up at him. "You keep that head up," he ordered, tipping her chin with his thumb. "Don't you dare hide that angel face from the world."

Claire's already pink cheeks turned as red as the balloons she was clutching in her hands. "Thanks, Gerard."

"But we could have gone *anywhere*," Hughie complained. "And we're still in Cork."

"Say it one more time and I'll burn your tent with you in it," Gibsie snarled, glaring at Hughie. "You think I'm messing? Keep upsetting her and see what fucking happens—"

"Whoa, whoa, whoa," Feely interjected, stepping between the boys. "None of that shit on Cap's birthday." Turning to Gibsie, he added, "Tone down the testosterone. You're peaking on the crazy with the death threats, Gibs."

"Hughie's right," Lizzie decided to throw her two-cents into the mix. "This is a disaster."

Claire's eyes filled with tears and she hurried off through the woods in the direction of the camping site, mumbling something about a fly being in her eye.

"Oh my fucking god!" Gibsie roared, clearly livid. "If any of you have a problem with being here, then get back in your cars and *leave!*" Gesturing behind him to where Claire had hurried off, he added, "Think very carefully about your next move, because if you're coming, then you're going to be *happy*. You're going to *smile,* and you're going to have a good bastard *time*. You're going to eat the cake, you're going to sing all the happy fucking birthdays, and you're going to *thank* that girl for spending the last bloody month organizing this trip for your unworthy asses!" Exhaling heavily, he looked around at us. "We left our heavily pregnant cat at home for this, and Claire's anxious enough about Cherub without all of you breathing down her neck, so if you upset her, again, I will legit take leave of my senses and lose the fucking plot." Eyes bulging, he added, "Don't push me, because I'm already halfway there!"

"Alright, lad," Hughie coaxed, holding his hands up, eyeing Gibsie warily. "You won't hear any more complaints from me."

Gibsie nodded stiffly before turning his glare on Lizzie. "And *you?*"

"For Claire's sake, I'll suck it up," Lizzie bit out.

"Good." Readjusting the slab of beer in his hands, Gibsie said, "Now, if you'll all excuse me, I need to go and find somewhere to take a shit because I've been holding one in since we left Ballylaggin – and I had a curry last night, so you can only imagine the pressure I'm under right now."

"You go do that, lad," Feely mused, slapping a roll of toilet paper on top of the case of beer in Gibsie's arms before he hurried off into the bushes. "We're all shiny, happy people here."

"Now listen up," Johnny said, drawing everyone's attention to him. "I personally couldn't give a shite if you're happy to be here or not. I don't care if you're being a pack of spoilt brats because we're still in Cork. I don't care if you don't particularly like one another. I don't care if you're in a fight with each other. I don't even care that it's my eighteenth. I. Don't. Care. Not one iota of fucks do I give about any of that crap," he growled, glaring at Katie, Hughie, and Lizzie. "I *care* that I have two days left with my girlfriend – *two days* – and then I'm gone for the summer. We've had a hard year. We've had surgeries and funerals, fires and loss. We've seen more hospitals and tears than you could comprehend in your little pea brains, and suffered some serious fucking upheaval. This is our break – our little time out from all the shite back home, so you are not going to mess this up for me, and you're definitely not going to mess this up for *her*. Are we clear?"

"As a whistle," Feely replied.

"Not *you*," Johnny shot back. "*Them*."

"Jesus, you're right," Hughie said, looking embarrassed. "I'm sorry, guys."

"Yeah," Katie agreed, red-faced. "We were being selfish."

"Me, too," Lizzie sighed. "Sorry, Shan, I didn't even think about what this trip meant for you and Johnny."

"*A lot*," Johnny bit out. "It means a lot for us."

They all nodded in understanding.

"Then let's get this show on the road," Feely declared, grabbing an armful of bags. "Onwards and upwards."

Ignoring the huffing and puffing around me, I focused my attention on ogling my boyfriend, appreciating the way the blue swimming trunks he was wearing hung low on his indented hips. There was this deep V between his hipbones, a clear sign that he took very good care of his body, and a trail of dark hair from his navel that disappeared beneath the waistband of his shorts. His thighs were just so thick with muscle – his calves, too. Everything about Johnny was just so tight, and toned, and *huge*.

"Like what you see?" he asked, catching me staring.

I blushed beetroot red. "Uh, sorry?"

Chuckling softly to himself, Johnny closed the boot of his car and grabbed our bags off the ground. "Come on, my little peeping-tom," he teased, slinging an arm over my shoulder. "But don't feel bad for staring." He leaned close to my ear before whispering, "I've been doing some peeping of my own."

"Yeah." I rolled my eyes. "Sure you have."

"Are you kidding me? You're wearing a white vest and no bra. You're lucky I didn't crash the bleeding car on the way up here, I was staring at you so hard," he shot back with a wolfish grin. "I was winding that car window down and *willing* the breeze to get you."

"Oh my god," I laughed, wrapping an arm around him. "You're so weird."

"Yeah, that's probably true," he agreed with a chuckle. "This is going to be a good trip, Shan."

"Yeah." I sighed contently. "I think you're right."

"You're doing it wrong again!" Lizzie hissed, shoving at Gibsie's chest when he attempted to help her and Claire erect their tent. "You're so bloody clueless."

"Do you see mine and Feely's pitched tent over there?" Gibsie bit out tightly, threading the pole through the fabric. "Looks a lot better than yours, doesn't it? Because I *know* what I'm doing, so get off my back!"

"But the instructions say you're supposed to do it this way," Lizzie continued to argue, waving a sheet of paper in his face. "Would you just put that damn pole down and look at this! Come on, don't be thick and just look at the instructions!"

"Oh, yeah sure. No problem—" Grabbing the instructions out of her hands, Gibsie balled the paper up and threw it in the river. "That's what I think of your instructions."

"Why did you do that?" Lizzie demanded, slapping his chest again. "I was trying to show you—"

"Because I can't fucking *read* them," he roared in her face. "And I don't need you to show me anything."

"Guys, stop," Claire warned, stepping in between them. "Liz, don't push him."

"It was a picture," Lizzie screamed right back at him, stepping around Claire to get up in Gibsie's face again. "I wasn't mocking your learning difficulties."

"No, of course you weren't," he shot back with a sneer. "You were just calling me thick and clueless for the fun of it." Bristling, he shook his head and continued threading the pole through the hoops in the fabric of the tent. "It's all just shits and giggles for you, isn't it, Liz? You can say whatever the hell you want to anyone and we're all supposed to just *take* it because you have *issues*."

"Don't you dare, Gibs," Lizzie hissed, eyes narrowed, as she continued to shove at Gibsie, pushing him backwards. "Don't you fucking *dare* bring that up!"

"Guys, come away from the bank," Claire ordered in a worried tone. "You're going to fall into the river."

"Why not?" Gibsie demanded, backing away from Lizzie, and moving precariously close to the edge of the water bank. "You clearly have a huge one with me, so why don't you just get it off your chest?" he taunted. "Once and for all."

Panicked, I looked around for Johnny but he was gone back to the carpark to collect the last of our things with Hughie.

"Just stay back," Katie whispered in my ear, placing a hand on my shoulder. "Those two are like a volcano that's been waiting to erupt for years." Sighing, she added, "And you don't need to be near it when it happens, Shan."

"Whoa," Feely called out, sprinting out of his and Gibsie's tent and moving towards them. "Let's just take it back a notch, everyone—"

"You know what he did to *her*," Lizzie snarled. "You know what he cost me!"

"I'm not *him*!" Gibsie roared at the top of his lungs, throwing his hands up in the air. "I had nothing to do with that!"

"What the hell is going on?" Johnny and Hughie demanded in unison as they jogged through the tree line towards the camp. "Hey – stop it, the pair of ye!"

"Gibs, get away from the water—" Hughie started to call out, but his voice was drowned out by Lizzie's high-pitched scream.

"He's your family!" Lizzie screamed and then shoved at Gibsie's chest. "And you're just like him!" Like a scene from a horror movie, I watched as Lizzie shoved Gibsie again, causing him to tumble over the edge of the bank.

The moment Gibsie fell into the water, all hell broke loose.

"Oh my god, he's drowning!"

"Get him out!"

"Gibs, hold on, lad!"

Panicked, I moved to jump in after him, but I couldn't because I didn't know how to *swim*. With my heart in my mouth, I watched as he completely froze up in the water, eyes wide and full of terror, before he started to sink like a stone. He didn't even flail or flap around. He just *froze*.

Johnny, Hughie, and Feely all ran past me then, jumping into the river after him.

"Gerard!" Claire screamed, rushing towards the bank. "Gerard!"

"I'm sorry," Lizzie choked out, looking like she was in shock. "I didn't mean—"

"Why would you do that to him, Lizzie?" Claire began to scream. And then she did something I never expected her to do. She *slapped* Lizzie across the face. "He's afraid of water, you heartless bitch," Claire continued to scream. "And you know he is."

Lizzie shook her head, looking like she was in the first stage of shock. "I didn't mean – I didn't – I swear—"

"You're okay, buddy," Hughie coaxed, holding Gibsie's pale face in between his hands and out of the water, as Johnny swam back towards the bank with his trembling frame slung over his shoulder. "We've got you," Hughie continued to say in a soothing tone, treading the water, as Feely hauled himself back onto the riverbank. "We're right here. You're with us, okay? You're not back there. That's it – good job, lad. Just keep nice and calm . . . "

"Have you got him?" Johnny demanded, breathing hard, as he thrust Gibsie's limp body towards Feely who was lying on his stomach, leaning over the edge of the bank, with his arms stretched out to take their friend. "Don't let him go, Pa—"

"I have him, Cap," Feely replied, grabbing Gibsie under the arms. "I won't let you go, buddy."

Gibsie looked like a frightened little boy, frozen in shock, as Feely hauled him out of the water and onto the muddy bank.

He collapsed on his hands and knees at the edge, and the sounds that were coming from his throat were gut-wrenching. It was almost like the keening noise of a wounded animal.

"Good, man," Feely panted, dropping down beside Gibsie and placing a hand on his back. "Shh, you're safe."

Johnny hauled himself out of the water next, followed swiftly by Hugh, and then all three of the boys were kneeling beside Gibsie, whispering words I couldn't make out in his ear.

Frozen to the spot, I watched as Gibsie scrambled away from the river bank on his hands and knees, not stopping until his back was pressed to the trunk of a nearby tree. He was shaking violently, with his head bowed, and his hands clasped loosely around his knees, clearly wrestling to get his breathing under control.

"It's okay, Gerard," Claire soothed as she knelt in front of him with a towel in her hand. "Shh . . . " With aching tenderness, she gently dabbed at his face and hair. "I'm right here with you." Moving onto his shoulders, she gently dried him off with the towel before wrapping it around his shoulders and cupping his pale face in her hands. "Deep breaths." Pressing her forehead to his, she stroked his cheeks and whispered, "I'll keep you safe."

"Is he okay?" Katie asked, sounding concerned. "Gibs?"

"He'd be a lot better if all of you *stopped* staring at him," Claire hissed, shifting her body so that Gibsie's face was hidden from view from the rest of us. "He's not a fucking circus!"

*Whoa . . .*

"Gibsie, I'm sorry," Lizzie blurted out, tears streaming down her cheeks, as she rushed towards him. "I swear, I didn't mean to—"

"Get away from him!" Claire snarled, taking a defensive stance in front of a boy who was more than twice her size. "Get back. All of you!"

"I didn't mean it," Lizzie choked out. "I swear—"

"Just give it a bleeding rest," Johnny growled, climbing to his feet. "You could have *killed* him."

"I know, and I'm so sorry!" Lizzie sobbed, shaking her head. "I didn't mean it—"

"You never mean it," Hughie muttered, stalking over to Katie, who was holding a towel out for him. "But we're all getting really tired of hearing that excuse, Liz."

"I said I'm sorry—"

"Well, sorry doesn't bleeding cut it this time."

"You can chalk that down, Cap."

"You could have killed him! What part of that don't you get?"

"Guys, stop," I choked out, feeling a huge swell of sympathy for Lizzie, who looked genuinely remorseful – and seconds away from a nervous breakdown. "She didn't mean it."

"She meant it, Shannon!" Hughie snapped.

"Hey – don't snap at her," Johnny warned, coming to stand in front of me.

"I wasn't."

"You fucking were!"

"Alright, lads, just simmer on down," Feely interjected. "Lizzie knows she was wrong, she's clearly sorry, so there's no need to start throwing shit at her – or each other."

"But she—" Hughie started to object, but Feely cut him off.

"You're perfect now, Hugh?" he asked, arching a brow. "And you, Kav?" He turned to Johnny. "You've never lost your head in a fight?"

"We've never tried to drown anyone," Hughie shot back, glowering at Lizzie.

"She didn't try to drown him," Feely stated calmly. "Don't be so fucking dramatic. She lost her temper and pushed him. He fell in and panicked. We know why. It's shit, it's sucks, it happened, now let's get *on* with it."

"And I'm so sorry," Lizzie sobbed.

"They know," Feely replied. Turning to Lizzie, he crooked a finger and said, "Come here."

"Wh-what?"

"I said come here," he repeated in a no-nonsense tone of voice. "Now." Stunned, I watched as Lizzie complied without a word and walked over to him. "Now, you and I are going to go for a walk and let them all cool off," Feely said, taking ahold of her hand. "And we're going to come back when everyone here remembers that they're not perfect angels."

"O-okay." Sniffling, Lizzie nodded and let Feely lead her away from the campsite.

"Are you okay?" I asked, following Johnny as he walked over to our tent and crawled inside. "Johnny?"

"I'm grand, Shan," he replied, digging a towel out of his bag. "I'm just a bit rattled." Sinking down on his knees, he toweled off his chest and back before sighing heavily. "This day is a bleeding disaster."

"Not necessarily," I offered, scooting onto my knees to watch him clean up.

"They're all fighting," he grumbled, dragging the towel through his hair.

"We're not," I whispered.

He paused and lowered the towel. "True."

"And we're together," I added, smiling.

He smiled back at me. "Another truth."

"What happened back there, Johnny?" I asked then, desperately trying to keep my eyes off his lower half when he slipped his wet swimming trunks off and tossed them out of the opening of our tent. "Can Gibsie not swim?"

"He *can* swim," Johnny corrected, rummaging around for a clean pair of boxers. "He just panicked."

"Why?"

"His father and sister drowned when he was small," Johnny muttered, brows furrowed, as he concentrated on pulling on his jocks. "They got into trouble out at sea or something like that." Shrugging, he added, "He's had an issue with water ever since."

"Oh my god," I strangled out, heart cracking clean open in my chest. "When did this happen?"

"His Holy Communion day, I think? So that would have made him seven?" Johnny replied, tone hoarse. Giving up on pulling his jocks up his wet legs, he kicked them back off and covered himself with a towel instead. "It was a long time before I moved down to Cork. He's only ever spoken about it once to me, and that was when I was eleven, so it's all a bit hazy, but I remember him telling me that his parents were going through a shitbomb of a separation at the time. I'm not sure of the ins and outs of it, but it was really bleeding messy, babe – affairs galore. Anyway, they all rallied together for the day that was in it and threw a massive joint party for both Gibs and Hughie."

"Hughie?"

"Well yeah, it was his communion, too, Shan," Johnny explained. "And their two families have always been close. They were practically raised together."

"Oh." I nodded. "Okay."

"Anyway, his stepdad Keith had spent a fortune to have the party at this flashy hotel by the coast for Gibs," Johnny continued, "and his father wanted to outdo him, so he rented a boat and took a bunch of them out on the water."

"Oh no," I croaked out, covering my mouth with my hands, not sure if I wanted to hear the rest of this story.

"They got into some sort of trouble," Johnny said. "I don't know all of the details, but Gibsie and his sister Bethany got knocked overboard."

A sob tore through me. "No."

Johnny sighed sadly. "Their da went in for them, but he didn't come back out." Releasing a heavy sigh, he added, "His sister didn't either."

*Oh my god.* "What about Gibsie?" I strangled out, dabbing at the tears trickling down my cheeks. "How did he get out?"

"That's the part he won't tell me," Johnny muttered. "I know it has something to do with the Biggs family – and maybe even Claire? But

I presume one of them swam out and saved him." He shrugged again, looking a little helpless. "He doesn't talk about it, and I don't push."

"How old was she?"

Johnny paused and thought about it for a moment before responding. "Gibs was seven, so she would have been two or three?"

My heart broke. "She was only a baby?"

"Yeah." Johnny exhaled a heavy sigh. "She would have been about Sean's age."

"Oh my god." I shook my head, struggling to comprehend what I'd just heard. "I can't believe this."

"We all have our secrets," Johnny replied quietly. "We're all a little fractured, Shan."

"Can Gerard and I have your keys?" Claire's voice filled my ears seconds before her head popped through the opening of our tent. Without a word, Johnny grabbed his keys off the tent floor and handed them to her. "Thanks," she replied before disappearing once more.

"Do you think he should be driving after what happened?" I asked, worried.

Johnny shrugged. "Probably not, but he needs space," he told me, brows set in a deep frown as he focused on plucking wet strands of grass off his shin and then tossing them away. "He'll go for a drive with her, she'll do whatever she does that brings him back down, and then he'll bounce back again."

"Claire?"

"Claire," he confirmed with a nod.

"I think they have secrets," I admitted, shifting closer to him.

"I think you're right," Johnny agreed. "But whatever he needs right now, he'll get that from her." Shaking his head, he added, "I can't give it to him."

"What about you?" I asked in a gentle tone. He was trying to put on a brave face, but I saw the concern in his eyes earlier – the sheer helplessness. "What do you need right now?"

Johnny reached over and pulled me onto his lap. "I have everything I need right here."

"Do you think they'll sort it out?" I asked then.

"Who – Claire and Lizzie, or Gibs and Lizzie?"

"All of them?"

Johnny shrugged. "Yeah, they'll be grand. He'll come back in an hour or two, all smiles and jokes. He'll brush it under the rug, and that will be that."

"You think?"

"I know him, Shannon," he replied. "That's how he copes. Humor is his thing."

"I don't want everyone to be mad at her," I whispered. "She's going through a lot."

"Shan—"

"I'm serious," I told him, begging him with my eyes to hear me. "Please, just don't hold a grudge over this."

"I'm raging over what she did to him," he admitted honestly.

"I know," I coaxed, straddling his hips. "But when she comes back with Feely, can you make an effort? For me?"

He stared hard at me for a long moment before blowing out a breath. "Fine."

"Thanks." I smiled. "I know you find Lizzie hard work – and she is – but there's so much more to her than meets the eye." I reached for his hand and squeezed. "She's all prickles, but there's a good person under that. She's a lot like Joey in ways. She makes it very hard for people to love her, but it's a defense mechanism. Trust me, I know."

"I'll take your word for it," Johnny grumbled, not looking impressed.

"So, you'll be nice to her?"

"I'll be nice," he confirmed grimly. "For you."

"I got you a present," I said then, trying to steer the conversation into gentler waters. "It's really nothing special, but I can give it to you now, if you want?"

"You got me a present?" Johnny's brows shot up and he craned his neck back to look at me. "Shan, you didn't have to do that."

"It's your eighteenth birthday," I replied. "Of course, I got you a present." Rolling off his lap, I held a hand up. "But fair warning, it's nothing as amazing as that flashy car your parents bought you."

"She's sweet, huh?" he chuckled. "She purrs like a dream."

"Uh-huh." Entirely uninterested in talking cars with him, I reached into my bag and rummaged around until my fingers found the book inside. "I made it myself," I told him, as I pulled out the scrapbook and thrust it into his hands. "And if it's bad, or you don't like it, you can just throw it away – I swear I won't mind." Clasping my hands together on my lap, I shrugged, feeling nervous. "Happy birthday, Johnny."

"You made me a book?" His voice was deep and gruff as he opened the cover and stared. "Of me?"

"Well, it's more of a scrapbook," I explained. "Detailing your career from the minis all the way up to here—" I reached over and flipped to the back page to where I had photocopied his letter of acceptance from the Irish rugby academy and taped it inside. "It's like an itinerary of your life in rugby." I blew out a shaky breath. "Is it okay?"

"Shan . . ." He shook his head and flicked through page after page of newspaper clippings and photographs of him from the age of six to eighteen. "Where did you find all this?"

"Your Mam helped me," I told him. "When I told her what I wanted to make for you, she took me up to the attic where she has at least thirty boxes of newspapers and trophies and god knows what else."

"She does?" he asked, not taking his eyes off the book.

"Yeah." I nodded. "It's like a shrine to you in that attic. I've never seen so much memorabilia belonging to one person in my life." Shrugging, I added, "You're kind of famous, Johnny Kavanagh."

A small smile ghosted his lips and he tapped his finger against the book. "I love this."

I sagged in relief. "You do?"

Nodding, he closed the book and looked at me. "And I love you."

"I love you, too," I replied, smiling back at him.

"I mean it, Shan." His tone was serious; his eyes blazing with heat. "I really do mean it."

"I believe you," I whispered, heart fluttering with excitement.

"If I could take you with me, I would," he choked out, setting the book back down and pulling me onto his lap once more. "I don't want to leave you."

My heart sank. "You have to go, Johnny."

He wrapped his arms around me and buried his face in my neck. "I'm so sad."

"Don't be sad," I begged. "Be *happy*."

"I am," he croaked out. "But I'm just . . . I don't know what I'm going to do without you. I feel like I just got you, and now I have to leave—" His words broke off and he groaned into my neck. "I'm not ready to give it all up."

"Give what up?" I whispered, trailing my fingers through his hair. "Hmm?"

"My youth," he admitted quietly.

"Johnny, you're still young," I coaxed.

"I'm not talking about my age," he mumbled. "I'm talking about you – and those fuckers out there," he added, pointing a finger at the tent opening. "And your annoying little brothers." He shook his head and sighed heavily. "I'm not ready to give it all up, Shan."

"You can do this." I forced the words out of my mouth when all I wanted to do was scream *don't go* instead. But I wouldn't be selfish with him. He needed to do this, and I needed to support him. "And it's only for the summer."

He stiffened for a moment before nodding. "Yeah, I know."

"Do you want the rest of your present?" I coaxed, desperate to cheer him up before we both ended up miserable. "Hmm?"

"There's more?"

Smirking, I pushed him onto his back and whipped his towel away. "If you want more?"

"Oh fuck," he growled, nodding in appreciation, as his hands moved to my hips. "I definitely want more."

Later that night, everyone seemed to have calmed down and were genuinely enjoying themselves. The tents had been pitched, the cake had been eaten, the arguments had been put to bed, the apologies had been accepted, and the sullen faces had been replaced with loose, drunken smiles – courtesy of the half dozen slabs of beer and other alcoholic concoctions on offer.

Sitting around a campfire at the edge of the river, with Johnny's arms wrapped around me, I listened intently to the banter and jokes that were going ninety. Gibsie and Lizzie had formed a silent truce of sorts and were sitting on either side of Feely, acting like nothing had happened between them earlier. I wasn't sure what to make of it if I was being honest, but I had to admit that pretending to get along with one another was a lot better than outright war. Claire was sitting on Gibsie's other side, and Hughie and Katie had just returned from a twenty-minute *toilet break* behind a nearby tree, looking all flushed and barely put together.

As I stared into the amber flames, I felt a sudden pang of guilt for feeling so happy. My mother's face flashed into my mind, followed swiftly by the image of Joey's haunted eyes the last time I saw him. The emotions that swept through me were so overwhelming that it caused me to flinch and drop the bottle of beer I had been sipping.

"And we have a lightweight," Gibsie cheered from across the fire, clearly back to his happy-go-lucky antics. "Little Shannon," he tutted, grinning. "Spilling your drink on the fifth bottle?" He shook his head, feigning disappointment. "What are we going to do with you, huh?"

Recovering before my grief could get the better of me, I blinked back the sting of tears in my eyes and slapped on a bright smile. "Cut me some slack," I joked, forcing humor into my voice, as I set my bottle upright on the ground. "It's my first time drinking."

Chuckling, Gibsie turned his attention back to Feely who was playing on his guitar and belting out a verse of Tim O'Riordan's "The Langer Song". All of our friends were singing along with him, laughing their arses off in the process, but I couldn't focus on the funny lyrics or the sound of Feely's beautiful voice because my mind was stuck on my family.

"What's wrong?" Johnny whispered in my ear and the smell of alcohol on his breath hit me like a wrecking ball. He was slurring a little from the empty slab of Heineken beside him, and even though he was his usually gentle self, my father's face just wouldn't leave my mind.

*"What's wrong with ya, girl?"*

*"What's fucking wrong with you now?"*

*"Go to sleep now, Shannon. Just close your eyes and it'll all be better in the morning . . . "*

"Shan?" Johnny asked again, dragging me back from the edge of my depressing thoughts.

"Hmm?"

"What's wrong, babe?"

"What do you mean?"

"Your body went all funny," he slurred, thankfully keeping his voice low enough so that only I could hear him. "You got stiff and then you went all jumpy-jumpy, and then you laughed, but it wasn't *your* laugh . . . it was like a 'ha-ha-ha, I'm laughing, but I'm not really laughing' kind of laugh."

*Whoa . . .*

"Are you okay?" he pressed, nuzzling my cheek with his nose. "Are you tired? Do you want to go to bed or something? In my dick tent?"

"Your *what*?"

"My pitched tent," he slurred.

"No, I'm fine."

"Uh-oh," he mumbled. "That's a bad *word* . . . Am I in trouble?"

"No, it's just the smell of alcohol," I admitted, turning my face so that I could look at him. His eyes were glassy and his cheeks were flushed. He looked *happy*. He looked like everything my father *wasn't,* but that smell was still *there*. Still on *him*. "It was on your breath and you just—"

"Reminded you of him?"

I blew out a shaky breath and nodded guiltily. "Sorry."

"I'm not drunk, Shan," Johnny slurred and then scrunched his nose up. "Okay, I might be slightly drunk," he amended, clearly *very* drunk. "But it's only 'cause it's my eighteenth."

739 • CHLOE WALSH

"I know," I hurried to soothe him, feeling terrible. "And I want you to enjoy yourself, Johnny—"

"I know I'm talking a bit funny – I can hear my own voice and that's never a good thing . . . hang on, what was I saying?" He shook his head and focused on my face once more. "Oh yeah – that won't happen to us." He reached up and cupped my cheek. "I will never hurt you, baby," he whispered, brushing his nose against mine. "Never ever, ever – not in a trillion, zillion years."

"I know," I breathed, heart-racing.

"You're my little darling," he slurred. "My whole heart's inside of ya."

My heart hammered in my chest. "Johnny . . ."

"You'll never be her," he continued to ramble. "And I'll never be him."

"You promise?"

He nodded. "I promise a million, billion promises."

Shivering, I slowly relaxed against him. "I love you, Johnny Kavanagh."

"And you know that I love you back, my little, blue river," he slurred. "Now, I know I'm fairly langers, but I could be a thousand percent langers and you'd still be safe with me." Smiling loosely, he added, "And you'd still be the best thing these eyes have ever seen." He pointed at his own eyeballs. "Yep, these ones *love* looking at you. Fuck, now I'm hard again."

"I thought you said you were only slightly drunk?" I questioned, stifling a giggle and oh *yep*, he was definitely hard again. I could feel him growing beneath me.

"Shh." He pressed his finger against my lips. "You're drunk."

"No," I laughed, feeling myself loosen up with his playfulness. "*You're* drunk."

"I'm horny," he declared gruffly. "And that's not sensible." He shook his head. "Nope, that's not a good plan, Shan, because I'm a Johnny with no johnnies."

"Johnny!"

"I know I'm hard," he continued to ramble on. "I can feel my dick trying to break out of my shorts to get to you, but I don't know exactly *where* my dick *is* right now, do *you*?"

"Yeah, I can feel it rubbing against me," I chuckled. "I promise, it's still in your pants."

"Oh, thank god," he sighed a huge gasp of relief. "I keep thinking it's gonna be gone." Squirming, he added, "They put a lot of needles near it, Shan."

"I know, baby," I soothed, trying not to laugh at him. "It's terrible."

"It *was* fucking terrible," he told me, nodding eagerly. "All the blood, and the blue balls, and the . . . " He shrugged and stared down at *my* lap for several beats before groaning loudly. "Ah shite – look, Shan! It's definitely gone."

"Oh, Johnny." I shook my head and kissed him. "You're a big dope."

"Hmm." He pulled my bottom lip into his mouth and sucked. "Sorry," he apologized, releasing my lip with a loud pop. "I just wanted a small taste of you."

*Oh god . . .*

"Lads, lads, lads, shut up, will ya? I have a song for ye!" Gibsie announced as he jerked to his feet, only to fall over the log he had been sitting on and land on his back in a heap. "Feely – strum me a chord, will ya?" he called out as he lay on the flat of his back with a cigarette balancing between his lips. "Good man yourself."

Everyone screamed with laughter as Gibsie cleared his throat and started to sing his own drunken rendition of Richie Kavanagh's "My Girlfriends Pussy Cat" at the top of his lungs. Smirking, he locked eyes on Claire, and I knew right there and then that he was directing every word to her. He was singing these words at her and he wanted her to know he meant the *opposite* of the lyrics.

"I'm a great sailor," Johnny declared, distracting me from Gibsie's hilarious *meow* noises. "Did you know that?"

"No." Smiling, I turned fully in his arms now. "You like to sail?"

"I'd love to sail," he purred, reaching down to squeeze my ass. "Down your river again."

"Oh." Awareness dawned on me and I blushed bright red. "Well, in that case, you're an excellent sailor."

"I know, right?" he said with a proud grin. "Years of practice."

I scrunched my nose up. "Uh, yeah . . . "

"Oops." He slapped a hand over his mouth. "I fucked up."

"Yeah," I agreed. "You kind of did."

"Should I get the dick boat out?" he asked, eyes wide.

"No, Johnny," I laughed, too amused to be put out by his overshare. "Not here."

"Well, I only sail one river now," he amended with a frown. "That's yours—" He paused to point at me. "In case you were wondering."

"Okay," I chuckled. "I got that. Thanks, though."

"No, thank *you*," he purred before heaving out a loud sigh. "I need a piss."

"Uh, okay?"

"I can't," he replied, looking forlorn.

"Why?"

"Because I'm *hard*."

"Oh my god—" Chuckling, I wrapped my arms around his neck and cuddled him. "You make me so happy."

"I'm gonna make you proud when I'm gone," he declared, wrapping his arms around me, and tipping half of his bottle of beer down my hoodie in the process. "And I'm gonna keep my dick in my pants."

"Uh, thanks?"

"Sure, sure," he agreed, still slurring. "Oh shite, babe, did I make you wet?"

"Uh, just a little bit," I confirmed, wincing when the liquid trickled down my back. Slipping my hoodie off, I rolled it into a ball and threw it in the direction of our tent. "That didn't go as far as I planned," I noted, eyeing my hoodie less than five feet from where we were sitting. "Maybe you should have thrown it for me."

"Don't worry about it," Johnny replied encouragingly before downing the last of his bottle and then staring into the rim of the bottle, looking all lonesome and cute when nothing else came out. "Looked like a perfect line out to me."

"It *would* look that way to *you*," I chuckled, thoroughly enjoying this version of him now.

"Where was I?" Johnny asked, looking confused.

"You were talking about keeping your dick in your pants when you're away with the team."

"Ah, that's the one!" He winked and nodded in approval. "And then I'm gonna make all my big plans with you when I come home."

"Oh, you have big plans?"

"Big, big ones," he confirmed. "I like kids, do you?"

"Uh, yeah, sure." I blinked. "I like kids, Johnny."

"Then we'll have some," he announced. "I'll do the rugby thing, and you'll do the vet thing, and then we'll settle down and cook up some babies." He smiled. "Good talk."

"You think I'm going to be a vet?" I asked, completely bypassing the crazy baby talk. "Me? A vet?"

"Of course," he slurred. "You're so smart, baby, with your science and your way with all the animals. My dog loves you. Brian loves you. My dick loves you. Fuck, you'll be the sexiest vet I've ever seen."

"But I only told you that once," I whispered, thinking back to one of the random conversations we had at night when Johnny slipped into my room. "I can't believe you remembered that – and especially in your current state."

"You only ever have to tell me a thing, one time, and it sticks." He tapped his temple. "I keep track of all your words right there."

"You're a brain box," I teased. "Do you know that?"

"I am," he agreed. "It's like *whoa* in my head all the time."

"That's because you're so smart," I reassured him. "You're always thinking."

"Hmm."

"What's the hmm about?"

"I'm not smart with you," he slurred. "It goes away when I'm with you."

"Is that bad?"

"It's so fucking good," he groaned. "I just ... fuck, I need to stop talking."

"No, keep talking," I coaxed, curious. "Tell me what's going on in that head of yours?"

"In my head right now?"

I nodded. "Yeah, right now."

"Your tits, your ass, your legs, and your perfect pussy," he came right out and said. "I just wanna fuck you, and eat you, and lick you, and touch you, and ... Jesus, I don't even know what else there is to do to you, but I know I wanna do that, too."

"Johnny," I breathed, trembling.

"Maybe you should get drunk," he suggested then. "Maybe that way I won't get in too much trouble?"

"Yeah." Trembling, I reached for my bottle. "Maybe I should."

Hungover didn't begin to describe the battering my head was taking when I came to the following morning, withered up on the floor of our tent. My stomach was conducting a civil war against my upchuck reflexes and I didn't dare move a muscle, terrified of who might win. Laying perfectly still, I opened my poor eyes, groaning when the sunshine attacked my ability to see straight.

"I'm dying," I whimpered, praying for some salvation, or at the very least a little divine intervention. "Dear god, save me."

A pained groan came from somewhere close by, and with great effort, I managed to turn my head to the side and find Johnny. He looked as bad as I felt and was squirming in what looked like physical pain. "Make it stop," his deep voice begged. Twisting onto his stomach, he face-planted the floor and then groaned loudly. "Close the curtains or something, Shan, fucking anything—" Burying his face in his pillow, he pleaded. "Just make the sun stop shining."

"I can't," I wailed, feeling terribly sorry for myself. "I'm on the way out here, Johnny."

It must have taken great effort from him, but I felt a heavy arm slump over my stomach, and then his fingers were trailing over my flesh in small circles. "At least we'll go together," he coaxed, face still buried in his pillow. "We've had a good run of it."

"But I'm naked," I croaked out. "I don't want to die naked."

"Won't matter when we're dead," he declared, equally naked beside me.

Hungover as I was, I couldn't resist the urge to sweep my gaze over his naked form, eyes lingering on his bare ass. "Did we, uh . . . " Shivering, I folded my arms across my bare breasts. "Did we do it last night?"

"Do what?"

"Have *sex*?"

"No sex." Giving my hip a little squeeze, he buried his face back into his pillow, and star-fished the floor. "Just sleep."

Unconvinced, I peeked around for the evidence of a foil wrapper, only to panic when I didn't find one.

"But we're naked," I croaked out. I tentatively shifted my hips and felt that familiar ache.

"I know," he mumbled. "Now sleep, Shan. *Please.* I have to drive us back home in a few hours and I'm trying to sweat the Jameson out of me, baby."

"Oh, okay." Squirming from the ache between my legs, I mirrored his actions and carefully rolled onto my stomach, watching him sleep.

My silence lasted all of seven minutes before I reached over and poked the ridiculously large bicep flexed around a pillow. "Hey – are you sure we didn't have sex?"

Groaning under his breath, Johnny attempted a sleepy nod. "Hundred percent."

"I feel like something's been inside of me, Johnny," I squeezed out, shivering as my body drowned in the feeling of being thoroughly satiated. "Maybe not full-on penetration," I amended. Tingling ripples of pleasure and excitement darted through me at the thought. "But there was definitely something *inside* me."

"Yeah," Johnny replied, peering up at me through one squinted blue eye. He held up his hand and twiddled his fingers. "These."

"Oh." Heat crept up my body. "Okay."

"Night, love you," he mumbled, closing his eyes once more.

"But it's morning."

"Shh . . . sleep."

Feeling needy, I braced myself and slowly wiggled over to his body. He was burning up, his skin hot and welcoming. Snuggling in to his side, I stroked my cheek against his shoulder.

"I'm trying to die in peace here, Shannon," he groaned. "And you're giving my dick notions."

"I'm cold." Shivering, I sidled closer to his big body that resembled a furnace 24/7.

"It's like thirty degrees outside," he noted, lifting himself up on his elbows to look at me. "You can't be cold."

"I am," I argued, shivering. "I'm perished."

Rolling onto his side, Johnny gave my body a slow appraisal from head to toe. "Ah, shite," he grumbled, throwing a thigh over mine and dropping his head on my chest. "That's my plan for the day gone out the window."

"What?" I whispered, greedily welcoming his warmth by wrapping my arms around him and holding him close. "What's wrong?"

He clamped a hand on my hip and exhaled a contented sigh. "I can't be getting notions of dying when you're looking like that."

# Goodbye For Now

## JOHNNY

"I'll call you every day," I vowed, as I stood in the middle of Dublin airport with my flight number being called over the intercom. "And I'll send you a million texts."

"But it won't be the same."

"I know, but we'll make it work," I promised.

"How?"

"We'll figure it out, okay? But I need you to stop crying," I begged. "Please."

"I can't help it. My heart is breaking here."

"I'll be home soon," I coaxed. "It won't be forever."

"No – no! Just no. You can't leave me, Johnny!"

"I have to go," I groaned. "Come on, don't make this harder than it has to be."

"You promise this isn't a forever goodbye?"

"I promise," I urged, patting his back. "Now, come on, Gibs. You're cutting off my air supply here."

"Fine." Sniffling, he released the death grip he had on my neck and took a step back, tears streaming down his cheeks.

"I can't believe you're actually crying," I laughed, and then quickly sobered my features when that only made him cry harder. "It's six weeks, lad."

"They're going to snap you up," he sniffled, wiping his eyes. "And I'll lose my best friend."

"You couldn't lose me if you wanted to, ya big eejit," I grumbled, pulling him back in for a hug. "Now, pull yourself together," I ordered, slapping his back. "Sean's watching you."

"Uh, yeah." Clearing his throat, he took a step back and puffed his chest out. "It's all good," he choked out, forcing a smile that looked like he was in physical pain. "I'll be fine," he added, voice breaking on the last note. "Ah, fuck it, this is too hard. I'm going out to the car." Sobbing, he high-fived me and mumbled, "Best of luck, buddy," before striding off through the airport, wailing like a banshee.

"Jesus," I muttered, rubbing my jaw, staring after my best friend. "The rest of you better not pull that shite on me." I turned to stare at my family, and gave my weeping mother a wary look. "I'll be back before the end of summer."

"See ya on the telly," Tadhg said, fist bumping me. "I don't like rugby, but I figure since it's you, I'll watch your games."

"Wow." I smirked. "How generous of you."

He shrugged. "Meh, we'll see how it goes. I might switch it off if I get bored."

"Bye, Johnny," Ollie said then, pushing Tadhg aside to hug my legs. "Don't let the airplane crash and explode with you in it, okay?"

Jesus Christ . . . "Yeah, okay." I patted his back. "I'll be sure to tell the pilot to not kill me."

"Thanks," Ollie replied, mollified, as he skipped away. "'Cause I'm going to miss you."

"I'm going to miss you too, lad."

"I'm proud of you, son," Dad said as he stepped forward and wrapped his arms around me. "More than I can say."

"Thanks, Da."

"I love you, Jonathan—" his voice cracked and he cleared his throat before adding, "very much."

"I love you, too, Da." Slapping him on the back, I took a step back and waited for my next mourner.

"My baby," Mam sobbed, throwing her arms around me. "My little boy."

"I'm 6'3, Ma," I coaxed, squeezing her tightly. "And eighteen. I'm a grown man."

"I don't care. You'll always be my baby," she cried, dragging my face down to smack half a dozen red lipstick kisses to my cheeks. "Now, you mind yourself over there, ya hear? Don't be taking any lifts off strangers. And only drink from bottles, not glasses, when you're out. And don't be letting any of the older lads on the team lead you astray—"

"It's okay, Ma," I soothed, resisting the urge to roll my eyes to the heavens. "I'll be in camp most of the time, so you have nothing to worry about."

"Don't be talking to any strangers, either," she added. "And if they look dodgy and they offer you anything, then you say no. Do you hear me, Jonathan?"

"Come on, Edel," Dad chuckled, physically removing my mother's arms from my neck. "He'll be fine. You raised him well."

"I'll see you real soon, okay?" I said, crouching down to speak to Sean who was tugging on the leg of my tracksuit. "I'll bring you back a big present."

"Onny," he sobbed, lip wobbling. "Me want Onny."

"I'll be back," I coaxed, feeling my heart crack in my chest. "I promise." Tipping his chin up, I wiped a tear off his cheek and smiled. "Are you going to take care of Sookie for me?"

Sniffling, he nodded.

"Good lad," I told him, ruffling his hair. "Now, no more crying because I'm going to phone you up, okay? I'm going to call the house and say 'Dellie, is my Seany there?'"

He smiled. "And me say 'my Onny there?'"

"That's right." Chuckling, I gave him a cuddle and stood back up while I still could and shouldered my carry-on bag. "I'll see you really soon."

"Come on, boys." Mam sniffled, shepherding the Lynchs like they were her own personal flock of baby lambs. "John's going to buy us something in the toyshop."

"Score," Ollie and Tadhg hooted as they barreled after my mother, with Sean and my father trailing behind.

"Yeah, I really need *you* to not do that," I choked out, feeling everything inside of me crack clean open at the sight of her midnight-blue eyes filling up with tears. "Otherwise, I'm walking right out of here and coming home with you."

"I'm s-sorry." With tears streaming down her cheeks, Shannon hiccupped a small sob and walked straight into my arms. "It's j-just—"

"I know," I strangled out, dropping my bag off my shoulder to wrap her up in my arms. Burying my face in her neck, I inhaled the smell of her, desperately trying to keep my shit together. "Me too."

"I love you," she whispered, fingers digging into my neck as she pulled my face down to hers and kissed my lips. "A crazy fucking amount."

"I love you, too—" my voice cracked and I exhaled a strangled breath before adding, "Most in the world." Cupping her face in my hands, I just stared at her, locking away the image of her face in my mind and then coming close to losing it when I thought about how long it would be until I saw her again. "I'm coming home," I told her. "Regardless of what happens." Brushing a tear from her face, I kissed her damp cheek. "I'm coming back to you, Shannon *like the river*." Heaving out another ragged breath, I stroked her nose with mine. "I promise."

"You t-take your time," she sniffled. "You g-go and shine, o-okay?"

I nodded sadly. "Okay."

"I want you to s-succeed," she continued to say, breaking me with her tears, and putting me back together with her words. "I want you to k-kick ass, and be the b-best damn outside center this country has ever seen—" she paused to kiss me. "But don't forget that you'll always be my 13." She sniffled and wiped my cheek with her fingers. "My binding 13."

I choked out a pained laugh, thinking about that stupid bet. "You heard about that?"

"Yeah." Half-sobbing/ half-laughing, Shannon smiled and nodded. "I won."

"Hands down." I kissed her puffy lips. "Undisputed."

"Now, I'm keeping 13," she told me. "So come home to me when you're done, okay?"

"I will."

# Summer Loving

## SHANNON

*Dear Shannon,*

*It's me – Johnny. I'm writing this so I can, once again, surprise and impress you with my mad letter writing skills. Ta-da? See, I told you not to worry about that knock I took on the pitch last weekend. It looked worse on the telly than it felt – and I still remember how to write, buy a stamp, and post a letter, so my brain's still working. I hope this letter finds you well. I'm praying that you're missing me just as much as I'm missing you. It wouldn't be fair otherwise.*

*I'm at the training camp in South Africa with the senior team. I'm rooming with Mick fucking Flanagan, baby – our CAPTAIN . . . which I feel stupid as fuck writing down in a letter, considering we spoke about this on the phone an hour ago.*

*I miss you.*

*Every bit of me misses every bit of you. I miss the feel of you. Sleeping alongside you. Talking to you. Driving around Ballylaggin with you in the passenger seat. Fuck, I'm pretty sure I'm starting to miss your brothers, too. That's how bad this time apart is getting for me. It's not just the sex I miss, either, Shan – though my dick misses you with a ferocity bordering on pain.*

*Are you well? You always tell me you're fine on the phone, but I can hear sadness in your voice. I don't say it because it's the same for me. I'm learning that I don't cope well when you're not around, Shan. I spend my nights stalking that bleeding Bebo account that Claire set up for you, and I tell you this without a single ounce of shame. \*By the way, I made my own account so accept me as your other half please\* . . . oh, and feel free to private mail me some* *nudes. I could do with some new material. My memory never seems to do you justice.*

*There's a beach here, about four miles from the team hotel, and every time I walk on the sand, I think of you. Of that day we spent at the beach back home.*

*You're in my mind all the time, Shannon. My heart, too. You did something to me all those months ago. I think you broke me, because I've not been right since. When we're apart like this, I feel unsteady, like I'm balancing a weight on my shoulders and my reward for not dropping it is seeing your face again.*

*So, yeah, there it is . . .*

*I'm going to tell you something in this letter, something I couldn't say on the phone or in a text because I don't think I could handle your immediate response . . .*

*I'm scared, Shannon. I feel like a fish out of water on this tour. The lads on the team? They're all so much older than me – with years more experience. They're real, grown-up men, baby, and I feel like I'm a walking transplant, some young fucker running on luck and borrowed time.*

*I've never felt that way before. I don't know what the hell I'm doing, to be honest. Most of the time, I'm two minutes away from throwing in the towel and catching the next flight home to you. I'm still here, though, because I made you a promise that I would shine . . . or sparkle, or whatever the hell it was that you asked me to do. There's talk of me actually starting this Saturday instead of coming off the bench, so maybe I'll get the job done then.*

*It's intense here, Shannon. It's like nothing I've ever experienced before. The U20's tour was a walk in the park in comparison to senior level. I started every single game – no pressure. But this? Jesus, my best is only middling in this quality of a team and that is enough to make me want to quit. I've never felt like quitting before – it's never crossed my mind. I'm working on trying to find my feet. Fighting for a jersey that's always been mine is unsettling.*

*Knowing that there's half a dozen world class players ready to swoop in and take that from me if I put one foot out of place is a pressure I'm struggling to manage. I'm on edge all the time, Shannon . . . Maybe I'm just homesick, or maybe I'm overthinking things, or maybe I just left my head back in Cork with you?*

*On the plus side, I've gained a stone in muscle. I'm over 6'4 now, too. But enough of my bullshit; how's your summer going? Is Gibsie okay? Has Joey been in touch yet? Is Sean saying any new words? What about Aoife? Any sign of her? How's my Sook? Those boys better not be drawing on her. Do you have a tan? Are you smiling? Christ, I miss you . . .*

*I know you tell me everything is fine when we talk on the phone, but if you're like me, and find it too hard to talk over a phone, then maybe you could write me back with another letter of your own?*

*You know what? I don't think my English essay in the junior cert was as long as this letter. What does that say about me? Note: I hope you're not worrying about those bleeding junior cert results. I know you kicked ass. Fuck, I love you. Did I write that down yet? Fuck it, if I haven't then here it is again. I love you Shannon Lynch. All of you. Every part.*

*Anyways, I'm running out of room to write on both sides of this paper so I'll take it as my cue to finish up. Oh, and could you ask my ma to stop calling so much? I know she's missing me, but it's getting out of hand.*

*Yours always,*

*Johnny. x*

*(PS: My dick is still in my pants, and my love is still a crazy fucking amount.)*

Carefully folding Johnny's letter back into its envelope, I tucked it under my pillow to join the others before reaching for the box sitting on my bed with my name on it.

Holding the box in my hands, I stared down at his neat handwriting and sighed longingly. Our communication these past six weeks had consisted of a steady flow of texting and late-night phone calls, letters, and packages, but it wasn't enough. Not by half. I could feel his anxiety dripping off the page and it hurt my heart. All I wanted to do was board a plane and *go* to him, but he would be home soon. A few days later than originally anticipated, but still, *home* was in sight.

"What did you get this time?" Ollie demanded, diving onto my bed, and almost giving me a heart attack in the process. "Aw, man, he sends you presents every day."

"Not every day, Ollie," I mumbled, blushing.

"You've had two packages a week since he left," Ollie groaned. "It's been six weeks. That makes *twelve* packages. I've had *one*."

"Because he's *my* boyfriend," I defended, even though I was grinning in delight. "Now back up so I can open it."

"It's because she lets him touch her boobs," Tadhg snickered from the doorway, where Bonnie, Sookie, and Cupcake were all nuzzling against his legs. "That's why she gets all those presents, Ol."

"Tadhg!" I choked out. "Don't say that."

"It's true," Tadhg laughed, scratching Cupcake's ear. "Deny it."

"First, you let him tongue kiss you, and now you're showing him your boobies?" Ollie groaned, clutching his stomach. "I feel a little sick in my guts."

"We don't do any of that," I lied through my teeth. "We only hold hands."

"Uh-huh," Tadhg snickered. "You keep telling yourself that, Shan."

"That's why he sent those tickets for the music festival he's taking her to when he comes home?" Ollie demanded. "So he can see her boobies?"

"Probably," Tadhg laughed.

Ignoring my brothers, I ripped open the box and grinned when I saw the green jersey with the number 13 etched on the back. Pulling it out, I held it to my chest, breathing in the smell of *him*. Shivering, I thought back to the conversation we'd had on the phone last week . . .

"You didn't!"

"Yeah, Shan, I did."

"You lie."

"Sometimes, but never to you."

"Impossible." I shook my head, not trusting this crazy talk. "Those concert tickets have been sold out for months."

"You underestimate my powers of persuasion, baby," he purred down the line. "I figured we could share a tent again."

"Oh my god, you're really serious, aren't you?" My eyes widened in excitement. "I can't believe this," I practically screamed as I did a little happy dance. "You actually got us Oxegen tickets!"

"Hundred percent, Shan," he replied. "It's all I'm thinking about. No parents. No annoying fucking brothers. No training. No drama. Just you and me, a tent, and some decent music for an entire weekend."

"Who's headlining this year?"

"Green Day and The Foo Fighters," he replied.

"God!"

"I know."

"But, Johnny, I'll never get in. It's over 18's."

"Again, you seem to be underestimating my powers of persuasion," he chuckled. "I'll get you in, Shan. Don't even worry your pretty head about it."

I rolled my eyes and then screamed in excitement. "We're really going?"

"Really, really."

"Just us?

"Just us," he confirmed before quickly backpedaling. "Well, no, not just us. Gibs is tagging along – and he'll probably bring Claire."

I grinned. "That's kind of a given, though."

"Guess who else is playing?" he said then.

"Who?

"Jimmy Eat World."

My mouth fell open. "No." My song. My life anthem. I had the chance to hear it live? "Oh my god . . . "

"That jersey is worth money," Ollie noted, dragging me from my thoughts. "Lots of it."

"Don't even think about it," I warned, hurrying to slip it on over my head before my scheming brother decided to try and swindle me out of my boyfriend's winning jersey.

On closer inspection of the jersey I was currently floating in, Ollie pulled a face. "Nah, it's only the U20's one," he told me, looking marginally disappointed. "Get today's one, Shan. That's the senior jersey – that's the money jersey."

"You're obsessed with money," I scolded. "It's getting out of hand."

"Nuh-uh," he shot back. "John says I'm a shark."

"And that's a good thing how?"

"He says it's going to be a good thing when I'm in court." Beaming, he added, "I'm going to be a barracker just like him."

"A barrister," Tadhg and I both corrected. "Not a barracker."

"That's what I said," Ollie huffed. "I'm going to be a barracker."

"Glad to see all those speech therapy sessions John's forking out for are paying off, Ollie," Tadhg shot back sarcastically. "You and Sean are something else."

"We are," Ollie agreed. "We're the best boys."

"You're a pain in my ass," Tadhg muttered, "that's what you are."

"You're just jealous," Ollie huffed. "Because you don't get to go."

"Oh yeah, I'm so jealous that I know how to pronounce my words and speak clearly," Tadhg drawled.

"Don't worry," Ollie soothed. "You still get to go to play therapy with us."

"I don't play at those sessions," Tadhg grumbled. "I paint."

"You should play," Ollie countered. "It's so much fun."

"I'm going on thirteen," Tadhg huffed. "I don't play anymore."

"That's a shame," Ollie told him. "You don't know what you're missing."

"Oh, shut up, you little twerp," Tadhg grumbled.

"They told you at counseling that you're not supposed to use your angry words," Ollie reminded him. "When you get cross, you're supposed to count to ten and breathe." He turned to me and smiled. "Deep breaths, isn't that right, Shan?"

"Yes," I agreed, holding back a laugh at Tadhg's outraged expression. "Deep breaths, Tadhg."

"Oh, go away and talk about your *feelings* to someone who cares," he shot back. "That breathing technique doesn't work when I'm mad."

"It is working," I promised, giving him an encouraging smile. He had turned inside out since moving in here. "Give yourself time."

"What time are your friends picking you up to go watch Johnny play?" Ollie asked then.

I glanced at my phone and smiled. "Now."

"*Now*," Tadhg mimicked, batting his eyes. "God, you're such a girl."

"I know," I countered with a laugh. "And *you're* a brat." Tilting my head to one-side, I smirked. "I hope you treat the girls in your year nicer than you treat me when you start at Tommen next month."

Tadhg snorted. "I'm not changing for anyone – and I'm not wearing a fucking blazer."

"Tadhg," I warned. "Don't curse."

"Well, I'm not," he snickered. "I don't care how cute Dellie says I look in one. I'm from the terrace, Shan, and I'm a hurler. I can't be walking around like all those posh, rugby fu—"

"Don't curse!" Ollie chimed in. "It's bad manners."

"You know what? The blazer will suit you when you start in a couple of years, you little kiss ass," Tadhg taunted. "*It's bad manners*." He rolled his eyes. "I don't know where we got you, Oliver Twist."

"Fine by me," Ollie replied, unaffected. "I'm going to be wearing a lot of blazers when I'm a barracker anyway."

"A *barrister*."

"Just like John," Ollie confirmed proudly.

"Well, I'm going to be a mechanic," Tadhg shot back. "Just like *Joey*."

"But Joey's not a mechanic," Ollie replied, frowning. "Joey's sick."

"Yeah," Tadhg huffed. "But once he's all better and comes home, he'll be a mechanic again."

"Is he coming home soon?" Ollie asked.

"No," Tadhg growled. "Because he's not better yet."

"Oh." Ollie's brows furrowed. "What's wrong with him again?"

My heart squeezed tight in my chest. I hadn't seen or spoken to Joey since the funeral back in May. He'd been in treatment for close to two months and was still refusing to let me visit him. "He's just resting," I forced myself to say. "He's really tired."

"Really?" Ollie scrunched his nose up. "I thought it was because he was messing with the helium."

"The *helium*?"

"Yeah." Ollie nodded innocently. "Freddie on my football team said that his mammy told Donal's mammy that Joey's in the hospital because he was messing around with the helium and the needles." He scrunched his nose up. "Why was Joey messing with needles and balloons? Wouldn't they pop?"

Tadhg glared. "It's not helium, you fool, it's heroi—"

"No, no, it *is* helium," I quickly interjected, giving Tadhg a pleading look. "Remember?"

"Oh, yeah," Tadhg agreed, cringing. "That's right."

"And he's really tired," I added, sagging in relief. "So, he's having a big rest."

"Yes." Tadhg forced a smile. "From minding us."

"Yeah, but he doesn't have to do that anymore," Ollie replied innocently. "Dellie does it now." He smiled brightly. "And John."

"You know what I miss?" Tadhg said, thankfully changing the subject. "Aoife's freebies from work."

"Oh, yeah," Ollie agreed. "She used to bring home all the best stuff to us." Scratching the back of his head, he looked around and asked, "Where'd *she* go?"

"Well, she's Joey's," Tadhg explained gruffly. "So, when he's not around, she won't be, either."

"Oh, okay," Ollie replied, happy to accept that explanation. "He should keep her, though. She's so pretty."

"Yeah." Tadhg nodded in agreement. "She's something else."

"Tadhg Lynch," I teased. "Are you crushing on *Aoife*?"

His cheeks turned bright pink. "No."

"Aww," I swooned. "You're so cute."

"Oh, fuck off," he shot back huffily.

"And you're even cuter now that your voice is breaking," I snickered. "My little Tadhg is growing up." Waggling my brows, I asked, "Should we have *the talk*?"

"About Johnny sneaking in and out of your room every night of the week when he was here? *Naked*," he shot back, not missing a beat. "That talk? Sure. Do you want to have it here, or down in the kitchen with his *mother*?"

I swiftly snapped my mouth shut.

"Yeah, that's what I thought," he answered himself, giving me a knowing smirk.

"Darren's driving down for the weekend to help Dellie while John's gone to the match," Ollie said then. "I hope he brings Alex."

"I hope Alex *doesn't* bring Darren," Tadhg countered with a devilish grin.

"Be nice," I chuckled. "He's probably going to have his car full of presents for you guys."

"And rightly so," Tadhg agreed. "He owes us five years' worth of them."

"True," Ollie agreed solemnly.

"You two are terrible," I laughed.

"Do you think he's nervous for today?" Tadhg asked then. "Johnny?"

"No," Ollie answered for me. "He's Johnny. He's not scared of anything – and he's got his dad with him." He smiled. "John."

"God, get over this fascination with John, will ya?" Tadhg muttered. "You're like a stalker."

"Like you and Dellie?" Ollie countered. "You *love* her."

"Yeah, I do," Tadhg shot back, unblinking. "A lot."

"Yeah, me too," Ollie sighed happily. "She's the best."

"That food," Tadhg added wistfully. "So much food."

"Shannon's getting fat," Ollie tossed out. "She loves Dellie's food, too."

"I'm a size 8, you thug," I choked out, offended. "I weigh 7 and a half stone. I'm not fat."

"You don't call girls fat, Ol," Tadhg groaned. "Remember what Joey told us? They're always skinny – even when they're whales."

"Oh, yeah," Ollie replied sheepishly. "But she's up that whole stone, remember? Dellie was crying 'cause she was so happy about it? Remember? The doctors said she was bones and skin and had to get the stones up or she'd get sicker."

"Skin and bones," Tadhg corrected with a pained sigh. "And don't worry about it, Shan. You're still a rake."

"I was never a rake," I huffed, feeling self-conscious. "Stop talking about it."

"We're all getting fat," Ollie offered with a smile. "It's not just you, Shan." He smiled and patted his thin stomach that was slowly filling out. "See?"

"Speak for yourself," Tadhg shot back, looking slightly stockier than his usual wafer-thin frame. "I'm getting muscle."

A car horn beeped three times then, signaling my spin to Biddies, and I leapt off the bed. "Oh, guys, I'm sorry, but I have to go," I told my brothers as I bolted out of my room and ran for the stairs, my smile spreading with every step I took.

"Enjoy, Shannon, love," Mrs. Kavanagh laughed when I tore through her kitchen like a bat out of hell, narrowly avoiding Sean, who was dressed as a chef and playing with his toy kitchen.

"Thanks, Edel. Bye, Sean," I called back before running outside and throwing open the back door of Gibsie's silver Ford Focus.

"Where's the fire?" Gibsie snickered and then grunted loudly when Claire slapped him in the stomach from the passenger seat.

"Filter, Gerard," she hissed. "Come on!"

"Oh, shit," he muttered. "I didn't even think—"

"It's okay, it's okay," I replied, hurrying to close my door and fasten my seatbelt. "Can we go now? It's his first starting cap for the senior team and I don't want to miss him."

When I walked into Biddies bar, I was greeted by a sea of familiar faces and Irish jerseys. The huge television screen mounted to the wall already had the match on. Green and white jerseys filled the screen. It was all I could see. *Fiji versus Ireland.* God, this was serious. This was *big*. I knew Mr. Kavanagh was standing in the crowds somewhere in that stadium halfway around the world, cheering on his son, waiting to bring him home to us, and the thought made me smile.

As I looked around at the people in the room, an extension of Johnny's family, I could see how much he was loved. These people were cheering him on. Trailing after Gibsie and Claire, I followed them to their usual table where I was greeted by Feely, Hughie, Katie, Lizzie, and the rest of his teammates from Tommen – minus Cormac and Ronan.

Anxiety was gnawing at my gut as I waved a shy hello to his friends and settled down on a chair at the table, knees bopping restlessly. Digging into the pocket of my denim shorts, I retrieved the fifty euro note Mrs. Kavanagh had given me and placed my order for a bottle of Coke with Gibsie, who was going to the bar.

Swamped in Johnny's unwashed jersey, I dutifully ignored the stares and hushed whispers being directed at me – partially because I was '*the daughter of that man who killed himself and his wife*', but mostly because I was '*young Kavanagh's doll*' – and focused on the television screen.

When the two teams jogged out from the tunnel and onto the pitch, the crowd in the bar went crazy.

It was surreal.

He was *there*.

On the television screen.

Number 13.

My heart beat so hard I had to press my hand to my chest to steady myself. Claire reached over and squeezed my hand in support.

"Just breathe," she encouraged, smiling knowingly at me, and I was grateful for the physical contact. I needed something to hold on to in this moment.

"Get in there, Cap, you fucking legend!" Gibsie cheered as he slapped three bottles of Coke down on the table for Lizzie, Claire, and myself, before knocking back half of his pint, eyes glued to the television. Clearly bursting with pride, he shook his head, smiling to himself.

And then "Ireland's Call" began to play, belting out from the surround sound, and a shiver ran down my spine.

*Oh Jesus . . .*

This was it.

*This was it!*

The camera zoomed in on the players, one by one, and when it landed on Johnny, the sheer volume of noise in the bar went clean off the Richter scale. Old men were banging their fists against the bar in triumph, cheering on their hometown hero. The man Johnny referred to as 'Fat Paddy' was literally dancing on top of a table with the owner of the bar. Feely was holding his head in his hands and staring at the screen in pure awe. Hughie was bawling his eyes out as he clapped for his friend. The rest of his teammates were going berserk. It was *insane . . .*

*"I'm going to be there one day," Johnny stated, tilting his head in the direction of the telly. "One of these days that's going to be me, Shannon."*

*"I know," I replied, believing every word. Biting down on my lip, I turned to face him and said, "Don't forget about me when you're a rich and famous rugby player."*

Shaking my head to clear my memories, I focused on the match as it unfolded on the television screen, never once taking my eyes off 13 green all through the first half and into the second.

Three minutes before the final whistle and Ireland was down by 3 points. On the edge of my seat, I chewed on my fingernails, jerking and flinching every time a tackle was made. Ireland was rewarded a turnover on the Fijian five-meter line, and the crowds in the stands went crazy, belting out the chorus of "The Fields of Athenry".

My heart sparked to life in my chest, adrenalin pumping through my veins, when my gaze honed in on Johnny lurking close to the scrum.

Making a break through the Fijian defense and their five-meter line, Johnny side-stepped their number 8, then ploughed forward, taking a spear from his rival jersey number just a second too late. Crashing over the line with his arm fully extended, ball in hand, he found touch on their try line. It was the final game of the tour and we had *won*. We won and he was coming *home* . . .

The bar erupted into a manic state of madness.

Gibsie threw himself across the table, knocking glasses everywhere, to hug the lads.

Meanwhile, I sprang from my seat, clapping so hard I thought my hands might break. With my eyes glued to the screen, I watched as the cameras zoomed in on Johnny's grinning face, as the men I knew he idolized surrounded him in celebration.

A single tear rolled down my cheek as I watched the boy who had saved my life on countless occasions finally reap the rewards he so justly deserved.

*Boy did good . . .*

"I need to pee," Claire announced, jumping to her feet. "Shan, will you come with me?"

I really didn't want to pee, I wanted to stay exactly where I was, watching Johnny's larger than life smile, but I reluctantly complied, allowing my best friend to drag me through the bar and into the ladies' bathroom. "Claire, my arm," I strangled out, tugging my hand free before she yanked it clean out of its socket. "What's the rush?"

"Okay, don't panic, but Bella's in the bar," Claire blurted out, sounding a little out of breath. Yanking the bathroom door open, she looked out and then closed it again before turning back to face me. "I wanted to tell you before you saw her and panicked. She and Cormac and a group of their friends walked in just before Johnny scored his last try. They're over by the bar." Blowing out a shaky breath, she rolled up the sleeves of her long-sleeved Irish jersey and narrowed her eyes. "It's okay, though, because I'm totally down for kicking her ass. I delivered babies with Gerard this summer. Nothing scares me anymore." She looked me up and down then and smirked. "You look so sexy in his jersey and those tiny shorts. It's going to drive Bella bonkers." She grinned devilishly. "By the way, you should totally wear this exact outfit when Johnny comes home on from the tour next week. He'll pass out when he sees how big your boobs have grown." Frowning, she added, "The pill is working wonders for your body, Shan."

"Oh my god, Claire, stop and focus, will you?" I strangled out, tucking my hair behind my ears as I tried not to panic. I hadn't seen Bella in months – not since that day at school. Anxiety churned inside of me and I clasped my friend's hand. "What do I do about Bella?"

"Nothing. I just told you that I'm going to kick her ass," Claire replied simply. "I've got this, Shan."

"I'm going to kick her ass," Lizzie's voice filled my ears as she stalked into the bathroom, looking furious. "That bitch has some nerve showing up here."

"Don't kick anyone's ass," I told my two best friends. "I'm serious, guys. I'm just going to leave."

"No, you're not," Claire shot back. "You belong here. That's your man on the telly."

"Yeah, but there's no point in arguing with her," I replied. "I don't want any more fights, guys. I'm tired of the drama. I just want a quiet life."

"Then you might want to remind Thor of that," Lizzie stated. "Because I think he missed the memo on fighting."

"Oh god," I groaned.

"*My* Thor?" Claire demanded.

"I guess he's taking that promise he made to Johnny about watching out for Shan seriously." Lizzie shrugged. "He's out there goading the life out of the pair of them."

"Well, she better not provoke him." Throwing the bathroom door open, Claire stalked back to the bar just as Gibsie was getting up in Cormac's personal space. He had a shit-eating grin on his face as he pointed to the television screen and laughed into his teammate's face, clearly taunting him with Johnny's success.

"And that is how it's done," I heard Gibsie laugh. "Come on, Ryan. Be a good sport and clap for your captain."

"Boys," Lizzie grumbled as we hurried after Claire. "Everything's a pissing competition with them."

"Yep," I croaked out, feeling anxious.

"Get out of my face, Gibs," Cormac warned.

Gibsie grinned like a maniac. "Make me."

"Gerard, don't be picking fights," Claire said when she reached his side. "You're on a warning, remember?" Fisting the back of his jersey in her hand, she tugged him back from Cormac. "You heard what our mothers said. If you get in anymore trouble this summer, you're not allowed to go to the festival next weekend." Releasing his jersey, she placed her hands on her hips and glared up at him. "And you're taking me."

"Of course, I'm taking you, Claire-bear," he purred, giving her a devilish grin. "I'll take you right now, if you want?"

"I'm serious, buddy." Grabbing his big hand in hers, Claire spun on her heels and stalked towards the door, dragging Gibsie after her. "I'm not going to be a single mother just because you can't stop chasing trouble and getting yourself thrown in the barracks. We have babies to raise, Gerard Gibson, and a concert to go to, so you're going to do what you're told. Now follow me!"

"Oh fuck, I love it when you boss me around, babe," he groaned, hurrying after her like a puppy. "Talk dirty some more to me."

"Get out the door, Gerard," she ordered, holding the door wide open. "Now."

"Yes, boss."

"Those two have the weirdest friendship I've ever witnessed," Feely, who had come to stand beside us, stated when Claire and Gerard left the bar. "Like ever," he added with a small shake of his head. "It's beyond strange."

I wanted to respond to him, but my attention was riveted to the girl glaring at me. Surprisingly, I held my ground and eye contact, staring back at Bella Wilkinson with my head held high.

"Let's go for a game of pool in the lounge," Cormac said to the boy standing next to him. "I'm done with this shit." Turning to Bella, he asked, "Are you coming?"

"No," she replied, not taking her eyes off me.

"Bella, just leave it alone—"

"What are you looking at, foster baby?" she sneered, glaring at me.

"You better take that back, bitch," Lizzie snarled, moving towards her.

"It's okay, Liz." Holding a hand up, I stopped my friend from pouncing, never once breaking eye contact with Bella. "Her words don't hurt me."

"You need to pack it in and leave her alone," Cormac warned, glaring at his girlfriend. "I told you, Bel, I'm not going through this with you again. If you're with me, you need to let this shit with her and Johnny go."

"I bet you're happy with yourself," she hissed, inclining her chin towards the television screen, ignoring her boyfriend.

"I'm happy for *him*," I corrected, not backing down.

"You must give one hell of a blow job to get yourself and your band of bastard brothers shacked up in the Kavanagh house," Bella continued. "Are you sucking his daddy off, too, foster baby?"

"Oh my god, you're fucking obsessed with him!" Cormac hissed. Shaking his head, he grabbed his jacket off the bar and stood up. "I'm right here, and you just . . . you don't even see me! All you're thinking about is him. I don't know what else I can do—"

"Of course, I see you," she snapped, tearing her gaze off me to look at her boyfriend. "I'm with you, aren't I?"

"Only because he's with *her*," Cormac shot back, eyes laced with pain. "They were all right about you, weren't they? You don't love me."

"Now you're just being a pussy," she tossed back. "Man up."

"I love you," he told her, red-faced. "I honestly do, but I can't keep doing this."

"Doing what?"

"Being second best," he growled. "I'm done with this shit, Bella. I'm done with being used. And I'm done with *you*!"

"You're not done with anything," she shot back laughing. "You'll come crawling back."

"I'm not cruel, Bella, and what you're doing to her is *cruel*," he told her, shaking. "What you're doing to me is worse." Swallowing deeply, he added, "I'm not coming back this time . . . This time, we're done."

"Then go," she dared him.

"Oh, don't worry." Shoving past Feely, Cormac stalked out of the bar. "I'm already gone."

The lack of feeling she had for her boyfriend was clear because when Cormac walked out of the bar, Bella didn't even flinch. She just continued to spew venom at me, throwing cruel comments and words like bullets intended to hurt me, but she couldn't do that anymore. Because I was *over* her. I was honest to god over Bella Wilkinson and every other mean girl that had targeted me from the age of three to now. What I'd endured this past year; burying my parents, losing my home, almost losing my brother to drugs, almost losing my *life*, it had changed me. I was different now, stronger, and she couldn't hurt me because I refused to hand that kind of power over to her or anyone else.

All the fear? I pushed it off my shoulders like a blanket, letting it fall away from my body, as I channeled the strength I *knew* was inside of me. There would always be another Bella, but just like my counselor told me, there wouldn't be another *me*, and that was my strength, my special power. I would never be a rocket scientist or a world-class rugby player, but I *was* a survivor, and a damn good one at that. So with my head held high, I looked her straight in the eyes and gave her something she would never ask for and probably never deserve. "I forgive you for what you did to me that day." She could keep her anger and cling to her grudge, but that didn't mean I had to. "And I hope you find some peace." With that, I turned around and walked back to my friends.

"Whoa," Lizzie mused, sinking down on the booth opposite my chair. "I don't know if you should be slapped for not giving that bitch what she deserved, or sainted for taking the high road."

"Sainted," Feely offered, sliding into the booth alongside her. "Definitely sainted."

"Guys," I mumbled, blushing. "It's no big deal."

"You are the definition of kill them with kindness and bury them with a smile," Feely told me.

"Screw the high road," Lizzie tossed out. "I would have kicked her ass."

"What did you do, Shan?" Hughie asked, tearing his lips away from Katie's to look at us. "Were you brawling?"

"Definitely not," I choked out, still trembling. "I'm not a fighter."

"Oh, I think you are," Feely replied. "Muhammad Ali right here, folks."

"She floats like a butterfly and stings like a bee," Katie chuckled. "A teeny-tiny bee."

"She KO'd Kav, didn't she?" Hughie laughed.

"Oh, he's on again – look!" I squealed, watching as Johnny filled the screen to receive a medal. "They're giving him Man of the Match."

"Shh, shh!"

"Shut up, ye shower of whores, he's talking!"

The volume was blasted to the maximum and the crowd in the bar went deathly quiet just as the reporter started speaking. "Jonathan, a massive congratulations is in order for a fantastic performance tonight. Your first start for the senior side and you scored two tries – and at only eighteen years old. Tonight must be a dream come true for you. Do you have any words?"

"I'm very honored to have the opportunity to represent my country," Johnny replied, still slightly breathless. "I'm well aware of how lucky I am to be in this position and for that I'd like to thank my parents for their commitment and support. My trainers and coaches at The Academy, my school for giving me the foundations that got me to this stage, and providing the concessions I've needed from time to time, and the lads I train with every day of the week, especially my three closest friends and teammates from club level; Gibs, Feely, Hughie. I wouldn't be here without their support, so tonight's performance was for them."

"Well, to top off a wonderful series win, you're also tonight's man of the match." The presenter placed a medal over Johnny's neck and shook his hand. "Congratulations, Jonathan."

"I actually wanted to mention one more person if that's okay?" he told her, still shaking her hand.

"Of course."

"I'd like to thank my girlfriend for her unconditional love and support. It's been a rollercoaster of a ride getting back from injury, and I can honestly say that I wouldn't be here today without her fierce encouragement." Clutching his medal in his hand, he looked into the camera and gave it a little shake before saying, "Shannon, I love you, and I'll be home soon."

"Aww!" Katie squealed, jumping clean out of her seat. "Shan, you're famous!"

"Fuck that, *I'm* famous!" Hughie cheered. "He said my name." Turning to Feely, he grinned. "Fucking Cap, huh? What a legend."

"I know," Feely laughed. "Gibs is going to lose his shit when he watches it back."

"Yeah, that boy is smooth," Lizzie begrudgingly sighed. "I'm made of ice, but I'm slightly melting here."

"Yeah." Nodding rapidly, I just stared at the screen, feeling my heart pound at a hundred miles an hour.

*Shannon, I love you, and I'll be home soon . . .*

*Shannon, I love you . . .*

*I'll be home soon . . .*

I didn't realize I was clutching my chest until Lizzie grabbed my hand. "Breathe, Shannon," she chuckled. "He's coming home."

"He's coming home, Liz." Biting down on my lip, I grinned at her. "He's really coming *home*!"

# The Boys in Green

## JOHNNY

Rugby united our country from the north to south, from east to west. For eighty minutes, there were no borders or politics to worry about. We were one nation standing behind twenty-three men going into battle. We were *one*, and that was a fucking achievement in itself.

"Ireland's Call" chorused around the stadium, setting alight a barrage of goose bumps across my skin. Heads held high, emotions over-spilling, nerves frayed, but united we stood. Ulster man with Connacht man, Leinster man with Munster man, exiles and hybrids, coaches and trainers, the back room and our families, roared on by the people, as we made our own little mark on Irish history, as we stood together, paving a path and opportunity for a better future. Respect at an all-time high, we stood together, we worked *together* for each other, and for the pride of our people – for *all* the people.

The Irish fans were the best supporters in the world. The whole fucking world recognized that feat. It didn't matter the sport or the occasion. They came in drones, regardless of the weather, and regardless of the score at the end of the eighty minutes, they returned the next week. This was what it was all about. These people made the feeling of pride burst clean out of my chest. We played for them, for our country, for each other.

Today was the proudest moment of my career. Wearing this beloved green jersey and number 13. I gave everything I had to my teammates, I left it all on the pitch, and at the end of the eighty minutes of the last game of the tour, we were victorious against Fiji.

Exhausted beyond comprehension, I forced my body to comply with my heart – a heart that was demanding I stay the fuck standing and *not* collapse in a heap on the floor – as I stepped off the bus and into the team hotel with my Man of the Match medal dangling from my neck.

Both led and flanked by my fellow teammates, I left the sanctuary of our bus and walked into the absolute mayhem that was the aftermath of an international match night. Being the youngest and least experienced person on the team, I followed my teammates lead by keeping my head up and staring straight ahead, trying to look unaffected by the madness when, in reality, I was shaking inside.

Flocks of fans were screaming in my face, pulling and tugging at my clothes, touching me like my body was public fucking property as we were ushered through the doors of the hotel and faced with even more screaming, diehard fans in the foyer. Phones and cameras were shoved into my face along with jerseys and pieces of crumpled paper. Reporters were shouting my name and then distracted by my captain as he accepted their questions. I ignored the media, turning my attention to the fans instead. Smiling for pictures, I signed every jersey, match booklet, poster, and piece of paper that was thrown at me, forcing myself not to grimace when countless pairs of lips smacked against my cheeks.

*"Johnny, you were amazing!"*

*"I'm staying in room 309 tonight."*

*"Kavanagh, can we have a picture?"*

*"I'll be in the bar later."*

*"Congratulations on your first starting cap, kid."*

*"God, he's so fucking sexy!"*

*"How does it feel to be compared to Ireland's greatest center?"*

*"Oh my god, he looked at me!"*

*"How are the ribs after that late tackle?"*

*"My kid loves you – can you take a picture with him?"*

*"The full eighty minutes, two tries, and man of the match, how are you feeling?"*

*"Look at the size of him in real life!"*

*"Your mother must be proud of you, laddie."*

*"This is my room key, big boy . . . "*

*"Are you proud of yourself?"*

*"I love you, Johnny Kavanagh!"*

Feeling swarmed and out of my element, I kept my eyes trained on the marker in my hand, doing my best to remain professional, as I scribbled my name across a rugby ball for a young boy.

"You liked the game?" I asked him, ignoring the group of women trying to pull at me. "Yeah?"

"You're my favorite," he replied, smiling up at me. "I want to be like you when I grow up."

*Fuck.*

"Thanks for coming," I said, standing in for a quick picture with him and his mother before slipping away, unable to keep up the charade another minute. Stars danced before my eyes, making it hard to see straight, as I battled through the hordes to get to my destination.

To get to my *father.*

I could see him up ahead of me, leaning against a table with a newspaper in hand, dutifully ignoring the madness around him. My heart was thundering against my ribcage; a mixture of adrenalin, desperation, and fear as I pushed through the crowds, ignoring everything and everyone in my path to get to him. Breathing through the panic, I closed the gap between us, letting my bag fall off my shoulder when I reached him. "Da," I choked out, shaking like a fucking child.

I watched his shoulders stiffen at the sound of my voice. I heard the small sigh that escaped his mouth. Turning slowly, he looked up at my face with a look of sheer pride on his face. "Hello, Jonathan."

"Da," I repeated, bowing my head, my voice a pained groan.

"I'm here, son." Three words. Three fucking words that brought me to my knees. "I'm right here," he whispered, wrapping his arms around me.

"Da—" I dropped my head on his shoulder, clinging to him like a child. "Get me out of here."

Two hours later, we were sitting in the back corner of a half-empty restaurant, and my heartbeat had returned to its normal rhythm. Grateful to have my father here with me after spending so much time away from everyone I knew, I listened intently as he gave me a summary of everything that had happened back home since I'd been away.

"Sean's really saying all those words now?" I asked between mouthfuls of steak. "Full sentences?"

"Most of the time, he's still waffling," Dad chuckled. "But he's trying. He's coming along in leaps and bounds."

"Well, shite." Stabbing a piece of potato, I shoveled it into my mouth and chewed thoughtfully before asking, "And she's really going to that counselor?"

"She's really going," Dad confirmed. "It's helping, Johnny. She's healing." I felt my shoulders sag in relief. Shannon had told me she was attending the sessions, but I didn't know for sure if she was telling me the truth. "She's starting to thrive, son. They all are."

"I miss her." Staring at the food on my plate, I continued to hoof it down, trying to distract myself from the god-awful pain in my chest. "I miss *home*."

"And we miss you," he replied. "But we're also extremely proud of you."

"Is she going out?" I croaked out, forcing the question out of my mouth. "Shannon? She's not too sad?"

"She's lonesome for you," Dad replied honestly. "I imagine desperately so, but she's putting on a brave face and getting on with things. She spends a lot of time with her friends. I suppose she's getting into the swing of being a teenage girl." Smiling, he added, "And your mother has her primped to within an inch of her life." He chuckled. "I've never seen so much pink and glitter in my life, son. It's everywhere. Makeup. Jewelry. Hair straighteners. Shoes. Dresses. I swear, every time I walk through the front door, there's another half dozen shopping bags clogging up the hallway."

"Oh, Jesus," I groaned. "She's treating Shannon like a doll, isn't she?"

"That's one way to put it," Dad laughed.

Grimacing, I took a sip from my glass of water before asking, "And how is Ma?"

"Her usual self," Dad mused, giving me a knowing look.

"She's in her element, isn't she?"

"Oh, she's loving having so many kids around to fuss over," he agreed, smiling fondly at the thought. "She misses her baby, though. All the children in the world couldn't fill the hole you made in her heart. Or mine."

"I bet." I chuckled, though it was a hollow sound. "I miss her, too."

"What's wrong, Johnny?" he asked then, picking up on my mood.

"They offered me a two-year contract, Da," I whispered.

"In France?"

"No." I shook my head. "In Dublin."

My father blew out a shaky breath and leaned back in his chair, food forgotten. "And the money?"

"Beyond our expectations given my age and experience," I muttered. "The kind of money I didn't expect to earn until my twenties."

His brows shot up. "The plan was to play for a French club for a year or two to gain experience before you signed for home," he noted. "They must think you're ready."

"Yeah." Setting my fork and knife down, I mirrored his actions and leaned back in my chair. "They must."

"They want you."

"They do."

"And you?" He tilted his head to one-side, studying me with intelligent eyes. "What do *you* want?"

"If I sign, I would have to move back to Dublin in September and finish out my leaving cert at Royce," I told him. "They're willing to work with me on my training schedule. I'd be a pupil of Royce on paper, but I guess I'd be more of an external student than anything, you know? Taking a few classes, keeping up with tutoring, and sitting my exams there."

"And what do you think about that?"

"I don't know," I replied honestly, still reeling from how fast everything was happening. "It's a lot to take in, Da."

"And you're hesitant?"

I nodded slowly.

"Because of Shannon."

*Yes? No? Maybe?* I shrugged helplessly.

"I see," he replied calmly.

*I doubt it.* I didn't think anyone could see what I saw in this moment. "I don't know." That was all I could say – all I could think. "I really don't know, Da."

"Dublin is a two and half hour car ride from Cork," he offered. "It's doable."

"It's not that," I croaked out, dropping my gaze to study my hands.

"Then what is it, Johnny?"

I opened my mouth to explain but snapped it shut again. I didn't have the words. I couldn't explain how I was feeling when I didn't understand it myself. "I'm lost," I finally told him. "I'm *conflicted*."

"Is this not what you want anymore?" he asked gently. "Because that's okay, too."

"I want it," I choked out. "Trust me, I want this, Da. Rugby is what I want to do with my life. That hasn't changed."

"But?"

"It's just . . . " I blew out a pained breath. "I don't know if I want it *yet*." I forced myself to look at him, expression guilty. "I don't know, Da. If I sign, then that's it. It's done. I have to give it all up."

"Give what up?"

"Tommen, my friends, Shannon, Gibs . . . " I shrugged, feeling lost and helpless. "I'll be a man."

"You *are* a man, Johnny."

"I know, but I just . . . I thought I had more *time*." I shook my head. "I didn't even realize that I *wanted* more time until they handed me that contract and I saw it all slipping away from me."

"More time to be a teenager?"

I nodded dejectedly. "How pathetic is that?"

"It's not pathetic," he corrected. "It's music to my ears. That's all your mother and I ever wanted for you – to just be *free*."

"I didn't do enough *stuff*, Da," I told him. "All of my friends were living it up, and I was always so focused on the game that I didn't join in."

"And you got the taste of it this year," he added, expression thoughtful.

"Yeah." I nodded. "And I know you're thinking this is about Shannon and that I don't want to sign because I'm afraid of leaving her, and to a point, that's true. I *don't* want to leave her, but it's mostly about *me*. About who I am and where I fit – and I need more time to do that. I didn't pay enough attention to my *life*. I didn't experience any of the stuff I now realize that I *want* to experience. I got a small stab at it, a few short months, and now it's gone."

"It's not gone," Dad replied. "You don't have to sign anything, Johnny. This is an adult decision, it's a commitment to your future, and it doesn't have to be made now. You can come home, son. You can continue working with The Academy, training with the U20's, and finish off your schooling at Tommen. We can decide after your leaving cert next year about college and where you want to play – if you want to play. Your future is yours, Jonathan. It belongs to you, not the coaches. You're still only eighteen years old. You can have that extra year, son. Your mother and I will support you no matter what."

"But I *still* want that contract," I choked out, feeling conflicted. "I want it so fucking bad, Da."

"And you're afraid of turning it down in case you don't get offered another one next year?"

Sighing heavily, I nodded. "Exactly."

"I don't see that happening, Johnny," my father replied. "You're too talented."

"It could," I warned him. "I could turn it down and get injured again. Worse than before. An injury I mightn't come back from. I could lose it all, Da. There are no guarantees in this sport. You know that as well as I do."

"I think you need to take some time out and think this through," Dad said. "When do they need an answer by?"

"I have a week to decide," I said wearily. "They're being amazing to me."

"Then you'll take every one of those days to think about it," he told me. "Nothing needs to be decided tonight."

"Really?"

"Really," he confirmed. "You're coming home next week, and then you have that music festival in Dublin with your friends that same weekend. Take that time to enjoy yourself, son. Go and be a *teenager*. Go mad. Have fun. Unwind. Get drunk – not too drunk or your mother will kill me," he quickly amended with a smirk. "But *enjoy* your life. We'll talk about what you want to do about the contract when you get home. We'll make a decision then."

# Guess Who's Back

## JOHNNY

"So, where is she?" I asked, excitement thrumming in my veins at the prospect of seeing my girlfriend after spending more than seven weeks apart. "Is she at the house? Claire's? You didn't tell her you were picking me up early, did you?"

"Excuse me, but can I be your priority for ten minutes," Gibsie demanded huffily. "I haven't seen you in almost two months, and all you can think about is getting your dick wet, you selfish bastard. You didn't even ask about my trip to Scotland last month."

"I missed you, too, lad," I chuckled, delighted to be back in his Focus, gripping the *Oh Jesus* bar, and silently praying for him not to kill us both with his deranged driving. "And your Toblerone is in my suitcase."

"Toblerone*s*," he corrected, narrowly avoiding an old lady crossing the road. "*Plural.* Don't even think about giving Hughie and Feely my stash." Swerving back on to his side of the road, Gibsie glanced in the rearview mirror and sighed. "Oh, thank god, she's still standing. For a minute there, I thought I clipped her with my wing-mirror."

"Maybe you should pull over and let me drive," I offered, trying to keep my breathing even and not freak the fuck out when he mounted the footpath taking a corner. "How the fuck did you get your full license?"

"My tongue," he replied smugly. "It's a wonderful weapon."

I grimaced. "Do I want to know?"

He shrugged. "Probably not."

Moving swiftly on before he scarred me for life with his indiscretions, I asked, "So how is your Aunty Jacqui and all the gang in Scotland?" Gibsie had family in Scotland. Every summer since as far back as I could remember, he took a week-long trip to visit his father's baby sister in Edinburgh.

"She's a wild one, lad," Gibsie chuckled. "I swear to god, I wasn't sure

I'd make it home in one piece. The woman can put a pint away faster than any man – and her friend Sharon is mad craic."

I didn't doubt it. I'd taken the trip with him back in third year and he wasn't exaggerating about his paternal aunt's wildness. It clearly ran in the family.

"You know that insanely good tattooist?" he continued happily. "The guy in Manchester – Dex Michaels? He owns Heaven and Ink."

I arched a brow. "The American guy on all the magazines and shite? He inks all the celebs?"

Gibsie nodded. "That's the one."

"What about him?"

A smirk crept across his face as he dived into his latest outrageous story, telling me all about how he had come *this* close to getting his calf inked by the high-profiler, celebrity tattooist until he checked for I.D. and got caught red-handed.

"You're such a dope," I laughed. "He was never going to ink you."

"He fucking *was*," Gibsie huffed. "I swear it was my backpack that let me down, lad."

"Your backpack?" I asked, frowning until awareness dawned on me. *Oh Jesus.* "Oh, Gibs, tell me you *didn't* bring that thing with you."

"I *know*," he groaned. "It was a rookie mistake."

"You took a *Fantastic fucking Four* backpack to a tattoo parlor." I shook my head and gaped at him. "What did you expect him to do, lad?"

"I expected him to ink me," he shot back defensively. "It's not like it's my first tattoo – *and* I look eighteen."

"True," I agreed. "But you also look *disturbed* when you walk around with that fucking thing strapped to your back."

"It's my *travel bag*."

"When you were *seven*."

"Well, it's his loss," he replied, smirking to himself. "I got my calf done when I came home."

"Good for you," I chuckled, shaking my head. "So, have you been keeping up with your training?"

He grinned. "I have indeed."

"And?"

"And I'm the shit," Gibsie chuckled.

"I know," I mused, thoroughly amused. "Keep it up and you'll be with me soon."

"Where there's a will there's a relative," he shot back, grinning wolfishly.

"So, where are we going now?"

"The beach," Gibsie explained, turning onto the coast road. "The tide is in, the sun is out, the water is warm, the beer is cold, and the best buddy is home. Today is a good day." He gripped the steering wheel a little tighter before muttering, "Just so long as no one tries to drown me again."

"I need to see Shannon," I told him, grimacing at the last part. "I love you, lad, I'm thrilled to be back with you, but I really need to see my girlfriend."

"And see her, you will," he chuckled. "She's at the beach with all the buddies."

"Yeah?" A huge smile spread across my face. "How does she look? Does she seem happy? Is she well?"

"She's definitely something," he replied with a smirk.

I frowned. "What does that mean?"

"You'll see," Gibsie chuckled.

"Holy shite."

"I know," he agreed with a nod.

"What the fuck?"

"I *know*," he laughed.

Shaking my head, I tilted it to one-side, watching as Shannon ran down the beach, screaming *mercy* at Claire who was hunting her down with a handful of seaweed. She was laughing and smiling, and all golden-tanned, and that beautiful brown hair was loose and blowing in the light breeze. But none of those things were what had my mouth hanging open. No, it was the tiny scrap of a red bikini she was wearing, filled out by a body that I didn't remember her having. I could have caught flies I looked so fucking dumbstruck at the sight of her.

Christ, something had happened to my girlfriend in the time we'd spent apart this summer. When I left for camp, I'd left Shannon behind in a loose t-shirt and even looser shorts. She was all pale skin and protruding bones. Standing here now, I felt like I had stepped out of Gibsie's car and into an alternative fucking universe.

Legs.

Fucking *legs*.

And tits.

Christ, she had *tits*.

And her ass.

She was still pint-sized, slimmer than the other girls, but holy shit was she filling out that bikini like a dream.

"That's not right," I choked out, tearing my gaze off Shannon to gape at Gibsie. "How does that happen in a couple of months?"

"Puberty? A growth spurt? Vitamins? Three meals a day?" Gibsie offered with a shrug. "She wasn't stressed out at home, or anxious puking every second minute? She's being taken care of? Shit, I don't know, lad. I don't even care. But she's glorious to look at, so don't look a gift horse in the mouth and just appreciate it."

"You've been *looking* at her?" I demanded, furious. "While I've been gone?"

"Ah, just the normal amount," he coaxed, as if the *normal amount* would placate me. "Look, look, they're wrestling with each other. Ah, lad. Fucking winning!"

Oh my Jesus, I had to bite back a groan at the sight of Shannon rolling around on the sand.

"Doesn't she look like sunshine?" Gibsie croaked out, slapping my chest. "Look at that fucking girl, lad!"

I knew Gibsie was talking about Claire in her little, yellow bikini, but I had eyes for no one but Shannon. It had been a long summer and I had no idea how to deal with all this new and exciting information – and visuals – frying my brain. I'd always been attracted to Shannon. She had always been beautiful to me, and incredibly sexy, but now? Those feelings had intensified to the point I could hardly think straight. I wanted to drop to my knees and worship whatever version of puberty that had paid a visit to my girlfriend. It was like waking up on Christmas morning and preparing to find the bicycle you'd asked Santa for under the tree, only to tear off the wrapping paper and find a top of the range BMX instead.

*Fucking winning . . .*

One look at her, and I was glad I had worked my body to breaking point this summer, spending countless hours in training every day, and coming home a stone heavier in muscle and an inch taller in height.

"Cap!" Hughie's voice filled my ears then and I turned to see him, Feely, Katie, and Lizzie standing around a disposable barbecue further up the beach. "Jesus Christ, it's him."

"He's back!"

"Hey, Johnny!"

I raised my hand and waved back to them, but kept my eyes on Shannon who was staring up at us from her perch on the sand beneath Claire.

"Shannon *like the river*," I called out to her, unable to stop the smile that was spreading across my face, as I climbed down the rocks to get to her. "Are you gonna come hug me or what?"

"Oh my god!" she literally squealed as she untangled herself from Claire and sprang to her feet. "You're back!"

*Tits,* that was all I could see as Shannon broke into a run.

"You're home!" she cried, barreling towards me. "Oh my god, Johnny—" her words broke off as she threw herself into my arms, all smooth skin and soft curves. Catching her easily, I hoisted her up, reveling in the feel of her legs around my waist and her arms around my neck. "You're back," she sobbed, smearing my entire face with lip-gloss, as she peppered me with welcome home kisses. "You came home to me."

"You knew I was coming home, Shan," I replied gruffly, feeling like my heart was bursting clean open. The loneliness I had been struggling to keep at bay while I was in camp hit me full force in the chest.

"But you're early?"

"I'm late," I told her, stroking my nose against hers. "I should have been here all summer." Unable to stop myself, I leaned in and kissed her, getting my first proper taste of her in what felt like forever. She kissed me back just as frantically. It was all tongue and clashing teeth and I swear to god, I'd never had a better kiss. "Jesus, I missed you so much," I told her, breathing hard against her lips. "I fucking love you." And I did. I loved her more than was good for me. I couldn't contain my emotions when it came to this girl.

"I missed you more," she whispered against my lips. "And I love you more."

*Doubtful.*

*Very fucking doubtful.*

"Okay, so I know you probably want to unpack when you get home, but I want my presents," Gibsie announced, shoving past me with my suitcases in hand. "You can continue mouth-fucking Little Shannon," he added in a cheerful tone, sinking down on the sand and unzipping my case. "I don't mind. But I'm just giving you a head's up that I'm about to root through everything you own."

"Hey – don't take them all," Hughie shouted, running up the beach towards us. "That's my Toblerone, you little bitch."

"Possession is nine-tenths of the law," Gibsie laughed, running off with an armful of chocolate in his arms. "Claire – grab the bag and run, babe. It's full of sweets."

"Welcome home, Johnny," Claire squealed, chasing after Gibsie with my carry-on bag in her arms. "Thanks for the sweets."

"Jesus," I muttered, reluctantly setting Shannon down on her feet. Stepping back, she folded her arms under her chest and I bit back a groan at the sight of her full tits pressing together in the tiny scrap of a bikini she was wearing. Her nipples were puckered and straining against the flimsy red fabric, clearly taunting me. *Jesus!* "Bring them back, you big

783 • CHLOE WALSH

eejit," I called after Gibsie, desperately trying to calm myself down and stop the semi in my jocks from flying full mast. "Some of those bars are for the kids."

"He *is* a kid," Feely laughed, closing the space between us. "Welcome home, Cap." Wrapping his arms around me, he clapped my back. "You were amazing over there."

"Yeah, Cap, welcome home," Hughie called out as he busied himself with digging in my luggage. "It's great to see you – holy shit, you got all their signatures on this?" He pulled out a New Zealand jersey and waved it around, eyes wide. "Can I have this one?"

"Yeah, I got two more for Feely and Gibs," I told him, grimacing at the memory of how much slack I had taken from my teammates for getting those jerseys signed from our oppositions. I didn't give a shite, though. I was still in school and playing with and against most of my childhood heroes. "There's a few Fijian, Australian, and South African jerseys in there, too."

"You were a good investment," Hughie mused, pulling out his pick of the bunch. "I knew it the day you stepped through the doors of Scoil Eoin with your Dublin accent and *fuck you all* attitude." Passing a handful of goodies to Katie, who was waving at me, Hughie continued to rummage around in my personal property. "I said it to Feely and Gibs that very same day. I told them this city boy is so intense, he's either going to hit the drugs or hit the big time." Shrugging, he added, "We voted unanimously that we were down for the ride, either way."

"Wow, Hugh," I deadpanned. "Thanks."

"No bother, lad," he replied. "I'm deadly proud of you, by the way."

"We all are," Lizzie announced, coming to stand beside Feely. "Welcome home, Captain Fantastic."

"Thanks . . . I think?" I replied, giving her a wary look.

"I'm being sincere," she replied, smirking. "It's good to have you back – for Shannon's sake. I'm not pushed. I could give or take you, if we're being honest."

"*There* she is." Winking, I added, "And it's good to see you, too, Viper."

784 • KEEPING 13

"Can we go for a walk?" Shannon asked then, slipping her hand in mine, blue eyes dancing with excitement. "Just us?"

Fuck yeah.

"You can't take him yet, Shan," Hughie objected. "We need to talk rugby."

"She can take me wherever she wants," I shot back, trailing after my girlfriend.

"You're whipped, Cap," he called after me. "In the worst kind of way."

Stumbling blindly into the tiny alcove between the rocks with Shannon's lips on mine and her fingers digging into my shoulders, I didn't have time to think about what I was doing or whether this was a good idea or not. My head was too clouded to think rationally, everything inside of me was completely wrapped up in this moment – in the way she made me *feel*. I was aching all over, the need to be inside of her unbearable.

"Are you sure?" I strangled out, breathing hard against her lips, as she reached between us and pulled on the waistband of my shorts. "Shan, I don't have anything on me."

"It's okay," she breathed, nodding frantically. "And I'm so sure."

"Really?"

"I'm on the pill now, remember?"

*Fuck.*

Tugging on the flimsy ribbons on both sides of her briefs, I groaned into her mouth when the fabric fell away from her body before quickly freeing myself from my shorts. "What do you want me to do?" I whispered, making short work of the tiny bra, and then shuddering when her full breasts fell free. "Christ, baby, your body is so different."

"Just be with me," she begged, hooking an arm around my neck and hoisting herself up my body. "Be *in* me."

Instantly, my hands were on her thighs; my dick *straining* to get to her. Pressing her back against the rocks, I closed the space between us, covered her mouth with mine, and slid home.

"What—"

"Was—"

"That!" we both finished at the same time, eyes wide and locked on each other.

"What just happened?" Shannon squeaked out, as she slipped her bikini bottoms on and tied the ribbons back together.

"I don't know," I replied with a shake of my head, breathing hard and fast, as I rearranged my shorts. "But whatever that was—" I tilted my head to one side and grinned at her, "we should do it again."

She flushed bright pink and quickly re-tied her bra. "I missed you."

"I could tell," I teased, lowering myself down on the sand beside her. Pressing a kiss to her shoulder, I nuzzled her neck, drowning in the intoxicating smell of her. "I missed you too, Shan."

"No, I mean I really, really missed you, Johnny," she whispered, climbing onto my lap. "Terribly."

"I know." Shivering, I wrapped my arms around her. "It was the same for me."

"Don't go away for so long again," she mumbled, burying her face in my neck. "Or if you do, take me with you."

I flinched at her words. "I need to tell you something."

She stiffened in my arms before whispering, "I'm listening."

"They offered me a contract."

Her body turned to stone in my arms and her fingernails dug into my shoulders. "In France?"

"No." I blew out a ragged breath. "In Dublin."

She was quiet for so long that I wasn't sure she had heard me, but then she whispered, "Did you take it?"

"Not yet," I replied hoarsely. "But it's a two-year contract, with a lot of money." I released another pained sigh before adding, "They want me to transfer to Royce and finish out my leaving cert there. I would have to move back to Dublin in September."

"Are you going to go?" she asked in a small voice.

"I wanted to talk to you first."

"It's what you want, right?"

"I've been working all my life for this," I admitted.

She shivered violently. "Then you should go."

"I should?"

"You should."

"But I don't want to leave you," I confessed, voice torn.

"I know," she replied, voice shaking. "But it's okay that you have to."

"Shannon—" I shook my head and buried my face in her neck.

"It's okay, Johnny," she sniffled, stroking my hair. "This is *good*."

"My head knows that," I choked out. "But my heart is fucking devastated."

"Let's talk it through," she said in a steadier voice than I was capable of finding given the circumstances. Leaning back, she cupped my face in her hands and looked at me with tear-filled eyes. "I am so proud of you," she told me, tears trickling down her cheeks. "You're the best person I've ever known, and I want this for *you*." Stroking her thumb over my cheekbone, she whispered, "You warned me a long time ago about this and I accepted it then. I accept it *now*. This is your future, Johnny, and you are going to chase it." She kissed me hard before continuing, "And I'm going stand by you and support you, no matter what, for as long as you want me."

"I will *always* want you," I vowed. "Fucking always. Don't even say it like that, Shan. *Christ*."

"What I mean is, if I'm the only reason you're afraid to sign, then you need to do it," she explained. "I mean it, Johnny. You're not losing me. You can have both. I promise."

"I just don't know if I'm ready for it," I croaked out, voice thick with emotion. "I thought I had more time."

"It's because you're so amazing, and now the whole world knows just how much." She gave me a watery smile. "They all want you."

"I only want you," I mumbled, pressing my forehead to hers.

"You have me," she replied softly. "Contract or not. I'm entirely yours."

# Festivals and Fangirls

## SHANNON

When I woke up on the second morning of the music festival in Dublin, it was with a heavy heart and a belly full of dread. For the longest time, I just laid on my side in my sleeping bag, watching Johnny sleep beside me. I studied every inch of his beautiful face, taking in every freckle and scar, and the way his thick, dark lashes fanned his cheekbones when he slept.

Memories of yesterday filled my mind and I smiled to myself, thinking about Johnny and Gibsie as they jumped around like a pair of lunatics to The Saw Doctor's "N17". With their arms wrapped around each other, they had chanted the words back to the band and leaped around like two crazed idiots. It was *hilarious*. They had both been extremely drunk and enjoying each other's company, uncaring of what they looked like in the moment, as they belly bashed one another and tried to out-jump the other. "N17" had rolled into "Joyce Country Ceili Band" and then "I Useta Lover" and they had danced along together, singing the words to each other like an old married couple.

Even though I was incredibly excited to take on the day and see all the other amazing bands and artists on offer, I didn't want to leave the tent this morning. Because tomorrow, we would have to go home. Because tomorrow, he would have to give them an answer. I didn't know what he was going to do. His father had told him to take a few days to mull it over and decide when we came home from Dublin, and that's exactly what Johnny was doing. We hadn't spoken about it since that day at the beach, and I was fairly sure neither of us wanted to bring it back up until we really had to. But the thought of him leaving permanently made my heart squeeze so tight in my chest, it was hard to breathe. Putting on a brave face, I danced, sang, and laughed my way through our day yesterday, but I was lonesome now. I was missing him before he even left.

"You're staring," he whispered, eyes still closed.

I smiled. "You're supposed to be sleeping."

"I can't."

"Why not?"

"Because I can feel your eyes on me." Smiling, he cracked an eyelid open. "Hi, Shannon."

"Hi, Johnny."

Stretching out his long limbs, he reached over and pulled me onto his chest. "We need to get a tent for home."

"Oh yeah?"

He nodded and kissed my hair. "With a padlock on the opening to keep your brothers and my ma out."

Sighing in contentment, I nuzzled my cheek against his bare chest. "You always make me warm."

"You always make me hard."

I rolled my eyes and smiled to myself. "It's been raining all night."

"Are you wet?"

"Stop," I laughed, slapping his chest. "You're being terrible."

"I'm only messing," he chuckled, snatching my hand up to entwine with his. "It's only a bit of summer rain, Shan. The sun will be out soon." Pressing a kiss to my knuckles, he said, "I love this."

"You love what?"

"You," he replied. "This." He shrugged. "Being here now."

Twisting onto my stomach, I looked up at him. "I love this, too."

"Do you want to stay forever?" he offered lightly, but I could see the pain in his eyes. "We can hide in this tent and never come out?"

"I think Gibsie would have something to say about that," I replied, giving him a smile.

"Yeah." Johnny sighed heavily. "Should have left the fucker at home. He was demented yesterday."

"He's fun," I laughed.

"He's insane," Johnny corrected.

"Come on, you know you love him," I teased.

"Yeah," he grumbled. "I'm fond of the little bollox."

"Johnny?"

"Yeah, Shan?"

"We'll be okay, won't we?"

"Yeah." He cupped my cheek in his hand. "We will."

"No matter what?" I whispered, leaning into his touch.

"No matter what," he replied gruffly.

The roof of the tent started to shake rapidly then, and Gibsie's voice filled my ears. "Hey, Cap? Are you getting your hole – I mean, are you making sweet love, or can I come in?"

"Yes, I am," Johnny growled. "Now fuck off."

The zip lowered on our tent opening and his blond head popped through. "Morning, family."

"I said I was making sweet love, asshole," Johnny snapped, sitting straight up.

"I know," Gibsie laughed, crawling inside. "That's how I knew you weren't."

"I could have been," Johnny argued.

"Nope," Gibsie shot back. "The tent wasn't shaking."

"Morning," Claire chirped as she crawled in after him, with a full face of makeup and her clothes on point. "How are my favorite lovebirds? Ready for another amazing day?"

"Do you have batteries I can take out?" Johnny asked her. "Your optimism is *endless*."

"I'm a sunny-side up kind of girl," she told him.

"We're hungry," Gibsie admitted with a sheepish grin. "We ran out of snacks in our tent."

"Because you didn't bring any," Johnny grumbled, flopping back down and taking me with him. "Like I told you to."

"Ooh, you have gummy bears?" Claire asked, rummaging around in our bags. "Wow, I thought you didn't eat junk food, Johnny."

"I don't," Johnny yawned. Rolling onto his side, he draped an arm around me. "They're for Shan."

"Aww," she swooned. "You're so considerate."

"Could you be – and leave?" Johnny muttered under his breath.

"Don't be cranky," I scolded, pinching his nipple.

"Do it again," he purred. "*Lower.*"

I blushed. "Johnny—"

"She can pull on your dick later," Gibsie announced. "Right now, we have places to be and drunk to get."

"*Drunk to get?*" Johnny shook his head. "Lad, you really need to start listening in class."

"Get out of the sleeping bag and come have fun with me," he ordered. "Or I'm going to fart on your girlfriend. And trust me, it's going to be a ripe one. I was on the cider all day yesterday."

"He's telling the truth," Claire added, gagging. "His farts are chronic, guys. I thought he was going to blow us up last night."

"You were farting, too," he shot back. "Like a ripper."

"I know," she replied, not missing a beat. "I had to try and drown out yours, didn't I?"

"God, the two of you are beyond fucked up," Johnny chuckled.

"Get up, or I'm releasing the beast," Gibsie warned. "Do it now or I might slip a salmon out while I'm at it."

"Ew, Gerard," Claire snickered. "That's so wrong."

I arched a brow. "A salmon?"

"He's talking about taking a shite," Johnny confirmed, jerking out of his sleeping bag quicker than a cat. "I'm coming, so go take your salmon and swim it down a river somewhere else."

Gibsie grinned. "Like your girlfr—"

"Say it and I'll kill you."


"Oh look, Gibs," Johnny roared above the noise of the crowd as Green Day took to the stage and started playing "Basket Case". "It's your anthem."

Laughing, Gibsie gave him the middle finger and continued to bounce around like a demented jack-in-the-box, bare-chested, with

Claire on his shoulders. She didn't look scared – quite the opposite. She had every faith in him not dropping her head-first into the masses. I found that strange considering the boy had already lost both of her wellies and her t-shirt in the crowd. It didn't seem to faze Claire one bit, though. She had her hands in the air, laughing and singing along with the band and the sixty thousand or so people surrounding us.

"Come on, Shannon *like the river*," Johnny said, crouching down in front of me. "Get your ass up here."

"Wh-what?"

He grinned. "Climb on."

"But I—"

He pulled me onto his shoulders as the band began to play the achingly familiar guitar rift. Scrambling for friction, I dug my fingers into his scalp as Johnny stood back up, towering over the people around us, and giving me a perfect view of the band on stage. "Oh my god!" I screamed through fits of nervous laughter as he clamped his hands down on my thighs and began to jump around. "Johnny – ah!" Cowering, I hunched forward, wrapping my arms around his neck, clinging to him. "Please don't drop me."

"Never," Johnny called back. He was shirtless, with his t-shirt hanging out of the back of his shorts, and had a baseball cap slung on backwards, as he chanted the lyrics back at the band with me on his shoulders. I knew he was getting plenty of looks from everyone around us – especially the girls. *People recognize him,* I realized. It was obvious in the way they sneakily tried to snap pictures of him on the sly. Johnny didn't seem to notice, though. Either that, or he just didn't care.

Feeling incredibly free, I threw my hands up in the air and laughed.

"Shannon!" Claire laugh/screamed my name and I reached out to grab her hand, laughing as all four of us screamed out the words of the song.

Cameras were flashing all around us, but for once I didn't care.

We were young and free and together.

Tomorrow would come, bringing with it all of the terror that came with an unknown future, but for now, I was happy. I was content. I was at the best music festival in the world with the only boy I would ever give my heart to.

When Jimmy Eat World took to the stage, I almost had a panic attack. I lost my mind even more when they started to play "The Middle". It was at that exact moment that I knew I was going to be okay. That I could do this. I could live this life with him. No matter what he decided, I would find a way to cope, because sitting on Johnny Kavanagh's shoulders, with his arm wrapped around my legs and his hand on my thigh, I knew there was no other place I wanted to be. I belonged with this boy and he belonged with me.

For their final song of their set, the band started to play "Hear You Me". I glanced over to Gibsie and Claire who were completely focused on one another. Gibsie had one arm hooked loosely across the front of her legs, while he held a plastic cup of whatever the hell he was drinking in the other hand. A cigarette dangled from the corner of his mouth as he slowly rocked from side to side amongst the crowd.

I didn't miss the way that every few minutes, Gibsie smoothed his hand from her calf to her ankle. I also didn't miss the way that Claire rewarded this move by tightening her thighs around his neck and dropping a hand to stroke the side of his jaw.

I didn't think either one realized they were openly petting each other. They just seemed to be completely in sync with one another on both a physical and emotional level.

Turning my attention back to the band, I listened to the lyrics, feeling that familiar surge of sadness swell up inside of me at the thought of my mother. A tear fell onto my cheek as I sang softly to myself. The feel of Johnny's hand squeezing my thigh drew my attention back to him. "I love you," he mouthed, craning his neck to look up at me.

Sniffling, I mouthed, "I love you, too."

Keeping his eyes on mine, he continued to mouth the words of the song, swaying us gently to the music.

Stroking his cheek, I leaned down and pressed my lips to his, not an easy feat given that I was sitting on his shoulders, but I had to kiss him. I just *had* to. The hand Johnny had on my thigh moved to cup the back of my head as he kissed me back, right there in the middle of a field, surrounded by sixty thousand people and Jimmy Eat World singing to us.

"You tired, Shan?" Johnny asked later that night. It was pitch dark, and I was sitting on some railing or other I had found to rest on. Johnny was standing right behind me, keeping a protective arm wrapped around my stomach, while we waited for Claire and Gibsie, who were queuing up at the mobile chipper.

Johnny was still shirtless, having given me his t-shirt to wear when the sun went down and the chill set in. Resting my head against his warm chest, I released a sigh of contentment. "Hmm."

"Hmm?" Resting his chin on my shoulder, he swayed absentmindedly to the music still playing in the distance. "What's hmm?"

"I'm just taking it all in," I told him.

"Johnny Kavanagh?" someone called out then, causing us both to turn in the direction of a group of much older girls.

"Oh my god, it *is* him," one of them screamed. "I told you!"

"Hey," Johnny replied, words slightly slurring from the beer he and Gibsie had been necking all day, but tone as polite and professional as always.

"Oh my god, you were amazing against Fiji," another girl told him – one with the biggest breasts I'd ever seen in real life. "*So* amazing."

"Can we get a picture?" another asked.

Johnny hesitated, tightening his arm around my stomach.

"It's okay," I said with a small nod, encouraging him to take the picture so we could get back to *us*.

Smothering a frustrated sigh, he slapped on a professional smile and walked over to the girls.

"Can you take it please?" one of them asked, holding her digital camera out for me to take.

Nodding, I hopped down off the railing and took the camera from her. "Okay, I have the flash on so it should work. Smile."

Johnny looked extremely uncomfortable, but he smiled as the group of six girls all draped themselves around him.

I snapped four pictures of them and then held the camera out for the girl to take back.

"Thanks so much," she gushed, staring up at my boyfriend like he held the moon. "He's amazing."

"Yeah." I forced a smile. "He is." *And he's mine.*

"I'm sorry about that," Johnny said, tone low, as he waved them off and hurried back to me. "That was fucking embarrassing."

"Don't be sorry for people loving you," I told him.

He shook his head and helped me back onto the railing. "They don't love me, Shan."

"They adore you," I corrected, pulling him closer to stand between my legs. "And that's okay."

"Maybe," he conceded, clamping his hands down on my hips. "But they don't love me."

"Oh?" I arched a brow. "How are you so sure?"

"Because I know what it feels like when someone loves me." He tipped my nose with his finger. "And that's not it."

Heat crept up my neck. "Johnny—"

"I know what I'm going to do, Shan," he whispered. "About the contract? I've made a decision."

My heart hammered wildly in my chest. "Really?"

He nodded slowly. "I have to do this for *me*," he whispered. "I need to. It's what's right for *me*, you know?"

"I understand," I breathed, feeling the weight of the world settle down on my shoulders.

"You'll love me no matter what?" A shudder rolled through him and he clenched his eyes shut. "No matter how hard it gets?"

"No matter what," I forced the words out of my throat, knowing that I was agreeing to break my own heart in the process. "You sign and you shine."

"And you'll be okay?" he pushed. "No matter what?"

I forced a smile. "I'll be fine."

"I'll marry you," he said then. "When we're older and everything settles down." Taking my hands in his, he placed them around his neck and leaned in close. "Just stand by me," he said in a voice thick with emotion. "*Stay* with me." His hand squeezed mine. "And I'll make you proud. I'll do right by you."

My breath came out in a pained rush. "Johnny . . ."

"We'll have a family," he continued to say. "One of our own, and I'll stand by you right back. In whatever you choose to do. No matter what."

"This won't break us," I croaked, touching my brow to his.

"Nothing can break us," he whispered. "I promise."

# A New School Year

## SHANNON

It was September 1st 2005.

A brand-new term, and my first day of fifth year. Deciding to take the leap year option with Lizzie and Claire, I walked through the doors of Tommen for my second to last year of secondary school, dressed in a brand spanking new uniform – ironed to perfection, courtesy of Mrs. Kavanagh – with my best friends at my side.

Everything was different now. I wasn't the same girl from nine months ago. I was a completely different person, with a new home and a new family. All because I made the reckless decision to take a shortcut through a rugby pitch and crash into the boy who had changed my life. The boy who had *saved* my life.

"This is going to be our best year yet, girls," Claire declared, looking her usual pristine self, with her hips swaying and her blonde curls bouncing as she walked. "I can feel it in my bones."

"No. Just ... no, Claire," Lizzie grumbled, trudging along beside her, looking like the angel of fury. "It's way too early for your demonic optimism."

"Ladies," Ronan McGarry purred, stopping in front of us when we reached our lockers. "I heard you three took the gap year."

"I hope *you* didn't," Lizzie shot back, releasing her glower on him.

"I did." He smirked. "You'll be seeing a lot more of me." Turning his attention to me, he winked. "Hey, Shannon."

"No." My lip curled up and I had to repress the urge to gag. "Just ... *no*."

Ronan's face reddened and he stalked away, clearly furious.

"That was epic," Claire laughed, throwing her arm over my shoulder. "Johnny would be proud."

"Yeah," Lizzie agreed, cracking an actual smile. "He would've loved to have seen you put that toe-rag back in his box."

"Don't," I groaned, stomach twisting up in knots. "I don't want conflict this year. I just want to get on with my life."

"Aww," Claire squealed then, distracting us both. "Look at him."

Swinging around to see who she was pointing at, I smirked when Tadhg stalked towards us, scowling.

"Oh, that boy is going to break some serious hearts," she added, pressing a hand to her chest. "I want to eat him up."

"Yeah, look at those baby first-year girls checking him out already," Lizzie chuckled, pointing to a group of young girls openly staring at my baby brother. "He's going to be the man."

"No, he's not," I said, horrified. "He's not even thirteen yet."

"Look at the cute first year!" Shelly and Helen said in unison as they rushed over to us. "He is so cute."

"That's Shannon's brother," Claire explained. "And yes, we're aware that he is beyond adorable."

"Hey, Tadhg," I said, giving him a bright smile when he approached. "How are you finding everything—"

"Don't talk to me," he warned, giving me a horrified look. "Jesus Christ, you're my *sister*. You don't know me when we're here."

"You're in the wrong area," I shot back, eyes narrowed. "The first-year locker area is downstairs."

"Whatever." Rolling his eyes, he shouldered his bag and turned around, heading back towards the first-year common area, growling, "This school fucking sucks," before quickly backpedaling to us. "By the way, *you* can absolutely talk to me," he said, winking up at Claire, who was towering over him.

"Uh, thanks?" Claire laughed, grinning down at him.

"Anytime, blondie," Tadhg replied before sauntering off.

"Oh, yeah," Claire snickered. "Give him a couple of years, and he's *definitely* going to be the man."

"Who's the man?" Gibsie asked, sidling up to us with Hughie and

Feely in tow. He waggled his brows at Claire and grinned. "Are you talking about me again, Claire-bear?"

"Nope," Lizzie answered for her. "You have competition this year, Thor."

"Oh, please." Gibsie made a pshhing sound and waved a hand in front of himself. "I'm the only competition around here." Looking thoughtful, he added, "I'm basically my own competition."

"Hey, blondie?" Tadhg called out from down the corridor, causing all of us to turn and look at him. "Nice legs." Turning to Gibsie, he smirked. "You better up your game, lad. Because it's *on*."

"Oh my god," Helen and Shelly giggled. "He's got spunk."

"Too much of it," I muttered under my breath.

"That little shit," Gibsie hissed, stepping around us to hunt after my little brother. "You better keep your pre-pubescent eyes off my baby mama, fucker. Or you won't have balls to drop!"

"I have bigger balls than you, fatty," Tadhg called back, laughing his ass off. "Just ask your mother."

"I'm not *fat*!" Gibsie roared. "And you leave my mother out of this!"

"I'm coming for your girl, Gibs," Tadhg continued to taunt, thoroughly enjoying driving Gibsie crazy. "Fair warning."

"I'm going to kick you all the way back to primary school," Gibsie snarled. "*Fair warning.*"

"Simmer down, Gibs," Feely laughed, dragging him back by the scruff of the neck. "He's a first year."

My phone started to ring in my pocket, distracting me from Gibsie's comical outrage, and I hurried off to one-side to answer it. "Hello?"

"Shannon *like the river*," Johnny's familiar voice purred down the line, setting my pulse racing. "How's my girl?"

Grinning, I bit down on my lip and swallowed a moan at the sound of his husky voice. "Hi, Johnny."

"Hi, Shannon." He chuckled softly down the line. "How's your first day going?"

"Good, how's yours?"

"Productive."

I smirked. "Oh really?"

"Yeah," he replied, and there was a teasing lilt to his voice. "See, I had this amazing dream last night about my sexy girlfriend."

Leaning against the locker, I glanced around to make sure my friends weren't listening before whispering, "Keep talking."

"She tiptoed into my room in the middle of the night," he continued. "And then she climbed under the covers . . . and when she took her clothes off, she started doing things to my body that made those pretty cheeks of hers turn pink."

"Oh, wow." Squirming, I blew out a shaky breath. "That sounds like a great dream."

"It was the best." A pair of arms came around me from behind, pulling me flush against a chest of hard muscle. "But it wasn't a dream, was it?"

Grinning, I spun around and openly ogled my boyfriend in his Tommen uniform, looking like the best thing my eyes had ever seen. "No, it wasn't."

"These late-night visits are getting out of hand, Shan," Johnny purred, stooping down to press a hot kiss to my lips. "I almost slept through my alarm for training, and Ma was watching me like a bleeding hawk when I came down for breakfast." Grinning, he added, "I think she might be onto us."

"Oh, you think?" I laughed.

"Hmm." Nodding, he leaned down and kissed me again. "We're going to have to get a little more inventive this year."

Sighing in contentment, I wrapped my arms around his waist and hugged him, thanking god that he had made the decision to delay his signing for another year so he could finish off his leaving cert here at Tommen. *With me.* It gave us one more year together before the big decisions had to be made. It gave us breathing space. It kept us together for a little longer, and I was savoring every one of those minutes. I felt guilty for being so ecstatic that Johnny had decided to stay. I also felt a huge swell of guilt and responsibility for him making that decision. I had feared he was staying out of duty to me, or because he was scared I wouldn't cope. When he explained that *he* wasn't ready, that *he* didn't feel like he could walk away from his life yet, and that he had thought it through with his usual precision and attention to detail, I relaxed. He *needed* this year. Some more time to just grow up and live a little before he moved on to the pros. He was talented enough that he was in the position to make that kind of decision and still have the full support and backing of not only his trainers at The Academy, but the Irish coaches, too. Of course, his mother was beyond delighted to have him home for another school year, but I had a feeling her excitement was quickly wearing off considering she had upped her spy patrol on our relationship, roping Sean into the mix, too.

"What's that for?" Johnny chuckled, dragging me from my thoughts.

"I just missed you," I whispered, nuzzling my cheek against his chest.

"You saw me this morning, Shan," he reminded me. "And at dinner yesterday evening." His voice turned huskier when he added, "And last night, when you had your lips—"

"I remember," I choked out, blushing. "You don't need to give me a verbal recap."

"You need to control that ward of yours," Gibsie announced, drawing our attention to him. "I'm serious, Johnny," he added, still scowling. "He is getting right on my tits."

"He's a kid, Gibs," Johnny drawled, arching a brow. "You can handle him."

"Oh, I *know* I can," Gibsie replied, still glowering. "But my version of handling him is very different to yours, and will most likely land me in a prison cell. Therefore, it's a good thing you decided to stick around until June, Cap, because you're going to need to stop *me* from bulldozing this year."

"By the way, Johnny, I saw your mother and father go into the office earlier," Helen said. She blushed and batted her eye lashes as she spoke to him. "I hope everything's okay."

"Yeah," Shelly agreed, joining in on the eyelash batting. "I hope it's nothing serious."

"Why are you two still here?" Lizzie asked in a flat tone.

"Liz," Claire snickered. "Be nice."

"I am being nice," Lizzie countered. "I could have said *fuck off*." She gave the girls a pointed look.

"You should buy a muzzle for that one, Claire," Shelly huffed, glaring at Lizzie. "She has issues."

"Big ones," Helen agreed before they stalked away together, arm in arm.

"Was that necessary?" Claire asked, still laughing. "They're harmless."

"They're *annoying*," Lizzie corrected. "And catty, *and* bitchy."

"They are," Gibsie agreed. "And we only have room for one catty bitch in this group."

"Thor, you better not start with me this morning," Lizzie warned. "I'm trying to be cordial here, but your face is just setting me off."

"Oh, Jesus, come on, Shan," Johnny muttered with a shake of his head. "It's too early for their shite." Catching ahold of my hand, he tugged me down the hallway after him.

"What do you think your parents are doing in the office?" I asked, hurrying along next to him.

Johnny shrugged. "Sorting out your brother's enrolment, I suppose."

"Yeah." I blew out a shaky breath, feeling nervous and anxious for him. "Do you think he'll be okay?" I asked. "Do you think he'll make friends and settle in here at Tommen?"

"There's only one way to find out," Johnny mused, pulling me to a stop just outside the girls' bathroom. "Here we go," he added, tone light and full of humor, as he pointed to the front entrance.

My breath hitched in my throat when my eyes landed on the boy standing in the doorway, dressed in the Tommen uniform, looking hard, and beautiful, and a little lost. A gear bag was slung over one shoulder, and a hurley was clutched in his other hand. His white shirt was untucked, his red tie was hanging loosely. His blonde hair was ruffled, and his expression was one of *fuck the world and everyone in it*. He looked thinner, darker, more haunted, but his green eyes were sharp and focused again.

"Oh my god," Claire choked out, running up to us, clutching her chest. "Is that—"

"Joey," I filled in with a small nod. "Yep."

"When did he get out?"

"Last week," Johnny told her.

"But you guys never said," she replied, frowning.

"We weren't sure what he was going to do," I explained, clutching Johnny's hand as I stared at my brother. "If he was going to take Johnny's parents up on their offer."

"But he's here!"

"Yep," Johnny and I both replied. "He's here."

"Who is *that*?" Shelly squealed, joining us once more. "Sweet baby Jesus, I'm in love."

"He's the new sixth year," Helen explained with a dreamy sigh. "The new boy of Tommen."

"Well, shit," Gibsie mused, coming to join us. "This year is going to be eventful."

"It's going to be something alright," Johnny replied.

"Yeah," Gibsie laughed. "Let the madness begin."

# THANK YOU SO MUCH FOR READING!

Johnny and Shannon's story has concluded but
Joey and Aoife's continues in *Saving 6*.

For updates on release dates, check out
**chloewalshauthor.com**.

Keep reading for an exclusive **bonus chapter**
of Johnny and Shannon before
the music festival . . .

# Tender hearts ... and chicken

## SHANNON

### BEFORE THE MUSIC FESTIVAL ...

He came back to me.

Finally.

After almost two months apart, Johnny was *home*.

The moment I saw him, I wanted to climb onto his lap and stay there forever. I didn't care about the logistics of it all, or my basic human needs, I physically craved Johnny Kavanagh to the point where I wanted to crawl *into* him and stay there forever. That was how intense my feelings for him had grown. How uncontrollably in love I was.

Even now, as I sat in the passenger seat of his car on the way to town, it wasn't enough. I couldn't seem to get *close* enough. The very real worry of his possible departure at the start of the school year was enough to send me spiraling into a panic attack, but I forced my fears back. I pushed through my anxiety, determined to live in the moment with the only boy I'd ever loved. Determined *not* to hold my boyfriend back from his dreams. After all, I owed him so much more than my life. I owed him *my* dreams. Because I was beginning to have those now. Actual dreams of my own.

"So, I know that I said I wanted us to have dinner together, but I have a feeling that's not going to happen," Johnny announced when we pulled up outside Spizzico's restaurant on Main Street and he killed the engine. Drumming his fingers on the steering wheel, he blew out a frustrated breath before gesturing to the familiar silver Ford Focus parked two cars up. "Bleeding Gibs."

I laughed because, in all honesty, what else could I do? "He really missed you this summer, Johnny."

"Yeah," Johnny sighed heavily again. "And I really missed him, but I really *need* time with you, Shannon. Time on our own. Without my ma or one of your brothers lurking around the corner."

"We'll have time," I coaxed, reaching across the seat to place my hand on his jean-clad thigh. "All the time in the world."

My words seemed to settle something inside of Johnny because when he looked at me again, there was a boyish smile in place. "All the time in the world, huh?"

I squirmed in my seat, feeling shy and aroused all in one breath. "You tell me."

"Oh yeah," he agreed, tone taking on a husky note, as he unfastened his seatbelt and leaned across the seat. "We'll have it all and more." His fingers brushed my chin for the briefest of moments, tilting my face upwards, and then his lips were on mine. Searing me with the kind of heat and affection that I would never recover from.

Falling into his kiss, I could do nothing but unfasten my seat belt and scramble onto his lap, fingers knotting in the fabric of his crisp white shirt, as our lips collided.

"Hi, Shannon," he groaned in approval against my lips, as his hands snaked out to clamp down on my hips.

"Hi, Johnny," I breathed, peppering him with kisses. He smelled so *good*, felt so *strong*, touched me so *right*. He was *everything* to me. "I love you."

"I love you more," came his grunted response when my tongue swept over his neck to taste him. "You look incredible tonight . . . hmm fuck . . . Did I tell you that, baby?"

Yeah, he'd already told me that.

At least five times.

Warmth crept over my skin when his hands moved from my hips to graze my bare thighs. "You're so beautiful," I whispered, lips trailing from his neck to the curve of his shaved jaw. "You make me so happy."

"Ah, Jaysus, Shan, you really need to stop saying these words to me," he groaned, hips flexing beneath me. "If you don't, we're never going to make it to dinner."

"And my baby's on a feeding schedule," I cooed teasingly, pressing one last kiss to his lips before pulling back to grin at his flushed expression. "Don't worry, Mister Rugby, I would never keep you from dinner." Grinning, I added, "After all, your stomach has been talking since we left the house."

He offered me a wolfish grin in response. "They do serve a fucking fantastic chicken, Shan."

"Uh-huh." Rolling my eyes, I climbed off his lap and laughed. "You and your chicken."

When we made it inside the restaurant and were shown to our table, it wasn't just Gibsie we found had highjacked our date night. Our entire friendship circle had decided to attend. And contrary to his earlier protests, Johnny was thrilled to be reunited with his friends – and most importantly, his other half.

With his arm slung over my chair, and his thumb trailing over my bare shoulder, Johnny snickered into his glass of water at whatever Gibsie, who was sitting on the other side of him, was whispering animatedly in his ear.

Feeling more content than I had in weeks, I looked around the table at our friends and smiled to myself.

Claire was gushing about what a wonderful father *Gerard* was to their litter of furball babies to Katie, Hughie and Feely, who were sitting opposite us.

Katie and Feely looked thoroughly amused by her antics, while a despondent-looking Hughie slumped forward with his head in his hands, eyes locked on his untouched food.

"Hugh, you are their uncle," Claire declared when her brother offered no response to her suggestion of a naming ceremony for their kittens. "You have to be there."

"Claire, if you don't pack it in, I'm going to stab myself in the eye with this fork," her brother grumbled, looking entirely unhappy about the whole ordeal. "Seriously. I can't take another fucking second of this."

"Well, I think it's a great idea," Katie chuckled, digging her boyfriend in the ribs with her elbow. "Of course we'll attend the naming ceremony for your kittens, Claire."

"*Thank you,* Katie." Claire beamed back at her. "I'm thinking about holding it the Sunday before we go back to school. I'll bake some scones for afterwards, and Gerard makes the most amazing—"

"Don't tell me you're encouraging it," Lizzie chimed in when she returned from the bathroom, tone dripping with sarcasm, as she slumped down on the chair next to Hughie. "Claire, they're cats. Cats don't need baptismal ceremonies."

"It's not a baptismal ceremony," Claire defended, cheeks reddening. "It's a naming ceremony."

Lizzie cocked a brow. "There's a difference?"

"Yes," both Claire and Gibsie chimed in unison.

"Kill me now," Hughie grumbled, still staring down at his plate.

"It's weird and it's stupid."

"Listen here," Gibsie interjected, turning his attention on Lizzie. "Be a bitch to me all you want, but not her."

Lizzie narrowed her eyes. "Did I say you could speak to me, *Thor*?"

Gibsie narrowed his eyes right back. "Did I ask for permission, *Viper*?"

Johnny shook his head, and Katie sighed heavily. Meanwhile, Feely continued to eat his meal. "Don't fight, guys," I began to protest, but it was too late.

The gloves were off.

Like the habit of a lifetime, the pair broke into a full-blown argument, where Lizzie tore proverbial strips out of Gibsie, and he tossed back sarcastic remarks that only seemed to incite her rage further.

"I'm not doing this again," Hughie announced, surprising everyone. "I'm not." Shoving his chair back, he stood abruptly. "It's bullshit and I'm done."

Having said that, he reached into his wallet and tossed a wad of notes on the table before walking out.

Wordlessly, Katie rose from her chair and hurried out of the restaurant after her boyfriend.

Hughie's storming out seemed to do the trick because it stunned Lizzie into silence, giving Gibsie ample opportunity to poke his tongue out at her and give her both middle fingers from under the table, while he mouthed an impressive array of obscenities at his favorite nemesis.

"Well, *that* was a slight overreaction," Claire declared, drumming her nails on the white linen tablecloth. "Moody much?"

"What's up there?" Johnny asked, directing his question to Gibsie.

"No fucking clue, Cap," Gibsie replied, reaching across the table to snatch up Hughie's untouched plate of chicken wings. "He's been like that all summer."

"Gerard's right," Claire chimed in, snagging a chicken wing off her brother's plate that Gibsie set down between them. "Seriously, Johnny, it's been mood swing central at my house since we got back from your birthday camping trip."

"Shite," Johnny muttered, rubbing his jaw. "I didn't know."

"How could you?" Feely offered in a good-natured tone. "You were busy setting the rugby world ablaze all summer."

# JOHNNY

"I love this song," Shannon declared later that night when we parked out at the house, as "This Year's Love" from David Gray drifted from the stereo.

"So, what's the story with Hugh?"

"Honestly?" She turned in her seat to give me her full attention. "I have no idea."

"That was fairly strange, though, yeah?" I thought back to the night's events. "I've never known Hughie to storm off like that." My brows furrowed as I racked my brain for the cause. "You're sure he's not on the outs with Katie? They barely spoke to each other all through dinner."

"I don't know."

"You don't know?"

"No." Shannon shook her head, expression guilty. "I know I should be paying more attention, but honestly, I've spent most of my summer either watching you on the television, waiting for you to come home, or worrying about Joey." She chewed on her bottom lip before adding, "I know that probably makes me a terrible friend, but I honestly don't have any more room, Johnny."

"Any more room for what, baby?"

"Pain," she whispered, blue eyes locked on mine. "Sadness."

My chest squeezed tight at her words. "Shan."

"I'm happy," she hurried to say, her words a breathy rush. "I'm so happy, Johnny. For the first time in my life. I feel *safe*. I feel *alive*, *good*, and I just . . . I don't . . . I want to stay in my happy place. Just for a little bit. Is that really bad of me?"

"No, Shan, that's not bad." I shook my head and smiled. "There's no one else on this planet who deserves a reprieve from pain than you, baby."

Her eyes searched mine for a long moment before she exhaled what sounded like a relieved breath. "Thank you."

"For what?"

"For understanding." Unfastening her seatbelt, she crawled onto my lap. "For being the kind of boy who doesn't storm out of dinner and leave me behind."

"To be fair, I have been known to storm out on occasion," I offered with a chuckle. "But I would never leave you behind, Shannon like the river."

"I believe you," she whispered, snuggling into my chest. "I really believe you, Johnny Kavanagh."

"Good," I replied gruffly, tightening my hold on her small frame. "Because when it comes to you, Shannon Lynch, I'm all in."

"Me too."

"Where you go, I go."

"Promise?"

"I promise."

# Glossary

| | |
|---|---|
| **Bluey:** | Porno movie. |
| **Jammy:** | lucky. |
| **Jammiest:** | luckiest. |
| **Corker:** | beautiful woman. |
| **St. Stephen's Day:** | Boxing Day/ December 26th. |
| **Bonnet:** | hood of the car. |
| **Boot:** | trunk of the car. |
| **Pound Shop:** | Dollar store. |
| **Burdizzo:** | castration device |
| **Messages:** | groceries. |
| **Mickey/Willy:** | penis. |
| **Spanner:** | idiot. |
| **Feis:** | a tradition Gaelic arts and culture festival/event. |
| **Hole:** | often said instead of ass/bottom. |
| **Solicitor:** | lawyer. |
| **Daft:** | silly. |
| **Daft as a brush:** | very silly. |
| **Poitín:** | Irish version of moonshine/illegal, home-brewed alcohol. |
| **Wheelie Bin:** | Trash can. |
| **Jumper:** | sweater. |
| **Cracking on:** | hooking up. |
| **Runners:** | trainers/sneakers. |

| | |
|---|---|
| **Wellies:** | rubber boots worn in the rain. |
| **Fair City:** | Popular Irish television soap. |
| **On the hop:** | skipping school. |
| **Cooker:** | Oven/Stove/Hob. |
| **Rolos:** | Popular brand of chocolate. |
| **Eejit:** | fool/idiot. |
| **Gobshite:** | fool/idiot. |
| **Lifted:** | arrested. |
| **Sap:** | sad/pathetic. |
| **Rebel County:** | nickname for County Cork. |
| **Primary School:** | elementary school – junior infants to sixth class. |
| **Secondary School:** | high school – first year to sixth year. |
| **Leaving Cert:** | the compulsory state exam you take in your final year of secondary school. |
| **Junior Cert:** | the compulsory state exam you take in third year – midway through your six-year cycle of secondary school. |
| **Playschool:** | pre-school/nursery. |
| **Junior Infants:** | equivalent to kindergarten. |
| **Senior Infants:** | equivalent to second year of kindergarten. |
| **First Class:** | equivalent to first grade. |
| **Second Class:** | equivalent to second grade. |
| **Third Class:** | equivalent to third grade. |
| **Fourth Class:** | equivalent to fourth grade. |
| **Fifth Class:** | equivalent to fifth grade. |
| **Sixth Class:** | equivalent to sixth grade. |
| **First Year:** | equivalent to seventh grade. |
| **Second Year:** | equivalent to eighth grade. |
| **Third Year:** | equivalent to ninth grade. |
| **Fourth Year:** | Transition Year: equivalent to tenth grade. |
| **Fifth Year:** | equivalent to eleventh grade. |
| **Sixth Year:** | equivalent to twelfth grade. |

| | |
|---|---|
| **GAA:** | Gaelic Athletic Association. |
| **Culchie:** | a person from the countryside or a county outside of Dublin. Usually used as a friendly insult. |
| **Jackeen:** | a person from Dublin. A term sometimes used by people from other counties in Ireland to refer to a person from Dublin. |
| **Dub:** | a person from Dublin. |
| **Frigit:** | someone who has never been kissed. |
| **Gardaí Síochána:** | Irish police force. |
| **Garda:** | policeman. |
| **Shades:** | police. |
| **Hurling:** | a hugely popular, amateur Irish sport played with wooden hurleys and sliotars. |
| **Camogie:** | the female version of hurling. |
| **Scoil Eoin:** | the name of Johnny, Gibsie, Feely, Hughie, and Kevin's all-boys primary school. |
| **Sacred Heart:** | the name of Shannon, Joey, Darren, Claire, Caoimhe, Lizzie, Tadhg, Ollie, Podge, and Alec's mixed primary school. |
| **St. Bernadette's:** | the name of Aoife, Casey, and Katie's all-girls primary school. |
| **Grinds:** | Tutoring. |
| **Fortnight:** | two weeks. |
| **Chipper:** | a restaurant that sells fast food. |
| **Craic:** | fun. |
| **Gas:** | funny. |
| **Mope:** | idiot. |
| **The Angelus:** | Every evening at 6pm in Ireland, there is a minute silence for prayer on the television. |
| **The craic was ninety:** | Having a lot of fun and banter. |
| **On the lash:** | going out drinking. |
| **On the piss:** | going out drinking. |

| | |
|---|---|
| **Swot:** | nerd/academically gifted. |
| **Spanner:** | idiot. |
| **Yolk:** | nickname for an illegal drug. |
| **Hatchet craic:** | Great fun. |
| **Langer:** | idiot. |
| **Fanny:** | Vagina. |
| **Scoring:** | Kissing. |
| **Shifting:** | Kissing. |
| **Shifting Jackets:** | Lucky piece of clothing, usually a jacket, when trying to pick up a girl. |
| **Langers:** | group of idiots and/or to be extremely drunk. |
| **Tog off:** | change into or out of training clothes. |
| **Child of Prague:** | a religious statue farmers place out in a field to encourage good weather. (An old Irish superstition.) |
| **Rosary, Removal, Burial:** | the three days of a Catholic funeral in Ireland. |
| **Spuds:** | potatoes. |
| **A slab of beer:** | a box of 24 bottles of beer. |
| **Get your hole:** | have sex. |
| **Ridey:** | a good-looking person. |
| **Strop:** | mood-swing/pouting/sulking. |

# Epic, emotional and addictive ...

The power and pain of first love has never been more
deeply felt than in Chloe Walsh's extraordinary
stories about the irresistible Boys of Tommen, which
will give you the ultimate book hangover.

## Collect them all!